THE OTHERWORLD BOXSET

BOOKS 1-3

EMMA HAMM

I0740167

Copyright © 2019 by Emma Hamm
All rights reserved.

Cover by: Magdalena Korz
Editing by: Amy Cissell
Formatting by: AB Formatting

No part of this book may be reproduced in any form or by any electronic or mechanical means, including information storage and retrieval systems, without written permission from the author, except for the use of brief quotations in a book review.

HEART *of the* FAE

Emma Hamm

Copyright © 2017 by Emma
All rights reserved.

Cover by: Natasa Ilincic
Editing by: Amy Cissell
Formatting by: AB Formatting

No part of this book may be reproduced in any form or by any electronic or mechanical means, including information storage and retrieval systems, without written permission from the author, except for the use of brief quotations in a book review.

GLOSSARY OF TERMINOLOGY

Tuatha dé Danann - Considered to be the "High Fae", they are the original and most powerful faerie creatures.

Seelie Fae - Otherwise known as the the "Light Fae", these creatures live their lives according to rules of Honor, Goodness, and Adherence to the Law.

Unseelie Fae - Considered the "Dark Fae", these creatures follow no law and do not appreciate beauty.

Danu - The mother of all Tuatha dé Danann and considered to be an "earth" mother.

Nuada - The first Seelie King, often called Nuada Silverhand as he has a metal arm after losing his own in a fearsome battle.

Macha - An ancient Tuatha dé Danann who is known as one of the three sisters that make up the Morrighan. Her symbols are that of a horse and a sword.

Redcap - A troublesome faerie, frequently found in gardens harassing chickens.

Máthair - "Mother"

Will-o'-the-wisps - Small balls of light that guide travelers into bogs, usually with the intention for the humans to become lost.

Brownies - Friendly, mouse-like creatures who clean and cook for those who are kind to them.

Pixie - A winged faerie whose face resembles that of a leaf.

Changeling - Old or weak faeries swapped with human children, usually identified as a sickly child.

Gnome - Generally considered ugly, these small, squat faeries take care of gardens and have an impressive green thumb.

Dullahan - A terrifying and often evil faerie who carry their heads in their laps.

Bean Sidhe - Also known as a banshee, their screams are echoing calls that herald the death of whomever hears them.

Hy-brasil - A legendary isle which can only be seen once every seven years.

Merrow - Also known as a Mermaid, merrows have green hair and webbed fingers.

Merrow-men - The husbands of their female counterparts are considered horribly ugly with bright red noses, gills, two legs, and a tail.

Boggart - A brownie who grows angry or loses their way turns into a boggart. They are usually invisible, and have a habit of placing cold hands on people's faces as they sleep.

Pooka - A faerie which imitates animals, mostly dogs and horses.

Kelpie - A horse like creature who lives at the edge of a bog. It will try to convince you to ride it, at which point it will run underneath the water and drown the person on its back.

Selkie - A faerie which can turn into a seal, as long as it still has its seal skin.

PROLOGUE

Once upon a time in a hidden land beyond human reach, there lived a king and queen of the Seelie Fae. They desperately desired an heir to the throne, but had not been blessed with children. In his frustration, the king journeyed across the sea to the cursed home of the Unseelie.

He made a deal with an ancient crone, half spider and half woman. If she would give him a child, then he would bring peace to their lands. The crone was pleased and promised when he returned to his wife, she would bear him a child.

The Queen carried not one, but two children. Twin boys, both heirs to the throne.

Many years passed. Their lives were filled with light and love. They had forgotten that the Unseelie do not make deals without payment, and stopping a war paid for one boy.

Not two.

Their first-born son grew into a warrior. His blade was unstoppable, his aim always true, his speed lightning quick. Their second born son grew into a scholar. He knew every whisper on the wind, every lie and story, every bit of knowledge that made the kingdom run smoothly. The King and Queen were certain the brothers would rule the Seelie Fae together.

They had not seen the jealousy growing within their youngest son's heart, nor had they seen the doubt growing in the eldest.

In a fit of rage, their youngest son buried a blade in his brother's back. The wound was superficial and might have healed if it hadn't revealed a nightmare.

Their son, their perfect first born, was flawed. Gemstones and crystals grew out of the wound, marring his strong body, and marking him unfit to rule their kingdom. Embarrassed and appalled, they did the only thing they could.

Banishment.

The disgraced prince was sent away to a phantom isle which could only be seen once every seven years. He begged his family to allow him to remain, but they had no pity for the man who had hidden his true nature.

The first-born son of the Seelie King faded into myth, then legend.

Then nothing at all.

CHAPTER ONE
THE BEETLE

Blood covered her hands. The metallic smell burned her nostrils and overwhelmed her senses. Although she'd finished the surgery an hour ago, she still saw the gaping wound, the splayed open flesh, and the iridescent shimmer of the blood beetle feasting upon sinuous muscle.

Sorcha sat on the back stoop with her hands dangling off her knees. The chickens pecked at her soft leather shoes; the jabs helped to ground her. This weightless feeling always happened after a long, grueling attempt to extract a beetle.

"Shoo," she whispered. One chicken shook its head, feathers ruffled in displeasure. She was certain the nasty redcap rode one of them. The faerie was secretive in his pranks, and likely thought she couldn't see him, but Sorcha always caught glimpses out of the corner of her eye. "There are tastier things than my feet."

She tapped her foot against the ground. The chicken clucked loudly and beat its wings against her legs, rushing to the other side of the pen. Even though Sorcha fed them every morning and night, she would bear the brunt of their anger.

Chickens were vindictive little things.

"Sorcha!" A feminine voice shouted. "Get back in here!"

She stood, wanting desperately to dust off her skirts but knowing she would only smear blood on them. To waste new fabric would be the worst kind of sin. She stared down at the blood flaking off her hands, lips pressed in a thin line.

"It will have to do," she muttered.

Their three-story home was at the edge of town, the only suitable location for a brothel. The stone walls were sturdy and clean, and the wooden roof free of rot. It was by no means elegant, but it was suitable for its purpose. For Sorcha, the cobblestone steps felt like stairs to the gallows.

Sorcha dunked her hands into a bucket of clean water near the door. Her sisters had meant it for cleaning, but if they wanted her to rush, then they needed to make the trek to the river once again.

She scrubbed her hands together, tainting the water with blood. It turned as red as the muscles in her father's back that had been revealed when she pressed her blade deeper…

"Sorcha!"

Snapping out of her stupor, she wiped her hands upon the plaid wrapped around her waist. A breeze pushed red curls in front of her gaze, obscuring her vision. She huffed out an angry breath and shoved them back.

There was blood caked underneath her nails.

"I'm coming!" she shouted, pushing open the door.

The room beyond was still. Papa's room was always quiet, but now it was silent as a tomb. Sorcha prayed every night it would not become one.

She knew how to prevent children from being conceived, how to birth a child, and all the ailments that might come after for both mother and babe. She had guided countless women through the trials of labor and treated many a croupy cough.

But she wanted to be a *real* healer. Her soul yearned to do more, to set bones and find cures for diseases. Shelves of books lined her bedroom, each containing detailed notes for every herb, every technique to heal, even the right faeries to beg for help.

It was a shame the faeries had stopped listening a long time ago.

Trophies of Papa's travels decorated the walls of his room. A bear pelt covered the stone floor, a dark wood desk contained all his notes and a balancing scale to count his coins. His pallet bed covered almost the entire back wall, heavy curtains shrouding him from Sorcha's view.

"Sorcha, his fever is back," her sister said.

She rushed to his side.

Rosaleen was the youngest in the brothel and innately kind. The longer she stayed here, the quieter she would get. Kind people never lasted in this profession. They were either lucky, and some nobleman took them as a mistress, or they disappeared forever.

Rosaleen's heart-shaped face was pale with fear. She had tied her blonde ringlets with a leather thong, but a few escaped to bounce with her movements.

Such a pretty little thing would surely capture a nobleman's favor. Or a soldier's, at the very least. What man wouldn't want a mistress such as her?

Sorcha pressed her hand against Papa's forehead and tsked. "We completed another treatment, and I thought rest would stave off another fever. I'm sorry, I was wrong. Can you get him hot water, please, Rosaleen?"

"Will it help?"

"It will. A spot of tea fixes a great many things," Sorcha lied. He wouldn't heal tonight, in a fortnight, or even in a year. He wouldn't heal at all. But Rosaleen was a delicate creature and lying eased her worry.

Sorcha watched her sister rush from the room with a troubled gaze.

"Good riddance," Papa coughed. "They fawn over me as if I'm already dead."

"They're worried," Sorcha replied with a smile. "And they have a right to be."

"There will be another man to take my place. A business like this won't be empty for long."

"But will he be as kind? Will he be as understanding?"

"I am neither of those, and the girls shouldn't expect another man to be."

Sorcha helped him sit up, her hand sturdy and strong behind his back. She remembered him as a tall man, broad and capable of taking on the world. He had thrown men out of this establishment without breaking a sweat. Now, he was skeletal. Each inhalation rattled and exhalation wheezed. His hands shook, and his eyes remained unfocused.

While he caught his breath, she plucked at the bandages and poultice packed around his ribs. "How does it feel?"

"Sore," he grumbled. "Damn beetles are always moving."

"At least we got rid of another hive mother."

Papa snorted. "It's something, but it won't save me."

No, it wouldn't.

A blood beetle infection was a death sentence, and no one had figured out how to cure it. They came from the skies. Swarms of green locusts, so beautiful the villagers wore their wings as jewelry in the first year. Then, they laid their eggs inside people. There was no catching up with them after that.

Sorcha sighed and laid her hand over one of the many bumps on Papa's back. The beetles lived underneath the skin, eating flesh from the inside out. They multiplied while feasting slowly upon their hosts, but at least they didn't spread until they exhausted their food supply.

Sorcha had figured out a way to extract them. She cut through skin, muscle, and sinew, carefully pulling the beetles out from behind. She then burned them and buried their ashes. It was the only way she could be certain they wouldn't fly off and infect someone else.

The bump underneath her hand shifted.

"I felt that one," Papa huffed. "How long do I have girl?"

"A few more months. I've been trying to keep up with their reproductions, but your body won't take this much trauma for long."

"That's what I thought."

The door eased open and Rosaleen poked her head through. "Can I come back in now?"

Sorcha rubbed Papa's back. "Yes, come on in. Can you pour the water in a cup for me, please?"

Pottery was scarce at the brothel. No one wanted to sell household objects to prostitutes, so they made do with what Sorcha received as trade from her midwifery. The mangled clay cup was lopsided, but it held water without leaking.

She packed yarrow into the cup and gave it a swirl. "Here you go, Papa. Drink up."

"Is this that bitter tea you keep making me drink?"

"It keeps the fever down and helps stop the bleeding."

"I don't like it." He sipped and made a face. "I think you're poisoning me."

"I think you're being a child. Drink it all—" she paused. "*All* of it, Papa. And then go back to sleep."

He grumbled, but laid back down on the bed without too much of a fuss. Sorcha drew the curtain so the light wouldn't disturb him.

Rosaleen stared at her. The weight of her gaze was like a physical touch. There wasn't much for Sorcha to say. She didn't want to ruin their happiness—and income—by giving a date to their father's death. They needed to stay strong, and later they could grieve.

She tucked her little sister under her arm and guided her from the room. "What's the matter little chick?"

"I'm worried about Papa. Aren't you?"

"You let me worry about him. I'm the healer, aren't I?"

"Midwife."

The word stung.

"I'm doing more than the healers would. They'd be bloodletting him when the beetles already do that. He doesn't need any leeches. He needs the beetles removed."

"They're still not listening to you?"

The sisters walked into the kitchen and main living space for the women. When they first moved to this city, only the family had lived in this building. Their Papa was a born businessman, and he set his sights on expanding their clientele. Now, there were thirteen women living and working under their roof.

The twins snuggled up near the fire, their heads pressed together as they shared secrets. Sorcha's herbs hung from the ceiling to dry for later use. A worn table stretched from end to end, two benches serving as seats. They stored a cauldron in the back room and brought it out for supper to hang over the fire.

Briana, the eldest of their sisters, swung the opposite door open. Masculine laughter and shouts echoed from the front of the house. "Rosaleen, you've a customer out front."

"All right," she squeezed Sorcha's waist. "I'll be back later. You'll be fine without me?"

"You worry too much," Sorcha replied. "Go on then. Make some money."

As the tiny blonde skipped past, Briana gave Sorcha a measured stare. "You're keeping yourself busy today, I hope? There's a long line of appointments, and I don't have time to watch over you today. You'll fend for yourself if you're sticking around."

Sorcha had never been like her adopted sisters. Her witch of a mother taught her too many things and her young mind had absorbed the information. Sorcha had more uses than whoring, Papa used to say. People paid more for healing than they did for bedding. And besides, no one wanted to risk laying with the devil's spawn. Papa never thought she was a witch or cursed, but she was whip-smart.

He made the decision for her to walk the path of a healer. From that day forward, she dedicated herself to helping others and tried to avoid the same fate as her mother. The acrid scent of burning flesh was seared into her memory.

Sorcha ducked her head and nodded. "I'll be at the guild meeting most of the day and then need to stop by Dame Agatha's."

"That poor woman is pregnant again?"

"Seems so."

Briana tsked. "That man needs to give her a break, or she'll go to an early grave. Speaking of, I'll need you to restock our own stores. We can't have any children running around."

"Of course. On the way back, I'll gather more mealbhacán, but the wild carrot tastes awful."

"I don't care what you gather, or how bad it tastes. Just make it useful."

Briana must have had a difficult client, Sorcha mused. Or perhaps it was the teeming mass of energy behind her. Men always grew excited on the Solstice.

She raced up the rickety wooden stairs, trying not to make eye contact with any of the male customers below. They lived in a large city, and most people knew her. She wasn't in the market for entertaining.

"Sorcha! When are you going to let us love you like we love your sisters?"

Only when she crested the first flight of stairs did she pause and lean over the railing. The long tangled mass of her hair hung over the edge. "Oh, Fergus. Someday you will make your wife jealous with talk like that."

"She knows I'm loyal to her!"

Briana stood behind the man, waving her hands frantically.

Right. Sorcha wasn't supposed to insult the customers, or they'd leave. She puffed out a breath that stirred the red curls in front of her face, conceding. "I'm a healer, Fergus. I don't partake in your festivities, but a man certainly can dream!"

He let out a hearty laugh, his cheeks stained red. "Ah, and dream I do, my lovely lass!"

She raced up the rest of the stairs. Her skirt whirled in an arc behind her, the blue plaid fluttering with her movements. The last thing she wanted to hear was that Fergus, of all men, dreamed of her.

They all slept on the top floor, away from the rooms where they brought clients. A place they could call their own was important. However, the more women they brought into their family, the less room they had.

Sorcha didn't work in the brothel, so her room was the smallest. It had once been used as a storage closet, but now held a small cot and stacked chests. Books, herbs, and all manner of magical objects were scattered around the room.

The first chest creaked as she opened it. She reached into the dark depths, her fingers skimming over well-worn objects, until she closed her fist around her greatest treasure.

Her mother had passed down her knowledge along with sacred objects. Many feared Paganism—considered it the work of the devil. They named those who practiced it *witches*. Sorcha knew better.

She pulled out a stone carved with a white dove. Pressing it to her lips, she whispered, "Good morrow, Máthair."

Not a day passed when she didn't miss her mother's laughter, her calloused hands, and the scent of cinnamon in her hair. She hadn't been a witch, just a healer who knew how to ask favors of the Fae.

Sorcha dropped the stone back into the chest and picked up a ceramic pot. Her mother had lovingly painted tiny flowers all around the edges, each stroke created with care and precision. She measured out a small bit of sugar and scooped it onto the windowsill.

"Share a taste of sugar with me," Sorcha said, "in celebration of our dutiful work."

Like her mother, Sorcha respected the old ways and the Fae. She believed in them where others did not. Her room was always clean, and her books always neatly packed away. All without Sorcha touching a single item. The brownies took care of her, and she took care of them in return.

She scooped up her medical notes and tucked them into a bag she slung over her shoulder. Patting her hair, she gave up on tying it back. The nest of curls would be free before she made it to the guild.

Tugging hard on her bodice, she pressed her hand against her chest. A hag stone—bored through with natural holes by running river water—hung around her neck. Another gift from her mother, so she could always see through the glamour of magic.

She turned and made her way back down the stairs.

Rosaleen was already exiting her room, closing the door gently behind her. Her hair stuck up in all directions, like a dandelion puff. She glanced over her shoulder and shrugged. "I wasn't expecting that one to be so quick. He paid for a half hour, so I suppose he can sleep it off."

"Someone new?"

"He wouldn't say who he was. Looks like a nobleman. His clothes are too fine to be working class."

Sorcha pulled up her sister's sleeve which was dipping dangerously low on her shoulder. "Fancy catching this one for good?"

Rosaleen blushed. "Oh, he's much too fine looking for me."

"And you're a rare beauty. He would give you a good life, away from working so hard."

"I couldn't leave all of you."

"None of us would think less of you for it. You'd be safe, well-fed, and you could visit. If he's kind, think about it."

"He was certainly kind," Rosaleen tucked a strand of hair behind her ear. "And I can appreciate a man who doesn't take much work."

Sorcha chuckled and touched a finger to Rosaleen's chin. "Think about it, little chick. Go get yourself cleaned up."

"The tea is downstairs?"

"Ask Briana. There's a few tonics left, and I'll bring back more."

They walked down the stairs together, giggling as Rosaleen told stories about the customers she'd already had that day.

"Will you be gone long?" Rosaleen asked as they reached the

ground floor.

"Briana's asked that I make myself scarce. There's a lot of customers, and I don't need to be underfoot."

"We might need you if anyone gets too rowdy."

"The men don't pay for healing anyways. I'd rather find customers who will at least trade."

"Not Dame Agatha?" Rosaleen's eyes glinted with mischief.

"You were listening!"

"Just through the grate while he was getting ready. I haven't heard a single rumor about Agatha being pregnant again, so what are you really going to do? Are you hiding a man?"

"Not everything is about men, Rosaleen." Sorcha lifted her bag and pawed through it. "I'm just visiting the shrine, that's all."

"I thought you were done with the faeries?"

"No one can be *done* with faeries. They will always be there, and someone has to leave offerings."

They had argued about this since they were children. Papa and his girls lived in the city where people had forgotten their ties to the land. Sorcha had grown up on the moors. She knew will-o'-the-wisps by name and had spied on goblin markets. She left offerings for brownies and whispered secrets to the Tuatha dé Danann.

If she had never seen these things, she might have questioned whether faeries were real.

Shaking her head, she pushed her way through the crowd of men in the front room. Briana hadn't been wrong. They were unusually busy, even for this time of year. Perhaps someone had spread word of the mysterious brothel filled with golden women.

Rumors said that Papa's daughters came from a line of goddesses. They were all unnaturally pretty with milk-pale skin and heart-shaped faces. Their full lips were always red and didn't leave berry stains on men's skin. Loose blonde curls never needed a hot iron, and they were graceful as dancers.

There were some who wondered about their odd duck of a sister. In comparison, Sorcha was a startling red rose among daffodils. She was taller than her sisters with waist-length red hair and tight-ring curls that billowed around her like a cloud. Freckles dusted her skin from the top of her head to the tips of her toes. And everyone found her slightly pointed ears to be unnerving.

Faerie touched, the villagers used to say. Her mother must have had a changeling child she refused to give back. Or perhaps that was just a sign she was touched by the devil, like her witch of a mother.

Whatever the reasoning, Sorcha was odd, strange, unusual.

She pushed past the last man and stepped out onto the streets. A horse and buggy waited out front, the emblem of an eagle painted on its side in gold. She reached into the pocket of her dress and pulled out a small shriveled apple.

Soft velvet lips plucked the fruit from her palm, and the horse nickered with happiness.

"You'll be waiting for a while, my friend," Sorcha said with a grin.

"Hey, woman!" A whip cracked over her head. "Ain't nobody ever told ye not to touch a stranger's horse? *Get* out of here."

She ducked away and disappeared into the crowd.

It was market day. The teeming mass of people all seemed to have something to sell. Unwashed bodies pressed against her, but all she could smell was fish, meats, and fresh fruit.

"Eggs for sale!"

"Flowers for your lady?"

"Fabric in every color!"

Sorcha kept her bag close to her side and tried not to make eye contact. She didn't need any trouble from the suspicious villagers who made the sign of the cross when she passed. Stalls lined the streets with food, billowing cloth, even jewelry from the far reaches of the land. Some vendors she recognized. Others she did not.

A minstrel played his flute, filling the square with a jaunty tune.

Sorcha recognized the song and covered her grin. The words were highly inappropriate. His hat on the ground overflowed with coins, so others must have appreciated the jest as much as she.

He winked at her when she placed a single coin with the others.

A woman selling dried herbs caught her arm and pressed a small jar of honey into Sorcha's palm. "For Danu."

"I will leave it in the forest," Sorcha tucked it into her bag. "For anything in particular?"

"Good health."

Nodding, she continued to push through the crowds of people. It wasn't the first time someone asked for a blessing. They weren't willing to follow the old ways themselves—too risky—so they'd ask Sorcha to leave them for her. If she was caught, she'd be burned at the stake by the same people who handed her gifts to take to the Fae.

A few others passed her bits and pieces to leave as offerings. A small packet of sugar, a dried bunch of lavender, a tiny jar of fresh cream. Little things that the faeries appreciated and might leave blessings for in return.

That was the deal with faeries. Their favors could not be bought or bribed. One had to continue leaving gifts and someday, maybe, the faeries would gift them a blessing.

Another woman grabbed Sorcha's arm and pulled her away from the crowd. A dirty kerchief covered her head and a moth-bitten brown dress hung from her thin frame. "My daughter won't stop crying. She's screaming the nights away, and my husband plans to leave her on the hill tomorrow night saying she's a changeling. Is there another way?" Her swollen eyes brimmed with tears, cheeks scrubbed raw and nose stuffed.

Sorcha patted her hand. "Bring her to the river and hold her in the water. No need to put her underneath it, just her legs will do. If they look the same, then she's no changeling. If they look like birch branches, then you know you're housing a faerie under your roof."

"The river?"

"Faerie magic doesn't work under flowing water and the glamour will break. If she's no Fae, then bring her to the brothel. I'll have a good look at her and see if I can give you something to help her. And you, get some sleep."

"Bless you, lady. We have nothing to pay you."

"I don't ask for payment. Leave an offering for Danu when you can and apologize for blaming her children for your child's illness."

The woman wrung her hands. "And if it is a changeling?"

Sorcha frowned. "Then you'll leave it in the woods and hope they bring your child back."

She pulled away and continued her journey with a troubled mind. Many families thought their sickly babe was a changeling, but rarely was it true. There hadn't been a changeling in this area for as long as she could remember.

Yet, offerings to the Fae had diminished in the past years. With the blood beetle plague, the rising of other religions, and more outsiders in their lands, faerie stories faded into myth.

The people forgot the shrines. Cattle and lye tainted the holy waters. Many people didn't leave cream and sugar on their doorsteps. No one remembered the old ways, and they were paying for that.

Sorcha shook her head. She hoped it wasn't a changeling. Often, the Fae swapped out children for a reason. It was an unwanted, ugly babe, or it was an ancient faerie who needed a quiet place to die. Neither of those were a fair trade for a human child, and leaving it on a hill didn't result in gaining their child back. The faerie would die alone on the hill, cold and unwanted once again.

But it was the only solution she knew.

She tried not to let her eyes linger upon the shadows at the edges of the street. Families cast out the infected from their home. The fear of spreading the blood beetles giving way to panic. She couldn't stop her eyes from searching for them at the edges of the crowd.

Her gaze caught on a painfully thin man. He scratched at a bulge on his cheek which shifted every time he touched it.

Sorcha shivered and hurried along her way.

The Guild building loomed at the end of the street. It looked nearly as impressive as the church. Imposing and tall, the walls stretched so high she had to shade her eyes to see their peak. One of the more prestigious patrons had paid for full stained glass windows. On one side, a healer looked down at her with disapproving eyes. On the other, a priest held his hands solemnly before him.

Taking a deep breath, she hiked the bag higher on her shoulder. Noblemen worked here, their fine velvet clothing easily ruined by her dirty touch, their jewelry blinding her with its opulence. She was not a welcome visitor.

She walked up the steps, counting each one as she went. By the time she reached thirty, she was at the front doors.

"This time will be different," she told herself. "They will listen to you. You'll make them."

Sorcha pushed the doors open and stepped onto the marble floors. Her footsteps echoed, those closest to her glancing up at the intrusive sound. She didn't let herself meet their gaze. She knew from experience their expressions would turn to shock and then anger. How dare a woman tread among their favored kind?

Confidently striding to the end of the building, she halted in front of a bespectacled man peering at ledgers. He didn't look up.

She cleared her throat.

"What is it this time, Sorcha?"

"I've come to speak with the healers' guild on the matter of blood beetles."

He didn't argue. They'd fought enough battles that minstrels should sing of their war. He lifted a hand, sighing. "Third hall on the left."

"Thank you."

She told herself to stay calm. Yelling at these men would only make them dig their heels in further, and she wanted to help. The blood beetles weren't going away, but maybe, just maybe, she could help the infected survive longer.

Her stomach rolled.

There wasn't any reason to be afraid. They couldn't lock her up or call her a witch. That would mean admitting they believed in magic, and these were men of science. The worst that could happen was that they would laugh at her.

It shouldn't bother her as much as it did. Her pride had always been a personal weakness, and one she had yet to tame. Sorcha wanted them to say she was right. Just once.

She pushed the door open and stepped into the hall.

A group of men gathered around a body laid out on a long table. A blanket draped over the dead man's legs, but that modesty seemed unnecessary when they had his rib cage cracked open.

"Gentlemen," she called out, "another blood beetle victim?"

The man standing at the head of the table raised his gaze. "Sorcha. I thought we threw you out last time."

"You *did*. And yet, here I am again. I have information on extracting the blood beetles I thought you might find helpful."

"I doubt anything a woman has to say would be helpful."

The room was as cold as his voice. She swallowed her anger and stilled her shivers. "I have taken detailed notes, as you requested last time, including drawings of my findings. As you have one of the afflicted before you, I would be happy to perform a live demonstration."

"Child, I appreciate your dedication, but you were never formally trained. We have no need for a midwife's opinions over the domain of men."

"Are women not afflicted as well?"

"I fail to see how this improves your argument."

"You dismiss me because I cannot understand the domain of men. However, it also affects the domain of women. According to your logic, I would understand that far better than you."

He sighed, bowed his head, and braced himself on the table, clearly taking measured breaths. "Sorcha. I should not have to explain this to you."

"What is there to explain? I have information that may be useful. You should listen."

Their collective gaze burned. She had known they wouldn't want her in the same room while they studied. It still frustrated her beyond reason.

"Why won't you listen to me?" she asked. "It's not a difficult thing to do. I am certain you can hear me as none of you are so advanced in age that I must shout."

Her eyes strayed towards the corner of a room where a handsome man stood. Geralt. His ink-dark hair glinted blue in the strong light trickling through the glass ceiling. His lips quirked to the side in a smirk, and his cobalt eyes sparkled with humor. Supple breeches hugged his well-shaped thighs, a white linen shirt billowed at his elbows, and a green brocade vest hugged his broad chest.

He swaggered forward. "If I may, gentlemen?"

Sorcha held in her snort of displeasure. She had been the one speaking, yet he did not direct his question towards her.

The doctor removed his glasses and snapped his handkerchief in the air. He pressed it against his nose, as if Sorcha brought with her a rancid stench, and waved his hand. "Please do."

"Sorcha," Geralt said as he strode forward. "It's not that we don't value your opinion, we certainly do. It's just that we are very busy and on the brink of great discovery."

"That you can remove the beetles? I've told you this every time I've come here."

"No. We have found a way to prevent them from breeding within the human body."

She ground her teeth together, so hard her jaw creaked. "That's impossible."

"It's not. I understand how badly you want to help us, and we appreciate it. But I am begging you," he held his hands clasped before him. "Give us more time. More *uninterrupted* time."

"I don't have time," Sorcha growled. "And neither do the rest of our people. The blood beetle plague gets worse with every season. You and your fellow *doctors* hole up in this room day after day, and you never find any kind of resolution. You take bodies like you're one of the *Dullahan*. All for nothing!"

Her shouts bounced off the high ceiling and struck the men like falling arrows. Some had the decency to flinch. Others remained stoic. Geralt's eyes narrowed upon her, and for once, Sorcha thought she had finally angered him.

The spark of fire disappeared.

"We are doing the best we can," the cajoling tone returned to Geralt's voice. "You are the bravest, most daring girl I have ever met. I appreciate your tenacity." His hand pressed against her spine and turned her from the room.

"I'm not leaving yet, Geralt. I can at least watch the examination. Perhaps I might have—"

"Sorcha," he interrupted. She could feel each finger burning through the fabric of her dress. "Perhaps you can explain why you don't have time to wait? I would like to offer my help."

"I don't want your help."

"But I want to give it. So please, walk with me."

She peered over her shoulder at the body. "If they would just listen, for once in their stubborn lives, I might be able to teach them something!"

"Not today, lovely. Not today."

He propelled her from the room with such ease Sorcha wondered if he had cursed her. More likely he was overpowering her. Geralt stood a head taller and didn't mind using his greater weight to his advantage.

There was little else she could do. Sorcha wanted to stay but would only make a larger scene if she did. Perhaps someday they would let her linger, even in the corner or in the shadows.

But she was just a midwife, and therefore, a lesser being.

Geralt leaned down, his lips brushing her ear. "Now, what is wrong with your father?"

"You know what's wrong with him. He's infected."

"I know he's infected, but you've never used him as an excuse before. What has changed?"

"It's progressed."

Geralt nodded at another nobleman. The other did not return the gesture. Old blood rarely acknowledged new riches. "How far?"

She stopped in her tracks. "Why are you even asking? You don't *care* how he fares."

"Of course I care." He pressed a hand against his chest. "I have always cared, Sorcha."

Everything was spiraling out of control. Her gut clenched and her fingers curled into fists. "This is not why I am here, Geralt. I'm not having this conversation with you in the middle of the Guild."

"Then let us walk outside."

"We've talked this through so many times. Enough!" Her exasperated shout echoed. Men stopped in their work and glanced towards them.

Her face turned bright red, the ache a weakness she resented. The last thing she needed was for these men to think she was hysterical. She already shouted enough.

Sorcha ducked her head and marched towards freedom, reminding herself to stay calm and composed.

"Sorcha!" Geralt called after her.

She rushed forward, bursting through the front door, and jogging down the steps. He caught up with her. The harsh tug of his hand on her arm would leave bruises.

"Would you at least listen to me?"

"I think I've heard it enough times." She shook herself out of his grip and rubbed at her bicep.

"You would have everything you desire," he said as she walked away. "You'd have a home, a husband, children."

"Is that what I'm supposed to want?"

"A man who adores you. Who whispers poetry in your ear every night and devotes himself to your happiness."

It sounded so good that she paused. He spoke of a life every woman desired. A loving relationship with a man who supported her every whim and passion. But she knew Geralt well. He wanted to believe he was that man, yet his eyes lingered upon the curves of other women. He drank more than he admitted, and above all else, he wasn't as good as he thought.

"I desire a useful man. One who can help us in our hour of need." She glanced over her shoulder. A curling red lock brushed across her face in the stiff breeze. "Words are of no use if no one is left to hear them."

"You want me to be the hero?" His jaw tightened before he growled, "I can't save everyone."

"No, you cannot. You're not a healer. You pay to be in that room among the brightest minds to satisfy your morbid curiosity," she lashed out. "Why won't you believe *me* when I say I can help?"

"You are a woman! What help could you provide?"

There it was. There was the anger, the red rage she saw so rarely. He buried his temper deep inside until it boiled over his edges.

"My sex doesn't change how much I know."

"You're naturally weak. You cannot help that, and we all understand. Why can't you?"

She drew herself up, squared her shoulders and gripped her plaid. "I am not weak because of my femininity. I do not look down upon you for not knowing how to birth a child or the right way to guide a woman through her first menses. Perhaps you should ask yourself why you feel the need to look down upon me."

A crowd gathered around the edges of her vision. This wasn't the first time she had screamed at a man in the street. Or a woman for that matter. She gritted her teeth.

"You can't change the world, Sorcha."

"I would if I could." She turned away from the town, from the villagers hiding smirks, from confused, handsome Geralt.

A crash shook the entire kitchen. Clay plates rattled, and a mug fell to the floor, shattering with an echoing clatter. The shutters slammed against the stained-glass windows with thunderous bangs.

The brownies flinched. They lifted their pointed, furred faces towards the ceiling. Nervous chuckles floated in the air with the bubbles from their dishes.

Oona, the only pixie in the kitchen, lifted her violet gaze and sighed. "The master's angry tonight."

"He was angry last night and the night before that!" The gnome walking into the room could look a sheep in the eye. His face was eerily similar to a bowl of mashed potatoes, with winged eyebrows always drawn down in an angry frown. He waddled to Oona and dumped a basket of flowers on the table. "For dinner."

"Thank you, Cian. Are you bringing the master his supper tonight?"

"That grumpy thing up there? Howling like he plans to tear the whole castle apart? I will not, under any circumstances. He's been too angry lately. The boy can go hungry."

"He has a right to be angry."

"No one has a right to be angry for that long."

Oona turned, lavender wings fluttering in the air. High arched eyebrows lifted even higher. The leaf-like fan of her forehead vibrated in anger. She shook a long finger at Cian, the extra digit giving her tsking weight. "You know as well as I why that man is angry. His own brother banished him here. His twin! After trying to kill him, more than once, need I remind you."

Cian crossed his short arms over his wide chest. "I have never felt bad for a king, and I don't plan to start now."

"Not a king." She shook her head. "A man who might have been king, if circumstances were different. Those he loved betrayed him, hanged him, and sent him to this isle with us. The least we can do is bring him supper."

"You bring it to him, then. I don't need to get thrown across the room like last time."

"He wouldn't dare."

"Few would," Cian nodded. "You're a frightening woman, pixie."

"And don't you forget it." She reached out and rapped him on the head with a wooden spoon. "Now, where is the master's dinner?"

He blushed, the red color highlighting on the peaks of his wrinkled skin. "Didn't get him one."

"Cian!"

"What? I told you I wasn't bringing him dinner!"

"There's not enough time to find him something to eat," she huffed. "And what do you think I'm going to do? Bring him pollen and honey?"

"Why can't he eat what we do?"

"Because he's a direct descendant of the Tuatha dé Danann. You think they eat like us?"

Oona spun and frantically searched the kitchen for anything she could bring to their howling master. He wasn't a picky man. He rarely ate at all, but he couldn't eat flowers, and he certainly couldn't drink only cream.

She ended up with her hands full of bread, honey, and milk. It was the best she could do although it wasn't likely to cool his anger.

Oona blew out a breath which stirred the petals of her hair, then marched from the kitchen.

The stone steps to the master's quarters always made her nervous. No railings prevented her from falling straight down the center. Looking down the stairs, she gulped. The fall would kill her, so she was certain to tread carefully while making her way to the master's quarters.

The peak of the tower opened to a walkway suspended over open air. Wind whistled past her ears. The vines in her hair turned to whips striking against her cheeks and neck.

She strode across the walkway while holding her breath. A stone door blocked the master's side of the castle from everyone else, protecting them from his rage.

Oona placed her shoulder against the door and grunted as she pushed.

Sounds of shattering glass and splintering wood filled the room beyond. Her hands shook as she traversed the broken landscape of furniture and vases. The master had gone through his seating area and beyond into his bedroom.

She paused a moment and stared at a crooked painting. The Queen stared down from the wall with a soft smile on her face. Now, three ragged strips were missing. The sagging canvas warped her face along the sliced edges.

"Master has never harmed you before," she whispered to herself. "What happened tonight?"

The sounds of the master's wrath silenced at her words. He'd heard her.

Oona took a deep, steadying breath, and walked towards his bedroom. She tentatively pushed the wooden door open with her toe, holding her breath.

"Master?" she asked.

"Go away."

She peered into the dim light. The curtains hung over the windows, covered in dust, and tied down at the bottom to hold them tight. Shadows formed around a four-poster bed with one post snapped in half.

She could make out his dresser, the chandelier swinging on the ceiling, even where his rug began. But she could not find him.

A bell rang in her mind. It warned her to leave and not let him lure her into his darkness. To preserve her own life and let him go hungry.

Her heart said the opposite.

She lifted her hand, snapped her fingers, and a warm faerie light danced in the air.

"There you are," she said. "I could hear you from downstairs and grew worried. You did quite a number on the front room."

"Go away, Oona."

He huddled beyond the bed, folded in on his great height until he was little more than a ball. His face turned away from her light as he always did when he saw her.

Not for the first time, she wished he would look at her without prompting.

"Master," she shook her head and marched to his dresser. "What have you done with your cloak?"

"I didn't think I would have visitors."

"Well, we share a castle. There's more of us than there are of you. What would you have done if the will-o'-the-wisps wandered up here to clean?"

"Frightened them away."

She reached into the top drawer and pulled out one of his many hooded cloaks. "Frightened them away. They already tremble when you walk past. Do you want them to run?"

"They should."

"I don't."

"You find no value in your own life."

Oona tsked. "That's cruel and unlike you. What happened, Eamonn?"

The glow from her faerie light reached him. He lifted a hand to cover his face and the other to reach for the cloak. "Not now."

"Yes, now." But she gave him the hood, watching the silk trickle from her fingers like black water. "You can't keep breaking furniture. We have a limited supply. Shipwrecks don't wash up every day."

He pulled the cloak over his shoulders as if his muscles had stiffened. Oona knew better. Once he lifted the hood over his face, she knelt on the floor.

"Don't—"

She didn't listen. She reached out and pressed her hand against his. "What happened?"

Eamonn turned his hand, letting her fingers dance over his palm which now held an open wound. "Another careless mistake."

"Oh, master. It's just a cut."

"You know it's more than that."

She glanced down, peeling her hand back from his. His flesh had parted from the meaty muscle of his thumb in a diagonal to his pinky. No blood welled from the wound. Instead, sparkling violet and blue crystals grew in the golden glow.

The wound would never heal again.

Oona curled her fingers over the disfigurement. "It's not as bad as the others."

"No, but it is a reminder of what I am."

"You are our king."

"I am an abomination and a pathetic excuse for Seelie royalty."

She linked her fingers through his. "Those are your brother's words, not yours. You are not ugly, nor are you deformed. In every way that matters, you are a Seelie Fae."

"Except physical perfection. I can never be king."

"Rules like that were meant to be changed. It isn't right that you're here and *he's* sitting on your throne."

Eamonn pulled away. He rose with creaking knees to his massive height. Oona was not a small pixie, but the Tuatha dé Danann were giants among men. The hood covered his face, and his hands glimmered in the light. His entire body was a geode cracking open with every slice to his flesh.

"Leave," he growled.

"Are you going to be all right alone?"

He turned his back on her. "I always am."

With a breaking heart, Oona solemnly left the room. She was careless on the stairs and nearly tumbled to her death before she made it back to the kitchens. Tears streamed down her cheeks.

Cian peeked in through the garden door. "What's he done now?"

"Nothing. He's done nothing but chosen to be alone."

"Ah, good riddance. All he'd do is break things down here. I like my garden the way it is."

He disappeared, and her heart stung as if she had swallowed something bitter. She looked up at the ceiling and shook her head. "He shouldn't be alone. He doesn't deserve to be alone."

CHAPTER TWO
THE TWINS

A branch launched back and smacked Sorcha across the face. She flinched, another twig pulling at her hair until she whimpered. She paused and tried to untangle herself, huffing out a breath.

The trees held fast, tangling her curls around their thin branches and twisting at her scalp. Her plaid stuck on the lower branches, and her arms were held down by vines.

"I don't want to let go of my anger," she growled. "It's healthy! No man should tell me what to do."

Anger rose again at the memories. Even her tromp through the woods hadn't cleared the red haze obscuring her vision. How dare he suggest she still her tongue, and then follow up those words with yet another suggestion of marriage? He *must* be mad.

"Let me go!" she grunted. "I'm *calm*."

Another harsh tug made her wince.

Sorcha sucked in a slow breath. Her cheeks puffed as she exaggerated the movement. "See? I'm not angry and won't desecrate this place with my…" she paused and grimaced. "With my trivial issues."

How had she forgotten? This was a sacred place, a haven for all who needed it, and here she was waltzing in wearing anger like a cloak upon her shoulders.

She hung her head in embarrassment. "My sincerest apologies. I will not make the same mistake again."

The trees groaned their approval. She shook her head and her hair slid from the confines of branches and leaves. The curls bounced against her cheeks, untangled and smooth. Her dress fell heavy against her legs, her plaid swaying with the sudden movement.

Her lips tilted in a soft smile. "I have learned your lesson, Danu, and I will remember it."

Nudging a branch aside, she stepped into the clearing. Green moss carpeted the ground all the way to the stones piled in the center. An artist had carved a triskele long ago; the three linked swirls faintly glowed on the granite. Water bubbled in between the mounds, smoothing the stones into perfect spheres.

She felt the warmth of the Fae here. The lingering effects of magic and nature made the tips of her pointed ears heat.

She pulled the bag off her shoulder and placed her offerings upon the stones. "Great Mother of old, I bring you gifts from those who seek your favor. Aileen, Eithne, and Nola leave honey, lavender, and sweet mead." As she spoke, Sorcha placed her hand upon each item. "I have brought you my mother's pin. It sparkles in the sun and reminds me of this place. I would like to leave it if it pleases you."

A warm breeze spiraled around her. It lifted her hair and teased the end of her nose. Dust motes danced and butterflies stirred into motion. Their wings flashed brilliant colors as the sunlight played across them.

Danu was pleased. Sorcha tilted her head towards the sun and let its heat soothe her soul. Although she was here, in her favorite place, dark thoughts still shoved to the forefront of her mind.

There were too many things to worry about. The blood beetles. Papa. Geralt. Her sisters. The list went on and on until she was drowning.

"Danu," she whispered, "my mind is troubled. I do not seek help, as I know you cannot always give it, but if there is a spare moment of your time… listen to my fears."

The air in the glen stilled as though something or someone was leaning forward in anticipation.

Encouraged, Sorcha sank to her knees and dug her hands into the moss. "The blood beetle plague is spreading ever faster. My own father has contracted the infection. I have the knowledge to extend his life, but I cannot stop him from dying. I fear I am only prolonging the inevitable.

"My sisters will not last long without his guidance. The man who takes his place will be unlikely to view them as people. I do not wish for them to lose their business or their home. They have done what it takes to survive here in the city. There is no shame in their profession, but there will be many who seek to take advantage of us in our father's absence.

"The Guild members refuse to listen. They sit in their ivory tower and poke at dead bodies while so many people die. They have gone so far as to say that because I am a woman, I do not have as much knowledge as them. I do not have the patience, nor the endurance, to continue. I will say something foolish or headstrong, and they will never listen again.

"Please, great mother of all and protectress of the Tuatha dé Danann, hear my plea for help."

Sorcha leaned down and pressed her forehead against the soft moss. She held her breath as she waited, but expected no response. No matter how many times she cried out for help, the Fae always ignored her.

It wasn't in their nature. Even the Seelie court was fickle, their rules keeping them strictly away from humans. The Tuatha dé Danann were separate from those rules. They were the beginning and the end, the start of all Fae. But that didn't mean they liked humans any more than their brethren.

Her heart thundered in her ears. Was that a giggle in the forest? Unlikely. Although, if it was, perhaps the Fae were listening.

She waited until her knees ached and her back screamed for relief. The moss turned cold beneath her fingers, the water glimmering in bright droplets upon her nails.

"Please," she whispered again. "Just this once, please, listen to me."

A branch cracked. That was no giggle, nor was it caused by the wind. Sorcha's spine tensed further, and she squeezed her hands in the moss. Could it be possible? Could this be the moment Danu finally answered her?

Loud thuds echoed nearby, the pawing of a large creature she could not see. Sorcha flinched. The breeze picked up. Its heat scorching along her shoulders and whistling in her ears.

"Women do not belong on their knees, child."

The voice sliced through her consciousness like a well-sharpened blade. It was the rustling of leaves, the gong of sword striking shield, the crunch of teeth biting through an apple. Sorcha's hands began to shake as she pushed herself up onto her elbows and lifted her gaze.

Her eyes caught upon hooves that sparkled and faded into human feet. A swath of rich green fabric tumbled down atop them. The tail of a golden belt lashed out and settled against rounded hips.

The woman was tall. So tall she rivaled the surrounding trees. Her mane of red hair hung heavy to her waist, the color so vivid that Sorcha's eyes burned. Harsh angles defined a face not delicate, but strong. Verdant eyes glowed as she stared at Sorcha.

"Are you hard of hearing, girl? Stand up."

Sorcha stood, albeit slowly. "You aren't Danu."

"Astute for a woman so willing to bow."

The pieces fell together. The sound of stamping hooves, the red hair, the triskele carved into the stones. Sorcha's brows drew together. "You're Macha, aren't you?"

"And you're at my shrine."

Every muscle in her body seized. There were many myths regarding Macha, and all claimed she was dangerous. A sister to the Morrighan, Macha was known for her strength on the battlefield. She would paint woad upon her skin and hack through any man who stood in her way. The fanciful tales claimed she had a steed made of fire and trapped dead men's souls within her blade.

"I meant no disrespect," Sorcha said as she dropped her gaze. "Please accept my sincerest apologies. I will leave."

The blade at Macha's waist shone sunlight into Sorcha's eyes. Lifting a hand, she held her breath and stepped backward. Each step brought her closer to freedom and the promise of life. This was no kind Fae before her.

"I did not give you permission to leave, human."

Sorcha winced. "What would you have me do?"

"You asked for help. I'm interested in providing it."

"I—" It was bad luck to not accept a Fae's favor. Except this didn't feel like a gift. This felt like an offer which would require a price. "I don't make deals with faeries."

"Yet you came to what you thought was my mother's shrine? You begged for a favor just moments ago, but nothing is free. Here I am, Sorcha of Ui Neill. Ask your favor of me, and perhaps I shall be kind."

Her mind raced through the details she remembered of this Tuatha dé Danann. Macha was a war Fae, but also was known for protection. She had once been a kind and motherly figure before mankind tried to kill her and her babe.

There was a small chance that Macha would help. Sorcha was a strong woman, capable, and frustrated by the limitations men placed upon her. Her frustrations would call out to a faerie such as this.

None of this guaranteed safety. In fact, Sorcha might argue the exact opposite was more likely to happen.

Faeries weren't trustworthy creatures.

"I wish to stop the blood beetle plague," she said. "If there is a way to save my father, to prevent other deaths, I would like to know it."

"You are a smart girl. No promises, no questions, just a statement I cannot interpret in any other way." One of Macha's brows lifted. "I like you."

"I did not come here to beg for help from the Fae. Nothing comes without a price, and I have very little to give."

Macha's gaze turned stormy, and she strode towards Sorcha. Closer and closer she came, growing ever larger until they stood toe to toe. Sorcha's neck ached as she tilted her head. The faerie was easily seven feet tall and her hair made her seem even larger. The cloud of color sparked with static electricity.

"You want something that you are incapable of without help. You have to ask for it, Sorcha. Ask for my assistance, and I will give you all you desire."

"I don't know your price."

"And you won't until we strike a deal."

Sorcha sucked in a deep breath. Their chests brushed, a zing of magic traveling through her and sparking at the points of her ears.

"Will you provide a cure for the blood beetles?"

A soft sigh brushed across Sorcha's face and smelled of crushed grass. "Yes, I will. And I will do even more. So long as you are on this journey to find your cure, your father will remain alive."

Sorcha thought she might faint. "Papa?"

"It is the least I can do. I am sending you on a quest, little human. Far from your homeland, from your family, from everything you know. Centuries have passed since I last saw the cure you seek. Even I am uncertain where it lies, although I have my suspicions."

"If you don't know where it is, how am I supposed to find it?"

"There are others who know." Macha cupped Sorcha's chin, her hand so large it touched both pointed tips of her ears. "You will start by finding my children. Their names are Cormac and Concepta. Use their knowledge wisely."

"You want me to find two faeries? Here?"

"They were banished from the Otherworld and remain in yours."

"Glamoured or invisible?" Sorcha asked.

Macha's hand clenched, squeezing Sorcha's jaw until her eyes watered. "Glamoured to look as you do. They will appear as nobles, but they should be the only twins living in the same manor. Find them, and you'll start your journey."

"What do I say to them?"

"That I asked you to find them, and that they owe me a favor. Tell them what you seek. They will guide you."

Sorcha wasn't so certain that was the truth. Two unknown Fae who owed a favor to a Tuatha dé Danann? Her breakfast rose dangerously high in her throat.

Air filled her lungs as Macha stepped away. The myths had not prepared her for the cold gaze of a Fae. She wanted to flee from that angry look. What had she done? Had she somehow insulted this faerie of war before she had even started?

"Thank you," Sorcha said, "for my father. He has suffered for far too long."

"I care little for human life, but I can see how important it is to you. As such, it is my pleasure."

Though it made her sweat to ask, Sorcha swallowed hard and murmured, "What is your price?"

Endless possibilities unfolded before her. The Fae might ask for a child, for Sorcha's life, or something as simple as an unnamed favor.

She wasn't certain how much she was willing to pay. Many faceless infected people may not be worth a life enslaved. But for her father? He had saved her from begging, took her out of the slums and into the city, gave her a life.

How could she say no?

Macha bent and dipped her fingers in the holy water of the shrine. She licked the droplets and smiled. "You will endure hardship, pain, and perhaps even death. I will enjoy watching your struggles as payment."

"What kind of quest are you sending me on?" Sorcha heard her own voice as though underwater. Distorted and slow, it echoed back upon her.

"One that benefits the both of us," Macha replied. "You get your cure. I get my children back."

"What does the cure have to do with your children?"

"Nothing at all. But in finding your cure, I trust you will bring my children back to Tír na nÓg."

"The land of youth?" Sorcha stumbled over the words. "The Otherworld?"

"I am growing tired of explaining my decisions to you. Leave now, or I will run you out of this shrine and rescind my offer."

Sorcha scooped up her bag and spun on her heel. She could not risk the Fae changing her mind. This was a chance to save her father! To save *everyone*.

At the edge of the clearing, she paused. One foot crossed the threshold of the shrine and into the forest beyond. The other remained in the enchanted glen.

She looked over her shoulder at the faerie who watched her with calculating eyes. Macha reclined on the mossy ground, her fingers playing in the burbling water of her shrine.

"Why are you doing this?" Sorcha asked one last time.

"I, too, have been at the mercy of men, more times than I wish to recount. My mother would tell you the best way to answer them is to remain steadfast, quiet, and continue doing the right thing." Macha's eyes flashed brilliant green. "I am not a woman, but sword and shield. I will carve my own path, or I will force others to create it for me."

"What does that have to do with me?"

Their gazes met and Macha smiled. "You are the same, little human. They tell you time and time again you are a pool of still water. Yet, we both know underneath the surface a tempest rages. I will enjoy seeing your claws grow."

Unsettled, Sorcha plunged into the forest. Branches pulled at her clothing and tugged at her hair. She did not let them hold her. This was no longer a safe place, no longer a haven.

Her breath sawed out of her body in ragged gasps. She had made a deal with a faerie. What had she been thinking? Such a contract was binding.

What if she didn't find the cure? Sorcha stumbled out of the forest and fell onto her hands and knees near the carriage road. Had she agreed to go on a wild goose chase for the rest of her life? Would she spend eternity searching for an impossible thing?

She couldn't breathe enough air. It stuck in her throat and made her chest ache. Her ribs expanded, her mouth opening and closing as she tried to breathe.

Logically, she knew this was a panic attack. Some part of her mind recognized her imagination carrying her away from sanity. Her body did not recognize this, vomit rising from her stomach.

She coughed as she expelled her breakfast violently. Mucus hung in streams from her nose and mingled with the drool dripping from her lips.

What had she done?

"Inhale, Sorcha," she muttered. "One breath. Two breaths."

In and out, she counted every heartbeat and movement of her lungs. Birds chirped in the trees nearby. Twenty-seven chirps before they stopped. Carriage wheels creaked and stones crunched under their weight.

Her fingers curled in the soil. She would be all right. There was a cure. There had to be a cure, because faeries couldn't lie.

Now it was up to her, as it always had been, to save her people. Her family. She could find the one thing that would save them all and kill the blood beetles. Her life had meaning again, other than just being the midwife who serviced both a brothel and the entire town.

"Is that Sorcha?" The sound of the carriage paused. Hooves stamped the ground, making her flinch. "Sorcha, darling, what are you doing?" —the voice was familiar—"It is not safe to be on the road in the twilight hours."

"Dame Agatha. It is so good to see you again."

"Well, I should hope it would be under better circumstances than finding you on the side of the road! Get up, child."

The words were too similar to the faerie's. Panic fled to the back of her mind, resolve and purpose taking its place.

A red carriage had paused in front of her. The wheels gleamed with gold paint, along with the emblem of a rose. A delicate flowered curtain was drawn back from the small window and framed Dame Agatha's aged face.

"How are you feeling?" Sorcha wearily asked her least favorite patient.

"Well, I was just about to call upon you, Sorcha. I have exciting news!"

"You're to be blessed with a child?"

"Again!"

"Again," Sorcha repeated with a sigh. Her lie had been the truth after all. "Congratulations are in order, then. I suppose you'll be stopping by the brothel soon?"

"Oh goodness, no, I'll need you to come to *me*."

Dame Agatha had never come to the brothel for any of her treatments. She considered their home to be a den of miscreants and thieves, no matter how many times Sorcha assured her it was the safest place in Ui Neill.

She wiped her mouth on a sleeve, trying her best to ignore the acidic taste of vomit on her tongue. "This is not your usual carriage, Agatha."

"Oh goodness, no. A dear friend loaned this to me. I'm going to visit them! Certainly, you've heard of the MacNara twins. Lovely folk."

Sorcha froze. "Twins?"

"Oh, you haven't heard of them yet? They are new to this area, but the nicest family you'll ever meet. So giving! So *progressive*."

She glanced towards the forest. "Thank you, again, for making this easy on me."

Movement stirred branches nearby. Sorcha thought she saw a flash of unnatural green and the glint of fiery hair.

"Agatha? Might your friends have need of a midwife?"

"Well, I don't see why not. You know I love having you meet my friends, Sorcha. Not your sisters, of course. I'm certain you understand why. But do come with me! It will be so refreshing to have a new face at these boring social gatherings."

Sorcha looked down at her earth-stained dress and the dark stain of vomit on her sleeve. Her sisters would be far more presentable, even after a hard day's work. It was a shame Agatha would never realize that.

"It would be my honor, Agatha." Sorcha stepped onto the footrest and opened the carriage door. Black cushions and waxed wood covered the interior of the impressive carriage.

"You can tell me what you think of names for this newest little one."

"Ah, how many is it now?"

"Nine, child. You should know. You've delivered them all!"

"Right," Sorcha said as she settled onto the seat across from Agatha. "My apologies, I lost count at seven."

"Truthfully, so did I. What do you think of Derval?"

Their carriage ride was dreadfully boring. Sorcha kept a smile plastered on her face and showed more teeth than was necessary. Agatha continued to prattle on without caring if anyone was listening. By the time they reached the stately manor of the MacNara twins, Sorcha was certain they had debated every name under the sun.

She was ready to get out of this cramped space. The scenery passed by at a slower pace than Sorcha could have seen if she was walking. The company turned out to be less than agreeable, and the destination could not live up to the promised entertainment.

But she would be a fool to not take this opportunity while it lasted.

They slowed to a stop, and the driver struck his hand against the ceiling. Sorcha opened the carriage door and stared up at the splendorous home. White marble gleamed in the splashed pink of the setting sun. The house was four stories high with rare glass windows. Twin staircases rose from the ground, meeting in a half circle that led to the red front door.

"My goodness," Sorcha whispered.

"It is quite a sight, isn't it?" Agatha said as she stepped out of the carriage. "They are impressive people with more wealth than they need. If they continue spending it on such things, I say let them keep it! Give us *plebeians* more sights like this." She winked. "It does a body good to see real beauty."

Normally, she wouldn't agree. But the stately manor might change her opinion if it was as beautiful on the inside as it was on the outside.

Agatha smoothed a hand down the silk of her gown, which was an unusual choice for visiting nobles who were partial to velvet and fine embroidery.

Did the other woman know the twins weren't human?

Tentatively, Sorcha asked, "Agatha, why are you meeting with the MacNara twins?"

"Oh," she lifted a hand and fanned her face. "They invited me to their manor, so of course I said yes. It's good to meet one's neighbors."

"They are hardly our neighbors, Agatha. They live half a day's ride from us."

Sorcha noted the way Agatha's eyes slanted to the side. The other woman pressed a hand against her throat as though she might still the pulse fluttering there. "Can you keep a secret, dearest?"

"Yes," Sorcha said, but she already knew what Agatha would say.

"The gossips aren't always right, but it's said the MacNara twins have some… gifts. I know in my progressed age that having a child will be difficult. But I already love this one as much as the rest, and I want it to survive."

"You want to make a deal with them."

"It's not a deal with the devil, my goodness! They're blessed."

"They're faeries, Agatha."

A measured stare filled the silence, stilling Sorcha's bitter tongue. "They are *not* faeries, Sorcha. There's no such thing as faeries, but there are blessed people."

Blessed? Sorcha wanted to smack some sense into the woman. Faeries were not blessed creatures hailing from the Heavens. They were earthen spirits making deals which required payment. Why couldn't Agatha see the truth in these thinly veiled secrets?

For all she wanted to get started on this journey, Sorcha didn't want Agatha's life to hang in the balance. They shouldn't stay here. Surely, the cure could wait until the new babe arrived. The thought left a foul taste upon her tongue.

"It's a bad idea to make deals with things you don't understand," Sorcha said. "Perhaps we should go."

"Nonsense. We've made it this far, and I refuse to turn back." Agatha lifted a hand when Sorcha opened her mouth. "I won't hear any more of it, Sorcha. I've made my decision. You can come with me or not, though I will feel sorely abused if you do not come with me. I invited you, and here you are. I've never known you to be a woman who goes back on her word."

So, she was frightened to go on by herself. With a lifted brow, Sorcha reached out and took Agatha's arm. "All right. Let's go."

The unrecognizable footman stayed with the carriage. As the women crested the stairs, the hair on Sorcha's arms lifted. She glanced over her shoulder at the footman who had eerily not moved in the slightest.

"Sorcha?" Agatha asked.

"Everything is fine." At the last possible second, Sorcha swung the hag stone around her neck into her hand. She lifted it to her eye and blinked.

He sat perched upon the carriage with natural grace, his long legs covered by fine, black cloth and a stately jacket pressed into crisp folds. She might have thought him human if he hadn't been missing his head.

"Dullahan?" she whispered.

She dropped the hag stone and rushed after Agatha who was already entering the MacNara estate. The inside of the building was as stunning as its exterior. White walls gleamed with gold filigreed wallpaper. A grand stairwell of white marble and light gray swirls spiraled from the ground floor and higher.

A butler greeted them and draped Agatha's pale blue cloak over his arm in a swath of color. His mustache twitched when Sorcha walked through the door, her slippers trailing mud across the pristine floor.

"Sorcha, isn't it lovely?" Agatha's voice echoed in the room. "They are gracious hosts to allow us entrance to such a grand palace."

"Hardly a palace," she responded. Although the home was beautiful, it was lacking a certain human touch. There were no portraits, no artwork, nothing but blank walls and empty space. In fact, it looked as though no one lived there at all.

The butler grunted his disapproval.

"Agatha, please don't go anywhere without me." Sorcha glanced around nervously.

The Dame's heels clicked upon the marble floors. Sorcha's own feet remained silent. Her leather slippers hardly touched the ground as she raced to the other end of the room. Snagging onto Agatha's sleeve, Sorcha steered her back towards the foyer.

"Dearie, you're far too concerned about my well-being. I may be in the delicate stages of pregnancy, but I assure you, I have carried many a child to term."

"I remember, Agatha."

They passed by the stairs just as a voice slithered through the air. "And who, may I ask, are you?"

The overwhelming scent of oranges filled the air. Sticky and sweet, it coated her lungs with citrus.

Sorcha glanced up at the head of the stairs. A woman stood there, far too beautiful to be human. Unbound golden curls fell in waves to her waist. A red silk dress caressed her body as she shifted, the deep V between her breasts leaving little to the imagination. Gold chains laced across her body, dipping down her torso, and framing her shoulders.

"Oh, my," Agatha murmured.

Sorcha swallowed hard. "Agatha, perhaps you should tell her why we're here."

"I know why the old woman is here," the MacNara twin said. "What I don't know is why *you're* here."

"I invited her." Sorcha felt the Dame tremble. "I assumed your hospitality would stretch farther than just my presence."

"You were wrong." Concepta's hand curled around the railing of the stairwell. "But you have done it, nonetheless. I'll speak with your friend alone."

Agatha spluttered, "Well, I *never*. She is my companion. You must not separate us."

"Ivor, please show our guest to the blue room."

"I absolutely am not leaving without Sorcha." The butler walked up and placed his hand against Agatha's spine. "Take your hand off me, sir! Sorcha? *Sorcha*."

"It's fine, Agatha," Sorcha replied. "I don't mind meeting with Lady MacNara. Please rest your feet in the blue room. I'm certain Ivor won't mind providing you with tea and biscuits."

The unimpressed stare the butler gave her suggested that he had not, in fact, planned on providing tea and biscuits. Sorcha narrowed her eyes.

He sighed. "It would be my pleasure, Dame Agatha. Please follow me."

They filed out of the room. A flash of silk was the last bit of her wayward patient she might ever see.

Sorcha sighed again. Faeries were proving to be even more difficult than the stories had claimed.

"Well?" Concepta asked from above. "Are you coming or not?"

"Are you in a rush, Fae?" she asked as she made her way up the steps. "One might think an immortal would be more patient."

The faerie bared her teeth. "And one might think a weak little mortal would know how to watch her tongue."

Sorcha reached the top of the stairs and shrugged. "I've never been good at that."

"You should learn." Concepta lunged forward, anger turning her eyes from crystal blue to raw amber. Sorcha gasped as the faerie's hand wrapped around her throat, gripping the other woman's wrists, but unable to break free. Concepta shoved her backward until Sorcha's spine hit the wall with a harsh crack, her eyes losing focus as pain bloomed behind her eyes.

She blinked. There was something off about the faerie's face. It twisted and warped in anger, shimmering with sparkling light in one moment and lined with rage the next.

The snarl that tumbled from Concepta's mouth wasn't human. Guttural and raw, it vibrated in Sorcha's ears.

"You reek of my mother, human." Concepta's lips brushed Sorcha's ear. "Are you another of her pets? What foul poison have you come to spread?"

Black spots crept at the edge of her vision. Her mouth gaped open, and a wheeze escaped her lips.

"If you cannot speak, I'm afraid I'll have to tell my mother you died without ever delivering her venomous message."

Sorcha pushed her thumbs into the sensitive tissue of Concepta's wrists. The pressure points allowed her the barest breath which she used to whisper, "Your favor."

The faerie's eyes widened. "What did you say?"

The grip upon Sorcha's throat lessened enough for her to cough and gasp, "Your mother said you owe her a favor."

"And she's using it for a little human?" Concepta shook her head. "Good guess, but not very believable."

"She said you knew how to cure the blood beetle plague."

"She said what?"

"Faeries can't lie," Sorcha rasped. "I know this as well as you. *Tell* me how to cure it."

Concepta released her and backed away. Her laughter sounded like hammers striking metal. "Oh, this is a pleasurable thing. You simply must meet my brother. He will like you."

There would be bruises on her throat. Delicately, Sorcha probed the muscles of her neck. They throbbed as if a noose had tightened across her airways. Faeries were strong, she noted, far stronger than any human.

She coughed. "Please."

"Yes, yes." Concepta waved a hand in the air. "Fine, then. Come meet my brother first. He'll want to know what's going on."

Was this it? Would she finally be able to save her father? Hope raised its head, filling her chest to the brim with happiness as fragile as a dandelion seed. It couldn't be this easy.

Could it?

The image of her Papa, skin moving with beetles, propelled her forward. The hallways were blank sheets of paper. White walls, white floors, gold filigree but nothing that suggested anyone lived here.

"Is this a new home?" she called out.

"No."

"Do many faeries live here?"

"Yes."

Odd, but Sorcha could see the sense in it. What faerie would decorate a human home with images of their family? A headless portrait would look out of place if not simply morbid.

She kept a hand around her neck as they twisted through empty room after empty room. A breeze trailed by. The distinct outline of a hand tugged at her gray skirt, pulling her forward.

Twin doors stood open at the end of the hallway. Beyond that, an oasis grew. Vines tangled from a ceiling which looked like a giant birdcage. Hydrangeas bloomed and filled the air with their sweet scent although they were not in season. An ornate fountain spewed mist into the air, white lilies twirling at its base. Brightly colored fabric spilled across the ground and was dotted with pillows.

People laid out upon the cushions. They held jeweled goblets in their hands, red wine pouring down their cheeks and onto their chests. Harp music gently wafted on the breeze from a musician in the far corner.

A man stretched near the fountain. His sculpted chest was bare to the sun, skin slicked with oil and well-tanned. Silk pooled around him, pants or skirt she could not discern. Red rubies wrapped around his throat and dangled on his forehead from a golden headpiece. A chain hung from his ear to a piercing in his nose.

The tingling sensation of magic pricked her skin. Sorcha clutched the hag stone at her neck.

"I wouldn't do that if I were you," Concepta said.

"Why not?"

"You don't know what kind of Fae live here, little human. If you peer into our world, you will run from this place screaming."

"As you are Macha's children, I assumed you were of the Seelie court."

"You know very little of our kind. Seelie or Unseelie is not a breed." Concepta flicked a glance towards her. "It's a choice, whether you want to follow the rules or you don't."

She watched as the faerie picked her way through the lounging people. She draped herself across the fountain next to her brother and dangled her fingers in the water. Sorcha thought she looked very much like her mother. It didn't seem like a safe observation to voice.

"Brother," Concepta said. "I brought you a gift."

"You know I dearly love gifts," Cormac murmured. "But human

playthings break so easily."

His gaze felt like a physical touch upon her skin, lingering on the swells of her breasts and the apex of her thighs. A slow smile spread across his face, teeth stained green by the viscous drink he nursed.

"I am not here for your entertainment," Sorcha replied. "I was sent by your mother."

"And Concepta didn't kill you yet? You must be a very impressive warrior."

"I am no fighter, Lord MacNara. Macha said you owe her a favor and I am here to collect."

He tsked. "Oh, sister, this is boring. Take her away."

How could he say that when he hadn't even listened? The glee in Concepta's unnatural eyes suggested she had known this would happen.

Her father needed her. Her sisters needed her. Gods above, the entire world needed help, and Sorcha had the rare opportunity to do so!

The faerie woman moved to stand up, but paused when Sorcha flinched forward.

"Wait!" Sorcha shouted so loud that even the music stopped. "I was told you know how to cure the blood beetle plague. I will do anything for your knowledge."

Cormac leaned forward and pointed a jeweled finger at her. "Anything?"

It was a sharp question, capable of slicing through flesh and bone. Was she willing to do anything?

"Yes," she said firmly. "Anything."

Concepta trailed a finger down her brother's arm. "I told you she wasn't boring."

"We're going to help her?"

"Yes."

"Even against our better judgment?"

"We have better judgment?"

Their hands met and fingers intertwined. "It's against the rules, sister."

"I like to break rules."

"It will cause trouble."

"For us?"

"There are always ripples."

Concepta lifted their hands and pressed a lingering kiss against his knuckles. "Then we will ride the waves they cause. I think this one will be worth the trouble if she succeeds."

"What makes you think she can?" Cormac cast a disbelieving glance at Sorcha. "She's just a slip of a girl."

"I am strong," Sorcha interjected. "I have brought countless children into this world. I know the cruelty of man first-hand, and I fear very little. There is much for me to lose if you don't help me."

The words seemed to catch Cormac's interest. He canted his head to the side and asked, "Like what?"

"My father."

He snorted. "My father was a king among mortal men, and he did little for me. Try again."

"My sisters. They live with my father, and if he dies of the blood beetle plague, they will become ill as well. I will not watch them die."

"You love your sisters?"

"More than I can say."

"In that, we see eye to eye." He released his hold upon Concepta's hand to trail his fingers through her golden curls, dragging a thumb across her lips. "Fine, we will help you."

"You know how to find the cure?"

"Our mother does not lie. We know how to cure the blood beetle plague."

Her heart stopped. The relief surging through her veins made her knees weak. "How?" she whispered. "Please tell me how, and what I need to do."

"Oh, it's not as simple as just telling you. We don't *have* the cure.

We only know where it is."

"Is it an object?"

"In a way," Cormac chuckled. His sister laid her head in his lap, then kicked her feet into the air. "The cure comes in the form of a person, at least for you."

"A person?"

"One simple being whom you will return to us."

Concepta rolled to her side. "You'll bring him back to the mainland, and then you'll have your cure. Eventually."

"Why would I bring a person here? What does that have to do with the blood beetle plague?"

"You don't need to know the information. All you need to do is travel to Hy-brasil."

"The cursed isle?" Sorcha blinked. "It can only be seen every seven years. I don't have time to wait seven years!"

"Then it's lucky for you that the time to see that isle is actually…" Concepta looked up at her brother. "Now?"

"In a few weeks."

"In a few weeks," she repeated. "And then you can see the isle. You can get our faerie, by whatever means necessary of course. Bring him back, and you'll have your cure."

Sorcha shook her head in confusion. "You're not making any sense. Do you have the cure or not?"

"We do."

"Then why aren't you giving it to me now?" She huffed in frustration. "Your mother said you owe her a favor."

Concepta's eyes sparked yellow again. She lifted herself into a crouch upon the stone lip of the fountain. "Are you saying I'm a liar?"

"We both know faeries can't lie."

"My mother's favor saved your life. You owe us another, which means you will bring back that pathetic excuse for a Prince! And if he screams or cries when he sees me I will bite off his tongue with my teeth."

A harp string snapped. Sorcha startled at the sound and turned to see all inhabitants of the room had fled. The musician was the last, the fabric of her dress caught on her own instrument.

Sorcha's teeth chattered against each other. "What are you going to do to him, if I bring him back?"

"That is none of your concern," Cormac said. "Do we have a deal?"

She was making too many deals with faeries all in one day. Her gut screamed that this was a bad idea. Macha was one thing. The revered Tuatha dé Danann valued female life and strength. These two? Some thread in their mind had unraveled, leaving gaping holes where insanity grew.

She watched Concepta crawl into her brother's lap and stroke the flat planes of his chest.

"She will say yes," Concepta said.

"Will she?"

"She can't let go of a future where she is the 'hero.' So many people have told her 'Sorcha, you are just a woman. You cannot do what you think you can do.'"

"Humans are idiots."

"Humans are more than idiots. They are good only to feed the earth when they die."

Sorcha swallowed. "I don't want to hurt anyone."

Concepta's head snapped around, glaring over her shoulder with cat-like eyes. "You've hurt people your entire life. A stillborn child you couldn't save, a screaming pain-filled night of a woman who did not desire a babe, a changeling you *left* near the woods."

"I did what I had to do. I have never killed anyone."

"But you will. Someday, everyone does. Whether by choice or not, we're all killers. It's far past time for you to accept that."

Sorcha straightened her spine. She was no murderer. If this woman wanted to prove something with her cruel words, then all she managed to do was set Sorcha's resolve. If she had to choose between an unknown man and her family, Sorcha would always choose her family.

"All right. I'll bring him back."

"Alive," Cormac added.

"Alive and well. I will convince him to return, and I won't force him."

Concepta giggled. "You can try. I don't think he'll come back at all. Still, it will be fun to know someone is bothering him. You'll leave now."

"Excuse me?"

"Now."

Ivor the butler appeared at her side. Sorcha squeaked when he grasped her arm. She stared down at the normal human hand and couldn't shake the feeling that there were only three fingers touching her bicep.

"Wait!" she cried out. "I have to say goodbye to my family."

"You're boring me again," Cormac grumbled. "We said you will leave now."

"I need my things."

"What things? You won't need things where you're going."

"Personal items, clothing, a promise that I'll return. I *cannot* leave without letting them know where I am going."

Ivor pulled at her arm.

"Stop it!" Sorcha screamed and raked at his hand with ragged fingernails. "Let *go* of me, you brute. Have some pity. I don't want my sisters to think I'm dead!"

Cormac lifted a hand. "Wait."

The butler froze, and she heard the jarring cough of his breath.

"Say that again," Concepta ordered.

"I don't want my sisters to think I'm dead." Tears burned in Sorcha's eyes. "They'll worry about me, and I cannot abide that."

Cormac trailed his hand along his sister's jaw, caressed his hands down her flushed skin, and followed the V of her silken dress. She smiled and closed her savage eyes. "We will allow you to say goodbye. We know the rarity of a blood bond and cherish the love that blooms between siblings."

The pull on her arm returned, and Sorcha did not look back upon the twisted twins who had freed her. She had a chance to do something right and help those in need.

As she stumbled down the steps, Ivor shoved her into the carriage with Agatha who was pale as snow.

"Are you all right, my dear?" she asked.

"No," Sorcha replied. "But, I think I will be. We're going home."

She glanced out the window and watched the rolling green hills become a blur. The faerie carriage sped towards the city with unnatural speed.

CHAPTER THREE
THE SHIP

Briana huffed as she followed Sorcha. "You can't leave!"

"I have to, and I already told you why, so please stop trailing along behind me. I have to get my things."

"You haven't even told us where you're going." Briana's voice thickened with unspoken emotion.

"I don't know where I'm going."

The Dullahan coachman had brought her straight to the brothel. He didn't speak, and she wasn't about to lift the hag stone to her eye again, but she understood his quick gestures. She didn't have a lot of time to make her goodbyes.

It was easier that way. Her sisters were prone to hysterics, especially when they weren't getting what they wanted. Sorcha had been their crutch for a long time.

Although they were all close, she was the one they went to in times of struggle. That meant she heard all their secrets, their stories, their gripes about each other and the life they lived. She kept them all safe, childless, and made certain every bruise or scrape healed. They weren't likely to admit it, but Sorcha was an integral part of their lives.

She would miss them so much.

Briana snatched a nightshirt out of Sorcha's hands. "Absolutely not! I'm not blind. You show up in some fancy carriage with a coachman, a *coachman*, and then you think I will believe you're off to cure the beetles? Sorcha! If you wanted to go off with some well-to-do nobleman, you know we'd be happy for you. Why are you lying?"

"I'm not lying."

"There you go again. Is it Geralt? Is that why you don't want to tell us?"

Sorcha scooted past Briana and stuffed another skirt into an oversized pack she could carry over her shoulder. It was better than smacking her sister in the face. "I can't believe you would even suggest I would accept Geralt's proposal!"

"He's rich. He's got plenty of land, and he's obviously in love with you, though I can't understand why he's still wasting his time when you so clearly won't come to your senses."

"I'm not marrying Geralt." Sorcha grabbed an armful of her journals and dumped them into the bag with her clothing.

"Why are you taking those?"

"I might need them."

"You can come back for them. Surely whoever you are going to see will let you come home? We don't mind letting you keep this room." Briana let out a frustrated grunt and ran her fingers through her hair.

She wanted to keep the room, too. There were so many memories within these walls. Sweet and cherished moments where her sisters had shared secrets and weathered nightmares.

Sorcha devoured all the details she could find. The marks on the door where she'd kept track of Rosaleen's growth. The flowerpot on the windowsill, now empty, because Briana had insisted the plant would grow back. The carved trunk her father had worked so long on, even though it looked more like scratch marks than the whale he said it was.

Life had a strange way of pulling her away from here. Every moment of her life, she had spent rushing away to faerie glens and leaving offerings. Now there was a chance to see the Otherworld in person, and she was so frightened to leave.

"Briana, I love you. I don't know if I've said it enough, but I do."

Her sister's face creased in worry. "What are you doing? What choice have you made, Sorcha? You can trust me."

"I already told you," Sorcha brushed her hand along Briana's cheekbone, memorizing the shape of it. "The faeries offered me a deal to cure the beetle plague. I won't see Papa die."

She left her sister in the room and lumbered down the stairs. The pack was too heavy for her, but she refused to let any of it go. The books were important. Every herb, every poultice, every bit of her mother's teachings was in those books. Where she went, they went.

Three flights of stairs felt like a full day's hike. Heaving the pack to the floor, she quietly made her way to Papa's room.

Knocking, she called out, "Are you awake?"

"For you, always."

Sorcha smiled, blinking back the tears welling in her eyes. She slipped into her father's room and closed the door behind her. Shadows hid the salt tracks on her cheeks.

"You're leaving," he said.

"You heard?"

"How could I not? Your sister was screeching like a banshee."

She settled onto the edge of his bed. "You always said at least one of us was a changeling child."

"Yes, but I always thought it was you."

"I made a deal." She blurted the words out and let them hang in the air between them. "There wasn't another way. The Guild won't listen to me, you're getting worse, and the beetles are spreading. Someone had to do something, Papa."

"And that someone had to be you?"

"Are you so surprised?"

He pushed himself up onto his elbows, gray-streaked hair plastered to his skin with sweat. This was the reason why she would risk her life. This man, who had given up so much to give her a chance.

Papa slicked his hair back, huffing out a tired breath. "I woke up this morning, and the beetles were worse than ever. I coughed up blood for the first time, and I know what that means. I didn't tell you because I didn't want you to worry. Then, this afternoon, they stopped moving. I don't know why. I don't know how. But they stopped and my first thought was that you had something to do with it."

A tear slid down her cheek. "Papa—"

He lifted a hand. "I'm not finished. I didn't raise you for the beginning bit of your life, but I saw a good girl when I met you. I never met your mother, but she obviously raised you right. The others are spoiled, vain, cruel to each other. You have never been like them. I knew from the moment you set your heart on curing me, you would find some way to stop this. I'm glad it's you. I'm sad you must leave me to do it, and I hope you didn't trade your soul for my old life. But I will stand by you if this is what you want."

"Oh Papa," she choked as she threw herself into his arms.

She hadn't done this since she was a little girl. It was far more difficult to fit in his lap now that she was full grown, but she tried her best. He rubbed her back as she fought back tears.

"It's not a shameful thing to want to save your family, Sorcha."

"They think I'm running away to be with a man. As if I would leave you? Them? I love you all too much to leave without good reason."

"And they love you. It's why they're so upset."

"What am I going to do without you?"

He chuckled. "I imagine you'll do just fine. Do you know where you're going?"

"You believe me?" She lifted her head from his shoulder. "You don't think I'm crazy or lying?"

"You've always seen faeries, Sorcha. I thought you were crazy when you were little, but then I started noticing things myself. Tiny hands used to tug your hair all the time. You stayed the night with Rosaleen, but your dresses were all perfectly pressed and folded on your bed. Strange things happen around you, child."

"Most would say I'm a witch." She wiped at her eyes, catching the salty tears upon her fingertips.

Papa shook his head, the deep grooves in his forehead standing out in stark relief. "You're no witch any more than your mother was. Faeries are picky who they choose to help, so I'd say you're lucky. Not cursed."

She didn't want to let him go. She wanted to stay curled up against his chest forever, or until he stood up as a strong man again.

Her chest heaved with silent sobs. "I don't know what I'm doing, Papa. Is this the right thing to do?"

"Does it feel like it?" He tapped her chest. "In here?"

"Yes."

"Then it's the right thing to do, and family be damned. You'll return to us someday, I'm certain of it."

She wasn't. Sorcha had a sick feeling deep within her belly that this was the last time she'd see him. Her hands shook as she cupped his cheeks.

"Goodbye."

He pressed his palm against the back of her hand, holding it against his heart. "Goodbye, sweet girl."

If she stayed for a moment longer, she would never leave. She threw herself from the bed in a whirlwind of movement and rushed out the door.

"Sorcha?" Rosaleen called. "Sorcha, are you really leaving?"

"Tell the others I love them!" she shouted and scooped up her bag.

The front door slammed behind her so hard the shutters shook. The Dullahan started, a bland expression on his face.

She tossed the bag into the carriage and lunged in behind it. Her fist slammed against the roof.

"Go!"

The whip cracked, an unnatural sound of creaking bone. Tears fell freely down her face as the carriage raced away from the brothel. Her sisters poured out of the house, their shouts echoing in her ears for miles down the road.

What had she done? Saying goodbye made her want to shatter into a thousand pieces. But a deal was a deal.

Sorcha had never been away from home. She'd only been alone once in her life, for three full days after her mother's corpse had stopped smoking. Those were dark memories. Thoughts her mind had hidden, so she wouldn't dwell upon the past.

Now, she'd be alone for an undetermined amount of time. Would she handle it well? Her heart felt like it was going to jump out of her chest. Short breaths expanded her lungs. Swirls of darkness blinked in front of her eyes.

She focused on the landscape flying past. They headed towards the sea, and she hadn't been to the ports since she was a girl. Her father had specifically avoided setting up a brothel near sailors. He said they were too frequent customers who never paid their debts. It was easier in a city where rich men might find their way down a dark alley.

Rolling green hills calmed her mind. Stone walls bisected the fields, built to remind everyone where their land was. Each stone glistened with moss, worn with age, touched by hundreds of passersby. White dots of sheep speckled the land.

Every now and then, they would pass over a stone bridge. Streams ran underneath them, housing trolls and goblins for the night. Sorcha could almost feel them, hidden in their hovels under the ground.

These emerald lands had always called out to her. This wasn't just a field. It wasn't just grass and sheep. This was home.

She pressed her head against the side of the carriage. The jolting movement thumped her skull against the wood every now and then, but even that didn't dull her torment. The land rooted her in the now, in the moment, in everything that wasn't the loss of her family.

She would see them again, Sorcha told herself. Even if it took years to get back.

Lush fields gave way to small homes with cultivated gardens. Then cobblestone paths snaked through the towns which grew larger and larger as they reached the ocean. She could smell salt and brine upon the air.

The carriage slowed as it passed through throngs of people in ragged clothes. Women with scarves over their heads avoided meeting her gaze, and men in moth-eaten wool leered at the carriage. Sailors who had seen better days wandered the docks, and farmers with dirt-streaked cheeks peddled their wares. Children snuck their hands into pockets for even the smallest of coins.

The wheels clattered as they passed by another brothel. Sorcha didn't recognize any of the women hanging out of the windows, but there was something in their haunted eyes that chilled her to the bone. These were not prostitutes looked after by a kind man. Run down, exhausted, and used, their bodies told the sad story of their lives.

Some part of her, equally chilled, wondered if that could be her future. Eventually, her skills wouldn't be necessary for the brothel, or they would find someone who would do the same things without the burden of room and board. Where would she go? There were no jobs for women like her. No husbands for a woman favored by the Fae.

She leaned back against the soft cushions of the carriage and refused to look back outside.

The ocean breeze coiled through her window, tangling in the loose strands of her hair. She could smell the fish, the seaweed, the salt of the ocean, and the sweat of men. She could hear the crashing waves as if she had put a seashell to her ear, but this was the real thing. These waves were just outside. All she had to do was lean forward one more time. Haunted eyes stared back at her, even though her eyes were closed.

"I will not become them," she whispered.

The carriage wheels squealed as they lurched to a halt. The Dullahan pounded the roof of the carriage, silently demanding she leave.

Sorcha let out a long, steadying breath. "You can do this, Sorcha.

You've done harder work before. All you have to do is step outside this carriage."

She curled her hand around her pack. Her fist clenched hard until the leather straps dug into her palms. Courage was never an easy thing to find even when necessary for survival.

The door banged open, and the Dullahan stared at her with dull eyes.

"Yes, I know," she said. "Give me a moment, please."

"It's time for you to go." His lips moved, but his voice came from his hands.

Sorcha shivered. The last thing she needed was a reminder that the man standing before her was actually headless, and that he was holding said head to speak with her.

"Where am I to go?"

"Find the ship with the yellow belly. It's Fae marked, and will take you to Hy-brasil."

"And when exactly is the isle visible?"

The Dullahan narrowed his fake eyes. "You have six days."

"Is that doable on a ship?"

"I'm no sailor, girl. Ask the captain."

He held out his hand for her to take. Sorcha couldn't force herself to touch him. The sparkle of malevolence in his gaze made her nervous, and she wondered if he would make her touch his head.

She leapt from the carriage on her own, shouldering the heavy weight of her pack with a sigh. "Thank you for the safe journey."

"You thank me for following my masters' orders?"

"Well, yes." She tucked a strand of hair behind her ear. "You may have been following orders, but you didn't pause overly long and it wasn't too bumpy of a ride. I didn't even get sick along the way. For that, I have you to thank. Not your masters."

His face twisted in confusion. "You are a strange human."

"You're not the first to say that. Oh," she shook her head. "I almost forgot."

Sorcha reached into her pocket and pulled out a small jar of honey she had neglected to leave at the shrine. In the rush to leave her home, she hadn't put it back in the kitchen where it belonged.

Now, the golden liquid felt wrong to keep. She held it out to the Dullahan with a soft smile. "Thank you."

"What am I supposed to do with this?" He held the jar close to his waist for his real eyes to look at.

"I don't know. It's a gift. Do you like honey?"

"I'm not the kind of Fae that likes honey."

"Then gift it to another, or enjoy it on your morning bread." Sorcha shrugged. "It matters little to me."

She walked past him, but noted the strange expression on his face. If she didn't know any better, Sorcha would have thought he was wistfully inspecting her gift. The Dullahan weren't known for their kindness. They announced death to all those who crossed their paths and cracked whips made of human spines.

Perhaps he'd never received a gift, she thought as she glanced over her shoulder.

Sorcha lifted the hag stone to her eye as he turned the carriage around. The candles still flickered inside, skulls grinning in decoration, the beautiful wood fading to stretched skin. Creaking wheels revealed human thigh bones spinning round. And the Dullahan himself, head seated in his lap with lips stretching from ear to ear, was staring back at her.

She lifted her hand in farewell just to have the satisfaction of seeing his confusion one last time.

The crowd swelled around her. People from all walks of life wandered the docks this afternoon. They drifted through the waves of people as a boat surfed upon the waves.

Colors and sound assaulted her senses. Vibrantly dressed women called out to her. Men shouted in the distance to raise the sails and hoist the anchors. A fish flopped on the ground where a woman hammered its head until it stopped moving. She moved onto the next while another woman sliced open its belly.

Sorcha's stomach lurched. Turning away from that side of the street, she struggled to make it to the docks. That was where she would find the captain. It had to be.

"Excuse me, sir?" she touched a man's shoulder. "Where might I find a ship with a yellow belly?"

"Why are you asking me?" he looked her up and down. "I don't give out charity to the likes of you."

"Charity?" Her mouth gaped open as he walked away from her.

Sorcha tried many times to find someone who could point her in the right direction. Women tried to hire her for work. Men mostly ignored her as if she didn't exist. One man even made her stand in front of him and shout to get his attention.

None of them wanted to point her towards a ship marked as the Dullahan had claimed. Did it not exist? She wanted to stand on a railing and scream. Someone in this gods forsaken port town must know where a ship with a yellow belly was!

The sun dipped low on the horizon and Sorcha gave up.

Weary and discouraged, she dropped her pack on the last dock and let it hit the wooden plans with a loud thunk. Heaving a sigh, she sat and swung her legs above the water.

"I just want to find a ship with a yellow belly," she moaned. She slumped forward and held her head in her hands. "It can't be *that* hard to find."

But it was. No one wanted to help her. Everyone's eyes were suspicious, and they thought the worst of her without asking who she was, why she was here, or what purpose she had in life. Why would people do that?

Her small sheltered town seemed so far away. Its people were backwards and dimwitted, but they were kind. She missed it already, and it hadn't even been a full day.

Sorcha sighed and tugged on her hair. "You can't give up. Too many people are relying on you."

She couldn't force herself to move. Her legs were aching from walking the docks all day. Pinpricks danced across her shoulders and spine from the heavy weight of her pack. Blisters seared the bottoms of her feet.

She might want to continue, but her body was telling her no. There was no possible way for her to get up and keep going. She hadn't even found a place to sleep.

"A stunning thing like you must charge a pretty penny for a night."

Her mind drifted for a moment. Would it really be that bad to entertain what her sister's had done for years? It seemed horrible in her mind, to give up her body for a few coins and a warm bed. But they didn't seem to mind.

No. She couldn't do it. She wasn't as strong as her sisters.

"Far too much for you," she retorted. Sorcha bared her teeth angrily and glanced up at the sailor staring down at her.

Dark hair and eyes blended into the night sky. A full beard masked most of his expression, although the gleam of teeth suggested he might be smiling. Dreadlocks pulled the rest of his hair away from his face.

His broad shoulders and chest were bare, and she imagined he was quite cold. A pelt of hair covered him from neck to dark pants. He wasn't wearing any shoes.

Sorcha's lips pursed. "*Far* too expensive."

"I wouldn't judge a book by its cover, sweet thing. Just how badly do you want somewhere warm to sleep?"

"Not that bad." She jerked her pack close to her side. "In fact, I'll go find a place myself. Thank you for reminding me it's growing dark."

"You sound like you aren't from around here, so let me tell you a few things. The docks aren't safe at night. Even for whores."

"I'm not a whore."

"Why else would you be on the docks? Respectable women stay up there," he pointed towards the candle light of the city. "The rest come down here to play with the likes of me. You look tired, hungry, and travel-stained. You either are a whore, or you will be soon enough."

Sorcha felt as though she needed to defend herself, or at least the title of whore. "My sisters run a successful brothel in Ui Neill. I don't take kindly to a man making less of their profession. And as for your knowledge," she struggled to her feet, "I'm looking for a particular ship. I need to travel far from here."

"A passenger?" he chuckled. "Sweetheart, you have to lie better than that."

"I am *not* lying. I was told to find the captain of a ship painted yellow and that he would take me to where I need to go."

"What do you want with the Saorsa?"

She smiled, the name was fitting. "The ship is named Freedom?"

"Who are you?" The man crossed his arms over his chest and frowned at her. "The Freedom doesn't take passengers."

"I'd think that would be the captain's decision."

"I am the captain."

The words echoed in Sorcha's mind. It couldn't be. Him? She looked him up and down. "You don't look like a captain."

"Have you ever seen a captain before?"

"No."

"Then you're a rather poor judge, aren't you?" His feet slapped against the dock as he turned away from her. "Oh, and by the way, being polite to a captain is a good start."

Sorcha stared at his back in shock. That was the captain? He couldn't be serious. She hadn't just ruined her chance at getting to Hybrasil without even asking him if he'd take her?

She licked her lips and shouted, "The MacNara twins sent me!"

The captain froze. "Excuse me?"

"The MacNara twins sent me to ask you for safe passage. I need to go to Hy-brasil, and they said you are the only person who can get me there."

The moon floated in the air behind him, outlining his figure with silver. "They were right, but I'm not going to the phantom isle."

"You're my only option. I have to go, and I need you to take me. I cannot apologize enough that I was rude, but it's imperative I go."

"You can't even see the isle."

"You can in six days," she said. "The Dullahan told me. Please."

He turned back towards her and crossed his arms. "What are you paying?"

"I have nothing to give."

"Anything in that pack?" He pointed at her bag.

"Personal items, mostly journals. I'm a healer. I can help in any way while aboard."

Hope blossomed. He was sizing her up as though she was a person, not just a piece of meat. That had to mean something. Perhaps he would take her.

At this point, Sorcha would swim to the damn isle if it meant progress.

A caw startled her. Sorcha flinched and looked at the sky. Outlined in darkness and stars, a raven called out again.

"I thought those only flew during the day," she whispered.

"Damned Fae," the captain grumbled. "All right. Fine. Onto the ship with you, but you will help the entire trip. And don't you forget what I've done for you."

"I won't service your men on the trip. I'm to have my own quarters."

"You'll be sharing mine," he grunted as he walked away from her. "Having a woman on board is bad luck enough. I'll be keeping an eye on you."

Sorcha grabbed her pack and swung it over her shoulder. Blisters be damned, she would make it to this ship. "My name is Sorcha. What's yours?”

“Manus.”

“The great?” She grinned. “It’s an apt name for a captain.”

“Now you’re complimenting me?” He glanced at her once she caught up. “Women are so damned difficult to understand. One minute you’re blistering my ears off, and the next you’re calling me after some historical figure.”

“You didn’t know the name Manus means great?”

“It’s a name. Who knows what their name means other than themselves?” He must have noticed the pout of her lips, because he added, “What’s yours mean?”

“Radiant,” Sorcha said with a soft smile.

Manus growled again and pointed at a ship out to sea. “That’s mine.”

“How are we to get there?”

“By boat.”

“I don’t see any other ships.”

“You ever been to the sea?” he said, lifting a brow. “You take a rowboat to the ship, and then we’ll climb aboard.”

One more thing she had to do, and then she could rest. Sorcha took a deep breath. This man could be lying to her. She certainly couldn’t see the bottom of the ship to determine if he was telling the truth.

“Okay,” she said. “Show me the way.”

Sorcha rolled to her side, eyes stuck together with sleep, her mouth dry. A scratchy blanket covered her legs and the overwhelming scent of tallow candles made her sneeze. She rubbed at her nose. The slight movement made her stomach roll.

“Oh, right,” she muttered. “I’m on a ship.”

She hadn't been bothered last night by the constant movement of waves. She'd been too tired to even notice there were men staring at her when the captain brought her aboard. Her pack was handed off with little complaint, and she didn't even ask where the captain would sleep. She face-planted onto the cot and propriety be damned.

Her stomach clenched hard, and her throat seized up.

"Ugh," Sorcha moaned as she burped. The ocean was making her entire body rebel now.

It took surprising effort to swing her legs over the edge of the cot. The whole time she held onto her mouth as though the effort would keep the bile in her stomach down. Another burp rocked her body forward. Bile burned the back of her throat.

Shaking her head violently, she lunged from the cot and pulled at the door. The fine details of the room didn't matter. The soft, polished statues stared with vacant eyes as she fled from the room and slammed her pelvic bone into the railing.

Vomit streamed out of her mouth and down the side of the ship. Sorcha hadn't thought there was anything left in her stomach. She didn't remember eating anything at all yesterday, but she couldn't stop the vomit.

"Ach, you didn't even have the decency to hit the water."

She recognized that voice. Her cheeks stained red, and she wiped at her lips. "I've never been seasick before. I apologize if I ruined your ship."

The man swaggering towards her didn't look at all like the captain she remembered. Tall and lean, he looked more like a pirate in a book.

Gold hoops swung from his ears. His hair and beard were so dark they gleamed blue in the sunlight. Richly tanned skin glistened with sweat like polished bronze. He had traded his worn pants for a fine cotton shirt tucked into a wide belt above tight black breeches. Knee-high boots—the leather folded over at the top, covering his knees—cracked against the deck of the ship as he strode towards her.

Sorcha was tongue-tied.

"Manus?"

"Don't recognize me, pretty thing?" His sleeves billowed as he lifted his arms. "A far cry from how we met, yes?"

"Very," she agreed. "I can hardly believe it's you."

He smiled, teeth flashing brilliant white against the dark tan of his skin. "Ah, that is the greatest compliment you might have given. You found me in a rather compromising position last night."

"One you are not proud of?"

"I'd never say I wasn't proud. Though you might have thought I was whoring, with good reason considering the words I said, I was actually visiting the one woman who's stolen my heart." He winked at her blush. "She is the only creature who can stand me. Sequestered on the land because the sea refuses to be her mistress, at least safely. I understand why my ladies fight over me, but, alas, I cannot choose between them."

The dramatic rendition of his life dissolved Sorcha's remaining seasickness. Her weak smile bolstered her strength, and she pushed herself away from the railing. "I'm certain they both miss you when you're gone."

"Neither of them miss me overly much, but it's kind of you. If you're feeling better, I ask that you join me in the center of the ship."

Sorcha's brows furrowed. "Why?"

"The ocean isn't a safe place, sweet thing. We're sailing into Fae waters, and I'd hate for you to be snatched up by a murúch."

"There are merrows here?" Sorcha flinched away from the railing.

"It's why the ship is painted yellow," Manus said. He walked towards her, slid an arm around her shoulders, and pulled her away from the railing. "Come, let me show you."

He reached into his pocket and placed a single sprig of heather on the railing. "A gift for the lovely ladies who guide my ship to safe waters."

Sorcha held her breath. She had always known faeries to take gifts that were offered, but they were always glamoured. Her gifts had disappeared. Running water erased the effects of magic, and she wouldn't need to use her hag stone to catch a glimpse of the Fae here.

A hand reached up from the edge of the ship. Impossibly pale, its long fingers were joined together by iridescent webbing. Rainbows sparkled upon the merrow woman's hand as she reached for the purple sprig. She was gentle as she pinched the blossom between her fingers and took it over the edge of the ship with her.

Sorcha's breath released in a great gust of air. "Was that?"

"It was."

"But the ship is so tall!"

"We put slats on the edge so they can climb it."

"Isn't that dangerous?" she asked. "Won't they drag you down into the ocean?"

"Myths aren't always the truth, Sorcha. We bring them gifts, and they give us safe passage. My men know the rules. If they wish to marry, then the marrows must be willing."

She blinked, surprised that anyone honored the Fae as she did. He read her expression well. The grin on his face was decidedly pleased as he sauntered away.

Free from watchful eyes, Sorcha lunged back to the railing. She squeezed her hand upon the polished wood and stared down into the waves.

A woman clutched the side of the ship, her wide dark eyes staring back at Sorcha with shock. Hair as green as seaweed tangled down her back in wet strands. She held the sprig of heather in her webbed hand. They blinked at each other until the merrow gave her a wide sharp-toothed grin and flipped off the ship. The bright flash of a green tail waved in the sunlight, splashing into a wave with one final twist.

Sorcha's knees went weak. A merrow. A *real* merrow had been so close she might have touched her. No hag stone had limited her vision. No glamour had hidden her true form.

Breathless, she tangled her hands in her hair and spun towards Manus. "That was a real merrow!"

"I know," he said with a chuckle.

"No. Manus that was a *real* merrow."

"I saw her as well, sweet thing."

"That was a faerie, without a glamour, and she wasn't even frightened of me!"

He tilted his head back and boomed with laughter. "Ah, I was right to bring you aboard. I know a faerie lover when I see one. Come with me, Sorcha. I have something special to show you."

Manus wrapped an arm around her shoulders when she reached him. The weight steadied her against the gentle sway of the ship. It was massive in her eyes. The deck teemed with twenty men, all rushing from one end to the other. White sails snapped in the wind and stretched taut to guide them across the waters.

They stepped up to the bow and stood behind the masthead. Sorcha leaned against the railing to peer at the wooden woman's face.

"Is this a faerie?"

"It is," Manus replied. "So we always remember who has given us this gift, and who guides us in safety."

"You are close with the Fae, then?" Few people would admit their ties to magic. Faeries were viewed as a superstition and believing in them to be child's indulgence.

"No one is close to the Fae. I deliver items for them. And sometimes people, like yourself."

"People? What do the Fae want with people?" Sorcha hadn't heard this particular secret before. She'd read every book there was on the Fae and spoke at length with anyone who had experiences with them. No one had ever said the Fae requested people be brought to them.

"There's always something here and there. A famous musician, an artisan," he cast a glance in her direction, "a midwife."

She stiffened. "How do you know that?"

"I carried you and your things to my room last night. I deserved at the very least a peek at your belongings."

"That's a terrible thing to do."

"You could have been an assassin, sweet thing. I protect my men and my ship."

Sorcha couldn't blame him for that. She would've done the same thing if a strange man walked into her brothel. It still felt like a violation of privacy.

She tugged at the hag stone around her neck. "What did you look at?"

"Just a few of the journals. As soon as I realized you were a healer, I let the rest be."

"You didn't take anything, did you?"

"Of course not." He looked offended. "I am neither thief nor pirate. What would I have stolen from you that the sea cannot give?"

Sorcha released the breath she held. The sea rolled, shaking the boat with one great lunge. Sorcha held onto the railing and stared into the dark waters where a shadow moved. "What was that?"

"That was what I wanted to show you," Manus said. "Have you ever heard of a guardian before?"

"Like a surrogate parent?"

"Like the species."

Sorcha raised a brow. "No."

He moved to stand behind her, lifting a hand above her shoulder and pointing towards the horizon. "When the Fae mark a ship, it is guided not just by merrows. A guardian is assigned to the boat. They are half woman, half whale. Their twisted features are terrifying. They can rip a man in half just with their hands."

"You're joking."

"I'm not. They guide our ships towards the Otherworld and ensure nothing else comes with us."

She wanted to shiver, but his hand was on her shoulder. He would know she was frightened. That was exactly what he wanted. Pulling her leg like this was cruel.

"I don't take kindly to men trying to scare me," she said. "I don't believe you."

"You should. The guardians are a very real threat, and it is my suggestion that you stay away from the water until we get to your destination."

Sorcha shook her head. "Which is?"

His hand shifted slightly to the left. "Do you see that?"

How could she have missed it? Mist and storm clouds created a wall in the middle of the ocean. A bolt of lightning cracked through the sky, and although they were too far to hear the thunder, she swore she could feel it.

"We're going there? Why?"

"Because that is the only way into the Otherworld," he said as he walked away.

"Hy-brasil is not in the Otherworld!" Sorcha shouted.

"It's on the border, darling. And you have to get close enough to see it."

She wanted to reach out and punch him. Or grab onto his dreads and toss him overboard. Guardian.

Sorcha snorted, but walked away from the railing. The last thing she needed was another scary story in her head. She had grown up with the Dullahan, trooping faeries, changeling children, and all other manner of frightening Fae.

Grumbling, she skirted her way past sailors on their hands and knees scrubbing the deck. They were eerily silent in their work. Their eyes followed her all the way back to the captain's cabin where she shut and locked the door.

Now that the seasickness had subsided, she got a good look at his quarters. And what stunning quarters they were.

"A four-poster bed?" she muttered. "What need does a man have of a four-poster bed out to sea?"

It wasn't very large, hardly enough room for two people, but it took up a remarkable amount of space. A wooden red desk was shoved in the corner. It didn't look like anyone used it at all. There were no papers, no inkwells, nothing to suggest that Manus ever sat at the desk.

Sorcha peered underneath it.

"No chair?" she muttered. "Of course it would be for decoration only."

Brown sheepskin covered the floor, soft against her bare feet. She curled her toes in its thick wool.

Someone pounded on the door. Whirling on her heel, she called out, "I'm not taking visitors!"

"Good!" Manus shouted back. "We're going to be heading straight for the eye of that storm. It's moving away from us, so we're going to put some effort in to catch it. Stay in the cabin! I don't need you falling overboard."

Her lips curled as she mimicked him. "I don't need you falling overboard. It's a good thing you're helping me captain, or I'd have half a mind to trip you into the ocean!"

A chuckle echoed through the door, growing quieter and quieter until it disappeared.

Sorcha huffed and crossed her arms over her chest. She should feel tired, but the long night's sleep was plenty. One might think that a sea captain would have an entertaining room, but there was little here.

Where was the treasure? The maps of wondrous places? At least trophies from all the places he had traveled. The man had a Fae-marked ship, for heavens sake.

She gritted her teeth and rummaged through her pack. There was one thing that always settled her mind, no matter where she was.

Soft vellum covered the worn leather journal. Its parchment paper curled at the edges, darkened with age and brittle with age. She lifted it to her nose and inhaled.

It still smelled like her. No matter how many years her mother had been dead, her books still smelled like her. Aged paper, lavender oil, sunshine, and the faintest hint of clover.

As always, tears pricked her eyes.

"I miss you," she whispered against the journal's spine. "I left Papa yesterday, and I hope it was the right decision. You always told me to be brave and kind. I think that's what this journey is for."

She turned the page and lost herself into a naturalist's recounting of healing. She read of teas which could stop bleeding, setting bones, cleaning wounds, walking a woman through every step of pregnancy. Sorcha's mother had unimaginable knowledge that she wrote down every moment she could.

It would never be enough. She would always want to devour her mother's words and wished she could remember her voice. Ten years was enough to forget many things about a person.

If Sorcha tried very hard, she could remember the way sunlight turned her mother's rosy hair to fire. How Sorcha had spent hours counting the freckles on her mother's arm when she had been ill. But she couldn't remember the tone of her voice, the whispered stories, or what she sounded like when she told her daughter "I love you."

Sorcha sniffed and blinked away tears.

Shaking her head, she patted the journal and placed it back inside her pack. "You'll stay there," she whispered. "Safe and sound."

Slapping wings smacked against the porthole of the ship. Sorcha flung herself back against the bed and stared at the giant raven poking its head into her room.

"Excuse me?" she gasped. "Who are you?"

It cawed at her, cocking its head to the side and staring at her with a single yellow eye.

"No," she said as she rose to her feet. "Absolutely not. I do not need a feathered friend in this room with me."

The raven didn't listen. It hopped from the porthole down onto the desk.

"No!" Sorcha said again.

She flapped her hands at it. There wasn't anything to shoo it away with, and now it might be too late. Ravens were intelligent, but she wasn't certain it could fly out the porthole. If she scared it into the air, then she might never get it back down. She eyed its wings.

"You're mighty and quite large," she said. "I think if you were flying that your wings would hurt me."

It tilted its head to the other side and jumped one hop towards her.

"Ah," she gasped. "Please don't do that."

The raven hopped backwards.

"No," Sorcha shook her head. "Don't do that either."

The raven froze and met her gaze.

"Can you understand me?"

It squawked at her.

Overwhelmed again, Sorcha tried to back away from it. Her heel caught on the edge of a rug, and she tumbled hard onto the floor. The bang of her tailbone hitting solid wood made her wince just as much as the sudden lightning bolt of pain.

The raven lifted its wings as though it might fly into the air.

"No!" Sorcha lifted one hand, the other rubbing firmly at her bottom. "I'm fine. *Please* don't do that."

It seemed to hesitate, wings still poised for flight.

"Really, I'm fine. I just didn't expect you to understand me. Are you the captain's?"

The raven's reaction was immediate. Its wings snapped down at its sides, its head rose from its feathers to an impossible height, and it croaked angrily at her.

"Did I insult you?" she asked. "I apologize. This is the captain's quarters. It's not that big of a stretch."

However, talking to a bird and expecting to be understood was a stretch. They were unnaturally intelligent, so it wasn't all that surprising that it reacted to her words.

She narrowed her eyes. "Am I making this up in my head? Yesterday, I was safe in my family's brothel, and now I'm hurtling towards the Otherworld. Or can you really understand me?"

It flapped its wings.

Sorcha rolled onto her knees and achingly rose to her feet. "I'm losing my mind. First, I make a deal with a faerie. Then I think ravens can understand me. What's next? Guardians are actually real?"

She snorted at the thought. The captain was trying to frighten her into staying in her cabin and away from his men. She understood that he might want her to stay out of the way, but he could have done it in a much more sensible way.

The raven croaked again and hopped towards the porthole. It pecked at the wood, the harsh thumps repetitive and strangely intentional. Between each jab, it would turn its head to stare at her.

Was it trying to get her to go to the window? She took a few hesitant steps forward. If the bird could understand her, did it want her to look outside?

"I'm losing my mind," she said.

Sorcha inched by the raven, keeping an eye on its movements in case it lunged at her. The bird stayed very still. She hooked her elbows on the edge of the porthole and leaned out.

The ocean waves didn't quite reach the window, but the salt spray misted her cheeks. The sun had set while she'd read. The moon spread its rays across the waves, turning them silver and frothy white.

It was beautiful. Untamed and wild, the ocean was the last bit of the world which remained a mystery. A wave crested against the ship, and the splashing water sounded like music.

"It's hard to believe such a place is so dangerous," she whispered.

She reached a hand towards the next wave. Sea water splashed, bitterly cold and bracing. Bubbles caught between her fingers and popped as she lifted them towards her mouth. She licked the salt from her skin with a soft chuckle.

"See?" she glanced over her shoulder towards the raven. "It's not all that dangerous."

A soft thump against the side of the ship startled her. She looked down into the black waters but could see nothing in their depths.

Sorcha narrowed her eyes and leaned further out the porthole.

Something in the darkness shifted. She couldn't see what was there, or where the movement came from, but the murk changed.

She scooted even farther out the porthole, her hands braced against the side of the ship.

In the darkness of the ocean, within arm's reach, an eye blinked—larger than a dinner plate and black as night. She could see it now. The entire impossible length of the creature stretched out larger than the ship.

Sorcha's mouth gaped open. Her fingers turned to claws. The guardian's head alone was larger than a horse! It was faintly human in shape, but its skin was ghostly pale and speckled. Its mouth was a large gash that spread across its face nearly to the ear canals on both sides of its head. Hair grew in a mohawk from the peak of its skull and stretched so far into the waves that Sorcha couldn't begin to guess its length.

It blinked its eye again. Lips stretched into what she hoped was a friendly smile, and Sorcha heard the thump again. The creature's long spindly finger was stroking the side of the ship. It paused at the top of the yellow paint and then traveled underneath the boat.

A soft whine escaped Sorcha's lips.

"Okay," she whispered. "I'm going back inside now. Please don't flip us."

She didn't want to startle the guardian, so she moved inch by inch until she fell onto the floor of the cabin. Only then did she allow herself to hyperventilate and shake her hands in the air. When did she lose feeling in her hands? Her heart beat so fast she thought it was rising into her throat.

"It's real," she whispered over and over again. "It's really real. That exists in the oceans. I'm never going swimming again."

The raven bobbed its head and made a sound like laughter.

"You stop it. You didn't see that thing."

The raven didn't stop laughing, even when Sorcha threw a pillow at it.

With all the new sights, and the rocking of the ship, Sorcha was certain she wouldn't sleep again. Nightmares would keep her awake. The possibility of the future would keep her awake. There was no possible way that she could slip into the endless night. But she did, and her mind did not plague her with dreams.

CHAPTER FOUR
THE PHANTOM ISLE

The ghosts of his past walked with Eamonn across the ramparts of the castle. They tugged on the cloak wrapped around his shoulders, tangled in the high peak of his braid, clutched at his wrists and pulled him back towards the gloom.

He shook his head, trying to toss aside memories like water shaking from his skin. He was not so lucky. His mind held him captive and replayed old memories from his childhood.

His father stared with eyes cold and unfeeling. The blade in his hand glinted in the glaring sunlight that traveled up the sharp edge to the point. It swung down, slicing across Eamonn's face and spraying blood across the battlements.

His mother turned away from the sight. His brother's smirk scalded into his memory and branded his mind.

Memories were his prison. Torment his penance for years of foolish attachments and familial trust.

Storm clouds rolled overhead. Slate gray and heavy with moisture, they threatened lightning and thunder that would last for days. The weather grew angry with him. Together, they would rage against each heartbeat—each breath—that kept him alive.

He dug his fingers into the cracked stone of the barely waist-high wall that was the only barrier between him and a hundred-foot fall. In his youth, he would have feared cutting his skin. Now, he listened to the scrape of crystals cutting into granite that crumbled under his clenched fist.

A low rumble of thunder rocked the isle of Hy-brasil. Far below the castle walls, tiny dots of sheep and faeries scattered towards the safety of caves. They would wait out the sky's anger there. Perhaps they would build a fire, drink mead and whiskey, and tell stories from their youth.

All while their master stood upon the highest tower and roared at the sky.

Eamonn heard a voice just like his own on the wind. Deep like the thunder, but even more dangerous—his twin brother's voice.

"This was your doing," Fionn said. "You are responsible for all their suffering and the suffering of hundreds more. You made me do this, Eamonn, and now we all pay the price."

He shook his head. "I did not choose this life. I did not force your hand."

The wound upon his throat throbbed, and the geodes in his neck cast violet light upon his fists. He still felt the biting rope, fraying at the edges, and swaying in the breeze.

He released the catch of his cloak, and let it fall to the stones. It fluttered in the wind, stretching out as though it were cloth wings.

Leather leggings hugged his thighs. The sewn strips dipped into craters of geodes and grew taut over peaks of pointed crystal. No shirt covered his bare chest, allowing the wind to whistle through the valleys of disfigurement. Abdominal ridges rose above the line of his pants, the bumps of his ribs bisected by gashes of violet wounds. His left shoulder was almost entirely gemstone, the large chunk limiting his movement. Spindly veins of opal traveled across his chest, down one thick bicep, and stretched to follow the line of his spine.

The deepest wound wrapped around his neck. The perfect circle was two fingers wide and created a hollow valley of jagged crystals. It deepened his voice to a gruff rasp.

Like his shoulder, veins of opal sliced across his face. Two twin lines started above his eyebrow and at the peak of his temple. They cut across his eye, skipped only at the opening of his mouth, and met at his throat. The crystal at his lips limited his speech and caused him to speak from one side of his mouth, giving him a permanent sneer.

He shaved his head on both sides, leaving only the top to grow freely. He wore it in a braid, letting it swing to the middle of his back. The golden hair was the last bit of beauty he had left.

Eamonn had once been the most desired Seelie man any woman had ever seen. The strength of his body, the legends of his battle prowess, and the startling blue of his eyes had wooed many to his bed.

The memories of beautiful women turning away when they saw his true form and the nightmare he had become plagued him.

He walked to the end of the rampart, and let his toes hang over the edge. His eyes drifted shut as the wind brushed his cheeks. It whistled through the crystals and sang a song only he could hear.

He may not be dead yet, but the time was nearing. Soon, soon he could let go.

"Master," Cian's voice cut through the raging storm within Eamonn's head. "If you planned on jumping, you'd have done it a long time ago."

"Leave."

The gnome never listened. Eamonn could hear his footsteps as he padded down the ramparts.

Cian cleared his throat. "Now it seems to me you're frightening the pixies in the gardens. They're staring up like your body is going to come crashing down on them any minute, and I need them collecting the pumpkins before the storm starts."

"Make them gather in the rain."

"Their wings will get wet, and we both know how difficult they are when they have wet wings. So why don't you take a few steps back and stop their trembling." Cian paused, and then added, "Or jump off and save us all the trouble of worrying."

The gnome had such a way with words. Eamonn shook his head and held out a hand. He kept his back turned towards Cian, knowing most of the damage to his body was reflected on his chest and face.

"My cloak," he grunted.

"I've seen you before, boy. There's no need to hide."

"My cloak, Cian."

He knew they all had seen him. Eamonn had accidentally strayed too far from his tower many times. The pixies had caught him washing in the waterfalls. The brownies found him in the training grounds. They were all stuck on the same isle. There weren't a lot of places for him to hide.

None of this meant he felt comfortable around them. His disfigurement was a disgrace to the royal line. The truth was branded into his mind after they hung him for seven days. Old wounds like that cut to the quick and rarely healed.

Cool fabric met his outstretched hand. Eamonn's eyes drifted shut for a moment, thankful that the gnome had followed orders. He would never say it. There was no purpose in congratulating someone for doing what they were told.

He swirled the cloak in a wide arc and settled it over his shoulders. Heat enveloped him with unwelcome arms. Eamonn hated the cloak. He hated hiding, but this had become his existence. He was no longer the handsome man he once had been.

"Storm's coming," Cian said as he walked up to Eamonn's side. "And you're still standing at the top of your castle leaning over an edge that could crumble at any moment."

"Would it be such a loss?"

"No. We'd get along just fine without you, but I'd have to dig a new hole in the garden, and I hadn't planned on doing that until next spring."

"Ever so gentle, Cian."

"I don't have to be gentle with you. The warlord prince of the Seelie

Fae should have thicker skin."

Eamonn twitched the edge of his cloak over his newly mangled hand. "That was a long time ago."

"Take one step back, and I'll tell you who I was before I came here."

"I know who you were," his toes curled over the edge. "Gnomes have always been good thieves. You stole from the wrong person and pay your penance here. Hy-brasil was and always will be a prison. Nothing more."

Cian planted a hand firmly against the base of Eamonn's spine. The sudden touch made him lock his muscles holding himself in place without twitching or revealing the sudden shock that raced through his veins. The gnome did not push, nor did he pull. He kept his hand against Eamonn's back relaxed but threatening.

"I was no common thief. I stole to make a living and feed my family. Your people view gnomes as little more than slaves. We work in your gardens, feed *your* people, while the rest of us go hungry. My children went to bed with their stomachs aching, and my wife withered away into nothing. I stole a single piece of bread from the kitchens of a lowly Seelie lord. For that, they banished me here—never to see my family again."

Eamonn remained silent. He knew the Seelie court was corrupt. It had been his desire to change those ways, even as he fought in the wars that upheld them. He had not been the king, however, and had little power to change anything then. Now, he never would.

His silence spurred Cian on. "I don't like you, Tuatha dé Danann. Not because of what you've done here, or even who you are, but for what you stand for."

The hand against Eamonn's spine flexed. His own hands slowly curled beneath the cape. If Cian pushed, Eamonn could catch himself on the half wall. He would need to have faith that the castle wouldn't crumble under his weight.

"I lost everything I ever had, because your people consider themselves above everyone else. It was a damned piece of bread, and I was banished from the Otherworld like I'd murdered someone. I wanted to feed hungry mouths, to get paid for the work I did. And look what happened to me!"

Eamonn felt the slightest nudge against his back.

"You got nothing to say to that?" Cian growled.

"There is little I could say which would change your mind."

"You're right. There's not."

The hand against his spine withdrew, and the gnome backed away. Eamonn straightened and squared his shoulders. He would not bow. He would not yield. Though he was a disgraced prince, he might have been king of these people.

He would not break.

Cian's feet struck the ground in hard echoes as he returned to the door which led to the rest of the castle. Creaking floorboards fought with the thunder. He stopped at the door and turned.

"You know," the gnome's words flung into the night like sharp assassin blades. "If you weren't such a prick, I might respect you. You don't even flinch."

"I fear nothing and no one. Leave, gnome, before I throw you from the tower instead."

The door slammed shut. A bolt of lightning sizzled through the air and struck the top of the tower. Thunder crashed so loud the pixies in the gardens below screamed and fled in terror.

Throughout it all, Eamonn stood silent and unmoving.

Long ago, he had been a pillar for his people. They called his name as he rode through the streets. They threw flower petals at his feet in hopes he might look upon them. Now, they ran in fear.

He tilted his head back and let his rage roar at the coming storm. He poured all the feelings of neglect, anger, fear, and self-hatred into the sound. It purged his blackened soul.

Eamonn twisted away from the edge of his castle and fell to his knees. Staring down at his ruined hands, he set his resolve towards living.

He would begin his work again, turn his mind and passion towards saving his people in whatever way possible. Storms like this always brought shipwrecked cargo. He would wait to see what his people would find upon the rocky shore.

Death would wait a while longer.

Less than a week at sea, and Sorcha was ready to kill herself. She held onto the railing and breathed through her nose. In and out. Slow and intentional inhalations, or she would vomit again.

Manus tried to make her eat, but she couldn't keep anything down. Even the ale tasted like bile. It exited her body as fast as she could drink it.

The ship coasted over a very large wave and crashed down the other side. Turning green, Sorcha moaned and leaned over the rail again. Watching the waves didn't help, but what else was there? Waves upon waves, that was it.

Her vision blurred. The muscles of her stomach clenched, trying to force out what wasn't there. She'd emptied her stomach of everything but thin bile hours ago. Now, dry heaves threatened to kill her.

The part of her brain which was a healer screamed she needed water. Not ale. Not whiskey. Water. Fresh, clean water that would hydrate her body. There was so much water surrounding them, and none of it was safe to drink. She licked her dry lips and wished for death.

"Sorcha! I need you away from the railing."

She lifted her head and tried not to shake. "Can't do that, Captain."

"Now!"

"I can't," she whispered. "I can't even move."

A wall of dark skin and beaded hair stalked towards her. "When I give you an order, girl, you best be following it. Get up."

"No."

"Get up!"

Sorcha leaned over the edge of the railing and prayed to whatever gods were listening. Take her now. Make it end. She didn't care how. If only she could stop throwing up for just a few moments, she would consider herself blessed.

Manus grabbed the back of her skirt and yanked her up. Her knees shook, muscles quaked, body bowed as she retched.

"Enough!" he shouted. "We are sailing directly into that storm I showed you, and I will not have you wrapped around the railing. The Fae wanted you in Hy-brasil, and that is where you are going. Now get back to my quarters!"

He released his hold, and she fell onto her hands and knees. "If I could stand to be in that room with that horrible raven then I would be there!"

"Raven?" Manus shook his head. "Damned thing can't leave well enough alone. I don't care who's sharing the room with you. You will be out of sight until we are through the storm."

"Why can't I stay on deck?" She looked up at him, eyes wide and skin pale. "I'll stay out of the way. The fresh air helps."

"I'm sure it does, pretty thing. But that storm is going to hit us hard. Waves will crash right over the deck, and at least in the cabin you can hold onto the bed. Make sure you grip the posts tight. Don't let go until I come for you."

He held his hand out for her to take. Sorcha eyed it as though it were a snake which might bite. Going back in that cabin would make her vomit even more violently than before.

But she didn't want to end up in the ocean during a storm either. Sighing, she slapped her hand onto his. "I hate the ocean."

Manus chuckled. "So many people do. She's a cruel mistress, and a temptress when she wants to be."

"A tempest you mean?" she asked while stumbling to the cabin.

"That, too, but it's unlikely we'll see a tempest while out here."

"What do you call that storm then?"

He opened the door and shoved her through. "I call that a widow maker. Stay safe."

Manus slammed the door so hard the floor quaked. The raven flapped its wings, slapping them against the table in anger.

"Yes," she murmured. "I agree. The man is charming, but he's also rude."

The ship tilted at a drastic angle. The entire frame shook with the impact of the bow hitting the water. Swearing, Sorcha tripped and landed on her hands and knees again.

"Apparently, he wasn't joking," she muttered.

Standing proved impossible as the ship rocked back and forth. Moaning with seasickness and fear, she crawled to the bed. Her hands fisted in the dark blankets which slid off the frame rather than pulling her up onto it.

Sorcha curled her fingers around a post and hauled herself up. Her stomach heaved again. There was nothing to vomit, but she still leaned over the edge of the bed.

Another great wave tossed the ship against the hard walls of the ocean. Sorcha's pack thumped against the wall, and a stone weight on the captain's desk fell onto the floor with a heavy crack.

She squeezed her eyes shut and hugged a pillow to her chest. There was nothing she could do but wait out the storm. She couldn't go out on the deck and help, she didn't know how. There were no men who needed healing, not yet. All she could do was follow orders and stay out of the way.

It went against every fiber of her being not to help, but she should stay where she was.

She heard the shouts before the ship rose, straight as a tree. She clutched the posts of the bed and whispered prayers.

"Please," she called out. "I do not wish to die so far from my homeland, from my family, from the earth. Faeries of the water and sky, help us."

The raven took flight, cawing its agitation and anger. The ship shifted again and landed hard on the waves which seemed to turn to stone. Sorcha screamed.

One of the posts snapped with a harsh crack. The wooden piece went flying into the air, tossed by the waves and their uncontrolled jouncing. Someone hit the door to the cabin hard, the frame vibrating with the man's weight.

Sorcha reached out her arms. "If we're going to die together, I might as well name you. Bran!"

The raven's head snapped towards her, as if it recognized the name. "Come here!"

The ship rolled again, and the man leaning against the door shrieked as thunderous water ripped him away. Sorcha watched the handle rattle and whispered a prayer for the man to remain on the ship. Anything to keep them all safe.

Bran darted towards her as the ship crested another wave. Sorcha reached out an armand held him close to her chest. One hand gently stroked his breast feathers, the other clutched the nearest post and held on for dear life.

"I didn't think I would die like this," she whispered, treating the raven as her confessor. "I always thought it would be at the stake. Rumors called my mother a witch. She spoke with the faeries and kept the old tales alive. Because of that, they burned her. I still remember every moment of it."

She pressed her face against his back. Bran tilted his head and tucked his beak against her throat.

"I'm not a witch. I'm not odd, or frightening, and I don't have any knowledge that can't be learned. Nothing will ever stop me from believing in faeries or leaving them gifts because they were here first. We need to take care of them, because they take care of us in return. Not for payment, but because they are kind and good and everything humans have lost. And because even as I'm hurtling toward my death, I can't stop thinking about them."

The ship shuddered and froze. Sorcha listened to the groaning wood, the rivers of water splashing off the sides, and the pounding rain striking the deck. They had stopped moving.

A great deafening cry vibrated the entire ship. The high-pitched screams of men joined it. Sorcha realized with horror that the guardian had grabbed the ship in her mighty hands. She could imagine the wide split mouth gaping its terrifying scream, the thin pale hands clutching the Saorsa as if it were a child's toy.

They were going to die.

She closed her eyes and breathed in a slow, deep breath. She had failed on the very first leg of her journey. But then again, this had been an impossible task from the start. The Fae didn't want her to find the cure to the beetle plague. They wanted to watch a theatrical attempt by a foolish human girl who had trusted them too easily.

Hands slapped against the side of the ship. Tiny scratching sounds which were too small to be the guardian's massive fingers.

Sorcha peeled open one eye, clutched the raven tight to her chest, and glanced at the porthole.

Green hair snaked through the opening, and dark eyes stared back at her. Rainbows danced across the merrow's fingers as she reached through. When their gazes caught, the merrow paused and cocked her head to the side.

The raven struggled, squawking angrily until it wiggled free. He snapped at the air with his beak and flew towards the merrow.

"What?" Sorcha muttered.

Were they not going to die? Bran grumbled at the merrow who tilted her head to the other side. She reached out and brushed a long finger down the raven's beak, and then released the edge of the porthole. Her green tail shimmered as she pulled herself further up the ship.

"Are we saved?" She could hardly believe she uttered the words.

The angry look Bran cast towards her was answer enough. They were being saved by the very creature she was so terrified of. Now, she understood why it was so important to have a guardian in faerie waters.

Sorcha placed her hand against a post and rose on rubbery legs. She had barely been able to walk on the ship before the storm. Now, she didn't trust her balance at all. Her hands were shaking, and she feared the guardian would drop them. She didn't want to end up back in the water after that experience.

Carefully, she made her way towards the door. Manus's voice echoed in her head. Do not go outside. Don't open the door. Stay inside the cabin where it is safe.

Yet, she also heard the screams of his men. She heard the thumping crash of bodies landing against solid wood and the rushing waves of water cresting over the deck. There were people who needed healing.

It didn't matter that she was afraid. Fear was a beast she could conquer as long as she could save just one life. This was what she was born to do.

Sorcha tugged hard on the door which resisted her movements. She threw her weight into the backwards motion and inched it open, bit by bit.

Men slumped all across the deck. Some had piled across each other, moaning and rubbing their wounds. Blood slicked her door, a red handprint catching her eye.

Merrows dragged themselves up the sides of the ship and across the deck. A few had curled around sailors and were gently patting their cheeks. They didn't speak. Instead, they hummed their concern. Their voices were deep and calming.

Sorcha stumbled towards the nearest sailor and dropped to her knees. "Where does it hurt?"

"Everywhere," he groaned.

"Where is the worst?"

He gestured towards his chest. Sorcha reached forward without hesitation and ripped his shirt open. A bright bruise already formed, purple and angry.

She danced her fingers over his ribs and watched his reactions. He flinched from the tenderness, but didn't respond overly much to her prodding of the bones. There was the slightest of groans when she palpated his stomach. Sorcha hesitated and did it one more time. She didn't feel any swelling from internal bleeding, but the number of bruises was concerning.

"Are you having trouble breathing?"

"Leave me, girl."

"Answer the question, sailor. Can you breathe?"

Another hand touched hers. Webbed fingers spread across the bruising of the man's chest and gently pulled Sorcha's hands away.

Sorcha stared in fascination as the merrow wrapped herself around the sailor. The long green tail twined through his legs and down to his calves. Her chest pressed against the man's spine and her iridescent webs glowed as they smoothed across his skin. She placed her chin on his shoulder, humming the deep base of the merrow song.

"Sorcha," Manus said. "Come with me."

She looked up at the captain's hand he held towards her. "What's happening?"

"I told you the Fae take care of us. Now, come on."

Manus's hand was just as cold as hers. He pulled her up and held onto her elbow when she swayed. "Were you injured?"

"No."

"Good."

He pulled her towards the bow of the ship. She glanced over her shoulder, watching more merrows swarm over the railings. Two dragged a man up from the ocean. They slammed him down on the deck so hard that Sorcha winced, but the hard strike made him cough up the seawater in his lungs.

They were not just saving the survivors, she realized. Three more merrows pulled up another man and laid him gently on the desk. They rocked back and forth over his body, keening their grief.

"They mourn the dead?" she asked.

"Of course, they do. We work with them, and we will mourn theirs before we set sail again."

"They had casualties?" Sorcha glanced around, trying to find the merrow bodies.

"You won't see them on the ship. Merrows turn to sea foam when they die. It's a cruel death, but it's better than letting sharks eat them."

Sorcha swallowed hard. "I'm sorry to hear they lost loved ones."

"Well, I lost good men as well. Feel sorry for the lot of us."

She blinked and looked up at him. His cheeks were red and splotchy, his eyes casting glares in her direction even as he propelled her forcefully towards the end of his ship.

"Are you angry at me?" she asked.

"I never should have taken this foolish mission. The journey to Hybrasil is dangerous, and I was fully aware of that."

"And that is my fault?"

"You asked to come here, freckles."

Sorcha jerked the arm he held. "How dare you blame this on me? I did nothing wrong!"

"You made a deal with the wrong faerie." He thrust her towards the bow of the ship and the wooden Fae staring off into the skyline. "I lost good men because of you. I won't blame you for their deaths, but I'm damned well getting you off this ship."

She stumbled, catching herself hard against the railing. The storm was subsiding, though the waves still churned with uncontrolled anger. She couldn't see anything in those secretive waves, the water dark and foreboding.

The island was within sight. Tall cliffs framed one side and led down to a rocky shore. A castle loomed over the small isle, crumbling towers and decaying wood structures giving the land an eerie, abandoned feel. It looked like a better abode for ghosts than people. Certainly not faeries.

"Hy-brasil?" she asked.

"You wanted to go to the island. There it is." His feet struck the deck hard as he walked away.

"Wait!" Sorcha spun. "How am I supposed to get there?"

"That wasn't part of our deal. As you can see, I have enough to worry about here."

"Can I borrow a rowboat at least?" She raced after him and caught the edge of his sleeve.

"Borrow? How are you going to bring it back? Swim to the isle if you need to get there so badly, freckles, or stay on the ship and return with us. I don't care."

"You want me to *swim* to that isle?" Sorcha jabbed a finger at Hy-brasil. "Do you even know what's in the water here? You said this was the gateway between the Otherworld and ours, so how many more faeries are there? We can both be certain I won't find just merrows!"

"Then stay on the ship, and I'll bring you home."

He whirled on her. His chest rose and fell in exaggerated rage while his hands opened and closed. Sorcha narrowed her eyes. He wasn't just angry at her. He was frightened. The storm had cost him much, and he was second guessing coming here at all.

They had to go back through the storm, she realized. This wasn't about the initial danger, but that they had to turn around and do it again. Maybe it would be easier returning to the human world, but she doubted it.

He would lose more men. More merrows would die. And she was pestering him with ferrying her over to the island which had caused all this trouble in the first place.

Sorcha released her anger with a soft sigh. "I understand, Manus. I do. But I need to bring my things with me, and they cannot get wet."

"I never said I'd ensure the safety of personal items."

"They're my mother's books," she called out as he turned away from her again. "They're the only thing I have left of her, and I will not let them go."

He hesitated. She watched his shoulders lift in anger, and then curl forward in defeat. "You're set on going, then?"

"I have no other choice. You know that as well as I. The faerie punishment for backing out of a deal is worse than a swift death at sea."

"I have a charm which will help your pack stay dry. It was a gift from a selkie, and I expect to have it back someday."

Sorcha twisted her fingers together. "I will do my best to return it once this is all over."

"I won't hold my breath."

Manus motioned for one of his sailors, the most mobile of the bunch strewn across the deck like autumn leaves. The raven burst out of the captain's quarters, its cry echoing as it launched into the air. She watched him stretch his wings and fly towards the isle.

Apparently, the raven was traveling to the same place as Sorcha. She turned her gaze to the land mass and suppressed a shiver. There was something about that place which felt *wrong*.

The air was too still. The ocean didn't crash against the rocks, but sluggishly avoided touching the land. Even the elements had forsaken Hy-brasil. There was more to the phantom isle than the legends sang, and Sorcha was afraid to find out what.

She braced her feet as the guardian gently set them down. The ship remained steady, bobbing as if there had never been a storm. Sorcha wished she could forget as easily as the Saorsa had.

Footsteps marked the return of the sailor who held her pack at arm's length. He held it far out in front of him, the pack dangling from his fingers as if he didn't want to touch her.

Sorcha recognized that expression. It was the same look her mother had been given for months before they burned her. They blamed her for every bit of bad luck. A neighbor's cow died, a child caught a cold, the well ran dry, all were the markings of a witch who had cursed the town. Sorcha's mother had been the one they chose to burn.

She snatched her pack out of the man's hands with a muttered curse. "I didn't call the storm, you imbecile. Give me that."

The sailor flinched away from her.

Good riddance. He could be frightened of her if that helped him make sense of the storm, but she wasn't about to let him treat her like a witch. Sorcha was a good person. She would have healed them all if the merrows weren't here.

She swung the pack over her shoulder and held her hand towards Manus. "The charm?"

He pulled a small bag from his pocket. The burlap was completely dry. Not even a single drop of water clung to its checkered pattern.

"This will do. Stick it in your bag and swim as fast as you can."

"Will the charm wear off?" She stuffed the small bag in her pack between her most precious books.

"It's unlikely to wear off. And freckles? A word of warning: where there are merrows, there are merrow-men. They'd like a pretty thing like you to stay with them, and most of their wives are here with us. No one will be able to stop them if they get ahold of you."

"Thank you," she gritted through clenched teeth.

He didn't stay to watch. Manus left to tend to his men, while she stood on the precipice of another decision. The water was another dangerous part of her journey. The ocean had yet to be kind, and its inhabitants were likely even worse.

Her eyes strayed to the haunted isle that had spawned straight from her nightmares. Hy-brasil, the phantom isle spoken of in legends and myths for centuries. Many believed it was a utopia, a place where men of highest intelligence and scholars of world renown were sent.

It looked like a ruin.

She carefully hoisted herself up on the railing and balanced with a sail rope in her hand. This was it. There was no going back once she jumped off this ship and landed in the waters below.

Papa's eyes swam in front of hers. His painfully thin body, the grating cough that kept the others up at night, the dangers of what might happen should she fail and he die. The beetles would infect her sisters next; they were the nearest food source. The families nearby might also fall. And she wasn't there to help prolong their lives.

Sorcha lifted her foot to hang in the salty air for a moment before she took a deep breath and leapt off the edge.

She hit the water with a stinging slap. Her skirts billowed up into her face and tangled with the long strands of her hair. The pack weighed her down, pulling her towards the bottom of the ocean with surprising ease.

Bubbles erupted from her mouth as she pumped her arms. Fabric tangled around her feet and trapped them. She couldn't kick. She couldn't breathe.

Frowning in concentration, she almost didn't notice the movement in the depths. Calm yourself, she thought. Calm was the only way to deal with the Fae. Panic would only lead to poor decisions.

She let her body relax although her lungs burned. Salt water stung her eyes when she opened them. Sorcha glanced down and held in a gasp when she saw red eyes staring back at her.

Deep at the bottom of the ocean, the merrow-men waited. They lacked the necessary tails to keep up with their brides. Instead, they had legs like a human man. Green scales covered their bodies which were hard with muscles. Gills and fins popped up with little rhyme or reason, giving them a grotesque appearance. But it was their faces that disturbed her the most.

Large fish-like mouths gaped open as they inhaled her scent in the water. Jagged teeth lined their gums. Their eyes bulged when they realized it was a human woman in their realm. Frilled fins fanned out around their faces and evil grins spread wide.

One curled his fist around a trident and pushed off the ocean floor.

He was swimming towards her. His webbed feet made him a much more effective swimmer, and her own pack was steadily dragging her to the bottom.

Sorcha wouldn't let that happen. Determined, she reached down and ripped the bottom of her skirt. Two great, heaving pulls split the fabric down each side. It wasn't much, but it was enough.

Her legs now freed she swam with all her might. Muscles burned, lungs screamed, eyes watered, but she eventually broke through into the sweet air.

She gasped in breaths that shocked her lungs. There wasn't enough air in the world to satisfy her cravings, and every inhalation tasted metallic. She rolled onto her back—still sucking in air—and kicked towards the isle.

The merrow-man was still coming, she reminded herself. She couldn't rest just because she could breathe. It was time to swim. Once she made it to the island, she could rest.

Only then.

When she finally caught her breath, she rolled onto her stomach and lifted her arms above her head. One arm at a time, one kick at a time, counting under her breath each stroke that drew her closer to Hy-brasil.

She couldn't stop for even a moment, or the pack would drag her under the water. Her stomach churned from too many dips beneath the waves. A belly full of salt made her more nauseous, but there wasn't even bile left to vomit.

She'd seen no sharks, but the stories said she wouldn't until it was too late.

Above her head, the raven circled. Its caw snapped her eyes open as she paused for a moment to breathe.

"Bran?" she whispered.

Again, the corvid's cry jolted through her body.

"Right," she muttered. "I have to swim."

The isle grew closer and closer, even as the sun began to set and the ocean turned red. She could make it if only she swam a little…bit…more.

Her feet touched land.

A sob lurched her body forward. She slipped underneath a wave, but it didn't matter that she couldn't see. All she could taste was salt but there were rocks and sand beneath her feet. She didn't have to swim anymore, and she didn't have to lose her mother's journals.

"Thank you," she whispered as she pulled herself onto the jagged shore. "Thank you so much."

She curled her fingers in the sand and mud. The grit digging into her nailbeds made even more tears stream down her cheeks. She had made it to the phantom isle through storms, giant whale creatures, and merrow-men.

Sorcha had really done it.

She laughed through the tears and rolled onto her back. The stars twinkled in the night sky. They were so beautiful. The land was so beautiful.

It no longer mattered that there was a mysterious castle looming overhead. It didn't matter that ghosts likely traversed with silent feet all around her. She wasn't swimming anymore, and the ground didn't move here.

Letting out a ragged breath, her eyes drifted shut. Just for a moment, she told herself. She could rest for a moment before she had to get back up and find the Fae the MacNara twins wanted.

Stars danced beneath her eyelids as she settled into the sand.

CHAPTER FIVE
THE BEAST

Cold air brushed her skin. Sorcha rolled to her side, murmuring in her sleep. Gritty sand touched her face and sucked into her lungs as she snorted awake.

She bolted upwards, scratching her nose with frantic hands. She coughed out sand and brushed dried salt off her cheeks. Her skin burned, raw and dry. Her lips cracked as she inhaled, blood leaking into her mouth and stinging her swollen tongue with the taste of iron.

Where was she? Her gaze danced over worn stones and bits of driftwood.

"Right," she whispered. "The boat…the storm…the swim."

Sorcha tucked her knees to her chest and hugged them close. There would be no more tears. She couldn't afford to lose her sanity; there was too much left to do.

Her mind settled, and she glanced around. What had awoken her?

Something snorted to her left. The muscles of her back seized, and she slowly turned her head.

A smooth, whiskered face blew air at her again. The seal's eyes were large and dark, surprisingly friendly. The warm air smelled of fish and rotten seaweed mixed with the musky scent of her newfound friend.

At her movement, the seal slapped a flipper against its belly and chortled.

"Oh," she said in surprise. "Hello."

It leaned in close and snorted at her again. When she flinched back, it let out another coughing laugh and rolled onto its back. Each smack against its side caused blubber to wiggle.

"Aren't you a funny little thing?" Sorcha wasn't certain it was so "little." The seal was already larger than her, and she was certain it wasn't full grown. Its long whiskers tilted up at her words.

It snorted at her one more time then turned to leave. Its body vibrated as it lurched across the shore, slipping into the water with more grace than it exhibited on land.

A thought sparked. "Are you a selkie?"

The only response was a quiet chuckle as the seal sank beneath the water.

Her muscles screamed in protest as she rose to her feet. The long muscles of her thighs seized, and her toes pointed as the arch of her foot clenched.

Sorcha whimpered. The pain was excruciating, but she couldn't stay on the sand. Stinging sunburns already covered her cheeks and arms. If she stayed out any longer, she would blister.

Water. She needed water. Her lips cracked as she opened them and wheezed out a breath.

She continued making soft sounds of discomfort as she pushed herself upright. She waved her arms for balance and settled. Coughing, Sorcha nodded her head.

"Step one, standing. Accomplished."

Her feet seemed so far away. She furrowed her brows and looked at her toes. When had she lost her left shoe?

Right about the moment a merrow-man had pointed his trident at her with a dangerous gleam in his eyes. She groaned and held a hand to her head. The headache pounding behind her eyes nearly sent her to her knees.

"Who is that?" a feminine voice asked.

"I don't know. She must have washed up from a shipwreck."

"That never happens."

"How am I supposed to know then? Banishment is the only way to get here, but faeries can't banish *humans*."

The second voice was far more masculine. Nasal and harsh, it made the pain behind her eyes spike higher.

"Please," Sorcha whispered. "Do you have any water?"

"Can she hear us, Cian?"

"Humans can't hear us when we're glamoured. She's hallucinating."

Sorcha stepped forward towards the sound, searching for the owners of the voices. "I *can* hear you. I came to Hy-brasil to speak with a faerie who lives here."

A scoff echoed across the stones. "There's plenty of faeries around here, human child. But there aren't many who will talk to you."

"Excuse me?" She blinked. "I need to talk to a Tuatha dé Danann who resides here. The MacNara twins sent me."

"Well, that changes things," the feminine voice said. "We might help you with that."

"We absolutely will not!" The other voice, Cian, was the male. "The master will have our heads, and I've gone toe to toe with him too many times. I will not be part of this."

"Please," Sorcha stepped forward and stumbled on a stone. She landed hard on her knees, crying out when the jagged rocks tore through her tender flesh.

"Look at her, *Cian*. We can't just leave her here."

"Don't be saying my name! Leaving her here is exactly what we'll do. We're not helping a human. Don't touch it! Woman, you'll be the death of me. She might be ill."

"But—"

"No buts! Stop helping people so much and think of your own hide. Humans don't belong here. Let it slip back into the water and forget about it."

Sorcha touched the gaping wound on her knee. Blood dripped from the torn flesh, already scabbing over, and encrusted with salt and sand. "Her," she whispered. "I am female, not an it."

"Could've fooled me," Cian grunted. "You look like something I'd scrape out of the ocean and toss to the side. Good luck making it to the castle."

Footsteps pattered across the granite stones. They were leaving. She gasped and stumbled to her feet, bracing her legs wide for balance. They couldn't leave, not yet.

"Wait!" she called out. "Please, wait!"

A blast of air heralded the approach of a Fae. Warm lips pressed against her ear and the feminine voice whispered, "I'll take care of you if you can make it home. One foot in front of the other, dearie."

The faerie presence vanished.

Sorcha lifted one leg and placed it before the other. She was unsteady, weak, and drained, but determined. Each movement splintered through her body in needles of icy pain.

"My body will not stop me," she whispered.

The longer she moved, the more her muscles loosened. Pain turned to ache, ache turned to exhaustion. She relaxed, and the fog cleared from her mind.

The haunting isle revealed tiny details of beauty she had not seen from the ship. The rocky shore was hazardous, true, but there were also small sparkling barnacles stuck to the stones. A pathway hewn into the side of the cliffs led up to emerald fields similar to her home.

And why wouldn't it be similar? This was still Ui Neill, she reminded herself. A mirrored reflection, but still the same structure of land and earth. The Otherworld was not so different from her own.

She hefted herself up on the first rock and caught her breath. Tiny purple flowers poked out between her fingers. The sun reached its peak, the heat causing mist to rise from the surrounding fields. It wasn't natural to see clouds this time of day, but there they were.

Sorcha pulled herself up on jutting stones and the marked pathway until she stood at the top of the hill.

Green filled her vision near to bursting. It was overwhelming to see such beautiful landscape. Her heart clenched and her fingers curled. Rolling hills covered in the most vibrant grass she had ever seen stretched as far as the eye could see. White dots of sheep lifted their heads every so often, smaller lumps of wool leaping through swirls of white fog.

Above it all, the castle loomed. The high peaks of towers looked like swords striking the gods.

Ravens flocked overhead. Their screams reminded her why she was here and how far she had come. She paused, hands on her hips, and lungs heaving.

"Not much farther now, Sorcha," she said to herself. "Then the real job begins."

Gravel crunched beneath her feet as she marched towards the castle. Her skin itched as if there were hundreds of eyes watching her journey. She supposed there could be. Fae were invisible to humans, and there were many on this isle.

She couldn't envision this as a prison. It was far too beautiful, too plentiful, too…human.

Skittering sounds of running feet rushed past her. Sorcha rocked forward with the force, her skirts stiffening with sand and salt. Her tangled hair stuck to her face as she whipped around.

No one. Not a single person stood around her, but she could feel the crowd. Hands tugged her clothing and grazed across her arms and pack.

She swallowed. "Thank you for your hospitality. I need to make it to the castle. Could you help me?"

It was a shot in the dark. The Fae standing around her might not want her to go there. They might want to toss her over the edge of the cliffs and wipe away all traces of humanity. Sorcha wouldn't blame them. Humans were rarely kind to the Fae.

Instead, gentle hands cupped her elbows and encouraged her to lean against them. The sores on her feet were so painful, she didn't hesitate to accept the invisible support. Tears pricked her eyes at their kindness.

"Thank you," she whispered. "I cannot thank you enough."

They helped her fly. Her feet skimmed the ground as they carried her towards the castle. The front door used to be red, the paint peeling from the top. Golden rivets tarnished with age were lodged around the frame, and a bronze lion held the knocker in its mouth.

Light filtered through the cracked door. She stooped and peered through the broken wood. An empty room stood beyond. White sheets covered the furniture, and cobwebs stretched from ceiling to floor.

Sorcha stuck a foot out and nudged the door open. Its groan echoed through the room and bounced up the grand staircase leading to the second story. A cobweb drifted on the air where she had torn it from its place on the door.

"This is the castle of Hy-brasil," she whispered. Sorcha reached up and caught the cobweb, transferring it and the spider to the wall. "Sorry."

Twitching her skirts to the side, Sorcha stepped into the castle with wide eyes. Dim light caught upon dust motes, turning the room to starlight.

"She made it," a familiar voice grumbled.

"I did," Sorcha replied. "You're Cian, are you not?"

"Humans aren't meant to know our names. I didn't give you that, ungrateful wretch."

"But I have it now, and I made it to the castle."

"With help."

She shrugged. "Does it matter? I'm here all the same, and now I would like to speak to the Tuatha dé Danann."

"The master isn't taking visitors."

There was a faint outline of a short figure in the shadows of the stairwell. Dust had settled upon his shoulders, far too round to be human and shuddering in anger. Sorcha narrowed her eyes on him and committed the little details to memory.

"I'm afraid I cannot give him that choice. Bring me to him."

"I'm not your errand boy."

"Then tell me the way." Sorcha put steel into her voice. She willed sharp edges into the words, so he would have no choice but to obey.

The Fae man grumbled. "If you think that will scare me—"

"It should," she interrupted. "You don't know me, gnome. You take a great risk in underestimating me."

She threw the words out in hopes her memory served true. Gnomes were short, squat creatures with round bodies and rolls of fat. The dust settling revealed a body type very similar to that.

Cian shivered and tossed the dust back into the air. "Good guess."

"Tell me the way to your master."

"What will you give me in return?"

"I will make no more deals with the Fae!" Her shout hurt her ears. "*Now.*"

"Up the staircase then, girl. Keep going straight to the throne room. You can't miss it."

"Throne room?" She coughed in surprise.

"What, did you think the master would be in his receiving room? The throne room, girl. You want to see the master so bad? Perhaps you should prepare for what you will meet."

She refused to look towards him. Clothing stiff, body aching, face burning from sun and salt, she ascended the stairs with her head held high. She would not break nor would she yield.

Sorcha resolved to be stronger than she had ever been before. Stronger than when she helped her first patient's child into the world. More capable than when her father fell ill, and her sisters needed her to be the stable one. More brave than the first time she cut into a stranger's body and pulled out beetles hoping they wouldn't turn and attack her.

The Fae would not look at her with pity. The master was even less likely to give her any kind of clemency. She would need her wits about her. Sorcha knew convincing a Fae to leave this isle would be nigh impossible.

But she had to try.

The staircase led to more ancient stones. One wall had crumbled to dust revealing a room filled to the brim with tattered paintings. She didn't pause, although her curiosity piqued.

At the end of the castle, another stairwell descended. Chandeliers covered in cobwebs dripped spiders instead of gems. The white marble floor had once been a remarkable sight. Now, cracks ran like rivers through a canyon, marring the once opulent surface.

Stairs led up to a dais covered by moth-eaten gray fabric. The throne loomed in the darkness, outlined by antlers and horns jutting out in all directions. Sorcha could only see heavy boots leading up to thick, muscular legs. Shadows blanketed the rest of him.

The Tuatha dé Danann was a man.

"I have journeyed across the sea, through hardships and storm, to make a deal with you, m'lord." She hesitated before the throne, unsure whether she should continue.

His boots shifted. A heel nudged enough to reveal a perfect footprint in the dust. How long had he sat there? Had he been waiting for her?

"I no longer make deals with humans."

There was something wrong with his voice. It was the grating edge of rock against the bones of the earth. It scratched down her spine and made her palms tingle. She gasped.

"The MacNara twins sent me, and they said you would—"

"The MacNara twins?"

"Yes, m'lord. They said you would help."

"Did they? Perhaps they mistook me for someone else."

"I—" she stuttered over her words. "A-are you connected to the human world at all? Do you know what's going on out there?"

"I have no concern for human strife."

She gathered bunches of her stiff skirt into her fists. "We're suffering from a blood beetle plague. We cannot survive if we do not have the cure, and the MacNara twins said they would help if I brought you back to them. I beg—"

"I see little begging," he growled.

Sorcha's mind whirled. He wasn't letting her finish! How could she beg if he wouldn't give her the chance to speak?

"The blood beetles eat humans from the inside out. We cannot stop them on our own, and I need you to—"

"Need?"

"Yes!" she exclaimed. "Need. There is *no* other way to find a cure. The twins promised me that all I have to do is bring you back—"

"They lied." The shadows bunched and coiled.

"Fae cannot lie."

"Then they twisted the truth. I can tell you now, girl, the MacNara twins do not have the cure for the blood beetles. Now go."

Her chest clenched in horror. They *had* to have the cure. She hadn't traveled all this way only to discover that the faeries had tricked her.

"Go?" she repeated. "Where will I go? This is an island!"

"I don't care where you go. Hy-brasil is no place for one such as you."

Had she failed? He remained in the shadows, barely moving except his damned foot that created more mysteries than it solved. Sorcha only knew his voice grated on her nerves, his imperious nature made her palms itch to smack him, and his refusal to help suggested he was a heartless creature with no care for others.

How dare he?

"My *family* will die if I do not find this cure."

"You are so concerned over death, I wonder if you have any other thoughts in your head."

Sorcha's mouth gaped open before her cheeks flushed bright red with anger. "Do you have any concern over the welfare of others?"

"Little for those who threaten my staff."

"The gnome at the door?" She swung an arm wildly in the direction from whence she came. "He is one of the rudest, most foul creatures I have ever met! I will not apologize for my tone nor my words."

"Humans rarely have any sympathy for the Fae. Yet, you seem to think I owe you a boon for…what? Existing?"

"Are you so cruel you cannot feel even the smallest amount of sympathy for my people?"

The damned boot she had been staring at shifted again. A surge of triumph straightened her spine.

"I am known for my cruelty. And, it seems, so are you," he growled.

"Your judgment is cast quickly for a man who will not even show his face."

"The sight of my face is not one for the faint of heart."

"Then you willingly admit to being a coward and a boor?"

"A coward?" His voice deepened, slicing through the darkness and cracking against the stone. It shook her ribs and vibrated through her body. "You dare accuse me so?"

"I dare much for the well-being of my family." Sorcha's voice shook with righteous indignation but she shivered in fear.

The shadows quaked, and the drapes around the throne billowed as he stood up…and up…and up.

Her brow wrinkled in worry as she stared at his great height. Good lord, how big was he?

A cloak concealed much of his figure. Like great leathery wings, the dark fabric billowed as he stepped down the stairs towards her. Each measured step clunked hard. The cracked marble creaked.

He didn't have to rush towards her to intimidate. The sheer size of him made her shiver in apprehension. Broad shoulders, trim waist, and a hood covering his head were all she could make out, even at this close distance. Sorcha held her breath and stood her ground.

She would not show fear.

He stopped only when his toes were a hair's breadth from hers. Sorcha stared into the darkness of his hood, her head barely reaching his biceps. She set her jaw and squared her shoulders. Whatever he would say could not be worse than their previous words.

"You know very little of me, human." His breath brushed her hair, carrying the scent of mint and citrus.

"I can confidently say I find your morals, and thusly your character, to be *abhorrent.*"

"On what are you basing these accusations?"

"You have forced your servants to call you master. You hide your face and intimidate a visitor seeking help. And then, you go so far as to refuse to provide aid to those who need it. Those, sir, are the facts upon which I judge you."

"Have you no care nor discretion for your own survival? You berate a creature of superior strength!"

"Superior? Sir, I find you *lacking* in every sense of the term."

His aggressive way of arguing made her think she had gotten through his thick hide, but she had been wrong.

His spine straightened, and his shoulders squared. The cloak drew tight across his chest and he stepped away from her. He took the air with him, stealing it from her lungs, as a blast of cold air pushed her back, such was his anger.

"Go," he said.

"I have nowhere to go," Sorcha repeated. "If you would stop being so stubborn—"

She didn't think. She reached out, grasped ahold of the cloak he wore, and yanked.

The fabric slid from his shoulders and revealed his horrific face.

Light speared across the misshapen form. Multiple marks gouged the flesh from his cheeks, forehead, and chin. She might have forgiven a scar, for they suggested heroic deeds. Even a birthmark or disfigurement from childhood could have been easily overlooked. But this?

Open wounds had turned to fissures in the stone of his face. Crystals grew from them, some violet, some precious gems, and a hint of color-changing opal, all jutting from his flesh and tainting whatever humanity he may have once held. They stretched far up the sides of his head, shaved other than a crop of hair at the top.

He might have been a handsome man once. His jaw was square, his lips full, and his eyes a piercing blue that stared straight into her soul.

Sorcha gasped as she met his gaze. Ice froze her veins and fear made her teeth chatter. And yet, warmth bloomed deep in her belly. His eyes were beautiful, expressive, and filled with so much pain.

"What happened to you?" she whispered.

He lunged towards her. With a gasp, she threw her hands up to cover her face. She knew that look. Sorcha had grown up in a brothel. The desire to strike a woman was easy to recognize in a man's expression.

He didn't hit her. Instead, his hand wrapped around her wrist with a punishing grip. Stone bit into the sensitive flesh, and she whimpered.

"Is this what you wanted to see?" he growled, so close to her face that their noses touched.

"I meant no disrespect."

He didn't give her even a moment of respite. He dragged her from the throne room so quickly she slid across the floor until she got her bearings. Only then did she jog to keep up with him.

Sorcha yanked on her arm. "Let me go!"

"No."

"Let me go, I said!"

"I heard you." His voice rumbled down the hallway and sent footsteps skittering.

"Where are you taking me?"

"You argue that you cannot leave this cursed isle, then insult me in the next breath. So, princess, I am taking you to your room."

"Room?" She dug in her heels, forcing him to drag her. "Is there a decent available room in this spider-ridden ruin?"

His fingers squeezed the delicate bones of her wrist, making her gasp in pain. "Are you afraid of spiders?"

"I'm afraid of very little."

"Good."

Sorcha winced as his shoulder struck the broken door. No wonder it had cracked nearly in half. The man treated himself like a battering ram rather than a person.

Stones dug into her heels as he yanked her outside, but she refused to yelp. He did not get the satisfaction of knowing the journey was just as painful as his stony grip.

"I can walk without you dragging me!" she shouted.

"I can hear without you screaming."

He picked up speed, then she couldn't speak anymore. Her breath tasted like blood as her lungs worked overdrive to keep up with him. The straps of her pack dug into her shoulders and arms. Her feet grew numb as the skin scraped off, and still he dragged her towards the opposite end of the isle.

By the time they reached his destination, she was ready to fall over. Dehydration and hunger weakened her mind and body.

He pointed to a small hut in what appeared to be a moor hanging on the edge of the ocean. Mist swirled across the swamp and moss.

"Your new abode," he growled.

Sorcha forced her eyes to narrow, to take in the details that her mind wanted to ignore. The hut hovered over the water on stilts and stretched out into the bay. Heather grew up to the salty water, crumbling and dying at the edges.

The hut's image wavered, as though she were looking through hot air. Runes appeared etched into the wooden walls and along the ramp leading to it. She suddenly understood the blinking lights hovering in the air near it.

"That's a hag's hut," she said.

"Astute."

"Those are incredibly dangerous for anyone who does not practice magic. I cannot stay there."

"You can, and you will."

He grabbed her arm again, swinging her around onto the ramp and shoving her shoulders for good measure. He waved a hand in the air. Glimmering light rose from the ground into the sky.

Sorcha lurched forward and hit an invisible wall.

"What did you do?" she croaked as she slammed her fists in the air. "What did you do!"

"I'm keeping you here. Survive, human. Eventually, I might listen to your inquiry."

He turned and walked away.

Sorcha nearly choked on her own tongue. He walked away? He left her with the most dangerous of evil magics behind her, and then just walked away?

"How dare you?" she screamed. "Don't leave me here! You cannot!"

He could, and he did.

She pressed her hands and forehead against the shield he placed at the edge of the dock and sighed. There was no possible way she would even attempt to stay in that hut.

Sorcha turned and glanced at the runes which kept blinking in and out of sight.

"Think. What are your other options, Sorcha? How can you fix this?"

She scanned the surrounding area, stepping towards the edge of the ramp to peer into the water. White glowing eyes blinked back at her.

"Not the water then," she murmured. "So…um…"

The runes on the door glowed a bright red, but were dulled to a rusty hue from the splatter of aged chicken blood. Sorcha recognized the arcing patterns upon the wood.

"The hard way it is."

She secured her pack on her shoulders and stepped up the ramp. The hag stone between her breasts slid free. She pressed it to her lips, then held it to her eye and watched the spells melt away.

It was a relatively simple protective curse. There were parts of her mother's books which spoke of pagan rituals. This spell she recognized from the pages of a black book she never should've read.

Her fingers itched to try out what she had learned, to dismantle the circles drawn by witches of old. However, such aged curses were useful. Now she could be certain there was at least one place on the isle she was safe.

Sorcha reached out and dragged her finger straight down the first rune. The second, she traced the circles and lines without hesitating. And the last, she turned her hand in the air as though she twisted a doorknob.

A harsh crack echoed in the air, and the door swung upon.

Without the hag stone, the interior terrified her. Eviscerated chickens hung from the ceiling in various states of decay, their blood covering the floor until it shone as if polished, and here and there, startlingly white feathers made downy islands in the gore. Human skulls decorated the walls with candles inside them, making the eye sockets glow. Knives, hatchets, and scythes hung on wall brackets while chains dangled above them.

Through the hag stone, the room was entirely different. Although it was a small, single room hut, it was a home, albeit dusty. A dining room table with one place setting was in one corner. Dried fruit balanced in the center, mummified with age. There was a desk in another corner piled high with papers and adorned with ink wells. A small, but quaint bed was against the farthest wall below a window shining in the moonlight.

Sorcha swallowed hard and steeled her nerves.

"Faeries of this household, I mean no disrespect. I am a weary traveler who searches for a place to rest my head. This home is safe, it is warm, and I vow I will touch nothing which is not mine. If your hospitality stretches so far as to gift food and drink, I will assist in cleaning this household."

For a moment, she heard nothing. Silence rang as loud as her words. She could only hope she had not offended whatever brownies or redcaps remained.

She twisted her fingers and listened. Her patience was rewarded. Soft chirping sounds heralded faerie movement. Pattering footsteps started towards her, and she felt the slightest of nudges against her thigh.

Looking down, she saw that a line on the floor had smudged.

"Salt?" she whispered. Or at least something similar. The white powder now held a fingerprint in it, marring the smooth line.

When she looked back up, the room was no longer frightening nor haunted. It was merely a room to the naked eye.

"Thank you," she said. "Your kindness knows no bounds. I will honor the words I spoke before entering."

She made her way to the bed and dumped her pack on the ground. Her back groaned with the movement, balance shifting with sudden lightheadedness. She wasn't done yet.

Her hands knew where the small jar of sugar was, even if her mind wasn't entirely functioning. Sorcha rummaged through her pack and came up with the tiny clay jar. It always paid to have some kind of gift for the Fae. She'd learned this lesson time and time again until her pockets were always full.

For good measure, she also snagged a tiny coin. The dim moonlight gleamed off the edges, for she had polished it many times over. Sorcha called it her lucky coin, and it seemed appropriate to give away now.

"I will share what little I have with you," she murmured. "They are small, but I believe I may find more tomorrow. Not as payment, I know your ways."

Chairs screeched as she turned, rocking as they thumped onto the floor. Sorcha blinked at the table now clean of all dust and removed of dirty plates.

"Well, you didn't have to go through all that trouble."

A mug appeared out of thin air and plunked onto the table.

Sorcha was stunned. She wanted to hold the hag stone to her eye just to get a look at the hidden faeries. They couldn't be more terrifying a sight than their master.

"You are too kind," she breathed. "I will leave my things above the fireplace. Please enjoy them, and I'm sorry there's not more."

Hardly five strides carried her to the other end of the hut. She leaned, blew the dust off the hearth, and set her items down. The brownie in her small room at the brothel liked to climb. She always hid little gifts in the rafters just to give it a reason for adventure.

They were naturally curious creatures, something she always respected about them. Brownies, although sometimes a nuisance, were helpful. They wanted to do everything they could, and when they couldn't, lost their minds.

Her brow furrowed. She hoped that wasn't what she was dealing with here. House brownies easily turned to boggarts if they didn't keep busy. And the room had been dusty…

She turned. "Are you brownies?"

There was no response.

"It will not make me think ill of you. It's merely easier for me to know what you might like in the cupboards. The brownie at my home was fond of honey, but I met a boggart once, and he was much fonder of fresh bread."

The cup on the table tilted.

Sorcha smiled. "A boggart then. I'll do my best to steal something from that nasty Tuatha dé Danann's kitchen. We'll have this place shining, and then I'll bake fresh bread, as long as you don't pull the covers off me."

She watched the mug dance back and forth. Apparently, that was the correct thing to say.

The soft swishing sound of her skirts lulled her senses into a stupor. Sorcha stumbled to the bed and fell face down. It didn't matter that cobwebs tangled in her hair or that the layer of dust was so thick it bounced with her and then returned to the mattress. She was so exhausted, she could even sleep through the boggart placing clammy hands on her cheeks as it checked to make sure she was alive.

She slept for the rest of the afternoon, through the night, and well into the morning. However, it felt only a few seconds until she was blinking her eyes at the dappled sunlight shining through the hut window.

Blinking, she groggily realized that a soft sound had awakened her. Tapping, like a spoon against ceramic, although that couldn't be right. She remembered very clearly that she was in a hag's hut which had seen better days. Even the boggart couldn't have gotten a tea set in such a short amount of time.

Sorcha sat straight up in bed, the tangled mat of her red hair sticking out at odd angles. The room had completely changed overnight. The dust and dirt was piled in a corner, the floors revealed to be rich warm wood. The furniture gleamed and the fireplace was scrubbed clean of all grime and smoke stain.

Something clinked again, drawing her attention to the kitchen table near another window. Two chairs framed it, one currently occupied by a short woman with a mop of white hair. An aged, though clean, kirtle touched the floor. Tiny pink flowers decorated the pale fabric, and must have been hand-painted. Her white hair smoothed into a large bun, but strands of frizzy curls had freed themselves.

The strange woman set her spoon on the saucer and sipped at her tea.

Sorcha blinked. "Am I still in Hy-brasil?"

"I believe so. If I'm in Hy-brasil, then you must be here, too." The strange woman had a nice voice. Comforting, like that of a warm blanket on a chilled autumn day. It was familiar although Sorcha couldn't put her finger on why.

Large, brown eyes watched her every movement as Sorcha fiddled with the blanket covering her legs. "I don't remember tucking myself into bed."

"Oh, I assume that was the boggart, dearie. Although, I'd say she is well on her way back to brownie now, thanks to you."

"Thanks to me?"

"You gave her something to do, and that's all brownies want."

Sorcha's mind raced, and realization dawned on her like a hammer. "You're the voice I heard on the shoreline. You were with that gnome!"

"It's a good memory you've got there." The woman set her teacup down and smiled. "You can call me Pixie."

"Is that what you are?"

"It is. Are you surprised?"

"I've never met a pixie before," Sorcha said as she gathered the blankets at her chest. "It's an honor, ma'am."

Pixie chortled, the laugh booming out of her chest and shaking the table. "Oh, but you are a sweet little thing! So polite. Boggart, I think you were quite right. She's a fair treat in this horrid place."

"Boggart? Is she here?"

"Of course, dearie. She doesn't want you to see her yet. She came all the way up to the castle, a rarity I might add, to tell us how pleasant you were. You've made her happy giving her something to do and a place to clean. Losing her hag was a terrible blow."

"I—" her head was spinning. Sorcha couldn't keep up with what Pixie was saying, let alone the strange turn this adventure had taken. "I apologize if this seems rude, Pixie, but what are you doing here?"

Pixie sat up straight, setting her cup down so hard the saucer chipped. "How presumptuous of me! Dearie, if I have frightened you in any way, do allow me to apologize. I've come to take you up to the castle, get you some tea, and then…" Her nose wrinkled. "Perhaps a bath if you are amiable?"

"I can honestly say that would be appreciated."

Sorcha pushed the covers back and stretched her aching spine. The pain of her journey had dulled to a persistent stiffness, but it was significantly better than before. Her skin still felt like it was covered in a thin layer of filth, and her hair didn't move when she shifted. Sorcha winced, she needed a bath as soon as humanly possible.

She looked down and frowned. "Who changed me into my underthings?"

"Boggart, dearie. Had quite the time of it as well. You're much larger than she."

"Yet another thing I need to thank you for, Boggart. I'll be sure to cook two loaves of fresh bread for us tonight."

A faint squeak from the corner radiated delight.

Sorcha hobbled towards her pack. Muscles screamed as she bent down to find clothing, so much that a soft whimper escaped her lips.

"Oh, there's enough of that," Pixie grumbled. "We'll throw a cloak over you, and you'll be covered to decency. We don't have the same ridiculous restraints as humans. A body is a body."

"And a body grows chilled," Sorcha pointed out. The idea of leaving without having to tie up the back of her gown sounded lovely. Usually her sisters helped, and she had little reason to change clothing on a ship full of men. Here, she would need help.

"A body will last until it's stuck in the bath."

"I suppose you're right," she stood up only to groan again. "But I still need to find something to wear."

"We have plenty, dearie." Pixie stood up and hopped towards her, surprisingly spry for a woman who looked so old. "Let me help you put your cloak on. It pins at your throat now, doesn't it? There. It's lovely.

We'll get you warmed up and fed in a moment!"

Pixie planted her hands on Sorcha's shoulder blades and shoved. For a glamoured being, her strength was impressive. Before Sorcha could blink, they were already outside and moving down the ramp.

Why was it that faeries dragged her around so much? Sorcha's eyes watered in the bright sunlight. "What time is it?"

"Mid-day, dearie. You've been asleep for some time."

"It was a long journey," she said.

"I imagine it would be! Coming from the human world all the way here. You're a brave little thing and polite."

"No braver than the next person." Sorcha tried to focus on the words, staring around her at all the new sights. There were people everywhere. Men and women, dressed in clothing styles from a hundred years ago or more, but still people. They tended the fields, drove herds of sheep out of their pens, laid in the grass, and pointed out clouds to each other. "Are these all faeries?"

"Indeed, they are."

"Why didn't I see them yesterday?" A man walked past them and doffed his shepherd's hat. Sorcha nodded back politely and tugged her cloak tighter around her waist.

"We tend to be shy around humans. One never knows how they will react. Boggart was adamant you were kind, so the others were less hesitant to be seen."

"Word travels fast around here," Sorcha mused.

"It certainly does."

Another man walked past them, his eyes lingering too long upon the gap at the bottom of the cloak which revealed the delicate lines of her ankle bones. Sorcha blushed, and Pixie smacked the back of the man's head as he passed.

"Cretin," Pixie muttered. "No respect for the womenfolk. Those selkie men need to be taken to task."

"That was a selkie?" Sorcha spun to stare at his back. He glanced over his shoulder and winked at her.

"We're not on a tour. Attention back towards the castle, please."

"But—"

"No buts! You aren't meeting a selkie today, or ever, if I have my say."

Sorcha furrowed her brows. "Are they dangerous?"

"To a person's sanity."

"He didn't seem all that bad."

"None of them do." Pixie guided her around the back to the castle, nudging her this way and that until she opened a small wooden gate. "The Fae are notoriously interested in humans. Far more than we should be, I might add. Stay away from faerie men, and you'll be much happier."

Sorcha stepped into the garden beyond the gate and inhaled the sweet scent of growing herbs. It was too early in the year for any plant to be bearing fruit, but tomatoes hung swollen and bright red. Basil spiced the air with a heady flavor while carrot tops tickled her toes.

"This garden is beautiful," she whispered.

"I'm sure Cian will be pleased to hear that."

"The gnome?" Sorcha skirted around a patch of turnips. "Cian is a gardener?"

"Most gnomes are. They're good at it, too. The earth listens to them, you see, and that makes it a lot easier. Come on!"

Sorcha glanced up and realized she'd fallen behind. Pixie was holding open a plain brown door framed by gray stone. Steam billowed out in hot, rolling waves.

"Where does that lead?"

"To the kitchens, dearie."

"I didn't see the kitchens before."

The cobblestone floor was cold against the soles of her bare feet. She curled her toes and held onto the door frame. The scent of pastries, bubbling stew, and strong tea made her head swim. Her stomach clenched in hunger.

Three women puttered around the kitchen. One leaned over a large cauldron, tasting the soup within. Another kneaded dough into a familiar shape while the last ducked behind a curtain. Trickling water striking a basin rained through her senses.

"Come on, dearie," Pixie said. "We'll get you all cleaned up, and then fill that belly of yours."

Sorcha tiptoed around the curtain and gaped at the large metal tub beyond it. "This is too fine for the likes of me."

"*Nonsense.* There's nothing better than bathing in hot water. In you go."

"I would be fine in a stream—"

"In."

The steely order had Sorcha unclasping her cloak. The fabric fell to the floor with a heavy thump, followed by her white underdress.

"Should I even be here?" she asked. The hot water stung the scrapes on her knees but made her muscles loosen their tight knots. She hissed her pleasure as the steam coated her face.

"Why shouldn't you be? Lean forward, and I'll get your back."

It had been a long time since someone helped Sorcha bathe. She remembered her mother scrubbing vigorously at her dirt-streaked skin. She was always red for days after her baths. In contrast, Sorcha's sisters were far less vigorous when she moved in with them.

"Your master didn't seem keen on having me linger," she said as the sponge slid over her skin.

"Yes, I heard he was rather…harsh with you."

She snorted. "Harsh is one way to describe it."

"He's a good man, but he has a temper."

"Was that his temper? I thought he was merely a brute, leaving little to make a good impression."

Pixie grabbed another bucket of water. "The master can be difficult, but don't let first impressions sway you. If you judge him harshly, he'll do the same for you. Hold your breath."

Water cascaded over her head and down her shoulders. Sorcha stared into the muddy water while clumps of earth swirled with her movement. Bubbles popped, releasing the scent of lemon into the air.

"Have you known him long?" Sorcha asked. The haunting vision of his marred face and electric blue eyes rose in the water.

"For as long as he's been alive. The master was a handsome child." Pixie paused. "And is still a handsome man."

She wanted to disagree. The words were on the tip of her tongue to say he wasn't handsome at all, that his exterior matched his interior, but she paused. Sorcha had always been quick to judge others. Perhaps now would be a good time to practice patience.

"I couldn't say," she said. "He didn't seem interested in helping me. That didn't add to his appeal."

"Help you? Whatever could the master help you with, dearie?"

Pixie moved behind the tub and tugged Sorcha backwards. Her spine hit the warm metal, and a soft sigh slipped from her lips. The weight of her hair slid out of the water and dangled to the floor. A slight tug suggested Pixie planned to work all the snarls into smooth curls.

"My people are dying," Sorcha said. "A plague is sweeping across our lands, and I can't cure it. No one can. Our doctors are baffled, our herbalists are stumped, and even the mystics shrug their shoulders and say the gods are angry. There is nothing to be done."

"And our master?"

"I was sent here by other Tuatha dé Danann. They said if I brought him back they would give me the cure. My father is dying, and my sisters are likely to grow ill afterwards. I had to do something."

The rasp of the brush lulled her senses. Her eyes drifted shut as the comforting rhythm reminded her body she had endured a significant journey.

"I'm sure if you told the master all that he'd help."

"He's already said no, but he doesn't know how determined I am."

"It's a good trait to have."

"Is it?" Sorcha laughed. "Perhaps I could bring you home with me, and you could tell my neighbors that. They only put up with me, because I'm a healer."

"A healer?" the Pixie's voice sparkled. "We don't have one of those."

She wanted to reply, but her muscles were so relaxed that all she could manage was a quiet murmur. The bath was exactly what she needed, although she hadn't known it before. Every ache disappeared. Every worry dissolved. She focused upon the repetitive movement of the brush, and let her mind quiet.

All good things came to an end. Eventually, the water chilled, and Pixie made it to the top of Sorcha's head.

"Come now, let's get you dressed." Pixie passed a gentle hand over Sorcha's head.

Tears pricked and water blurred the edges of Sorcha's vision. She hadn't expected to find people who were so genuinely good-hearted. It was nearly her undoing.

"Thank you," she whispered and stood. The water sluiced off her body, pouring in waterfalls from her breasts, lingering in the valleys of her hips.

Pixie tsked. "You need to gain weight, dearie. You're positively *thin.*"

"I'm not from royalty. I'm working class."

"That doesn't make a difference to me. Come here."

The towel in Pixie's hands snapped as she held it out. Another strange moment. No one dried Sorcha off after her bath except herself. Even her mother had let Sorcha wrap herself in a towel before scrubbing her hair.

The soft towel dragged over every inch of Sorcha's body with expert precision. Pixie didn't hesitate as if she had done this her entire life.

"Pixie?" Sorcha asked. "What did you do before you came to Hybrasil?"

The other woman hesitated for a moment. "I was a lady's maid to the most beautiful of Seelie women."

"Who?"

"The Queen Neve, of course."

"Queen?" Sorcha let out a long breath through her teeth. "That's a high-ranking position."

"Queen usually is."

"No, I mean the Queen's maid. That must have been an incredible experience. I envy you."

Pixie looked at her with shock in her eyes and burst into laughter. "Dearie, you are a delight! I have never in my life had anyone envy me for being a maid." She laughed so hard that she handed the towel to Sorcha. "High ranking for being a Queen's maid. The thought!"

With a soft smile on her face, Sorcha finished toweling herself dry. "It's a rather remarkable position, you must admit."

Twisted shadows danced behind the blinds and between the maids drifting through the room. Sorcha tilted her head to the side and watched the wings, feathers, and misshapen forms revealed by their shadows. They likely weren't aware she could see their true forms.

She hoped, someday, they might walk without the glamour in place. Their fear was warranted. Humans didn't react well to strange creatures. Sorcha refused to believe she would recoil from their appearances.

That would require she stay. She shook herself. Staying on this island wasn't a part of the plan, and she had to believe the Tuatha dé Danann would at least listen. Her journey was of great importance. He had to see reason.

"Pixie?" she called out. "Where is your master today?"

"Training in the yard, I would suspect. That's where he usually is."

"Training?"

"Oh, yes," Pixie said as she returned. She held a pale green gown in her hands, the swath of fabric nearly touching the floor. "He's a very impressive warrior, although I'll let him tell you those stories. I believe this will look lovely with that hair of yours."

She reached out and traced a finger across the dress. Velvet, the material of nobility.

"I cannot wear this," Sorcha said. "I'll ruin it."

"No one else is wearing it. You might as well ruin it or the moths will."

Yearning flooded through her, sparkling at the ends of her fingertips as she reached for the gown. She'd never worn such fine fabric before. The brothel prided itself on providing well-groomed, beautiful women to its customers, but the velvets were saved for her sisters when important clients came to visit. Sorcha had always worn wool and cotton.

Her fingers trailed over the fabric, pulling it into her arms. "Thank you."

"I enjoy decorating pretty things, dearie. Now put that on, and we'll get you some food."

Sorcha dragged the dress over her head and tied the towel along the wet length of her hair. Someone had set up a feast on the table. Fresh fruit, vegetables, lettuce, and bread overflowed their bowls. A jug of cold water sat within easy reach.

She fell onto her seat and stared in disbelief. "This is for me?"

"Well, it's not much," Pixie sniffed. "But it must do for now."

"This is more than I ever would have asked for. You should have sent me on my way with an apple."

"We have better hospitality than that. Eat up."

Sorcha shoveled food into her mouth and gulped glass after glass of water. Her stomach could rebel later. This was more food than she'd seen in weeks. The water tasted like the first snowfall.

When her belly ached and her throat closed at the thought of more, she pushed her plate back and sighed.

"I hate to be more of a bother," she began, "but do you have extra flour and butter? I'd like to make bread for Boggart, but have no supplies."

"For Boggart?" Pixie repeated. "Brownies prefer honey, dearie."

"She's not a brownie anymore and seemed very excited about bread."

"I suppose that hut has a kitchen, doesn't it? All right, then. We'll give you enough to stock your kitchen, and then you won't be a bother here."

The faeries filled her arms with everything she could need. So much food that Sorcha needed a pack which was quickly produced and stuffed to the brim.

They were kind and gracious almost to the point of suspicion. Sorcha's brows drew together as she left the kitchen with a shaking head. It made little sense for them to change their minds so quickly. One day they were invisible, and the next, they were making friends? It all seemed rather odd.

"What are you doing here?" The grumpy voice behind her was familiar.

Sorcha turned and met the gaze of Cian, the gnome. Not the glamoured human, not the invisible voice, but the short, squat gnome. Rolls of fat poured into the vague shape of a face. Two eyes, a nose, and a wide split mouth on pasty pale skin, all underneath the wide brim of a brown hat. He had shoved himself into clothing, buttons threatening to pop off under the stress. He wore no shoes, because his toenails were so long they curled into the ground.

"Cian," she said with a hesitant nod.

"You don't even have the good sense to run screaming?"

"I have your name. Why would I scream?"

"Gnomes are frightening creatures. We used to eat humans."

"'Used to' is the operative phrase there, I imagine," she said as she nudged the fence gate open with her hip. "Thank you for reminding me that not everyone here is as kind as the faeries in the kitchen."

"Brownies. They always want to take care of something. They'll smother you to death if you let them!"

She had come to the same conclusion. The gate slammed shut behind her, and she skirted back down the lane towards the hag's hut.

The faeries were kind, but almost too kind. She didn't remember the stories about brownies, but fully intended to put Boggart to good use. Plying someone with bread for information was easy enough, though perhaps a bit devious.

It would work out best for them both in the long run. She needed more information, and Boggart was the perfect person to ask.

CHAPTER SIX
THE DINNER

"She asked for what?" Eamonn's voice echoed in his chamber.

"The ingredients for bread, master."

"She didn't ask for the bread itself?"

"No. She said she wanted to bake the bread for Bronagh herself."

He leaned back in the high chair of his desk. Steepling his fingers, he pressed them against his lips. "Why would she want to do that? The boggart is hardly something to waste her time on."

"Perhaps she considers Bronagh *worth* her time, master."

He hadn't thought of that. Boggarts and those of the lesser Fae were traditionally beneath the Tuatha dé Danann. Their jobs were clear. Slaves, footmen, sometimes maids if they were pretty enough. Never in his life had he seen anyone take the time to treat them with respect.

The suggestion that the human cared was ridiculous. She had been so furious, charging into his throne room like she owned the place. Her eyes spat fire, while her words seared his pride. He refused to believe her as kind as Oona thought.

There was a warrior in her.

Oona bustled behind him, cleaning every inch of his quarters. She was good at that. He had never seen another pixie so willing to do a maid's job. She was the best, and the only acceptable maid to bring with him to this cursed place.

He much preferred the pixie without her glamour. The old woman's disguise grated on his nerves. Pixies were lithe creatures, with a cap of flower petals instead of hair. Hers was a pale dusky lavender, matching the shimmering wings she wore draped around her shoulders.

"Where is she now?" he asked.

"The same place as last night. The hag's hut."

"She went back?"

"Without complaint, I might add."

Eamonn leaned forward and pressed his elbows against the desk. "Why?"

"To cook bread for Bronagh."

"Yes, but why else? There has to be a reason."

Oona sighed. She crossed around to the front of his desk and knelt before him. "You will hurt yourself trying to understand the human. You know full well it's impossible."

"I cannot accept that as truth."

"Then you will go mad. Let it go, master. Some things you will never understand."

He couldn't let it go. He closed his eyes and saw her flashing green eyes. Emeralds and rainforests hid in her gaze, equally dangerous and cutting. It was strange he would remember her eyes, since the rest of her was unimpressive.

No self-respecting Seelie would ever entertain royalty while looking like they rolled in a pig's pen. The woman had been disgusting. Seaweed stuck in her hair, clothing wrinkled and smudged with dirt. One foot bare, the other covered by a threadbare slipper.

Yet, she'd held herself with the grace of a queen.

Perhaps that explained how she'd bewitched him. She was an enigma, an oddity, a strange creature who made little sense. She shouldn't exist, and yet, here she was.

"No human has ever come to Hy-brasil, have they?" he asked.

"Not that I know of, master."

"So how did she get here?"

"I wouldn't know. It's not my place to question how people arrive, only to take care of them when they do."

He snorted. "Cian made quite the impression."

"That was my fault," Oona winced. "I said his name in front of the girl. I didn't think she could hear us while we held our glamours, but somehow she did."

"He's angry at you?"

"When is he not?" She stood up from his floor and scowled at him. "You're stalling. What are you going to do about her?"

"Who?" Eamonn lifted an eyebrow and leaned back in his chair. For good measure, he lifted his booted feet onto the desk.

"Stop teasing me! It's bad for my health. You know full well who I'm speaking of. She's a nice little thing, and it's not settling well with me that you were so rude."

"Did I ask for an opinion?"

"No, but I'm giving one. She is the sweetest little thing that has washed ashore in nigh two hundred years. You need to apologize to her—" Oona lifted a hand when he opened his mouth, "—apologize, and then invite her to stay here. It's not safe to live in that hut."

Eamonn wanted to fly across the table and strangle her. Apologize? To that miscreant who shouldn't be on this isle to begin with? He had more things to worry about than the feelings of a silly little girl.

Memories of his brother flashed through his mind. His throat tightened as it had when the noose cinched tight across his Adam's apple. The gems at his neck cast a dim glow across his clasped fingers.

Oona made a soft sound of distress and looked away. "I meant no disrespect, master."

"I'm certain you didn't. You have always been one of my favored servants, and for that I spoil you. Do not make me regret that."

She bowed and turned to leave. He met her gaze as she hesitated by the door. "Master, if I may be so bold, perhaps we no longer wish you to see us as servants. We see you as family, my dear, and someday we hope you'll see us the same."

Her skirts swirled as she raced from the room.

He frowned. Was that how his people saw him? As a mysterious figure who cared little for them?

Long ago, when he was young and drunk on the idea of power, he had thought that way. Eamonn stood, clasping his hands behind his back as he wandered to the portrait of his mother. Her golden hair fell straight without a single strand out of place.

He remembered her like this. Always perfect, no matter what the situation. Even when they hanged him.

"What would you do, Mathair?" he murmured. "The girl is a problem. A distraction."

She was the last thing he needed. There were only a few more months to prepare. Even then, he wasn't certain if he would manage. Eamonn walked a path leading only to death.

But a fair, red-headed lass haunted his steps. She had only been here for one night, and already he had not slept. What more would she do?

"Perhaps she is a witch," he said. "A temptress sent by my brother to ensure I never return home."

The thought was likely. Fionn would do anything to keep the Seelie throne.

Growling, Eamonn spun on his heel. Long legs carried him to a wall carved with the image of a great bird. He pressed his palm against a loose stone, pushing hard until the wall gave and revealed a crystal embedded within the structure. Gem touched gem, and the wall shifted.

Beyond, a room glowed, filled to the brim with Fae artifacts. Magic swirled in the air. It danced upon his skin, skittering across the crystals of his face and neck. He was not cursed; Eamonn had tested that immediately once the affliction made itself known. But magic enjoyed touching him all the same.

Brushing the dust motes aside, he reached for a small handheld mirror. Carved roses twined from the handle and bloomed at the top. He thought it rather frivolous. Magical objects always were.

"Show me the red-headed lass." He leaned forward and breathed on the glass. The mirror swirled with mist and cleared. No longer reflecting the room, it revealed to him the interior of the hag's hut.

"What?" he growled. "There must be trickery here."

That was not the girl who had marched into his throne room with anger burning her cheeks. The beauty spinning in circles looked more like a Fae lady.

Her hair, which he remembered as matted and soiled, spun around her in a wide arc. Curls bounced with her movements as she hopped from side to side, arms held as if a partner swung her around. The green velvet dress hugging her curves spun in a perfect circle as she twisted and turned.

He recognized that dance. The humans practiced it at Beltane. The women bent and swayed with lively music.

She danced alone. Her hands clapped in time to music that did not play, and the smile stretched across her face spoke of pure glee.

Eamonn's lips quirked to the side. She was a horrible dancer. Far too bouncy, no control over her limbs or facial expressions, and obviously untrained. Yet, there was still something compelling about her joy.

"This is not the muddy creature with the personality of a shrew," he murmured. "What other secrets do you hold, little human?"

The mirror heard his request, and the image shifted closer as the woman stopped dancing. Her ears were slightly pointed, he realized.

"Curiouser and curiouser."

The burning need in his stomach expanded, blossoming into a full-blown red haze of want and desire. He had to find out more about her. Where she came from, why she was here, what her plans were.

Eamonn brushed aside the wonderment of how she was raised, who had taught her the secrets of the Fae, and why her ears were tipped with faerie points. These were frivolous things which held little weight. They weren't important.

She wasn't important.

And yet…he lifted his head and shouted, "Oona!"

The pixie hadn't gone far. He heard the door open and her voice call out, "Yes, master?"

"Invite her to dinner."

"Master, she requested privacy tonight."

"What?" He dropped the mirror and strode into his parlor. "She said what?"

"She requested that Bronagh and she have a quiet evening to get to know each other."

"Why?"

Oona shrugged. "I would imagine she wishes to rest after her long journey."

"No, she's too smart for that." Eamonn couldn't imagine she didn't have some kind of plan. She was far too dedicated to her cause. Perhaps he was thinking too much like a warrior, and not enough like a man. "How much does Bronagh know about the castle?"

"As much as anyone, I would imagine. She used to live here."

"Would she remember many of its secrets?"

"Maybe?" Oona blinked and twisted her hands together. "You don't think the girl has any ulterior motives? Master, she's been very kind."

"Even the kindest of people can be coy. And clever. I would like to be certain she isn't plotting anything sinister."

Oona threw her hands up in the air. "She's the least sinister person I've ever met!"

"And that would make her an incredible spy, wouldn't it?"

He lifted an eyebrow and reached for his cloak. He would find out just how dangerous this woman might be. Although his people might think him indifferent, they were all he had.

With an embellished swirl, the cloak settled upon his shoulders, and he strode across the battlements.

"You see, Boggart, it's rather easy to make bread," Sorcha said as she kneaded the dough into a rough shape.

The answering squeak made her smile. It wasn't a very supportive squeak, nor did it sound as if the faerie believed her. No matter. The bread would taste wonderful.

Homesickness overwhelmed her as the smell of flour and baking bread filled the small hut. Her sisters loved fresh bread, and Sorcha always made certain it was ready for them at the end of the night. They never wasted a scrap. The scent made the brothel feel more like a home rather than a workplace, and giggles had lifted their spirits to the rafters for hours every night.

She missed them more than anything else. Her eyes drifted towards the moon peeking through the window, and she sent a silent good night to her siblings.

All her hopes and wishes lifted into the air and drifted out to sea. She prayed they were healthy and happy. She hoped Rosaleen had taken up that kind nobleman and now lived in wealth and comfort, and Briana remembered to relax. Sorcha made the sign of the cross over her chest and breathed her worry into the moonlight.

"Please keep Papa alive."

She couldn't force those things to happen, not from here. Sorcha resorted to wishes and dreams. Perhaps the Tuatha dé Danann would hear her and see that her family would think kindly upon her choices.

A squeak interrupted her thoughts.

"Oh?" Sorcha turned and placed a hand on her hip. "And just what is that supposed to mean?"

Boggart still refused to speak although Sorcha was certain it could. Soft chirps were its only form of communication, and it remained glamoured.

Sorcha scanned the hut, trying to find whatever had made Boggart speak. The bread was over the fire, but it wasn't burning. No bugs had come in through the open window. The fire was roaring at the correct rate and wouldn't run too hot.

Nothing was amiss. Sorcha shrugged and shook her head. "I'm sorry. I don't know what you're trying to tell me. This would be easier if you would speak."

Another squeak, much louder than the first, echoed in the room.

"I don't know what you *want*, Boggart."

Multiple squeaks came from the creature who shimmered into view. Boggart dropped its glamour and revealed its true form. Skinny, wrinkled, and lightly dusted with white fur that smoothed over bare breasts, she resembled an albino rat. Her head hardly reached the top of the bed.

She pointed a knobby hand at the door. Sorcha noted that Boggart's fingertips were bulbous before glancing where she pointed.

"The door?"

A crashing boom rocked the wooden frame, bending the wood inwards. Sorcha flinched. Her hip struck the clay pot containing all her flour which exploded onto the floor. White puffs fluttered into the air and covered the floor in an impressive starburst.

She cursed and stooped. Her frazzled mind said scoop the flour into her hands and back into the pot. Sorcha dropped to her knees and pulled it all towards her, fruitless in her attempts to clean.

The banging on the door wasn't stopping.

"Who is it?" she called out.

Perhaps the broom would be a more appropriate way to clean this. She looked dubiously over at the straw covered in cobwebs. She'd ruin the flour if she used that. There had to be something cleaner.

Boggart shrieked, bouncing up and down while pointing at the door. Impossibly, the knocking turned thunderous.

Sorcha leaned back, placed her flour covered hands on her thighs, and stared at the ceiling. When had her life turned into babysitting and terrifying moments? She refused to be frightened of someone who couldn't enter the hag's hut, protected by the spell splashed in chicken's blood.

"Boggart, stop screaming."

She didn't listen to Sorcha. Instead, Boggart screamed even louder. Its high-pitched whine dug at Sorcha's ears, a headache blooming inside her skull.

"Please stop knocking!" she shouted. "I'm coming! I just need to take care of this before I—"

The knocking stopped.

Sorcha let out a relieved sigh. She'd taken care of the deep bass. Now she had to make Boggart be quiet.

Leaving the flour for later, she charged towards the panicking Fae. Sorcha knew how to calm children down. In fact, it was one of her better talents. Boggart couldn't be any different from that. She was the same size as one.

Sorcha slid her hands underneath Boggart's armpits and picked her up. Like a child, Boggart wrapped her legs around Sorcha's waist immediately. Panting breaths brushed against her ear, but at least Boggart stopped screaming.

"Shh," Sorcha whispered as she rocked back and forth. "It's all right. Everything is fine. You can stop screaming now, little love."

Although her fur appeared wiry, Boggart was as soft as a rabbit all over her body. Unlike Cian, Boggart wasn't wearing any clothing. One of her feet moved restlessly against Sorcha's stomach.

She only had three toes, Sorcha realized with delight. Three thick, bulbous toes that ended in blunt little black nails.

The pounding started up again. Boggart squeaked and nestled her pointed nose in Sorcha's neck.

"Shh, it's all right," Sorcha repeated as she walked them towards the door. "Nothing is going to happen to you. It's probably Pixie with more food."

She hoped.

With the faerie wrapped around her like a second skin, Sorcha stepped over the massacre of flour and grasped ahold of the door ring. She sent a silent prayer to whatever gods were listening. If this was a will-o'-the-wisp or something equally terrifying, Sorcha would faint dead away.

"Best be safe," she whispered.

She opened the door just a crack, enough to see who was behind it but not let them in.

The dim twilight made it difficult for her to see anything. It was just a blank space on the other side of the door. No walkway, no moon, nothing but black.

Sorcha arched a brow. Now that was unusual.

Something shifted in the darkness, bringing her focus much closer. That wasn't darkness at all, but a black cloth so dark it appeared to be night.

There was only one person on the island who would wear that.

Sorcha nudged the door open the entire way and peered upwards. Outlined by the moon, the master of the isle stared back at her. His cloak made it impossible for her to guess where he was looking, but she could feel the heat of his gaze as if it was a physical touch.

"Good evening," she said. Her words were biting and quick. He was the last person she wanted to see tonight.

"What is that?"

Sorcha blinked. "You must be more specific."

"In your arms."

"Oh," she glanced down at Boggart, who tightened her hold upon Sorcha's neck. "This is Boggart."

"I know who it is, but why isn't she glamoured?"

"You frightened her."

"*I* frightened her?" he growled.

"That incessant knocking would frighten even the bravest of beasts."

The fire crackled, an ember shooting across the room. Its light cast a brief glow across his features, revealing a glint in his eyes which made Sorcha shiver.

"But not you." His voice was a physical caress, dancing down her spine until it curled her toes.

"I am neither man nor beast, sir. You'll find women are far more difficult to frighten."

She turned away from him. He was ruining all her plans. Now Boggart was too scared for bribery, and Macha knew how long it would take until Sorcha could get her information. The tiny creature was fragile.

Anger coursed through her veins until a flush burned her cheeks. She wanted to fly at him, to scratch at the ugly crystals marring his face and scream that he had no right. The ridiculous, pompous, overbearing ass that he was.

Through all her raging emotions, her hands remained gentle upon Boggart. She soothed the creature with soft circular motions and laid her on the bed.

"There, there," she murmured. "You stay here and I'll make him go away. Will that help?"

Boggart nodded.

"Good. Hide under the covers, and I'll come get you when he's gone."

This would be easy. It was exactly what Sorcha wanted, and now she had an excuse to usher him away. Hopefully, Boggart would then calm down, and Sorcha could sweet-talk her for information about the very man she was forcing to leave.

She wiped her hands against her skirt and marched towards the door with renewed purpose.

"I'm afraid I must ask you to leave," she said.

"No."

He said the word as if it ended the argument. As if just by imperiously inserting himself into her life, he could dictate what he wanted, however he wanted it.

She blinked at him. "Excuse me?"

"No."

"Might I ask why you are refusing to leave my doorstep even though I have requested that your presence no longer darken it?"

"This isle, and everything on it, is under my command. I do as I please."

He moved to step over the threshold. Sorcha ground her teeth, the muscles of her jaw flexing in anger. "If you take one more step, I will activate every protection spell on this cursed hut and expel you from this room."

His foot hovered just above the interior of her home. "You wouldn't dare."

"I would dare much, sir, against a man who seemingly does not understand boundaries. You must ask a woman if you may enter their abode, and when granted approval, you may do so. If they request you leave, then you remove yourself. As far as lording over all who linger on this isle, I must inquire who named you king. They must be sorely lacking in wits."

If he continued, she would figure out how to activate those spells. She was no witch, but he had no way of knowing she was bluffing.

He inclined his head. "You are correct. My apologies, my lady, I was out of line."

Sorcha found herself incapable of words. This man never ceased to surprise her. He was an ass, of that she was certain, but she hadn't expected an apology. Let alone an admission of guilt. Was he capable of self-reflection?

She cocked her head to the side, looking him up and down. "What did you say?"

"I have not been in court for many years. My manners are not what they used to be." He swept his cloak to the side, crossed an arm over his waist, and bowed. "I humbly request your presence at dinner this evening."

"I'm eating here."

"The castle can offer much finer dining."

"Be that as it may," Sorcha gestured towards the fire, "dinner is already cooking."

"Then as forward as it is, I request you allow me to stay. You need not provide food, merely company."

Sorcha panicked. She didn't want him to stay! How was she going to get Boggart to speak? Stammering, she pointed towards the bed. "I'm afraid Boggart is quite frightened of you. It wouldn't be polite to allow you to stay when—"

"Boggart is not afraid of me." The head of his cloak shook. "She's afraid I plan to take you away from her, like I did her hag. Might I come in?"

"I—." She quirked a brow. "Why did you remove the hag?"

"She was dangerous. Her spells were reaching the castle and wreaking havoc among my people."

"You were protecting the faeries?"

"That is my job. They take care of me, and I protect them."

Sorcha breathed in a slow breath, letting it out with a huff. There were no more arguments, no more walls she could erect. He was being polite. It would be rude to refuse him entry now, and he already thought she was little more than a peasant.

It would not do.

She gestured towards the table, "All right then. Come in and seat yourself. There should be enough for all three of us."

He ducked, entering the hut like a storm. He was far too big. Sorcha gaped at his head which nearly touched the ceiling, and the wide spread of his shoulders, which he had to tilt to fit through the door.

It was no wonder his castle doors were two wide. The man wouldn't be able to fit through anything less.

"I'm afraid I do not have a grand palace to offer, or even complete dining services," she said as she walked towards the bed. "But two seats will have to do."

"I've eaten in worse conditions."

"Have you? I was under the impression 'masters' rarely ate outside their splendorous castles." She leaned over the bed and pulled the blankets away from Boggart's face. "He's eating with us, but has promised I can stay."

"I am no king, nor have I always lived here."

Sorcha lifted Boggart into her arms and started towards the table. The faerie clutched at her dress, tiny claws digging through the fabric and into her skin.

"A curiosity I have no desire to satisfy. I will not pity you, sir, if that is your aim."

"I do not ask for pity, but for patience. It is I who am out of line. I remember manners, but they are no longer second nature. I'm afraid I lost them long before I came to this isle." He sat on her chair, the wood creaking ominously for a few moments before silencing.

She hooked her foot around a stool and dragged it towards the table. She must have been a frightening sight, limping towards him with wood screeching, carrying Boggart who looked more monster than beast. He didn't flinch in the slightest, Sorcha noted with disappointment.

Boggart plunked down on the stool and let go of Sorcha's dress hesitantly. She let out a little huff when Sorcha left her side, watching her master with beady eyes.

"I will not call you 'master'," Sorcha said as she pulled the bread from the fire. "Do you have another name?"

"Some call me Cloch Rí."

"The Stone King?" Sorcha quirked a brow.

He reached a hand forward, placing it in full view on the table. The crystals revealed on each peak of knuckle were just as startling as the first time. Violet-toned and ragged-edged, they turned his hand into more rock than fist.

"Ah," she murmured. "Appropriate then."

She set the bread down with a cloth underneath it. Steam rose into the air, the warm comforting scent easing the tension in her neck. She added cheese and fresh strawberries to a plate beside the bread.

"Cian keeps an impressive garden," she said as she sat down. The hut was suddenly too small, the air too close.

The cloak still covered his face, but she could feel his gaze. It lingered upon her hair, following the spirals of her curls across her shoulders and arms. Highly inappropriate. He had said he wasn't a gentleman, and she believed him.

"He wouldn't like you using his name so freely."

"No, I suppose he wouldn't. Perhaps, that is why I use it." She reached forward and broke off a piece of bread, the steam rose into the air in wispy swirls.

"You do so because it might anger him?"

"Annoy him. I would never use his name against him."

"Many humans have said the same thing, and they always use the name."

"Do you think I am like most humans?"

"I have yet to meet one who shatters my perception of your species."

Sorcha popped the bread into her mouth, chewing to give herself time to think. "You think very poorly of humanity."

"I have been given little reason to think otherwise."

"I could say the same about your people."

Boggart reached for a loaf and tucked it underneath her arm. She gave them both a suspicious glance before hopping off her seat and stalking back towards the bed. Her little chirping grumbles suggested she didn't appreciate such tense conversation when she planned to enjoy her dinner.

Sorcha agreed with her. Mealtimes should be peaceful. A time for family to enjoy each other's company after a long day of work. But there was something about this man that pushed all her buttons, and she couldn't help but argue.

"What grievances against the Fae could you possibly have?"

"Abandonment, for a start. You entered this world with full intention of molding it to your will, and then you disappeared."

"Disappeared?" His hand clenched on the table. "Your people ran us out of our *lands*."

"I find that difficult to believe when you yourself stated that the Fae are far superior to humankind."

She watched his fist tighten until she heard the creaking of stone and crystal. Slowly, he released his hold in tiny movements. When his palm lay flat upon the table once more, the hood of his cloak tilted to the side.

"You are quick-witted for a human. It is…intriguing."

"That sounds like a compliment." She reached forward for a strawberry and took a large bite. She would count this as a successful battle in their ongoing war. He might have won the first by throwing her into a nightmarish cottage, but she had recovered quite nicely.

The strawberry burst in her mouth. Sweet flavor coated her tongue, filling her senses with the taste of sunshine and summers spent hunting in the fields. For hundreds of years, Sorcha's family had foraged the land for survival. Her mother had whispered the tales in her ear as they sucked the juice from these red bellied fruits.

Some of the ichor within the strawberry overflowed her lips, dripping syrup down her chin.

Sorcha didn't see him move, but she felt the touch of his hand as though he branded her. His calloused thumb traced the line of liquid from chin to mouth. It rasped over her sensitive lip, catching every last drop of sticky juice.

One of the crystals on his palm scraped her jaw. Cold to the touch, it was a lightning bolt of sensation against the sudden, flaming heat of her cheeks.

She parted her lips in a silent gasp. The smooth texture of his nail touched her top lip, dipping into the warm breath she expelled before withdrawing.

She was undone, unmade, reborn as something else entirely. Her hands clenched in her lap as she stared in shock at the Fae who dared to touch her without asking, to slice through her stalwart resolve, and stitch the beginnings of attraction into the fiber of her being.

They stared at each other, frozen in time. Moonlight speared through her window and pierced the lining of shadow covering his face. It danced along the deep gashes of crystal, like a stone she had once cracked open to reveal the geode inside.

His eyes held wicked intent that stole the breath from her lungs. Vivid blue, like a crystal clear sky, like the azure waves of the ocean, they saw straight through her.

He wanted her, she realized. He wasn't playing a game; his emotion was too raw and hungry. She had seen the expression upon men at the brothel before, even sometimes cast in her direction, but never had she felt the emotions reflected in herself.

Her stomach clenched. She dug her fingernails into her palms and forced herself to swallow the remaining strawberry.

Sorcha's eyes followed his hand as he lifted it towards his mouth.

The chair screeched as she shoved to her feet. "Boggart, have you finished?"

A squeak from the corner suggested the little faerie still had a long way to go, but Sorcha was quite done with tonight. She looked back towards the massive shadow seated at her table.

"I'm afraid I have to ask you to leave, sir. As you can imagine, my journey has been trying, and I'm finding myself faint."

"From your journey," he repeated as he stood.

She was once again overwhelmed by the sheer size of him. Her head barely reached the center of his chest. She knew his hands were massive, and that she might wrap her arms around his shoulders if she tried very hard.

Sorcha blew out a breath. "Indeed. It was a grueling week-long sail, and then I swam the rest of the way here. Merrow-men are not kind while chasing their prey, so if you would please," she gestured at the door, unable to finish the sentence when the weight of his gaze pressed upon her.

"I have been scolded once tonight on respecting a woman's wishes. I should not like to experience it again." He swept into a low bow, his cloak spreading across his shoulders like wings.

"Yes, a shrew is not likely to keep her mouth shut."

He chuckled. "The only shrew in this house is the boggart."

Sorcha listened for the angry shriek, but Boggart had nothing to say to the comment. Perhaps she agreed.

Still, it made her cheeks flame all the hotter. She rushed to the door and held it open. "Thank you for the interesting conversation."

He moved like a shadow, silent and smooth, hesitating only briefly in front of her. She inhaled the scent of mint and beeswax.

"It has been an enlightening, albeit short, evening," he said before leaving the hut.

Sorcha sagged against the doorframe. All the energy he carried swept out with him and emptied her body of the adrenaline rush she rode. It had been a brief conversation, but her legs shook and her hands trembled.

A zing of awareness jolted up her spine. Spinning, she leaned out the door and shouted, "Stone!"

He paused, one foot on the dock to her hut and the other on his cursed isle. "Pardon?"

"You said some call you Cloch Rí. I shall call you Stone until you give me your true name."

"You think I'll ever give you that kind of power over me?" His voice wavered with humor.

"I would bet my life on it, Stone."

"I look forward to your attempts, Sunshine."

She hoped he smiled, although it seemed unlikely a man such as him knew how to twist his lips in happiness. There was a certain pleasure to making a man smile. She had forgotten what this was like. The courtship, the laughter, the teasing, everything that made butterflies take flight in her belly.

He started up the hill that led to his castle. The moon rose behind the imperious structure, silhouetting the jagged spires and crumbling peaks. It was a ruin, a relic of a time long ago when this isle might have been a sight to behold.

There was something hauntingly beautiful about this place. The emerald hills glimmered with dew in the silver moonlight. Fireflies danced above the wheat fields looking like magic kissing the land. And its king, the disfigured monster of a man, outlined as a shadow striding across his domain.

"You're being fanciful," she said. "Stop it, Sorcha. Go to bed."

She couldn't. She stayed where she was, pressed against the doorframe, watching him walk away from her.

A small hand tugged her skirt. Sorcha glanced down at Boggart's strange, elongated face. Bread stuffed her cheeks, bulging them to the side and preventing her from squeaking.

Boggart tugged again and pointed towards the bed.

"Yes, it's bedtime. Where are you sleeping, little one?"

The faerie pointed at a small lump of moth-eaten blankets in the corner.

"Is that where you want to sleep? The bed is plenty big enough for the both of us."

Boggart took off for her corner and burrowed underneath the blankets. Her long, whiskered nose poked out of the mound, sniffing for a moment before disappearing again. Sorcha could hear the slight sound of munching.

She must have taken the rest of the bread with her, Sorcha thought with a smile. Shaking her head, she disrobed and hung the velvet dress from the window. It was too nice to leave on the floor or fold into the chest in the corner.

Tomorrow, she promised herself as she got into bed. Tomorrow, she would explore the island and speak with its inhabitants. She would not be distracted by the handsome king. She needed to convince him to come back to the mainland with her and damned if she would fail.

The air vibrated with the sound of wings, wind brushing over her face as she snuggled into the pillows. A raven croaked as it landed on her windowsill.

"There you are, Bran," she murmured quietly, so as not to disturb Boggart. "I wondered where you'd flown off to."

He croaked.

"Of course, I worried. We survived a near-death experience together. And no, I can't seem to sleep."

The raven tilted his head, staring at her with one dark, beady eye.

"It has nothing to do with him!"

He flapped his wings, settled onto the windowsill for the night, and turned his back to her.

"That's just rude," she grumbled. "I'm not lying to you. I slept for a full day when I first arrived here. I'm not tired in the slightest."

Perhaps it had something to do with the master of the isle. His gaze like ice, with molten heat in its depths.

She shivered and pulled the blankets high over her shoulders. Huffing out a breath, she resigned herself to a difficult night with little sleep.

CHAPTER SEVEN

The Healer

Sorcha crested a hill. Her breath was ragged and dripping sweat stuck long strands of her hair to her brow. She'd wrapped a bedsheet across her body as a makeshift pack. Her own was too large to bring on an adventure across the small isle.

The white sheet was a stark contrast to the old dress she wore. She found the floor length gown in a chest left behind by the hag. Moths had gotten to it, chewing holes through the fabric and leaving the edges ragged, but there was nothing functionally wrong with it. She wouldn't ruin it any further, and who needed fine clothing every day? The velvet was lovely, but not practical.

She prided herself on being a practical woman.

Hiking the sheet higher up her shoulder, she blew out a breath. A curl bounced from its confining tie.

Sorcha groaned. At this rate, by the time she crested the small mountain there wouldn't be any hair left in the tie. The unruly curls demanded freedom.

Gravel crunched under her borrowed boots. There used to be a path here, the ground worn down by centuries of feet. The earth had grown back over the years, smoothing the marred ground, and covering the path to the peak.

She scrambled on hands and knees to the crest. Air sawed from her lungs and her knees wobbled, but she had done it. Plunking down near a cairn, she yanked the wayward curls back into their tie.

Bran cawed overhead, his voice shouting in the air.

"Yes, yes," she muttered as she pulled hard. "You could have done this in half the time. Need I remind you feathers are far faster than flesh?"

He circled above her, dipping and diving as if to mock her exhaustion.

"Must be easy being a raven. Those of us down here have to struggle our way up the mountain. You can soar over and far beyond."

She released the knot across her chest that held the pack with a relieved sigh. Food was only a slight weight, but she was still sore. Her muscles needed to move, to release the tension and stiffness that hindered her movements.

Perhaps a mountain had been a little more than she could handle.

Rubbing her shoulder, Sorcha pulled out the small jug of water and a block of cheese. It wasn't much, but it would do.

She kept a *sgian dubh*, a knife, strapped to her ankle for moments like this. Dicing the soft cheese, she lifted it to her mouth and glanced down the mountain.

Everything seemed so small from up here. The land stretched out before her, dotted with sheep-like stars in the night sky. Tiny people worked diligently on their land. From here, she could see they had cast aside their glamour. Wings sparkled in the sunlight, warped forms bent over the fields. She knew if she walked within a few feet of them, they would put their glamours up so fast she never would get a peek at what they looked like.

It was the only mountain on the isle. Its peak was even with the top of the castle. Quiet and lonely, this respite gave her moments to think while remaining distant from all the people here.

No one wanted to speak to her about their master. They were as elusive as the man himself, answering her questions in vague responses that weren't quite lies. Perhaps he had warned them away from speaking to her. Perhaps they were loyal to the mysterious man.

Sorcha scowled at the tiny figures. They were equally quiet about their own information. Everyone was polite, kind, and giving, but they didn't trust her.

Glamours were still in place. They brushed her off when she suggested she might help. They whispered behind her back when she left although they likely thought she couldn't hear them.

The master, Stone, remained elusive. She saw him in passing every now and then but didn't feel the weight of his gaze. He didn't repeat the heated experience which had left her dry-mouthed for days.

Her knife slipped in her hand and cut her thumb. Hissing out an angry breath, she sank the blade into the ground.

"Get your head out of the clouds," she scolded herself. "That man is hardly worth your time or effort. Just get him off the isle and to the mainland. And stop hurting yourself while daydreaming."

She ripped a piece of fabric from the bottom of her dress, muttering about foolish, wool gathering girls. Tying it around her thumb, she cinched it tighter than normal as punishment.

Sorcha planned to spend the entire day upon the ridge. She was getting nowhere with the locals. They wouldn't give her any information about their master, which meant she had to go directly to the source.

The source was dangerous. The source burned like fire, with ice cold eyes that made her mind freeze in the wake of his hold. She would have to watch him constantly. There would be no more strawberry incidents, or anything of its ilk.

A voice whispered in the back of her mind that she wanted another such experience. She wanted more than boxat. For a calloused finger to become a hand, to feel what those crystals felt like against her skin.

"Foolish girl," she muttered.

It was impossible for such thoughts to come to fruition. She'd get herself in trouble, lose focus. Or worse, lose herself.

Stones skittered behind her, cracking together and rolling down the mountain in a great avalanche of sound. She rolled onto her side, peering towards the noise.

Snow white hair blew in the faint breeze. Heavy skirts tangled between Pixie's legs, catching her as she struggled to the top. Her normally calm face was bright red with exertion.

"Pixie!" Sorcha called. She jumped to her feet and ran towards the Fae. "What are you doing up here?"

"Oh, dearie, why do you have to choose such a place to get away from us all? It's awfully far away and my old bones can't take it."

"Somehow, I doubt you're as old as you portray yourself," Sorcha replied with a grin.

"You wouldn't know," Pixie said with a grimace. "Dearie, I hate to ask a favor of you, but something terrible has happened."

Sorcha's smile faded at the worry and anguish in Pixie's voice. "What happened?"

"It's little Doo—I mean—" Pixie caught herself and shook her head. "Pooka! It's little Pooka, he's fallen out of a tree and broken his arm. A terrible thing, nasty break, and he's the only child on the island. It's broken through the skin, dearie, and we don't know how to set the break. He's bleeding something awful."

"Did you put a compress on the wound?" Sorcha scooped up her things and swung them over her shoulder. "How bad is the break? Just how far is the hand pointing away from its usual position?"

"I, I don't know! I didn't look at it closely, in truth. The break was so terrible and the boy was in so much pain…"

"Come on then." A thrill of excitement rushed through her veins. Although Sorcha knew it was likely a terrible thing, she always felt this way before any kind of surgery. Her hands tingled to touch wounded flesh. Her mind fired with ideas on how to solve the problem of pain.

Sorcha's strange mind was both a blessing and a curse. She knew there were countless ways to heal a broken bone, but only a few that worked. If the bone had broken through skin, she would need to set it, then wrap it to encourage healing from the inside out.

She followed Pixie down the mountain at a much faster speed than she'd ascended. Both women rode a wind of anxiety and worry. If the boy bled badly, he might not be alive by the time Sorcha made it to him.

She hoped that wasn't the case.

They reached the hills and ran. Pixie no longer seemed like an aged woman for she flew over the grass.

"I have one thing to ask," Pixie said as they reached the castle. "The boy is young and impressionable. You cannot heal him without seeing his true form."

"Then so be it," Sorcha replied, breathless. "Open the door, Pixie."

"No young man wants to feel scorn from a beautiful woman. I beg you to hide any reactions you might have to his appearance."

"I have already seen both Cian and Boggart, Pixie. There is no reason to worry. Just let me see the boy."

Pixie sighed and swung open the kitchen door.

The room beyond had descended into chaos. The central table was clean of food and utensils. Faeries rushed in wide circles, to and from a small body laid out on the wood. Sorcha saw the faint impression of fur, wings, and scales before everyone erected their glamours.

All but the boy.

He crouched on the table and whined, his face warping through hare, dog, and horse. Pookas imitated animals, but she had never heard of one switching so many times.

Sorcha kept her face steely as she made her way to his side. He opened his mouth with a growl, fanged teeth shining in the candlelight. She had seen animals do that before when they were in pain.

She reached out a hand. "Shh, little master. I will not hurt you."

He growled again, but his lips closed. Again, his features changed. His nose dipped down, his pupils turned to slits, and whiskers grew upon his cheeks.

"Can you control it?" she asked. "I'll need you to pick a form before

I can heal your arm."

He turned his face from her, scooting on his butt towards the other side of the table.

There was little time. Blood smeared his front and slicked the table. Red like hers. Red like a human.

She lunged forward and wrapped a hand around his ankle. The other Fae hissed at her movements reminding Sorcha just how dangerous the situation was. These people liked her, but they did not trust her. This was the one youngling they had. They would not tolerate mistakes.

"Easy there," she whispered. "Let me see your arm. I can help."

The boy stared back at her with mistrusting eyes. He had a reason to, she supposed. Sorcha had had very little opportunity to earn his trust.

"I know I'm a stranger," she breathed, turning her voice into a coo. "You are right to be scared. It is a good thing for you to be wary of those you do not know. I can make your arm feel better if you'll let me."

He inched towards her. The movement was slight, but it was there.

Sorcha let out a relieved breath. "That's right, come to me. What a brave boy you must be. To break your arm like this, you must have been doing something terribly heroic."

"No," he grunted through blunted teeth. "I was climbing a tree."

"Oh, well, that is very heroic! There are plenty of heroes who climbed trees. Do you know any of them?"

Pooka shook his head and moved the rest of the way toward her. She gently positioned him so his legs hung off the edge of the table. He moved his hand from the broken arm, stark white standing out amidst all the blood.

"It's hurt real bad," he whimpered.

"Yes. Yes, it is. But I'll help. While I'm working, I'll tell you a story." She gestured over her shoulder, and Pixie leaned in. "Yarrow, as much cloth as you can, and perhaps a little liquid courage. Is there anything different about Fae bodies I should know?"

"Not that I can think of. Is he going to survive?"

"Of course, he is," Sorcha leaned back in shock. "I'm here now."

The collective sigh rocked through Sorcha. Why would they think the boy would die? A severed limb, or perhaps impalement yes, but a broken arm? He hadn't bled out. She could certainly heal him.

She hesitated and asked, "What did you do before?"

"Well," Pixie glanced at the boy and lowered her voice. "Usually, we'd let it be and hope it healed on its own. A wound like this usually festered. We'd do what we could with honey compresses, but most times we'd lose them."

"You don't have to worry about that anymore. I'm here."

Sorcha shouldn't have said the words, but she did. These people needed her strength, her courage, her understanding. They didn't need to know she planned on leaving as soon as possible. Or that she was leaving at all.

She turned back towards the boy and plastered a smile on her face. "Have you heard the story of Macha?"

"Yes," he said with a sniff. Two large tears rolled down his face and dripped onto his bloodied pants.

"Did you hear how she cursed the line of Ulster?"

"No."

"Good. Listen to my voice and nothing else, all right? This will hurt, but I want you to hear the story and not focus on the pain."

They had waited a long time to come get her. The muscles of his arm had wrapped around the bone's new position and did not want to release. Thankfully, it was a clean break. She was gentle with the sensitive bone and ragged edges of flesh.

Sorcha viewed the entire injury before deciding she would need to stretch the muscles before they would allow the bone back in its place. Theoretically, it would be easy. For her.

The boy, she worried about.

She set about the surgery in the best way she could. The entire time she told the story of Macha. How she had married a mortal man and carried his child. How the foolish man had bragged about his wife to a rival king who forced her into a foot race. When she beat him, and lay near dying on the finish line, she cursed nine generations of his family to experience the pain of childbirth.

Although the pain must have been great, he listened. The boy repeated sentences of the story as she made three passes of stretching the muscle. He asked her questions as she snapped the bone back into place with an audible crunch. He bit back tears as she packed the wound with yarrow and wrapped it tightly with cloth.

They were both covered in blood and exhausted by the time she finished. She tugged the knot of his sling and nodded. "That will do. You have been brave enough to claim the title of hero, young Pooka. It's been an honor."

He sniffed hard, but straightened his spine. "It didn't hurt a bit, ma'am."

On impulse, she leaned forward and wrapped an arm around his shoulders. "I couldn't have asked for a better patient, sweet boy. Now ask your mother to tuck you into bed with a full jar of honey."

"I'm not allowed to have that much!"

"I think under the circumstances, you've earned it."

A very tall woman, thin as a birch tree, stepped forward. Sorcha stepped back to give her room and made eye contact.

The woman's glamour shimmered and fell. An adult Pooka looked far different from her son. She was an amalgamation of all mammals. Patches of light and dark fur blended together until she appeared more patchwork quilt than person. Her elongated nose and face were faintly horse-like. This must be his mother.

"Thank you," she said in her deep voice. "I cannot thank you enough."

"You would have done the same for me, if it came to that."

"All the same, you are welcome in my house any time."

Sorcha nodded. She waited until the kitchen emptied, and then sagged against the table. Exhaustion made even breathing difficult, her lungs working overtime. Her hands ached. She held them out, flexing her fingers in and out.

"You did well," Pixie said.

"I must see him every week for at least a full moon. That wound could still become infected."

"I'm sure his mother would appreciate it."

A piece of bread with sliced meat appeared in Sorcha's line of vision. Startled, she glanced up.

"Thank you." She held up her bloody hands. "Perhaps a basin of water first?"

"Come with me."

Sorcha stood on wobbly legs and followed Pixie through the gardens. Cian was absent from his usual post, a blessing she was thankful for. Bantering with the gnome would be difficult when she could hardly see straight.

They crossed a small wooden bridge in the garden and onto another part of the castle grounds Sorcha had yet to see.

It was peaceful here. Water burbled out of an aged fountain. The stone woman inside it poured water from a wound on her chest. She clutched the sword which had plunged between her ribs and held her sword up to continue fighting. Flowers grew wild in this section of the gardens. They tangled with each other, creating walls of roses and thorns.

"I didn't know roses grew this time of year," she mumbled.

"This island differs from what you're used to. Faerie-touched lands bear fruit even in the strangest of times. Why else would we have strawberries this late in the year?"

"Fair point."

"You may wash in this fountain."

"This one?" Sorcha gestured. "This looks far too nice to be a washing fountain."

"Long ago, it was a place of worship." Pixie's expression fell. "No longer."

Sorcha could see it was a sacred place. Blooms of every color stretched as far as she could see. The roses grew with wild abandon, vines stretching all around them. And the woman herself appeared eerily familiar.

She leaned forward to peer at the face. "Is this Macha?"

"It is. I thought it fitting you wash in her waters."

"I won't desecrate sacred ground."

"You're washing innocent blood from your hands. You saved him while telling her stories. Macha will appreciate that."

Sorcha supposed she was correct. The red-headed woman was fierce. Perhaps she would appreciate a little blood in her waters more than she would wine or gold coins.

She leaned down and dunked her hands into the cool stream. It ran over her hands with a soft, trickling sound, easing the aches from her bones. She saw another face in the ripples. A pointed face with wild hair, eyes flashing an unnatural green.

Macha was watching her. The Tuatha dé Danann winked at her, disappearing when Sorcha released the water she held in her cupped hands.

Her purpose burned bright in her mind. These people may be kind, but they should not distract her. Papa needed her. Rosaleen, Briana, and all her sisters needed her to stay focused. A small boy with a broken arm shouldn't so easily sway her.

But he did. They all did. With their thoughtful gifts, their easy going attitudes, and the magical way this isle captivated her. Sorcha had always been an outsider among her family. The witch's child who knew too much. Here? She was just another human girl who could not possibly understand all the wondrous things around her.

If given the choice, she would choose this life over her old one. It wasn't an option, but was entertaining to muse upon at least. She sighed and turned back towards Pixie.

"I am exhausted and my bed sounds like a respite I have earned. If you don't mind, I will take your gracious offer of food."

"Of course, dearie." Pixie handed the sandwich to her wrapped in a cloth.

When had she gotten a cloth? Sorcha stared down at the bundle in her hands. She was missing details so large as this?

She shook her head to clear it. "Perhaps a good sleep will clear my mind."

"Unlikely. It's a rather confusing place for a human such as yourself. I'm impressed you've lasted this long without losing your head."

"Do others?"

"You're the first human who's shown up on our shore," Pixie said with a smile. "You're new to us, although some have experiences with humans. We're all going through some learning."

"I appreciate your patience." Ironic, the words that slipped off her tongue. Hadn't a certain king asked her to do the same for him? And she had mocked him.

"You may wish to walk around the castle to get to the hut."

Sorcha arched a brow. "Why? It's faster to go back through Cian's garden."

"A walk is good for your health."

"I already climbed a mountain today."

"Yes, but the sights one sees on the other side of the castle are rather rare. You won't be seeing it on top of that munro. Eat your food on your walk. I promise you'll feel better if you go the long way."

The strange smile on Pixie's face made Sorcha nervous. The faerie had been kind thus far, but there was still plenty of time for trickery. Narrowing her eyes, she nodded. "All right. There are no games afoot?"

"The Wild Hunt doesn't start for another month yet, dearie. You're safe."

Sorcha continued eating as she rounded the castle. The rose garden didn't stretch very far. Her fingers itched to pull at the weeds, to take on the challenge of taming such a beast. Yet, she also knew that fatigue and roses did not play well together. She was more likely to bleed than succeed.

Once free from the tangled mess of blooms and thorns, the emerald hills stretched in front of her once more. The castle had grown into the landscape. Moss covered the stones at the base of the walls, meshing with the green grass until it was nearly impossible to tell them apart.

She waltzed past a sheep which lifted its head and baa'd.

"Hello," Sorcha nodded. "It's always a pleasure, mistress wool."

The fluffy animal gave her a rather unimpressed look and chewed. She had always liked sheep. Their odd, sideways pupils and all. They enjoyed having their cheeks scratched, and Sorcha loved their pleased expressions.

The bread disappeared by the time she made it halfway around the castle. Pixie had been right. The fresh air was doing wonders for the exhaustion that surged through her body. Each step beat back her drooping eyelids and trembling fingers.

A cracking sound echoed. Too far to cause her to jump—close enough to pique her curiosity.

"What is that?" she muttered as she picked up her pace.

The sound was strangely familiar. Not something she had heard often, but the ping of metal striking metal wasn't easy to forget.

Once, two men had gotten into a duel outside the brothel. Briana had been in the middle of it, rolling her eyes and ignoring the two men fighting over a prostitute. She called them both foolish, slammed the door, and told the girls to pay them no mind.

Sorcha had never been good at that. She had raced up the stairwell, stuck her head out the window, and watched the two men fight. They had been sloppily drunk and incapable of standing straight. Two strikes of sword against sword, and they both gave up.

This didn't sound like that kind of fight.

The closer she came, the more fierce and violent the strikes of metal became. Each clank rang in the air with the resounding quality of a gong. She counted fifteen by the time she reached the top of a hill and stared with open mouth.

This was a new part of the castle. Sturdy wooden fences marked off a section of field, packed down by stamping feet. Straw dummies hung from posts, their guts hanging out from too many hits. Targets lined one end of the fences, painted in circles of red to guide arrows home.

It was the men which caught her attention. A strange dark man stood in the center of the field. Half his head was shaved, dark hair falling nearly to his waist on the other side. There was a smudge of black across the shaved half of his face. He wore little more than breeches. Long and lean, his tanned skin was slicked with glistening sweat. A tapered, wicked spear glimmered in the sunlight, held with ease in his strong hand.

The other was eerily familiar. Sorcha gasped and dropped into the high waving grass, so he wouldn't see her.

So, this was the master of the isle.

Stone, as she now called him, was even more impressive without his cloak. He was massive, easily reaching seven feet tall, although she would've bet her life he was taller than that. Strangely, it didn't make him blocky. His body was as lean as the other man's. Broad shoulders tapered to a trim waist and long muscled legs. He wasn't wearing his cloak. He wasn't wearing anything other than a matching set of brown breeches.

She could count his rippling abdomen muscles even from her great distance. Bulging pectorals and flexing biceps caught her attention as her mouth went dry. He, too, was slicked with sweat. They'd obviously been fighting for some time.

Her gaze caught on the sword in his hand.

"Now, that's a sword," she whispered.

The gold handle sparkled with red stones. The blade itself was clearly well-made, a line down the center hollowed to allow blood to flow freely. It was massive, a broadsword rather than a rapier.

He lifted it as though it weighed less than a feather.

Sorcha's breath caught and her mind went blank. So that's what Pixie meant when she said he was handsome man. In his own way, he was indeed.

The damage to his body was far more extensive than his face or hands. A starburst wound bisected his right shoulder and spread in webs. It looked as if someone had cracked through stone. There were hundreds of small fissures that crawled over his shoulders, across his chest, and down to his stomach. Small scars revealed more parted flesh and burgeoning stone.

Their lips moved though she couldn't hear them from where she hid. Stone lifted his blade and dropped into a fighting stance.

The dark man raced towards him, a grimace on his face that was frightening. He leapt into the air with sword held above his head. Stone shifted at the last second, whirling to keep pace.

They didn't fight in any way she'd ever seen before. Her lips parted as she watched.

It was as if she watched dancers. Although Stone was clearly the larger of the two, he spun in the air and blocked each parry easily. The stones did not seem to hinder his movements. In fact, he used them to his advantage.

The other pivoted off a target and thrust himself high into the air. It was a killing blow if he landed where he wished. Stone kept his sword at his side and grasped the descending blade in a crystal fist. He used the momentum to pound his fist into the other man's face.

Sorcha winced at the cracking sound and forced herself to remain in place when the dark man dropped to the ground. He rolled on his shoulder, ending up on his feet, and shaking his head.

Blood dripped from his nose, but he appeared to be laughing.

"That was where you got the crystals on your knuckles from," she whispered.

Stone had punched so many people, or things, that he had worn the flesh from the crystals underneath. That was the closest thing she could think of, for surely a curse was the cause of his affliction. Stone was clearly Seelie. No one else would be as beautiful, even with such disfigurement.

What did it all mean?

She shook her head and sank deeper into the grass as the two men clapped each other on the shoulders. She could already hear the scolding tone he would use when he realized she had spied on him. Or perhaps he wouldn't scold at all. Perhaps he would draw her into those strong arms, those rock-hard muscles. What would he smell like? Like musk and man? Or like straw and grass?

The unknown man cupped his hands around his mouth and shouted, "Why your highness, I do believe we're being watched!"

Sorcha's cheeks turned bright red. She ducked until her chin touched the ground. Surely, they couldn't see her? The grass was tall enough to cover her twice over if she laid down like this.

There was a grumbling reply she could not quite understand. Peeking up over the grass, she locked eyes with the strange new arrival. She could see his grin all the way from where she was.

He waggled his fingers. "Hello, red-headed lass! You're a long way from home."

Sorcha supposed she could stay laying in the grass until they gave up, but he would still know. She had been spying like a little school girl who didn't know any better. She might as well grit her teeth and be an adult.

Standing, she inhaled a deep breath, ready to accept her punishment. She might enjoy punishment, if Stone would be the deliverer of said punishment. But, the last thing she needed was another repeat of their first night, and his hands on her skin or body.

She didn't look up as she walked towards their practice range. Head down, she counted each step and curled her hands into fists. She could do this without embarrassing herself. She was looking for more yarrow.

Pooka would need it, and the stores were low.

Why would Pixie send her all this way if she was only going to embarrass herself? Surely, the faerie had known her master was practicing.

Sorcha almost stopped in her place. That was exactly why the Pixie had sent her here. What was she up to?

By the time she reached the fence, heat flushed up her neck to her face. Sorcha worried her cheeks might be smoking.

She looked up directly into a caramel colored chest. Her gaze traveled farther up, catching on the dark "smudge" on his face that wasn't dirt at all. Tiny dark feathers covered one side of his face, his eye that of a raven, not a man.

She recognized that yellow eye. Full of intelligence, far too human, and watching her with chagrin. The raven had been far more than just a beast after all.

"Bran?"

He swept into a low bow and looked up through the curtain of his hair, grinning. "My lady. It is a rarity to see such bewitching beauty on Hy-brasil."

"If anyone would know, it would be you." She curtseyed in return. "My apologies. I was looking for yarrow."

"Ah, then you had no luck?"

"I'm afraid not."

"I believe there is some directly behind you, fair lady."

She glanced over her shoulder and cursed. "There certainly is."

There went her lie. The Fae could sniff it out anyways. They were incapable of lying. She flicked a glance towards Stone, who stood as still as his namesake with his back to her.

"I had no idea you would be practicing," she began. "I was told a walk would clear my head after dealing with the Pooka. You did hear about the boy, didn't you?"

A droplet of sweat traveled down the valley of Stone's spine.

Muscles bunched on either side, stymied only by the protrusion of crystals. "I had not."

"He broke his arm while climbing a tree. I've set the bone and packed the wound with yarrow, but they will need to watch for infection."

"And why are you telling me this?"

Bran cleared his throat. "I'm glad to hear the boy is well. I apologize for lying all this time to you, beautiful thing that you are."

"You've followed me since the MacNara twins," she murmured while casting a curious glance towards Stone, who still hadn't turned.

"I rarely trust the MacNara twins, and when I saw one such as you entering their home? I had to follow you. My honor simply wouldn't allow for anything else."

She wasn't certain he had that much honor. A man who hid himself from a woman in the form of a raven was unlikely to be a gentleman. From the top of his half-shaved head, to the bottom of his taloned feet, this was a man she'd have a hard time trusting.

"You, sir, are surely a rake."

"Me?" He slapped a hand to his chest. "I have never been called such a thing!"

"Bran," Stone's voice cut through the banter. "Enough."

He glanced over his shoulder, revealing the uninjured side of his face. Sorcha noted how he angled his body away from her. As if he were trying to hide. There was no cloak for him to cover the injuries, at least not that she could see.

The man was strange. So easily risen to a challenge when she could not see him, but now he appeared almost frightened. Embarrassed, perhaps? She had placed him in an awkward situation. It was likely he hadn't wanted her to see his disfigurement.

She wouldn't have wanted anyone to know. Sorcha couldn't imagine how he felt knowing that his skin was so severely marred.

She swallowed hard and nodded. "Thank you, Bran, for pointing out the yarrow. I'll take my leave, gentlemen."

Dipping into a curtsy for good measure, she cursed herself for listening to Pixie. With burning red cheeks, she snatched the yarrow and rushed away from the castle. If it took her the rest of the day to get to her hut, so be it. She refused to stay any longer in the presence of a man who so clearly didn't want her there.

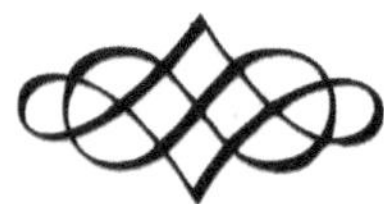

Eamonn slammed the door to the castle, hands shaking in anger. How dare she? That woman had no right to walk around the grounds as if she owned the place. All other Fae knew to leave him be when he was in a rage. He would wear himself out with sword and shield, but they were not permitted to view him.

Growling, he swiped a vase from its stand. The shattering crash only eased a small fraction of his anger, but it was something. Shame overwhelmed him.

She had seen him.

When Bran said they were being watched, Eamonn had turned with the expectation that Pixie was coming to announce some other chore he needed to do. But it hadn't been any of the faeries he would have guessed.

She stood in the middle of the field with goldenrod brushing her fingertips. He had named her aptly. Sunshine caressed her hair and shoulders like a lover. Her hair swirled around her like a dust devil made of fire. Her freckles flecked her nose and forehead as if the sun couldn't help but kiss her cheeks.

She was so beautiful. And he?

Eamonn walked past a shattered mirror and growled. He was little more than a monster.

"She's even prettier when in a human form," Bran's voice echoed down the hallway. "I'm surprised you let her stay, considering the circumstances."

"Leave, Unseelie. You have overstayed your welcome."

"I always do. And yet, here I am."

The fluttering of wings buffeted his ears, and Bran materialized down the hallway before him.

Eamonn clenched his fists. "How does she know your name?"

"Jealous?" Bran picked at his fingernails. "Or anxious?"

"No human should know the true name of a Fae."

"Does it make you feel better to know she guessed it?"

"No," he snorted. "But it does speak to your mother's intelligence. Naming her son so predictably will be your downfall."

"My mother is plenty intelligent. She created you, now didn't she?"

Eamonn bared his teeth.

The other Fae hardly seemed intimidated. "Easy there, Stone King. I have no quarrel with you."

"You've done enough." He brushed past the raven and slammed open the door to another abandoned room. There were hundreds in this castle, filled with relics of a time long ago. They held little meaning to him. Which meant they were far more interesting to break.

"Come now, how can I make it up to you?" Bran trailed after him. "I so hate it when you're mad at me."

"The only reason why you are here is to train with the best."

"And you are the best. But we can't train together if you're just trying to kill me."

Eamonn crushed a stone head between his fists. "In my experience, that is the best way to learn."

It was thoroughly satisfying to see the Unseelie Prince's eyes bug out of his head. Bran was whip-quick and wiry, impossible to defeat from a distance. But Eamonn was strong, made even stronger by the crystals that decorated his skin like armor plating.

"What has you all riled up?"

"She saw me." He smashed another piece of a statute, the remaining hand from one of his other rants.

"So?"

"She *saw* me. I hadn't planned on ever letting her see me."

"That would be impossible anyways. She lives on the isle now."

"She lives in a hut off the isle, specifically so that she would not have the potential to see me."

Bran couldn't understand. Not really. For an Unseelie, he was highly attractive. Most his features were unchanged. Sure, the raven eye in the man's head was unsettling, and he would never have passed for a Seelie Fae, but he was pleasant enough to look at. Handsome for his own people.

Eamonn would never be considered handsome again. Beyond that, he was so flawed that the throne he had coveted for so long had slipped from his grasp. He would never be king and his twin, that treacherous, backstabbing fool, would forever sit upon Eamonn's throne.

"What if I trade you a secret?" Bran's voice danced in the air.

"I don't make deals."

"Not a deal. I've somehow wronged you, although I can't understand why. I'll willingly gift you this secret on a very small condition that you take that poor girl out of the hag's hut."

Eamonn paused. "Why would I do that?"

"Because she deserves to be in the castle. She's lived a tough life, from what I can tell. I'd like to see her pampered."

"She doesn't want to be here. I've offered her dinner every night in the dining room, and she insists upon eating with that boggart in her house."

The raven man hoisted himself onto a cabinet, crouching at the much greater height. "Brownie."

"Excuse me?"

"The boggart is no longer. She's turned back into a brownie."

"That's impossible." He shook his head. "It's only rarely done, and a human girl isn't going to bring a faerie back from the brink of madness."

"Shows how little you know." Bran shrugged. "It's a good secret, too. A shame you don't want to trade for it."

Eamonn shook his head, brought his elbow down upon a stone soldier tipped onto the floor. The satisfying crack echoed so loudly through his own skull that he saw stars. But it helped. Oh, did it help.

He wanted to break more. To wallow in self-pity that she, of all people, *Sunshine* had seen his true form. He hadn't been able to turn around, for fear of what he'd see in her gaze.

Horror? More than likely. When he had been driven from Seelie that was what their expressions had been. Horror that the king wasn't a man at all.

Beast.

Betrayer.

Secret? His mind drifted towards the tantalizing bit of information Bran held over him. Eamonn, like the rest of his faerie race, had never been able to resist hidden knowledge.

Breathing hard, he glanced over his shoulder. "What kind of secret is it?"

The calculating look in Bran's raven eye made Eamonn shiver.

Bran leaned forward, hands dangling over his bent knees. "I know her true name."

Just the mere thought of Sunshine's name sent him reeling. What would it taste like on his tongue? Likely as distracting as the rest of her. But Eamonn was certain the merest hint would be a droplet of pure honey coating his mouth.

What a deal it was. Moving her from the hag's hut cost little. There were plenty of available rooms, far away in the depths of the castle. He would have someone placed outside her door, to make sure she didn't wander where she was unwelcome.

It was insane. Making deals with Unseelie Fae had never ended well for his family. Look at where he was now! And this was the son of the very Unseelie who had cursed their family for all time.

Still…it was her name.

He scratched the crystals on his jaw, pondering the thought. He could do much with a name. He could compel her to leave the island.

No. He would never do that. Could never do that. She was too intriguing, too interesting, far too strange a human to leave. He wouldn't allow her to wander far from his side, not until he figured her out.

"All I have to do is move her from the hut to the castle?"

Bran leaned forward with a wry grin. "Well, set her up in a nice room at least. I want the girl to be taken care of, not placed on a shelf to gather dust like the rest of your nice things."

"I can't promise to take care of her."

"I didn't ask for that. She's capable of protecting herself. She made the swim across the sea to get to you."

"To get to the isle," Eamonn corrected. "She didn't know I existed."

"And that's where you're wrong, Cloch Rí. She's been looking for you the whole time, and you've been a thorn in her side."

"She wants me to end a plague."

"For now. But who knows. If you let her closer, she might want more."

"Since when do you play matchmaker?"

Bran hopped down from the cabinet, sauntering towards Eamonn on clicking clawed feet. "Do we have a deal?"

Eamonn glanced down at the hand offered. Bran had one human hand, and one beast. He held out the clawed hand, taloned with three fingers like the foot of a raven.

Although his mind screamed he could find out this information on his own, Eamonn reached forward and clasped the talon. For good measure, he dug the crystals of his palm into the leathery flesh. "We have a deal. Now what is her name?"

The wild smile returned to the raven man's face.

"Sorcha."

"Sorcha." The voice whispered on the winds and tingled in her mind. It swept through her window and through her hair, tangling in the red strands.

She recognized the voice. It belonged to a terrifying woman. Tall, stately, wild red hair matching her own.

Sorcha leaned out the bedroom window and peered across the moors. Will-o'-the-wisps danced merrily above the bog. The scent of peat moss filled the air, earthen and musty. She wrinkled her nose.

Perhaps she only wanted to hear her name. After seeing Macha's face in the fountain, she worried the Tuatha dé Danann had more to say. Was her family all right? She had only made a deal for her father, not her sisters. Had the worst happened, and the faerie come to tell her the bad news?

The thoughts plagued her throughout the evening. Homesickness was a bitter taste in her mouth, leaving bile rolling in her stomach and an empty hole in her chest. She missed them. Briana would know what to do with a man who wouldn't listen. Rosaleen would charm him with her innocent curls and girlish laughter. Papa would give him a pipe and set him down to talk about adventures and traveling.

Sorcha? She would hover in the corner, waiting until someone asked for something. She was far more comfortable taking care of others than she was being the center of attention.

"Sorcha." The wind whispered through her window. "Sorcha, come to me."

Something tugged deep in her belly. The compulsion to move was not a choice, but an order. Her feet slid across the floor even as her mind wailed that she didn't want to move. She didn't know who called out to her.

She watched as if someone else moved her hand, turned the door handle, and pushed the door open.

Macha stood in the midst of swirling white lights. They sparkled upon her shoulders and cast a cold gleam upon her eyes. She lost all color, standing in the moonlight with shadows twining through her hair.

"Lady Fae," Sorcha said. Her feet halted at the edge of the dock. "I had not thought to see you here."

"No, I imagine you didn't. Why else would you have washed your filth in my fountain?"

"It was the blood of a child. One of your children."

"I do not call all faeries my children, nor do I lay claim to a Pooka." She spat the last word as if it were a curse. "The Unseelie can have their animals. Mine are among the Seelie."

"Is that how you would be known? As a mother who cast aside her offspring?"

"You have become daring. That is good. You will need to be strong for this task."

"What more could you possibly ask me to do?" Sorcha's jaw dropped. "I'm already trying to cajole him to come to the mainland."

"Where is your success? I watch you making friends, not convincing the lord of this isle to leave."

Sorcha couldn't argue with that. She hadn't done much. "I'm trying to befriend him so I might convince Stone that—"

"Stone?" Macha raised her eyebrows. "You've named him?"

"Well, yes. How else are we supposed to converse?"

The waters rippled as Macha stepped forward. Will-o'-the-wisps scattered, darting over the lily pads to safety. Ragged-edged clothing revealed glinting weapons strapped to her arms and thighs.

Sorcha swallowed hard. She would accept her death if it came now.

There was no honor in forcing a man to leave his home, and she refused to give up that part of herself. Stone deserved to make the choice.

"You are a coward," Macha whispered. She reached out and ghosted her fingertips across Sorcha's throat. "You hesitate, because you wish him to make this decision for you. If you fail, it is not your fault. It is his."

"That's not true," her throat convulsed. "I don't want to force him to make a decision he isn't prepared for."

"While you wait, your people are dying."

"My family?"

"Your father, as promised, is alive. The blood beetle plague is spreading, and you are forgetting your purpose."

"I couldn't forget that."

"It does not matter to me whether you fulfill your deal. But the deal still stands. If you do not bring the master of this isle back to the mainland, then I will release my hold upon your father's health. I need not remind you how poorly he was doing when you left."

Sorcha's entire body shook. "It's only been a few weeks."

"You might not be entirely in the Otherworld, but you are on the border. Time moves differently here."

"What?"

Macha stepped back from her, a tired and knowing smile on her face. "Take care, little human. I will do my best to help you, but time is not on your side."

Sorcha stumbled backwards, barely catching herself on the edge of the dock. What was she saying? Her mind whirled.

"How long have I been gone?" Sorcha cried out. "How long, Macha?"

"That is not for me to say. Hurry, child."

"Macha! Answer my question!"

The water rippled as magic brushed its surface, then the Tuatha dé Danann disappeared.

Tears burned in Sorcha's eyes, streaming down her cheeks as she panicked. Had she been gone for months? Years? How could she have forgotten that time was different here?

But she wasn't in the home of the Faerie. Not really. Hy-brasil straddled the line between Otherworld and her world. She couldn't have been gone more than a few months, could she?

"What must they think of me?" she whispered. "I did not desert you! I would never do that."

But she had. Sorcha had let memories of her family become substitute for the real thing. In doing so, she forgot the warmth of their touch, the sound of their voice, the lingering support of their embrace.

"I'm so sorry. I should never have lost myself in the magic of this place."

CHAPTER EIGHT
THE STORM

Sorcha paced in front of the kitchen door. She'd spent the entirety of two days mulling over Macha's words, replaying what she might say and how he might react. The problem was she didn't know. Stone was a rather unpredictable person. First he was horrible, then he was kind, then he wouldn't even look at her.

The last thing she needed was to go back to the "toss her out of the castle" route they'd started their relationship with. He had shown an ability to be a gentleman. Now she needed to use that to her advantage.

Her first thought was to dress up. She'd put the green velvet dress back on and twirled around in front of Boggart asking how she looked. Brown patches were showing up all over Boggart's body, and she stroked one on her forearm before clapping.

But that hadn't been right. Sorcha wasn't trying to impress him with her beauty. She needed him to take her seriously. The blood beetle plague was a terrible affliction, and he needed to understand how dire the circumstances were.

She switched to the outfit she usually conducted her midwifery in. Stains decorated the front of the white apron and rips frayed the ends. She thought it rather suited the conversation.

Boggart hated it.

The little faerie then found the perfect dress or at least that's what her chirps sounded like. It had been Sorcha's mother's. Pale yellow with tiny hand-embroidered white daisies along the hem, it snugged tight to her waist while sweeping the ground. Sorcha rarely wore the dress for fear she might harm the delicate fabric.

Still, she tried it on. Worn cotton swayed against her thighs, delicate lace brushing the tops of her feet. The square neckline allowed the wind to brush over her skin, the tight sleeves complimented her strong arms.

Sorcha didn't second guess her choice until she stood outside the kitchens. Now, she paced back and forth wondering what her plan was. Did she think he would say yes just because she wore a yellow dress?

Of course, he wouldn't. He was a man who called himself master. A peasant girl in a pretty dress wouldn't change his mind that easily.

A grumbling voice lifted. "Are you going in or not, girl?"

"I'm thinking."

"What could you have to think about that would make you trample my rutabagas?"

"Hush, Cian."

The click of his jaw snapping together made her flinch. She should know better than to issue an order while using a Fae name.

Sorcha winced, "I'm sorry, Cian. I rescind that order."

His mouth flew open so fast she thought he might unhinge his jaw. "How dare you! This is precisely why humans shouldn't have our names!"

"I agree," she interrupted, stopping him mid-rant. "I never should have used it. That was careless of me."

Cian grumbled but turned back to hoeing the patch of lettuce which she swore had popped up overnight. The man was magic with the garden. Sorcha wished he lived near her sisters. Maybe they wouldn't have given so much money to the marketplace.

Squaring her shoulders, she marched into the bustling kitchen.

Most of the faeries still kept their glamour around her. They feared her reaction to their true form, or worried they might frighten her.

Whatever the cause, it irked Sorcha to no end.

Already bristling, she searched through the steam and heat waves to find Pixie. The old woman was one of the Fae who remained glamoured. That little tidbit Sorcha liked least of all.

"Pixie!" she called out.

Everyone paused for a brief second. Sorcha knew what was running through their minds. The human was here. Be more careful than before. Even though they liked her, even though she had saved one of their own, tension appeared where there hadn't been before.

Pixie rushed towards her, wiping her hands on a towel as she went. "What can I do for you, dearie?"

"Where is your master?"

"The throne room, I would imagine."

Sorcha growled. "Why is he always in that damn throne room when I need him?"

"He's expecting company."

"Company?" Sorcha glanced around the room with surprise. "You're preparing a feast?"

"Yes. It's a rarity that we have visitors."

"Who's visiting?"

"I don't think I'm supposed to say," Pixie glanced over her shoulder at the brownies frantically cooking. "You should remain in your home tonight. It would be safer."

"Who's coming?" Sorcha repeated.

Pixie did not respond. Instead, she turned on her heel and hustled back towards the table where she'd been decorating tiny pastries.

Frustration surged through her and gathered in her clenched fists. Sorcha didn't like being left in the dark. Who was coming? This was a cursed isle impossible to even see for another seven years, so who would have the power to find it?

There were so many questions no one would answer. No one in this room, at least.

All the more reason to go bother the master of the isle.

Resolve settled upon her shoulders like a well-worn cloak. She wouldn't be intimidated by visitors who might frighten her. She'd met the terrifying Macha—a woman who rode through battle and cleaved men in two. There were few worse than that.

Her footsteps echoed down the hall as she marched towards the throne room. She vaguely remembered where it was, although she caught herself turning into empty rooms.

One held shattered stone statues. Her foot caught upon a head, empty eyes staring up at her and carved so realistically that she expected it to blink. Unnerved, Sorcha backed out of the room as though the statues might call out for help.

Rounding a cobweb covered corner, she finally saw the grand entrance. This time, she paused to really look at it.

Carved white marble arched over the double doorway. Tiny flowers, slithering ivy, even beetles crawled from the floor and arched into the ceiling. This wasn't just an intimidating entrance, it was a work of art.

The green double doors stood open, golden rivets and foil outlining each individual plank. It was the only thing in the castle not falling to pieces.

She brushed her hand along the worn wood as she passed. It was clean, much to her surprise. Every tiny piece of the grand ballroom shone as bright as the sun.

Although cracks still traveled through the floor, this was now a place of rare beauty. The chandeliers dripped rubies and emeralds, light striking the gems and casting colored shadows upon the floor.

Sorcha gasped. She hadn't realized paint covered the walls. The Wild Hunt stretched on either side of her. Fae in chariots, armored and terrifying, chased down human and animal alike. Larger than life, they seemed to move on their own as she stared.

All this stretched towards the throne where the king lounged in wait and cast in shadow. New curtains hung from the ceiling, blood-red and so silken they dripped onto the floor. The staircase to reach him was made of pure gold.

"You are early." His grumbling voice raced down her spine in shivers and trembles.

"I hadn't realized I was expected."

"It's you?"

He stood. His great height at once overpowering and overwhelming even though she was still far from him.

Sorcha was intensely aware of her simple appearance. She should've chosen the emerald gown—she might not have looked so out of place. Her mother's dress looked more like a wildflower placed incongruously in a porcelain vase.

Each thunk of his footsteps made her blush burn hotter. What had she been thinking? Of course, he would entertain guests in a finer way than he lived. She was a *fool*.

Embarrassment did not suit her. Sorcha reminded herself that she was a midwife, not a princess. This was her best dress before Pixie had given her something else to wear. There was nothing to be ashamed of.

She lifted her gaze, and her mouth went dry.

A warrior stood before her. Commander, chief, lord. She sucked in a rasping gasp as he strode towards her across the wide expanse of marble.

He wore elven armor. Each dark silver plate meticulously hammered to fit the movement of his arms. The symbol of a stag embellished the wide leather chest piece. Chainmail swayed against his thighs, knee-high boots striking the floor with hard purpose.

Metallic threads wove through his long braid that was tied off with golden clasps. The sword she had so admired was strapped to his side.

"You should not be here," he growled.

"I see that now."

"I am expecting visitors."

"Yes, yes, it appears so." Sorcha was tongue-tied.

He was so handsome, so overwhelming, so otherworldly that she was incapable of finding her own thoughts. She turned to leave, but paused when he reached out and grasped her arm. Crystals bit through the delicate fabric.

"All is well?"

She shivered. "That depends on your definition of well."

"How can I help?"

"You have to come back to the mainland with me," she whispered while staring at the door. "I cannot linger here any longer."

"You know my answer."

"Then I will have to force you." Sorcha whipped around, her green eyes sparking with anger. "You did not tell me that time passed differently here! My family could be dead in a few days, have you no care for that?"

"Who told you?"

Her heart stopped. His words tumbled over and over in her mind. Sorcha's throat closed as she asked, "Why didn't you?"

"There wasn't an appropriate opportunity."

"The first moment I stepped into this throne room and told you my purpose, you should have let me know that my chances were limited. I *cannot* give up. My family needs me."

"Family is who you choose, not who is in your blood."

Sorcha wrenched her arm from his grasp. "Then I choose *them*. A thousand times over, I choose them!"

"You have been given a good home here. In time, I would move you into the castle—"

"In time?" She pressed a hand against her mouth and backed towards the door. "As if it's some kind of reward for good behavior?"

"I had to make sure you were trustworthy."

"Trustworthy? Do you have some kind of initiation people must go through before you lower yourself to call them friend?"

"No, it's not like that."

"Then what is it like, *master*? What must I do before you consider my family worthy of your attentions?"

She was even with him now, four steps up the stairs. He lifted one foot and placed it on the next step, hesitating in the face of her anger.

"I cannot leave this isle. I cannot help your family, even if I wished to."

A choked sound escaped her lips. "Even if you wished to?"

"That's not how I meant it—"

"I understand perfectly how you meant it. Thank you for making things so clear."

"*Wait.*"

She whirled and raced from the throne room. Sorcha rounded a corner, pushing through back rooms until she recognized where she was. She had to avoid whatever horrific guests he might be entertaining. She didn't want to know what beasts consorted with such a horrible man.

He had no care for her family. And if he had no care for them, then he didn't care what happened to her.

It shouldn't sting as much as it did. She barely knew the man, although he had become a regular figure in her thoughts. She'd even given him a name.

Foolish, she berated herself. Childish. Friendship with him was wishful thinking.

She hurtled down the steps, pushing through the kitchens without pause. Pixie shouted behind her. Stopping would only result in more anger, and Sorcha couldn't deal with any more.

A storm cloud brewed on the edge of the isle. It barreled towards her as she sprinted directly into its electric power. Storms didn't bother her, not when she knew shelter was so close.

The sweet scent of peat filled her lungs. Bleating sheep scattered as she charged through their midst. The tie in her hair loosened in the breeze, flying free to let her hair stream back in a banner of bright red.

Her lungs ached, but she did not slow. She wouldn't stop until she could slam the hut's door behind her. The crash might stop her whirling thoughts.

A tear slid down her cheek. She dashed it away with an angry slap, leaving a mark of red against her freckled jaw. Then another slid free, this time hitting her face so painfully that she realized it wasn't tears at all.

It was rain.

The clouds unleashed their fury. Rain pounded the ground and echoed in her ears. Thunder rumbled in the distance. Lightning cracked far off in the ocean, a bolt zig-zagging from the sky and into the water.

She squinted and kept running. Her mother's dress would be ruined, and it was another thing she could blame on him.

How love-starved was she that she would trust such a monster?

The raging storm echoed the tumultuous emotions beating in her breast. He had no right. He had no right!

She lost her way in the sheets of rain. The hag's hut was barely visible below the small cliff she stood upon, but she would not let that deter her. The rocks were slippery and dangerous. She skidded down, sliding her hands into cracks and crevices, gripping with strong fingers. A small, romantic part of her whispered that this might be what it felt like to touch the geodes of his skin.

She grunted and yanked a stone from the ground. It tumbled down the small cliff side and splashed into the foaming waves. Good riddance. She shouldn't be wondering what he might feel like. She shouldn't be wondering anything about him at all!

Sorcha would leave this isle empty-handed and find another way to save her family. There had to be more she could bargain. She could promise her life to Macha just to get away from this place.

From him.

Lightning cracked and struck the ground above her head. Sorcha flinched, glancing up to see the bolt strike a tree hanging onto the edge of the small cliff. Blinded, she hugged herself close to the rock and whispered a silent prayer.

The tree screamed. Sizzling electricity raced through her, standing her damp hair on end. Then she heard it. The creaking groan, the snapping cracks of roots being pulled from the earth, and the rumbling of stone.

She looked up although she already knew what she would see. The aged tree released its precarious hold on the cliff and plunged towards her.

Sorcha tucked her body closer to the stones, wedging her side into the cliff and shredding the delicate skin of her stomach. The roots slid past, the trunk smashing against the stones but not touching her.

She breathed a sigh of relief. Then, a falling branch whooshed past where she pressed herself into the niche of the cliff. She lifted her head at the wrong moment and shrieked as a flame-red strand of hair wrapped around the slick wood.

It yanked her backwards, tossing her into the deep mire where ocean met bog. Sorcha hit the water with a loud slap. Her back burned, and her mind screamed. She hadn't taken a breath before striking the water, her body sinking like stone.

Bubbles obscured her vision. Air twisted, leaving the tree which dragged her further and further down. She reached her hands for the surface, dark waters swallowing her whole.

The tree hit the muck with a muffled thump. Billowing mud floated up like smoke. Sorcha watched with horror as the surface blurred and disappeared. She twisted—chest aching—and grasped onto the tangled bit of hair.

She tugged, but there was too much for her to yank free. Her fingers felt along the strand until she touched the tree branch. Something slithered through her grasp.

Sorcha flinched backwards in fear, stopped by a yank against the back of her skull which twisted her around. The foggy water was too dark for her to make out more than vague shapes.

But which way was up?

Her heart thudded painfully. She didn't remember which way was up. The branch was attached to her, so directly above it would be the surface? But the tree angled down. Didn't it?

She tugged on her hair again, frantically placing her feet against the branch and pulling hard. She felt more than heard the ripping, but it wasn't enough.

This wasn't how she wanted to die. People didn't often swim in Ui Neill; they were too far away from the selkies to have that bloodline in their midst.

She wanted to die on rolling green hills or in the middle of a field of heather. Why did it have to end like this?

I love you, she thought. I love you so much, Papa and all my sisters. I wish it could have been different.

Black spots blurred the edges of her vision. At some point, she would have to suck in a deep breath. She would breathe in murky water, and that would be the end.

Sorcha had always been a fighter. She wouldn't suck in the salt water until the very last second or until she passed out. Her body convulsed, arguing with her mind that she needed to breathe. She squeezed her eyes shut, so she could forget for one second that she was underwater.

Just a moment longer, she thought. Just one more moment to enjoy being alive. To feel the cold water on my fingertips and remember that she *lived*.

A warm hand wrapped around her arm. Her eyes snapped open. It was too dark to know whether the shadowy figure was a merrow-man, but she didn't care anymore. She just wanted to breathe.

Heat spread from the gentle touch as it slid down her forearm and found where she still clutched her hair. An odd scrape of scale abraded her skin, slicing through the lock of hair easily.

No, not scale, she realized. Crystal.

She clutched onto his shoulders with clawed hands and desperately kicked. If she could just get to the surface. If she could just inhale.

His hand wrapped around her jaw, forcing her head down. She didn't want to look down into that darkness. Why wasn't he moving? Didn't he understand that she was moments away from inhaling water and—

Warm lips wrapped around hers. He squeezed her jaw and her mouth opened for a moment. He exhaled. She breathed in his air desperately. The pain in her lungs eased.

It wasn't enough, but it would do. Sorcha squeezed her eyes shut and hooked a leg around his waist, anchoring herself to him. She tried not to take too much of his breath, he'd need it to get them back to the surface. But it was addicting.

The crystal running down his upper lip sliced through her own lip. She winced at the pain and drew back. Salt stung the wound.

With her securely held in his arms, Stone pushed off the bottom of the ocean. They shot through the water like an arrow from a bow. She held tight to his broad shoulders, ripples of muscle shifting beneath her fingertips.

They broke the surface, and she gasped in air. It was too much, she choked violently and hung onto him for dear life. He wasn't even breathing hard. He simply waited until she stopped coughing and then rolled onto his back.

When she struggled, he brushed the wet strands of hair from her face. "Easy, relax. Let the ocean take you back to shore."

Sorcha coughed again, "I can swim on my own."

"Let me do the work, Sorcha. Stop fighting me."

She felt as though a bolt of lightning had struck her. That was exactly what she had been doing since the moment she reached this isle. Fighting him, in every conversation, in every rule he made. And yet, he still saved her.

Waves rocked them, white caps growing dangerously high as the storm raged above them.

"I trust you," she whispered and let her body go limp.

He wrapped a strong, bare arm across her shoulders and drew her back against his chest. Crystals bit into her spine from his gaping shoulder wound, but she refused to complain. He swam them back to shore with the grace of a selkie. The waves rocked forward, seaweed brushed her legs, and the wound on her lip bled freely.

"What were you thinking?" he growled.

"I wasn't."

Lightning cracked overhead, casting his face in a grim light. Sorcha turned away from the disappointed expression. She had already disappointed herself, she didn't need him to be, too.

"Obviously."

The wind rushed overhead, pushing waves up and over their heads She shivered violently.

He cursed. "We're almost there. Just a few more moments."

How had she been carried so far out? Sorcha hadn't noticed the tree moving, but it must have slid along the ocean floor.

His feet touched land, and Stone dragged her forward into his arms. The steely bands wrapped around her as if she weighed nothing.

The bulging muscles of his chest were distracting. Not a single hair covered his skin, not even on his arms. Up close, the crystals were so much angrier. The wounds carved into his skin and deep into his flesh. It was a miracle he could even move.

"I can walk," she rasped.

"Enough."

"I'm not so weak as to—"

"I said enough, Sorcha."

She looked up at his severe face, unable to resist tracing the smooth line of his jaw. "That's the second time you've called me by name. I don't remember giving that to you."

The muscles under her fingertips bunched. "I have my ways."

"Obviously."

Shivers rocked her body, and it didn't escape her notice that he tucked her tighter against him. Sorcha shifted until her head was underneath his chin. He was so large she could tuck her knees into his armpits and still be comfortable.

"Why are you so much bigger than me?" she asked, teeth clacking with chills.

"What kind of question is that?"

"I just want to know. All the other Tuatha dé Danann are the same. Y-you're all larger than life."

"I'm not that much bigger."

"You're a veritable giant compared to me."

"We're not human," he grumbled. "That's the only answer I have."

Sorcha glanced over his shoulder, brows furrowing in confusion. "Why aren't we going to the hag's hut?"

"I'm taking you to the castle."

"I was told to stay away from the castle—your guests are dangerous."

"They are."

"I think I've had enough of danger for one night."

Stone jostled her, tossing her up higher against his chest. He was like a furnace, and she couldn't understand how. The water chilled her skin and made her bones ache. Why didn't it affect him in the same way?

"I'm not putting you anywhere they might find you."

"Who are they?"

"That's not for you to know."

Sorcha shook her head. "I might be freezing, but that hasn't changed my curiosity. I thought this isle was only visible every seven years."

"It is."

"Then who are these people who suddenly arrived? Are they shipwrecked, like me?"

"No."

"Do they live on a different part of the isle?"

"No."

"Are they selkies or merrows come to visit?"

"Stop asking questions," he said.

"No," she said, repeating his favorite word. "Why are you shirtless?"

"I'm not foolish enough to attempt swimming in armor. Silence. These visitors can hear very well, and they would be too interested in a human girl. Keep your mouth shut, and trust me to take care of you."

Strangely enough, she did.

Sorcha tucked her hands underneath her chin to conserve what little heat she had left. She had survived many winters, but never had she been this cold. The biting rain washed away the salt water on her skin slicking her body with freezing drops. The wind howled and shoved at their bodies although his steps were sure and steady.

She owed this man her life. Sorcha wasn't sure how she felt about that. Tricking him into coming back to the mainland seemed wrong. He didn't deserve that mistreatment.

If she was being truthful with herself, it was unlikely she ever would have tricked him. Stone was an intelligent man beneath all that brawn. A noble Fae who had taken up the throne in this forgotten place.

They didn't disturb any other faeries along their journey to the castle. Most had sought shelter from the raging storm. Others remained in the castle to wait out the rain. Storms always seemed to keep everyone from their labor, even the faeries.

He rounded the stone castle walls to the place where she'd seen him training with Bran.

Teeth chattering, she bit out, "Is Bran really the raven who has been following me?"

"So it would seem."

"Why would he waste his time following a human?"

"I've asked him the same question."

He entered through a narrow door and slammed it shut behind them, sudden silence and darkness making her heart pound again. "And what was his response?"

"I do not control the Unseelie Fae. No one can."

The darkness made it seem almost as if she were underwater again. Shadows made shapes vaguely familiar, but difficult to piece together. She recognized this room when lightning struck again, spearing light across the room.

Broken statues littered the floor. The haunting faces stared at her with vacant eyes.

Sorcha shivered and tucked her face against the crystals of his neck. Their jagged edges dug into her cheek but she did not care. The pain anchored her, driving away the fear with knife-sharp points and cold, smooth plains.

His hands clenched on her shoulder and legs. "Not far now."

"Where are you taking me?"

"Somewhere safe."

"There's nowhere safe on this isle," she whispered, her breath whistling through the circular wound on his throat. "Everything is dangerous, and one must decide whether to live in fear, or courage."

"We all know you've chosen courage, little human. Foolishly so."

"I'm not as fragile as you think."

He didn't respond, suggesting he disagreed with her. Sorcha was thankful he didn't argue his point. She couldn't debate him right now, not when her body was shivering so violently she worried she might jolt right out of his arms.

They rounded one last, shadowed corner and reached a dead-end. A carving on the wall caught her attention. A warrior held her sword aloft, driving back creatures of the night which Sorcha could only imagine were the Unseelie. Their twisted and warped forms disappeared into the smooth marble.

Her face was beautiful and hard. Her armor carved so meticulously that Sorcha could see individual links of chainmail. The sword itself appeared so realistic that she might pluck it from the woman's hand and swing it herself.

"It's beautiful," she whispered. "But I don't see a doorway."

"Humans. You look at things so superficially."

Stone jostled her forward, forcing her to grasp onto his neck with a gasp. Their gazes locked for a moment as their noses touched. She felt the warm fan of his breath grazing her mouth. Electric blue eyes burned her flesh and seared her to the bone.

"Look." A crystal brushed against her mouth. "You need to remember this."

She wasn't certain she'd ever forget the cold slide of stone warmed by the heat of his body.

Sorcha ripped herself from his captivating gaze and glanced over her shoulder. He pressed his thumb into the grooved pommel of the sword. She heard a soft click, the rasp of sliding stone, and then he pushed.

It wasn't just a carving; it was a door.

He wrapped his arm around her again, and she kept one arm looped around his neck. She wanted to be upright for this hidden secret. She wanted to remember.

Darkness lay within the room, not with tendrils of fear but a soft quiet that eased the soul. The slight burble of water reached her ears trickling from some unknown stream. Heat brushed against her skin in an almost physical touch.

Sorcha released a slow breath. "I can't see anything."

"I'm going to put you down," he said at the same time. She heard the creaking of crystals. "Patience, little human."

He set her down on a smooth bench. Sorcha couldn't see the color, but she could feel the texture as soft as velvet. She ran her palms over the edges, the bumps of carvings, dipping into hollows and valleys.

Impulsively, she toed off her sodden shoes. Soft moss cushioned the arches of her feet as she placed them back onto the floor. It was not wet with rain as she'd expected.

Sorcha tilted her head, listening for the pattering sound. It was there, but far away, as if she was in the very belly of the castle. She couldn't believe they were in a dungeon. No dungeon had a door so fine nor moss so soft.

Where were they?

Yellow light flashed, blurring her vision in bright sparks of color. The beautiful room before her couldn't be in the castle! Lush moss carpeted the circular room and ivy covered the walls, making it seem more forest than room. A canopy of blushing roses hung in tendrils over a bed piled high with furs. In the center, a carved woman stretched towards the ceiling atop a still pool studded with white flowers. Her wings spread wide for flight and were so detailed that Sorcha could see the veins stretched across them.

"This place is too fine for me," she said.

"There's no such place."

Her jaw dropped. What did he mean by that? He couldn't be saying she was worthy of such a room? This was fit for royalty or a high-born Fae gifted in the arts.

Sorcha glanced down at her calloused palms and shorn fingernails feeling well and truly out of place.

"I can't—" he paused and glanced at her then down at his chest. "I have to ready myself for these pests. I trust you can warm yourself?"

"Is there a place for a fire?"

He gestured towards one of the ivy-covered walls. "Everything you need should be in the room beyond."

"Oh." She didn't know what else to say. He'd saved her, brought her to this haven, and then…was leaving? Who did that? "It's very difficult to understand you."

"I don't know if that's a compliment."

"Neither do I."

He stood surrounded by green, and she couldn't help but wonder who this man truly was. She caught glimpses of him, but never the full portrait.

He held his hands limp at his sides. Drops of water dripped from the strands of his hair, running down the shaven sides, and disappearing into the crevices filled with gems. He couldn't meet her gaze, and as she watched, his hands clenched and relaxed.

"You aren't comfortable with me looking at you," she said. "That's why you didn't wish to speak when I saw you training."

"I know what I look like."

"What do you liken yourself to?"

"A monster. These," he gestured towards the shoulder wound and his throat, "are unnatural. Marks of disfigurement that make me less Fae, less of a man."

"I don't see how something such as that could make you less of anything. They are startling at first, but the shock fades, and I hardly even notice them now."

"It is a beautiful lie." He swept into a low bow. "I'd forgotten how refreshing it is to hear such words. Thank you for not telling me the truth."

"What?"

He swept out of the room so quickly she felt only the breeze of his passing.

Sorcha was left with the trickling water, the soft movement of roses, and complete silence. She sat upon the bench and stared at the ceiling, at the surrounding splendor. She was utterly alone for the first time since arriving.

Drawing her knees to her chest, she blew out a quiet breath. When had she last been alone? Surely it must have happened, but she couldn't think of a time. Her sisters had always been home. She'd traveled to the MacNara's with Agatha, had left with the Dullahan, spent days upon the ship. Even in the ocean there had been merrow-men and the Guardian.

She refused to let her thoughts turn dark. Heat should be her first task. She needed to get out of these wet clothes or she would catch cold.

The healing thoughts helped. She could diagnose herself like a patient, the segmented thoughts easy to follow.

Sorcha stumbled to her feet and brushed the ivy aside. She'd never seen a washroom such as this. More vines covered the walls, blue flowers unfurling their petals and filling the air with a heady floral scent. A large circle cut into the ground, warm water constantly pouring from a small hole in the wall.

"A hot spring," she murmured.

There was a small chamber pot in the corner, along with a vanity table filled to the brim with hairbrushes and pastes she did not recognize.

None of this was for her, she reminded herself. She should warm her shivering body and then jump into bed. There was no need for pampering, nor did she have any idea what those faerie treats would do to her.

She stripped the sodden fabric away, pausing a moment to stare down at her mother's dress. Seawater was likely to stain it, but she could at least try to save it. Tears pricked in the corners of her eyes.

"I miss you," she whispered. It was the same feeling every time. She missed her pagan rites, Beltane, the whispered faerie stories her mother had been so good at telling.

Steam rose into the air in wispy tendrils, begging Sorcha to warm herself. She turned and dipped a toe into the water. The shocking warmth made her gasp, then moan as she sank into the water to her shoulders.

Her shivers ceased immediately, coaxed to stillness by the gentle lapping waves of water. She could stand in this pool, and it would only come up to her breasts. This was safe water.

Curious, Sorcha scooped a handful and touched it to her tongue. Fresh water. Not a hint of salt tainted the taste, nor was it sulfuric as many hot springs could be.

"This place continues to grow stranger by the hour," she whispered.

Tipping her head back against the stone lip, she let her mind quiet until her skin pruned. Even then, she took a while to leave the comfort of the bath. It was as if she was the last person on earth. Silence calmed her anxious thoughts, steam whisked away old aches and pains, and the water held her in a gentle embrace.

She could spend the rest of her life like this.

When her eyelids drifted shut more than they stayed open, Sorcha dragged herself out of the warm bath. Blearily glancing around the room, she realized there was no drying cloth available.

She sighed. Hopefully, Eamonn wouldn't come waltzing back in while she stood stark naked in the center of the room. She dunked her mother's dress in the water and wrung it out a few times.

Leaving the yellow fabric on the edge of the bath, she peeked through the ivy to make sure no one was in the room. Of course, faeries could glamour themselves. She narrowed her eyes.

"Hello?"

No one responded.

"If there are any servants in here, I'm going to come out and I have nothing else to put on. Please don't…stare."

She chided herself as she dashed across the moss. Who was going to stare at her? They probably thought she looked as ugly as she found them.

Leaping into the large bed and snuggling beneath the furs, she hummed contentedly as the softness brushed her skin. The furs dried the water away and trapped the heat until she was in a cocoon of warmth and comfort.

She sighed happily, but took stock of her body just in case. The shivers had left, but she could already feel her nose clogging. She would have a slight cold, but hopefully nothing would settle in her chest.

If she was lucky, she would escape this entire ordeal unscathed. If she wasn't, she would need to make compresses and drink as much tea as she could.

Sorcha could hope that her body wouldn't have any adverse reactions. There wasn't time for her to fall ill.

Eamonn sat in the shadows of her room, berating himself for returning here. He hadn't planned on this. Especially not on this night.

The emissaries from the Seelie court rarely came to visit. He found it curious they chose now, of all times, to show their faces. Was there a spy in his court of fools? He couldn't think of anyone who would pass secrets to his brother, but it wouldn't be the first time. He would need to interrogate a few to ensure his safety. For the good of everyone, his brother could not know what happened on this isle.

They always made him angry. These glittery giants, women and men, dressed in full armor under the pretense that they wished to visit an old friend. None of them cared how he lived before his banishment, and they didn't care now.

He thought the entire thing suspect, always had, but it was not within his power to deny them. If his brother wanted to keep an eye on him, then he could. But Eamonn wouldn't make it easy on him.

Armored and silent, he stared them down. The throne room changed to ballroom, a slap in the face to the brother who was not king. They brought their own musicians, their own people, everything that they thought he didn't have. The only thing Eamonn did was have the room cleaned.

Let them think he lived in splendor and enjoyed his life here on Hybrasil. Eamonn enjoyed the thought of his brother's anger.

And when it was all done, he had meant to go back to his room. To break whatever he could in an attempt to cool his anger and embarrassment.

But he found himself here.

Staring at her.

Her hair fanned out around her head like the petals of a red rose. Streaks of sun-kissed skin paled to milk white, beautiful and unique like the rest of her. She was soft in sleep. Softer than he'd ever seen her.

There was always a hard edge riding on her shoulders. Lines formed between her brows, expressive with all her emotions. She was an open book.

His lips quirked. She wouldn't like how easily he read her.

One hand tucked beneath her cheek, pale lashes spread out and casting shadows. He sat himself in the darkness and counted every freckle on her face. It was the first time in years he had calmed down without crushing marble, shattering pottery, or snapping wooden frames.

He didn't know how she did it. Even while asleep, there was something infinitely calming about her mere existence.

Should that frighten him? He felt as though it should.

She stirred in her sleep, yawning, and slowly opened her eyes.

He waited for the flinch, the jump, the terrified shriek that would make his ears rings for days. So many Fae women had reacted in a similar way.

She did none of that. Sunshine, Sorcha, did none of those things. She blinked a few times, focusing on his form in the shadows, and then a soft smile spread across her face.

In that moment, she gutted him. No one had looked at him like a person in such a long time, without pity or fear. She just opened her eyes and smiled at him. As if he was finally where he belonged.

"I had a feeling you might come back tonight." Her voice was raspy as if water filled her lungs. Right on cue, she coughed into her fist.

"It's not unusual to fall ill after attempting to take your life." Why did he say that? Eamonn dug his fingers into the crystals on his opposite wrist. Always picking a fight, especially when worried.

"Oh, hush, you know that's not what it was. I need my things," she said when she stopped coughing. "I have a tea for this."

Eamonn gestured towards the small table he had set next to the pile of furs. "Anise, honey, and mulled wine."

She glanced over at the steam rising from the porcelain cup and back to him. "Yes. Thank you. That's exactly what I needed."

"Don't look so surprised. Healing humans is not so different from the Fae."

"I guess it isn't." She pulled herself up, catching the furs against her chest and shoving the heavy mass of her hair back. "You know the healing arts?"

"A small amount. I watched my nursemaid as a child."

"Clever."

"I never claimed otherwise." He watched her sip the tea, her face scrunching up. "Bitter?"

"I just don't like the taste of anise. Never have."

"It will help."

That soft expression returned to her face, eyes half-lidded and lips quirked to the side. "Yes, it will."

He didn't know what to say when she stared at him as if he brought all the stars in the sky to her. It was tea. Nothing more, nothing less.

They stared at each other until his heart raced. Eamonn couldn't piece together *why* he was so affected. Then his eyes traced the line of her shoulders. Bare and pale as the moon. Tiny freckles dotted her skin, more than he had counted on her face. He hadn't seen those.

How badly did he want to connect those dots? Enough to clench his fists and lock the muscles of his legs, restraining himself from leaning forward and tugging the furs away. He had forgotten to bring her anything to wear.

Bless his forgetfulness.

"Are your visitors gone?" she asked.

"Excuse me?" His mind had been elsewhere. There were freckles dotting her arms, so it would make sense if they spread to her legs as well. Was she freckled everywhere?

"Your guests, the dangerous ones. Have they left?"

"Yes."

"Is it safe for me to wander your halls again?"

"I—" he shook his head to clear it. "No, it's never safe to wander the castle halls. There are many hidden secrets and spirits who keep them."

"I haven't met a spirit yet, just faeries."

"Then you are lucky."

"This place is one of the strangest I have ever seen. Spirits wandering the castle at night. Faeries in the kitchen. You do keep strange company, Stone."

His name hovered on the tip of his tongue. Just once, he wanted to hear her say his name. His given name. But he knew how dangerous it would be to tell her. A human in possession of a faerie's name was bound to use it.

Even that danger would be worth hearing her lilting voice caress the syllables of his born name.

If he was any other man, he might have told her, but he buried the desire for the safety of his people. Eamonn was a creature bred for war and destruction. He could not take the risk.

She leaned forward and coughed again. He clenched his fists, reminding himself that she could take care of herself. She was human and not worthy of his instinctual reaction. To protect. To care.

His father's voice echoed in his mind. She was beneath him. A base creature on par with the lesser Fae. Ignore her struggles, but use her as a servant or slave when the time was right.

He'd never believed those words.

Eamonn stood and settled next to her on the bed. Her bare back shook, ribs expanding until he could see the bumping lines before hacking out air in the next second.

His hand was so large against her skin. It spanned the entirety of her back, rubbing gently back and forth. He did not pound—that wouldn't help—just tried to comfort as his nursemaid used to do.

"Thank you," she said on a sigh. "I'm sorry. I didn't expect a simple dip in the sea to affect me so."

"That was more than a dip."

"Venture?"

"Mistake." He caught himself again. Why was he so cruel to her? He couldn't understand why he tried to make it an argument every time she spoke. Other than to see the red peaks of color on her cheekbones that he so thoroughly enjoyed.

Eamonn didn't clench his fists this time. He reached and ran a finger over the high arches of her cheeks, tracing the spaces between freckles.

"What are you doing?" she whispered.

"I haven't the faintest idea."

He could get lost in those eyes. Green like ivy leaves, like moss when the sun first strikes after days of rainfall. How was she holding him captive? Had she cast a spell on him?

Or maybe he was simply so starved for attention he couldn't help himself. She was the first person to see him as a man, not a monster.

How could he stop?

Eamonn leaned down, eyes darting between her wide gaze and pouting lips. He'd never noticed her lips before. Berry red, thinner than most but still pleasing. Would she taste like the raspberry color staining her mouth?

"Master?" Cian's voice cut through the silence, jolting him to his feet and back to reality. "I'm sorry to interrupt, but there's been an unexpected complication."

"How so?"

"It's the visiting Unseelie, sir. He's requesting an audience, demanding really, and said he won't take no for an answer." Cian rubbed the side of his head. "He nearly took my ear off pulling at it."

"Bran," Eamonn grumbled. He glanced back at Sorcha, who clutched the furs to her chest. Her eyes were wide, her chest heaving.

That was the fear he'd expected. He should've known that although she may someday trust him, she was unlikely to ever *want* him. What a fool he was.

Eamonn nodded, and then eased off the bed and away from her. Without glancing back, he ducked out of the room. He'd made enough of a scene to want to hide from her for the rest of his existence. Bran had done the right thing by causing a mess only Eamonn could fix.

Damned Unseelie usually ended up being right.

CHAPTER NINE
THE UNSEELIE COURT

Sorcha moved permanently into the green room after her incident at the cliff. Boggart panicked, rushing around the hut and shattering plates until Sorcha caught her and explained the faerie was coming with her. That soothed her troubled mind although she didn't let go of Sorcha's leg for a few hours.

The faeries helped get all her things to her new room. She insisted everything go in the bathroom. The clothes remained in the drier bedroom. She didn't want to ruin the pristine image by filling it with wardrobes.

Thankfully, the faeries agreed.

Sorcha spent hours in the room, enjoying the quiet solitude. Boggart mostly stayed with the other brownies in the kitchen, having found a new appreciation for a large space to work with. She brought every meal to Sorcha and spent time listening to her talk. She still didn't speak.

The warning Macha had issued rang in Sorcha's ears more often than not. She'd tried to find Stone for several days, but he'd disappeared. She suspected he was in one of the castle towers. Pixie had whispered the suggestion a few times, but no one would tell her which tower.

Time was ticking. Every day passing by felt like a nail in her father's coffin. She had to do something! But there wasn't anything to do—not as long as the master of the isle hid himself from everything and everyone.

She sat on the edge of the faerie fountain, watching minnows dart towards each other. Every tiny movement flashed their silver bellies as they playfully zipped away from her fingers.

It was late, and she should be sleeping. The longer she stayed on this isle, the less she felt the need for rest. Energy sparked in the air. It made the hair on her arms stand up and her body yearn to move, to dance, to do anything other than fall asleep. Again.

There was so much more she could be doing.

"But they won't let me," Sorcha breathed with a sigh. "They think I'm some well-to-do lady with no need to be in the garden."

She snorted. She had mucked stalls, pulled weeds, and stuck her hands where they shouldn't be. The scars on her arms and legs were proof enough.

They'd heard it all. Every time she argued with them, the faeries shook their glamoured heads and sent her back to her room, or for a walk in the fresh air, or heavens forbid suggest she might need something else to eat.

Sorcha ran a hand over her soft stomach. She'd eaten enough in the past month to feed three people, and still they said she was too skinny.

A minnow swam towards her swirling finger, tapping it before dashing away.

Sorcha smiled. At least the animals were welcoming. Even a few of the sheep had taken a liking to her, and they didn't mind when she trudged through the fields with a dirty hem. The faeries would not make her a lady. She had no use for being a lady.

All she needed was their master to agree to return to the mainland.

"Sorcha," a voice whispered on the wind. "Sooorchaaa."

It exhaled her name, elongating the syllables until it sounded like a long drawn out moan. Frowning, Sorcha peered into the shadows. No eyes blinked back at her, no faeries stood in her doorways.

"Hello?" she called out. "Is anyone there?"

"Sorcha."

"Yes?"

A soft breeze brushed against her face and stirred the hair hanging around her cheeks. This room was closed in the depths of the castles, with no windows or cracks where the wind might sneak through. A breeze was impossible.

And yet, there was one.

She reached out her hand, fully expecting to meet a solid invisible body. It was not a solid beast, nor was it a faerie hiding in plain sight. This was truly air tangling around her.

Again, her name whispered through the room. This time it was accompanied by movement on the wall furthest from her. Ivy shifted in a waterfall of movement as if a hand brushed against the other side.

Sorcha rose from the fountain and gingerly made her way to the wall. She was certain there was nothing behind that wall. She'd checked a hundred times, running her hands over the plain stone as she checked for secrets the faeries may have hidden.

The ivy shifted again.

She held her breath and reached forward. The leaves were cold to the touch, far colder than the room.

"Sorcha," the voice whispered. "Come to me."

Magic swirled through the room. The ivy rustled, then suddenly blasted the greenery away from its surface. A burning white light grew so bright that Sorcha tossed an arm over her eyes. The sound of ringing bells filled her ears.

Then all was silent.

Sorcha dropped her arms, blinking at the swirling wall of darkness before her. The wall had turned into water. Dark water, like the bottom of the ocean that had nearly killed her.

She shivered. What kind of magic was this?

"Sorcha," the voice warped as it passed through the liquid portal. "Sorcha, come to me."

Her stomach dropped, but she couldn't quell her own curiosity. Someone was calling for her. Were they hurt? Was it someone she knew?

She reached out and touched the wall. It quivered and quaked. A small piece of it broke off, floated over her shoulder, and popped in the center of her bedroom.

"Strange," she whispered.

Everything here was strange, and she found that it didn't shock her anymore. Watery portals, faeries in kitchens, boys made up of a menagerie of beasts. What else could happen in this strange and unusual place?

"Sorcha, there is not much time."

She glanced over her shoulder. No faeries stood in her doorway. No whispers suggested they were listening. Would anyone know if she disappeared?

Someone would have an opinion about this. The angry lord of the castle would notice she had disappeared without his say-so. A rebellious part of her wanted to plunge through the portal just to anger him.

"Why is that considered rebellious, Sorcha?" she asked herself. Her voice bounced back through the portal, echoing her words. "You're curious. Go through the portal."

"Yes," the whisper repeated. "Go through the portal."

"It could be dangerous."

"It is dangerous."

"But that has never stopped me before."

"You are brave."

"What if this is an Unseelie?" she peered through the waters, trying to see if anyone stood beyond.

"It's definitely Unseelie."

"They're unpredictable."

"They're everything you ever desired."

"How so?"

Apparently, the voice didn't want to answer questions, as it didn't respond. She waited to see if it would speak again.

It didn't.

Sorcha understood what it was doing. The voice, or owner of the voice, wanted her to go through the portal, and it wanted to convince her to do so. This couldn't end well. She had read countless tales where faeries lured humans into their worlds. The Unseelie were not kind to humans.

"This is a terrible idea," she whispered. "You're going to end up hurting me, or trapping me in the otherworld forever."

"We wouldn't do such a thing."

"You want to do harm."

"We want to provide knowledge."

"What could you know that I do not?"

The wind coiled around her ankles and wrists. "We know much, little human. Your beast is not what he says he is."

"My beast?"

"Stone." The voice moaned the word, dragging out the syllables as it had her name. "He is not who he seems to be."

"Then who is he?"

"Come to me, Sorcha. I will explain all you desire to know."

Her scalp tingled.

This was a trap. This was an Unseelie who wanted to lure her into the Otherworld and toy with her.

How did the stories always end? The human would lose their minds in the depths of the Unseelie kingdom. They would find themselves slaves, left to the mercy of the hideous creatures crawling through the muck and mire.

But so many of these creatures were different than the stories. The Seelies weren't what she thought. Could it be that the Unseelie were also not how the myths portrayed?

Taking a deep breath, she plunged into the portal.

The liquid clung to her body, sticking to her hair and clothing. It pulled at her. Did it want to drown her? The sticky fluid clawed at her lips and eyes, but never sank into the wide gape of her scream.

Cold sank into her body until she was certain it would freeze her. She would die here, and the Unseelie would win. Her toes curled, her fingers grew numb, and the coils of her curls solidified.

What a fool she was.

The bubble of portal popped and threw her out. She gasped, tumbling onto a stone floor, air whooshing from her lungs on impact.

Laying on the ground, she tried to find her bearings. Dim, grey light revealed shadows but no solid forms. The floor was solid stone, so she wasn't outside. The air was stale. It tasted like dust and something she couldn't quite name. Rotten, but sweet. She could hear a soft sound above. A dull shush, a scrape of something heavy brushing against stone.

That was impossible. There couldn't be anything above her, not something that weighed enough to make that sound.

Curling her hands into fists, she squeezed her eyes shut and counted to ten. She was brave. She was strong. Fear would not force her to curl into a ball and weep.

Sorcha's fingers began to shake.

"Sorcha," the voice called out to her again. This time it wasn't through the portal, but echoing from above. "Look at me."

"I wish not to."

"Look at me!" The voice boomed so loud that Sorcha flattened herself against the floor in fear.

Cold seeped through the front of her dress. She blew out a breath and wondered what Macha would do. Would she draw her sword and threaten the Unseelie's life?

Probably, but Sorcha was not Macha. She couldn't condemn anyone when she hadn't spoken to them, judged their character, heard their story. There was no reason for her to be frightened of this creature who commanded her gaze. She placed her hand flat against the floor and pushed herself onto her back.

A monster anchored herself to the ceiling above Sorcha. At first, she couldn't make out the shape hovering in the air. It was too large, too much of a blob made of shadow.

Then she made out the bulbous stomach, bloated and larger than three horses combined. Eight legs stuck out from the wide belly. They shifted as she watched, smoothing across the stone ceiling, and creating the sound she had heard.

Attached to the body was the torso of a woman. Heavily muscled, so pale she was almost blue, with long lanky hair that hung down towards Sorcha. The smile spread across the creature's face split from ear to ear.

"Hello, Sorcha of Ui Neill," the monster murmured. "Welcome to Caisleán dorcha."

Not just Unseelie then, Sorcha realized. This was their castle, the home to the royal family of Unseelie beasts. The family who were kings and queens of monsters.

She swallowed the scream rising in her throat, and instead stared in horror at the dead body trapped in a white blanket of webbing. "Lovely to meet you."

"Is it?" The woman cocked her head to the side. "You look positively terrified."

"I am."

"Then why don't you scream?"

"I do not wish to offend."

"A scream is a gift." Thin legs scraped the ceiling as she untangled herself. Muffled thumps echoed, one leg striking the ground near Sorcha's legs. More followed, thumping again and again until the creature was looming over her. "It is an agreement that I am a terrifying creature whom you respect and fear."

Sorcha swallowed hard.

The woman leaned down, until she nearly touched Sorcha's face with her own. A hairy leg balanced her right next to Sorcha's ear. "I wish to hear you scream."

She couldn't contain it. Sorcha squeezed her eyes shut and screamed out her fear and terror. This beast wasn't just going to scare her, she would devour her whole.

No stories whispered this creature's name. Nothing had hinted to the little midwife from Ui Neill that something like this ever existed. Faeries were strange, yes, but they were never so deformed as this.

A leg stroked Sorcha's stomach. She pushed backwards but knocked her head against a thick leg. The tiny fibers of hairs brushed the back of her neck. Trapped. Sorcha was trapped. There was nothing she could do but scream and scream.

"Enough!" The booming shout splintered through her skull in tiny points of pain. "You have done me a great honor with such terror."

She traversed over Sorcha, heavy belly brushing against Sorcha's side. She swallowed the gorge that rose in her throat. The stomach was smooth, not hairy like her legs. A red splotch of color resembled an hourglass on her belly, but Sorcha had never seen the arachnids in Ui Neill.

The creature pressed her hands against Sorcha's chest, forcing her to stare up at the ceiling. Shock tied her tongue in knots. The creature only wanted to hear her scream? What other purpose did she have for dragging Sorcha here?

Of course, there might not be a purpose at all. The Unseelie might have found herself bored and merely wanted a plaything. But how had she known where Sorcha was?

The cobwebs on the ceiling moved.

"Please, don't let there be another," she whispered.

"There isn't." The creature's voice lifted in amusement. "It's my dinner."

Sorcha narrowed her eyes and cried out. There was a man tangled in the webs. At least, she thought it was a man. The spider woman had wrapped him up so tight, she could only see the outlines of pectoral muscles and the bulging thigh muscles that strained against his ties.

"He'll quiet down eventually."

The webs covered his face, preventing him from breathing. "He's going to suffocate."

"Yes, he will. That is the point."

"What a cruel way to die."

"It is better than poison that travels slowly through the blood. At least now he will calm down then drift off into sleep."

"Why not just snap his neck and be done with it?"

The movement of the woman paused, and Sorcha felt the weight of her gaze like a physical touch. "Would that be your preference?"

"If you plan to eat me, I would like not to be alive at all."

"I don't plan on eating you. Little girls like you make terrible meals. Not enough meat on your bones. Besides, humans are always so bitter."

Sorcha lifted a hand and pointed. "That's not human?"

"No, that's Seelie. I prefer a lighter diet while I'm watching my figure."

"You're watching your figure?"

"Isn't every woman?"

Sorcha couldn't imagine what figure the creature was talking about. It was hard to force a ball into sensuous curves.

"Why have you brought me here?" she asked.

"All in good time. Get up, girl."

She looked back up at the man who was tangled in the creature's web. His struggles were slowing, a few twitches here and there were the only way she knew he was still alive.

"I think I'll stay here."

"You want to watch him die?"

"No."

"Then get up."

Sorcha couldn't find an argument. Sighing, she rolled onto her knees and told herself to forget about the man in the ceiling. He was beyond her help, no matter how much she wanted to cut him down and breathe air back into his lungs. She, too, was at the mercy of the monstrous woman.

"What shall I call you?" Sorcha asked.

"You may call me Your Queen."

"Queen?" Sorcha gasped. "Are you—"

"Yes.

The queen of the Unseelie Fae stood before her, and Sorcha was acting as if she were some beast she needed to squash beneath her heel. She was lucky to still be alive.

Falling onto her knees, she pressed her thumbs to her forehead. "Forgive me, Your Majesty. I am a lowly beast indeed to not recognize royalty."

"I asked you to get up. Do not make me ask again."

Sorcha scrambled to her feet again. What did this creature want of her? The darkness stirred, casting out mist in great billows that swirled around the Queen's legs.

Her legs moved in synchronization Sorcha realized. Not like a real spider which sometimes could seem jerky in their movements. This woman moved with a natural grace. Each leg lifted and was placed so gently that the sound they made was quiet and dull.

"Are you done staring?"

"What?" Sorcha looked up to see that the Queen was staring back. She was immensely tall. Easily two of Stone's great height. "My apologies."

"Stop apologizing."

"I—" she cleared her throat. "I understand."

"Good. Now, follow me."

She didn't want to follow this creature deeper into the darkness. Who knew what waited for her there?

The Queen saw her hesitate. "I'm not going to kill you, child."

"You have yet to answer why I am here."

"Because I bade you come."

"That's not an answer."

The Queen sighed. "There is much at play here. You have stepped into a world where you will make a decision that will ultimately affect all the players on the board. I will not leave the fate of the Fae in the hands of an uneducated human. Follow me."

"What do I have to do with that?"

"All will be revealed in time. The web is large, and there is much to explain."

Sorcha watched the spider woman disappear into the darkness with her jaw open. There was much to explain? She was just a midwife. What did she have to do with the fate of the Fae?

She wouldn't go with the Queen. They had obviously coaxed the wrong person through the portal.

Giggles echoed behind her, coming closer and closer through the fog and darkness. Shivers danced up her spine. What manner of Unseelie stood behind her? Was that the wind on the back of her neck, or was it the breath of yet another monster?

She bolted after the Queen, steps loud and uncontrolled.

The entirety of the castle was dark. Some small sconces decorated the walls, lit with green fire that did little to cast light in any direction. She couldn't see, but she could hear the queen.

Thump. Thump. Shhh. Thump. Thump. Shhh.

It was a horrible sound. The dragging of a thick body by legs too thin and hairy. Sorcha shivered again, knowing nightmares would plague her for years to come.

The Queen's chuckle bounced from ceiling to floor. "Good, you are smart enough to follow."

"I'm smart enough to not be left behind."

"Ah, yes. My children are far too curious for their own good."

"Your children?" Sorcha glanced into the shadows. "How many do you have?"

"Seventeen Tuatha dé Danann children, and hundreds of lesser

Fae."

That alone was intriguing, and went against everything Sorcha knew. "You have children who are both Tuatha dé Danann and not?"

"We are not the Seelie Fae. There is value in lives which are not human in appearance."

"Do the Seelie Fae not agree?"

"No."

She had suspected as much. The legends always spoke of creatures that looked like humans as kings and queens. So few people saw any kind of faerie that didn't look like a human.

A stairwell appeared before them, the stones swept clean and glistening in the green light. Sorcha blinked, trying to bring everything into focus. It was difficult here, where magic was so thick that she could see it like a fog.

"Do you not wear glamour?" Sorcha asked. "All the faeries I have met thus far have worn a glamour."

"Seelie, I take it?"

"Most."

"All. An Unseelie would never hide their true form. The Seelie hide to protect human's delicate sensibilities when the reality is that we are all beautiful, powerful beings. Humans should run in fear."

"You would give them nightmares for the rest of their lives."

"Will your dreams be troubled?"

"Without a doubt," Sorcha shivered. "I will never sleep again for fear you will hover above my bed."

"You flatter me."

That was not her intention, although she was relieved her words had complimented the Queen. Sorcha merely told the truth.

A scrying pool on a large altar stood in the center of the room they entered. Shards of black glass made up the floor. Sorcha stared at it and swore she saw dark fire reflected beneath. Wind brushed across her ears bringing with it the screams of tortured souls.

The Queen skittered towards it, hunching over the bowl, and rocking back and forth. Sorcha wasn't certain she had ever seen a spider move like that. Was the queen even part spider? Was she merely wearing the skin of one?

The Ballad of Tam Lin burst into her mind. The Queen in that story had turned his lover into a spider. He held onto her great abdomen, her legs, her great eyes. For days, he hung on as she changed into dozens of creatures.

Sorcha couldn't help but wonder if this chosen form was symbolic.

"Come," the Queen said. "Gaze into my pool, and I will show you all you desire."

"I desire very little."

"Humans lie every day. You desire so many things that you cannot even breathe for the wanting."

"I want health and happiness for my family. That is all."

"Oh, little human. You desire so much more than that. It is healthy to want."

"I care for others."

"You care for yourself. The desire to heal others builds your confidence, solidifies your reason for being. You have yet to discover who you are. Come."

Sorcha stared at the Queen's strong hands gripping the edge of the stone bowl. "I'm afraid to know what I want."

"Everyone is."

She stood on the precipice of something great, but she didn't know what she would find. The Queen offered something without cost.

"What do I have to do?" Sorcha asked.

"Listen and learn."

Small, black dots appeared on the Queen's forehead from her eyebrows to her temples. At the same time, every dot blinked.

A whimper escaped Sorcha's mouth as she realized the dots were eyes. The Queen, like many spiders, had multiple eyes that all stared with expectation at the human on the stairs.

What did she have to lose? Thoroughly uncomfortable, Sorcha stepped towards the scrying pool.

"What would you have me learn?"

"Everything."

The Queen leaned forward and dunked a finger into the clear water. It swirled, dark magic dropping like ink and spreading rapidly. Black swallowed the bowl of water and wisps of white smoke rose into the air.

"You are entangled in the most important plot of this millennia, and there is so much you need to see."

"Why?"

"The Fae are a tricky lot. Our legends speak of so many beautiful stories. Of heroes who swing blades that cleave giants in two. Of heroines who seduce a man with one glance and drag them to the bottom of the ocean. But we are not a group of people who enjoy death and destruction. There are as many species of Fae as there are stars in the sky."

Whispers echoed her words, three voices overlaying the Queen's.

"Who are they?" Sorcha asked.

"My children."

"Where?"

The Queen glanced over her shoulder and nodded. Three women stepped forward, lashed to the ceiling by thin threads of web. They had rings pierced down their arms where the threads looped through. Pale as snow, their eyes were blind. No color lived on their bodies at all. White hair, white eyes, white skin so pale it was blue.

"Three daughters," Sorcha nodded. "You are blessed."

A smile spread across the Queen's face. "Blessed? You don't have children, do you?"

"No, your highness."

"Children suck the lives out of their mothers. They drain them until they are little more than husks. But they are good for the soul."

One of the wraith-like women stepped forward. The Queen petted her head and pushed her towards the scrying bowl. "What secrets do you have to share with the little human?"

The pale woman cocked her head to the side, unseeing eyes blinking slowly. "I share the state of the Seelie Fae."

"Why?" the Queen asked.

"It is important she know the situation in Tír na nÓg. She must know what the people do and how they suffer."

The daughter stepped forward and reached out her arm. The Queen looked at her with no emotion, wrapped her strong around the limb, and snapped it in half.

Sorcha cried out as blood poured into the scrying pool. White bones poked through torn flesh and fragments of hanging muscle dipped into the water. Through it all, the daughter did not flinch nor cry out.

"What are you doing?" Sorcha screamed. "Stop!"

"You do not understand our ways. Watch and learn. That was what you promised me." The Queen patted her daughter on the head again. "Thank you. Go back to your sisters for healing."

She stepped back into the fold. The other two reached for the thick threads of webbing and pulled hard. They lifted the injured woman into the air by the rings on her arms. She dangled for a moment, suspended above the ceiling before a long spider leg reached out and pulled her through the webbed ceiling.

"What was that?" Sorcha whispered.

"My husband."

"There are more of you?"

"It takes two to make children."

"What manner of Fae are you?"

"Do not waste the blood of my children. Look into the scrying pool, and see the truth of the Seelie Fae."

Sorcha wanted to follow the injured woman to insist that she might help. Of all people, she could set a broken bone, wrap the injury, pack it with herbs so it didn't get infected. But these were Unseelie Fae. They would not want her help.

Swallowing hard, she nodded.

Black water swirled with blood. She placed her hands on the side and leaned over until she could peer into the depths.

"What am I looking for?" she asked.

"There are images even in the darkest of places." The Queen placed her large hands on top of Sorcha's. Her flesh was frigid. "See the truth."

A dwarf appeared in the water. His beard tangled around his ankles, and he fell onto the ground. He reached out to stop himself, but a whip cracked through the air before he touched the ground. His face twisted in pain, then he lay still.

Another man walked towards him, golden hair swinging at his waist. The golden newcomer was perfect in every way. His skin glittered in the sun, his eyes strikingly green. He held the whip coiled around his wrist and nudged the fallen dwarf with a look of disgust.

"What is he doing?" she asked.

"They use the dwarves to mine for copper and gold. When anyone tries to leave, they whip them until they either return or die."

"Why?"

"They want the gold but are not willing to work for themselves."

The image shuddered, shifting to reveal a beautiful pixie. Her forehead arched up into points, looking very like an autumn leaf. Blushing colors painted her skin, furthering her autumnal look. Black eyes swallowed any white that might have existed on a human, but still seemed kind.

The pixie winced and rubbed her hand over the opposite wrist. Skin burned red around a brand in the mark of a trinity knot.

"What is that?" Sorcha asked.

"The faeries are branded depending upon who they call master. Each of the lesser Fae are born with this mark, but it can stretch and distort as they grow. It will be burned again into their bodies if it is difficult to tell who's mark it is."

"Why brand them? Why not simply know who works for you?"

"So that the faeries can't slip away in the dead of night and disappear."

Sorcha's mind raced. She knew what that meant, what darkness the Unseelie suggested brewed in the Seelie lands. "They're slaves?"

"They most certainly are. Their king has turned them into little more than beasts to trade. They are born, bought, and worked to death long before they see their families grow."

"It doesn't make any sense," she muttered. "Why force your people to be unhealthy? It isn't the mark of a good king if he cannot provide a good life for all his people."

"Were you under the impression that the wise king is a good one?"

"Wise king?"

The Queen snorted, retreating from the altar with great thudding steps. "It is the name he has given himself. Wise, for his knowledge is vast."

"Knowledge does not mean intelligence."

"Astute for a human child."

"You are not the first to say so."

"One last vision especially for you, Sorcha of Ui Neill."

Brows furrowed, Sorcha leaned over the pool and stared into the dark waters.

A woman appeared, painfully beautiful and holding her hand over her belly. Her waist-length blonde hair swept nearly to the floor. Silver silk fabric poured from her shoulders to sweep the crystal floor.

"Who is she?" Sorcha asked.

"Elva, the most prized concubine of the king. Her mother was one of my most prized followers." The Queen tapped the water with her nail. "She has just realized that she may be pregnant."

"Isn't that a good thing?"

"That is not up to me to decide. You will need to know her name.

You say you are a good person, midwife. This is one who you could save."

Sorcha looked up. "Why would you want me to save any of the Seelie?"

"I am not a heartless creature. There are some who deserve to live, and others who I would relish crushing their skulls beneath my hands. Elva is one whose true name I give to you in full confidence you will use it well."

Another of the Queen's daughters stepped forward, and Sorcha winced in preparation for the next dark deed. She couldn't take much more of this. The Unseelie were always rumored to be twisted and depraved, but how far did that insanity travel?

Did they feast upon it rather than food?

"Peace," the Queen whispered. "You have seen enough bloodshed."

The Princess reached up and held a mirror towards her mother. Vines tangled around the handle. It was as large as Sorcha was tall, and the Queen held it as if it were nothing more than a handheld mirror.

"Do you know our history?" the Queen asked. "Do you know the difference between Seelie and Unseelie?"

"Your kind gave up honor and law to live wild and free."

"Yes. And do you think we made the wrong choice?"

Sorcha didn't know. She shrugged, frowning in concentration as she mulled the question over in her mind. "Who am I to judge others for the choices they make? If a soul is born to be wild, it will only grow angry with a leash wrapped around its neck. If a soul prefers order, then it will shrivel with too many choices. Neither is wrong."

"You do not see darkness as evil?"

"Nothing is evil. The very idea was created by those who won wars and wished to paint their poor choices as the right thing. No one goes into war or battle thinking they are evil."

"You speak with the tongue of a philosopher."

"I am just a midwife."

The Queen's face split open in that jagged edged smile again. "Come closer, Sorcha. This mirror will show you the future."

"I do not wish to see my future."

"I wish to see it."

Sorcha frowned and remained where she was. "You want to see my future? Why am I so important to the Queen of the Unseelie Court?"

"Look."

She wanted to. Every fiber of her being screamed for Sorcha to look into the future and see what would happen. Who didn't want to know what their end would look like? How much time she had left?

But what would she find? If she stayed on Hy-brasil her family would die, and she would've done nothing to prevent it. If she returned home without Stone, it was likely she would die from the beetle plague. There was only one suitable ending, and it was slowly slipping out of reach.

Sorcha shook her head. "I have no wish to see my future. I will stand before the mirror if you need to see it, but I will not look."

"You have no desire to see the end of your life?"

"Of course I do," she said. "I want it more than anything, but I am also frightened of it. I make my own choices, and I would rather believe they have not already been destined."

The Queen's expression softened, a strange look on such a monstrous being. She lifted a hand and beckoned Sorcha forward. "Then I will look for you, child."

Sorcha's footsteps echoed in the altar room. Each steady sound beat in tune with the pounding of her heart. She closed her eyes as the mirror began to move, then turned her back.

Even the air seemed to hold its breath. The Queen was silent as she watched the images casting light on the floor. They twirled and moved at Sorcha's feet and she watched them with rapt attention, but could not make out what they meant.

One of the daughters gasped, and a thick body moved above them. Sorcha held still until the cold sank into her bones. Her toes ached, her fingers trembled, and her breath fogged the air.

"So that is your choice," the Queen said. "You are an interesting woman, Sorcha of Ui Neill."

"Is it an agreeable choice?" She wanted to ask why she was making a choice at all. Thousands of reasons danced through her mind, but none seemed important enough to tempt a Queen. Of course, even the wing-beat of a butterfly could change time.

"It is agreeable to me."

"And to me?"

"I do not know you, human child. How should I know what you will find agreeable?"

Sorcha licked her lips. "May I turn around?"

"Do you wish to?"

"No."

"Then why are you asking?"

"I have never flinched away from something I was afraid of."

Thumping from the ceiling made the cobwebs twang. They vibrated as the great king of the Unseelie Court descended from his throne. He was so much louder than his wife. She prayed it was because he did not care to be quiet or dainty. She had a feeling she was wrong.

Sorcha slowly turned, holding her breath so hard her lungs hurt. She would not scream again. These creatures could try to frighten her time and time again, but she would not scream.

He stepped from the ceiling, long legs clacking as they struck the ground. Armor covered the hairy appendages that rubbed together with a grating sound. Like his wife, the king was too muscular to be attractive. His body bulged, swollen with meat and strength.

"This is the girl?" he grumbled. His eighth leg touched the ground and he lurched towards his wife, rubbing a leg against hers. "Did you find out what you need to know?"

"I found out enough."

"If I may," Sorcha asked. Her voice wobbled. "Will you now tell me why you summoned me here?"

"You're going to find out soon enough. You are welcome to leave now, human girl."

Sorcha wasn't sure if she should. The entire situation was scarring and terrifying, but there was something strange about the faeries.

"You aren't telling me everything," she murmured. "Why are you meddling in my life?"

"The master of your isle does not know there are Unseelie living in his household. You must be careful, for you do care for them."

"Who?"

"Oona is her given name, and as she is of my Court, I gift her name to you."

"Who is she?"

"Your Pixie."

So, her name was Oona. It was a beautiful name for a beautiful creature, and Sorcha was honored that the Queen thought her trustworthy enough to gift it.

"That still doesn't answer my question."

"I have no intention of answering."

"Fair enough," Sorcha murmured. "I'll have to ask Bran if he has any idea."

The Queen froze, and the King stiffened. He cocked his head to the side and lifted a long finger to point at her. "What does this Bran look like?"

Sorcha gestured at her face. "Half raven, half man. He has feathers, a raven eye, and the leg of a bird."

Echoes of laughter came from all directions of the room. They bounced atop the ceiling and shook the webs.

The Queen shook her head, still chuckling. "Ah, you have met my ugliest son then."

Ugly? The royals in front of her were anything but pretty. How could Bran be considered the ugly one?

The King shook his head. "Unseelie do not value beauty in the same way the Seelie do. He is too human, too weak, and can only change his form into a raven. Pathetic excuse for a child, but then, he is the youngest. We do not have to worry about him taking the throne any time soon. Be gone, human. Tell my boy to come home soon. His sisters miss him."

One of the albino daughters lifted her hands as if she were pleading. Were these creatures even capable of such emotions? Did they miss their family, or did they miss the way they might torture them?

Sorcha didn't plan to stay and find out. Bowing so low that her forehead nearly touched the floor, she whispered, "It was an honor, Your Majesties."

"An honor?" The Queen tsked. "Oh dearie, the Unseelie do not like lies. You may want to run, for my children are hungry and your fear tastes sweeter than wine."

Sorcha did not have to be told twice. She'd counted each step as she followed the Queen and knew the way back to the portal.

Spinning, she raced down the stairs taking them two at a time. It didn't matter that she might trip and fall. Breaking her neck would be a blessing if it meant freedom from this hellish castle.

Breath sawed in and out of her lungs until she tasted blood. Screaming laughter chased her, goblins and trolls whooping and hollering as they tracked her. Down the corridors she flew until she couldn't hear them anymore.

She slowed to a walk, holding her ribs as they ached from overuse. Why did she ever wear the dresses Pixie gave her? They were too tight!

Oona, she corrected herself. Pixie's name was Oona.

She smiled at the thought. Oona might not be pleased, but it was a beautiful name, and Sorcha would never use it without permission. It was the third Fae name she held. How lucky a woman was she?

The portal room remained untouched. Fog swirled across the ground, lifting in tendrils that looked like hands reaching for help. Sorcha walked through them. She had to remember that these were Unseelie Lands and did not live by the same laws.

She couldn't help those who were suffering without condemning herself to the same fate.

Sorcha pulled her cloak around her when cold air drifted underneath its folds. She shivered and peered into the darkness to find the watery portal, or even the barest hint of leaves.

There. In the deepest shadows between leaves and branches, she recognized a familiar stone wall.

Brushing aside ivy and moss, she placed her hands against its cold stone surface.

"There you are," she said. "It's time to go home."

Nothing happened. She scraped her hands all over the edges, but couldn't open the portal. Nothing seemed to work. No gemstone in a sword that she could push, no whispered words.

"Oh, what have you done?" she whispered into the night. "How am I supposed to go home now?"

"Portals are magic, you know," a familiar voice echoed. Deep and baritone, she had only heard it once before.

Sorcha turned on her heel, pivoting to glare at the Unseelie Fae who stood behind her. "Bran."

"Sorcha."

"What are you doing here?"

"I should ask you the same question. Don't you know that the Otherworld is dangerous for humans?"

"I could say the same for Unseelie. It's worse here, so I've heard."

"Ah, there are so many bad stories about my kind." He grinned, his raven eye dancing to and fro while the human eye remained locked on her. "Not all stories are true, little human."

"You've been kind thus far." She pressed her spine against the wall.

"I would ask you continue to do the same."

"I hear you met my parents."

"And some of your siblings as well. I would never have guessed you came from such parentage."

"Where did you think I came from? A bird?"

"Certainly something that suggests the same species," she gritted through clenched teeth. "You lied to me. You didn't tell me you were an Unseelie prince!"

"I was not aware that you were privy to such knowledge."

Sorcha blinked in shock, her jaw falling open. "How dare you even say such a thing? You traveled across the sea with me! You followed me from the MacNara's, and you teased me in front of Stone. I would even go so far as to muse that you were behind him moving me into the castle."

"Do you think I'm looking out for you, I wonder?"

"Why else would you be following me?"

"Because the MacNara twins paid me to? Perhaps I wished to infiltrate your 'Stone's' castle. Or maybe I wanted to drag you here to be my slave." He cocked his head to the side. "There are plenty of reasons and none of them kind."

"And none that I believe."

"Is that so?"

"You are far too smart a man to be bought, even by the MacNara twins who appear to be intelligent and manipulative people. You don't want to harm Stone; you practiced with him like an old friend and teased him quite mercilessly. And if you wanted to drag me back to Unseelie with you, why haven't you? Why wait until your mother summoned me?" She tilted her chin up, refusing to be cowed by this dark man.

"Ever so brave," he whispered. "You are a remarkable little human. Did you know that? There are few who would dare stand up to me in such a way, but you didn't even flinch. You are quite the match for him."

"For who?"

"No one."

She arched a brow. "Really? That's what you have to say?"

"No one, everyone, someone." He shrugged. "There are plenty of people of whom I could be speaking. The long and short of it is that you need to go back home before he finds out where you've gone."

"Stone?"

"Yes."

"You—" she bit her lip. "You know him?"

"No one knows him."

"But you know him more than most."

"Yes."

"Perhaps you might answer a few questions for me."

Bran's raven eye narrowed. He crossed his arms over his chest and the bird eye looked her up and down. He was measuring her or trying to see a way through her lies. Finally, he waved a hand for her to continue.

"Your mother made me look in the scrying bowl. There were faeries that the Seelies used for slaves. Branded, mistreated, living out their lives as if they were not worth even the slightest of things. Is this true, or was this some kind of Unseelie trick?"

He snorted. "The Seelie like to make their people labor until they break. They believe in bloodlines and power more than respect. Don't let them fool you. They preach honor and then stab each other in the back."

"Is Stone treating the faeries on the isle like slaves?"

"Do you think he is?"

She pondered the question before shaking her head. "I don't think so. I've seen no behavior that might support such an accusation. But I do not see him often, and secrets hide in the shadows."

"I know Stone well enough to say that he's not treating them like anything. He's a solitary creature. Rare for a Fae."

"Is it?"

"We're creatures who like the company of others. Even the

Unseelie enjoy each other's company. Stone has never been like that. They say he used to tent away from his men on the battlefield. He was the first to reach enemy lines, and the first the enemy found if they came looking in the night."

"And now?"

Bran cocked his head to the side. "Ask a more direct question."

"Is he the same man now as he was back then?"

"No, but not in the way you think. He has become harder and softer with time."

"How is that possible?" She wanted to know the answer so much it burned in her belly.

He shook his head. "That's a story I can't tell you. You must ask him if you want to know that badly."

"How can I ask him? I rarely see him!"

"That might change soon." Mischief and hidden knowledge sparkled in his eyes.

"You know something I don't know."

"I always know something humans don't know. You're a lucky little thing to be living in a time of such burgeoning change."

Sorcha's mind raced to keep up with the Unseelie Fae. His words made little sense, but she knew he mostly spoke in riddles. There was something he didn't want to tell her. Something she needed to figure out for herself.

"Are you lying?"

"I cannot lie."

"Are you hiding the truth?"

Bran's face split in a jagged-edged smile. His raven eye locked upon her gaze while the other glanced away. "Faeries always hide the truth. It's too easy if we don't."

"I would argue it's much better if you don't hide the truth. You might get the results you want."

"Where's the fun in that? It's better if the ending is chosen by free will rather than our own design."

"Why get involved if you don't have a specific ending you want to see?" Sorcha shook her head, knowing he wouldn't answer her question. "Can you open the portal, Bran? I'd like to go home."

"Home?" He tilted his head to the side again. "Curious choice of words."

"Slip of the tongue. My home is with my sisters."

"Perhaps now, but not for long." He nodded at the portal. "All you have to do is see through the glamour, and you can go home."

"How am I supposed to—ah." She pulled the hag stone from between her breasts and placed it against her eye.

The stone turned to a watery portal through the small hole in the hag stone. Light shimmered from its surface. The ivy beyond had not been pulled back, leaving the room obscured and difficult to see, but it was there.

She knew it was.

"Thank you," she said as she turned.

Bran had disappeared. There wasn't time to figure out what he was hiding. She took a deep breath, stilled the disquieting sadness in her heart, and left the Unseelie lands behind.

CHAPTER TEN

THE KISS

Leaving the Unseelie castle was more difficult than entering. The cold touch of the portal sent gooseflesh across Sorcha's skin. Magic such as this should never touch a human. It slid along her body like the foreign touch of an unseen person.

Sorcha shuddered, unnerved by the cold, clammy sensation. It was over soon, or would be as soon as her left foot slid free. Ivy brushed against her face until she blew out a breath that stirred the greenery.

She fluttered a hand in front of her face, parting the curtain of ivy and entering the enchanting bedroom.

Nothing had changed. All her things were exactly where she had placed them. The blue flowers glowed with a soft light emanating from their petals on the far wall. The faerie fountain stared placidly off into the distance, hardly comparable to the real thing.

How could she ever look at this place with the same eyes? This island was beautiful, but the shadows now moved, and the bed looked like a prison.

She sighed and unhooked the clasp of her cloak. It fell to the ground with a wet thump although she didn't remember getting it wet.

Exhaustion overwhelmed her. She couldn't remember a time when it wasn't hovering in the corners of her mind like an unwelcome house guest. She never remembered inviting the bone biting feeling, but it never seemed to leave.

A soft sound interrupted her thoughts. Sorcha couldn't pinpoint where it came from in the room. Everything was how she left it, right down to the emerald leaves overlaying the walls.

Again, the shushing noise echoed in her ears. It was the distinct sound of fabric sliding against fabric. The movement of a human body.

Or perhaps that of a Fae.

She sucked in her breath and froze, shifting until the portal was no longer at her back. The air was too still, laced with violence and aggression. She'd never felt danger so powerfully.

Her heart beat. She breathed so quietly she hardly inhaled at all. Darting eyes searched for the cause of the sound as she wondered what had followed her onto the isle.

A shadow peeled away from the wall, rushing towards her so fast that Sorcha didn't have time to react. A pillar of darkness surrounded her. She slammed back into the stone wall, ivy tangling in her hair and around her shoulders.

Sorcha turned her head to the side and squeezed her eyes shut. She couldn't, wouldn't, look death in the eye. Taking one last deep breath, she caught the scent of lemons, mint, and whiskey.

Stone?

His shaking hand brushed a coiled red curl away from her face, tucking it gently behind her ear.

"Where were you?"

The question reverberated in her mind, but she couldn't find the words to answer. Questions of her own overpowered her tongue. How had he realized she left? Why was he here? What had happened while she traversed the Otherworld?

Was he drunk?

He stumbled, rocking sideways before catching himself with a forearm slammed against the wall above her. "Where *were* you?"

Again, he asked the same question. Anger made his words harsh, but she caught the distinct tones of worry underneath the growl. Why would he worry about her? She added the question to all the others she would never give voice.

"Unseelie lands," she whispered.

"And why wouldn't you ask me?"

"For what?"

"Guidance. Protection. An answer to whether or not it was too dangerous for an unarmed, weak, human woman in the Otherworld?"

Sorcha gulped. "I was unaware I might need any protection. There was no point when I felt like I was in danger. Until now."

"You think you are in danger from me?" His head tilted and a spear of light slashed across his eyes. Twin lines wrinkled between his eyes, vibrant blue nearly glowing with anger.

She couldn't respond. Her fear spiked the air with static electricity, making the hair on her arms raise. Of course, she was frightened of Stone. He loomed over her until all she could breathe was his scent, and all she could see was the powerful set of his barreled chest.

"Sorcha." He said her name as if it was a prayer. "You never have to be afraid of me."

He lifted a hand and traced the outline of her face. Crystals scraped across her forehead, past the sensitive skin of her temple, down the soft curves of her cheeks. She couldn't breathe as he thumbed the plump rise of her lips.

He swayed again, eyes squinting in concentration. "You are so flawed. So unlike my people who would have scrubbed these markings from their skin long ago."

"Markings?"

"These," he touched the peaks of her cheeks, her forehead, and the dip of her upper lip.

"Freckles," she whispered. "We call them freckles."

"I've never seen them before, though I know their name. The Fae have smooth skin, like porcelain, as if an artist had painted them with one tone. But you…you have so many colors."

"Colors?"

"Your hair, your skin, even your eyes have flecks of green, blue, yellow."

"You've noticed all of that?" She couldn't stop asking questions. Shock twisted her tongue, asking questions she didn't mean to voice.

"I notice everything you do. You haunt my steps and my dreams. You've bewitched me, Sorcha, and I want my soul back."

"I don't know how to give it back to you."

He leaned closer, his breath fanning over her lips. "I wonder if you taste like the sun."

"You're drunk."

"Yes, I am."

She didn't move as he leaned down and devoured her.

He tasted like whiskey and peppermint. Her eyes fluttered shut as the textures of his mouth slid against hers. Soft lips, like velvet, nibbled at her own. She couldn't breathe, didn't want to, even as his arms slid down the wall and slipped around her shoulders.

Teeth nibbled at her full bottom lip. No, she realized, not teeth. The harsh edge of crystal biting into her swollen flesh as he pressed harder.

She inhaled in surprise, and he took advantage of the opportunity. His warm tongue swept into her mouth, bringing with it an explosion of flavor. Spices, foreign to her senses, made her drunk as their tongues tangled.

Strange, she hadn't thought it would be like this. And then she didn't think at all.

He tasted her, unmade her, whispered endearments she didn't understand against her mouth. The crystals sliced at her skin, splitting open her lip, and pouring the metallic taste of blood into her mouth.

He didn't stop. She didn't want him to.

Warmth poured over her like a wave. She couldn't think. He was everything and nothing, tying her to the ground by the electric heat of his mouth. His hands slid over her shoulders and massaged her muscles until she relaxed against the wall.

"I knew you would taste like sunshine," he whispered against her lips. "I knew it from the moment I first set eyes on you."

"Another flaw?"

"Entirely."

He dedicated his attention to sipping from her lips. To licking, and sucking, and tasting every inch she would allow him. Hot breath slid across her cheeks, crystals cold and scraping, a sharp contrast to the soft flesh of his skin.

Teeth worried at the sensitive peaks of her ears. Her knees went weak, mouth dropped open in pleasure even as her eyes snapped open. Her nerve endings came alive. Heat rippled through her from the points all the way to her belly.

"What—" she gasped.

A pleased, masculine growl rumbled in her ear.

His hands traveled down her arms, smoothing across the skin he found so flawed. Somehow, she didn't think he meant it as an insult. She'd seen the Fae for herself, so perfect they looked like stone. Perhaps he saw something alive in her. Something real.

She arched her back as one of his hands trailed across her collarbone. He nibbled at her ear, scraping both teeth and crystal against the sensitive flesh. His hands traveled farther, fingers trailing along the gaping, oversized neckline of her dress. She thought surely her mind would fracture from the pleasure as his hands ghosted over the soft swells of her breasts.

Until the air went cold.

His breathing changed. The hot gusts of breath stilled to calm, measured inhalations. He pulled a long strand of web from her shoulder, the sticky filaments stretching out across his fingers.

"What is this?" he growled. "And you say you had no need for protection?"

"It's not what you think."

"You lie." His eyes narrowed further, an entirely different beast staring at her through the windows of his soul.

"I didn't speak with anyone," she whispered, cowering against the ivy. "Stop looking at me like that."

"Like what?"

"Like you want to hurt me."

"I promised I wouldn't hurt you, and I will hold true to that vow. No more lies, little human. Why were you in Unseelie lands?"

She swallowed. How much should she tell him? The Queen wouldn't want her running her mouth, and the information she held was a secret. Sorcha still didn't know who had opened the portal from this side or if it was entirely the Queen's doing.

But he would know if she lied. She wasn't certain how the Fae knew, if they tasted it in the air or could read body language. If he knew, then he would continue to push until she told the truth.

Sorcha had never been a good liar. "I don't know why I was there. The portal opened from this side, and there was information the Unseelie Queen wished to share with me."

"That portal can't open on its own."

"I don't think there are any Unseelie here."

His eyes darkened, storm clouds brewing in the vivid blue. "Oona."

"What?"

He didn't answer. The heat of his body disappeared, leaving her shivering and alone in the room.

"It's probably better he left," she finally said with a shaking sigh. But she didn't believe the words. How could she when her body was quivering with unfulfilled pleasure?

Was that how it felt for her sisters? Surely, it couldn't; they had no attachment to the men who came to the brothel.

A memory surfaced of a blond man with his arms wrapped around

Briana. Sorcha had caught them in an alcove outside the brothel, whispering words of endearments, the likes of which she'd never heard before. The soft press of lips to skin, the sound of gasps and sighs.

Maybe they did know what this felt like, Sorcha thought. Maybe they'd had it ripped away from them so many times they forgot to tell her.

Or they didn't want to share. The moment felt so infinitely private that Sorcha wasn't sure she could breathe a word of it. She tucked the memory into a hidden part of her soul for a time when she felt lost or discouraged.

For a single moment in time, she had felt what it meant to be cherished.

Her mind flared to life as the heat in her body disappeared.

"Oona!" She gasped.

He'd left this bedroom with clear intent in his eyes. Anger had radiated from his skin like a physical being, his crystals glowing and shimmering with rage. Stone had promised he would never hurt her, but Sorcha had no way of knowing whether he promised the same to the faeries under his protection.

She burst into motion, rushing from the room, and swinging herself over the bannister and down the stairs. There was no time for exhaustion, no hesitation, nor second thoughts. Sorcha had to warn Oona, to rush her from the castle until she could figure out a way to calm him down if possible.

As much as Stone knew his people's families, he didn't know them well enough to guess where they were. Most of the pixies on the isle slept with each other in Macha's garden. They said it kept them safe and protected.

Oona wasn't like the others. She slept in the kitchens with the brownies, to make sure that her domain was clean every night.

If Sorcha had observed Stone correctly, he would go to the pixie grotto first. Then he would go to the kitchens.

She ran shoulder first into a door, busting through it so she could shorten her path to the kitchens. Stone's legs were longer. He would be much faster, but he was operating through rage and nothing else. Sorcha was still thinking clearly.

Rooms filled with covered furniture and shattered wood flickered through her vision as she ran through each long dead room. Spider webs tangled in her hair and dust covered her shoulders as she made the last jump and threw open the door to the glowing warmth of the kitchens.

"Oona," she frantically called. "Oona! Wake up!"

A small mound in the corner shifted, and the pixie sat up. She didn't don her glamour immediately. The round face didn't match the persona Oona had chosen for herself. The high peaks of her forehead resembled an oak leaf, violet tinges blushing the high tips and trailing down her shoulders onto her wings.

"What? Who is it?"

"Get up, Oona! He's coming!"

"What?" The pixie burst into movement, throwing blankets into the air and rushing towards Sorcha. "Where is he coming from?"

"I'd assumed he would go to the grotto first."

A roar shook the door, coming from Macha's fountain.

Oona glanced over her shoulder. "You are correct. And now you know I am Unseelie."

"Yes."

"I did not mean to lie, but there are so many secrets in our world. The Queen wanted to see you, and I could not refuse."

"Oona, he's almost here!" Sorcha wrapped her hand around Oona's forearm and tugged. "You're coming with me. I know where to put you until he calms down."

"I won't put you in harm's way."

"I'm the only person in this castle that has nothing to fear from him. He gave me his word. Come with me!"

Oona glanced at her in shock. "He promised what?"

"If you don't come with me now, I will carry you. Get *moving*."

"The master has never given anyone a promise of protection. Explain yourself, dearie."

Sorcha blew a breath at her hair. "Oona, I order you to follow me now."

Using the faerie's name was harsh, but Sorcha could hear his footsteps pounding towards the kitchen. Their time was short.

Oona's spine straightened, and fire flashed in her eyes. But she followed Sorcha when she turned and raced back the way she came.

Sorcha tried to make their trail difficult to follow. She took them through different sections of the castle, hoping a long chase would quell some of his head. They passed broken statues, scuttling spiders, and ripped paintings of faeries she would never meet.

"We're almost there," her harsh whisper barely audible over the pounding of their feet. "So close, Oona. Keep up."

The faerie ran faster.

Sorcha slid around a corner, skidding until her spine hit the wall with a harsh thunk. The air whooshed from her lungs, but she forced herself to keep going. She didn't know what Stone planned on doing. The fear in Oona's eyes spoke volumes, and it was enough for her to steal the faerie away.

Her gut said Stone would regret any judgement he made in anger. These faeries had dedicated their lives to him. They weren't slaves, they weren't servants, and he had no right to harm them. Even if they made mistakes.

She slammed into the carved wall and pressed the stone in the sword's pommel. The grating grind echoed. Stone's enraged shout was far closer than she hoped.

Sorcha grabbed Oona's shoulders and shook her. "You listen to me. There's a bathroom in the back corner with a hot spring. Get into the springs and do not come out until I come get you. Do you hear me?"

"You're putting yourself in danger for no reason, dearie. Don't worry yourself with me. I've lived a full life."

"And I would have you live more. Oona, I order you to hide in the hot springs."

The faerie's spine stiffened, and she disappeared into Sorcha's bedroom.

"Now that's taken care of." She stepped farther away from the carving and the groaning stone slid back into place. "Let's deal with the last bit."

She slid her fingers around the sword pommel, wiggling and gripping until she felt it give away. The tiny nub of stone slid into her hand with little complaint.

"And you're coming with me." Sorcha stuck it between her breasts for safe keeping.

Then she turned, pressed her spine against the carving, and waited.

She didn't have to wait long. He came barreling around the corner like a bull, sides heaving and crystals casting violet light onto the floors and walls.

He pointed a finger and shouted, "You defy me?"

"I do."

Stone walked towards her, each step a deliberate movement filled with aggression and power. She likened the movement to the first night she'd seen him. Intimidation was his purpose, and the first night she had been frightened.

She refused to be this time. Sorcha tilted her head back and met his gaze with a set jaw. "I'm not letting you get to her."

"She is mine to punish. An Unseelie living under my roof has no right to live."

"She is no one's but her own. You have no right to punish her for begging my help. If you want to punish someone, then punish me."

He hesitated. "You?"

"I walked into that portal without anyone telling me to. If you require someone to scream and shout your anger at, then it should be me."

"You didn't know what you were doing."

"I knew precisely what I was doing! I was raised with stories of the Fae. I left offerings and sacrifices to your people since I was a child. Unseelie lands are legend, and I assure you, I know all its dangers. I did not eat or drink. I spoke to as few people as possible—"

"You spoke to unknown Fae?" he interrupted.

"I spoke to those who were necessary, and Bran helped me back. What more do you want, Stone?"

Angry breaths expelled from his body in short huffs. "You should have asked for my help."

"Which you couldn't have provided. You are stuck here with the rest of them."

"I would have given you a weapon to take with you!" he shouted

Sorcha matched his tone and screamed back, "I wouldn't have used it! I heal people, I don't attack them, Stone."

"My name is not *Stone*!"

The walls creaked as his thunderous shout struck the walls. The carvings behind her quaked, and the floor shook with the force of his rage. He turned from her, his shoulders shaking with anger.

And fear, she realized as the light of his crystals dimmed. He had been frightened for her and waiting for her to return had only caused the fear to fester.

Sorcha's own anger dimmed.

"Then what would you have me call you?" she whispered quietly as she stepped forward. "Master? King? Lord? There is nothing else for me to say."

"I would have you call me by name, if it were possible."

"And why isn't it possible?" Daring to reach forward, she placed her hand against his back. Though fabric covered his skin, the dips of crystal gashes were easy to find. She slid her fingers into the wounded valley to hold him in place. "You already know my given name."

"A human in possession of a Tuatha dé Danann's name is far too powerful."

"Why? Do you fear I might order you to kill someone for me? To steal?"

"I fear that you would ask me to lay the world at your feet." He glanced over his shoulder, blue eyes searing through her calm resolve. "And it would be all too easy to do."

He stepped forward, her hand sliding from his back, out of the grooves of crystals that bit at her fingers. Then he walked away from her, each footstep measured as if he were trying not to run.

She did not stop him, nor was she certain that she could. The sheer force of his power frightened her. But it was the blunt terror of his words that held her in place.

Would she ask for the world?

Sorcha didn't know.

It was some time before she walked back into her bedroom. Sorcha's mind whirled with the possibilities of what he had meant, what that meant for their relationship. Was that a declaration of intent?

Did he feel something for her? Did she feel something for him?

She wasn't certain. She knew that his eyes haunted her dreams, that his tortured body was intriguing rather than fearsome. Did she want him? The violent reaction of her body to his suggested she might.

How would that even work? He was so much larger than her, surely he would crush her if she even attempted to have relations with him. And a part of her questioned whether she wanted him or the protection he could provide.

Would that make her a whore like her sisters? Was payment the requirement that divided easy women and business women?

Sorcha feared she would never know. And did it matter? Her sisters gave pleasure and reassurance to those who might not have it in any other way. If they derived pleasure from their job, then they should continue it. She would not judge them.

She pulled the small stone from between her breasts, staring down at the carved marble gemstone. Her mind stilled, thoughts narrowing down to one question which loomed above all others.

Would he have hurt Oona?

The stone slid easily back into place, and the heavy door receded into the wall. Sorcha longed for the day when the grinding of stone against stone would cease. When it had been used so much that the passage was smooth and silent.

She toed off her shoes, moss soft against her aching feet. She hadn't run this much in ages, between her bolting steps in the dark castle and then the rush through the portal. Her body wasn't certain how to handle the rush of adrenaline followed by bone-deep exhaustion.

Along the way to the bathroom, she pulled off each piece of her clothing. The outer kirtle dropped to the ground, the heavy skirts and belts holding each piece in place. Underclothing stuck to her skin where blood and fluid had leaked through each layer of fabric.

Sighing, she brushed aside the ivy and found Oona waiting by the door with a brush in her hand.

"Relax," Sorcha said. "It's just me."

"Oh, thank heavens," the pixie dropped the brush to the ground. "I wouldn't have hit him, dearie. I just...I just—"

Sorcha lifted a hand. "If his intent was to hurt you, then you have every right to protect yourself. Now if you don't mind, I'm very tired."

"Of course, dear."

Oona reached for the final ties of Sorcha's underclothes, quickly untangling the strings, and stripping the heavy weight from Sorcha's body. Sorcha stepped into the hot spring, sighing as her muscles eased.

"Did you bring the water from here?" she asked as Oona turned to put her underthings away. "The first day?"

"No. No, this is a royal room. These rooms are off limits for lesser Fae. Not without permission or company."

"But I'm not a high Fae."

"Perhaps you are," Oona looked at her intently. "You've the pointed ears, although far smaller than any I've ever seen. Are you sure you aren't a changeling?"

"My mother would have told me. She was a friend to the Fae and would have raised their child with pride." As much as she wanted to be Fae, Sorcha doubted there was the barest hint of it in her bloodline.

"And you have no ancestors who came from Underhill?"

"Not that I know of, and I've never had any sway with the elements. The earth is just earth, the air just air."

"Then you must not be Fae." Oona shook her head. "I don't know what you are child, but you aren't entirely human. This room was not meant for creatures such as me. It's said that all living things would grow ill and shrivel if they weren't meant for such a room."

"Are you certain it's not just a myth?"

"Most things are myths, but there's a shred of truth in every story. The magic here has deemed you worthy of staying within its walls. How, or why, I have no way of knowing."

Neither did Sorcha. It didn't seem right that she stayed in a room like this. It was too fine, too beautiful, and she had never lived in beauty like this before. Why should she start now?

Oona bustled out of the room, muttering about masters and faeries, and Sorcha could hear her opening chests for sleep clothing.

Sorcha's fingers ghosted over the tips of her ears, wondering if perhaps she had a bit of Fae in her, after all. But wouldn't they know?

Perhaps it was something she would never know or understand. Sorcha scrubbed her skin with a brush, the thick bristles turning her skin bright red and digging out all the crust underneath her nails. The water hardly changed color at all. It seemed to clean itself, replenishing from the free flowing spring.

Oona brushed aside the ivy that acted as a bathing screen, a light silk nightgown in her hands. "Come on then. You've had a busy day."

"I'm sorry." Sorcha looked up at her, wet hair tangled at her shoulders and spread out in the water like a fan. "I'm so sorry that I used your name without permission. I didn't want you to get hurt, but it's no excuse for treating you like that. I keep using faerie names even when I know how powerful they can be."

"There's no harm done, child." Oona's lips quirked to the side. "You saved my life."

"Still, I would like to give my name in apology. I trust you to use it well."

Oona's eyes nearly bugged out of her head. The nightgown fell from her hands and landed on the floor like a dying butterfly. "Why ever would you do that? Dearie, that is a dangerous thing to do. You should not give any Fae your name! Ever!"

Sorcha stood from the water, wrapped a cloth around her body, and held out her hand. "It's nice to meet you, Oona. My name is Sorcha of Ui Neill. And it would please me greatly if you would refer to me by name from now on."

Tears slid down Oona's cheeks. "I couldn't. It's not right."

"Please. I'm so far away from family and friends, and I consider you as close to me now as any other. I would like to hear you call me Sorcha, for it is my given name and should be spoken often."

"Sorcha," the faerie whispered. "You are the first human to ever give me their name."

"Use it wisely."

"And only with love," Oona said. She stepped forward and wrapped another cloth around Sorcha's shoulders, rubbing briskly. "Now let's get you dried off and into bed."

"Do you want to talk about the Queen?"

"Let me take care of you. I have no wish for nightmares, my dear."

Sorcha could almost feel the aching pain of loss. Oona was banished here, and likely would never see her family again. The resolve set inside Sorcha grew all the more strong. She would find a way to send Oona back home. To send all of them home.

They deserved to see their families. They deserved to be free.

Eamonn stormed into the highest tower of the castle, rage simmering underneath his skin. How dare she? How dare she defy him, in his own castle, without even a hint of fear in her eyes?

She should worry that he might snap her pretty little neck. And he could!

He held his hands out, staring down at the palms that had taken so many lives in his long life. He could feel the shifting of flesh, the crack that echoed through his fingers when a spine gave way. There was not a gentle bone in his body.

At least, that was what he had believed.

But even with the multiple bottles of whiskey clouding his mind and judgement, he had been gentle with her. The crystals on his hands hadn't broken through her speckled skin.

He tossed his head, shaking the long braid down his spine. Speckled wasn't the word. Flawed, as he had told her, wasn't the word either. Those freckles were captivating little stars decorating her skin like the splatter of a painter's brush. She was the most unusual creature he had met.

The voice of his twin brother, Fionn, echoed in his mind.

"But you always loved the humans, brother."

Eamonn growled. "You have no place here."

"You'll hurt her, like the rest of them. Those hands weren't capable of preserving such delicate bodies even before you broke. Ruined, maimed, beast that you are."

The old doubt filtered into his conscience. He wanted to be the kind of man who was capable of touching a woman and not worrying that she might break. He wanted to stroke soft skin, to squeeze and pet, but he knew what dangers lay down that path.

And it infuriated him.

Roaring out a frustrated call, he swung a heavy fist at the newest chair in his living quarters. The wood splintered beneath the weight of crystal and bone. Small shards burst into the air, slicing through his forearms.

The now familiar ache forced him to pause and tilt his hand. Meaty flesh split farther and crystals grew through muscle and skin. They glimmered, reflecting the light as if to mock him. They were beautiful, yes, but they were ugly at the same time.

He dropped his hand in disgust.

"That temper tends to get you in trouble."

Eamonn's jaw ticked at the familiar voice.

"Why were you in Unseelie lands, Bran?"

"Am I not supposed to be looking after your newest lady conquest?"

"Why?" Eamonn added steel to his voice, not allowing the other Fae a chance to argue further. Bran would talk around a subject until he was blue in the face.

"I had business there."

"You should not be following her."

"Why not?" Bran stepped out of the shadows, a sly grin on his face. "I do what I want, Prince. Just as you do."

"You should have been protecting her if you were there."

"She was fine. Managed well if you ask me. The only thing that caught her up was the portal." Bran's raven eye winked. "And if we're being honest, opening that on her own was an impossible task. She wouldn't have gotten it open without any Fae blood."

"You don't think she has any?" Eamonn wasn't so sure.

"Dry as a bone, that one. I thought perhaps she might, but any power would have surfaced on that ship we came over here on. She's not Fae."

"Then what is your explanation for the ears?"

Bran shrugged. "Physical deformation. She is strange though, I'll give you that. She knows how to manage the Fae and always says 'thank you.' I haven't had a human thank me in what feels like centuries."

"They forgot about us. That's why we left."

"All but her." Bran nodded towards the now broken furniture. "I'd hazard a guess you did something you're regretting?"

"Go away, Bran."

"I'm here now. I don't think I want to leave until the end of this story. What do you plan on doing with her?" Bran walked towards one of the lounge chairs, splaying his body across it without a care in the world. He pointed towards the comfortable seat. "This one is off limits. Break the others."

Eamonn sighed, tension and anger giving way to annoyance. "I'm finished."

"You say that, but then you always end up flipping the chair I'm seated in."

"That's because you annoy me so much."

"I don't follow your rules, Seelie. It's just the way I live my life."

"And you waste your time annoying me?"

Bran kicked his feet in the air, holding his hand out for a drink he knew Eamonn would share. "It's not like there's much going on back in my court. And here you are, on the brink of making the next step towards your future."

Eamonn lifted a glass and the bottle of whiskey from his desk, pouring a healthy amount into the crystal. "You think I'm on the brink of something? What other future do I have than rotting away on this isle?"

"Well, you don't *have* to stay here." Bran leaned out and grabbed the drink. "You're just choosing to."

"That's not true."

The raven eye rolled in its socket. "If you haven't put that piece of the puzzle together, then there's not much I can do to help you, brother."

Eamonn narrowed his eyes, glaring down at the reclining faerie. "Do you know something?"

"I know a lot of things." Bran sipped the whiskey. "This is quite good."

"And you will not share?"

"You already know it, Eamonn. You're just refusing to admit that you know it. Use that brain of yours. If the crystals haven't affected your head yet that is."

Eamonn stared for a moment, his mind whirling with possibilities until it settled on the information Bran was using. He shook his head. "That was a long time ago, and I am no longer king."

"Ah, but you are the oldest son."

"And unfit for the Seelie throne." Eamonn held his arms out, crystals sparkling in the dim candlelight. "Do I look like a Seelie Fae? Do you really think they'd follow me?"

"I think all the things you used to say were compelling to the faeries who only knew slavery. If you kept whispering in their ears of freedom, they might just follow you rather than your brother who treats his subjects like cattle rather than people."

"There is still the matter of the Tuatha dé Danann."

Bran drained the rest of the glass. "Do you think that's an issue? They always chose you, Eamonn. You were the favored son from day one. Or did you think your brother hated you simply because he was born with darkness in his heart? Hatred is learned, Eamonn, and it festered inside Fionn for years before he stabbed you in the back."

"I would have been a good king," Eamonn said. "But I never would have been a *great* king."

"Times change." Bran hopped onto his feet, circling the room, and eyeing the crystal decanters on Eamonn's desk with a calculating raven eye. "What are you going to do about the girl?"

Eamonn slumped onto the remaining chair. "I haven't a clue."

"Send her home?"

The glass in Eamonn's hand shattered.

Bran cocked his head to the side. "Unlikely then. Well, if you will not send her home, then just what do you plan on doing with her?"

"I have yet to decide."

"I have an idea."

"Do you?" Eamonn's head thumped against the back of the chair, and he stared up at the ceiling. "Please, advise me Unseelie Prince."

"Remind yourself what it feels like when a woman wants you. It might do you a world of good."

"She doesn't want me. She's frightened of me, yes. But any other emotion has never passed through her at the sight of me."

"Curious. It didn't look like that when you tried to consume her."

"I what?" Eamonn's face flamed with embarrassment and anger. "You were watching."

"I'm always watching," Bran tapped the black feathers circling his eye. "But more importantly, I could see what you did not. Alcohol may cloud your mind, but it does not mine. She wants you, my friend. Almost as much as you want her."

"And what do I do with that? You ask me to plan for war, and then to distract myself with a woman." Eamonn tossed the remaining shards of glass onto the floor. "A man can only do so much, Bran."

"I can help if you want. However, I'd much prefer the task of distracting your lady."

Eamonn growled.

"Calm yourself." Bran lifted his hands in surrender. "I jest. You need to wait for your brother to make the first move, and trust me, he will. Why do you think I was in Unseelie?"

Eamonn wanted to throw something at him. "Was this entire

conversation a way for you to circle around to what you found out in Unseelie? Out with it, Fae!"

"Not yet. I want to know what you're doing with Sorcha first."

"I don't like you using her name so freely."

"I think she's hardier than you give her credit for. No faerie blood runs in her veins, but there's something else there that gives her a spine of steel. What are you going to do with her?"

"I don't know," Eamonn groaned. "Give me peace and perhaps I will find out!"

"You gave her the queen's room, yet you do not know what you want her for." Bran tsked. "You're a confusing man, my friend. A supple woman, willing no less, just floors away from you, and yet, you hide in a tower."

"Are you quite done commenting on my love life?"

"That will never stop."

Eamonn stared at the ripped portrait of his mother and prayed for patience. He'd never been good at waiting. The battlefield wasn't a good training ground for patience. "Bran."

"Fine. Your brother has been keeping track of you, you know, and this girl worries him. He thinks a happy life might coerce you into returning."

"He is a fool."

Bran snorted. "A fool who is correct."

"She has no sway over my actions or decisions."

"You've left this tower more since she arrived than you had in your entire time here on Hy-brasil, and you are considering going to war with your brother."

"I considered that before she showed up."

"And now you have meaning behind the action. She would look pretty with a crown atop her head." Bran mimed placing a tiara on top of his half-shaved head.

"She's human."

"What's that got to do with anything? For once in your life, give up that stalwart honor and foolish sense of right and wrong! War is coming whether you choose it or not. Enjoy your last days of freedom. The bloodshed will begin soon."

The feathers on Bran's face ruffled and spread across his skin. His form shifted, morphing from man to beast. He let out one croaking scream before lifting into the air and flying out the window.

Good riddance, Eamonn thought. He couldn't handle one more minute of the Unseelie's constant suggestion he go back home.

What was left for him? A stolen throne, a twin who hated him, a kingdom who assumed he'd abandoned them. At least here there were people to take care of.

He clenched his fists as the pit of his stomach clenched. He missed home. It was a strange thing, to miss a place so profoundly that his heart ached. But this place held none of the beauty that Tír na nÓg could offer.

Standing, he paced in front of his mother's portrait. "Even you wouldn't want me home. You, who did nothing when Fionn hanged me in the square. Our own people cheered for days as I dangled, unable to die because the crystals on my throat protected me." He jabbed a finger towards her. "You didn't even cut me down."

The memory was a jagged thing, harsh and cutting even after a hundred years. She had tears her in eyes when their gazes met, but she had not helped her son. Her first born. Her beloved warlord prince who had cut down the world for her.

His mother had shown her true colors. As had his father, who hadn't even looked as his son hung from a fraying rope. Three days. Three days he swung in the breeze and endured the never-ending pecks of crows, the cries of vultures waiting to feast.

He had defied them all.

Death would not come for him. He would not submit to those who had betrayed him. Eamonn survived. He had always been good at that.

Fionn hated him, of that he was certain. Something festered deep within his twin's gut, and there was nothing Eamonn could do to change it. What brotherly love there once might have been, was long gone.

Eamonn braced his arms against the wall next to his mother and let his forehead touch the cool stone. What choice did he have?

The faces of the isle's Fae danced behind his lids. They had been banished for many things. Stealing from a Tuatha dé Danann. Worshiping a different ancestor than their master. Going home to visit family when they should have been working.

Nothing as serious as murder. They would've swung next to him on the gallows if they'd done such a thing.

There was no purpose to this place, other than a punishment worse than death. Fionn's voice echoed in his mind.

"Let him rot."

And that was exactly what he was doing. He might as well grow barnacles rather than crystals. Eamonn was doing nothing other than sitting and waiting for time to pass.

He glanced over and met his mother's cold gaze. "I'm coming home, Máthair."

Sorcha wound through the hallways, twisting the armful of lavender she carried into a purple crown. The brownies were busy cooking and had little time to entertain her. She'd tried to talk with one of the selkies, but he had to go fishing to replenish their stocks.

Every day that passed brought new frustrations and new boredom. Blowing out a breath, she stuck her tongue out in concentration as she finished the very end. Lavender made a beautiful flower crown, but the tiny buds sometimes fell off before she could finish.

She'd smelled the patch before she saw it. Rosaleen had always been searching for more lavender to hang in her room. She said it took away some of the more unpleasant scents.

Sorcha didn't have the heart to say that even lavender couldn't take away the scent of death. It wasn't what Rosaleen had been talking about, but Sorcha's struggles had been far different.

Crown finished, she placed it atop her head and let her red curls coil around it.

Soft slippers on her feet rendered her footsteps silent. If she came across anyone, Sorcha planned on telling them that she'd gotten lost. In reality, she was looking for the master of this isle. He had disappeared after one drunken, angry night.

Again.

She was growing tired of having to find him. Stone should be accessible for all his people, herself included. She had to convince him to come back to the mainland with her.

Every time she saw him, her tongue tied itself into a knot. She hadn't even asked the question again!

One part of the castle was off limits. The faeries said she was forbidden from entering the western tower. It was the master's and the master's alone.

But she had seen Oona slip into the shadows. She had carried food in her arms, for the master himself, but she had still gone into the western tower. That meant it wasn't off limits for them.

Just off limits for her.

She placed her palm on the cracked wooden door and glanced around. She couldn't see any faeries, and no one cried out for her to stop.

"Hello?" Sorcha said.

No one responded.

"Good enough," she whispered as she pushed open the door.

A blast of cold air pushed her backward. Purple petals tangled in her waist length hair and fell onto the floor. The blanket of cobwebs on the ceiling stirred. They bounced with the weight of the musty air and shadows danced upon the walls as spiders fled the light.

Sorcha blew out a breath. "There is nothing to be afraid of. Shadows are just that. Shadows."

Her own voice echoed, distorted and warped. She shivered, but pushed on.

She wandered for a while. The western tower was far larger than she expected. There were many doors down the long hallway into darkness. None of them opened, no matter how hard she pushed.

Eventually, she gave up trying. She stayed close to the wall and squinted in the darkness to make out where she might go next.

There, up ahead, was a light. Dim and with no source she could distinguish.

Sorcha squared her shoulders and crept down the hallway until she could press her palm against the door. The light was yellow. Candlelight?

A smile spread across her face.

"Got you," she whispered. "Let's see what you've been up to."

She tested the door, one hand on the handle and the other firmly against the wood grain. Unlike the others, this door was well oiled. Silent, it hid her presence as she slid it open inch by inch.

Sorcha peeked through the small crack. A candelabra glowed with the light of a dozen candles placed atop a sconce on the wall nearest her. There was a nice blanket of shadows behind a pillar. If she could sneak over to that, he wouldn't be able to see her.

Bravery, foolish bravery perhaps, was her middle name. Holding her breath, she darted through the door and ducked into the shadows.

Her heart pounded so forcefully she was certain he would hear it. He'd be so angry if he found her sneaking. Even his servants would berate her for hours if they discovered she had stolen into this forbidden place.

Sorcha furrowed her brows. She listened for some kind of sound. The movement of fabric, the exhale of a breath, the murmuring of voices.

Was he here?

She leaned around the pillar. The room was small, quaint even. Blue glowing flowers grew up from the floor, stretching their vines into the ceiling. Leaves larger than her entire body folded over the thick tendrils and swept the ground.

At the end of the room, a large stone loomed in the shadows. She had seen its ilk before. A sacred stone, the triskele carved into its surface marking it as a holy object.

He knelt before it wearing nothing but a small loincloth. His back was broad, sliced so many times that he glimmered in the weak blue light. Even his feet were broken, she noticed. The sole of one gaped open and a valley of violet crystals danced down it.

Her cheeks burned. He held his hands folded before him, long braid trailing down his back and completely still.

She should leave. This was a holy place, and her intrusion was not welcome.

Shame made her palms sweat. She had always been a curious creature, but she'd never waltzed into a church just to watch. This was sacrilege.

"Grandfather," he murmured. His voice was deep, like the shifting of the earth in the middle of the night. "Nuada Airgetlám, I beseech your help."

Grandfather? She ducked behind the pillar again and pressed her hands against her chest. He was the grandson of Nuada Silverhand, ancient king of the Seelie Fae, long thought dead? It wasn't possible!

"I am lost. I have followed your paths, listened to your wisdom, and still I am here."

The pain in his voice made her ache. Sorcha had never heard him speak in such a way. He was a private person, and she wasn't surprised that he kept his secrets close.

Her eyes locked upon the cracked door. He fell silent and her opportunity to do the right thing was now. She could slip out, forget that she had intruded, and tell herself she had eased the curiosity eating at her.

But now, here, she could satisfy that curiosity. It burned so brightly her thoughts burst into flame.

She gritted her teeth and twisted her fingers together. She would regret this.

A few moments more, she told herself. He had to leave eventually. Sorcha peered around the pillar again, watching as Stone leaned forward and pressed his forehead against the ground.

The strong muscles of his thighs bunched. His back flexed, tightening into a valley following the ridge of his spine.

"They know where I am. I have always said that if they find the courage to fight me, then let them come. My brother must find the man within if he wishes to wipe me from the Otherworld. And I have remained alone."

She pressed her chest against the pillar. Her fingers were freezing, but she couldn't pull away from the shadows. Her eyes stayed locked upon his prostrate figure.

"You raised me to be a weapon. I was untouchable with your sword at my side, and then you allowed me to be cut down by my own blood. Through all this, I endured. I existed. But now, I do not know what path you wish me to take.

"There is another here. A woman who survived the journey from Uí Neill to Hy-brasil. I thought such a thing impossible for one so frail, and surely the mark of your children is upon her."

Sorcha held her breath. She wanted to know what secrets he held regarding her presence.

"She is a distraction I do not need. If I wish to be prepared for my brother's attack, then I should ignore her. Or perhaps send her away."

He sighed, as if the thought pained him.

"He sent more men. I entertained them for a time in the throne room, but their eyes wandered. They searched for the best place to attack. The easiest way to draw blood and strike at my heart. I'm confident they found nothing."

He hesitated, and she leaned forward to hear his quiet words.

"I have no fear of pain. My hands are stained with the blood of kings and the ashes of old gods. But I fear what my brother might do to her, should he find out about her existence."

His head dipped forward in thought.

"She is strange. Unlike the creatures I am used to, or the ones remember from Seelie. Breakable and yet strong. Flawed, yet somehow perfect and uncommonly kind. I don't know what it is you would tell me to do, Grandfather."

Sorcha knew what she wanted Nuada to tell him. Try anything you want, for our time is fleeting.

Her heart raced as her mind played through the possibilities. He was not an ugly man. The crystals were unusual and dangerous, but they didn't detract from the harsh angles of his face. Her sisters would run from him in fear.

His height alone would be a problem. And if he was so tall, there may be issues with fitting together…in more intimate ways.

She cocked her head to the side and looked him up and down. It was worth taking a chance. He was a beautiful man.

Stone sat up, his back and shoulders flexing. Shadows danced across the imposing muscles, flickering to life only to disappear as he shifted.

"I fear touching her with my hands. I am an unyielding man, created to do violent things. Laying with a woman, being kind to a woman, is not in my nature."

Her heart shattered all over again. Did he truly believe he was incapable of being gentle?

Green light trickled from the top of the triskele to the bottom. Great drops of emerald fluid leaked from the edges of the stone and slid to the ground.

"Peace, grandson." The voice was smooth honey wine, the comforting voice of the wind after a long journey home. "The course of love is no easy path to tread. The sky may tremble, and the wind may howl, but the only person who can sway your decisions is yourself. What do you feel when you look at this girl?"

"It is like nothing I have ever felt before."

"Do you like the way it feels?"

"It makes me feel weak," Stone growled. "One look from her, and I am ashamed of myself, of my decisions, of the path I walk."

"And what path is that?"

"I walk towards my death. My birthright was taken, and I will not allow another to take what should be mine."

The green light flared so bright that Sorcha had to duck behind the pillar.

Nuada's voice rose, "And whose choice is that, grandson?"

"My own."

"Do you wish to die?"

"No."

"Then my suggestion is for you to live. As much as you can. Experience life, experience courage and honor in ways you were never given as a young man. You are still a being capable of brutality, but that does not define you. The Fae are infinite creatures, capricious and volatile. It is far past time for you to discover other purposes for yourself."

"You approve?"

Nuada's chuckle echoed in the room, and the green light faded. She watched the nearest pillar until the light completely disappeared from its gray stone. Only then did Sorcha peek from her hiding spot and glance towards Stone.

He remained kneeling in the same spot, head heavy. His hands flexed upon his thighs but he did not move. He did not speak.

He did not know she was there.

Sorcha turned and let herself out of the altar room. She wasn't certain she breathed a single breath as she raced down the hallway and out of the western tower.

What had she heard?

She pressed her spine against the wall and leaned her head back until her hair caught in the cracks of stone. She didn't know how to take this new information. What would she do now that she knew of his affections?

His words rang through her skull over and over again. She made him weak.

Was that a good thing?

CHAPTER ELEVEN

THE KELPIE AND THE KING

Sorcha rubbed her eyes, yawning as Oona dragged her down the hallway.

"Where are we going?"

"The master has asked for you, dearie."

"The master?" Sorcha asked. "Why would he be asking for me this early in the morning?"

"It's not for me to say."

"Do you know?"

"Haven't the faintest idea! It's just a lovely thing that he's asked for you. He doesn't ask for anyone."

"And here I thought that might be just the tiniest bit frightening."

Sorcha didn't know what to think as she walked through the hallways in nothing but her faded cotton nightgown. Her hair stuck out in all directions, curls creating a nest of hair that hardly bounced as she moved. She spent more hours than she could count taming the wild beast of her curls before bed. Even so, she always awoke the next morning with the wild mane tumbling in all directions.

"Wait, hang on," Sorcha grumbled as she twisted her arm. "I'm hardly dressed for meeting with Stone."

"Stone, is it? You've given him a nickname?"

The sparkle in Oona's eyes made her uneasy. "I won't call him master. But it's hardly proper to meet him in my nightclothes."

"Oh, faeries don't have the same delicate sensibilities as humans. You're fine as you are."

"I most certainly am not!"

"No matter, if we go back now, we'll be late. And I can promise you, the master won't appreciate us being late."

Sorcha blew out a breath to stir the curl in front of her eyes. "Why should I care what upsets the master?"

"He's been so nice to you lately, dearie. You should be kind in return."

"He's been kind?" She wracked her brain, trying to remember even the slightest bit of kindness he had shown to her lately. But try as she might, she couldn't remember even seeing him. "I hadn't noticed."

"You didn't notice the daisies on your bedside?"

"Those were from Boggart."

"Nor the sweetmeats that are far better than the kitchen has ever made before?"

"You were trying new recipes. I watched you bake them."

"There were far more dresses in your clothing chests than I remember."

Sorcha shrugged her shoulders. "I found another dress in the hag's hut that were my size. I'm failing to see how the master has been kind. You aren't helping, Oona."

"If you just looked, you could see that he had a hand in all of that."

"I see just fine," she ducked underneath a low hanging beam that Oona could fit underneath easily. "But he's been hiding again."

"Oh dearie, he's never hiding. He's just making sure you're comfortable in every way he can."

"Somehow, I doubt that," she grumbled, a flash of guilt heating her cheeks for a moment. She was being ungrateful, perhaps even childish, but *knowing* his emotions for her somehow made this all so much more difficult.

Oona shoved her around a corner, through a room she didn't recognize, and out a side door of the castle. Sorcha spun around, hands on her hips.

"I didn't even know that door existed." How could she? Once closed, it blended into the worn stone. "Strange."

"Is it?" Stone's deep voice traveled like a physical touch down her spine.

"Oh!" Sorcha spun, pressing her spine against the cold wall of the castle. "I didn't know you were there."

"Obviously," he said as he stepped from the shadows. Black breeches covered his legs, his ever-present dark cloak covering his form and blending into the shadows. "Although one begs to understand why you wouldn't be looking for me? Oona must have told you I requested your presence."

"She said you summoned me." Sorcha stuck her chin into the air. "I don't like being summoned and dragged out of bed."

His gaze lowered. The burning touch of such a bright look made her knees weak and her hands clutch at the wall for support. He looked as if he could see straight through the thick cotton nightgown. It showed her ankles, which was more than enough, but somehow it felt as though he could see all of her.

Sorcha tugged it higher up her neck. "Why did you want to see me?"

"I thought perhaps we could share breakfast."

"Breakfast? And I couldn't get dressed to do that?" She shivered. "It's nearly time for the first snow fall."

"I would gladly take the blame for your shivers, if only it was my decision to not allow you further clothing." Sorcha watched with wide eyes as he swept the cloak from his shoulders and held it out to her. "If I may."

"So chivalrous," she commented.

The crystals marring his face had lost most of their strangeness. She now saw him, the man beneath the scars and cruel curse. Still, she wanted to wince when she saw the new cut along his jaw.

She swept the cloak over her shoulders, his lingering warmth enveloping her. She inhaled and without thinking blurted, "Why do you always smell like mint?"

His startled laugh was a balm to her homesick soul. "Why do you ask?"

"I didn't think it was a Tuatha dé Danann trait. Bran does not smell like mint although I believe he is the same species as you."

"You think Bran and I are the same?" The brow not held still by crystals arched.

"Well, yes. Although he has more physical deformities, it does appear that you are similar in structure and build. You are not just any Tuatha de Danann."

"Astute. You notice things most humans would not."

"Why do you smell like mint?"

He chuckled again. "You aren't letting that go, are you?"

"I must have my curiosity satisfied."

She watched as he held out an arm for her to take. Strange, she thought, that he could swing so quickly from raging bull to well-bred gentleman. Sorcha arched her own brow.

"I will give you your answer," he acquiesced, "if you walk with me."

"What happened to breakfast?" she asked as she slid her hand over his forearm. Crystals bumped underneath the fabric of his flowing white shirt.

"You seem less inclined to eat."

"I rarely miss a meal. I would not say no to good food, even if the company may yet sour my appetite."

A hearty laugh rang in her ears as he guided her from the castle. "You think very little of me, don't you?"

"On the contrary. I think very highly of you and become disappointed when you do not live up to my standards."

"Ah, and what standards are those?"

They stepped onto a dirt pathway leading them towards the ocean. The cold, autumn air bit at her cheeks and turned her nose bright red. This had always been her favorite season in Ui Neill. The grass would eventually turn brown, the leaves flaming the same color as her hair. Although she would miss the summer, autumn always had a special place in her heart.

How long had she been gone now?

She blinked away the sudden tears in her eyes and forced a grin. "If I told you my standards, you would certainly try your hardest to meet them. And then, however would I meet the real you?"

"The real me?"

"You are not the terrifying man you portray yourself as."

The muscles under her hand bunched. "Why do you say that?"

"Oona says you've been leaving me gifts." It was the only excuse she could think of to say. Sorcha didn't believe he was the one who had left them in the first place. Boggart and the other brownies were far too kind. They liked any excuse to see her happy.

"Yes, the daisies were difficult to obtain this time of year."

She stopped, so startled that her feet forgot how to move. Sorcha stared up at him, mouth agape. He paused when her hand slid off his arm, glancing down at her with a questioning expression.

"That *was* you?" she whispered.

He flushed. "Come on. If we're late, you'll miss it."

"Miss what?"

"Your surprise."

"I thought this was just breakfast."

"It's a little more than that." He shook his head and held his arm out again. Obviously impatient, he waited for her to decide.

"I—" she glanced down at his arm and back up at his face. "Why are you doing this?"

"I thought that would be rather obvious." His gazed dipped towards her mouth, blue eyes flashing with an emotion she couldn't—

wouldn't—name.

Sorcha couldn't reply. Instead, she reached out and held onto his arm again. Her fingers slid over the craggy bumps and valleys, callouses whispering over the silken fabric. They both shivered at the contact. If he asked, she would say it was the cold.

He didn't ask.

They wandered across the fields as the sun turned pink on the horizon. The birds awoke, singing their morning songs to each other. Though chilly, it was a clear morning with not a single cloud in the sky.

"Hurry," he murmured.

They picked up speed, clambering over rocks and across seaweed. He held her steady over every bit of their journey, never letting her slip or tumble to the sand.

His handprints burned into her sides, even when he wasn't touching her. Sorcha marveled at his strength. He could lift her without appearing tired or showing any strain. Both his hands could span her waist.

How was it possible that such a creature existed, and yet so many humans didn't know they were there?

She shook her head and pulled herself up onto a rocky incline. Catching her breath, she turned back to look at him as he hefted his bulk over the stone to join her.

"Where now?"

He pointed behind her. Tilting her head, Sorcha turned and gasped.

A waterfall tumbled from a rocky cliff into a vast pool of water. Glamour hid it from her view until she nearly fell into its edge. She hadn't even heard the crashing thunder of water striking the ground. White foam bubbled where the waterfall met still pond.

Great stones jutted towards the sky, moss growing upon their granite surfaces. It stretched as far as her eye could see. And at the base, white horses stamped their feet in the ripples of water and tossed their heads.

She had never seen anything like it before.

"It's beautiful," she whispered.

"I thought you might like it."

"I do. It's a rare gem in a world that could use so much more beauty."

"It gets better," he murmured in her ear. "How much do you trust me, Sorcha?"

"Very little."

His chuckle danced across her skin in bubbles of sensation. "Ah, you must do better than that, lass. How much do you trust me?"

"Enough."

"Close your eyes."

She stiffened, but complied. Curiosity had always gotten her in trouble, and she wouldn't back away now. Besides, it seemed as though he was far more interesting than he let on.

Strange, but she hadn't thought that a Fae could capture her attention so wholly. There had been many men in her town, but none of them so intriguing. So odd. So unusual.

The words rang in her ears. Of course the strange witch's daughter, the midwife who thought she was more, fell in love with an impossible man. *In love.* The words burned even thinking them.

His arms reached around her, chest pressed against her spine. She moved forward and back with each great inhalation, rocking on the waves of his own making.

She gasped as his fingers traced the outline of her chin. Delicately, oh so delicately, he touched her. As if she might shatter with just the mere breath from his lips.

His fingers lingered at the stubborn thrust of her chin, joining together to spread across her full bottom lip. The butterfly touch trailed up her cheeks, his thumbs anchoring at her jaw.

The slightest graze whispered over her eyelids.

"Your eyelashes feel like feathers," he whispered in her ear. "I have very little poetry for women such as you. I cannot ever compare your body to artwork, or sing you songs of lovers in a hidden grove. My experiences limit my words and talents."

"I never wanted poetry," she said on a soft sigh. "I only wanted a man who could see me for who I am."

"Then open your eyes, Sorcha of Ui Neill. And see the world as it truly is."

She blinked, opening her eyes as if she had never seen the sun. And, had she ever seen it?

The veil of the world shattered through the ointment he pressed against her closed lids. Colors were suddenly so much *more*. The white horses grew long manes and water dripped from their foaming snouts. Webbed toes stamped the ground, their tails flicked back and forth.

His arm around her waist was suddenly more solid. More real. The crystals were more than just stone, they were imbued with magic that she could see as sparkling light dancing atop his skin.

"Oh," she whispered. "What did you do?"

"I opened your eyes." He nudged her backward, holding her against his chest and letting her stare without worry of balance or fear of falling. He had opened her eyes to the world she had never seen.

"I had no idea all this was here."

"Glamour is a strange thing. Faeries place it upon everyday objects without even realizing what they do."

One of the horses tossed its head, glancing at them with dark green eyes.

"Kelpies?" she asked.

"Yes."

"Aren't they dangerous?"

"Not to me."

"And to me?" She tilted her head back, looking up to catch his expression.

He stared back at her. His brows smoothed. and his lips curved into a soft smile. The crystals marring his eyes, lips, and skull were made more beautiful by her new sight.

"Never to you. Not as long as I stand by your side."

She felt his low hum against her spine. It wasn't quite a song, nor did she think he had the voice to sustain such a melody, but a rumble that came from deep within his belly. The kelpie nearest to them lifted its head.

It ambled closer, shaking its wet and dripping head. Seaweed tangled in its mane, and foam erupted from its nostrils every time it snorted.

"Have you ever wanted to touch a kelpie?" he asked.

"It's dangerous. They'll drag humans down into the bottom of the ocean and drown them."

"But, have you ever wanted to touch one?"

"Yes," she answered. "Without question, I have always wondered what they felt like."

He stepped forward, sliding his feet under hers until he walked for the both of them. His arm around her waist was comforting and strong. "Then let us fulfill that wish."

The kelpie tossed its head as they moved, watching every twitch, every step, every breath that Sorcha took. It ignored Eamonn, perhaps the only creature in existence that was able to ignore the crystals and jagged edges. Its head swayed as she walked closer, a strange translucent glimmer spreading across its body.

"What was that?"

"That is what a glamour looks like to a Fae."

"That?" It looked like a bubble stretched across the kelpie's skin. Light reflected off the surface in rainbows. "But it's so beautiful."

"Did you think it wouldn't be?" His hand slid under her arm, guiding it up into the air. "Deceitful things are not always ugly."

"Shouldn't they be?"

"Not necessarily. Sometimes, we hide our true selves to spare humans the grievous injury of our appearance."

Sorcha looked over the kelpie, seeing the strange webbed feet, the scaled skin, the seaweed hair and did not flinch. She could understand how some humans might be afraid of it. The legends said it was dangerous, and it likely was. It was different, uncomfortable to even be around.

But that was what made it so lovely. Sorcha had been the oddity in her town, and she knew how deceiving appearances could be.

She stepped out of Stone's comforting warmth. Her nightgown stuck to her skin as mist clung to the sodden fabric. The cloak felt heavy upon her shoulders, but did not slow her determined pace.

Her palm met the cold, wet snout of the kelpie. It huffed, bubbles foaming between her fingers.

"Hello," she whispered.

It cocked its head to stare up at her. A strand of seaweed fell across its forehead. Sorcha didn't hesitate. She brushed it aside and stroked her hand across damp scales.

"There. Now you can see me."

Stone's voice rumbled, "I've never seen a human treat faeries so kindly."

"I've never seen a human treat faeries like anything at all." Her heart clenched. "We have forgotten what it means to be connected to the earth, to the waves, to the creatures who care for all of those things."

"It is why we faded from your world."

"And I hope you know that your kind is dearly missed." The kelpie's skin was faintly like that of a snake, albeit a cold, wet one. Sorcha couldn't stop petting the creature nor did it seem to want her to stop. Every time she pulled her hand away, it would bounce its head.

"Is that so?" Sand suctioned to his feet as he walked away. Sorcha tracked the slurping sounds to the rocks where he settled. "I see no signs that humans even remember us."

"Myths and legends teach us lessons. Tales of your kind frighten children, and I can't say how many people have thought their babe to be a changeling. They remember you, and they blame many things upon faeries that are their own fault."

Sorcha could not change the minds of people who were so set in their ways. She wanted to, but she also wanted to remain free of fire.

"And you stayed true to the old ways?"

The kelpie snorted on her hand and turned to provide its back. She knew what it wanted and shook her head. "No, my friend. I have no wish to visit the land beneath the waves. Go back with the others."

Sorcha patted the broad back and made her way towards the flat rocks Stone sat upon. The water had yet to splash them although it wouldn't have mattered. Water already weighed her dress down from mist gathering at the hem.

Shivering, she tucked the edges of his cloak underneath her legs. "My mother followed the old ways. She taught me how important it was to leave milk on the windowsill, offerings at the hidden forest shrines, and to always respect the way of the Fae."

"Smart woman," Stone said. His eyes remained trained upon the kelpies rooting through the pool's still waters. "Would that others listened to her wisdom."

"They thought she was a witch, because strange things happened around her. Faeries helped when they could. I don't think they meant to make her seem suspicious or strange. They just wanted to help."

"What happened to her?"

Sorcha shivered again, placed her chin onto her knees, and sighed. "They burned her at the stake for worshiping devils. It took her nearly an hour to burn, because it was so misty that they had to keep lighting the pyre over and over again. I was lucky they didn't feel like burning a child that day."

His bright eyes locked upon hers. "They burned a favored of the Fae?"

"I don't think she was favored. Just one who recognized that our world would never be the same if she gave up on her beliefs."

"And for that, they burned her." Stone shook his head. "Your people are barbarians."

"There is kindness in even the darkest of places. My father plucked me from my village and brought me home. He took me as a daughter, told his children that I was their equal. People such as him exist, but it is so easy to focus on the bad."

Stone grunted. "You have a unique way of looking at the world."

"How so?"

"You twist even negative things into positives. You refuse to think ill of anyone, even those who have wronged you. I have never seen such a creature."

Sorcha shifted, mist playing across her face in small ice cold pricks. "And you? How would you have dealt with a dead mother and a people who betrayed you?"

He reacted as if struck. His gaze snapped away from hers, fists clenching in sudden anger. The muscles of his jaw worked. "Revenge."

"Revenge?" Sorcha shook her head. "What good would that do?"

"I find wiping out those who have wronged you tends to soothe the soul."

"It cannot soothe the soul in the slightest and even suggesting so is cruel. The implications of revenge are that no mercy will be shown."

"Would you show mercy to those who killed your mother?"

"You have experience with this," she said. Her eyes searched his for the truth and found a lingering pain she recognized. "What happened to you?"

"The Fae are not kind creatures. We do not allow for weakness to show among our people."

"The brownies accepted Boggart back into their family with arms open wide. Even after she fell from their ranks and returned with her tail, quite literally, between her legs. Tell me again, Stone, that your people do not allow for weakness."

The ragged sigh that rocked his shoulders tugged at her heartstrings.

"The Tuatha dé Danann do not allow for weakness. The lesser Fae are far more…" He paused, seeming to struggle for the words.

"Kind."

"Kind," he repeated with a nod. "Yes, they are capable of forgiveness, which is more than I can say of my people."

"Can they really not forgive? Or do they choose not to?"

His hand touched the angry wound of crystals that wrapped around his neck. "I do not have an answer for that question, Sorcha."

She couldn't stop staring at his throat. The markings were too familiar, yet she couldn't pinpoint what might have caused such a wound. She had seen a man nearly decapitated once, his family had brought him to her in hopes that she might help. There hadn't been any possible way for her to bring him back. But these markings weren't that.

A memory surfaced of bright red skin, bruises spread in spidery tendrils, and the vacant eyes of a thief who had been in the wrong place at the wrong time.

Sorcha had been too young to understand that the hanged man was dead. She ran through the crowd and tried to help him stand up. The gasps of the crowd would always haunt her, even more so than the dead eyes of the man.

She rose onto her knees, turning towards Stone with her gaze locked upon his neck. She gave him time to back away, to brush her hand aside, to tell her to stop.

He didn't.

Her fingers settled upon the cool surface of the crystals. The ones here were smoother than the others, like the polished gems of a crown. She dipped her fingers into the crevice. Magic, so cold it burned, tingled underneath her nails as she followed the angry line to the back of his neck.

"This was among the first," she whispered.

"How did you know?"

"The stones feel old."

"Worn down by time and the elements."

"They hanged you," she observed. "I recognize these marks, although I didn't piece it together until now. How did you survive?"

His massive hand touched just below hers, fingering where skin met rock. "I didn't think I would. The crystals prevent anything from killing me. I hung there for three days before they finally cut me down."

"What did you do?"

"I existed."

Sorcha shook her head. "Surely it was more than that? Living isn't a reason to kill someone."

"It was for my family."

"Family?" Shock jolted through her body until she thumped back onto her heels. "Your family did this?"

"I told you, the Tuatha dé Danann do not forgive weakness."

"What weakness? The crystals? How are they a weakness?"

Suddenly enraged, she surged forward again. Her fingers traced the ragged edges of crystal that bisected his face. She touched the top line at the edge of his shaved skull. "This is the mark of a brave man who has endured much hardship."

Her finger traveled down to rest just above his brow, "And this is the beginning of a journey." She trailed over his eye and hesitated at the high rise of his cheekbone. "The mark of self-discovery." To his lip where the crystal made it difficult to him to smile or speak. "Of bravery." Her thumb touched his chin, "Of stubborn pride."

He chuckled, "Stubborn?"

"I recognize familiar flaws."

"Yes, you are certainly stubborn, little human."

"So much so that I refuse to give up on bringing you back with me. I have to save my family, Stone."

He growled, and she shrieked as his arms wrapped around her and lifted her into his lap. Encircling her with crystal and the scent of mint, he stared. "You refuse to give up on this cursed adventure?"

"It's not cursed. Macha sent me herself. I made a deal, Stone. And I don't think she'll let me give up any time soon."

"Macha," he grumbled. "She is ever meddlesome. Far too interested in humankind if you ask me."

"I didn't ask for this."

"You shouldn't have made a deal with Macha."

"It was the only way to save my family." She reached up and cupped the good side of his face, leaving the raw edges free to her gaze. "I will not regret making this deal, because it led me to meet the most magical people, a wondrous land, an enchanted place filled with all the delights I never would have seen otherwise."

He tilted his face in her palm. Light sparked off the edges of crystals and nearly blinded her. "I am glad you will remember this place fondly."

"And she brought me to you."

Stone stiffened in her arms, his eyes snapping open, burning into her soul. "Why would you say that?"

"You are the most intriguing man I have ever met."

"Monster."

"Man." She pulled him closer, pressing her forehead against his and tasting mint upon the air. He had endured so much, had survived it, and all she could think was that she'd finally met someone who could understand her.

This was a man who had seen what perceived differences could do, in the most drastic of terms. His own family had condemned him for his appearance and had disregarded his suffering.

She wanted to fix him so much, her heart ached.

"I am sorry life has been so cruel. You should never have suffered, but you are strong and kind underneath all those layers of stone and gem."

"It made me strong," he growled, his breath fanning over her lips.

"Oh, yes. You are very strong."

She heard the creaking of his teeth grinding against each other.

"You should flee this isle and tuck yourself back into bed."

"Why?"

"I am not the kind of man you want to fall in love with, Sorcha."

"Who said anything about love?" She surged up, pressing her nose against his and her chest flush to his crystal shoulder. "My time here is finite, unlike your long-lived kind, love only makes this more difficult. All I can ask is for memories that will fill my thoughts with magic. You've done that for me already, Stone."

He growled. "My name is not Stone."

"Then would you tell me what it is?"

Her heart stopped as his broad hand pressed against the small of her back. He cupped her head and slanted his lips across hers, pulling the breath from her lungs as his tongue tangled with hers. Heat spread across her skin like a powerful desert wind.

She wrapped her legs around his waist, knees tucked against his ribs. It didn't matter that the crystals dug into her thighs or that her lungs screamed for air. The taste of mint, lemon, and man coated her tongue and made her lips tingle with new desires.

He groaned, clenching his fist at the back of her head. Her hair tugged, little needles of crystal biting the back of her skull. She should tell him it hurt, but the warmth of his kiss was overwhelming. He didn't just kiss or taste.

He claimed.

Sorcha gripped his crystal shoulders and let her mind free. She focused upon the feather-light touches stroking the dip of her spine. The lingering pass of sharp crystal and velvet-soft lips. The hypnotic rhythm of his darting tongue.

He pulled back, and they both gasped in air. His hands fisted in the material of his cloak wrapped around her, but he did not pull or rip. She thought he might, considering how his hands were shaking.

"I thought I had imagined that first kiss," he whispered.

"Did you?"

"I was drunk."

"You smelled of whiskey."

"I wasn't entirely in my right mind."

"I noticed," she smiled. It was impossible not to touch his face, now that she knew he wouldn't flinch away. The crystals were a tantalizing texture against the heat of his skin. "Would you have hurt Oona?"

"I have no way of knowing. The Fae are…precipitous at the best of times."

"Easily angered?"

"Emotions do not come naturally to us, and when we do feel, it is a thousand times stronger than any other species."

"Ah," she whispered as he pressed his lips against her fingers. "That is why Boggart changed so much when she lost the hag."

"And when she met you."

"I am no paragon nor miracle maker."

"No, but you are infinitely kind, and you always remember to thank us for our services. Do you know how much that means to a faerie?"

"It's what I would want them to do for me," she replied. "They have given me no reason to not be kind. Their hearts are good and their intentions pure, no matter the cause. This has been my dream since I was a child, to sit here on the edges of a pool with kelpies and faeries surrounding me."

"Then I am glad I could make your dreams come true." He said the words as if she had given him a gift.

She rolled off him, planting her butt back on the cold rocks with a small smile on her face. "Did you say something about breakfast?"

"In truth, I forgot it at the castle."

"Did you?" Sorcha burst into bright peals of laughter. "Stone, that was the entire point of this trip!"

"The entire point was introducing you to the kelpies," he grumbled. But he smiled that sideways smile she recognized.

She pressed a hand to her stomach. "It was a magical experience

I'm not likely to forget. Can I come back and see them again?"

"As long as you are with one of the Fae."

"Why?"

"Kelpies serve their purpose. They are not good at resisting temptation." He stood and held out a hand for her to take. "And you are most certainly tempting."

She grasped his hand and did her best not to wince as the crystals on his palm dug into her skin. "But they aren't dangerous to the Fae?"

"Not at all. They recognize us as one of their own. You, however, are human."

Sorcha tucked a strand of hair behind her pointed ears. "My father used to jest that I had faerie blood, because of these."

"If you had faerie blood, the kelpie would have known it. He tried to get you to climb atop his back."

"It didn't feel like he was trying to kill me." She glanced over at the male kelpie who flicked his seaweed tail in their direction. "It felt different from that."

"They have their purpose, and they know it well. He would have pulled you underneath the waves if you'd let him."

Sorcha didn't respond, but placed her hand on top of Stone's forearm and let him draw her from the magical place. Her mind stayed with the kelpies, wondering if he would have harmed her after all. It didn't seem like that was the intention.

Those dark green eyes had seemed almost sad. Sorcha couldn't believe it wanted to hurt her. Rather more that it simply wanted to show her something remarkable.

Flour burst into the air in great white clouds. The brownie it struck stared in horror at the mess covering her apron, then narrowed her mouse-like eyes and twitched her elongated snout.

"M'lady!"

Sorcha covered her mouth with a giggle and let the remaining flour drop back into its bag. "Sorry." She shrugged.

"You are not sorry! I watched you pick it up and throw it right at me."

"You said you needed flour."

"I said I needed help cooking. You're making a mess." The brownie tsked. "Whatever are we going to do with you, child?"

"Perhaps give me something to do rather than bother you."

"Is that your game?" The brownie sniffed. "Working around the kitchens is no place for a lady."

"I'm not a lady. I'm a street rat turned midwife who lives above a brothel. How many times do I have to tell you? Give me something to do with my hands!"

"I most certainly will not."

"You could use the help," Sorcha trailed the brownie around the table, tapping her soft head as she went. "I can bake bread, I can peel potatoes, I even used to make soup for the entire family. I think I could figure out how to make even more than that."

"I'm not doing it."

"Why are you so stubborn?"

The brownie whirled and brandished a wooden spoon. "Why are you so persistent? Go make yourself useful somewhere else, child!"

"Where? In the gardens? Cian's already chased me out *three* times today."

"Did he use the pitchfork?"

Sorcha rubbed her behind. "Yes."

"Good. That's the only way to get nasty little things like you to stay where they're told."

Sorcha groaned and plopped down on a chair. "What am I supposed to do then? Wait around until someone gets hurt? That's dangerous you know. I'll just start causing accidents to ease my own boredom."

"You wouldn't dare," the brownie said as she slipped off the apron and beat it with the spoon. "You're too kind for that."

"Yes, I am. But I have given it a good hard thought."

"Thoughts aren't actions, love. Now would you get out of my kitchen? I've got to make a day's worth of meals for all the faeries, and you aren't helping."

"But I want to help!"

Steam rose in the air from the big pot of soup the brownie was working on. She waved a hand and knives chopped the vegetables, measuring cups scooped up milk and salt, even the dish cloths Sorcha had ripped down rose back into their place.

Magic made everything so much easier. It felt almost like cheating.

Sorcha sighed and banged her forehead down on the center table.

"You're getting my table dirty."

"I'm resting," she murmured against the grain. "Isn't that what you all keep telling me to do?"

Oona's voice joined them, thoroughly amused. "Resting is what you're supposed to be doing regularly. Somehow you forget that."

"I've rested so much that I don't even want to sleep at night."

"Well, dearie, that's the life of a lady."

"Then lady's lives are boring, and I want my old one back."

Oona rubbed her back as she passed, leaning down to whisper in her ear, "We need to go back to your room. Now. But you cannot seem suspicious. No one can know."

Now that was exactly what Sorcha needed to spice up the day. She sat up straight and plastered a fake smile on her face. "Oona, I think I have a new idea for decorating my room. Would you come with me and suggest plants that might grow?"

"You want to plant things?"

"Of course, but I'll need your opinions. I can't understand what would grow here and what wouldn't."

The brownie turned and gave them both a suspicious glance. "What are you up to?"

"Nothing," Sorcha said. "I just want to redecorate."

"Oona, you be careful with that little human. She's a menace!"

Oona smiled, "Oh, she's a dear little thing. Just bored is all. I'll take her out of your hair, if it pleases you."

"It does," the brownie grumbled. "And make sure she doesn't come back any time soon!"

As if she would go back into that kitchen run by a stuck-up mouse.

Oona hustled her from the room with a hand on her back. Sorcha should have been alarmed at the speed they raced towards the portal, but excitement coursed through her veins.

"Don't you run the kitchens?"

"Not anymore. The master said that's only for people he can trust to not put poison in his meals."

"Rude!" Sorcha blurted. "He knows you're loyal."

"He does, but I betrayed him, dearie. It was the right thing to do. Now, open this wall so we can get inside. It's of the utmost importance."

The fear in Oona's voice rattled Sorcha. This wasn't an exciting trip, or even something that she would speak of again. Her brows furrowed, and she pressed the stone pommel hard.

"Is everything all right?" she asked as they raced into her bedroom. "Did something happen to one of the faeries?"

"They're fine. It's you I'm worried about. You've been summoned."

"Summoned?" Sorcha snorted. "By who? The master again?"

"By the king."

Her ears stopped working. All she could hear was a painful ringing sound. The crashing of bells and funeral dirges.

"The king?" she repeated. "How does the king know I exist?"

"I don't know, my dear. But he knows and you cannot refuse him"

"Who is the king of the Seelie now?"

"His Highness the Wise." Oona spit on the floor. "And may he rot forever in his castle. He does not respect the lesser Fae, and I wouldn't trust him as far as I could throw him. Pathetic excuse for a man. And dangerous. You must be careful with your words."

"I won't go." Sorcha shook her head. "He's not my king; I don't have to answer."

"He is everyone's king. If you don't go, he will send someone to hunt you down. The Wild Hunt is nothing compared to the creatures the king can call down upon you."

Then she had to go. There were no other options, but Sorcha still wracked her mind trying to figure out a way to escape.

"The king?" she repeated. "What would he want with me?"

"Midwives are scarce, and rumor has it his most favored concubine is pregnant."

"Concubine?" Sorcha repeated. "Does he not have a Queen?"

"Not this king," Oona muttered. "He has chosen to rule alone."

"Isn't that a bad idea?"

"It's a terrible idea! The Seelie queen has always tempered the king. She is the kindness to his justice, the heart of the people. She is giving and just. That has always been the way of it until His Highness the Wise took the throne."

Oona swung a cloak over Sorcha's shoulders, smoothing the fabric until it settled just right. Worry furrowed her leaf-like brow.

"You're making me worried," Sorcha said with a soft smile. She touched Oona's brow gently. "I won't do anything rash. And, as you remember, I'm a knowledgeable midwife."

"Don't say a thing about living on Hy-brasil," Oona advised. "He won't like that information very much. All we can do is hope his informants don't tell him how they found you."

"Why shouldn't I tell him about Hy-brasil?"

Oona guided her towards the carved portal and lifted her hands into the air. Delicate, twig fingers swung in the air as she called magic to life.

"No matter what you do, do not mention the master."

"Why can't I mention Stone? Or Hy-brasil?" Sorcha backed towards the portal and stared Oona down. "I need to know before I make a mistake!"

The cold touch of the portal slid up her ankle and calf before Oona bowed her head. "You'll figure it out when you get there, dearie. Just keep us all, and yourself, safe."

The pixie reached forward and shoved Sorcha's shoulder. She tumbled onto a cold marble floor, worry spinning her head.

She would know when she got there? What in the world did that mean?

"Ah," the cold voice made her freeze. "You must be the midwife."

It was so inhuman that she had no difficulty pinpointing to whom the voice belonged. The king himself waited on the other end of the portal, and Oona hadn't even mentioned that.

She placed her hands firmly on the floor, following the lines of gold in the polished stone all the way to the most extravagant throne she had ever seen. It was so tall it touched the ceilings, feathers and fairy wings turning it into a testament of Fae. Red billowing curtains stretched from the top all the way to the ground like theater curtains.

A man reclined in its center. This was all far too much show for a midwife, but the silver cape he wore trailed three men's length onto the floor. His white blond hair reached his waist, just touching the embroidered waistcoat he wore. Not a single stitch was out of place.

Guards stood at attention all around, their golden armor gleamed in the sunlight pouring from the open ceiling, nearly blinding her. They clutched swords the same height as Sorcha in their hands.

"Your Majesty," she said and bowed her head again. "I am the midwife."

"Good. I have use for your skills. Come with me, human." His voice was as cold as the bitter blizzards in the dead of winter.

She shivered and rose to her feet. "It is always a pleasure to provide services to those who require them."

"I'll keep that in mind when I need a new concubine." His feet entered her line of vision. Perfectly manicured shell-pale toes framed by his golden sandals. "Who can say no to a king?"

He lifted a hand, and her gaze locked upon his fingertips. Stained black as night, his nails were pointed. She had seen the cause before in a previous patient. By the time she arrived, the woman had already been comatose.

Opium addiction was a dangerous beast to tame.

The stained fingers slid underneath her chin and tilted her face to the light. She was hesitant to look him in the eye—kings could be quite strange—but Sorcha had never been cowed before.

She looked up and her world ended.

Stone stared back at her. Or not Stone, but what he might have been if crystals hadn't cracked through his skull.

Perfect cheekbones, flawless skin, full lips that she had seen quirk to the side so many times she knew each line and fold. His eyes frightened her most. Vivid blue, like the sky after a violent lightning storm and so familiar her heart hurt. Now, she saw cruelty reflected in those eyes. She missed the flawed fissures and frown lines surrounding them.

"You'll do," he said as if she wasn't about to faint. "Come with me."

Her feet stuck to the floor. He turned away from her with a flourish of his cape, and still she didn't move.

The king? How did he look exactly like Stone?

The Seelie King glanced over his shoulder and arched a perfect brow. "Are you so foolish that you do not understand an order when you hear one?"

Her Stone. Her kind, disfigured Stone was not reflected in this strange apparition before her. She suddenly understood why Stone reacted so violently when she mentioned family.

This man hadn't just stolen Stone's birthright. He'd taken a kingdom, a throne, mother, father, brother.

Even his face.

Oona's voice echoed in her mind. Do not let the king know where she came from. Do not mention the master. No wonder the pixie had been terrified.

Tears pricked her eyes. She had so misjudged Stone as a cruel man who saw no other solution than revenge for those who wronged him. This wasn't just a family squabble. His twin had ripped away his life and inserted himself into what was rightfully Stone's.

She wanted to smack the perfect face of the king. She wanted to drag her nails across his cheek, so he too might feel the pain and anguish he had caused.

But she couldn't. Sorcha needed to keep a cool mind to get through this alive. Under no circumstances would she risk Stone's life.

"My apologies, Your Majesty." She dipped into a curtsey, hiding her angry tears and red flush. "Please, lead me to the lady I might assist."

"You are far too presumptuous." He reached forward and fingered a lock of her hair. "I wonder what Fae calls you slave?"

It was too close. "No one, Your Majesty. I came from the human realm."

"And who let you into my kingdom?"

"I have always been close to the faeries. My mother left her offerings every week and passed along the respect in her bloodline."

"Respect." He let her hair drop as his lip curled in disgust. "Your kind has little understanding of the word."

The king turned, lifted an imperious hand, and walked away.

The air rang with clanging metal as the guards slammed their swords against their chest plates and followed their king. Sorcha tucked her arms against her sides and tried not to trip. The guards were so close to her that she could feel the cold air radiating from their armor.

It all seemed to be far more fanfare than necessary. They were all over two feet taller than Sorcha. Why did they need so many guards for just her? She wasn't likely to be able to fight one of them, let alone fifteen.

She caught glimpses of the Seelie castle from between the soldiers. It was as if the entire palace was made of light. White floors, golden ceilings, rays of sunshine that bounced until it hurt her eyes to look into some of the rooms.

How did they live like this? Everything was too perfect, too pristine. Her fingers itched to leave a smudged print on the glistening floor. Anything to prove that this place was real and lived in.

Sorcha glanced over her shoulder and caught sight of the faeries trailing after them. Brownies and hobgoblins, dressed in little more than burlap sacks. They held brooms and dustbins, sweeping up any dirt that might have fallen from their feet. More trailed after them with hand rags and water. Their gaunt faces were haunting and hungry.

His Highness the Wise, indeed.

Clenching her fists, Sorcha reminded herself where she was. This was his land, his palace, his kingdom. Although she wanted to free every faerie she found, she would only get herself killed. Or worse, reveal where Stone hid.

She didn't even know if he was hiding. Stone had spoken of revenge. Did he have a plan she didn't know about? Were the other faeries privy to such information?

Questions whirled through her mind until she could hardly think or breathe.

There were no answers in the pristine walls and sun-flooded rooms. She would have to wait until she returned home. Then she would corner Stone and force him to answer all the things he had not shared.

They marched through a pavilion, giant stone arches outlining the square. Flowers bloomed, larger than life and vibrantly colored, filling the air with a sticky sweet scent.

"Would you like a drink?" the king asked. "The honey from these flowers are said to be the most rare and exotic treat."

"No, thank you. I am not thirsty." She would not take any chances.

"Food? We have many things you may never have dreamed of before."

"No. I ate before I arrived."

A grin spread across his sculpted lips. "As smart as you are brave. You are an intriguing little human."

"I know the ways of the Fae," she said. "It is an honor to serve when I can, but I do not wish to linger here."

"You have someone to go home to?"

"No."

"You're lying." He licked his lips as if she had provided a most delicious delicacy.

"I rarely lie."

"I can taste it in the air. Humans are so easy to read. Your eyes dilate, your chest heaves with your guilty breath. You are a book that I can peel open and read every word."

She hated him. She hated every dark word that dripped from his tongue, because she knew he was right. He was nothing like his brother and that frightened her more than anything else.

They walked through the pavilion, and he rapped his knuckles against a marble door.

"My love," he called out. "I have brought you a gift."

"I do not wish for a gift!"

"You will want this one."

"Please, my king. I do not feel well today."

"Precisely." He shoved the door open and nodded towards Sorcha. "Enter."

"She does not seem to wish for visitors."

"It is not her choice. My concubines obey to my every whim and fulfil my every desire. I wish for her to be seen, and you will ensure she is healthy."

Sorcha curtseyed. "Then your wish is my command."

As she passed, he reached out and grabbed her chin. "If she

becomes ill after you touch her, no one will be able to hide you from my wrath. I will peel your skin back inch by inch, and I will keep you alive through it all."

"I wouldn't dare harm someone who needed my help."

Sorcha glared at him, meeting his gaze without flinching. This man could threaten her all he wished. She refused to bow to a man who treated his loved ones like slaves.

The king dropped his hand, chuckling. "I will leave three guards by the door. If they hear anything unusual, even the slightest of sounds, they will bring your head to me on a platter."

"I am doubtful my head would satisfy your pallet," she growled. "Might I suggest a more tasteful organ?"

The grin on his face was as feral as her words. The king turned, snapped his fingers, and left with half of his guards. More than three remained standing at attention.

Good. Perhaps the king realized just how dangerous a little human midwife could be.

"At ease, gentlemen," she muttered to the guards. "I wouldn't want you to faint in all that hot armor."

Sorcha didn't wait to see what kind of startled expressions they tossed her way. She stepped into Elva's room and slammed the door behind her. Let them rot while they waited to see what she might do. Sorcha didn't care. If they served such a horrible king, then they deserved the same fate.

Smoke curled around her waist like tendrils of fingers. Frowning, Sorcha turned and peered into the bright, sunlit room.

She had never been inside an opium den and had never desired to do so. Now, she knew what they looked like.

Red velvet hung in great sheets from their ceiling, tangling with golden wire twisted into leaves. Gemstones hung in sparkling tendrils from above. From floor to ceiling, smoke coiled around all the opulence.

Hookahs littered the floor, laying atop mountains of pillows and spilling liquid to the floor. Three faerie attendants lay stretched across the ground. Bark skin made them blend into the ground, their lips and fingers stained black by opium tea.

"Elva?" Sorcha whispered, using the faerie's true name on a whim. "I am a midwife."

"Midwife?" The bed rustled. The faerie woman pulled the curtains aside. "What are you doing here?"

"Your king summoned me."

Elva ripped the curtains to the floor. Her grace disappeared under the haze of drugs. "You are in grave danger."

"I am here to help you."

"If he invited you here, then he knows precisely who you are. And he knows where you come from."

The words made Sorcha freeze. The faerie had so many drugs in her system, that surely she wasn't revealing she knew about Hy-brasil. Or did she?

"I come from the human realm," Sorcha said. "I am here to make certain you are healthy. It is what your king wishes."

The faerie fell against Sorcha. "You do not understand. You do not know him. He wants to hurt me, so he brought you here. You need to go."

"What is wrong? Elva, you need to speak to me. If there is something I might do to help you—"

Black-tipped fingers pressed against Sorcha's mouth. The faerie's eyes were wild. "No. No, there is nothing you can do to save me."

"Save you?" Sorcha repeated. "Do you need saving?"

"What could be done for me was lost long ago, little human."

The panic made Sorcha nervous. She held the much larger woman in her arms and pressed Elva's head into her shoulders. Tears soaked through the fabric on her shoulder.

Squeezing her eyes shut, Sorcha pressed closer until their bellies touched. It had been nearly a month since she had seen Elva.

Smooth stomach met smooth stomach.

"Are you not pregnant?" Sorcha whispered.

"He wrapped me in silk and velvet. He called me his love and tore me from everything I loved."

"Where is your child, Elva?"

"Gone. With everything else."

"What happened?"

"Life." The faerie woman pulled back, swiping at her tears in anger. "Life for a Tuatha dé Danann royal. There is nothing you can do to help me, midwife. I made a deal with a devil and take a snake to bed each night."

"Elva—"

"I can help you."

"What?" Sorcha shook her head. "*I* do not need help. I need to make sure you are healthy, and perhaps that is why your king brought me here."

"He did not bring you here for me. He brought you here for a lesson to be learned. He does not believe that me losing the child was merely because it was my first and because faeries do not carry children well. You are his scapegoat. His reasoning behind the loss of his child."

"I will not give you anything to prevent childbirth." Fear twisted around Sorcha's tongue, slowing her words into a slur.

"We both know that is the truth. But he has never cared for the truth."

What a sad existence this woman lived. Sorcha tucked her arm around Elva's side and nudged her back towards the bed. It was unclear whether the woman was speaking from the heart or a drug-induced panic.

Either way, Sorcha's job was to heal. She couldn't mend the rift between Elva and her king. She couldn't even touch the pain that stained the woman's soul. All she could do was get her settled in bed and quiet her mind.

She tucked the faerie into bed and smoothed her hair from her sweat slicked forehead. "Where are you from, Elva?"

"Cathair an Tsolas."

"The city of light?" Sorcha smiled. "I've heard of the legends. It is a place constantly filled with the sun."

"It sparkles when you look upon it."

"Tell me of your city, Elva. I dearly love stories."

Elva whispered tales of a magical city filled with Tuatha dé Danann and faerie subjects. She laced legends Sorcha recognized with truths that spoke of pristine streets and people wearing the most outlandish costumes.

All the while, Sorcha cleaned. She lifted the dryads from their stupor and handed them out the door to the guards. The men seemed surprised that she would dare lay a hand upon any faerie.

"Not a word," she growled at them. "Take these ladies back to their quarters, or where ever you put them."

"They stay with the concubine."

"And I say they go. If you wish to argue, please tell your king to meet me here. Otherwise, put those women where they can sleep off the opium."

The guards stared at each other, shrugged, and two left with the faeries tucked under their arms.

Sorcha closed the door once more. Elva's privacy could be contained within these walls. No guards needed to gossip any more than they already were going to. The king and his favored concubine both relied upon opium. Enough that their fingers were stained with its poison.

The story of a beautiful city filled the air. It twisted in the smoke and filtered out the windows as Sorcha threw them open. Fresh air would do a world of good for this room.

She piled the pillows against the far wall and placed her fists upon her hips. There wasn't much else she could do in such a fine room. This wasn't built to be a comfortable living place, but a feast for the senses.

"You don't live in a very practical bedroom," she murmured. "Pretty it might be, but useful it is not."

Elva didn't stop mumbling her story. The words seemed to ground her. The opiates were slowly filtering out of her system as Sorcha puttered about.

She stuck her finger in a small groove in the wall. A door popped open, revealing what looked to be all the items she would need to clean.

"Convenient," Sorcha said. A bucket of water waited for her, along with a mop that looked as though it had never been used before. Why keep something in a closet if it would not be used?

Faeries. They would never make sense to her.

She poured the water onto the floor and scrubbed stains and smells. "*Elva.* Enough with the story, my dear, I think I know enough to believe I lived there."

"Humans can't live there."

"No? That's a shame. We're not all that bad."

"I'm beginning to see that." The fog had cleared from Elva's voice. Now, she sounded more ashamed than babbling. "What are you doing?"

"Cleaning."

"Yes, but why?"

"Because there is hookah oil smudged into your floor, and the entire place reeks of opium." Sorcha paused to blow a red curl from her forehead. "Don't you ever have anyone scrub the floors?"

"None other than you."

"Hmph. If you aren't going to do it yourself, you should have someone clean at least every once and a while."

"Why not you?"

"I'm not for hire." Nor would she ever be. The longer she was in this place, the less Sorcha liked it. How had Stone grown up in this place?

The thought filled her mind until it was all she could think of. Stone had lived here. He had grown up here. The king was his brother. And the king's concubine sat only a few feet from her.

Moving the mop once more, Sorcha stared down at her work. "Elva?"

"Yes?"

"Did you know that the king has a twin brother?"

"It's blasphemy to even mention that the king has a sibling."

"Does that mean you won't tell me about him?"

Elva rolled onto her side to watch Sorcha work. "I knew him."

"The king?"

"His twin."

"What was he like?" For once, she could speak about Stone with someone who wouldn't hide the truth from her. There were enough opiates in Elva's system to loosen her tongue. This might be the moment when she finally figured out his story.

"He was an impressive man. The king and queen took different routes to raising their sons. The eldest boy tended towards the wild and feral faeries. They feared he might turn Unseelie, so they convinced him to train his mind and body as a warrior. He was the most fearsome creature who ever lived."

"You speak as if he no longer exists." Sorcha couldn't clean and listen at the same time. She leaned the mop against the wall and sat down on a stool. "Is he dead?"

"Gone. And if you're lost to this world, you're as good as dead."

"Where?"

"Banished. Some say he still lives on Hy-brasil, but I have many contacts there. If he lived, I would know."

"Do you think he was murdered?"

"I wouldn't put it past the king to do everything in his power to keep the throne. His twin was the favored son. He was perfect until his brother destroyed him."

"So I've heard," Sorcha murmured. "You said you knew him?"

"As best as anyone could. He was older than I and always fighting the Unseelie. There was something wild in him that could not be tamed. He frightened me. He frightened most of the faerie women, but we all wanted him. You know, we used to call him the red stag?"

"The red stag? Why?"

"There was something in him that wasn't faerie at all. Something that spoke of beasts in the wood, whispers on the wind, magic in his blood that didn't come from the Tuatha dé Danann. He was dangerous, and I think his brother saw that in him."

Sorcha hung on every word. She leaned forward until she perched on the very edge of the stool. "What did the king think his brother would do?"

"He would change everything," Elva whispered. "He didn't see the lesser Fae as creatures made to work. He saw them as people, valued them as soldiers and friends. That is not the Seelie way."

"Is change such a bad thing?"

"I wouldn't know."

Sorcha's heart broke for this shell of a woman. Her feet carried her to the other woman's side. With as much gentleness as she could muster, Sorcha tucked her back underneath the covers.

"Try to sleep," she murmured.

"Will it help?"

"I don't know if anything will help. But I find that a good night's rest and quiet dreams always seem to ease the soul."

"My dreams are all nightmares." Elva turned onto her side, away from Sorcha's kind hands. "But at least I know that nightmares aren't happening, no matter how tragic they are to experience."

Sorcha stayed until Elva's breathing slowed into the steady rhythm of sleep.

What had this woman endured? What had they all endured?

She stood slowly, taking care to not shake the bed. They all had such tragic stories, such heartbreaking lives where hardships did not end.

Humans struggled throughout their entire existence. Poverty, death, illness, were all things that humans understood came with their humanity. Sorcha had never thought that faeries would also struggle. They were spirits of nature. Surely, they would live better lives?

She had been wrong.

"You got her to sleep?" The king's voice was quiet as he entered. "I don't remember the last time she laid herself down without a fight."

"She needed comfort."

"And you think I'm incapable of providing that," he murmured as he sat on the edge of her bed.

"It is not my place to judge, Your Majesty." But they both heard the hidden words beneath her quiet tones. Yes, she blamed him. She blamed him for a lot more than just Elva's unhappiness.

He stared down at the beautiful faerie he called concubine. There was something about his expression that made Sorcha feel as though she were intruding. He didn't glare, or grasp at her flesh. He simply stared at her with a soft expression and followed the line of her cheek with his gaze.

"I love her," he said. "I love her so much it hurts to breathe. But that is one of the hardest things about being king. If I marry her, I put her in harm's way. If I leave her as concubine, she stays safe, but she hates me."

Sorcha's tongue got ahead of her mind, words slipping from between her lips without permission. "I don't think it is the title that offends her."

"No," he chuckled. "No, it's everything. I am not my brother. I do not see the lesser Fae as creatures capable of having positions of power. I do not believe giving them free will benefits our people. The old ways have worked for a very long time. Changing things leads to unanticipated endings, and I will not risk the future of our people on the dreams of others."

"I asked her if change was a bad thing, and she said she didn't know. Now I ask you the same, King of the Seelie Fae. Do you believe change is bad?"

He looked at her with a troubled expression wrinkling his brow. "The Fae are unused to change. Perhaps you would be better suited to answer such a question."

"I think controlling the future with an iron grasp only limits the possibilities of tolerance and positive change."

"You are far too wise to be human."

"I am not Fae," she said.

"You are something else entirely." He looked back down at Elva, fingering the edge of her blanket before standing. "I owe you a boon."

"A boon? From the King of the Seelie? That does not seem a wise choice to offer."

"And yet I offer it freely. Easing her troubled soul is worth more than just a boon, but I do not believe you will use such a gift in a way I will agree with."

He held out his hand for her to take. Sorcha raised a brow and hesitantly grasped his hand in hers.

She wanted to trust him if only because he looked like Eamonn. His palm was smooth against her calloused fingers. No crystals bit into her skin. No scars abraded the sensitive flesh of her wrist. He was perfect. Everything Stone was not.

Sorcha shivered. "Then I accept your boon with the understanding that I do not agree with your choices, King."

"You are not the first to disagree with me and you will not be the last. Know that I am grateful for your assistance, and will not forget it."

"I hope someday that is useful." She pulled away from him and scooped up her cloak.

"As do I, little midwife," he said. "For I fear you and I will face each other on different sides of a battlefield someday."

Sorcha glanced over her shoulder, hand on the door to her freedom. "Have you consulted with anyone to see your future?"

"I know my future without having to ask any of the Unseelie their opinions. Both of my endings result in killing myself. Either this flesh, or that of my mirror."

Something inside her clicked like a key turning in a lock.

He knew.

He knew she lived with Stone. He knew where she came from, and still he ordered her here.

And now he was letting her go.

"Why?" she whispered.

"The end will come whether you are involved in this story or not, midwife. I believe it will be far more interesting with your intervention."

"Why is it that all Fae seem to think that their own future is a story?" Sorcha said. "There is no *story* here. No one will sing of two brothers who destroyed each other!"

"How can you know that for certain?" The king waved a bejeweled hand. "There are stranger stories told to this day. Keep your head up, little midwife. Your journey has only just begun."

"I want no part in this story."

"You're already in it. War is coming. Tell my brother to enjoy his last few days of life."

CHAPTER TWELVE
THE HUNTER'S MOON

"Where are we going?" Sorcha asked. A blindfold covered her face, the velvet soft against her skin.

Stone had walked into her bedroom with it in his hands, a sheepish grin on his face. He refused to tell her where they were going, but she also refused to stop asking.

"Sorcha, just let it be a surprise."

"I can't do that. I want to know."

"You'll find out!" he said with a chuckle.

"But not soon enough!"

She didn't think he knew about her recent escapade into Seelie. He certainly hadn't mentioned it.

Sorcha had scrubbed her skin for an hour before she saw him. Clean water and lemon verbena washed away the scent of faeries and anything else he might have recognized from home.

Weeks passed. Sorcha took to begging him every night to return to the mainland with her. Sometimes, she thought he might bend. Other times, all she did was anger him.

He grew angry so easily.

But tonight, he was happy. Pleased, almost. The surprise he planned obviously meant something to him.

"Stone," she begged, "I want to know!"

"And you will, little human. Just not yet."

Sorcha tried to figure out where they were going. She knew each turn of the castle by heart, but got lost when he spun her in circles.

"What are you doing?" she asked with a laugh. "You'll make me *dizzy*."

"I don't want you to guess what direction we're going."

"I wasn't tracking our steps."

"You most certainly were. I could hear you mumbling under your breath." He leaned close, breath tickling her ear and sending shivers down her spine. "I refuse to let you ruin this surprise."

"I don't like surprises."

"You'll like this one."

He placed his hands on her shoulders and guided her down the hallways. Each step felt more and more unfamiliar until he finally tugged her to a stop.

His hands were so big. They covered her shoulders and dipped into the hollows of her collarbone. She was intensely aware of the soft circles he drew just beneath the winged bones. He seemed to stroke her skin without thought.

"You have been so kind to my people. And you have made a lasting impression upon all of us. I wanted to do something for you."

"Thank you," she said. "I don't deserve anything special though. I hope you didn't go out of your way."

"We only spent a few nights on it."

"A few nights? Stone!"

"My name is not Stone."

"I refuse to call you master."

He chuckled, hands sliding across her shoulders and tangling in the heavy weight of her hair. "Someday, I would like to hear the word cross your lips just to see how unnatural it sounds."

"You won't like it if I ever called you master."

"No, I wouldn't. I've come to expect you to surprise me, Sorcha. It would be a shame for you to fall in line like the rest."

The knot at the back of her head pulled, and the velvet fell free.

She gasped in delight. The throne room glimmered with light. The ceiling, free from cobwebs and dust, had a mirrored finish that reflected the candlelight. Smooth marble and great swaths of red fabric made the room seem fit for royalty.

Sorcha couldn't care less for the grand appearance of the room. It was the people her eyes locked upon and the sight of them that made her knees weak.

Every faerie on the isle had dressed in their finest. They did not decorate themselves with silk or velvet, but clean clothing and woolen cloaks. Their faces scrubbed clean, they had tied their hair in intricate braids.

They were not a people of royalty. They were not kings and queens, but men and women who lived on the land.

"They look out of place," she said with a chuckle. "And they are the most beautiful things I've ever seen."

"Good. You'll be seeing a lot of them tonight."

"Not for me," Sorcha turned with a worried expression. "You didn't bring them all together for me, did you, Stone?"

He winked. "You have lost your memory coming here, haven't you, Sorcha? As much as I would love to force my people to bend a knee to your beauty, that is not why they are here. It's Samhain."

"Already?"

She'd left home in spring, and it was Samhain already? Sorcha felt as though she'd only just washed up on the shore, and now autumn knocked upon the door of the human world.

The tangled mass of people parted, and Oona marched towards them. Her wings were on full display, red markings painted from her lip to chin.

"Child of the human world, would you do the honors?"

"The honors?" Sorcha tilted her head. "Do you celebrate the same way my people do?"

"Your people? Or your mother's people?"

She grinned. "My mother's people. My father and siblings were never ones to celebrate the old ways."

"Then light the fires for us, child, and honor the dead."

Sorcha tangled her fingers with Stone's for a moment, squeezing his hand. She looked over her shoulder as she descended the stairs. His gaze caught hers, pride and honor reflected in their depths.

"Thank you," Sorcha said.

"I knew it would be important to you."

"How?"

He shrugged. "I just knew."

Her fingers slid from his, trailing along the crystals of his palm and whispering across their twin callouses. She walked backwards down the stairs with a soft smile on her face. "And will you be partaking in the festivities, my king?"

Stone's jaw dropped and Sorcha reveled in his surprise. He seemed unable to speak. A state she found surprisingly suitable to her tastes. With a wicked grin on her face, she turned to Oona and followed her to the altar.

"The Wild Hunt is tonight?" Sorcha asked. "Are we safe here?"

"This is not the Otherworld, but it is not the human world either. The Wild Hunt does not touch upon these shores," Oona replied. "But we still honor the ride and dream of seeing their might once again."

"We won't even see them?" Sorcha had hoped to catch a glimpse. Now that the ointment had cleared her eyes of glamour, it would be a treat to see what the faeries saw. The Wild Hunt, led by their great horned king, had always been fascinating.

Her disappointment was great, but it was also a blessing. She didn't know what Cernunnos, the leader of the Wild Hunt, would do if he saw a human in the faerie prison.

Thick branches with green leaves still clinging on their twigs created an altar where Eamonn's throne usually sat. The roots of the tree wrapped in a circle on the floor, creating a base that was strong and steady. Offerings piled near to overflowing all around it. Milk, honey, and more food than any Tuatha dé Danann could devour.

"It is a good offering," she said.

"This year has been better than most. We have much to be thankful for."

"As do I." She reached for a goblet filled to the brim with wine and poured it on the roots. "To many years with family and friends, may we all last the night without nightmares and the next year without pain or strife. I thank my ancestors, the gods above, and the gods below. We come to this place to celebrate Samhain and seek shelter from the Wild Hunt."

Something stirred within her breast. A memory, or an age-old knowledge passed down through generations. She remembered the words as if her mother whispered them in her ear.

Sorcha lifted a finger and traced runes into the air. "Spirits of the East and Air, I welcome you into our circle and bid you well tidings. On this sacred night of Samhain, come dance with us."

Faeries stirred behind her, pixies lifting into the air and buffeting her spine with their breeze. Her curls blew over her shoulders. Blue light lifted from the runes she drew. She gasped. Never before had she seen a Samhain ritual like this before.

Leaning forward, she struck flint and steel to light the candle at the base of the altar. "Spirits of the South and Fire, I welcome you to feast with us on this sacred night."

The candle flared, and the air turned hot. She told herself not to wipe at the sweat on her brow, that it would insult the faeries who enjoyed the heat.

She dipped her fingers into the goblet to her left and flicked the droplets of water. "Spirits of the West and Water, I welcome you to drink and be merry with us tonight. Join our revelries on this sacred Samhain eve.”

The air turned muggy. Her dress stuck to her back, and her hair felt heavy with the weight of water in the air. A kelpie snorted although she had not seen any in the crowd.

A small pot of dirt was the last and final piece of her ritual. She rubbed the dirt between her fingers, feeling the ancient knowledge it held.

“Spirits of the North and Earth, I welcome you to this hall and ask that you tell us stories from ages past. Speak easy and loosen thy tongue on this sacred night.”

She felt the powerful cheer of the faeries before it made her ears ache. Sorcha grinned, unable to keep her own happiness from bubbling forth. This was a good night. A blessed night. A peaceful night.

Her chest squeezed tight and her eyes lost focus. There was one more candle that should be at this altar.

She reached forward, traced the outline of leaves that died and withered as she watched. She struck the flint and steel one more time, lighting the dead tree on fire.

The faeries fell silent.

“I welcome thee, Morrighan, and your sisters to our fold. Lady of Fate, War, and Fear, you are welcome within these walls.” Sorcha lifted a goblet of wine, tilted her head back, and closed her eyes. “Morrighan— hail and welcome!”

A deafening cheer followed her words, but she did not hear it. Instead, Sorcha heard a pleased chuckle and smelled the wheatgrass scent of horses.

“Well done,” Macha murmured. “Feast and stay safe from the Wild Hunt.”

Oona wrapped an arm around Sorcha’s shoulders and gave her a shake. “Well done! It’s almost as if you were born a druid priestess!”

“A what?” Sorcha opened her eyes in shock. “What did you call me?”

"Oh, dearie, you have *druid* in you. I knew there was something strange about you. Only a priestess would know that ritual. And someday I'll ask who taught it to you, but for now, drink!"

Another goblet of wine pressed into her hand. Holding two, she watched Oona dance a merry jig towards Cian who watched with a sour expression. When the pixie reached him, he sighed and held up his arms. They spun in wild circles around other Fae until everyone in the hall was dancing.

Sorcha stood with her hands full, watching the merriment with shock. A bubble of laughter escaped her lips, effervescing until she couldn't contain it any longer.

A crystal hand plucked one of the goblets from her grasp. "Well met, priestess."

"I am no priestess," she shook her head. "My mother may have been, I'm realizing now. It was from her book that I gathered that knowledge."

"That kind of precision comes from years of practice."

"I can honestly say that I have never performed a Samhain ritual quite like that. Do you think it's because we're closer to the Otherworld?" She gulped a mouthful of wine as if that might help clear her head.

"No. I think it's because druids pass knowledge through maternal lines. And because you were born a priestess."

"My mother always wished I was a changeling, that faerie blood would have been something to be proud of."

"Your mother wouldn't wish you to be a changeling, they have sad lives. We've already confirmed you're not Fae. Perhaps there are a few things we might consider."

"We?" Sorcha glanced up.

His ocean eyes stared down at her, curiosity and kindness reflected in their depths. "If you are so inclined to find out who you are, I offer my services."

"What help can you provide?"

"There is a library."

"Here?"

"Yes."

Sorcha placed her hands on her hips. "When were you going to tell me?"

"When you asked."

"And if I never asked?"

Stone's lips quirked to the side. "Then you would never know."

"You are a cruel man," she said as she handed her goblet to a passing faerie. "Do you dance?"

"I did."

"That sounds as if you no longer dance."

"It is no longer graceful," he patted his hip. "The crystals prevent much movement. Fighting is one thing, grace is innate when you're fighting for your life. Dancing does not come naturally."

"Good," she said. Sorcha lifted her skirts high enough to show her feet and pointed. "I have two left feet. I cannot dance well at all, and it's very likely that you will be thankful for the crystals because otherwise I might crush your toes."

"I don't have crystals on my toes."

"Then you will when I'm done with you." She winked. "Perhaps you would care to look at your dance card for a free space where I might write my name?"

He arched a brow. "Can you even pen your name?"

"Not all humans are illiterate." She shook her head. "You know I can read, Stone."

The growl that rumbled from his throat sent shivers down her spine.

Sorcha gasped as broad hands slid around her waist and pulled her against his chest. She splayed her fingers against his heat. His legs framed hers, inner thighs pressed against her hips. Her stomach was flush against his—crystals biting through the thin fabric.

"This is hardly proper," she whispered.

"Humans do not dance as the Fae do."

"This is how you dance?"

"Well, not particularly."

She glanced up and caught the sparkling laughter that danced in his eyes. He cocked his head to the side, lifted a hand, and gently tucked a strand of hair behind her ear. His fingertips were feather-light against her skin. He traced a circle against her neck, trailed down the slope of her shoulder and arm, lifted her hand until it rested against his bicep.

She couldn't breathe, couldn't even think as he followed the same path on the other side of her body and curled his fingers around her hand. His other palm flexed against her spine.

"This is the proper way to dance with a woman," he said.

"Is it?" Sorcha heard the breathless quality to her voice, the sultry notes that dripped from her tongue.

Heat flashed in his gaze, a blush spreading across his cheeks. "Perhaps you have never danced with a man."

"Boys, yes. A man?" Sorcha's eyes followed the ragged edge of crystals, the barbaric braid swaying from the peak of his head to his waist, the linen tunic belted by sheep skin. "Never a man such as you."

He pressed gently against her spine, and they spun into the crowd. Faeries waltzed around them as a band struck up a tune.

Sorcha would remember none of the fluttering colors and magic sparking in the air. How could she? He stared at her as if she were the world. As if she plucked the stars from the sky and wove them into the strands of her hair.

Stone used his body like a weapon. He spun her in circles until she didn't know which way was up and which way was down. He only stopped when she stumbled, falling into his arms.

She liked being pressed against his chest far too much. He was safe, and broad, and so much more than any man she had ever met before.

She said something, it could have been anything, she didn't know what. But he tilted his head back and laughed so hard that the corded muscles of his neck stood out in stark relief. The crystals gaped at the wound caused by his hanging, and she couldn't see the disfigurement anymore.

He was beautiful. An instrument of power and symbol of strength.

Stone spun her into his arms, pressing his cheek against the top of her head before unraveling her. He pressed her spine against his chest, dipping until he could whisper in her ear, "How did you know I was to be king?"

"You carry yourself as if you were meant to rule."

"And Oona told you."

He would taste the lie, so she said nothing and glanced over her shoulder. "Does it really matter how I know, Stone?"

His expression turned so fierce that she thought he might crush her. Instead, he traced his finger down her cheek and pressed his forehead to hers. "Eamonn."

"What?" she gasped.

"My name is Eamonn."

Before she could comment on such a gift, he spun them in wide circles around the room until she tossed her head back and laughed. This was perfect. Every single moment was perfect and sweet.

And he was perfect. Every broken bit of him was perfect for her.

He had brought together all the people who meant something to her. Every faerie who had given her gifts, kindness, laughter, peace. They were all here in their finest outfits, and it didn't matter that they had no silk nor velvet to share.

Their hearts beat as one. Samhain had never been celebrated by such a strong family of people.

They passed the day in each other's arms. Every now and then, they would stop for food and drink. Sorcha's feet ached, but she didn't want to stop dancing. So she would stuff her face, tease the faeries she saw along the way, but she never strayed far from his side.

There was an impending sense of doom, something she couldn't explain or understand. Although this night felt as though they found each other for the very first time, tomorrow was uncertain.

Her siblings' voices whispered in her mind. This was how a woman became a mistress. Fall in love with the wrong man, and disaster was sure to follow. He should be a king! And Sorcha? She was a midwife from so far away that he wouldn't even know the name of her town.

Sorcha brushed the voices aside, not wanting to worry about the future tonight.

Another voice joined her siblings. *Tell my brother to enjoy his last few days.* She couldn't tell Stone—Eamonn, she reminded herself—that she'd met his twin. She refused to issue a warning she wasn't certain held any weight.

She had a boon from the king of the Seelie Fae. If he wanted to kill his brother, then she would use her boon against that. Eamonn would live. They could stay on this isle until the end of time.

And then the blood beetles would devour her family.

It was so easy to forget reality here. She understood the many stories of men and women who spent centuries in the Otherworld only to return and find everything gone. Life was so easy here. There were no responsibilities, no people to take care of, only herself and her own whims.

Perhaps someday she would forget the echoes of her family. Tonight, she certainly would. But tomorrow morning, Sorcha knew she would remember every bit of the guilt she sewed into her bones.

The music quieted as the sun dipped below the horizon. Her dress stuck to her skin, and her hair billowed around her like a red cloud. She leaned against Eamonn's side and stood at the window staring at the bright streaks of colored clouds.

"Have you enjoyed your Samhain, m'lady?" he asked.

"I believe this was the most enjoyable celebration I have had the pleasure of joining."

"What was your favorite part?"

"The company."

"Ah," he chuckled and scratched the back of his neck. "Present company excluded, I would hope."

"Hope? Why would you hope for exclusion from that grouping?"

Eamonn spread his hands wide. The pink light of the sunset played off the crystals. "I'm hardly fit to grace the halls of lords and ladies. The dogs may enter, but the wolves must stay beyond the door."

She hated hearing him speak of himself like that. So many years of torment and disapproval from family and friend led to self-hatred. She had seen it in herself.

It was so much easier to say he was wrong and ignore the emotions reflected in herself.

Sorcha reached forward and intertwined her fingers with his. "Even wolves can be tender, loyal, and brave-hearted. I would rather run with them in the wild than paint my face and try to blend into the walls."

He squeezed her fingers. "I forget who I speak with."

"A midwife?"

"A druid priestess with far more power than she admits." He pressed his lips against the backs of her knuckles. "I'd like to show you something."

"Another surprise? Eamonn, I might faint away if you keep up with this. I'm convinced someone has stolen your body and masquerades as a gentleman in your flesh."

His eyes flashed. "I enjoy the sound of my name upon your lips far too much."

A shiver trailed down her spine. "Then I shall endeavor to use it upon every occasion."

"Come with me."

She trailed after him into the depths of the castle. Past cobwebbed corners, stained glass windows dimming with the sun, and hidden alcoves where mist gathered. Up a stairwell she didn't recognize that curved dangerously with no railing. Out onto a catwalk so high that the clouds tangled in her skirts.

"Where are we?" she shouted into the wind.

"Are you afraid?"

"No! This is beautiful!"

His grin flashed as the stars blinked to life behind him. "Wild thing that you are, fear has no name for you, does it?"

"Fear is an enemy to battle. I know her well."

"Do not fall."

"Will you catch me if I do?"

"I will fly upon the wings of the Wild Hunt if need be."

She burst into laughter. "I thought faeries couldn't lie?"

He tugged her off the edge of the catwalk and into a hidden corner. The heat of his chest seared through the fabric of her dress. "I do not lie. If I had to call the Wild Hunt to save you, I would."

"I think I would fall to my death before you could manage."

"I'd find another way."

Sorcha grinned and shook her head. "What do you want to show me?"

Eamonn pressed his back against the wall and pushed. The sparkle in his eyes caught her attention before she noticed the wall had turned into a door. A warm glow lit the frame with orange light.

He pushed harder to reveal the fur rugs and walls lined with books.

"Oh," she whispered. "Is this the library?"

"No. These are my quarters."

"Yours?" Sorcha arched a brow. "Just what kind of woman do you think I am, Eamonn?"

She knew he would growl at her use of his name. She wanted to hear it again and again.

The deep baritone rumbled from deep within his chest. It was the call of a lion to its mate, the quiet huff of a stag in the forest, the gurgle of water underneath ice.

He reached for her, yanking her into his chest until her hands splayed against him. "Say it again."

"I have no need to call you by name."

"Say it."

"You brought me here for a reason, Eamonn." Sorcha grinned at the quake she felt behind her palms. "Why are we here?"

The disappointed breath that blew across her face smelled of mint. "You are temptation, little priestess."

"Hardly. I wasn't raised a druid."

"You don't need to be. Druid is in your blood, and I'm curious to see what you think of this surprise."

He didn't let go of her entirely. Eamonn slid his hands down her arms and tangled his fingers with hers. Silent, he guided her towards a bookcase and released his hold.

The tome he pulled from the shelf sparkled in the light. Its deep green cover and gold threaded words wavered under her gaze.

"Is it glamoured?" she asked.

"Not that I know of."

It was changing in front of her eyes. The green dappled as if sunlight was striking it through leaves. The letters shifted and moved until she couldn't read what the title was, let alone who had written it.

Eamonn held it out for her to take.

She stroked the spine, something inside her calling out to treat it like a beloved pet. It creaked as she opened the pages. Ink blots stained most of them, hand drawn pictures of herbs and instructions filling the parchment paper.

"Who wrote this?"

"I don't know. There's nothing on the pages."

"What?" Sorcha glanced up. "There's plenty on the pages. There's just no signature."

"I can't see anything written in that book. I have tried for years, but no matter how much I try, the pages remain blank."

"Interesting." With her nose buried, she meandered towards the chairs. "There's much here I've never considered. Mugwort, for example, is rarely used to cure nightmares. It's curious that it suggests using it while chanting… something. I can't read that part."

"You aren't quite ready for it yet, I imagine."

"Why?" Sorcha wrinkled her nose. "Why wouldn't I be ready for knowledge?"

"For the same reason I was not ready to be king." He plucked the book from her grasp and set it down on a small table. "We all must grow before we take on responsibility."

"You would make a good king."

"So you say, but I was not ready as a young man."

He circled her. Sorcha knew the expression in his eyes. The darkened edges, the attention to detail, the hunger that she had only seen in a wolf. She was being hunted, and she didn't know whether she wanted to flee or embrace the danger.

"I see many qualities in you that would make a good king. I don't know if anyone is ever ready to take on such a daunting task."

"How did you know I was meant to be king?"

"That's my little secret."

She felt his breath fan across the back of her neck. "I don't like secrets."

"Would you prefer that I lie?"

"I never prefer lies."

"Then I am afraid you must resolve yourself to be disappointed, Eamonn."

Sorcha stood perfectly still, fear locking her knees and curiosity stilling her breath. At the sound of his name, a single finger touched her throat. Her breath caught.

His fingernail scratched just enough to leave a mark as he trailed it down her neck and to her shoulder. He hesitated for a brief moment before hooking it underneath the yellow fabric of her dress.

He was giving her time to tell him to stop, she realized. A voice in her head screamed to leave, to run, that a faerie could not be trusted. But her heart knew what she wanted.

Him.

Sorcha sighed as the fabric of her dress slipped down her shoulder, baring milky white skin dotted with freckles. He groaned and traced patterns between the beauty marks.

"Do you know what they used to call me, Sorcha?"

"No." She couldn't think, let alone decipher what his words meant. Not when he was stroking the bare skin of her shoulder and the cold breeze brushed past her sensitive arms.

"The Red Stag. I used my blade like the antlers of the beast, leaving wounds dotting across my enemies' flesh. I carved my namesake in skin more times than I can count."

"Is that supposed to frighten me?"

"It is a warning."

"That you are dangerous?" She glanced over her shoulder, the fabric of her dress slipping even further. "I know that, Eamonn. You are the sword, the weapon, the soldier of the Seelie Fae."

He traced circles on her neck. "And the sword is far mightier than the pen for a time. But eventually a sword loses its weight, becomes a symbol more than a weapon. All warriors turn to the pen once they win their wars."

"Precisely why I believe you would make a good king."

His breath feathered over her arm. Crystals pressed into soft flesh, surrounded by the velvet heat of his mouth. A soft flick of his tongue stroked between freckles.

"Why does your whole body taste like sunshine?" he asked. "It's intoxicating."

"Does my whole body? I wasn't aware you had tasted every inch."

"There is no going back from this Sorcha. If you make this choice, I cannot stop."

"You are a large man, Eamonn, but you are not my first."

Sorcha reminded herself to breathe as his hands curled around her waist. He yanked her against him, pressed her spine against his stomach. "Who dares touch what is mine?"

"I am my own before I am any other's. But if you must know, I grew up in a brothel. A girl gets curious."

"A girl toes the line between right and wrong."

"Is there such a thing?" She spun in his arms, eyes sparking with anger. "Right and wrong suggests that there is only black and white. I refute that belief and instead replace it with my own. If I desire a man, I shall take one."

An answering anger sparked in his own eyes. Crystals lit with the fires of his passion. "And what do you desire?"

Every fiber of her being yearned for him to touch her. She wanted his fingers in her hair, his body pressed against hers—in hers—until she didn't know where he started and where she ended.

Sorcha wanted him. It didn't matter he was larger than her, or that he was Fae. She might regret it in the morning, but now she would enjoy every second of this poor decision.

She slid her hands up the wide plane of his chest, tangled her fingers around his braid and pulled him down. Their foreheads pressed together. She inhaled his air and breathed into him new life.

"I desire a king."

"Then a king you shall have."

He lifted her into his arms as if she weighed nothing. Sorcha had seen him swing a sword taller than her, perhaps she felt like a feather to him. She might have pondered such thoughts if he hadn't swooped down and devoured her lips.

Her body glowed with passion and desire so great that she feared it would never be satisfied. Something, or someone, uncurled deep within her soul. A woman she barely recognized, who knew how to take what she wanted and asked for the world.

Candlelight disappeared in curls of smoke as he laid her across a feather down bed. Inky darkness obscured him from her vision.

His hands trailed down her sides, following the indents of her waist and the flare of her hips. Cold crystal pressed against the smooth column of her neck. The highest points dug into her skin, not quite painful and sending shivers racing from each touch.

The tight bodice of her dress eased. Her lungs expanded and her back arched, pushing her chest into his waiting hands. He slipped his fingers under the gaping fabric, smoothing his fingers around her waist and pulling her into his chest.

Stones pressed against bare flesh. She sighed, the sound almost too loud as he surged up and captured her lips again. The erotic scrape of crystal mingling with his guttural groan sent shudders rocking through her body. He smoothed his hand over her bare spine, hand shaking as he held himself in check.

"Eamonn," she whispered. "I want to see you."

"No one wants to see this face."

"I desire to see nothing *but* you."

Candles flared to life all around the decimated room. Shattered furniture, shards of stone statues, and broken mirrors created a battlefield. The bed was all that survived unscathed.

Eamonn did not look at her. He turned the scarred half of his face away from her as if she might be insulted by the mere sight of him.

Sorcha reached out and sunk her fingers into the hollows of his cheek. She whispered fierce and hoarse, "How dare you hide from me, my king."

"Your king?"

"You hide from no one."

The words struck a fire deep within her belly. She would tear apart anyone who dared say this man was not a king. She had met the imposter who wore a stolen crown. No man could ever live up to the goliath who hovered above her and dimmed the lights for fear his face would lessen her passion.

Her heart beat like a pounding drum. She gentled her grip on his face, sliding down the well-known dip of throat and collarbone. Her fingers curled around the edge of his shirt and lifted it.

All the while, Eamonn's eyes watched her movements. So many emotions played across his face. Shame. Embarrassment. Wonder.

"What manner of creature are you?" he asked. "Fearless in your ability to see past this gruesome figure, and so selfless that you would allow a beast to lay hands upon you."

"You are not a beast," she said as she flung his shirt to the floor.

The caverns of geodes followed the lines of his ribs. She traced their edges, daring to dip into the crevices until crystals bit at her fingers. Sorcha outlined each wound, each grievous injury until she was certain she had marked each with her scent and her touch.

She sat up, pressing her chest against his and her mouth against his shoulder. She traced the mangled flesh and stone with lips and tongue.

"I claim you as mine, rightful king of the Seelie Fae." Sorcha sank her teeth into his skin, biting through flesh until the harsh edge of stone cracked her lips.

Blood smeared his shoulder. Marking him for all eternity.

He roared out in anger, or perhaps something far more dangerous. His hand flexed beneath the fabric of her dress and ripped. Crystals and warm skin traced the delicate line of her spine in apology.

"You toy with fire," he growled. "Once wounded, I never heal."

"Good. Perhaps any other woman who dares touch you will think twice."

The feral grin on his face beckoned the creature inside her, the woman who wanted to feast upon the Fae. "And you say you are not a druid."

"I like you better with your mouth shut."

"Shall I find something to keep it busy then?"

Sorcha couldn't respond. A fire burned in her blood, and need swelled until it crashed over her mind. She straddled his waist and arched her spine, offering her body as a banquet upon which he could feast.

Candlelight made her skin glow. He lifted shaking hands, gliding over the bumps of her ribs until he could take her in hand. She tilted her head back, unable to maintain eye contact when the crystals flared to life. Violet glowed behind her closed eyes.

She gasped as crystals slid over the tips of her breasts, cold and strangely hard. Her spine curved further, and she pressed into his hand. A long sigh hollowed her belly as he teased a silken tip between his fingers.

He followed the line of her throat with his nose. Teeth closed around her ear, his hot breath vibrating in her ear. She clenched her legs against his sides as wet heat rushed through her.

"Lie down," he drawled.

"No."

"Sorcha."

"I said no."

"Now is not the time to argue with me."

"What did I say about keeping your mouth shut?" she asked.

Sorcha locked her ankles and twisted her body. His brows drew down in surprise, but he obliged her request. Eamonn rolled.

He stretched his body across the bed and settled her hips over his. Cocking his head to the side, he asked "What now?"

A wicked grin spread across her lips. Sorcha smoothed her hands over his shoulders, pushing his arms away from her and onto the bed. She stroked across the bulges of his biceps, over the crystals on his forearms, and locked her fingers with his.

Her hips rocked, playing back and forth across his hardness. He was incredibly large, far more than a human man could ever dream of being. A small moment of worry made her wonder if he would fit.

She'd have to make him.

Sorcha whispered her lips over the mangled mess of his shoulder.

The crystals scratched into the surface of his chest nipped at her mouth. She danced her fingers across his ribs, smiling at his gasp as she trailed her fingers across his stomach.

She lingered at the band of muscles arching over his hip bone. Tiny nibbles sent gooseflesh raising before her eyes.

"Sorcha," he moaned. "Have pity on a man."

Hardly. She looked up at him, flicking a brow before biting down hard.

He clenched his fists in the sheets and threw his head to the side.

"Pity is for the weak," she whispered, "and you underestimated the woman you took to bed."

She slid her fingers beneath his breeches, brushing her cheek over his throbbing heat. The sheets whispered as he arched against her touch. He lifted himself so she might free him from the confines of clothing.

He was glorious. Sorcha was thoroughly pleased to see that faeries were built entirely similarly to men.

She pressed a kiss against his shaft and made her way back up his body. She straddled his waist and took hold of his hands.

"You have been on this isle for a long time. It would be careless if I did not ask how long it has been."

Blue eyes blistered with heat as she tucked his fingers against her ribs. "Too long."

"How long is that?"

"Long enough that I'm not putting a number to it."

"Then I'll be gentle this time," she whispered.

In truth, she wasn't certain she could wait. Her wet heat already slicked across him, and she couldn't stop the rhythmic canting of her hips. His arms flexed, and he pulled the dress over her shoulders.

Hands roamed down her shoulders, lingering upon the curves of her breasts and sliding across her thighs.

"Gentle?" he asked. "When have I ever asked for gentle?"

She had never felt like this before. He willingly gave her full control over the situation, and she wanted to devour him. She wanted to mark him for all eternity. To shred him until all he could do was whisper her name.

The newly discovered part of herself, the animal, the beast, wanted to see him on his knees. She understood what men felt like when they came to the brothel. She could order him to do whatever she wanted.

Sorcha leaned forward, sank her teeth into the lobe of his ear, then soothed the ache with her tongue. "What do you want, Eamonn?"

He growled and lifted his hips.

"Oh," she whispered. "Is that all?"

She reached between them and wrapped her hand around his hard length. He pulsed between her fingers, eager and wanting. As a reward, she slid her hand up and down until he was breathing so fast that he rocked the bed.

But not yet. She wasn't done with him yet. She paused, waited for him to catch his breath, then notched him at her opening. He was broad, too large, too thick, and far too enticing.

She wanted to see him as he entered her. She wanted to watch his eyes and brand herself into his soul.

"Eamonn," she whispered, knowing how much he liked to hear his name on her lips.

"Now, Sorcha."

A rush of heat tensed her belly, and she groaned. Throwing herself down, she seated him all the way to her core.

They both gasped, arched, ached for each other as two became one. The candles blew out as a gust of magic rushed through the room.

He filled her to the brink of pain. She stung, but the needles of sensation eased from pain into pleasure. Erotic tingles danced down her spine, multiplying as he groaned in appreciation.

Sorcha leaned forward. His breath feathered over her lips, and she couldn't bring herself to move. Not yet. She wanted to savor each moment that passed. Each clench of muscle that dragged him ever deeper.

A drop of sweat dripped down his temple.

"You feel like coming home," he whispered. The words tasted sweet against her lips.

She knew how long it had been since he felt like he had a home. He'd been the outcast for centuries. And now, he admitted that sliding into her body fulfilled that piece of himself.

The earth could have split open, and Sorcha would not have been able to stop. She lifted up and drove back down. She gasped, clenching hard as she set a rhythm that made him grip the sheets again.

He didn't touch her until she picked his hands back up. He gave her all the power, all the freedom to use his body as she saw fit. She pressed his palms against her breasts, dragged his hands to her mound and encouraged him to touch, to learn her body as she learned his.

Slow movements became frustrating. She braced her hands on his chest and sped up but her thighs were quivering and her mind fractured.

He growled and lifted her away. He spread her across the bed, her hair a wildfire of curls, as he plunged back into her.

The time for tenderness had passed. The animals inside them clawed to the forefront. They fought beneath the sheets, twisting for power and control. She sank her teeth into his shoulder again, fitting them into the marks she had already left. The howling in her soul grew louder as he reached between them and slid his thumb across her molten heat.

"Eamonn!" she shouted.

She tensed, her whole body reaching for the stars. Higher and higher he brought her, forcing her further than she had ever gone until she arched her back and cried out in release.

Her eyes opened wide to watch as he threw his head back and groaned. The crystals that wrapped around his throat pulsed, his arms shook, and his hips stilled.

They had battled, drawn blood, and in the end, they lifted each other towards the stars and emerged victorious. Both alive, and undone.

Eamonn fell onto the bed next to her, chest heaving.

He tucked her against him, a wide hand spread across her spine. Sorcha hid the smile blooming across her lips. It was strange how easily he lost the self-conscious way he carried himself. First, he stopped wearing the hooded cloak, then he grew comfortable with her seeing his scars, and now he didn't flinch when they were pressed against her skin.

A woman could get used to this. Even the stones on his hands didn't bother her. They had heated in their passions and warmed her back. She was cocooned—safe within his arms.

The sheets rustled as he shifted his legs closer to hers. His lips pressed against her brow, gentle so that he did not break her skin with the crystals. "Stay with me."

Sorcha shivered. "There's far too many meanings for me to guess what you mean."

"Stay with me here on Hy-brasil, for as long as you live."

"It's a bold command for a faerie. Your kind despise humans."

"You aren't human. You're druid, and beyond that, you are mine. They will love you, or I will bring them to their knees."

She sighed and pressed her lips against his collarbone. "You can't force people to accept change. And as much as I love this place, the faeries, this world you've shown me, I have to go back."

"Why? To save the small amount of people who care for you?"

"It's not just about my family, but everyone. The blood beetle plague is horrific, and I will not allow it to spread any further."

"And they promised to give you a cure, if you brought me back," he grunted. "They twisted the truth, Sorcha. They'll send you on another impossible quest as soon as we return to your land. And another after that. Faeries, especially the MacNara twins, cannot be trusted."

She rose onto an elbow, searching his gaze for the truth of his words. "You don't think they have the cure."

"I think they know of the cure, but they have been trying to meet with me for centuries. They toy with their puppets, force them to dance, and they do not care whether they snap the strings."

"I will break those strings," Sorcha growled. "How am I to save my people?"

"I don't know." He lifted a hand and tucked her wild hair behind her ear. "I don't know if it's even possible for you to save them. Plagues come and go, but humanity always survives them."

"People are in pain. I can't stay knowing that they're suffering and I might help."

"You have too large a heart for your body," he murmured.

She caught the hand he pressed against her chest, holding it tight enough that the crystals pricked her skin. "I can't, Eamonn. They're my family, my people, I can't let them live a life they don't deserve."

"Every time you open your mouth, it's as if you are plucking words from my soul. Promise to stay here, and I will return to your world with you. I will help you in your journey to find the cure for your people."

"You will?" Sorcha hadn't thought he would so readily agree. "Staying here is the easiest choice I have ever had to make. I will remain by your side gladly."

"It stings that I have to bribe you to remain here."

She had heard the words before. Men said to them to her sisters every day of the week. They paid women for favors and hoped that they loved them in return. Sorcha knew none of her sisters loved those men, but the way her heart hurt when she saw Eamonn told her this was different. This was true.

Laying back down, Sorcha tucked her head into the hollow of his throat and breathed in his earthy scent. "I stay because I choose to, not because you have agreed to save my people with me. You spared me the difficulty of deciding between you and my people. For that, I thank you."

He hesitantly wrapped his arms back around her. He pulled her closer to him until she couldn't tell where he began and where she ended. "No one should have to choose between their people and those they love."

"Speaking from experience?" She knew he was. She had seen the place he had grown up, the glistening palace walls and the silk draperies. His people needed him, missed him, desired to have a king worthy of their affection. Even the royals, Elva came to mind, wanted him to return.

"Yes."

Someday she would convince him to go back to Seelie. She would convince him to take his stolen throne, to place a crown atop his head, and become the man she saw inside him. His people would rejoice and cheer out his name.

But not until she saved her people. Only then would she convince the Seelie prince to return. Perhaps it was selfish, and likely the wrong choice, but Sorcha couldn't bear it any longer. Her people needed her. The guilt tore at her soul and their imagined screams of pain ate at her mind. This place, although beautiful, was not hers. She would willingly give up her old life if she knew that her family and people were happy.

Closing her eyes, she snuggled closer to his heat and resolved herself to sleep. He pressed a kiss against her head. She stayed awake until his breathing evened into the steady rhythm of dreams.

Sorcha rolled onto her side and reached for Eamonn. She hadn't slept well—a new bed was always difficult the first night. She kept rolling over to find him, worried that he might disappear into the night.

The Wild Hunt was afoot, and she feared he would be taken by Cernunnos and his bride.

Her fingers smoothed over the empty bed, sheets cold from the absence of his body. The spike of fear made her breath catch in her throat. Where was he?

It couldn't be the Wild Hunt. Moonlight filtered through the windows, mocking her thoughts. Surely no other Tuatha dé Danann would take him from this prison?

Mind catching up to the fear, Sorcha sat up and dragged her fingers through the tangled mass of her hair. She was thinking irrationally. This was the place they banished people. No one would remove them.

She took a took breath and forced her muscles to relax. She focused on the tips of her toes, willing relaxation to travel from the ends of her feet all the way up her body. Once her muscles released their tension, she felt significantly better.

There was still no answer to what had happened to Eamonn. *Where* he was? Perhaps he had gone to bathe himself.

She couldn't imagine why. A grin spread across her features in the twilight. He had proven himself quite a worthy man.

Her body ached in places she hadn't realized she had. Each throb of muscle and quake of limb reminded her that she had been well and truly claimed, and that she had laid claim to him as well.

Sorcha bit her lip and pulled the blankets up to her chest. Curls fell across her naked body, slipping on the silken sheets.

"Where is he?" she muttered. "I would like to repeat last night."

Clattering echoed from outside the door. On the stairs? She couldn't imagine why Oona would bring food or tea up. It was far too late, and if Eamonn asked her to make the trek up those stairs in the middle of the night, then Sorcha had words to stay to him. The man wouldn't learn a thing about his people.

Oona was an old woman! No matter that her body appeared young, she had enough years on her to deserve a bit more respect.

She slid her legs over the edge of the bed and hissed when her toes touched the cold stone.

"Eamonn," she growled. "Everywhere else in the entire castle has sheepskin so we don't freeze our toes off in the morning. Yet you insist upon punishing yourself even this early."

Dim light made it difficult to find her dress. The yellow fabric was ruined. He had ripped all the buttons off the back. But it would have to do for now. Oona wouldn't mind if a bit of her skin was showing.

The faerie had already seen every bit of Sorcha anyways.

She snorted. How strange it was to no longer worry about who saw her nudity. She had been frightened of revealing even the smallest bit of ankle when she first arrived. Now, she wasn't worried about waltzing around with her entire back unclothed.

The mind was a strange and wondrous thing, she mused. She slid the fabric up and over her shoulders, pressing it against her chest and maneuvering a makeshift tie around her waist.

Clattering became clanging, growing louder and louder as it reached the door of Eamonn's quarters. Sorcha's brow furrowed. She knew that sound, and yet she didn't.

It wasn't the sound of pottery or plates.

The door to the bedroom burst open, slammed against the wall with a thunderous bang, and fell off its top hinge. She shrieked and held her arm up.

"Sorcha!" Eamonn's shout was a welcome, if concerning, sound to hear.

"Eamonn!"

"Where are you, woman?"

He couldn't see her in the darkness. She ran towards him, wrapping her arms around the frame outlined by candle glow.

"I'm here," she whispered. "I'm here. What's wrong?"

Metal dug into her ribs. Her biceps met cold armor and the pommel of his sword pressed against her belly. He was dressed for war.

Eamonn wrapped his arms around her, pressing his lips against her hair. "Thank the gods. You're safe."

"I'm fine, what's happening?"

"When did you see my brother?"

The question chilled her to the bone. "What?"

"You saw my twin, Fionn, and you did not tell me. When was this?"

"Eamonn, I'm sorry. I should have told you. He summoned me and I knew it would cause problems if I didn't go. I didn't want to—"

He held her an arm's length away and mashed a finger against her lips. "I'm not angry with you. I just need to know what was said between the two of you."

"Nothing I thought you needed to know, or I would have told you immediately."

"He tried to convince you he would be a good king."

"Yes," she nodded. "He tried very hard."

"And he didn't succeed."

"No. I still believe you would be the better king, and it pained me to see an imposter sitting on your throne, wearing your face."

He tilted his face, wincing at her words. "You may regret saying that."

"He offered me a boon. He wouldn't dare harm me, not when I can command him."

"Dangerous for a king to offer such a thing."

"That's exactly what I said."

Eamonn tapped her chin with an armored finger. "Precisely why I find you so interesting, Sorcha. You think like a soldier."

"I think like someone who wants to survive. Why have you donned your armor?"

She watched him carefully as he pulled away. The armor creaked with his movements, groaning and shrieking plates scratching against each other. His spine stiffened, and he took a deep controlling breath.

"I always knew it would come to this. My brother has wanted me dead for centuries. I threaten his right to sit on that throne, even though I have been disgraced and banished. As long as I am alive, the people will always call for the High King of Seelie to sit upon the golden throne."

"As they should."

"It's not my choice, Sorcha," he said. "The world has made this decision for me. I am ruined, therefore, I am unfit to be king."

"Don't you believe change is worth considering? Perhaps the people who choose to be Seelie Fae no longer wish to have a perfect king."

"You say blasphemous words you could not hope to understand."

"I understand more than you know." She reached for his face, framing his cheeks with her hands. "Your people are dying under the control of a tyrant who shows them little kindness. They want you to come home. Even the Tuatha dé Danann."

"What do you know of such things?" A spear of candlelight spread across his face.

No, not candlelight, she realized. Fire from outside the window of the castle's tallest tower. Something was burning outside. She could smell the smoke now, acrid and burning her nose until she wanted to sneeze. She would not look.

"Elva was the faerie Oona wanted me to help. She said she was raised with you and your brother. She spoke very highly of you and the good things you might have done if you became king."

"Elva," he whispered. "That is a name I have not heard in a long time."

"The king made her his concubine."

"He had no right." The sudden anger in Eamonn's voice startled Sorcha.

"Was she yours?"

"No. She was another's, but he would not have claim over a Seelie woman if the Seelie king wanted her." He cursed. "How dare he meddle in such things? No wonder he is so hated."

Sorcha swallowed. "Eamonn, why are you in armor?"

"The king is here."

Of course. She should have guessed, but she hadn't wanted to think the worst had happened.

"Why?"

"You know why."

And she did. The king wanted to kill his brother once and for all. Sorcha ducked her head, stroked her hand across the smooth plates of his armor, and nodded.

"What do you need me to do?"

"Stay safe and out of the way."

"How?" She looked up at him for guidance. "I've never been in a battle before."

"Follow me. I will bring you somewhere I know you won't be harmed."

"And if you fall?" She didn't want to ask the question. The thought of him bleeding out on the battlefield without her assistance made a scream rise in the back of her throat. "I can help the wounded."

"I need you to stay out of the way. Follow me as closely as you can, and if we come across any of Fionn's men, do not interfere."

Sorcha nodded and followed as he rushed from the room. The weight of his armor must have been great, but he moved as if he wore nothing. It differed from the metal armor she had seen before. Interlocking pieces slid easily against each other and did not hinder his movements. No adornments made the armor "pretty." It was functional. Practical. Like him.

She held her skirts high as they raced through his chambers and out onto the dangerous parapet hanging above the ground. It was then that she saw the army.

Spread out across the isle she loved so dearly, men and women in golden armor lifted their swords and spears. The Fae who lived in the castle and served their true master stood around the castle in a weak line.

There were so few of them.

Sorcha stopped running, fisting her hands in the fabric of her skirts as tears dripped down her cheeks. They would die. Under no circumstances could such a small amount of Lesser Fae stand a chance against an army in full battle gear.

The faeries she knew and loved held kitchen pottery in their hands. Pots, pans, garden hoes.

A choked sob rocked her forward. "They don't even have weapons," she whispered. "Please have mercy on them. They don't even have *weapons*."

"Sorcha!"

She flinched at Eamonn's shout, rocking forward dangerously near the edge.

"Sorcha, get down!"

A man climbed over the edge of the parapet. Twin blades glinted in the moonlight. He used them as hand holds, puncturing wounds into the side of the castle. They knew where Eamonn was.

The gilded edge of his armor was sharp as a knife. He spun towards her, not Eamonn, and grinned at her look of fear.

"You're getting in the way," the faerie grunted. "Off you go."

He lunged, and she spun away. His hands caught in the fabric of her dress, and she fell onto her hands and knees. Stone bit into her palms. Hair fell in front of her face, obscuring her vision. His hands gripped her ankles, and she screamed.

Then he disappeared. Ripped away from her legs with a panicked shout of his own. She looked over her shoulder to see Eamonn lift the faerie over his head. Too easy. Too simple. His expression was cold and heartless as he threw the man over the edge.

The echoing scream sounded like the wail of a bean sidhe.

"Come." Eamonn reached out a hand for her to take. "We have to go."

"That man—"

"One of my brother's and not worth your guilt. Get up."

She wanted to vomit. Sorcha had seen death many times over, but never so carelessly handled.

For the first time since meeting him, she looked at Eamonn with new eyes. Somehow, she had fantasized about him as the hero in a fairytale, but he was a flesh and blood warrior whose hands and body were stained with death and war.

She fit her hand into his, knowing full well what it meant. She could not support death. But she would not turn from him either.

He pulled her to standing and nodded. "That's not the last of them, Sorcha. There will be more."

"I know."

"You didn't."

"I do now."

He gave her one last, lingering glance before racing towards the door to the main part of the castle. Sorcha followed, her heart thudding hard in her ears.

The clattering of his armor echoed in the winding stairwell. It bounced up the circular tower, growing louder and louder. The slamming gong of church bells. Funeral bells.

A body fell silently down the middle shaft of the stairs. Sorcha wouldn't have noticed it, for the female faerie did not even shout in fear, but air whistled through her armor and the thudding weight charged the air with electricity.

"They are following us," she said. Her words seemed too loud, disrespectful of the deaths she had just seen.

"Of course, they are. Stay close."

As they neared the bottom, Eamonn drew his broadsword. The rubies in the handle suddenly made more sense. The blade feasted upon the blood of its enemies, and thousands of souls were caught there.

Though the thought was fanciful, Sorcha still edged away from his sword.

"Are you frightened of me?" he asked. He did not look at her, instead he stared down the hallway and waited for her answer.

"Not of you, but of your weapon."

"You should be afraid of Ocras."

"The sword's name is Hunger?"

"It devours my foes and cleaves flesh and bone. She does not desire you."

"Her?"

Eamonn flashed a feral grin. "Of course. Women are capable of both beauty and pain."

"There are many who would argue with you on that."

"They would have to argue with Ocras."

"Are we running?"

"Not yet."

"Why are we waiting?" She didn't look down the hallway, not wanting to see what they would run towards until the last second.

"Just a bit more," he murmured. "Just long enough to give them time."

"For what?"

"Now."

He rounded the wall and charged down the hallway with a piercing shout. His roar made the walls shake and the ground quake with the force of his rage. As promised, Sorcha followed close behind but gave him enough room to swing his sword.

And swing he did.

Four soldiers waited for them. Two men, two women, golden armor molded to their bodies. Helms topped with bright feathers hid their species and made them appear all the more otherworldly.

They attacked all at once, and it was as if they struck a bull. Eamonn ducked into the first one, slamming his shoulder into the man's stomach. Metal crunched as he lifted an arm to block a sword slicing towards him. It struck his forearm and snapped in half as it cut through his armor and met crystal underneath.

Ocras sang as she swung through the air and sliced through the neck of a male faerie. It stopped halfway through, blood dripping down his armor as Eamonn placed a foot on his chest and shoved him away.

He didn't hesitate. He turned and lashed out, plunging the sword into another soldier's chest cavity. She shrieked and fell to the ground while holding her stomach.

Eamonn wrenched her sword out of her dying grip and caught the next attack on its blade. The weapons shrieked their fury into the air. The muscles on Eamonn's neck bulged, veins pulsing as he pushed the other back. Step by step.

Unlocking their swords by swinging his to the side, Eamonn sank the blade through the crevice where thigh met pelvis. The man fell with a cry, holding onto his leg.

The last woman ran. She raced down the hallway as if it might contain a new escape. Eamonn growled and pulled the stolen faerie sword from the man's leg, ducked his head, and calmly walked down the hallway.

Sorcha didn't know whether to be terrified or angry. The metallic scent burned her nostrils. Blood welled into the air until she thought she could see it hanging above her like a curtain of guilt.

She couldn't stand by and watch this happen.

Eamonn wasn't looking, so he couldn't stop her. She rushed forward and placed her hands on the faerie man's shoulders.

"Easy," she whispered. "I will drag you back to the wall. Do not make a sound, or he will turn around."

The man grunted and pressed his hands harder against his wound.

Sorcha, though small, had grown strong from manipulating the human body and hiking all across the isle. He was larger than her but small for a Fae. She tucked her hands under his armpits and dragged him a few feet until he could lean against stone.

She dropped to her knees next to him and brushed his hands out of the way.

"No," he grumbled.

"Let me. I'm a healer."

The wound was deep and cut through muscle. If he was lucky, he would live, but he would never walk again.

Sorcha would not be the one who told him that. Perhaps faerie healers knew more than she did about their bodies. The only thing she could do was stop him from bleeding out.

The tearing sound of her dress made Eamonn pause. She could feel the heat of his stare, his anger burning through her flesh.

Quickly, she wrapped the cloth underneath his thigh and cinched it as tight as possible. She knotted the fabric, ignored his pained whimper, and turned towards Eamonn glaring daggers at her actions.

"I won't let him die."

"Why? Some strange affection towards my twin?"

"Because he's just doing a job. I won't stand by when I can help, no matter what side he fights for."

"Soft heart."

Eamonn turned and flung the sword in his hand. It whistled through the air and embedded in the faerie woman's back who scrabbled at the door, then hung limp.

"Let's go," Eamonn said. He turned and yanked Ocras out of the other woman, holding out a bloodied hand for her to take.

Sorcha stood slowly, measuring him with a weighted stare. "You're angry at me."

"I am."

"Why?"

"He doesn't deserve your help."

"He's alive. That means he deserves my help. I will never stop wanting to heal people, and if you want me to then we can end this now. I help others. That's what I do."

She watched a muscle jump on his jaw. His eyes canted away from hers, staring at the wall until he finally nodded. "So be it. Come with me."

He did not reach out a hand, and she did not take his arm. They stood still in the hallway filled with blood, looking away from each other. A rift between them grew, splintering and splitting, a canyon tearing apart their tenuous alliance.

Sorcha should have been heartbroken. She should have been sad, but she was angry. How dare he be angry at her for trying to save another life?

Her heart whispered to be gentle. That the man standing before her needed as much healing as the man behind. His brother was here to kill him. Eamonn likely would not be looking for those who were just doing a job compared to those who wanted him dead.

Maybe they all wanted him dead. She had no way of knowing.

He glanced at her. She met his gaze as his eyes widened in fear. "Sorcha!"

She heard the crunching sound of armor moving before she turned. The faerie she'd saved stood behind her. She saw nothing but cold determination in his gaze and a knife that seemed to glow in his hands.

Time slowed. She heard her own exhalation and his hand began to descend. Sorcha ducked, her palms dragging across the plates of his armor. Her fingers slid across metal and gripped a sharpened piece.

She gasped as he fell against her, staggering in pain. She squeezed her eyes shut as hot blood poured over her hands. The jagged edge of armor bit into her fingers, but sliced into his chest even farther when she tried to move.

Her hands trembled, but she couldn't make them move. He gasped in her ear, the rattling wheeze of a dying breath. She knew it well. Sorcha had heard it many times, but never so close.

Eamonn might have killed the others, but she had killed this one.

"Sorcha." Eamonn's armored hands pulled her away from the body. It fell to the ground with a wet thud. "Sorcha, I'm sorry you had to do that."

"I didn't mean to kill him."

"You had to protect yourself, mo chroí."

"I didn't know what to do."

"The first one is always the hardest. But we do not have time for this."

"I should check for a heartbeat," she said. She tried to turn but he wouldn't even let her look at the body.

"No. No, we leave now, Sorcha. I need to hide you from him."

"From who?" Her mind felt foggy. All she could feel was blood on her hands, and she should have been comfortable with the feeling. How many times had she felt blood on her hands? Pouring from between a woman's legs. It was life.

But this was death.

"Sorcha."

"I thought you and Bran looked like you were dancing. It was beautiful to watch you spar. I was so impressed. I thought real battle would look like that, but it doesn't."

"Practicing is one thing. It's easy to make the movements look graceful when there is no blade striking at your throat. Real battle is gritty, messy, brutal. I'm sorry you had to see it."

"Mo chroí," she whispered. "You called me your heart."

He gripped her hand and did not answer. They raced through the halls, ducking around soldiers. The castle rang with the screams of Fae who had not gone to the forefront to fight the king's army.

Sorcha couldn't handle any more death. She squeezed her eyes shut and let Eamonn guide her across the floors. Perhaps he knew that she wouldn't look. Eventually, he swung her into his arms and charged through the endless doors and hidden rooms.

He burst through a side door. She curled against his chest and whimpered, wanting nothing more than for this battle to end. For her life to be back to normal. To wake up in her own bed and have this be nothing more than a wondrous tale for her sisters.

Wind brushed her hair across her face, cool and calming.

On the breeze, she heard a haunting song. A cry that trembled from a woman's lips, speaking of lost love and a death that came too soon.

Eamonn stood still.

"Bean sidhe," he said. "I have no quarrel with the Unseelie."

"Where is my brother?"

"I had assumed he returned to you."

"No twisted truths, Seelie king. I want my brother returned safely."

Sorcha felt his nod against the top of her head. "I have use for him yet."

"He will not fight for you. We do not need another war with the Seelie Fae on top of everything else which has happened. Bran wants a war. He does not speak for the Unseelie council."

"I have never thought he did. He gave up that life long ago."

"Good." The banshee wailed, and the wind picked up again. "See that my brother returns home safely."

"After he assists me."

"The deal is struck."

The cold touch of the wind felt like a woman's hand. It slid across her brow and down her arms. Sorcha heard a quiet whisper on the breeze.

"Hello, priestess."

What did the Unseelie woman know that Sorcha did not? The words weren't merely an observation. As if she had seen her before, or perhaps her likeness.

Eamonn touched her chin. "You must walk from here, mo chroí."

She touched her toes to the ground and balanced herself on his arm. "What are you going to do?"

"What I should have done a long time ago."

"You're going to fight him?" Sorcha shook her head. "Eamonn, more bloodshed will not fix this. You need to talk to your brother."

"You think he wants to share the throne? It's not possible for the Seelie Fae to have two kings."

"Surely, your parents had thought of this? You're twins, Eamonn! They must have known there would either be two kings, or you would sit upon the throne."

A shadow passed over his face. "They had always intended for us to share the kingdom. Fionn made his choice."

Another faerie name she had in her collection, although this one she did not want. The name of the king danced upon her tongue and tasted like soured milk.

She did not want this responsibility. She did not want this name that branded itself into her mind because she knew this was the first faerie name she wanted to use.

This was the only power a human had over a Fae. She had his name, and now she could command him to do whatever she pleased. Sorcha could walk into the fields of battle and scream for him to stop and he would.

But such responsibility meant she chose a side. It meant she trusted that Eamonn would make a better king, and now that she had seen him in battle she was no longer sure of that. He had changed much. All she knew for certain was that he was not his brother.

She could not decide if that made him worthy of a throne.

Eamonn stared down at her. "You have chosen?"

"I will not choose. I came here to save my people, my family. Not to become entangled in the faerie courts and their wars."

"I don't think you have a choice," he said. He traced a line from her forehead, down her nose, and across her lips. "You're here, Sorcha. That means you're involved."

"I don't wish to be."

"Wishes mean nothing to the Fae."

"I know." The words caught around the thick knot of a sob.

"I never meant to hurt you."

"Eamonn, tell me what is going on. Where are you taking me?"

"I'm not taking you anywhere, mo chroí."

He leaned down and caught her lips in a searing kiss. He poured himself into her, sinking tongue and taste until she felt the essence of him crawling underneath her skin. Their memories pulsed in her heart, and she knew this was goodbye.

Sorcha tangled her fingers in the long tail of his braid and pulled him towards her. She dug her nails into his skull, marking him as hers even further than she already had. Their teeth clacked together, blood welled at her lips, but she did not want to stop. If she stopped, her heart would break, and her being should shatter into a thousand pieces.

He pulled away.

"No," she whispered and squeezed her eyes shut. "No, Eamonn don't do this. You promised to come back with me."

"If you stayed." His thumb traced a line over her bottom lip. "And you aren't staying."

Taloned feet gripped her waist. Her eyes snapped open, and the ground dropped away.

"No!" she screamed. "No! Please, no!"

Her soul splintered, shouting that she didn't want to leave him. He shouldn't be alone when he faced the battlefield.

Great wings buffeted air against her head. She struggled, to no avail. The beastly bird did not release its hold upon her waist. Soon they were too high for her to escape.

The highest peak of the castle was nearly within her reach. Everything looked so small, even the armored faeries who attacked the front door and beat back those she loved. She could still hear the screams.

Eamonn stared up at her. Once she was too high and fell limp in the bird's claws, he turned and walked onto the battlefield.

The faeries of the isle parted like a sea in front of him. His tarnished and aged armor looked like stone as he moved through the crowd. The golden army stood in front of him, a wall of power and clear intent.

Sorcha wondered which one was Oona. From so high, she couldn't make out faces or traits she might recognize.

Eamonn's people were short and squat. Their forms warped and stretched with animal features, strange skin, oddly shaped bodies. They looked so different compared to the perfection Fionn brought with him.

These were the Tuatha dé Danann, the great faeries who enslaved those who did not deserve it.

The twins mirrored each other, standing at the forefront of their armies. Fionn sat upon a great white steed. The long tail of his hair whipped in the breeze. Eamonn stood with his legs rooted in the earth, his braid thin and still. They stared across a sea of blood and did not move.

"Bran?" she whispered into the wind.

A booming caw echoed all around her. She glanced down at the talons wrapped around her waist. Each claw was as big as her forearm. Rough grey skin covered them. She hadn't realized he could turn into such a massive beast. Another secret revealed, another to store away in her memory.

"Are they going to kill each other?"

The wind whistled past her ears, and she couldn't tell if the croak was for her or simply a grumble.

"Am I ever going to see him again?"

The Unseelie Prince didn't answer. He turned them both away from the battlefield and soared over the ocean.

Too far away for anyone to hear her sobs.

CHAPTER THIRTEEN

HOME

They traveled across the sea with great speed. Bran took them high over the storm's edge, moonlight giving way to sunrise.

Sorcha wanted to take in the beauty. She wanted to appreciate the world, because she would never see it this way again. Merrows jumped from the waves and called out to them. The Guardian swam through the depths as a shadow drifting aimlessly.

She took it all in, but her heart felt empty. Drained. She wasn't certain if it was even there anymore.

Her faerie prince was likely dead. If he wasn't dead, then he'd killed the mirror image of himself. Who could be the same after that?

Was killing a twin like killing oneself?

Bran's claws dug into her skin, shredding the waist of her dress. The pain was dull compared to the ache of her heart. She'd always thought she would grieve like Rosaleen did when she lost a lover she liked.

The blonde waif of a girl would wail and scream. Her cheeks would burn with the salt of her tears. The house would ring with the anger of her cries, the disappointment in herself, and the man who had left.

Sorcha was numb. There was nothing inside her at all. Just a dull throb where her heart used to be.

Bran's toes shifted. "I'm bringing you home."

She nodded, although he couldn't see her response.

He jostled her. "Did you hear me, midwife? I'm bringing you home. Wasn't that what you've wanted this whole time? To go home?"

Sorcha did not respond. Instead, she stared down at the waves and wondered how much it would hurt if he let her go. She had heard the higher one was, the more solid the surface of water became. If he let her go, she might strike hard enough that she wouldn't even feel it.

His toes clenched hard, squeezing the breath out of her. "It's not the end of the world, you idiot. You have a purpose, remember?"

"Excuse me?"

"I can tell you're moping!"

"I think I have a right to."

"You didn't even fall in love with him. You've lost a good friend. That means nothing."

"He has become a part of me."

The faint outline of houses appeared on the horizon. A familiar city. It felt like such a long time ago that she had stared across the table at humans. How long had it been?

Time moved differently in the Otherworld, and Macha had said it was the same in Hy-brasil. How much had her world changed?

Sorcha wasn't certain she would survive it.

Bran soared over the tops of buildings, past ships and sailors. No one looked up at the great winged bird carrying its human cargo. He took them to a small hut. Abandoned and falling down, it may have once been a home.

No longer. Sorcha listened to the soft sound of feathers as he brought them down to the ground. He placed her gently on the roof of the hut and hopped down to the dirt where he shifted forms.

Feathers melted into caramel skin. Black clothing formed over his body. Talons shrank into fingernails until only small points remained. A dusting of tiny black feathers still decorated his face, and the single raven eye glared up at her.

Bran held his arms out. "Time to get off."

"I can't feel my body," she whispered. "It's the strangest feeling. I never thought losing someone I loved could actually hurt my physical form."

"Come, Sorcha. I will tell you a story."

She didn't want to hear a story. She wanted him to take her back to Hy-brasil, so she could look after the survivors of Fionn's war. The hard look in his eye suggested he wouldn't take no for an answer.

Perhaps it was better in the long run. She scooted to the edge of the thatched roof and tumbled into his arms.

He set her down carefully, then placed a hand on her back and pushed her towards two fallen logs. She sat down hard. Her hands didn't feel right. They didn't seem to be placed on the ends of her arms in a way she could control. They almost felt backwards, but that wasn't right at all. She had used these hands thousands of times.

Bran reached forward and cupped the backs of her trembling fingers.

"I lost someone very dear to me. I spent my entire existence wooing her. Sticking twigs in her hair until she had to cut it to get them out. Putting frogs in her bed and mice in her slippers. I teased her endlessly, and still she loved me."

He sighed heavily.

"And then one night, someone took her away. There was nothing I could do, and I was promised she would be happy, but I would never see her again."

He squeezed her hand to bring her attention to his story.

"I thought piecing myself back together would be impossible. It certainly felt like it in the first few months. But I found a different purpose as someone other than the man who loved her. I found my freedom, respect for myself, and I realized that even without her I was still a good man. I could still do great things, and that she was just a reward for working hard."

He lifted her hands and pressed his lips into her palms. "You will find yourself again, Sorcha. And I believe it will be in healing your people with these hands."

"How am I supposed to heal them?" Her eyes were so dry she couldn't even blink. "He was the answer to finding a cure, and now he's gone."

"I'm certain you will find a way. You always have."

"Is he really gone? Am I never going back to that wondrous isle full of faeries that I love dearly?"

"Do you think they'll still be there?"

"I want them to be. I don't want there to be a war and all that death. Bran, how can I stop it?"

The hands holding hers disappeared. Cold air rushed around her body, stealing the breath from her lungs. She glanced up and found that she was alone.

The sun rose into the sky far above her by the time she found the courage to stand. Her knees shook. Her body trembled. Her lungs gasped for air, and still she did not feel like a person.

Pain should ground her body. It should remind her that she was alive. It didn't.

"Home," she breathed. "I want to go home."

She didn't know where home was anymore.

The landscape became more recognizable the more she stared. These fields were ones she knew like the back of her hand. Sorcha stumbled as she moved, but at least she was moving.

Each step brought her closer and closer towards the haven she remembered in her mind. A small home. Quaint, three stories of stone and wood and laughter.

Gods, how she needed the laughter.

Stones crunched beneath her feet, digging into the calloused flesh until she bled. She remembered vividly another time when her feet were aching. Sorcha had dragged herself throughout the known world, only to return to this place.

Chickens clucked. The air smelled sweet, like fresh baked bread and sticky honey. Sorcha stood on the rise of the hill beyond the brothel.

She inhaled again and trembled. The smell of bread turned stale, honey turned sickly sweet, and the scent of death made her vision blur.

There were boards over the windows of the brothel. Nailed crudely from the outside, locking her family within. The side door that led to the chicken coop was also boarded shut, and the chickens were living out in the wild.

"No," she moaned on a trembling wheeze. "No, please no more."

The tears came like a wave crashing over her head. She fell onto her knees and crawled to her family home, unable to stand but needing to help them.

She knew the painted markers on the windows. A red beetle, haphazardly painted as if the artist wanted to flee the area as fast as he could. Smart man. The blood beetle plague was apt to spread if they took to the air.

Sorcha didn't care. She didn't want her family to die alone, and she would not allow them to die if she could.

Like an old woman, she pulled herself up onto the fencing and stared at the stone walls. Flashes of anger, old and buried deep, fueled her.

She stepped forward. Each simple movement so difficult that she seemed to have forgotten how to walk. Step by step, shift by shift, she lifted foot and flexed thigh until she pressed her hands against the boards covering the door.

The wood bit into her forehead as she leaned against it, but she did not feel the pain. They were in there. The beat of their hearts called out to her.

"Rosaleen," she whispered. "Briana, Papa…anyone."

She didn't know how long she stayed there, hovering between life and death, choice and silence. Heat spread over her body, wrapping around her waist. It almost felt like arms holding her against a solid chest and breathing life into her body.

Healing would take time. But courage, strength, honor, these were things that had always been deeply embedded in her soul.

Sorcha lifted her head and yanked hard at the boards.

"Briana!" she shouted. "Let me in!"

She threw her weight against the door and began pulling at the hammered boards. Each harsh jerk wrenched her shoulders but the first board tore free. She continued to screech and shout, banging against the barrier that kept her from her family.

Finally, a voice came from the other side. Weak, but wonderful to hear. "Sorcha?"

"Yes, yes, Rosaleen! It's me! I'm coming in."

"Don't come in!" Her sister coughed. "It's not safe."

"I'm coming in whether you want me to or not. What happened?"

"We're sick."

"Is Papa alive?"

"Barely."

"Is anyone dead?"

"No."

Sorcha sobbed out a breath of relief. "Good. That's very good. Now, I'm going to pull at this last board and then I'm going to come in."

"You can't. You'll get sick too."

"Are the beetles still flying?"

"No."

"Then I won't get sick. I won't let you or anyone else die."

She wrenched the last board free and grasped the door knob. It wouldn't turn.

"Rosaleen," she groaned. "Unlock the door."

"I'm not letting you die for me."

"I won't die for anyone."

"You left us."

"I didn't have a choice. I was trying to find a cure and failed." Sorcha's throat closed and her voice turned hoarse. "Let me help you. Please, give me a purpose again. I promise that I will do nothing other than heal you."

Silence rang louder than screams. Sorcha held her breath and counted the seconds that passed by until she heard the click of a lock.

Rosaleen opened the door and peeked through the crack. "It's not pretty in here."

"I know."

"We're not pretty anymore."

"You will always be beautiful. Even when you are old and grey and wrinkled."

The door opened completely. Open sores spread across Rosaleen's body where they had tried to extract the beetles. Burn marks scarred her cheeks and circular brands traveled her arms like chains.

Sorcha ghosted her fingers over one. "What are these?"

"The healers said they knew how to stop the beetles for good. It didn't work."

Resolve straightened Sorcha's spine. A beetle moved underneath her sister's skin, traveling across the high plane of her clavicle. She could stop this. She could help, and Bran was right.

She had found her purpose, and she refused to give up.

Sorcha pulled her sister into her arms, hugging her tight. "I'm here, little sister. I'm going to keep you alive."

"Where were you?"

"The Otherworld."

"With the faeries?"

"Yes."

"We always thought you were a changeling."

Sorcha smiled. "I'm not. I'm a druid."

"Are you going back?"

Sorcha stared into the darkness of the brothel. Shadows moved, clung to bodies, and her sisters entered the room. Her father shuffled from his bedroom and leaned against the door frame.

Their clothing hung on their skeletal frames. Hollow cheeks and haunted gazes stared at her as if she were their salvation. Sorcha knew that she was. She would expend every bit of her energy healing them.

She kissed the top of Rosaleen's head.

"Yes. Yes, I am going back."

AFTERWORD

And thus ends the first part of *Heart of the Fae*.

I hope you enjoyed reading this just as much as I enjoyed writing it. This story was an adventure in every page, and the characters more beloved than any I have written before.

If you liked it, please don't forget to leave a review!

ACKNOWLEDGMENTS

There are so many people to thank for this book that I couldn't possibly write them all down. If I forget you, I am sincerely sorry and yell at me later.

Nata - This cover made the book what it is today. Your artwork inspires me to be a better writer and helped bring this story completely to life. I cannot thank you enough.

Amy - Your editing skills have no limit! Thank you for looking over this whopper of a book and for putting up with my constant changes. You were immensely helpful and I look forward to collaborating even more!

Renee - Seriously, what can I say that would express how much you are appreciated? You listen to me prattle on and on about this book MONTHS before I wrote it. And then you walked through every footstep at my side. This book is as much yours as it is mine.

Emily - Thank you for the constant support, the jokes that made me laugh, and talking me off cliff edges. I'm not really sure I would have put this book out into the public. Not to mention the knitwear that you've created based off this book series (www.withlovefrommaine.com)

Mom and Dad - From green hair, to constant complaining and stress, you've been there from day one. I am so thankful that I have family who supports me through every bad decision, every knee scrape, and every resounding success.

To my Readers - Every book you buy, every review you leave, every message you send means the world.

This is for you.

VEINS of MAGIC
Emma Hamm

Copyright © 2017 by Emma
All rights reserved.

Cover by: Natasa Ilincic
Editing by: Amy Cissell
Formatted by: Alexandria Bishop

No part of this book may be reproduced in any form or by any electronic or mechanical means, including information storage and retrieval systems, without written permission from the author, except for the use of brief quotations in a book review.

GLOSSARY OF TERMINOLOGY

Tuatha dé Danann - Considered to be the "High Fae", they are the original and most powerful faerie creatures.

Seelie Fae - Otherwise known as the the "Light Fae", these creatures live their lives according to rules of Honor, Goodness, and Adherence to the Law.

Unseelie Fae - Considered the "Dark Fae", these creatures follow no law and do not appreciate beauty.

Danu - The mother of all Tuatha dé Danann and considered to be an "earth" mother.

Nuada - The first Seelie King, often called Nuada Silverhand as he has a metal arm after losing his own in a fearsome battle.

Macha - An ancient Tuatha dé Danann who is known as one of the three sisters that make up the Morrighan. Her symbols are that of a horse and a sword.

Redcap - A troublesome faerie, frequently found in gardens harassing chickens.

Máthair - "Mother"

Will-o'-the-wisps - Small balls of light that guide travelers into bogs, usually with the intention for the humans to become lost.

Brownies - Friendly, mouse-like creatures who clean and cook for those who are kind to them.

Pixie - A winged faerie whose face resembles that of a leaf.

Changeling - Old or weak faeries swapped with human children, usually identified as a sickly child.

Gnome - Generally considered ugly, these small, squat faeries take care of gardens and have an impressive green thumb.

Dullahan - A terrifying and often evil faerie who carry their heads in their laps.

Bean Sidhe - Also known as a banshee, their screams are echoing calls that herald the death of whomever hears them.

Hy-brasil - A legendary isle which can only be seen once every seven years.

Merrow - Also known as a Mermaid, merrows have green hair and webbed fingers.

Merrow-men - The husbands of their female counterparts are considered horribly ugly with bright red noses, gills, two legs, and a tail.

Boggart - A brownie who grows angry or loses their way turns into a boggart. They are usually invisible, and have a habit of placing cold hands on people's faces as they sleep.

Pooka - A faerie which imitates animals, mostly dogs and horses.

Kelpie - A horse like creature who lives at the edge of a bog. It will try to convince you to ride it, at which point it will run underneath the water and drown the person on its back.

Selkie - A faerie which can turn into a seal, as long as it still has its seal skin.

PROLOGUE

Once upon a time, a rose fell in love with a stag.

She was nothing more than a seed when he first passed. She saw him and spread her roots deep into the ground. Small buds appeared the next time he walked by, and she bloomed so that he might lean down to smell her sweet scent. Her leaves unfurled and her thorns shrank so she would not frighten him.

But roses weren't meant to grow on salty shores. He bid her climb upon his antlers, where he could carry her. And though roses were meant to settle in soil, she tangled her roots around his tines.

He carried her for a time. She turned her petals towards the sun and danced in the rays. She grew thirsty, but did not tell him for fear he might put her down. She was the happiest she had ever been in her short life.

Waves crashed toward their home and threatened the stag's well-being. Although he did not tell the rose, he worried for their safety. A stag could swim for shore.

A rose would surely drown.

Then one day, when the waves were at their peak, a raven flew by. The stag called out to him and begged the raven to take the rose in his claws. "Bring her somewhere safe," he pleaded. "Somewhere she can stretch her roots again."

The raven took her gently, ignoring her sad cries and petals reaching for the stag. "You're going home," he said. "A rose cannot grow where there is no soil."

They flew across land and water, sea and surf. The salt spray burned her roots and knocked all the petals from her blooms. By the time the raven put her down in the forest, she had given up.

The old oak sighed, "You are not a rose. You have no thorns."

"I am a rose, though my thorns are dull."

The birch tree swayed. "You are not a rose. You have no petals."

"I am a rose, though my petals fell off."

The ash tree wept. "You are no longer a rose, but you can become something more. Sleep in my roots for a time."

When the rose awakened, she found that the ancient trees were right.

Branches grew from her hair and bark covered her skin. Roots tangled in her feet, but she was not the same as the trees. Her body was curved, her mind clear, and she could move far from their side.

"See?" The ash said. "You aren't a rose after all."

CHAPTER ONE
THE ROSE AND THE STAG

"Sorcha, my face itches!"

"Sorcha, my stomach hurts!"

"Sorcha, I can't breathe!"

Sorcha blew a tangled curl away from her face and stared into the rafters as if she could see her sisters through the floor. They claimed the plague had rendered them useless and refused to move from their beds, no matter how many times Sorcha reminded them that they weren't dying.

Yet.

Laundry obscured her vision, piled so high she could barely see over the edge, making her biceps shake with the weight. This was the first load of many that she would need to bring to the river. She was the only family member who wasn't infected by the plague, and the only one the villagers allowed to leave the brothel.

"Small blessings," she muttered before calling out, "I'll be right there, dearest sisters!"

"But Sorcha!"

"I know your discomfort is great, but I beg you, have patience! I need to put the laundry away."

"Is the laundry more important than us?"

She rolled her eyes. Her sisters had always been superb at

convincing their father how ill they were. It was a shame they couldn't convince their healer sister.

Sorcha reminded herself that they were gravely ill. The blood beetle plague wasn't something to brush aside. It was a silent killer. But she couldn't shake off the feeling they could at least be attempting to help. Even Papa got out of bed for dinner. He didn't make her carry plates all the way upstairs and bring them back down.

A cool breeze brushed her sweat stained nape. Its touch was welcome and pleasant though surprising considering nails held the windows shut tight.

Lifting a brow, she set the laundry on the floor and nudged the kitchen door open. Her father sat feeding a small brown bird on the windowsill, wooden planks leaning against the wall next to him.

Sorcha leaned against the doorframe and crossed her arms over her chest. Papa nudged the seeds forward. Patient, he let the bird peck and eat before setting more down. Closer and closer until the tiny nuthatch hopped onto his hand and ate from his palm.

"You have a rare talent," she said.

He glanced up with a smile. "I learned this from you."

"Did you?"

"When you were little you used to say, 'Papa. Birds are scared of you because you're big. If you make yourself small and quiet, then they will like you as they like me.'"

"I don't think you've made yourself small."

"Well, I've never been good at shape shifting."

The nuthatch shook its feathers and took one last bite, flying out the window on silent wings. Papa watched it with a melancholy expression.

"You miss the outdoors," Sorcha said.

"More than anything. What season is it now?"

"Spring is coming. I think we've seen our last snowfall."

"So soon?"

"It doesn't feel soon," she chuckled. "But we're all still here. And that's a blessing."

"All of us?"

"Yes. Who else are we missing?"

Papa turned on the window seat and gave her a measured look. "I may be ill, but I am not blind. You left something behind."

"Everyone leaves something behind after a long journey."

"Even when it's another world?"

"Yes."

Sorcha took a seat at the long kitchen table, pulling the stained kerchief from her head. A mane of red curls sprang free to billow around her. It still felt strange that nothing had changed in her childhood home.

The wooden table held the marks she had carved into its edges to distract herself from family quarrels. Herbs hung over the fire to dry, filling the air with the scent of basil and rosemary. A cauldron bubbled with soup for dinner.

The same and not. She noticed details that never would have bothered her before. Dust around the edges of the hearth. Cobwebs in the high peaks of rafters. Drafts of cold air that never seemed to disappear.

She blew out a breath. "Do you want me to tell you more stories of Hy-brasil?"

"Your sisters were calling for you."

"Yes, they were."

"You don't want to tend to them?"

"Not really." Sorcha plunked her elbows onto the table and cupped her head. "Does that make me a bad person? I should want to help my sisters. They're ill, and they deserve all my attention and care."

She heard her father stand and shuffle towards her. The bench creaked as he sat down next to her. His thin hand rubbed her spine. "You've been so dedicated in keeping us all alive, I thought something terrible must have happened."

"Why?"

"No one works with such fervor unless they're trying to forget something. Or someone."

"And I am."

"I know."

She turned her head to peer over at the man who had saved her life countless times. New wrinkles had appeared on Papa's face. Crow's feet deepened into folds of skin, his forehead lined with worry and pain.

"It's still hard for me to grasp how much time passed," she said. "A year and a day? Really?"

"I can say it over and over again, Sorcha. We thought you were dead."

"I'm sorry to have caused you worry."

"Stop saying that." He reached forward and pulled her hand away from her face, holding it in his tight grip. "You experienced an adventure that none of us could ever imagine. You tell us stories every night that fill our dreams with wondrous things. It is a blessing you have returned to us."

She couldn't think of it like that. Sorcha didn't want to think about Hy-brasil at all. The haunting memories of ocean eyes and crystal skin plagued her dreams. The hole in her heart tore wider with each passing day. She didn't know how to stop the ache, so she soothed it with family. But even their comforting presence did little to fix what was broken.

Sorcha squeezed Papa's hand. "I'm glad to help. It's good to be home."

"But it's not where you want to be."

"No."

"You want to be with him."

"Yes," she breathed. "Very much."

"Then you must go back to him."

"I can't."

Papa frowned. "Why not? You can go to the Otherworld, can't you? You can find a pixie to help guide your way."

"It isn't like that. Pixies will let the king know I have returned, and he will track me down. I don't even know if Stone is still alive."

She had resorted to calling him by his nickname, for fear the wrong ears would hear his true name. Humans weren't likely to get involved with faerie politics, but one could never be too careful.

Her heart throbbed. She hoped he was alive. His vigor and strength were such that he may have won the first battle with his brother, but she had seen the golden army and feared the worst.

"Does your heart say he's alive?" Papa asked.

"Yes."

"Then he is alive."

"Ever the optimist. Did the bird tell you he still had breath in his lungs?"

"Birds tell us many things. This one told me you have not been yourself."

Sorcha's lips twitched. "Did it?"

"You know it's the truth, dear one. You haven't even visited the shrines."

"I don't want to."

"Since when?" Papa dropped her hand and slammed his fist down on the table. "Those shrines meant the world to you, even as a child. What has changed?"

"I no longer believe they are useful."

"You're lying."

She remembered how the faeries tasted lies on the air. Perhaps her father had more faerie blood in him than she did. Sorcha arched a brow. "You think so?"

"There's a hard edge to you now. You break your back taking care of us, but I don't think you want to anymore. There was a time when I thought you would work yourself to death just to save us. Now, I wonder if you even care."

"Of course I do."

"Then where is your faith? Where is your request for faeries to come and aid you? Have you grown so arrogant that you think you can do it on your own?"

She shoved away from the table. Her legs needed to move, her mind racing as she walked the kitchen end to end. "I am afraid! Is that what you want to hear? I did not fulfill my half of the bargain, and as such, I broke a faerie deal. I cannot go to the shrine because I do not know what awaits me there."

"You think they will kill you?"

"I don't know!" Sorcha threw her hands up, catching an herb on her fingers and tossing it to the ground. She sighed and stared at the ceiling. "I'll go get the broom."

"No." Papa lifted his hand. "You will not. You'll leave this house and go to the shrine."

"What will happen if I don't come back? Who will pull the beetles out of your bodies and keep you alive?"

"We managed for a year on our own."

"Because I made that part of my deal!" Her shout rose into the rafters and a pigeon took flight. She sighed and rubbed her temples. "I'm sorry, I didn't mean to shout. I don't want to see you die, and I do not trust the village healers."

"Neither do I. But, I think the faeries still have plans for you. We're alive for a reason." He stood and pulled her hands away from her face. "You're a talented healer, Sorcha. But you aren't the only reason the beetles haven't killed us yet."

He was right. She had noticed how quickly they healed from her surgeries. The beetles weren't multiplying inside them as they were in her other patients. In fact, the entire brothel seemed stuck in a single point of time. They remained ill, with the same amount of beetles, but the sickness did not grow.

"I have nothing to bring them," she mumbled. "No sugar, no cream, no flowers from our gardens."

"Then you will bring them your apologies."

"Faeries don't care for my guilt. They care for offerings."

"Perhaps they will forgive you. I remember a time when people used to go to the shrines just to be with the faeries in nature. I don't believe everything is about giving them something. Sometimes, the giving is in being there."

"When did you become a philosopher?" she asked with a wry grin.

"About the same time I looked death in the eyes and he told me that my daughter saved my life."

Tears stung her eyes. "Oh, Papa."

"Don't you 'Oh, Papa' me. Get on with you girl, and pick some of those lovely greens on the way back."

"Dandelions?"

"I don't care if they're a weed, they taste delicious and they do my old bones good. Say hello to the faeries for me."

She cast a critical glance at the laundry and shrugged. "Why don't you come with me? You've never greeted them before."

"They wouldn't want me to start now. They'd see an old man stumbling towards them and think I'd lost my way. It's far easier for them to connect with a pretty, young woman. Now, off with you!"

Sorcha didn't wait for any further arguments. Her sisters would yell again, and then her opportunity would disappear. She raced from the kitchen, wrapped her cloak around her shoulders, and plunged outside.

Cold air sank into her lungs with fine, claw-like points. It made her gasp, charging her blood with electricity. She came alive when she left the brothel.

She had changed so much.

Papa wasn't wrong when he pointed out her lack of care. She'd missed her family dearly, but the distance had provided her with experience and perspective. Her sisters couldn't stop talking about trivial things, men, cleanliness, food and drink. Her father only spoke of his travels, though at least that was slightly entertaining. And none of them had the magical qualities of the Fae who she held dear in her heart.

The old fence door squeaked as she opened it. One of these days, she would fix the rusty hinge. She needed to fix the window shutters, the rotting holes in the roof, clean up the backyard… The list went on and on.

Perhaps she resented this life. For a time, she had lived in a castle, waited on hand and foot. Now she was the one who waited upon others.

"Have I fallen so far?" she questioned and cast a glance towards the silhouette of her home. "Do I resent them for being ill?"

Yes. The answer was a resounding yes that echoed in her head like a scream in a canyon.

She gripped the fence in her hands, glaring up at the house as if *it* was the problem.

"Sorcha! It's too cold to be outside." The smooth masculine voice made the hair on the back of her neck raise.

Plastering on a fake smile, she bared her teeth. "Geralt."

He strode toward her with all the grace of a dancer. Tight pants hugged his legs, accentuating what he believed to be his best feature. A grand cloak of black wool swept the ground behind him clear of fallen snow.

"You'll catch a cold, Sorcha, and who will take care of you while you take care of your family?"

"I manage quite well on my own."

"But you shouldn't have to." He stripped the leather gloves from his hands, finger by finger. "Please, allow me."

"I'm not taking your gloves, Geralt."

"You most certainly are! What kind of gentleman would I be if I let you wander without proper clothing?"

He reached forward and took her hand, pressing the gloves into her palms with a smile that made her want to smack him. She let the leather fall to the ground.

"Is this how you usually treat women? As if they don't understand when they need to take care of themselves?"

"They shouldn't *have* to take care of themselves."

"What if some of us want to?"

"Why ever would you?"

Sorcha snorted and rolled her eyes. "You'll never understand."

"Nor do I wish to. I enjoy taking care of those who are dear to my heart—"

"Don't." She lifted a hand to interrupt him. "I have no interest in hearing what you have to say. I have places to be, Geralt. Now, if you don't mind."

"I'll walk with you. Are you going into town?"

Certainly if a single woman were traveling, she must be going to town. Sorcha tried not to roll her eyes, and failed horribly. Where else would a single woman be going but to town? Ridiculous man.

"I'm going to the shrine."

"What shrine? At the church?"

"No. In the forest."

"Ah," he said and frowned. "You would never have admitted that before your disappearance."

"People change."

"Apparently so."

Her boots crunched through the snow, leaving the faintest hint of footprints in her wake. She wouldn't stand around and listen to him say anything else about her life. She had no interest in speaking with a man who wanted her to bend to his will.

"Where were you anyways?"

He didn't know when to leave well enough alone.

The hills were all white around them. No trees sprung up from the earth, only small mounds where stone walls stood. Even the sheep stayed close to their barns this time of year. No one wanted to wander too far from the safety of a fire.

Sorcha tucked her cloak tight against her body and ducked her head. Perhaps, if she was lucky, Geralt would leave.

"Did you hear me? I asked where you went."

She sighed. "You've asked me that same question a hundred times over."

"Yes, I have. And you have yet to give me any kind of answer."

"I'm not sure why I'm required to answer you at all."

"You aren't. I wish to know."

"Why?"

"I care for you, Sorcha. You know this."

If she rolled her eyes any harder, she'd see the back of her head. "You care for the *idea* of me! You don't know me."

"I do! I've known you since you were a child."

"You rode past me with your father a few times. That hardly counts as knowing."

The tromping sounds he made through the snow grated on her nerves. Didn't the man know how to be quiet? She wanted a peaceful walk to the shrine! Was that really too much to ask?

"I've been talking to Briana through the wall, and she told me where you think you were. The faerie world, isn't that the story you've told?"

"Briana talks too much," she grumbled.

"You know faeries aren't real, don't you Sorcha?"

She cast a sidelong glance towards him and stopped walking. He had no right to tell her what was real, and what wasn't. This man pushed too much, thought he knew far more than a simple woman, and she grew weary of men who thought so highly of themselves.

"Geralt, is the sky blue?"

"Yes." He hesitated as he answered, looking at her as if she had lost her mind.

"Is the grass green?"

"Yes."

"But it's white right now."

"Well, there's snow on it."

"Then how do you know there is green underneath?"

"Because I've seen it."

"And if you hadn't?" She gestured towards the fields. "If you had never seen green grass before, how would you know what color it was? Would you not think grass was white?"

"I'd move the snow."

She kicked her foot, toeing the ground until it revealed the yellowed dead grass underneath. "You'd be wrong then, wouldn't you?"

"What are you trying to teach me?"

"You haven't seen the faeries, but you seem to think you know about them. Before you judge the hills to be green, I suggest you attempt to see them first. Faeries won't like you entering their shrine without permission. I really must go alone."

His jaw dropped, and she didn't wait to see what he might do next. Geralt had tried for far too long to woo her. And as much as he would make a good, traditional husband, he would not be a good husband for her.

Women were two-dimensional to him. They fit into a little box of his own making so he could explain their reasoning and actions. Sorcha stunned him every time she opened her mouth. Perhaps that was why he found her so intriguing. But she thought it more likely that he wanted to tame her.

That would never happen.

Snow crunched behind her.

"If you keep walking towards me Geralt, I will put you on your back in the snow. Leave me be."

"You've changed!" he called out.

"Yes," she said. "I have."

Her father wasn't the only one to notice. The bitterness in her heart had spread so far that she couldn't control it. Pain made her angry, and this wasn't a physical pain she could mend with herbs or medicine.

Bran had been wrong. He said she'd put herself back together, find meaning in saving lives.

She had done exactly the opposite. Bitter anger festered in her soul until she looked at the blood beetle victims as weak creatures. Sorcha didn't like the changes in herself, but she didn't know how to stop them.

The forest appeared in the distance. A snow squall headed her way, small enough that it wouldn't touch her once she ducked beneath the trees. Snow-laden branches touched the ground. They looked as though they were bowing to her as she stepped into the shadows.

If only they were. She wished the trees could hear her, that a man might step out of their bark and beckon her forward. "Come to us," he would say. "Find our hidden secrets and faerie rings.

She shook her head. The villagers claimed she lost her mind. A strange man must have kidnapped her, done horrible things, and the poor dear had broken. Why else would she speak of faeries as if they were real?

"Forever misplaced," she grunted as she ducked beneath a branch. "Always the one believing in the wrong things."

The woods were quiet. Too quiet.

No branches pulled at her hair, warning her to hide her anger. No birds sang their songs. Only stillness and the muffled thump of snow falling from the trees.

Where were the faeries? Where was the wind that brushed through her hair?

Brows furrowed, she stepped into the well-known clearing with anxiety twisting her stomach. There was something wrong.

"Is it me? Have I offended you, Macha?"

Even the light had disappeared from this sacred place. No water burbled in the stones. The triskele carvings turned dull with age, no magical glow giving them life.

She hadn't thought this was how they would punish her. Silence was worse than the threat of death.

"Are you never going to let me see you again?" A tear slid down her cheek. "You can't hide from me. I can see through your glamour!"

No giggles danced on the wind. Nothing but silence.

"You're just going to cut me off?"

She wanted to scream. She wanted to rage at the faeries who thought she deserved this, but the truth rang in her head. They could never see her again and it wouldn't hurt them at all.

They ripped magic from her life and everyone she held dear.

Sorcha lifted her chin, locking her knees so she would not fall and embarrass herself. She would remain steady. Tears dripped down her cheeks, but she refused to admit that was a weakness.

Only those strong enough to feel let tears fall.

"I will not apologize," she pleaded. "I was gone longer than expected, and I did not leave willingly, but I had to take care of my family. It was not a slight against you or your kind that I did not keep this shrine alive."

A sharp pain dug into her ankle, twin points of agony that ground against the delicate bone. She gasped and glanced down. A bright green snake, as long as she was tall, rose out of the snow.

Its mouth closed around her ankle, impossibly wide with silver fangs that dug deeper and deeper into her flesh. It coiled, looping its thick ropey body around her shin.

Pain and numbness spread from the viper's fangs. It stared up at her with glittering cold eyes.

"Impossible," she slurred. Snakes couldn't move in the winter. Snakes like that didn't live in Ui Neill.

She tasted nightshade on her tongue. Her tongue thickened, lips growing numb. She knew the signs of poison well.

Eamonn lifted his face to the blistering cold wind. It whistled through the crevices on his cheeks, sinking deeper and deeper into his being. The freezing edge of winter was as much a part of him now as the exaggerated limp and useless right arm.

"Master!" Cian shouted through the shrieking wind. "We cannot keep going!"

"We must!"

They could not stop in the storm. Snow blew against them, pushing jagged edges of ice underneath their clothing. Relentless and angry, the Otherworld appeared determined to destroy them.

He pulled the hood of his fur cloak lower and tilted his head down. He would beat back the wind himself if it meant they would reach their destination.

There weren't many of them left. His brother had ridden onto the isle with single-minded intent. Destroy everything in his path and leave nothing but smears of blood and ash.

"M-Master!" Oona coughed the words, her lungs weak from days in the frigid tundra. "I can't go any further!"

"We have to keep going."

"I—"

The wind swept past his ears, drowning out any words she might have said. Anger heated his blood. The crystals around his neck flared with bright violet light.

"Oona, I don't have time to argue with you. We continue on towards the dwarven stronghold! It's the only place where we might find sympathetic faeries."

They didn't respond.

Growling, Eamonn spun on his heel. His cloak flared around him and cold air buffeted his chest. It sank deep into the crystal wounds lacing his body.

Oona sat in the snow, shoulders slumped and heaving. Cian knelt beside her with his hand on her shoulder, his expression one of complete loss.

They were all bundled up in whatever they could find. Fifteen people left from the hundreds who had lived on the isle. A mother and her child hung near the back, the tiny pooka still healing from an injury a midwife might have tended.

Boggart hung near the back, her thin frame quaking with every breath. She was too thin, too small for such a journey.

He imagined he could see an outline behind the faeries. A pillar of shadows that shifted and moved. Red curls hung about her face, vivid even in the ghostly form.

She stood behind them, watching over each staggered movement. She haunted his footsteps with the echoes of her voice.

"Take care of them," she whispered on the wind. "They need you."

Eamonn sighed and rubbed a hand over his face.

"We'll stop awhile."

"The dwarves?" Cian asked.

"Nowhere to be found, my friend. We're going in the right direction, but they don't want to make themselves known just yet."

"Damn dwarves. They'll let us freeze to death and rob the clothes from our back."

Oona whimpered. "I remember dwarves. They were kind creatures with hearts made of pure gold. They could sing magic that would let women spin gold from straw."

"You're delirious," Cian grumbled. "That wasn't the dwarves."

"You've never met a dwarf."

Eamonn didn't have time to listen to them quarrel about yet another faerie species. Rolling his eyes, he pointed towards the few who remained on their feet.

"You, find something for kindling. You, help me create a bank out of snow to give us some kind of shelter. You, gather up clean snow for water so we can boil it. You—" he pointed at the mother. "Take the extra furs and bundle him up."

"I couldn't, m'lord. The others need them just as much as us."

"Your boy's lips are turning blue. Let him have a turn with the furs first, and tuck Boggart in with him. We'll pass them around later."

Gods, he tired of the cold. He wished for a warm ale in his hand, an able-bodied woman on his lap, and the cold to disappear forever.

None of which were likely to happen. He had sent away the only woman he wanted in his lap, there was no ale, and frost was gathering around his lips again. He grunted and shook ice spikes from his shoulders.

The others quickly set up camp. They'd had enough practice over the weeks of travel. He looked back at them as he set his back to work, pushing the snow into some semblance of a shelter.

They huddled together for warmth and comfort. Not a single faerie kept a hand from each other. Even Cian reached out to smooth hair from a forehead, touching fingers to lips, whispering words of encouragement in ears.

He ground his teeth. They wouldn't offer anything to him. He was the master, the invincible Tuatha dé Danann who held the sky at bay.

If only that were the truth. He shook his head and pushed the snow until a thick, tightly packed wall sheltered them. Wind dashed over the top, blowing flecks in his face as he stood. It would do for the night.

The selkie looking for kindling returned, shaking his head. "There's nothing, master."

"Of course not," Eamonn grumbled. This cursed land was trying to kill them.

He raised an arm against the biting storm and charged towards their supplies. The sled made for perfect kindling, and it would be drier than whatever was buried underneath the snow. They could carry the food and water in their packs.

"Master!" Cian called out. The gnome was just a head traveling through the drifts, his body lost in the mass of white. "We need that!"

"We'll put everything in the packs."

"We can't carry any more on our backs!"

"We need to stay warm."

"Then we'll huddle in the shelter you made."

"Without a fire, we'll all die, Cian. It has to happen."

Cian reached his side, jumped, and grabbed Eamonn's arm. The weight pulled him to the side. "We cannot carry any more."

Anger surged through his veins, so strong that he saw red.

"Then I will carry it myself!" he shouted as he loomed over the gnome. "I will lose no more to this fucking cold!"

The storm raged on. Bitter cold winds pummeled their bodies, digging into their furs, and leaving ice crystals on their bare faces. Cian stared at him with a frown.

"We will lose people, master. It is inevitable."

"Not if I can stop it."

Eamonn turned and pulled the remaining packs from the sled. He set them with the others, marking their location in his mind so he could find them tomorrow. The snow would bury them.

The sled had served them well, and now it would do even better. He lifted the six foot frame and snapped it like a twig between his hands.

Cian sighed. "Well, you'll be wearing those."

"I said I'd carry them."

"It's a lot of weight. That's most of our food and water."

"Enough, Cian."

"I'm just trying to look out for you, master. You certainly aren't doing it."

"I don't need someone to look out for me," Eamonn growled. He cracked the remaining pieces and tucked them under his arm. "Let's go back and get the others fed."

They trudged through the snow. Cian spat into the wind as they reached the higher drifts, the wad froze before it hit the ground.

"What are you planning to say to the dwarves?" Cian called out. "They don't like your kind!"

"They'll like what I have to say."

"And if they don't?" The gnome hopped up to catch a glimpse of Eamonn's expression. "They aren't the most amiable lot."

"They don't have to like it; they just have to do as I say."

"Right, because that has a history of working so well with dwarves."

"They like my brother even less than they like me."

"That's not because he's your brother or even that he's the king. They don't like Tuatha dé Danann. They might not even let you in."

"Then we can all be thankful that I'm this large. I'll force my way in."

"Through solid gold doors?"

Eamonn lifted a crystal fist. His hand had been injured in the fighting, the bones turned to a solid mass of violet. He could still move it slowly, but it took practice. He considered it a small miracle and tried not to fear the change.

Cian audibly swallowed. "Point taken, master."

It took only a few moments to get the fire started in the center of the bank. Magic assisted to dry the wood, and soon a merry crackle sang over the howling wind.

Eamonn set himself apart from the others. He was furthest from the fire, allowing the others to soak up the warmth. Their small bodies needed it more than he did. Oona roasted vegetables with a pan from Cian's pack and a large packet of herbs, honey, and milk.

"Master?" she asked. "Will you join us?"

He shook his head and flashed a mouthful of dried venison.

They huddled together in a lump of Lesser Fae. The boy tucked himself so close to the fire that Eamonn worried he'd set himself alight. They were all exhausted, cold, and hungry.

He could do little more than shoulder the heavier burdens. He chewed his food, ignoring the worried glances Oona cast over her shoulder. The gnome must have told her about their conversation.

Worry ate at his mind. He didn't want to tell them the extent of his injuries. His hand was the least of his worries. Valleys and crevices stretched across his body in all directions.

He barely felt the cold. The numbing ice sank into his crystals and only barely slowed his body; it didn't affect him like the others.

It was worrisome.

Eamonn had never pushed the affliction as far as it could go. He didn't want to know what would happen when he was more geode than man.

He hadn't told them that Fionn's blade had caught him by surprise. Eamonn could still see his twin as he rode from behind and lifted his blade. Eamonn had felt him, like a cold wind that danced down his spine.

He turned, and the blade followed the same path their father's sword had. It dug along the dip of flesh and bone through his eye.

Eamonn took care not to show the others. He didn't want them to see the fractured half of his eyeball, the crystal splitting the orb. He touched it now and then, musing that he didn't even feel the touch. All the other wounds were sensitive, but not this one.

If he closed the other eye, he saw the world in fractured pieces. A few faeries turned in hundreds. Fire became a blaze that stretched all around him. He wondered if this was what madness felt like.

"Master?" Oona called out one last time. "We're going to rest. Join us?"

"No."

"It's warmer by the fire."

"Sleep well, Pixie. I'll take the first watch."

She grimaced. "The only watch."

"Indeed."

"You have to sleep sometime, Eamonn."

"Not tonight. We're too close to dwarven territory. I'll not be caught off guard."

He ignored the tears that welled in her eyes. He couldn't fall prey to her emotions, no matter how tired he was.

Soldiering was what he did. Their travels brought back memories of a time long ago when he had pushed his men towards armies of Unseelie Fae. They had scattered before his great sword, running from the Untouched Prince.

He had never seen the Otherworld with snow like this. The drifts were nearly as large as he was in some areas. He guided the faeries around the mountain-like structures and hoped it wouldn't tire them out too much.

Obviously, he had been wrong. They all fell asleep within moments of laying their heads down on the ground.

The fire crackled. The wind howled. And Eamonn remained so still that snow gathered on his shoulders in small lumps. Hours passed but his mind never quieted.

He didn't need the fire, for a fire lived in his memories. Sorcha, the one woman who had captivated his thoughts since the moment she burst into his throne room. She danced in his mind's eye, swaying to and fro with the fire. She wore the green dress, the one he was particularly fond of, and the flared skirt fanned around her like ocean waves.

Gods, how he missed her, but this was no life for a woman like her. He hoped she had gone home, found her family, and maybe a good man to give her children and warm nights.

The crystals on his throat throbbed. Any man who dared touch her would find himself at the end of Eamonn's blade. Perhaps it would be better if she were alone.

A shadow moved in the corner of his eye. Short, stout, and far too narrow to be a gnome, the dwarf slipped past the sleeping faeries.

Dwarves were shifty folk. They had sticky fingers, and no one could find them in the winding tunnel systems that made up the dwarven strongholds.

The shadow shifted again, but Eamonn did not move. Still as stone, he willed his body into complete silence. He didn't even breathe as the dwarf slid over a mound of snow and made his way towards their packs.

At least, Eamonn thought it was a he. The beard suggested "male" but one never knew with certainty until they spoke.

Eamonn stood and silently made his way towards the thief. His footsteps made no sound, and he did not reach for his sword, knowing Ocras would sing for blood.

His face twisted into a snarl as he darted forward. The dwarf had no chance, Eamonn's hands closed around its shirt.

"Oy!" the dwarf wriggled violently, trying to slide out of the jacket.

Eamonn twisted his fist, crunching crystals through the fabric, forcing the dwarf to remain still. "You're going nowhere."

"Le' go!"

"I don't let go of thieves."

"I ain't a thief!"

"You were stealing from our packs."

The dwarf stilled its struggles, narrowed its eyes, and shrugged. "I was just looking at 'em."

"Why?"

"Thought they might 'ave something interesting inside."

"But you weren't planning on stealing?"

"No, sir."

Eamonn arched a crystal brow. "Let me get this straight. You were just going to look at the packs?"

"Sure was."

"Just to see if something interesting was inside."

"That was the plan."

"And if you found something you fancied, you would leave it."

"You got it, mate."

"Even if it was a valuable sword?"

The dwarf's eyes dipped to the red gem on the pommel of Ocras. "Well, that might 'ave been a different story."

"You would have taken that."

"A pack of hungry peasants don't 'ave any need for valuable objects."

"So you would steal something worth money?"

"I wouldn't call it stealing," the dwarf quipped.

"You'd leave something behind for it?"

"Sure would."

"Like what?"

Eamonn could see that the question stumped the dwarf. It wiggled its feet and shrugged again. "I'd 'ave found something."

"Do you have any food on your person?"

"No."

"Any water?"

"Just snow."

"Then you have nothing worthy of trade. That's called stealing," he said as he leaned closer to glare into the dwarf's gaze. "And do you know what I do with dwarves who steal from me?"

The soft creaking of a bow being drawn carried on the wind. Eamonn stiffened and listened for the telltale rustle of feathers as an arrow was notched.

"I think you would say that you gave thieves whatever they wanted and let them go in peace," the heavily accented voice rumbled. "Now put the girl down."

Eamonn cocked his head to the side and looked the dwarf in his grasp up and down. "Girl?"

"What?" she pinwheeled her arms at him. "You couldn't tell? Come 'ere I'll show you what a girl looks like up close!"

The dwarf behind him barked, "Put 'er down."

"I don't think so," Eamonn twisted his hand until the girl yelped. "Now."

Eamonn glanced over his shoulder at the dwarf who planted his feet into the snow. His bow stretched higher than his head, and Eamonn was certain this one was male. His grey beard fluttered in the wind and silver-plated armor decorated his body.

Their gazes locked and Eamonn gave him a feral grin.

Oona stirred, waking from her slumber to blink at the standoff. "Master," she murmured. "Perhaps you should do what he says."

But he was already angry. So angry that he wasn't thinking straight and frustrated that the dwarves were already pulling weapons. What had he done to earn their hatred? They didn't know who he was. They had no right.

He twisted the girl's jacket until she grasped the neck and wheezed.

"Shoot the arrow," Eamonn said. "Show us the true nature of dwarven hospitality."

The dwarf didn't hesitate. He loosed the arrow that cut snowflakes in half and struck Eamonn right over his heart. The metal tip bent as it struck flesh and then crystal. Wood shattered into splinters that decorated the snow in tiny shards.

Eamonn felt nothing. He cared for nothing. All he knew was that the dwarf had attacked.

Cocking his head to the side, he dropped the girl onto the ground and snapped the metal tip from his crystal. "You cut my jacket."

The dwarf dropped his bow into the snow. "What are you?"

The smaller dwarf at his feet scuttled backwards. "Cursed."

"Monster," the other echoed. "You are not welcome on dwarf lands. We will drive you and your cursed people out."

"You can try," Eamonn growled.

Oona scrambled to her feet, holding out her hands. "No, please. He's no monster!"

"Explain what he is then, because the dwarves do not abide by black magic."

"He is your king!"

The wind whistled through his crystals and Eamonn stared the dwarves down. The little girl climbed towards the male, ducking behind him as if that would keep her safe. His hand hovered over Ocras, but he did not pull her free. Not yet.

"King?" The dwarf shook his head. "There is only one king."

"You are correct," Oona warned. "You stand before the High King of the Seelie Court. The firstborn son of Lorcan the Brave."

"Who, the Untouched? He's dead."

"I'm not dead," Eamonn said. "Far from it."

The dwarf shook his head. "Well, pull my beard. If it's really you, the lord under the mountain will want to see you."

"Wait just a minute," the female dwarf grumbled. "'Ow do we know it's really 'im?"

"You don't," Eamonn said.

Oona shuffled forward, hesitating when the dwarves backed away. "I am Fae, just as you. I cannot lie."

"You could believe that he's the high king, and he might lead you astray."

"I cared for him as a child. I sang songs to him when he slept, and I watched while they hung him. This is the eldest son, the one spoken of in song."

"And what do you want with the dwarves?" He directed his question to Eamonn with a nod.

He shifted, placing his hand against Ocras. His furred cloak parted in the breeze and revealed his crystal fist and misshapen torso.

"I wish to speak with the lord under the mountain regarding an army."

"For what?"

"For war against Fionn the Wise."

"You want to take back the throne?"

Eamonn shrugged. "I wish to see my brother's head on a stake."

"You have no desire for the throne?"

"We shall see how the story unfolds. The rest is for your lord's ears alone."

The dwarves turned their back on Eamonn and the rest of his crew. They wrapped their arms around each other and mumbled. One of their heads would raise to meet his unwavering gaze before they ducked back down.

Finally, they turned as one. "We'll take you underground."

"You'll feed and wash my people."

"We take only you."

"You take everyone." Eamonn's hand flexed on the pommel of his sword. "Or I'll insist upon justice for the attempted theft and find myself another dwarf."

"You'd never find another."

"If you think I cannot tear this mountain apart, then you do not know my reputation."

The male dwarf snorted. "Come on then. The lot of you."

Eamonn turned his back on them and gestured at Oona. "Wake the others. We're going underground."

CHAPTER TWO

THE MEDICINE AND THE BLADE

Sorcha couldn't breathe, couldn't think, couldn't feel. Black sparks obscured her vision as poison coursed through her veins. The snake sunk its fangs deeper into her ankle.

Blood dripped from the twin punctures onto the snow where it sizzled and sank to the earth. Swallowing hard, unable to feel her own tongue, she glanced down and watched seedlings grow from the perfect red circles. The snow melted around their fragile stems.

She blinked and the powdery white returned, its blood-stained imperfection swallowing the seedlings.

The snake squeezed her leg, unlatched its mouth, and wound its way up her body. The smooth scales rasped against her skin as it looped around her neck and opened its mouth wide.

Venom dripped from each fang. She felt the poison land on her cloak, burning through the thick fabric and sticking to her breast. It burned, but she couldn't lift her hand to brush it away.

Her gaze caught the slitted eyes of the snake. A low hiss vibrated through her skull and the air turned hot. She panted, but could not inhale enough air. Not while the creature swayed, tightening around her throat.

It looked away from her, pointing its flat head towards the forest beyond.

Delirious, she stared at the trees and watched the snow melt. Leaves unfurled and moss grew upon the trunks, so thick and lush that it rivaled any she had seen before.

The trees moved. They did not pull up their roots or bend. They parted like a wave as if the world ripped in half and a new path formed.

Sorcha furrowed her brows, struggling to stand and watch the phenomenon. The snake hissed in her ear and it sounded like words.

"Walk forward," it said. "Walk towards your destiny."

But she couldn't walk. She couldn't even lift a foot as the venom that tasted like nightshade froze in her veins. She was cold. So cold.

Snapping jaws closed around her jugular, sinking deep into the corded muscle of her neck and pumping more venom into her body. She felt it. Cold like ice and hot like fire all at the same time. It unthreaded from her neck and stretched in splintered pieces throughout her body.

"Go," the snake hissed again. "The trees know the way."

A tear slid down her cheek and she stepped forward. Whispers echoed in the trees. Not faeries, for she knew their voices well. The deep grumbles came from within the earth, tangled in the roots of trees. They groaned out legends, myths, and stories about a rose garden that grew between great oaks.

Sorcha listened as she walked through their path. Her vision warped, and she saw people in the shadows. Not faeries, not dryads, but figures wearing leather with their faces painted blue.

The sun set, and the moon rose at the end of the path—a full moon though she was certain it had already passed. Her head tilted to the side, baring her neck to the snake which hissed in her ear. The moon was dripping silver.

Fat droplets fell towards an altar at the end of the path. Sluggishly, they dripped into the basin. The water turned silvery-white, like milk with rainbows dancing upon the oiled surface.

"Drink," the viper hissed. "Drink and join the others."

"What others?" Sorcha asked, her words slurred.

The snake didn't answer. She heard her ragged breath mingling with the steady thrum of her heart. It sounded like the beat of drums.

It was drums, she realized, drums beaten by those standing among the trees. They weren't there, she thought. They couldn't be there because she could see through them. They held swords and spears in their hands. The sound came from striking blade against shield.

"Drink the moon?" she slurred. She could already taste the heady flavor. The cold ice water that would wash away the nightshade as she swallowed.

"Drink," the viper hissed again.

Sorcha stepped forward and dipped her hands into the altar. Underneath the milk white water, her flesh melted away. She flexed her skeletal hands, whimpering because there was no pain. Only a blank space where feeling should be.

She wondered how she was meant to hold the water in these hands. But as she scooped it in her palms, the flesh returned. She lifted the moon to her lips and drank deeply of its essence.

It slid down her throat like a balm. The physical effects of the poison washed away. Closing her eyes, she reveled in the return of sensation.

The viper's jaw snapped.

Sorcha opened her eyes and stared at the moon. Blood dripped from the top and turned it red.

"A bad omen," she said.

"Not for us," the viper hissed. "Never for us."

"Us?"

The phantoms stepped forward. Their hands trailed down her sides until Sorcha could no longer tell what was a hallucination and what was really happening. She could feel their fingers clutching her flesh.

They lifted the snake from her neck and stripped the clothing from her body. They plucked at her hair, pulling strands from her head. Their fingers were cold.

Shivering violently, she wrapped her arms around her nudity and stared at their painted faces. They warped, changing from man to beast.

To nightmares.

A woman stepped forward, twigs tangled in the long length of her wild hair. She was nude as well, twin circles painted around her breasts and runes carved into her skin.

"Welcome, sister." She placed a crown of ivy on top of Sorcha's red head.

"Sister?"

"We're all sisters," another voice rasped in her ear. "And now you have finally returned."

"I've never been here before."

"You have."

"No," Sorcha shook her head. "I would remember this place."

They traced circles on her skin, leaving blue paint in their wake until runes and markings she did not recognize covered her body.

Hands pushed her forward, towards another altar she had not noticed.

"Lie down," the voice behind her cajoled. "Lie down and join us."

"I don't know what is happening."

"Come home," they chorused. "Come home and finally be free."

"Free?" Tears gathered in her eyes, although she could not explain why. "I want to be free."

They pushed and pulled, stretching Sorcha out on the altar. The red light of the moon bathed her skin, its rays nearly as warm as the sun.

She heard the vines slithering over the stone altar before she saw them. Leaves softly rustled as they tentatively touched her legs and wrapped around her calves. They twisted around her arms and coiled in her hair.

"What is happening?" she moaned. "What are you doing to me?"

"We're waking you up," a voice sang. "It's long past time for you to join your mother."

"My mother is dead."

"Your mother is always alive."

Sorcha's mind spun as the painted women chanted. They linked hands and rocked back and forth. They spoke in a language she did not understand, but that didn't matter. The moon was shining, its rays red as blood.

She thought the moon had cured her of the viper's venom but she had been wrong.

The snake's scales rasped over her hipbone. It traveled up her belly, between her breasts, and arched until it loomed over her and obscured the red moon. It opened its mouth.

The women stopped chanting. All fell silent as a fat drop of venom landed upon Sorcha's chest.

"It is time," the women cried out. "Will you join us?"

"Yes," she found herself saying. "Yes I will join you."

The snake lunged forward and sank its fangs into her neck.

Sorcha jolted forward. She landed on her knees in the snow, curling her fingers in the cold. She patted her body down, feeling only her woolen cloak and thick layers of skirts.

"What?" she mumbled.

It wasn't possible. She had been in that forest glen with chanting women and a snake digging its fangs… She felt her neck for puncture wounds.

Two perfect scabs left raised edges on her neck.

"Hello, granddaughter." The voice came from the edge of the clearing. It sounded like the whisper of tree leaves and strangely familiar.

She glanced up at the man. A leather thong pulled his silver hair back. Furs covered his body, and he held a staff made of silver wood she did not recognize. He stared at her with a gentle expression and recognition in his green eyes.

She knew his eyes.

"You have my mother's eyes," she observed.

"That is because she shared mine. Just as you do."

"Who are you?"

"I am your grandfather."

"What happened to me?" Sorcha gestured at her neck. "Was that real?"

"In a way. The things that happen in our minds always have meaning and are not always simply in our heads."

"What was it?"

"An ancient ritual no longer practiced by our kind."

"Our kind?" She shook her head. "I'm sorry, I don't understand. Who are you?"

He strode forward and held out a hand. "My name is Torin. I am your grandfather."

She stared at his hand. Fine wrinkles stretched from the palm out to his fingers. They would have meant nothing to her before coming to this clearing, but she read them easily. A long life. A lost love.

Sorcha slid her fingers into his. "You are my mother's father?"

"I am indeed." He pulled her to her feet. "And you look exactly like her."

"You knew her?"

"I did."

"I did not."

"An unfortunate mistake I take full blame for. She should never have been allowed to leave when she was insistent upon staying so close to the Fae."

"Why did you let her?" Sorcha's heart clenched. "If you knew it was dangerous, why did you let her go?"

"She wanted to take you into the wilds of the world. Brigid was never afraid of anyone."

"Brigid," Sorcha repeated the beloved word. "You knew my mother."

"She was beautiful, like you."

"I am not beautiful."

He reached forward and tucked a wayward strand of hair behind her ear. "How do you feel?"

"Like myself."

"Not new?"

Sorcha flexed her fingers. "Perhaps a little new. What should I feel like?"

"Changed."

"Why?"

"You took part in the ceremony. You are not the same person anymore."

"Why can I not be the same person as before?"

"You gained much knowledge."

"And knowledge changes a person?"

"It does."

Sorcha wracked her mind for any differences, but she could feel none. She shook her head. "I feel the same."

Torin frowned and held out his staff. "Take this."

She took it.

"It's well made," she observed.

"Does it feel warm to the touch?"

"No."

"Hm," he pulled it out of her hands and pointed towards the forest. "Look at the forest. What do you see?"

"Trees."

"And?"

"Leaves."

"Hm," he grumbled again. "And listen to the air. What do you hear?"

She closed her eyes and exhaled. She tried to listen, but couldn't focus. Her hands were shaking, her heart beating so rapidly she forgot how to breathe.

Had she really been in the forest glen this whole time? Had the snake been in her mind? The women too?

He hadn't answered her questions. Instead, Torin had spoken in veiled truths and strange riddles.

Who was he?

She found it hard to believe a relative appeared out of nowhere. Her mother's family had never tried to contact her before. Nor did she remember her mother ever speaking of them. It was as if they didn't exist at all.

"Child?" he asked. "What do you hear?"

"The wind," she shrugged and opened her eyes. "I hear the same things as before."

"Try again."

"I fail to see what you are doing. Why do you want me to listen, look, and feel? What good will this do?"

"I'm trying to see what kind of druid you are."

"I am me." Sorcha lifted her hands palm up. "I am Sorcha of Ui Neill. I am a healer and a friend of the Fae. That is all."

"A druid is always something."

"Then I shall be the first to remain who I am."

"Your mother was one of the Banduri. A legendary healer and seeress."

"My mother was just a healer," she corrected. "A friend of the Fae, as am I."

Torin scoffed. "You can ignore your legacy all you want, but you are one of ours. You accepted it in the ritual and now you must learn."

"I don't take kindly to people telling me I *must* do things."

"You will learn!" He struck the staff upon the ground, and an echoing strike slammed against her ears. "You have no choice!"

"You will be silent, old man!"

Her scream echoed through the forest and shook snow from the leaves. A cry echoed hers, the aching grumble of a troll awakened from its slumber.

"Oh," he said. "So you are one of those."

"What did you say?"

"We call your breed of druid a 'Weaver.'"

Sorcha shook her head. "What are you talking about?"

"A Weaver's purpose is to tie together the lives of druid and Fae. To link those of us who keep watch over the land and its people. It is a rare gift."

"What do you want from me?"

"I want nothing from you." He flexed his hands on the staff, leaning against it with a soft smile. "I want to help."

"What can you possibly help me with?"

"Curing the plague. Returning home to your lost love. Finding the faeries and affecting the course of time."

Sorcha blinked.

What was he going on about? Did he really think he could change all those things with a little druid magic?

"The druids are long gone," she said. "How do I know you can do all you say you can?"

"Trust me."

"I find that trust has grown far more difficult to earn."

"Yes, after all you have gone through, I imagine it is."

"What do you know of me?"

Torin nodded towards the remains of the faerie stones. "I have watched you since the beginning. I know you went to Hy-brasil, that you fell in love with the high king. I saw him force you to leave the isle so he could battle his brother without fear you would fall."

Sorcha's heart leapt in her throat. Eamonn's image danced before her eyes. "Is he well?"

The question fell from her tongue like a drop from the moon. She wanted to suck it back in, to not ask at all for fear of what he would say. Her heart hadn't healed yet. It couldn't be torn open again so soon.

"He lives," Torin said.

Her knees buckled, and she fell back onto the ground. "He lives?"

"He fights for the throne."

"I told him to," she sighed. "I don't know if that was right or wrong."

"He will save his people, but you must save him."

"Why?" She looked up at her grandfather and saw an eye painted in the center of his forehead. Memories swam in her mind, images of a fearsome beast and her husband. "You work for the Unseelie Queen."

"I have contact with her, but a druid works for no one."

"Why am I so linked with the fate of the Fae?"

"You are his." Torin smiled. "And he is yours. The end does not happen without both sides of the coin."

"And his fate decides that of the Fae?"

"Precisely."

"Oh, Eamonn," she said quietly so that Torin would not hear the faerie's real name. The forgotten prince was so intertwined with the future and he didn't even know. "I should be there with him."

"Yes, you should. But not now."

"Why not now?"

"There are people you must save."

Sorcha threw her hands into the air. "Why does everyone keep telling me that? I cannot save anyone at all! The blood beetle plague is worse than before. I need a cure."

"Then you must ask for one."

"Why? Because you have one?" She scoffed. "No one has the cure. All I can do is watch people die and wish I knew how to help."

"I have the cure."

Sorcha froze. He had a cure? There was no possible way he could have a cure, but he didn't appear to be lying.

She rose to her feet and pointed at him. "You have the cure?"

"Yes."

"The faeries said they had it."

"The Fae you spoke with knew I had the cure. They would have traded that knowledge after you'd completed three great deeds."

"And you'll give it to me?"

"Yes."

"For what price?"

"Druids do not ask for payment. It is a gift to my granddaughter."

Sorcha shook her head. "No. Nothing is free. What do you want from me?"

"Our seers have looked into your future, and we wish for you to remember us kindly."

"Why?"

"You did not want to see your future when the Unseelie Queen provided you the opportunity. Have you changed your mind?"

Had she? Sorcha wasn't certain. So many other people seemed to know her future. Why shouldn't she?

"No," she conceded. "I do not want to know my path before I walk it."

"Then I give you this gift, granddaughter."

He reached underneath his cloak and pulled out a small vial. Gold filaments wrapped around the glass, leaving a melting texture on the outside of the orb. It was not of this realm, although she did not think it was from faerie either.

"This contains waters from the Cauldron of Dagda. They can give any human immortality, or heal any grievous wound. Make your choice wisely."

She took the vial and held it to the weak sunlight. Fracturing rainbows danced upon its surface, like the water of the moon. "I would never consider keeping it for myself. There are so many people this could help."

"Precisely why I feel no worry in giving it to you."

She clutched the vial in her hand and sighed. "And returning to the

Otherworld?"

"The Fae banished Druids from their shores long ago. I cannot assist you in returning. But if you create miracles as you travel, the faeries will find you themselves."

"One drop of this will save a life?"

"And it will always replenish itself."

"You believe Macha herself will find me?"

"I believe there are many ways to get to the Otherworld, and you will find at least one, if not many, in your travels."

Sorcha blinked. "Travels?"

"Do you want to just save your family? Or do you want to save the world?"

She thought about the question long and hard. Long ago, she would have said the world. She would have given up everything she had just to journey and have that appellation stamped onto her name. Sorcha of Ui Neill, the healer of the blood beetle plague.

Now? She shook her head. "If I could give it to another, I would. As soon as I find a way back to the Otherworld, I will hand off this burden to another."

Torin nodded. "I thought as much. You feel very strongly for him, don't you?"

"I do."

"Why?"

"I have no answer for that. He earned my trust and showed he is an honorable man. That is enough for me."

"Do you love him?"

Did she love him? Sorcha knew she wasn't herself without him. That she missed him so much her heart ached, and a great crater grew with every passing day. She could survive without seeing his face. She just didn't want to.

Sorcha sighed. "What is love but burning passion and fleeting moments? I knew him for a small amount of time and I cannot say if I love him or the idea of him."

"He loves you."

Her heart stopped. Her stomach clenched and her hands began to shake. She tucked them underneath her armpits and shook her head again. "What?"

"He loves you. Faeries do nothing by half, and he admired you greatly."

She wanted to go back to Hy-brasil. So much that she could barely breathe. But it wasn't there anymore. Her home, her people, all destroyed by a beautiful king and his golden army.

What could she do? There was nothing left for her there but a faerie who wanted his throne and whose brother wanted him dead.

She sighed. "I wish we had longer together, but I cannot go back. How would I even find him?"

"I have faith in you."

Sorcha turned to leave, but hesitated at the edge of the clearing. This place was always where her life changed. Glancing over her shoulder, she looked at her grandfather. A man who should have been in her life since she was a child.

"What can a Weaver do?"

He flashed a grin. "They're the reason the druids were banished from the Otherworld and hunted until we nearly disappeared forever. They knit the Fae together with humans, but they can also control them."

"They can control the Fae? They must need the faerie's name."

"Druids have a drop of faerie blood. Some can control nature, some change the shape of objects or themselves. But Weavers? Weavers can command the Fae without knowing their true name."

She clenched her hand around the vial that would save her people. Eamonn's face flashed before her. The ruined crystals of his body glinted in the light of his brother's sword. She remembered the mistreatment of faeries by the Seelie Fae and the corrupted castle of the Unseelie Queen.

Their pain and anguish called out to her.

She could leave this clearing and never return. She could heal her people and be renowned across the land. She didn't need the faeries' help. Sorcha could forget them entirely as they had so clearly forgotten her.

Her hands trembled, and she turned towards her grandfather.

"Show me."

A harsh strike of a hammer slammed against the back of Eamonn's knees, and he fell with a grunt, crystal cracking against stone. It annoyed him to hear the harsh sound that no normal faerie would cause. There was no pain, no discomfort, not even the smallest twinge from his knees.

How far gone was he that he couldn't even feel pain?

"So this is the high king?"

The deep voice of the Lord Under the Mountain rattled him. It was a voice Eamonn recognized, though one he had never expected to hear again.

Glancing up, his eyes caught upon the throne. The dwarf seated on the giant gold monolith was tall in comparison to the rest of his people. His beard was short, trimmed rather than left in a long braid. His hair hung to his shoulders which were free of armor and covered only by a sleeveless shirt. Black tattoos swirled in circular patterns from his shoulders down to his fingertips.

"Angus," Eamonn said. "How fortuitous."

The dwarf behind him shoved at his shoulders. "You'll treat the lord with respect!"

"I'll treat him with respect when he gets down off that throne."

The Lord Under the Mountain snapped his fingers. "Have you no care for the head that resides upon your shoulders? At any point, I can order the guards to remove it, and they will not hesitate."

"I'd like to see you try." Eamonn tilted his head back to reveal his ragged neck wound. "It's already been attempted a few times."

"Aye, I remember you swinging up there."

"I remember you dragged away in chains."

"'Tis a shame neither of us won our freedom that day."

The dwarf behind him inhaled. Eamonn thought it rather pathetic that he didn't realize sooner the two men knew each other.

Eamonn straightened his shoulders and placed his hands on his thighs. "Are you going to make me kneel for the rest of this conversation?"

"I rather like you on your knees."

"Just so you can finally look me in the eyes?"

Angus snorted and hopped down from the throne. His heavy boots echoed as they struck the ground. He paused in front of Eamonn, planted his hands on his hips, and shook his head. "Shame that you're right. You'll have to lose your legs just so you can't look down on me."

"As if you'd ever let me."

"All right, since you're so handsome. Stand up."

The dwarves surrounding them gasped as Eamonn rose to his full height. He slapped a hand against Angus's shoulder and grinned. "You're lucky I recognized you, otherwise we might have come to blows. You've changed, old friend."

"And what would you have done if you didn't? We'd have swarmed you."

"Unless you've got your pickaxes handy, I don't think it would have done much."

"No," Angus shook his head with a trouble expression. "It's gotten worse."

"It will only continue to worsen."

"It's no curse then?"

"No."

"Shame." Angus turned towards his people and waved his hands. "Off with you. I can take it from here."

"But sire—"

"I said no, Cait." He addressed her with affection. "You've done your scouting duty well. Return to your training."

She huffed and joined the others, glancing over her shoulder before leaving the throne room.

Silence echoed in the large underground hall. Eamonn's own people were tongue tied, staring at Angus and he as if they'd conjured magic out of their palms.

Cian was the first to break the silence. "What the bloody hell was that?"

"This is Angus," Eamonn turned with his hand on the dwarf's shoulder. "An old friend from my days serving the previous king."

"When you were fighting the Unseelie?"

He nodded. "Angus was one of the few dwarves who willingly joined the fight. He was a remarkable warrior."

"Still am," Angus quipped. "Don't you be questioning my capabilities."

"In my experience, sitting on a throne does little to sharpen the blade."

"You have little experience sitting upon a throne." Angus's voice took a hard edge. "That fool twin of yours is hardly an example of a good king."

"In that, we agree." Eamonn gestured towards the faeries he brought with him. "Food and lodging?"

"Absolutely."

While Angus called out for his people, Eamonn prepared his. "They'll bring you food and water. I don't know what kind of hospitality they'll offer, but I assume they'll at least provide beds. Get a good night's rest."

"I'll stay with you, boy." Cian straightened his cloak with a grimace. "I don't like the idea of you here without one of us by your side."

"Angus is trustworthy."

"And you don't always make the right decisions when you aren't thinking straight."

"This is my battle to fight, my friend." Eamonn clapped a hand on his shoulder. "It is appreciated, but I'll need you healthy for the rest of this journey."

He grumbled, but followed the tiny dwarf woman who led them all from the throne room.

Angus perched on the arm of his throne, looking Eamonn up and down with a critical glance. "You look like you've been rolling with the pigs."

"I've been on Hy-brasil."

"Same thing then."

"You could say that." Eamonn held his hands out at his side. "I came in peace."

"Ocras is out in the open. I'd dare say that wasn't your intention."

"One can never be too careful with dwarves."

"Now that is the truth." Angus bounced his knee before blurting, "Why are you here, Eamonn?"

"I want to kill the king."

The silence that followed was deafening. Eamonn clenched his fists and forced himself to remain still. Angus would not refuse him. It was sheer luck he had become Lord and not one of his many brothers. Angus knew first-hand what Fionn could do to the Seelie Fae.

The dwarf pulled a blade from his hip and dug it underneath his nails. "You're going against blood? Since when?"

"Fionn has crossed the line."

"He didn't cross the line when he tried to hang you?"

"Don't focus on my misgivings. He is my brother, Angus. I had no desire to turn my back on the only family I have left."

"So I ask again, what changed?"

"He attacked my home," Eamonn growled. "He attacked my people."

"Not that I don't appreciate the change of heart, but it doesn't sound like you. You've never cared that much. He played you. What the hell changed to make you go soft?"

He saw red hair stirring in the breeze, trailing over freckled skin so white it was nearly milk. Dirty fingernails with blood caked underneath from helping heal his people, even though he didn't want her to. Eamonn heard her name dance in the air and tasted sunshine on his tongue.

"I gained perspective."

"You met a woman."

Eamonn glared.

"In my experience, that's the only reason a man would change his entire outlook on life. She must be a stunning faerie to have convinced you to return home."

"She's not Fae."

"A human?" Angus's knife slipped and cut his thumb. Fat drops of blood dripped to the floor, but he didn't react. "You fell for a human?"

"I fell for no one."

"A human, Eamonn? One of the unwashed creatures who swarm their world and destroy everything in their path?"

"She's not like the others."

"Oh, none of them are like the others. That's how all the stories go until they turn on you and go back home. Just how badly do you hate yourself?"

"She wouldn't leave," he growled. The large hall suddenly felt tiny as the walls closed in on him. "Be wise, Angus, and still your tongue."

"I don't see her in your crew, thus I am correct. She left and now what? You want to take back the throne so she'll return to your arms? Grateful a king would want to place her on the throne next to him?"

A slow warning growl rumbled through Eamonn's chest. "Choose your next words carefully, friend."

"You'll attack me over a woman? How the tables have turned." Angus hopped from his throne and tucked his knife back into his waistcloth. "I cannot provide as much help as you'd like. Your brother has attacked the dwarves too many times."

"All I ask is for a few men to fight by my side."

"I don't have even a small number. I have enough to keep this stronghold safe while still helping out the other tunnels. You'll have to make due with five."

Eamonn grunted. "Five men? You want me to kill the king with five men?"

"You were a great general once. Think like that man again."

Angus had lost his mind. There wasn't a flaming chance that Eamonn could pull off the greatest assassination their people had ever seen with five dwarves, a gnome, a boggart, and a pixie at his disposal. No matter how renowned he was in battle, Eamonn would fail.

"I go to war," he gritted through his teeth. "And you say I should fight with five men?"

"I didn't say I wouldn't help in other ways." Angus rolled his eyes. "Easy there, Untouched. Your quick temper hasn't changed in all this time I see. Follow me."

"Where?"

"Ocras has served you well, but she won't be a match for thousands."

"And you have a sword that will be?"

"It's not just any sword. I have the sword of Nuada."

Eamonn's heart jumped into his throat. The sword of Nuada was a legendary blade, passed down through his grandfather's line. No one had seen it in hundreds of years. All the relics of the original Tuatha dé Danann had disappeared long ago.

Until now.

"You have the sword of Nuada?"

"I do."

"And you told no one until now?"

Angus scoffed. "Just who would I be telling? Your brother?"

"Why are you telling me?"

They descended a stairwell from the main throne room. Living space gave way to a giant cave system with networks of halls that disappeared deep into the earth. Pulley systems lifted dwarves up and down the great mines, all lit by a channel of lava that poured out of vats from above.

"Of all the royalty in the Seelie court, you're the only one I'd trust not to use this blade against my people."

"Why's that?"

"I fought with you, Eamonn. I've seen what you can do with a sword and I've seen how you treat the Lesser Fae. You didn't see us as base creatures." Angus's reflection in the polished stone walls revealed his grimace. "I hope I can trust your opinion to be the same now."

"It's been a long time. I fell into the affliction carried by my brethren."

"No longer?"

"You can thank the little human for that."

"Oh?" Angus's voice lifted in curiosity. "What's she got to do with all this?"

"She saw them as equals, even when I could not."

"I think I would like this girl."

"Most do."

"But still so foolish that she left you?"

Eamonn growled. "That was my doing."

"Ah." Angus maneuvered them around dwarven miners who stared up at the beastly man walking among them. Most shied away from meeting his gaze although a few glowered as they passed. "Then it is not she who is the fool."

He couldn't agree more. He had been a fool to force her to leave, but there had been no other option.

Eamonn refused to put her in harm's way. His brother would try to use her as a pawn. The Seelie would fight to capture her, to tear her from his side and do unspeakable things just to make her talk.

She was innocent. She did not know the ways of the Fae, nor did she know how to protect herself. Of all people, he would preserve that innocence with his last breath.

As they passed another group of dwarves, he flexed his crystal hand and told himself this would all be over soon. If he had the sword of Nuada, others would surely follow him. The dwarves may not fight, but there were many more creatures he could call upon.

They would follow the High King of the Seelie Fae to the pits of hell. Or he would force them.

And once all this was done, he could find her again.

Eamonn sobered at the thought. Time passed differently in her world. She may be an old woman, with wrinkles and frail bones. He'd never seen an aged human before. They weren't often found in the Otherworld.

"In here," Angus grunted. "And try to keep your wits about you, Eamonn."

The dwarf was right. Eamonn forgot too easily where he was. The dwarven strongholds were mazes that even the most intelligent of Fae could get lost in. He needed to pay attention to where they were, in case Angus left him in the dark.

Angus reached up and pulled a lever. The pail attached to it dropped, pouring lava into a trough that spilled out into the most incredible treasure room Eamonn had ever seen.

Gold stretched as far as the eye could see. Mountains of coins, gemstones, and armor piled atop each other as if they didn't matter in the slightest. These items should be displayed, placed in a setting of honor. A crown caught his eye, diamonds glittering in the solid metal.

"What is this place?" he asked.

"The place we put things we want to forget."

"You put the sword of Nuada in this room?" Anger raced through his blood, hot and hard.

"I *hid* the sword of Nuada in this room. Great beards! Would you calm down?"

He had never controlled his anger well. Long ago, when war was in his blood and rage flickered at the edges of his vision, he had rode the waves of anger like a captain guiding a ship. He'd gotten too good at convincing people he wasn't a split second from tearing out their throat.

"Just get it over with," he growled.

"Eager to get your hands on the weapon that could change the tide of war?"

"It is my grandfather's sword, and I still don't think you have it."

Angus arched a thick brow and plunged his hand into a mountain of treasure. Gold fell in an avalanche all around him, trickling down in great waves that sounded like dripping water. Each clink grated on Eamonn's ears until he could barely stand it.

He watched with rapt attention as Angus pulled his arm out of the pile and brandished the most beautiful blade in all of history.

Claíomh Solais. The Sword of Light.

Red stones glittered in the pommel of the sword, each like a tiny drop of blood. The gold hilt tapered into the open mouth of a wolf that swallowed the rest of the blade. It was a beautiful blade. Light glinted off the sharpened edge, runes scribed into the flat edges spoke of the battles it had survived. And won.

Angus pulled it back when Eamonn reached for it. "Not so fast. You know the legends of this sword?"

"Yes."

"Then you know what it can do."

"It carries the power of manipulation, controlling the minds of others once the blade is drawn. Yes, I know, Angus."

The dwarf grimaced. "I'm handing you a very powerful weapon, Eamonn. Please take this seriously."

"Do you know the legends?" Eamonn's lips split into a feral grin. "That blade will only work in the hand of the high king."

Angus pointed the tip at Eamonn's belly. "Kneel."

"No."

"Walk away."

"No, dwarf."

"Remove yourself from this mountain and never return."

"Are you quite done?"

Angus shrugged. "I wanted to see if you were telling the truth. Do you want to see if you're really the high king?"

Did he? Eamonn wasn't so certain. He'd spent a majority of his life avoiding his birthright.

He licked his lips and held out his hand. "It's far past time I accepted my heritage."

"You're certain?"

"Give me the sword, Angus."

Although Angus's face twisted in worry, he extended the hilt towards Eamonn.

Licking his lips, Eamonn reached forward and grasped the wolf head. Cold metal struck frigid stone, and fire raced through his blood.

He gasped and staggered backwards, holding the sword with both hands now in fear he would drop it. The wolf's mouth opened and closed in a frenzy as it tried to swallow the blade. The desperate thumping of his own heart echoed until Eamonn's eyes burned.

A pulse of magic filled the room, lifting the gold coins into the air and dropping them all with a boom that shook the walls of the cave. He clenched his fists around the haft of the blade and willed it to still. It would bend to his will.

The wolf exhaled and blue fire licked up the sword of Nuada. Twisting and hot, it burned the tips of his fingers. Crystals formed on the palm that had not yet been ruined.

Through it all, Eamonn gritted his teeth. He would bear it. If this was the price the blade had chosen, then he would pay it. His physical form would withstand the pain because he refused to break.

He heard the growl of a wolf in his ear and the pleased chuckle of his grandfather.

"Well met, grandson. Take the blade; it is yours."

Another blast of magic fluttered his cloak, and all fell still. Fire cooled. Wind quieted. All he could hear was the ragged breath of the dwarf and the creak of crystal as he peeled his hand from the sword.

"What kind of cursed magic was that?" Angus spat out.

"That was my grandfather."

"So, you are the High King of the Seelie Fae?"

"It appears so."

"I will not bow."

"I would not expect you to," Eamonn said. He pointed the blade towards the dwarf and growled, "What other relics do you have hiding in this place?"

Angus struggled, clasping a hand around his throat while his face turned bright red. His body twisted and crumpled to the ground as he fought against the blade's magic. "I will cut out my tongue before I tell you," he choked.

"Then be free, old friend."

Eamonn dropped the blade. Angus fell limp, panting as he stared up at Eamonn with a shocked expression.

"You've changed," the dwarf observed.

"Time is not on my side. Now, we will talk about the army you have hidden in this mountain."

"I don't have an army hidden."

Eamonn pointed the sword once more, arching a brow when Angus gulped. "Twisting your words will not deter me. We both know you aren't telling me the whole truth."

"I will not put my people at risk."

"Don't make me force you, Angus."

"The man I fought beside would never stoop so low."

Eamonn swallowed hard and cast his gaze from his oldest friend. "Then I suggest you choose wisely. There is no other choice I can make. Fionn must fall."

"The dwarves have no army."

"Then I suggest you find one. Quickly."

CHAPTER THREE
THE DREAMS OF WITCHES

The hovering drop of liquid fell from the vial, splashing against Papa's tongue. He was the last she treated and the most stubborn. Sorcha had argued with him night after night, but he refused. He always put his girls first, even though he had suffered the longest.

She didn't want to heal them all at the same time. Who knew what was really in the vial that her druid grandfather had given her? She didn't want to risk their health on the word of a strange old man.

Briana was the first, the bravest and most tired of being ill. A single drop on her tongue, and they waited. For days and days they waited until Sorcha finally cut into her sister's back.

She pulled out each beetle and stared in shock at the dead insects. They didn't move, they didn't struggle, they didn't even twitch.

The cure worked.

Sorcha treated the rest of the household one by one, then pulled out the beetles remaining underneath their flesh. The miraculous substance in the vial baffled her and never seemed to diminish.

Her father swished his mouth and swallowed. All his healthy daughters clustered around him, staring with rapt attention. They prayed that Sorcha was right and hadn't gotten lucky with all thirteen of them.

He looked into their expectant faces and shrugged. "They don't seem to be moving anymore."

Rosaleen shrieked and jumped into his arms. "You're cured! You will live, Papa!"

The other sisters leapt forward. They all clustered together in a great circle around their father, tears streaking their cheeks and laughter bubbling from their chests.

Sorcha smiled, tucked the vial back into its small case, and stepped back from the revelry. They would all live. It was a miracle that should fill her soul with happiness.

But she was still so empty.

She stirred the soup above the fire and let them have a moment. They deserved to be happy. Their lives unfolded in blank pages they could write upon, though they would hold scars for all eternity.

When had she become so cold? Was this a normal reaction for someone after coming home from the Otherworld?

She imagined it was. This place, these people, they all seemed so dull compared to the life she had seen. They didn't understand magic or the wondrous things it could do. Their minds were so focused upon themselves, rather than each other. The plain wood walls, dirty stone floors, and drafty rooms made her heart heavy.

Sorcha missed the faeries more now that she knew they lived. Now it wasn't that she had lost them. They had chosen to leave her behind.

She blew out a breath and pushed her hair back. Hy-brasil had taken everything she knew about herself and obliterated it. Now, Torin was trying to give her back some semblance of self.

Who was she now? Who was this woman who saw faeries, healed the blood beetle plague, and felt her heart grow colder by the day?

"Sorcha?"

Briana's voice snapped her out of her thoughts. Smoothing her sweaty palms against her skirts, she turned with a false smile. "Yes?"

Her family stood together and stared. Worried expressions crossed all their faces, except her father's. His crestfallen expression warned Sorcha that he could read her thoughts.

"What?" Sorcha asked. "What is it?"

"You won't be staying with us, will you?" Briana asked.

"No."

"You'll do the right thing and heal all those people who need help?"

"Yes."

"You're leaving us?" Rosaleen's lower lip quivered. "We just got you back!"

Briana stepped forward and cupped Sorcha's face in her hands. She searched Sorcha's gaze. "Did we ever really?"

She should have cried. She should have at least sniffed because her sister was right. Sorcha was physically here, but she had left her heart in the Otherworld.

"No," she said so quietly that only Briana could hear. "I fear you did not, sister."

Briana leaned forward and pressed their heads together. She smelled like herbs and sickness. Not the way Sorcha remembered her, but the scent that would forever stick in her mind.

"You were never happy with us, no matter how hard we tried."

"I wasn't meant for this life."

"You were meant to run with the faeries." Briana leaned back and pressed her lips against Sorcha's forehead. "My little changeling sister."

Their father stood. Sorcha caught his eyes over Briana's shoulder and flinched when she saw the tears gathering. "We've already packed your things and took the liberty of adding another pack with what little we've had saved up."

"I'm not taking your money."

"You're saving people by leaving us, child. We want to help in any way we can."

"I should help remove the beetles—"

"We've watched you, and Papa has already agreed to allow us to remove them without your help."

She frowned. They were all misty eyed, wanting to give her their hard earned money and leaving themselves at a disadvantage. Shouldn't she feel something?

"Thank you," she said. "I will return as soon as I can."

"Don't." Briana squeezed her arm. "We always knew we only had you for a short amount of time, and it was selfish of us to keep you this long. Go be…whatever it is you are."

She should hesitate.

She didn't.

Sorcha hugged Briana and the rest of her sisters. She pressed her palms against her father's cheeks and kissed him soundly on the cheek. "Thank you."

"Visit us."

"I will do my best." She whirled around and rushed towards the door, wanting to leave as soon as possible.

Her father's voice made her freeze with her hand on the door.

"And go back to him."

Her hands clenched. "I will try."

She fled her childhood home with two packs slung under her arms. She looked back only once as she walked down the street towards the sick-house. Her sisters waved from all the windows and her father propped himself up at the door.

They were good people. They would be all right without her.

She spent weeks in the sick houses of her small town. The healers called it a miracle. That God himself sent her to purge their people of the plague.

Sorcha let them give her whatever name they wanted. She fanned the flames of rumors hoping that one of the Fae would come investigate.

None did.

Geralt stopped her a few times, his cheeks red and concern running like river through his veins.

"Sorcha! Stop for a moment would you? You will run yourself into the ground!"

"I have people to help, Geralt," she shook his hand from her arm. "Let go."

"When was the last time you slept?"

"Days ago."

"Sorcha, I know you want to help these people but you're no good to them if you're dead." He pushed back the lock of hair that always fell in front of his eyes. "Let me help you. Go eat, sleep, and come back with clear eyes and clear mind."

"I'm not handing this vial over to anyone."

"Where did you get it, anyway?"

"The faeries," she lied as she checked the temperature of a patient, pleased that this one was still alive. The man had been so emaciated she thought he would die long before the beetles were extracted.

"There are no such thing as faeries!"

"You can believe what you want, Geralt. But right now, you're in my way."

She put her shoulder against his and shoved. He stumbled backwards, landing on a bed where she piled the beetle corpses.

His shout of disgust was music to her ears. She did not offer him help, nor did she turn to look at him no matter how much she wanted to see the shocked expression on his face.

Geralt gave up after that. His incessant declarations of love ceased, and he disappeared back to his family manor. He shouldn't have been around the plague victims anyways. He was more distraction than help.

Sorcha cleared her town of those infected and moved onto the next. She waded through healers crying out their remedies, through priests blessing the infected, and walked directly into the sick houses.

Everyone she touched healed.

Her patients spread stories of the red-headed woman who walked among them. They saw her pointed ears and said she was one of the Tuatha dé Danann casting pity upon their people. Others said she was a bean sidhe guiding their souls from the land of the living.

When asked, Sorcha merely smiled and inquired about their health. As cold as it seemed, she wasn't interested in getting to know her patients. This was a means to an end. Healing was a stepping stone to the next point of her life.

She got her patients down from hundreds to ten. Those who had been sick the longest no longer suffered from the blood beetle plague, but from the after effects. Their lungs were weak, their bodies frail, and she would see this through until the end.

"Sorcha?" the little girl she tended asked. "What's that sound?"

Laughter and shouting echoed down the halls of the sick house. Frowning, Sorcha stood and smoothed her apron down. "I don't know."

A bang on the front door, followed by laughter, was the last straw. No one had any right to disturb the ill.

Temper in full blast, she raced towards the door with her hands curled into fists. Another shout, female this time, fueled the flames of her anger further.

Throwing the wooden doors wide, she glowered at the group of men hovering over a bundle of rags.

"How dare you?" she shouted. People milling through the streets hesitated. "Have you no respect for the wounded?"

"Ah, hush healer," one man replied. "We're just having a little fun!"

"You are disturbing my patients. Get away from here."

"Or what?"

Sorcha reached into the shadows behind the door and pulled out a knotted staff. She had found it during her travels, and it felt right in her hands, settling between her fingers with the perfect weight. She used it to knock the riffraff off her steps.

The men chuckled. "Come on now, Red. You won't do anything with that."

"Won't I?" She charged down the step and swung. She held the end in her hand, letting the weight of the staff do the work her arm could not. The bulbous end struck the vocal man on the temple. He dropped like a stone.

The others gaped at her.

"Well?" She jabbed the staff at them. "I don't have all day, boys. Get off my steps!"

They picked up their friend and raced away laughing.

"Damned fools," she grumbled. "Too many of them in the city."

"You can say that again."

Sorcha started and looked down at the pile of rags. Or rather, the woman wearing the most disgusting clothing Sorcha had ever seen. Bits and pieces of fabric fluttered in constant movement as the woman stood.

Her black hair was so tangled, Sorcha would have shaved it all off. Dirt smudged across her face and underneath her nails. She speared Sorcha with her gaze. Mismatched eyes, one blue and one brown stared straight into her soul.

"Pity for the poor?" the woman asked. "Or rather, penance for the unworthy?"

"What are you going on about?"

"Have you a spare farthing?"

"I have no money to give."

"Pity." The strange creature spat upon the ground.

"Why were those men accosting you?"

"They claim I am a witch."

Sympathy flooded through Sorcha. The emotion startled her as she had not felt it in such a long time. She reached out and smoothed a hand down the woman's arm. "They have called me the same."

"Sure they have, healer. But they're right about me."

Sorcha drew her hand back with a gasp. Her hands shook with the desire to cross her chest. "What?"

"I'm a witch, and I willingly admit to consorting with the Fair Folk. I call upon them, and they listen to my desires."

Sorcha lifted a brow. "Really? You call upon the Fae and they do whatever you tell them?"

"Of course."

"Faeries don't do that."

"Perhaps not your faeries."

"Are you making deals with them? Over and over again? You're selling your soul doing that." Sorcha shook her head and turned back towards the sick house.

"You think you know the Fae?" the woman called out.

"I know I do." Sorcha paused at the top of the steps. "I spent more time in the among the Fae than you could imagine. Making deals with faeries is dangerous."

"Hey!"

The woman's shout echoed as Sorcha closed the door. Let her follow if she wished, but Sorcha would not argue. There was little she could do for a woman up to her neck in debt that would eventually be paid.

The door slammed open and footsteps echoed down the hall towards her. "I said, hey!"

"I heard you."

"Then why didn't you stop?"

Sorcha grabbed a towel from one of the racks. "I'm a busy woman."

"You've spoken with the Fae?"

"Yes."

"You lived with them?"

The woman was leaving dirt smudges on the floor that Sorcha would have to mop up. The other cleaners had fled when she said she had no more use for them. They likely ran from memories of the sick and dying, the tragic souls who lingered in torment.

Pursing her lips, she pointed towards the small kitchen. "That way."

"Why?"

"You want food and water?"

She didn't have to say anything else. The ragged woman spun on her heel and charged into the kitchen.

Sorcha leaned against the doorframe and watched the crazed witch rifle through her cupboards. She pulled out bread and cheese, tossed sugar onto the window sill, and clunked down a tankard of water.

Little manners, but she might have been pretty if she cleaned up. Sorcha could tell a beautiful woman hid beneath the grime. She couldn't tell her age, although it would have been hard even if she was clean. People who led hard lives always had haunted eyes that aged them.

"What's your name?" Sorcha asked.

"Aisling."

"Pretty name."

"I'd say you could tell my mother that, but she's dead."

"Any other family?"

Aisling paused with a mouth full of food. "No."

"Well, you can stay here then if you help out."

"I'm not asking for handouts."

"You just asked if I had money," Sorcha said.

"Didn't say I was going to work for it."

"You are incredibly rude, aren't you?"

Aisling flashed a toothy grin. "Dealing with the Unseelie will do that to you."

Sorcha sat down and watched the witch eat. What had driven her to make deals with the Fae? Was she so foolish that she didn't care for her own safety?

Perhaps Sorcha would never know. Aisling finished her food in record time, leaned back, and patted her stomach.

"You never remember how good food is until you go a few days without."

"You haven't eaten in days?"

Aisling shrugged. "Some weeks the good folks want more than others."

"You peddle witch's wares?"

"I speak to the faeries for them. Like you, apparently."

"The faeries don't speak to me anymore," Sorcha said as she shook her head.

"They cut you off?"

"Seems so."

"Is that why you're making a name for yourself?" Aisling leaned back and propped her feet up on the table. "You're trying to go back."

"In a way."

"You're trying to piss off the faeries so bad they take you back to punish you. You're really that crazy."

Sorcha blinked. "Crazy?"

"Faeries aren't kind to the ones they want to punish. If you mess up enough here, they won't take you back to the Otherworld and let you go your merry way."

"I have to get back."

"There's hundreds of ways to get to the Otherworld, and this is your choice?" Aisling leaned back and shook her head. "Not a good plan, healer. Find another way."

"What would you suggest?"

Aisling turned and stuck her hands into the folds of her clothing. She had pockets, Sorcha realized. Although she wasn't certain which flaps were pockets and which were just random bits of cloth.

The witch pulled out a worn leather book and held it out. "There's probably something in here."

"What's this?"

"Something I stole from the Otherworld. Maybe you'll be able to make some sense of it."

Sorcha took the worn journal and thumbed a page open. The blank parchment quickly filled with inked words. A signature she recognized, *Scribohai*, appeared at the bottom of each page.

"Wow," Aisling exclaimed from over Sorcha's shoulder. "It never did that for me."

Sorcha's eyes danced over the words, skimming through the dark magic spells that required sacrificial animals and the like. One word stood out above all others.

Portal.

She snapped the book shut and held it to her chest.

"Hey!" Aisling yelped. "I was reading that!"

"It's not for you."

"How do you know?"

"Because it didn't reveal the words to you. I know druid magic when I see it, and those were not for you."

"They looked like interesting spells."

"Every spell does, I'm sure."

Aisling yanked her rags and gave Sorcha a critical glance. "I don't know what you've gotten yourself into, healer, but it doesn't look like something you're prepared for. When you want to open that portal, call me."

The witch whirled around and sulked away. She held a stolen apple in her hand as if she dared anyone to tell her to put it down.

"Sorcha," Sorcha called after her. "My name is Sorcha."

Aisling's shoulders shook as she began to laugh. "Sorcha? Of course you're her. The entire Otherworld is abuzz with your name. I'd be careful if I were you, Sorcha of Ui Neill. The Fae are mad at you."

She watched the other woman slip out of the sick house, laughing the entire way.

What did the witch know that Sorcha didn't?

Worried, she tucked the book under her arm and went to complete her rounds. The patients didn't care she struggled with new information nor that her future suddenly became brighter. They wanted her to feed them, roll them off their sores, and empty their bedpans.

Sick houses were never short of work. She stowed the book away for later viewing and tired herself out. The sun had set by the time she completed her rounds.

She was weary down to her bones.

Sorcha stumbled into her room and washed herself thoroughly. Although the blood beetles no longer threatened her life, she had to worry about every other sickness.

Eamonn's voice whispered in her ear, "Humans are so fragile."

The memory made her smile. He did not understand how fragile humans really were. She had watched children die because they fell into a lake at the wrong time of year. Women fell ill because their corsets were too tight, and men died from a simple cut on their leg.

Death followed humans like a well-known lover. Sorcha could almost feel him breathing down the back of her neck, waiting for the moment when she made a mistake.

She eased her dress over her shoulders. Bruises covered her spine and back from the savage slaps and kicks some of the patients gave her. She was prepared for them to be violent. She would have been, too, if there were only a single window for her to stare out of while she waited for weeks and months to heal.

They designed sick houses for death. Sorcha swore that people died faster here than if they were outside. Although she left the windows open, the private rooms had none. The air grew stagnant and cold.

Her dress fell to the ground with a soft sound, and she finished washing. Each drag of the washcloth made her bite her lip. What she wouldn't give to slide into a warm bath and have Oona wash her back for her.

Sorcha stumbled to the bed and fell asleep almost instantly, praying no dreams would wake her. She was far too tired.

But the dreams came. Dreams of the most unusual origin.

She blinked her eyes open. Fog swirled in coiling billows and staircases led into a never-ending mist and disappeared. This wasn't a normal dream, nor did she feel the strange lightheaded quality of sleep.

Sorcha was awake, or at least aware, in the dream she wandered through. Frowning, she spun around.

A fine dress covered her legs. It wasn't something she ever would have chosen for herself, her first indication that a faerie meddled with her dreams.

Red velvet poured over her shoulders like blood. Bell sleeves touched the tips of her fingers and the wide skirt flared over her hips, so heavy and large that she felt the entire dress move as she shifted.

Her hair swirled as it piled on top of her head.

"Ah," a smooth voice said. "Look how pretty you are."

"Fionn," she growled.

"You remember me? How flattering."

Sorcha spun in a circle, trying to find him in the billowing mists. "How could I forget the King of the Seelie Fae?"

"You've grown bold."

"I've grown desperate."

A hand touched her waist. Strong and achingly familiar, she spun around in his arms to stare up at the beloved face. Eamonn looked back at her, vibrant blue eyes blazing. But it wasn't him, not really.

She flinched back from the mask Fionn had placed over his face. It was a macabre imitation of his brother.

"What's wrong with you?" she growled. "Why would you wear that?"

"Do you not like it? I thought it would be rather agreeable, considering how you favor my twin."

"You are a sick and twisted man."

"You and my twin are of the same mind when it comes to that." He pulled her into his arms. "It is good to see you again, midwife."

"Healer now."

"Of course. How could I forget? The little midwife who saved everyone from the blood beetles."

"You sound disappointed."

"I am. I always thought you would do more important things than save humans. There was an edge of greatness to you when we first met." He shrugged. "Either way. Won't you dance with me?"

"Dance?"

Sorcha felt the brush of fabric against the back of her dress. Gasping, she craned her neck to see hundreds of other faeries had joined them. Each more beautiful than the last, the Seelie Fae had joined their king in the dream world.

Music burst into the air. Violins and harps twining together to create a jig that no one could have sat still through.

She hated it. She hated it even more when he pulled her closer, placed her hand on his shoulder, and propelled her into the crowd.

"What do you want?" she growled.

"Can I not wish to spend time with my favorite human?"

"You hate humans."

"I don't hate you."

She glowered at him as they spun wildly among the other Fae. "You want something from me."

"Can you not enjoy the night before finding your way to politics?"

"I will not be stuck in this dream forever."

His expression changed, twisted into something awful. Something she recognized far too well. "You are too intelligent for your own good, midwife."

"You have told me this before."

He spun her in a wide arc around a tree that grew in the center of the room. Its roots groaned as they passed. "Where is he?"

"Who?"

"Don't play coy. You know of whom I speak."

"I couldn't even fathom a guess."

Fionn pulled her towards him. She struck his chest hard enough to knock the wind from her lungs. He squeezed her, painfully tight, in warning. "You know where he is."

"If I knew where he was, don't you think I would be with him?"

"He sent you away. He pushed you out of the castle and back into your life where you live in grime and ruin. Why else would you want to go back to the Otherworld? The human world is far too plain for you."

The cajoling expression was back on his face. If she were any other woman, he might have convinced her to stay here with him. He was painfully handsome, all high arched cheekbones and a dazzling smile.

Fionn had a dangerous edge to his looks. It was behind his eyes, she thought. Something behind those vivid blue eyes had twisted to hatred.

Her thoughts turned to the first night she had met Eamonn. To a throne room cast in shadows, and a slash of light across glittering eyes. He had the same eyes as his brother back then, filled with darkness and anger.

She reached up and feathered her fingers over the crest of Fionn's cheekbones, just underneath the azure rage. "You're so much like him."

The emotion in his eyes boiled, but he smiled down at her. "I can be anyone you want me to be, little midwife. Just ask."

"You can't be him."

"Why not?"

"Eamonn has learned something you have not."

"Which is?" he growled.

"He has learned how to let go of his anger."

Fionn tossed his head back and laughed. She shook in his arms, each rumbling chuckle pulsing through her body. The faeries dancing around them paused and joined in his laughter.

"Oh, little midwife. You are thoroughly entertaining. You think my brother has let go of his anger?" His smile warped into a menacing grimace. "Let's see how wrong you are."

He spun her around in his arms, yanking her back against his chest and twisting his hand in her hair. He used the rope of her braid to secure her. Pulling her head back, he petted the long column of her throat.

"Look."

She jerked, not caring that her hair pulled at her scalp. He had no right to contain her in such a way. She squeezed her eyes shut as a flicker of light burst through the fog, revealing images.

"Look, midwife. See the choices your lover makes."

Sorcha didn't want to open her eyes, but temptation clawed at her stomach. Fionn lied. Whatever he showed her would be a lie, so there was no harm in looking.

She peered into the fog. Swirling light and colors accosted her senses, and then sound filtered through.

Clanging strikes of steel against steel. The harsh crack of a whip, and the song of the wind as it whistled through crystals and stone.

A sword sliced through the thick layer of mist. Eamonn stepped from the whirling colors of fire and brimstone like a warrior victorious. Blood splattered across his armor and dripped through the valleys of his wounds.

But he was alive. And he was well.

Sorcha breathed a sigh of relief that was short lived as he advanced towards her. Fionn held her still as Eamonn brandished his sword and snarled.

He charged towards them with an unfamiliar blade glinting in sunlight she could not feel. Sorcha gasped and screwed her eyes shut as he lifted his blade, flinching against Fionn's shoulder.

"Oh no," he murmured in her ear. "You don't get to close your eyes for this. Watch."

His fingers dug into her cheeks, forcing her to turn for the last moment when Eamonn plunged his blade into her chest. The ghost sword sank through her torso and she gaped up at the man she loved. His face twisted into a grimace of cold, calculated hatred. There was no pain, for dreams did not have pain, but he stared down as if she were nothing more than an animal.

"He sweeps through my armies, killing hundreds of good men with families waiting for their return," Fionn growled.

She stared up into the glittering eyes and wondered what had happened. He had been so against death, at least when she left him. Crystals were digging into one of his eyes, freezing it in place until all it could do was stare with cold rage.

"He doesn't care about our people. He only cares about the throne and his personal vendetta."

"That isn't him." She shook head head. "He cares about the Lesser Fae. He cares about them all."

"You are so sweet. So naïve. Do you see that sword in his hand, little midwife?"

Eamonn pulled the blade from her chest. A wolf's mouth swallowed the steel, glittering red eyes staring at her as he pivoted away from the faerie he had just killed.

"Yes, I see it."

"That is my sword. My rightful sword from our grandfather."

She knew who their grandfather was. Had seen Eamonn kneeling at an altar, asking the ancient Tuatha dé Danann for guidance. "That is the Sword of Nuada?"

"It is. And only the true King of the Seelie Fae can wield it." His grip tightened on her waist, squeezing until she whimpered. "And I am the true king."

"Apparently not."

"You dare threaten me so?"

"I am so tired of faeries saying that to me," she growled and wrenched herself out of his grasp. "I am no weak maiden who fears you. You would be wise to fear *me*, would be King of the Seelie Fae."

He tossed his head back and laughed again. "And why should I?"

"I know your true name, Fionn the Wise."

He froze, glaring at her as if she had done the unthinkable. "Using that name brings you down a dangerous path."

"I have used faerie names before, and I will again. Now release me from this dream."

"Tell me where he is."

"I will not. Fionn, let me go."

She could feel him fighting against her words. The weight of his will fell over her shoulders as if he were pressing down upon her.

He grinned. "You have to mean it, midwife. You have to really mean to strip my own thoughts from my mind and force yours in their place."

"Let me out of this dream, Fionn."

"Again!" All the faeries surrounding them echoed his laughter. "Again, little girl. Maybe with more practice you will control the King of the Seelie Fae!"

"Now, Fionn. I bend you to my will. Let me go!"

"No!"

He spun on his heel and advanced. His hand fisted in her hair, twisting the strands until she yelped and her knees gave out. She landed on her knees at his feet.

His handsome face twisted with cruelty. His lips touched her cheek as he leaned down to whisper in her ear, "You will never control me. Now tell me where my brother is."

Sorcha winced as he pulled hard on the long tail of her braid. "I will never tell you."

"That's fine," he chuckled in her ear. Magic swelled around them, pressing upon her shoulders and into her mind. "Then tell me where you are, sweet midwife."

Sorcha fought against the desire to tell him everything he wanted to know. She struggled in his grip to no avail. Panic welled in her belly until all she could do was tilt her head back and scream.

"Fionn, let me go!"

She lurched up in bed, her hair a tangled mess around her and the scent of stale sweat filling the tiny room she slept in. The fire had died down. Shadows danced in her visions as the faerie magic dissipated.

Sorcha pressed a hand against her chest and tried to catch her breath.

"I did it," she gasped. "I controlled him."

But had she? She wouldn't ever really know, although she suspected he wasn't finished with her yet.

Her pillow suddenly seemed less inviting. Nightmares waited down that path, and she wasn't certain she had it in her to battle Fionn again. The King of the Seelie Fae was much stronger than she'd given him credit for.

Shivering, she pulled the blankets around her shoulders, left her bed, and stoked the fire back to life. Light would banish the nightmares from her mind. Sorcha threw open the window for good measure, hoping the sickly sweet scent of fear would leave on the wind.

What battle had she won? And what was Eamonn doing?

"He needs me," she said as her heart clenched.

He needed someone to remind him that there was good in the world. That he needed to be that good for others, or he would find himself walking the same path as his twin. But she couldn't do that from Ui Neill.

Her gaze caught on the leather-bound book the witch had given her.

"No," she told herself. "You will not stoop to dealing with the Unseelie. There are other ways to get back to the Otherworld."

None that were so quick, however. Sorcha chewed on her bottom lip and stared at the easiest solution to her problem. Eamonn didn't have much time, and neither did she. The Seelie king was coming for her. She needed protection and Eamonn needed a conscience.

Grumbling, she tossed the blankets from her shoulders and picked up the book. Magic hummed against her fingers as if the book knew she wanted to use it.

She flipped it open and ran her fingers down the center seam. Words appeared on the blank parchment, words she shouldn't understand but somehow did.

This was dark magic, not just faerie favors or spells that might heal. Witch words appeared, calling upon powers that Sorcha could never understand. Nor did she want to. Runes, chicken blood, sacrificial lambs, and more danced before her eyes until her stomach rolled.

As if the book knew she had seen enough, the pages fluttered and settled upon what she wanted.

The portal.

"I'm just reading your pages," she muttered. "I'm not using you."

A voice whispered in her mind, "*Not yet.*"

Shivering, Sorcha ran her fingers over the words and tried to decide whether it was worth it. Shadows danced just out of her reach as Unseelie Fae slipped into her room.

She could see them out of the corner of her eyes. Twisted and warped, the goblins hunched over each other and held their breath. Would she do it? Would she take the deal offered in the form of stretched skin and ink?

The spell was rather simple, but it required more than one person. Sorcha couldn't drag one of her patients into this mess. She didn't even want to make the deal herself.

Another spell appeared on the edge of the page. A spell to find someone. A spell with a name already written in blood.

"Aisling," she muttered.

It was cruel, perhaps, to involve the witch in even more deals. But who better to assist opening a portal to the Otherworld than someone already up to their neck in debt?

Sorcha snapped the book shut and ignored the triumphant screams of the Unseelie Fae.

She had a witch to catch.

CHAPTER FOUR

The Hangman And The Portal

Eamonn swung his blade over his head, the metal singing as he brought it down onto the nearest elf. The unnaturally beautiful creature danced backwards and the sharpened edge traced a scraping line down his breastplate.

The elf grinned. His helmet covered only the sides of his face, leaving his eyes and mouth free.

"You won't win, beast," the elf crowed. "You can only fight for so long!"

"Haven't you heard the legends? I will fight until the last of you is dead."

"I'd like to see you try."

Unable to bear the creature's prattle for a second longer, Eamonn rushed forward. His opponents never expected him to come within range of their swords. Some were forward thinking enough to lift their blades, hoping they would cut through Eamonn's impenetrable skin.

They were always wrong. His crystals sliced through metal until it was nothing more than dust.

This elf was not intelligent enough to even try. He cried out, held up his hands, and froze when Eamonn caught him by the throat.

"Wait," the pretty creature gurgled. "Mercy."

"I have none for your kind."

Eamonn squeezed his fist until gore and meat covered it. Only then did he let the body drop to the ground.

The battlefield was a horrendous place to be. In the many years since he had been a general, Eamonn had forgotten what it was like. The true fear and crazed stares as men fought. The screams of the victorious mixed with those who clung to life, refusing to die quickly.

The Sword of Light hung heavy in his hand. It drew him down in a way Ocras never had. The runes written upon every inch of metal vibrated with power, stinging his palms and heating the crystal of his hand. He didn't like it, but it was effective.

A dwarf ran past him. Young, perhaps too young to be fighting, and screaming as an elf cut him down. Blood splattered into the air, filling it with iron and red mist.

Anger simmered just beneath Eamonn's skin. What right did they have? The High Seelie Fae were no better than the Lesser Fae. And yet, he saw the glee in the elves' eyes. They wanted to kill the dwarves. They wanted to see their blood on the ground but refused to lower themselves to allow even a speck to touch their armor.

The sword in his hand throbbed. Energy, like nothing he had ever felt before, surged through his arm and straight to his heart.

Claíomh Solais knew what to do. The runes glowed as its power flexed, pushed against his mind, and begged to be let free. The sword could make them pay. It could destroy them all.

Eamonn let it take over his entire being, lift his arm, and draw the blood it desperately wished to drink.

The blade carved through air and flesh. He dimly heard screams that rang in his ears, piercing and echoing with pain. A stream of blood dripped down his chest and underneath his armor, creating a river between his abdominal muscles.

How much blood covered him now? He didn't know.

He didn't care.

The sword cleaved through flesh and bone, separated limb from trunk. He stabbed through the lines of Fionn's army over and over again.

Time slowed. He did not know where he was, who he was, nothing other than the repetitive motion of his body. Parry, block, swing the blade along with his body. He was no longer a man, but a weapon.

Belatedly, he realized he had been fighting for a very long time.

Eamonn swore as he cut down the last of the elves. His shoulders ached from swinging the heavy blade that fought for control with each movement. His body wanted to rest after hours upon hours of battle. The Fae did not stop when they started a fight. They would continue until everyone was dead.

He swung too hard and the Sword of Light split through the last elf's torso. He stared into the man's eyes as he fell, clutching the gaping wound on his belly.

Shouldn't he feel something? Eamonn shook his head and stumbled backwards.

He only felt exhaustion. There wasn't room for pity in the empty spaces of his mind.

"Master?" Oona called out.

Why was she here? Eamonn spun, sticking the sword's point into the ground to balance himself. Bodies lay upon the battlefield, strewn like fallen red leaves in autumn.

He frowned. Had he done all this? Who had fought with him?

"Eamonn!" Oona's voice became frantic. "Answer me!"

"Here," he mumbled. "I am here."

A tiny winged body crawled over a mound of fallen soldiers, her expression melting into relief when she saw him. "Oh, my boy, we thought we lost you!"

"I'm fine."

"I can see that, but how?" She clasped her hands at her chest and gazed up at him, purple wings vibrating in fear. "Dearie, how did you do this?"

"Do what?"

"The dwarves retreated hours ago. You've been alone."

He glanced down at the sword. "I don't know."

"Sweetheart… Are you all right?"

"I don't think so, Oona. I am not myself."

She breathed out a relieved sigh. "Come with me, dearie. Let's get you cleaned up."

He stared down at her hand. Could he touch her? After he had spilled so much blood, was he worthy to touch the woman who had raised him?

"Eamonn," Oona gently said. "Let go of the sword and let me guide you from the battlefield."

Did he want to? Eamonn couldn't decide whether he wanted to put the sword back in its scabbard or if he wanted to run it through the pixie.

She closed her hand over his, so tiny and small compared to the crystalline structure of his fist. "Rest easy, my boy. The battle is done."

The battle is done.

The words rang in his ears over and over again until he sighed and thrust the sword into its sheath. "My apologies, Oona."

"I know blood lust runs in your veins, dearie. I've been raising those in your line since your father was a boy."

His father had suffered from what he called a blood rage. Eamonn knew the back of his father's hand much better than the front. He had never wanted to become that man.

He clenched his fists. "I have no wish to follow in my father's footsteps."

"And you won't. Come with me, Eamonn. Come and see your kingdom."

"My kingdom?"

"We're at the foothills of Cathair Solais. It is far past time for you to see the castle of your childhood."

"Has it changed?" He didn't know what he would do if it had changed. If the world had grown better in his absence.

"Only a bit."

Oona placed her hand on the small of his back as she guided him away from the carnage. He couldn't help but look down, attempting to force his mind to remember. What did their faces look like? What terror had they felt as he plowed through them?

He couldn't remember anything. Only a red mist that swallowed his view. Anything that walked through the mist, he had killed. Plain and simple.

"Where are the dwarves?" He slurred the words as he said them.

"They retreated."

"Why?"

Her fingers flexed against his spine. "They didn't want to get in your way."

"Smart."

"Has this ever happened before?"

Eamonn shook his head, then lifted her up and over a large pile of men. At her confused glance, he shrugged. "I don't want you touching them."

"So sweet, even after all of this." She patted his cheek. "It will be all right, you know."

"It has to be."

"I know you'll try."

They walked away from the battlefield and over to a cliff edge. The dwarves remained as far away from him as possible, he noted. Perhaps they knew when a beast walked among them.

He heard the whispers as he walked by. "The Red Stag…it's really him."

"I thought he was dead?"

"So did I. But there he is in the flesh. Did you see the way he carved up those elves?"

"Chopped them up as if they would be his dinner, he did. That blade of his wouldn't stop moving! Couldn't even see it."

Eamonn blocked them out, shaking his head and clearing the echoes of screams. He wasn't the same as he used to be. He didn't remember this red fog, and he certainly had never forgotten the faces of those he killed.

They plagued him for centuries. But now? He had to force himself to look at their faces, and even then couldn't care less that they were dead. They fought for the wrong side.

"Come here," Oona reached out her hand for him. "See your kingdom in the light."

His kingdom.

Eamonn inhaled deeply, took the offered hand, and stood to stare down at the Castle of Light.

It gleamed as only the golden castle could. Sunlight bounced off its smooth surface, but also absorbed into it. White and gold, the high peaks and pristine towers had never been dirty. They sparkled and blinded those who looked upon their surface.

The grounds had changed. A colorful garden stood in place of the maze he had run through as a child. He could see faeries walking through it even now, oblivious that a battle had taken place just above them.

He couldn't attack the castle. Not yet. There was much to plan, and his brother couldn't know how close he was.

Soon, he would return home.

"Let's go," he said.

He needed to address the dwarven army. Men fighting for Eamonn couldn't be afraid of him. He didn't want to rule like his brother.

He climbed off the rise and let the image of his home fade. The castle would wait for him; no army would destroy the legendary Castle of Light.

The sword at his hip bumped against his thigh, reminding him that there was much more at play here. As the high king, he had certain abilities his brother did not have. As long as he could figure out how to use them.

Dwarves huddled together in small family clumps. They weren't happy about fighting for him. They weren't happy about fighting for anyone but each other.

Cian rushed towards him, holding up a hand. "They aren't pleased with you, master. I'd go so far as to say they're frightened of you."

"I'm not surprised."

"I wouldn't be addressing them any time soon. Let their fear settle."

"What else would you have me do?"

"Walk?"

Eamonn glanced around them and lifted his arms. "Where do you want me to walk?"

"Pick up the bodies then. They're frightening everyone."

"What did they think they would find in war? Sunshine and flowers?"

Oona tugged on his arm. "Come with me, we'll go for a walk. It'll be good to ease your muscles."

"I don't want to walk."

"Master," she pulled again. "Please."

He recognized the panic in her eyes. She had worn the same expression when Fionn rode up to the castle on his white steed. She was hiding something from him.

Eamonn turned around and felt his heart freeze in his chest. Now that his mind had settled, he recognized this place and the rotting platform tucked into the side of the mountain.

He waded through dwarves that scattered as he approached. His booted feet touched the edge of the platform as he stared up into the blank space where a pole once stood and a rope had swayed in the breeze.

He lifted a hand and pressed it against his throat. The crystals pulsed with light, ancient pain vibrating through his body.

The breeze ruffled his hair. His long braid swayed, but his body remained still as stone.

Voices whispered in his ear from long ago.

"That's the monster."

"That's the one who betrayed us all."

"Look at him! He's so ugly now."

"I can't believe I ever let him touch me."

They had forsaken him. Not just the people who had professed to love him, but his own family.

He would never forget the haunted gaze of his mother who pressed her fingertips to her lips and said nothing. Did nothing. Watched her eldest son swing from the end of a rope with tears in her eyes, immobile and silent.

The crowd behind him held their breath as if they thought something remarkable was about to happen. The banished prince, the ugly man who had fallen from grace, stood before the gallows which had started it all.

He lifted a foot and placed it on the rotting planks. They held his weight as he ascended the stairs. Oona sobbed out a breath, the only sound in what remained of the battlefield.

Why did he suddenly feel so old? His bones ached almost as much as his soul. He tilted his head back to the sky and remembered ravens pecking at his eyes. He experienced every memory he had kept buried deep within his person so he would not feel this pain again.

But now he felt it. He lived every second of the days he swung from the end of that rope. The biting pain in his neck as the crystals sank ever deeper. The worry that perhaps he might never die, and they would leave him here.

He had survived. And so had his purpose.

Eamonn clenched his fists and turned towards the crowd of dwarves and the remains of his people.

"You all know my story," he began. "Some of you were there to watch while my own family condemned me for my face."

The temporary army stared up at him with shock, some with awe. To the younger faeries, he was a legend. A myth that parents told their children at night. The Untouched prince who carved his way through armies without getting a single wound.

"It was never my intention to come back here." He looked over the battlefield and shook his head. "It was never my intention to start a war. But someone reminded me that my people were being mistreated."

Oona sniffed and pressed a hand against her mouth.

He jabbed a finger behind him. "This is the very place they tried to take my life. They saw me as a monster, but more than that they saw what I stood for. If the royal family could be marked as 'flawed,' then the Lesser Fae were not half beasts. You are Seelie Fae, just as much as they are. I survived, and I know now that my purpose was to return here, on this day! To guide you back to your homes, to your people, to the rights stripped from you."

A few of the dwarves stood up.

"I will not allow my brother to destroy this land any further. You and your families deserve the recognition you are owed. I will place my life on the line for you as I did on the battlefield today. Stand with me, brothers and sisters of the Fae. Let me be your sword, for I will strike down any who threaten you. Let me be your shield, for I will weather you through this storm. Let me be the biting cold of winter and the blistering heat of summer, for I will cut through the forces of Fionn the Wise and bring you home!"

A thunderous applause shook the ground as the faeries all stood and stomped their feet. They screamed up at him, anger and rage fueling the flames.

He would bring them home. Or he would die trying.

"Don't get too comfortable," Sorcha grumbled. "I only asked you here to help because the spell requires two people."

"We both know why you asked me here, and it wasn't for that." Aisling grinned and tossed one of her new coins in the air. A full bag jangled at her waist, the last bit Sorcha had to her name.

"Just…" Sorcha blew out a breath and placed her hands on her hips. "Quiet. Please. I'm trying to concentrate."

"You're not doing a good job of that."

"And that is entirely because you won't shut your mouth."

"If you'd listen to me, then this might go faster."

"What!" Sorcha threw her arms to the sides. "Where am I going wrong then? What could you possibly have to say that the book can't tell me?"

Aisling hopped down from her seat on a nearby stump. Mud caked her bare feet which slapped against the cold wet ground as she hunched over a nearby rune. Tangled hair covered her face, twigs and leaves knotted into the heavy mass. She reached out and touched a ragged nail to the tail of the rune.

"This is wrong."

"That's exactly how it looks in the book," Sorcha grumbled. "It's not wrong."

"The Beacon cannot be curved. The lines must be straight for the rune to stay lit." Aisling moved, her hunched body crawling over the circle of runes Sorcha had carved into the ground. "Your Elk rune is quite good, but the Birch Goddess is missing its top."

"You're saying words I don't understand."

Aisling arched a brow. "And you want to be a druid?"

Sorcha's cheeks burned. She was horrible at this—at magic—at rituals foreign to her. How was she supposed to figure this out when no one was here to teach her?

And the witch before her seemed to know so much. Aisling said there was no druid blood in her lines, nor faerie for that matter, but she was innately capable when it came to spells. She crouched over the runic circle and pivoted, fixing all of Sorcha's mistakes.

"Thank you," Sorcha said. "I appreciate your help."

"Say that more often, and I might keep you alive."

"I already said it!"

Aisling looked over her shoulder and bared her teeth. "Then say it again."

"Thank you, Aisling, for helping me return to the Otherworld."

"And for keeping you safe."

"I fail to see how you are doing that."

"If you make this portal wrong, it will chop you in half when you step through." Aisling clapped her hands together. "Just like a cleaver on a fish head."

Sorcha's neck ached in response. She nodded. "Point taken. Are we certain it's fixed then?"

"Oh, now you're worried. Ridiculous. Just trust me, would you healer? This is what I do."

"How do you even know how to do this?"

"Grew up with it."

"You grew up with a druid?"

Aisling drew straight lines to link the runes together. "Sort of. I lived with a traditional witch. The old hedge witch type that made money off love potions and other lies. She had these books though, like the one I showed you. Books that spoke to me, and some that didn't."

She had to have druid blood. Sorcha couldn't believe anything else. If the books were revealing their secrets, then it seemed all too likely.

"They're druid books?" she asked nonchalantly.

"Guess so. If the one you have now is druid, the others are pretty much the same." Aisling leaned back and puffed out a breath. "It looks about right."

"About right doesn't sound as if you have much faith it will work."

"It should work."

"You're not giving me any confidence here."

"Well, I've never done this spell before, have I?" Aisling glared.

"The goal is to get you through alive. That's the best I can offer."

Sorcha nodded. She didn't want to interrupt the witch too much, but her legs bounced and her palms slicked with sweat. Just how much time had passed in the Otherworld? Would she even be able to find him?

Him. She could feel the bumps and grooves of crystal against her fingertips just from the thought of him. The soft sigh he let out whenever she leaned on his shoulder, or touched his hand without flinching.

Something deep inside her knew he needed support. Fionn's dream had solidified that, but she had known long before the dream. She had known the moment she left the isle that she took a piece of his soul with her.

"That will do," Aisling stepped carefully out of the circle. "We'll see once it's activated."

"That's it?" Sorcha stared down at the ground. "It doesn't look like much."

"Did you think magic would be all flashing colors and pretty lights? Of course it doesn't look like much. This is natural magic, not the crap those traveling peddlers pass off." Aisling held out her hand. "Now give me something of his."

"What?"

"We have to find him in the Otherworld, and the only way to do that is to have something of his. Don't you have a lock of hair?"

Sorcha wrinkled her nose. "I don't keep people's hair."

"Amateur. You should always have hair from everyone, just in case."

"Do you have mine?"

"Yes," Aisling said and patted the folds of fabric over her chest. "But don't worry. I have no desire to curse you."

"Not yet."

"You're learning. So you have nothing of his?"

Sorcha shook her head.

"Blast. This suddenly became a lot more difficult."

"It said nothing in the book about needing something of his," Sorcha said. She pulled the journal out of her back and leafed to the page with the portal drawing.

"I'm not surprised. That's just a way to *get* to the Otherworld. But it will put you down wherever it decides, and we need to make sure it's where you want to go."

"Then was this all a waste?" Sorcha snapped the book shut. "I cannot go anywhere in the Otherworld, I'll never be able to find him."

Aisling tapped a finger against her chin. "Just how close were you to this faerie?"

"Very close."

"Close enough that he might be thinking of you?"

"Time passes differently in the Otherworld. I don't even know how long it's been since we've last seen each other."

Sorcha rubbed her chest. The thought he might have forgotten her made her skin itch. What if he didn't want her back? He had sent her away to stay safe, but there was always the chance he sent her away because he was done with her.

"I can find someone that's thinking of you," Aisling muttered. "Are you ready?"

"Now?"

"Now."

Sorcha nodded, though nerves made her stomach rise into her throat. Too many things could go wrong. Bad endings ran through her mind over and over until she questioned the sanity of this. She didn't even know this witch!

Kneeling at the front of the circle, Sorcha scooped up a handful of dirt. "By earth, I open this portal between our world and the Otherworld."

Aisling crouched at the top of the circle, leaned down, and blew upon the next. "By air, I break the shields that separate our kind."

Sorcha spat on the next rune. "By water, I lift the veil and create the way into the Otherworld."

The witch hesitated only for a moment, a feral grin splitting her features. She lifted a hand and snapped her fingers. Fire danced upon the tips, crackling with unnatural energy. "By fire, I open the portal."

Aisling tossed the fire onto the last remaining rune which burst into flames. The circle melted into the ground as the elements combined. A glassy surface spread before them, and Sorcha stared down into the Otherworld.

It was just as beautiful as she remembered. Green grass so perfect that her eyes watered. Sunlight and faeries flying past the portal without even glancing up at the two women staring down at them.

Aisling sighed. "It never gets old, does it?"

"No. It doesn't at all." She missed it so much. Just seeing the land and the faeries made her soul squeeze. "Now what?"

"Now we find someone who's thinking of you."

"That could take a while."

"It most likely will. I can't imagine there's hundreds of faeries thinking of you all the time. No offense, healer."

"None taken."

Aisling spread her hands over the portal and hummed under her breath. "Spirits of the air, aid me. Seek the one who dreams of a red-haired lass, who whispers the name Sorcha of Ui Neill. Breathe into this portal your guidance and bring us to the place where they rest."

The surface rippled and zipped across the landscape until everything was a blur. It seemed to hesitate in some spots for a few moments, but then continued searching for a person thinking of Sorcha.

She blew out a breath. "Come on. One of you, please think of me. Please."

Surely she hadn't been gone that long? They couldn't have forgotten her already.

And then the mirror stilled, settling on a small patch of moss in the center of a forest. Emerald green and dotted with dew, the meadow was a small slice of heaven.

"Better go now," Aisling said. "I don't know how long it will hold, and if it's moving while you jump then you'll be tossed into the air."

"I just jump down?"

"That's all."

"Will it hurt?"

"I don't have a clue. Never been through a faerie portal before. Never even seen someone try it until you."

The flashing grin she gave Sorcha was not comforting. There was something about the woman that was strange and unusual. Not her looks, Sorcha had seen a fair bit of women who were rough around the edges. It wasn't the way she moved, or spoke, but something innate that hovered just out of reach.

Sorcha sprang into movement and tossed her pack over her shoulders. "How old are you anyways?" she asked.

"Me?" Aisling put a hand on her chest. "It's rude to ask."

"I find it hard to believe you're worried about my manners."

Aisling stood, placed a palm against Sorcha's spine, and shook her head. "I'm younger than you. Eighteen years to my name, and I already know more than most people find out in their entire lives. Say hello the faeries for me."

"You're how old?"

The witch shoved, hard, and Sorcha tumbled through the portal. She landed on her hands and knees, cushioned by moss. The jolt still knocked the breath from her lungs.

"Aisling!" she cried out. "I'm not done with you yet!"

Sorcha rolled onto her back and stared up at the portal which was steadily shrinking. A bird's nest covered head poked over the small window and waved. "Have fun!"

"How do I get back?"

The portal closed before the witch could answer.

"Blasted witch!" she grumbled. "I need to get back, eventually!"

She rolled back onto her hands and knees, pulling out the leather bound book. There had to be something within its pages that could help. The portal page flew past, but there were no inked words after that.

Plenty of spells appeared, all to protect herself against faeries and their ilk. Nothing that would help her get home, or even find the creature who had been thinking of her.

Sorcha rolled over, her curls spilling over her face and tangling in front of her. No faeries stared back at her. No birds sang in the trees, and no bugs flitted through the air.

All was still and silent.

She was home. Sorcha breathed in the clean, sweet air and felt the missing piece inside her slide back into place. This was where her soul belonged.

Tears stung her eyes and she couldn't catch her breath. She felt as if a lifetime had passed since she'd last walked in this wondrous land. Her fingers sank deep into moss that shimmered with dew.

There was someone here thinking about her. Someone she must have known, for who else would think of her in this place?

She swallowed. "Please don't be Fionn."

Sorcha rose to her feet, nearly stumbling. Should she call out? Should she let whomever was here know she'd arrived?

It was the only option. Although it seemed foolish in place like this, Sorcha knew it was the right choice.

"Hello?" she called out. "Hello? Who's there!"

A twig broke to her left.

"I'm not supposed to talk to strangers." The voice was young and made her sag with relief.

"Pooka," she breathed and turned. "It's me."

"Who are you?"

"You don't remember me? It's Sorcha, Pooka."

The boy had grown so much since she last saw him. He stood nearly as tall as her. He hadn't taken the form his mother chose, the patchwork woman had been uncomfortable to look at. Instead, Pooka had chosen a thicker form that leaned heavily towards canine features.

He squinted his eyes. "I don't know a Sorcha."

"I put your arm back together when you were little." She pointed at the appendage. "I told you stories of Macha to keep you quiet and said you were a brave man for handling so much pain with nary a peep."

She watched him rub the arm, exactly where he had broken it. She held her breath and prayed that he would remember. How long had she been gone? He was so different than she remembered.

"If you're really her, then what are you doing in the Otherworld?"

"I came to find your master."

"He doesn't need to be found."

"He does."

"Why?" Pooka gave her a suspicious look. "Are you going to stop him?"

"Stop him from what?"

Another voice interrupted, calling out, "Domnall! Where are you, boy?"

Pooka turned bright red. "You didn't hear that name."

"I wouldn't have used it against you anyways."

"Domnall! I thought I told you to gather mugwort, not to wander off into the forest and-" Oona stopped talking and halted behind Pooka as she caught sight of Sorcha. Tears filled her eyes. "Oh."

Sorcha's words stuck in her throat as all the emotions bubbled up. "Hello, Oona."

Tears dripped down her leaf-like cheeks as Oona launched herself into Sorcha's arms. "Oh my dearie! My girl, you are here!"

"It's been so long."

"Longer for us." Oona squeezed her so hard that she could barely breathe. "Oh my dear, sweet girl. How we have missed you!"

"Are you all right? You made it out of the castle?"

"Just barely."

"Cian?"

"Alive."

"Boggart?"

"Still with us."

"Good," Sorcha mumbled against Oona's shoulder. "Good."

"I cannot believe you're here!"

"Neither can I!"

Oona pulled away, framing her face and touching every part of Sorcha she could. "You're real."

"I'm real."

"How?"

"There's so much to tell you. But only once everyone is together. Where is he?" She watched Oona's face fall. The knot in the pit of her stomach clenched hard. "Oona?"

"Oh, dearie. It's been a long time since he sent you away."

"What happened?"

The leaves rustled behind them. Cian blundered towards them, shaking leaves from his shoulders. "I can't leave you two alone for even a second! You wander off like you have nothing else to do—"

He looked up and froze.

Sorcha waved. "Hello, Cian."

"What are you doing here?"

"I'm glad you survived the battle."

He huffed. "Yeah, well. You picked a bad time to come back."

"Why?" She looked around at the beloved familiar faces. "Why is this a bad time? What's happened?"

"The master," Oona said. "He's…not the same as he was when you left."

"What do you mean?"

"The king's forces seek us out. Somehow, Fionn caught wind that Eamonn was building an army. We have been fighting our way through the Otherworld to get to the Castle of Light."

"I'm sorry, why has this changed him? He's always been a warrior."

"You've never seen him like this, dearie."

"I've watched him kill for me. Have you forgotten I was there? I was with him when the battle started. He killed five elves and didn't even flinch. They couldn't touch him!"

Oona winced. "They're touching him now. I don't think he cares anymore if they touch him."

"What?"

Cian shuffled his feet. "What the pixie is trying to say is that he's falling to pieces. Solidifying more after every battle because the crystals strengthen him."

"He's throwing himself in front of the blade," Sorcha gasped in horror. "That won't make him stronger."

Oona played with her fingers, twisting them to and fro. "We've been trying to convince him of that, but he won't listen. He's certain he'll get his throne back and save everyone. But now you're here! Maybe you can convince him otherwise."

"I can try," she whispered. "But I don't know if he'll listen to me. How long has it been?"

"Five years."

She rocked back on her heels in shock. "Five years?"

"Five long years filled with fighting and hardship."

Pooka snorted. "And hunger."

"Have you been traveling all this time?" Sorcha asked.

"We haven't stopped since the battle."

She exhaled and tried not to think of their struggles. There would be time for that. She had all the time in the world now to be with them. But, there was something she had to do. And she couldn't wait any longer.

"Where is he?" Sorcha asked.

Oona pointed. "Through the woods in the glen."

"You're certain?"

"Yes."

Sorcha handed off her pack and smoothed her hands down her simple, blue skirt. "Please take this back to your camp. I'll join you later."

"You're going to him?"

"I am."

CHAPTER FIVE

The Reunion And The Throne

Leaves fell from the trees, green and bright. They smelled so sweet compared to the winter she had left.

Her hands trembled as she walked through the forest towards the glen where Eamonn stood. Would he even want to see her again? Had he missed her as much as she'd missed him?

Tiny orbs of light burst into the air from their haven atop the leaves. They trailed after her, landing in the curls of her hair and nesting deep within the coils. Perhaps they felt the rapid beat of her heart and heard the whispered promise of a story coming to life.

The forest was so quiet. Sorcha picked her way through the moss, avoiding every twig or stick that might give her away. She didn't want him to know she was coming. She needed just a few more minutes to control her breathing, feel the tingle in her fingers, and face the fear of rejection.

She brushed aside a tangled length of vine and there it was. The glen that glowed gold in the sunlight.

And him.

Eamonn sat on a stump in the center of emerald ground. An unfamiliar sword laid across his lap, and he stared down at it.

He had changed. The crystals had spread, but it was more than that. He was in the sunlight without a cloak, without fabric covering his face.

Eamonn was bare to the world, and he did not flinch away in fear.

She placed a hand against the nearest tree to balance herself. The dream Fionn had shown her was true. He had truly become more crystal than man, and yet he was still *hers*. She could feel it.

He must have been deep in thought, because he did not look up. She stepped onto a twig and let it crack beneath her heel.

"I asked for solitude." His deep voice sent shivers down her spine. "I need no company, Oona."

She couldn't speak. He sounded the same, even though time had passed. It was still him.

His shoulders hunched forward before he growled. "Oona, how many times do I have to tell you?"

Sorcha watched him stand while holding her breath. He turned around, and their eyes met. Lightning danced between them. The wind rushed into the glen, whipping the tail of his braid that was longer than she remembered.

But it was his eyes that held her. Like a physical touch, a whisper, a promise.

"You came back."

"Of course I did."

"After all this time, you came back."

He took one step towards her, a lurching step before catching himself as if he didn't know whether he had the right to touch her. She let out a choked sound, and then they were running towards each other. She didn't know which one moved first, but it didn't matter.

His arm wrapped around her, one hand lifted to cup her face and press her forehead against his, breathing her in.

"I thought I'd lost you forever." His breath fanned against her lips.

"How could I stay away?"

"You aren't safe here."

"Is life worth living if we are not together?"

Eamonn bent, lifting her by the hips until he could kiss her without straining. They poured their frustrations, their longing, their heartbreak into a single kiss that wiped those emotions away.

She wrapped her legs around his waist and dug her fingers into the grooves of his shoulders. He was solid and real, the man she had desired for so long. Finally, she could clasp him to her chest and breathe him in.

Her back hit a tree, the bark digging through the fabric of her dress, but she didn't care. Sorcha traced the angular curve of his jaw, down the strong column of his neck, into the deep crevices she didn't remember.

Eamonn kissed her as if he were a drowning man. Each lingering pass of firm lips and biting crystal healed her fragile heart. He didn't just take her lips, he devoured her.

He drew back for a second, pressing a raspy moan against her throat. "I should let you go."

"Please don't. I only just got you back."

Her words snapped the tether of his tight control. His hands were everywhere. Splayed open against her spine, pressing her closer to his body while sliding up the smooth length of her thigh. Her dress parted and warm air danced along her calves.

Every nerve ending in her body fired until all she could feel was him. He licked a trail of fire down her throat and across her shoulders.

This time was different than the first. He didn't hesitate or draw back, he did not allow her to take control. Somehow, she understood this moment was not about how much they missed each other. This wasn't just a reunion or a heartbreaking moment to remind each other they existed.

He wanted to brand her with his touch because he'd come so close to losing her.

The fabric of her bodice tore as he moved too quickly. Sorcha gasped and arched her back.

He licked a trail from the hollow of her throat to her breasts. She forgot how to breathe as he drew the tight pebbles into his mouth. Their first time had been so sweet she hadn't been able to think.

Now she felt as though she were adrift at sea and he was the only raft in sight. She clutched onto his shoulders and rocked on the waves they created.

His hand slipped underneath her skirts, slid up the back of her thigh and clenched the globes of her bottom. He pulled away from her chest, breathing into her ear, "I have missed you."

"Stop toying with me," she ground out. "Now, Eamonn."

"We've hardly gotten started."

"I will learn every inch of your body again, but I cannot wait any longer!"

He leaned back and arched a brow. "I forgot how demanding you were."

Sorcha yanked his braid so hard that his head jerked backwards. "I'm insulted you forgot anything at all."

"I didn't forget your taste." He leaned forward and licked her lips. "Sunshine and strawberries."

He fumbled with the clasp of his belt to free himself. Sorcha braced, knowing it had been a long time and that he was a considerably large man. But then, he hesitated.

Eamonn brushed her curls from her forehead and pressed a kiss against her temple. "Are you sure? There's plenty of soft moss to cushion your back, and time before the others find us."

This was why she adored him. Sorcha's eyes drifted and a smile burst free. "Yes, yes this is what I want."

"Thank the gods."

Her thighs clenched hard around his hips as he plunged inside her with one swift stroke. She had dreamed of this moment so many times but no dream could replicate the feeling of his hands so gentle on her hips. The crystals slashing across his abdomen rubbed against her belly with each grind of his hips against hers. He whispered endearments in her ears with each flex of his muscles.

"My sunshine," he groaned. "My light."

She framed his face and brought his lips to hers in a kiss so delicate it was painful. "Yours."

There was no way to get closer to him, and yet she wanted to. She dug her nails into his back, catching on new wounds. So much pain laced across his skin, but she could provide him a haven.

Her toes pointed, her head tilted back to brace against the tree.

"Eamonn," she gasped.

He traced his palm up the arch of her spine. Cupping the back of her neck, he pressed his lips to hers again. "I can't lose myself in you."

"Who says you can't?"

The groaned response was little more than noise, and he quickened his strokes. Each time, he came closer and closer to touching her very soul.

Unexpectedly, light exploded behind her eyes. The orgasm happened so fast she hadn't felt it building. Stars fell from the sky and burst free from her skin in one clenching moment that had her holding her breath.

He growled and buried his face in her shoulder as he found his own release.

Panting, she tightened her hold on him. He wrapped his arms around her, holding her so tight she could barely breathe. As she stared up into the dappled green leaves above them, she wondered how she would ever let him go again.

Her thighs clenched hard around his hips, drawing him ever closer. She couldn't shake the feeling that the moment she let go, he would disappear again. Tears pricked her eyes.

"Please let this be real." She pressed the words against the crown of his head. "Please tell me this isn't a dream and you won't disappear the moment I look at you again."

"Let us both hope this is not a dream for I would surely not survive the waking."

"Don't say that. Not so soon after you almost died."

"I cannot die."

"You aren't invincible, Eamonn."

"I am with you at my side."

He pulled back, and she looked upon his beloved face with fearful love. She traced his wounded brow.

"Your eye," she gasped.

"It is nothing."

"Does it hurt?"

"No more than the others."

Sorcha could see the pain in his eyes. He was afraid she would reject him for his differences. And she had forgotten how much his past influenced his future.

She leaned forward and pressed a chaste kiss against his brow. She hoped the butterfly touch would heal the scars on his heart.

"I am sorry for your pain."

His fingers flexed against her sides. "Mo chroí."

"Eamonn, don't get mad at me for what I'm about to do."

"How could I grow angry with you now?"

She drew back just enough to cock her arm back and slap him across the face so hard that the crystals on his cheek sliced through her palm.

He flinched and lifted a hand to his cheek. "What was that for, you mad woman?"

"Don't you *ever* force me to leave your side again!"

"There was a battle! You would have died if you stayed!"

"And that is not your choice!" Her shout echoed through the glen. "If you get to risk your life for me, then I get to do the same. And if you try to do that again I will find a way to put a sword through your heart."

He blinked at her in shock. "Did you just threaten me?"

"Never take away a woman's choice to stand by her man. Do you hear me?"

"I hear you."

"Say it again."

"I hear you, my fierce druid priestess." He traced the outline of her lips with his thumb.

"I mean it, Eamonn. Never again."

"I will always put myself as your shield. I have to protect those I cherish. And you are my heart, Sunshine."

His words dug into her ribs, wiggling their way through the icy exterior she had erected. "Then let me walk beside you and heal every wound."

Their lips clung together, breath mingling until all her tongue stung with mint.

"I am so glad to have you back."

"As am I."

He pressed his forehead against hers, rolling back and forth until the crystals made her wince. Only then did he step back, lowering her legs to the ground gently and holding on as her balance reset.

Moss sank between her toes. When had her shoes fallen off? She glanced around, looking for the worn slippers that had kept her feet warm all winter.

"Looking for these?"

Eamonn held them dangling from his fingertips.

"Yes," Sorcha said while holding out her hand.

"They're so tiny."

"I imagine they would be to you, I'm a lot smaller than most Fae." She hopped, trying to grab them out of his hand.

He let the slippers drop into her waiting hands. Sorcha marveled at how easy it was to slide back into this life. She had thought it would be harder, more difficult to connect with him.

It was as if she had never left.

Hopping on one foot, she pulled her shoes on. "What's happened while I've been gone?"

"I could ask you the same question." He waited until she was standing again before pulling her into his arms and carrying her to the stump.

Eamonn settled with her in his lap, his hands playing with the dip of her waist. She couldn't stop touching him either. Every new cut needed exploring, and she couldn't see all of him.

She sank her fingers into his hair and pulled hard. "What happened on the isle?"

"Fionn overran the castle. His men cut through most of ours, beloved people fell because they didn't have sword or weapon."

"How did you get out?"

"I don't know." He shook his head, dislodging her fingers from the crown of his head. "I don't remember it. Oona says I drew Ocras and took care of the problem, but will not tell me any more."

"Blood lust?" She had heard of such a thing in the legends, but hadn't thought it was real. Worry knotted her stomach as if a fist closed around it.

"Far worse than that, little sunshine. He retreated to the edge of the isle, but was obviously gathering his forces for another attack. There were so few left we fled into the Otherworld. There were many hard months as we struggled to find a new home."

"I thought our people couldn't return to the Otherworld? You said banishment is forever."

"It is, until the High King of the Seelie Fae decrees they are absolved."

Sorcha stopped breathing. She hadn't thought it possible such a thing was possible, although she was ashamed she hadn't thought of it herself. He was the eldest son, the rightful heir to the throne.

"You took a great risk," she said while shaking her head.

"I knew I was meant to be king from the moment I first took breath."

"You chose to forsake that life."

"That doesn't mean I cannot take it back."

His palms smoothed down her spine to calm her. But her brows furrowed all the same, and her gut twisted. "Eamonn, it will not be easy to take this path. Your brother won't give up, your people will be confused. You're suggesting splitting your people in two."

"I know that very well. I've spent the last five years fighting to regain independence and my throne."

"How has that worked for you?"

"I'm still in a forest, without throne or crown."

Sorcha had thought as much. She wracked her mind for an idea, something she could say to help. But she was thoroughly out of her element. A peasant girl from Ui Neill knew little to help a faerie king.

She cleared her throat. "What steps have you taken thus far?"

"I have an army of dwarves, and the few gnomes who have come to help the cause." He shook his head, lips twisting to the side in disappointment. "It is a very small army with little ability to fight Tuatha dé Danann and elves. Luck is not on our side."

"You're meeting them head on?"

"How else would you have me fight?"

She toyed with his braid, pulling it over his shoulder and rubbing the silken strands between her fingertips. "I wouldn't have you fight at all. You're a king, should this not be solved through the courts?"

"This is not something my brother and I can talk about."

"Why not?"

"He will not give up the throne."

She rubbed the fine strands between her fingers again, trying to remember all the legends and myths of the Fae. Sorcha had never been the storyteller. She much preferred using her hands to listening, and tended to doze off when the ballads were sung.

Sorcha wracked her mind for any story which might fit, settling on a legend she'd heard long ago. Cormac Ulfada, a wise High King of the human race, and his many intelligent decisions to keep his throne.

Her eyes glinted as an idea formed. "He doesn't have to."

Eamonn tilted his head to the side and regarded her with a curious expression. "What do you have brewing in that mind of yours?"

"These are your people, Eamonn. You have proven yourself to be the high king. Fionn has no real claim to the throne. Why should you have to fight for what is yours?"

"That is what we do. We fight for what is ours."

"But what if you didn't have to fight? What if your people made the choice for you? They will follow you without a war, without blood, without death. All you have to do, is give them the option to follow a more worthy leader."

He blinked at her in shock. "Just how much did you learn while you were gone?"

"Learn? I have been home with my father and my sisters."

"Are they well?" Eamonn stroked her chin, worry painting fine lines across his forehead.

"They live."

"You cured the plague, didn't you?"

The proud expression on his face filled her heart near to bursting. He believed in her when her own family hadn't thought she could make miracles happen.

"How did you know?" she asked.

"I always knew you would."

"With no help from you."

"Did you need my help?"

Sorcha shook her head. "No, apparently not."

He traced a finger down her forehead to the tip of her nose. "You have never needed me to cure the plague. You're perfectly capable of saving your own people."

"Am I supposed to say the same thing to you?"

"It would be appreciated."

"I don't agree with you, Eamonn. All this death seems unnecessary. How many people have to die before you trade thrones?"

He sighed and buried his face in her neck. She felt the hard press of his lips against her collarbone. "This is not something a human could comprehend. Tuatha dé Danann do not give up, and Fionn has desired the throne his entire life. He's not going to welcome me into his castle with a smile."

"Have you tried speaking to him?"

"Enough, Sorcha. Let me enjoy having you back in my arms for a few moments before you try to heal all my wounds."

She hugged him closer, her mind whirling with thoughts. Fionn had obviously been concerned about Eamonn's whereabouts. If he was invading her dreams, then he had an inkling his twin was closer than he wished. But just how close was Eamonn?

"Are we near the Castle of Light?"

He heaved a sigh. "Right above it, mo chroí. So close to my family home I can feel its magic in the air."

"What are you planning, Eamonn?" Her heart beat hard in her chest, so rapidly that he tapped his finger on her skin in time to the beats.

"Another battle to end all battles. I cannot keep fighting him like this. He has an endless amount of soldiers and they continue to draw closer and closer to our location."

"Then you need to find a stronghold."

"A stronghold?" He leaned back and stared into her eyes. "First you declare I must speak with him, and then you suggest a stronghold?"

"What about the Castle of Light makes it so special?" she asked. "Is it powerful? Are there people there who would aid you? Or is it merely the familial ties?"

"There is nothing special about the castle."

"Then let us find a new castle. A new place where those who have been wronged may flee." She scooted up in his lap, plans already forming. "If you refuse to speak with him, then build your army out of those who willingly fight for the cause. Spread word that you exist. That the high king wants to return to the throne."

"You are suggesting a coup."

"I'm suggesting much more than that," she said, excited as the idea formed. "I'm suggesting you create a second throne. A higher throne."

"I like the way you think."

"Not every man would listen to a woman."

"I know better than to ignore the wisdom of women. Though I do not always agree with you, mo chroí, I will never dismiss your opinions."

Her heart swelled with happiness.

Eamonn smiled, wolfish and full of mischief. "Now, why don't we stop thinking for a while?"

He tilted her back until her spine hit the soft moss. Prowling after her, he settled between her legs and smiled.

She grinned back, happiness bubbling in her chest. "The moss is comfortable."

"I wouldn't put you anywhere else."

"The sun is warm."

"It sees you and smiles."

"You feel so familiar," she said in wonderment and lifted a hand to touch the new crystals near his eye. "And yet, so different as well."

"No more talking, mo chroí."

She didn't for a while as she found each new wound and left her mark on his body once again.

"Here you are, dearie."

"Thank you, Oona." Sorcha took the offered bowl filled with rabbit stew. The mere scent of it made her stomach rumble. She couldn't remember the last time she had eaten, but that was what came with the job of healing.

They all sat around a small fire. Boggart sat in her lap, Cian and Oona bickering over the right way to cook rabbit. Sorcha had grieved with them when she first arrived. They had lost so many. Now, they all gathered to eat and forge their bonds all over again.

Small fires crackled in the shadow of the mountain range around them. Clusters of dwarves formed around each flame, little mingling occurring this late at night. Family groups, Sorcha guessed. The dwarves were silent folk and weren't interested in speaking with her.

Although, they were far more intuitive than the other faeries she had met.

A small female dwarf stumbled into Sorcha as she arrived, snorted, and muttered, "Now there are druids 'ere too?"

Sorcha had stared after her in shock.

They stayed away from her after that. She didn't know if dwarves were among those that banished her people in the first place, but she guessed it was likely they were a part of the decision. Druids were fearsome creatures to the Fae. Humans capable of magic defied all logic.

She tucked into the stew and tried to find Eamonn in the crowd. He slipped into his warlord visage as soon as he set foot in the camp. All of his attention poured into catching up with the dwarves he called "generals." She thought it more likely they were heads of their families.

Boggart tugged on her sleeve and pointed.

Sorcha followed the direction of Boggart's jabbing finger, finding the same female dwarf at the edge of the shadows. She didn't look frightened, but something else entirely. She was watching Sorcha with a hard gaze.

"Can I help you?"

"I don't think so."

"Are you hurt?" Sorcha asked. "I'm a healer."

"Druids don't 'eal dwarves."

"You have a problem because I have druid blood?"

"Your kind makes poor decisions. I remember the stories of when you 'ad free access to the Otherworld. Stealing magical objects. Using them against each other until you accidentally killed an important faerie.

I know all of it, and I don't trust you."

"Well," Sorcha put her bowl to the side and hugged Boggart tighter in her embrace. "Perhaps it would set your mind at ease to know I do not follow the old ways. I was not raised a druid, and magic is very new to me."

"Is it?" The dwarf nodded at her bowl. "Then why did you leave a bit of food?"

"I'm no longer hungry."

The little woman crossed her eyes and flicked her beard over her shoulder. "Go on. Do what you want to do with it. I'll watch to make sure you aren't up to any funny business."

"I don't want to do anything with it."

But that was a lie. The dwarf was reading her mind, Sorcha realized. Her fingers itched to pick the bowl back up and throw the remnants into the fire. She had always done that, even as a child. She always tossed leftovers into the flames, even food someone else might eat.

Words bloomed in her mind like the ink that appeared on the papers of her books. Baring her teeth in a grimace, she picked up the bowl and flicked the remaining food into the flames of the campfire.

"Feast, ancestors of old. I thank you for the food you have provided and the safe haven you offer for my soul. I honor your memory with this simple food. Blessed be."

The flames spun up into the air, and Sorcha saw people in the dancing spikes. Faces she did not recognize, but made her relax all the same. Each wore the blue woad the women in her vision had worn.

She clenched her hands into fists.

The dwarf tsked. "See? Druids never fall too far from the tree. You're lucky I'm not my grandfather, or I would 'ave already taken your 'ead from your shoulders."

"Why hasn't anyone else then? I see waves of dwarves as if I looked into the ocean, and not one of you has raised a finger towards me."

"Because we're all dying out there." The dwarven woman jabbed a finger at her family. "And if you can stop that, put an end to all this madness, then that means you get to live. Otherwise? Stay out of our way."

Darkness swallowed up the tiny woman as she fled back to her own campfire.

Sorcha shook her head. "Are they all like that?"

"They are when it comes to protecting what is theirs. Are you really a druid, dearie?"

Oona's eyes were massive. The moon reflected in their iridescent depths, twin limpid pools that Sorcha thought were all too hopeful for her liking.

"Yes. My grandfather found me while I was home."

"Family? From your mother's side?"

Sorcha hummed, Boggart's soft snore vibrating against her neck. "I don't know how much I trust him. He seemed to know far too much about my life, but didn't appear to care for my choices. It was all very odd."

"It's good to have people who understand you."

"He doesn't understand me. He doesn't seem to understand the world." She snorted. "I'd trust the witch more than him."

"Witch?" Oona startled. "Witches are dangerous creatures."

"Don't I know it. But she helped to get me here, and I think it's more likely that she has a little druid blood in her."

"The druids are returning then." Oona's voice took on a strange quality, a whisper in the wind. "It is as it should be. The Otherworld is returning to its previous state. The high king takes his throne. The druids walk back through the portals. The Lesser Fae join their families and leave their lives of hardship."

"We hope."

Cian plopped down on the other side of the fire. He shook himself and water sprayed from his rolls of flesh. "That boy won't listen to a damn thing."

"Eamonn?" Sorcha asked.

"Aye. He's got it in his head we'll be moving. A whole army! Moving from the nearest point to the castle we could be."

"Where are we going?"

"Ask him. He won't say a word to me."

Sorcha stood, searching for Eamonn across the campfires that dotted like stars.

"He's there, dearie." Oona pointed towards what used to be a solid platform, but now had rotting holes like gaping mouths. "In the place where all this started."

She didn't comprehend the words until she realized where they were. A platform, a great column of wood, and a man whose throat bore the mark of the noose.

"No." Sorcha shook her head. "No, it cannot be."

"He chose to remain here. To remind himself day after day why he is fighting so hard."

"This is where they hung him?"

"We're standing in the same spot his family stood all those years ago. They watched him swing from a rope for hours before going back to their castle and falling asleep." Oona sniffed. "I still don't know how they did it. They made me go back with them, and nary a one had even a nightmare. Their boy was left out to the elements, unable to breathe, and with all the beasts of the Otherworld chewing on him. And they didn't seem to care."

Sorcha couldn't bear it. Her feet moved her towards the platform where Eamonn stood staring up at the sky. No one was looking at him.

They were looking at her.

She was graceful as she picked her way through the crowds. Her skirts glowed in the moonlight, turning them silver and white.

"A ghost," someone muttered.

"A bean sidhe."

"No, a druid."

Her hair stirred in the breeze. Curls fluttered across her face as she stared at him. He didn't respond to her approach. The muscles of his back tensed, his fists curling in on themselves.

He knew. He always knew when she was walking up to him. And she was certain he knew she was about to argue with him.

Silently, she walked up the rotting stairs and placed a hand against his spine.

"Eamonn."

"You will not change my mind."

She smiled. "Why would I even try? It was my idea, mo chroí. We leave this place?"

"I will not stay upon this cursed land for a moment longer."

"Wherever you go, I will follow."

"It will not be an easy journey."

"Then it is good you have a healer who will help you along the way."

A great sigh rocked his shoulders. He turned to her then, pulling her into his arms and bending to rest his chin on her forehead. "I didn't think it possible to miss another person as much as I missed you."

"I would miss losing a limb. And that is precisely the way I feel when you are not with me."

"Thank you for standing by me."

"I will convince you to speak with your brother, Eamonn."

"You can try, but I will never yield."

She shouted in her mind words of encouragement. Not for him, but for herself. Sorcha knew, deep in the pit of her gut, that the only way to end this war without further bloodshed was for the two of them to talk. They had to understand there was only so much more war this land could take.

But for now, she would wrap herself in Eamonn's arms and pray that he understood.

He straightened, tucking her underneath his arm. "Men and women of Underhill!"

The dwarves all stood. Sorcha looked out over their ranks and wondered just how many they had lost. Five years of battle? Or was it five years of Eamonn fighting, and these people had only been here for a few weeks?

Old scars and new decorated their faces, worn armor weighed them down. Rust outlining the edges and chips marring the pristine surfaces.

"We have fought for a long time. You are a hard and true people, but now I must ask another boon."

A rumble of worry echoed.

"We leave this land tomorrow. I will not risk our troops and our lives any further. We go to our family's homeland. To the castle of old where the Tuatha dé Danann first touched the ground."

"Where?" someone shouted.

He squeezed Sorcha against his chest. "To the castle of Nuada Silverhand!"

The resounding cheer at these words could likely be heard all the way to the Castle of Light. They were going to Nuada's sacred home?

She glanced up at Eamonn. "Is that wise?"

"Where else would we go?"

"Anywhere. I do not wish to anger your grandfather."

"Neither do I." He released her, holding her hand and guiding her down the stairs. "But there is no other choice. As you said, the battle can only go on for so long. I need a new throne until I take mine back."

They traveled for days across the wide expanse of the Otherworld.

Sorcha began to recognize mountains and hills. The peaks she had climbed over as a child, now covered with sparkling glitter, traversed by faeries, and far more vibrant. Flowers reached for her with their leafy hands. Grass tangled around her ankles if she stopped for too long, stroking whatever skin it could find.

Eamonn set a blistering pace that left the entire company exhausted. He did not come to see Sorcha again, although she understood why. The dwarves took much of his attention.

The more she watched them, the more she wondered how he had gathered such an army. They didn't *like* each other, let alone him. Small squabbles quickly turned into giant brawls. Taking care of them sapped his energy.

He hadn't forgotten her, she was certain of that. After all this time, she was finally in the Otherworld. He was busy, not distant.

Sorcha kept repeating the words in her head. It became a poem, a hymn, that repeated over and over again in her mind until it stuck.

After all this time.

She turned to look back the way they had traveled. A long line of dwarves trailed down the mountain like a river. It was a rare day of sunshine that turned the fields to rolling waves of green grass. Stone outcroppings jutted from the earth, mimicking frothy white peaks.

Oona and Cian stayed close to her, the others from Hy-brasil not far behind.

Stones crunched behind her, but she didn't need to look. Pooka was far younger than the rest of them. His boundless energy sent him running ahead and back with updates on where they were going.

"We're stopping," he sullenly reported.

"Is that a bad thing?"

"Might be, depending on what you think of this journey."

The wind picked up and blew Sorcha's long strands like a banner in the wind. "What do you mean by that?"

"We've arrived."

"And so soon."

She looked back at him, crouched on a rock with a frown on his face. When had he gotten so old? She saw the worry lines that marred his expression and knew he had a reason to be afraid.

"Go help the others," she said. "We will need them all with us when we reach the castle."

"You want them in the front?"

"I think it would be wise to have his family near him."

"You think he considers us family?" Pooka shook his head and hopped to the ground. "You got a lot of big ideas in that head of yours, but you still don't understand Tuatha dé Danann."

"I think holding onto prejudices brought your kind to this point. Now go get them all and meet me at the front. How much further is it?"

"Far."

She pinned him with a censoring gaze. "Domnall."

"Over the rise," he grumbled. "You'll see it before you get too close. He stopped everyone so they could look at the castle before we go anywhere."

Oona huffed and puffed up to them. "Are we stopping?"

"No, sorry."

"Ah well, it was a hope anyways. Do we know when he wants to stop for the night?"

"He's reached the castle." Sorcha looked up at the jagged edge of the mountain they climbed. "It's on the other side of this crest."

"We best be going then."

"Pooka, how many times do I have to tell you to go help the others?"

"You don't get to order me around."

Sorcha turned on her heel and grabbed the boy by the ear. His yelp sounded eerily like that of a wounded puppy. "I tell you what to do because you need to learn how to respect your elders. Go get the others before I leave an imprint of my boot on your behind."

"You wouldn't dare."

"Try me, pup."

He glared for a few moments before his shoulders rounded in defeat. She gave his ear one more twist before setting him off.

Oona chuckled. "You'll have him fawning over you in no time."

"The boy needs to listen."

"The boy is halfway in love with you, and you hardly cast him a glance."

"Of course I don't." Sorcha rolled her eyes to the heavens. "He's just a child!"

"I wasn't suggesting you encourage him."

The two women started back up the mountain. Sorcha held out her arm for Oona to take, although she knew the pixie wouldn't admit to weakness. They linked together and clambered over the rocky path.

Oona was out of breath. Sorcha could feel her lungs burning. It was a shame she was so tired, for the landscape was beautiful, and she would have liked to pause and enjoy it.

The mountain was foreboding. Sheer cliffs dropped off into nothing, with no path to mark their direction. No one had been here for a very long time.

They passed a few dwarves who sat themselves on stones and pulled out their water skins. Red cheeks and sweat-stained faces revealed how hard Eamonn had pushed them. Too hard.

"Why does everyone seem so nervous?" Sorcha asked.

"It is said the castle is haunted."

"Nuada's castle? Why would it be haunted?"

"You know of the Fomorians?"

Sorcha had grown up on the stories of the beastly men who'd battled the Tuatha dé Danann. Centuries of war had thinned the numbers of both, although there were plenty of romantic stories in between. It seemed the two cultures loved to fight each other just as much as they loved to break the rules.

"I know of them."

"The human legends never said they crossed over into our world, but they did. Nuada's castle was the first they took, and they reigned there for a good century before they lost everything. So many people died there." Oona blew out a breath. "It is said that ghosts walk the halls with the heads of goats and bodies of men."

"So it's abandoned?"

"Far more than that. It's cursed. Even the Unseelie will not traverse its battlements."

"Wonderful. And what about a haunted castle sounded like a good idea to Eamonn?"

Oona tightened her hand on Sorcha's arm. "Nuada Silverhand was the last High King. You haven't put it together, have you? A king can be anyone in name. People will kneel before anyone with a crown. But the High King of the Seelie Fae is something else entirely. He is the true ruler recognized by the land itself. There can be many kings. There can only be *one* High King."

Sorcha blew out a long breath, forcing the tension in her body to ease. It made sense that Eamonn would be the high king. He was the first born son and did not bend to the old ways. He saw things in a way that would benefit the whole of his people.

What had she gotten herself into?

They crested the top of the mountain and Sorcha nearly fell to her knees. Nuada Silverhand's castle was built on the peak of the nearest mountain. Walls stretched from the cliff edges, supporting the ornate towers above. Tattered banners fluttered in the wind. Stone outcroppings melded into the castle, making the castle appear as if it grew out of the mountain itself.

The only way to enter was a crumbling bridge dripping stones like water. Crows sat upon it watching the meager army appear over the rise.

"It is terrifying," Sorcha observed. White birds rose from the castle battlements and circled overhead.

"I fear it will be even worse inside."

"How long has it been since anyone has lived there?"

"Centuries."

Sorcha sighed. "Then it will be falling apart."

"An army does better when there is something to do. He is smart to bring us here while waiting for more to come."

"Will they?" Sorcha glanced down at Oona. "It was an idea I had, but I do not know the ways of the Fae. Will it be likely that others will follow him?"

"I believe they will have no choice. The High King of the Seelie Fae commands us all."

Sorcha's eyes strayed across the crowds of dwarves. Standing like a mountain in the center of a field, Eamonn stared at the castle. She could see the determined set of his shoulders, the way his long legs stood strong and braced. Wind buffeted him, but he did not move, didn't react even when the dwarves set down their clanking packs.

He was just as worried as she was.

With a gentle squeeze, she released Oona and made her way through the throngs of faeries. This time, they did not whisper that a druid was among them. They merely watched as the strange redheaded woman moved among their ranks.

She stood next to Eamonn, tiny compared to his great height, and watched the strange birds circling overhead.

"We've made it," she said.

"Against all odds."

"It's far larger than I imagined."

"Long ago, this castle housed thousands of faeries."

"I can see how it would be possible." She reached out tentatively, unsure whether he would want her support. It didn't seem likely that he would want her hand. Instead, she linked her pinky with his. "Are we going in?"

"I don't know how dangerous it will be."

"Then perhaps just the two of us should go first?"

He shuddered as if the mere suggestion made him uncomfortable. "You will not go into that castle until I have made certain it is safe."

"I thought we already had this conversation."

"We have, and I say it again. This is not a safe place for humans, Sorcha. Remain here so I don't have to worry about you while I clear this castle of any remaining evil." He slid a finger under her chin and nudged until she looked directly into his gaze. "Do you understand, Sorcha?"

"When did you get so domineering?"

"About the same time I took being a king seriously."

"I don't like it."

"You don't have to. You just have to listen." He let his hand drop and headed back towards the dwarves. "Don't even think about it, Sorcha!"

Sorcha was damn well thinking about it. He should know by now she hated anyone telling her what to do. All she wanted was to set a foot on the bridge to see his reaction.

She glared at the missing stones and moss covered parapets. It would be so easy to pick her way across that and explore the massive castle. And really, what was he going to do? He wasn't even looking at her.

Part of her knew this was a bad idea. She could feel in her bones that something horrible might happen.

But her pride wouldn't let her forget his order. She gnawed on the idea like a dog with a bone until she blew out a breath and shrugged.

She'd have to go fast. The bridge didn't look like it could hold a lot of weight, but if she hopped between the large gaps, it should hold up. Lifting her skirts, she jumped from the nearest gap to the center of the bridge.

It groaned so loudly that she was certain it would break. The clouds beneath her weren't likely to catch her when she fell.

"Sorcha!" Eamonn's shout seared her to the bone.

The stones underneath her feet began to crumble. Heart beating, lungs heaving, she flew across the falling bridge. Each step she took felt as if it would be her last. The crashing of stones striking the ground beneath her echoed through the canyon.

The bridge in front of her quaked. Did that mean what was behind her had already fallen?

"Don't look," she muttered as she leapt from stone to stone.

Looking would only solidify how much danger she was in. She had to focus, had to get to the other side of the bridge or fall to her death.

Sorcha planted her foot on a stone that was already falling. She shoved, leaping into the air and rolling onto the other side of the bridge. Air exploded from her lungs and she shoved herself over.

Hair fell in front of her eyes, but she could still see him. Her massive faerie prince who raced across a bridge that crumbled to dust behind him. Eamonn's face was twisted in anger and concentration, sunlight sparkling as it struck the crystals of his body.

She held her breath as he let out a powerful roar and the bridge fell away beneath him.

"No," she breathed. It couldn't be. He couldn't fall and die now. Not because of her foolish mistake.

Wisps of smoke and debris puffed from the ground. It swirled like ghosts, the movement strange and unntural. Would he haunt this place with all the others?

A crystal hand latched onto the remaining edge of the bridge. His human hand followed, fingers gripping the stone so hard that it dented.

"Thank the gods," she muttered as she crawled over to him.

Sorcha leaned over the edge to flash a relieved smile. Eamonn did not appear amused.

"It's not over yet, sunshine."

She grabbed onto his forearm and blew her hair out of her face. "Never doubted for a second you'd make it."

"Let go."

"You're hanging off the edge of a cliff, let me help you."

He released the hand she grabbed and shook her off. "Back up, Sorcha."

For once, she realized it was probably a good idea to listen to him.

She slid backwards on her bottom to give him enough room. With one great heave, he yanked himself up and over the bridge, rolling to her side.

Eamonn dropped a hand on his chest that lifted rapidly with each breath. "Don't do that again."

She leaned over him, her hair creating a curtain around them. "You didn't have to follow me."

"Of course I did," he said as he smoothed a thumb over her cheekbone. "Are you done risking your life for curiosity?"

"Doubtful."

Eamonn groaned, rolling to his side and onto his feet. He waved at the dwarves that stood in a line at the edge of the cliff. Oona and Cian piled on top of a large rock, teetering dangerously at the edge as they waited to see whether they were all right.

They were lucky. Sorcha's stomach clenched as she saw the damage to the bridge. There was nothing left but the skeletal bones reaching out into the abyss of nothing.

"Would you look at that," she said. "Seems like we're stuck here for a while."

"The dwarves will fix it in no time. Once they figure out that they want to follow, they'll speak to the stones."

"Speak to the stones?"

"Did you think they tunneled through mountains?" Eamonn turned to her, his crystal eye glittering. "They ask them to move, and they do."

"Ah," she nodded. "As with everything here, I suppose I have to say that makes sense and move on. Are we going to the castle?"

"Absolutely not."

"But it's right there!" She gestured at the looming dark stone and high parapets.

"I can see that, Sorcha."

"It's where we were planning to go anyways."

"And it is dangerous. Faerie-cursed land is never friendly to humans."

"I've already been to Unseelie," she said, planting her fists on her hips. "You're telling me that this castle is more dangerous than the Dark Castle? If it is, then perhaps we should find somewhere else to bring your army."

"You've been where?" His eyes blazed with anger. "I'd forgotten about that."

"Yes, well, the Queen was awful." Another flock of birds burst into flight. The wind billowed around them, clearing out the dust from the collapse and revealing the decrepit walls. "Are you certain you don't wish to go in?"

"We're waiting here until the dwarves complete the new bridge."

"How long will that take?"

He waved again at the dwarves. She could see their mouths moving, but their shouts wouldn't carry over the deep valley between them. "As soon as they start building, it shouldn't take long."

Sorcha snorted. The dwarves were setting up camp for the night, and she didn't blame them. They would likely start building as soon as the sun rose again. Eamonn set a grueling pace and they were all exhausted.

They deserved a bit of rest.

She shook her head and started up a path. There were buildings all around the roads that splintered out from the bridge. She imagined these had once been homes as it seemed unlikely that anyone other than royalty and their immediate staff would have lived in the castle.

Ivy crawled up the walls of the buildings and the protecting battlements that surrounded the entire town. Gothic swirls and dramatic rooftop peaks suggesting this had once been a home for artists and craftsmen.

"Sorcha? Sorcha! What did I say?"

She rolled her eyes. "You said you would stay and wait for the dwarves. I don't fancy sleeping on a cliff's edge."

"Get back here!"

"No."

She heard his growl of frustration and the skittering of small stones as he followed her towards the central courtyard.

"I don't like ghosts," he grumbled when he caught up with her.

"There's no such thing as ghosts."

"We're in the Otherworld. Anything is possible."

"Then I should like to meet them."

"Please don't say that."

Sorcha grinned. "Is there someone following us, Eamonn?"

"No."

"I'm quite certain I can hear a third set of footsteps."

"Stop it!"

CHAPTER SIX
THE GHOSTS OF THE CASTLE

Paint flecked from the rotting wood of the railings once grand stairs overtaken by moss and vines. The doors were easily twice Sorcha's height, terrifying and imposing in their grandeur and age.

"Is this what it felt like?" Eamonn asked.

"What?"

"Walking up to the main door of the castle on Hy-brasil and wondering what was behind it?"

"Yes," she replied. "This is exactly what it felt like."

"I don't give you enough credit for your bravery."

"Or for my foolishness," Sorcha added with a grin. "I was just as impulsive when I walked into your throne room."

She placed her hands against the wood and shoved. Surprisingly, her hands didn't puncture the door. The echoing creak danced down her spine, but it swung open without falling off its hinges.

It was a start.

She peeked through the cobwebs and tangled vines. There were shadows dancing upon the walls, ones she didn't think came from the plants. Could they be goblins? They looked faintly similar to the hunched creatures she had seen in the Unseelie castle.

Eamonn's hand landed on her shoulder and nudged her behind him. "Let me go first."

"I thought you were afraid of ghosts?"

"Not so much that I would let you put your life before mine." His lips tilted to the side. "Have a little faith, sunshine."

"I never doubted you."

His scoff echoed as they walked into the great hall.

King Nuada Silverhand's castle was as grand as she imagined it. Stained glass windows framed the hallway, and colored lights danced on the white and black checkered floor, which was missing a few pieces of marble.

Vines grew over the walls, and giant blue hydrangeas poked through cracks and crevices. Gold glinted on the wall nearest to her. Sorcha stepped closer, shifting ivy to the side and stumbled back with a gasp.

Eyes stared back at her.

Eamonn caught her against his chest. "It's a painting."

"I thought it was… It looked so…"

He spread his hand wide against her belly and leaned down to chuckle in her ear. "Who is afraid of ghosts?"

"Apparently both of us. Whose bright idea was it to come in here when the sun was setting?"

"I believe it was yours."

"Right, queen of bad ideas."

"Come on, Sorcha. We've only stepped a few feet into the castle."

"Now you want to explore," she grumbled and detached herself from him. "What are those shadows?"

"The glass."

She glanced up. The stained glass high above them revealed outlines, human and faerie in nature, created by smoke and black tar. "Strange."

"An intimidation tactic most Fae recognize."

"I didn't think the Seelie Fae would be all that interested in marring such beauty."

A shadow passed over his face, his blue eyes piercing her with their intensity. "That wasn't created by the Fae."

"The Fomorians then?"

"Likely."

He turned and marched through the hall as if he owned it. And in a way, he did. As a direct descendent of Nuada, he was the only person remaining who could claim this haunted place.

He always seemed to end up in forgotten places, she mused. Their feet left slashing marks against the dust ridden floor. Some of the large blue blooms picked up their heads as she walked past, tiny vines stretching for her.

"The plants don't do that with anyone else." Eamonn narrowed his eyes at the offending greenery.

"Sure they do. They just want attention."

"From you."

She picked her way over a tree which had fallen through the wall and landed atop a stairway leading up. "They don't do it to faeries?"

"No."

He paused in front of a plant that had grown so large it covered the entire wall. "Come here."

"I don't know if I want to. They seem more interested in me than the other plants."

"I want to try something."

"I don't."

"Sorcha," he growled.

She gritted her teeth and let him grab her hand. "What do you think will happen? They're just plants!"

"They aren't just plants. They're guards." He furrowed his brow in concentration, holding her hand just above the nearest hydrangea. "These flowers aren't native to the Otherworld, and yet, here they are."

"You think I have something to do with that?"

The plant reached out a thin vine and wrapped it around her finger. Smooth and warm, it slithered to her wrist, gently stroking the sensitive skin.

"I think there's something behind this wall of plants," he murmured.

"Why do you think that?"

"The stairs stop here."

"They also keep going behind us. This could just be a wall."

"You said you have druid blood. Ask the plants."

Sorcha rolled her eyes. "Ask the plants, he says. As if that's possible."

The vine tugged hard on her wrist. Eamonn caught hold of her hips and pulled her back against him, but the plant did not let go. Another vine lashed out and wrapped around the other arm, this one significantly thicker and stronger.

She stared in shock as the leaves parted and green eyes met her gaze. The rustling wind brushed past her ears, but she could not feel it.

"Eamonn?" she gasped. "There's another painting."

"I don't see anything, Sorcha."

"Please be another painting."

The eyes crinkled at the edges in a smile. She had time to let out a small whimper before the vines pulled her arm even harder. Eamonn's hands slipped, crystals digging into her soft skin before the plants enveloped her.

"Sorcha!"

She stumbled out to the other side of the plants, which placed tiny leaves against her bottom and pushed hard. Wildly, Sorcha spun in a circle, praying the opening would still be there. She wasn't fast enough and couldn't catch even a glimpse of Eamonn through the tightly wound plants.

The wall rippled, leaves twisting and turning, flowers pushing through to stare back at her. Unnerved, she glanced over her shoulder.

"The throne room," she said in awe.

What else would the flowers guard?

Roses crawled over the walls, sinking thorns into stones, red sap oozing down the cracks like blood. Threads hung from the ceiling — remnants of once grand curtains — each strand humming as her gaze passed over them.

"They're your ancestors." A voice drifted out of the darkness.

"Torin?"

"I never strayed far from your side, granddaughter."

He stepped out of the shadows, his staff thunking against the cracked stone floor. Robes hung from his broad shoulders and braids twisted through his long grey hair. He looked different here. Stronger and more confident.

"What is this place?" Sorcha asked.

"Our ancestral home."

"This is the castle of Nuada Silverhand. I have no claim here." She hoped. A small part of her clenched, hoping he wasn't about to tell her she was a descendant of the great Fae.

"That is where you are wrong. You have more claim than Nuada did when he entered this place."

Torin circled her, his staff echoing in the chamber. The roses turned with him, twisting and twirling in the air, following his every movement.

"This is a Seelie castle."

"It used to be, but it was Fomorian before that. And afterwards as well."

"How is that possible?" she asked. "The Fomorians and Fae have never lived side by side."

"They did here for many centuries."

Her eyes widened. "The Fomorians band Fae lived in harmony?"

"They did."

"But that's not possible. All the legends say the Fae and Fomorians hated each other."

"The legends were wrong. It was here our people first started."

"Are you claiming druids came from the Fomorians? I thought we had Fae blood."

"We didn't come from the Tuatha dé Danann." He stopped in front of her and smiled. "It is why we're connected to the land, to the sea, and to the sky. A faerie and a human can make a faerie or a human child. Fomorians and faeries made something else entirely."

"They made druids," she said in wonderment.

"Indeed."

"Why did you wait so long to tell me?"

"Would you have believed me?"

Sorcha tossed her arms out to the side in disbelief. "I'm having a hard time believing anything lately. Why am I here, Torin? I might suggest this was your plan all along."

"Yes, I wanted you to return to this castle."

"Why?"

"You should be with your family."

"My family is back home. I left them to come here, so you must give me a better reason than that."

He stepped back, gesturing at the roses which bent to his will. They slithered away from each other, scraping across the floors and walls until they revealed a giant stained glass window in the shape of a sun. It was so big she thought it would rival a tree. Six men's height, or taller, spindly pieces all fitting together to create a masterpiece of art.

Light splintered through the room, revealing two thrones at the center. One blackened by fire and jagged, the other covered in roses and thorns.

"What is this?"

"These are the thrones of our people. Many have sat upon them, Nuada, Balor, kings and priests. But it is not the first king who shaped our world." Torin walked towards the blackened throne, placing his hand upon a knife sharp point. "Nuada Silverhand created an empire of Tuatha dé Danann. He fought, he battled, and he ruled as a good man." He placed his hand on the vines of the other. "Ethniu, his wife, was a

Fomorian who gave up her world to be with him."

"Ethniu?"

"The daughter of Balor, king of the Fomorians. She left everything she knew because of her love for Nuada. And as his first wife, she gifted him children the like of which the world had never seen. Children who became the druids. She feared him, loved him, and sat upon this throne to spread goodness and light."

Sorcha swallowed. "This is too familiar to me, grandfather."

"As it should be. Time repeats itself over and over again. Stories, legends, myths, they're all happening even now as we speak."

"You want me to be queen," she blurted. "Queen of the druids."

"Queen of the Seelie Fae."

The words sounded ludicrous even to her own ears. Her? Queen? Of all people, Sorcha was the last person to ever desire a throne.

"I am not royalty," she argued. "I am a midwife, and I am happy as such."

"You searched your entire life for something more than squalling babies, screaming mothers, and a brothel."

"That doesn't mean I want to be a queen," she growled. "It's ridiculous to even consider the thought!"

"You would make a good queen for the Fae."

"He'll never ask." Her heart shattered into a million pieces, but she meant every word. "He will be the greatest king they have ever seen. He will take a Seelie faerie as a bride and forget all about me. I will help his people, I will guide his thoughts, but he will never make me queen."

"He already has. He's brought you before his people, made speeches with you by his side, planted his seed inside you. What more could you want?" Torin slapped both hands down on the thrones.

"The words," she said. "I want him to say it. I want him to ask me to be his queen. Otherwise, I'm forcing myself upon him."

"Sorcha. Do this for your people."

"Who are my people?" she cried out. "Please, tell me grandfather.

To whom should I show my allegiance? The human family who raised me as a child? The faeries who took me in and showed me kindness? Or the druids who appear in my life unexpectedly and ask for impossible things?"

"You go with your heart. I can read you like a book, child. You want to belong somewhere, and I tell you now, you belong with us."

The words soared through her veins and took root in her soul. "Us?"

"Did you think we left you? Or that we brought you to a place that was not as much yours as ours?"

People stepped out of the vines. Each flower, each leaf, each stalk revealing a soul hidden in the shadows.

"We've been waiting for you," Torin said with a smile. "Centuries have passed since the last druid walked these halls. And now, you can take the throne. Nuada is not your ancestor, Sorcha, he left his wife to the mercy of the wilds. But Ethniu with her gracious wisdom, and her kind heart, married another. You are her descendant."

"You want me to walk in her footsteps?"

"I want you to take up your blood right. This place, this castle, these people are all yours."

"They are his!" Her shout echoed and a few of the spirits blasted back.

The throne of Ethniu shivered. Leaves quaked and buds pushed forward to bloom into bright red roses.

Torin gestured towards the movement. "This place is no longer that of the Fae. It can be something far more than that, and you are the only one who can take this step. Join us, my sweet girl."

"What would a Queen look like?" she asked. "What kind of ruler would I be? All I can do is control them."

"What do you think he plans to do?"

"To help his people."

"With Nuada's blade? That sword controls all who stand within its path. He destroyed an entire army on his own because they stood still and let him cleave their heads from their shoulders."

She swallowed. So that was how he had won. All this time, she wondered just how far he would go to gain back his throne.

Now she knew.

"The queen tempers the Seelie King," she repeated the words Oona had told her so long ago.

"She always has. But now is not the time for a tempered queen. Now, when the worlds are shifting and time is unraveling, we need a Queen who will speak for us *all*." Torin stepped forward and held out his hand. "Speak for the druids, for your people. For those who have a right to the Otherworld just as much as the Fae."

Sorcha stared into his eyes, wondering just how much of this was truth. He might be her blood, but she didn't believe for a second he wouldn't lie to her.

Torin had his own agenda. His words tasted bitter and dangerous. Would she go against Eamonn by taking her grandfather's hand?

He smiled. "I'm not trying to trick you, Sorcha. Few druids draw breath, and I would not see our people die out."

Something wasn't right. Brows furrowed, she reached for his hand and watched as hers passed through it. "You aren't real."

"I am real to you, to our people."

"But you aren't here."

"Didn't they tell you the castle was haunted?" The corners of his eyes wrinkled. "Druids are connected to the earth, tethered by their souls. We are not quick to fade from this realm."

"So you are all…" She looked around, catching the gaze of each druid lingering by the ivy. "You're all dead."

"Yes."

"Your souls are in the plants."

"And the dust, the glass, the mortar of this castle."

Sorcha's eyes filled with tears as she realized the magnitude of this decision. These weren't just trapped souls, they were her family.

"If I do this, will you be released?"

"No," Torin shook his head. "That is not what we want. We want to be here, with you, and give meaning to all the sacrifices we've made."

Sorcha lifted a hand and pressed it to her heart. The shifting spirits blinked in and out of existence. Torin wavered in front of her and the throne glowed. "None of this is real, is it?"

A few of the spirits spoke, their words like the rustling of reeds in fall.

"This is very real."

"No it isn't. This is the same as the altar, as the snake, as everything else you've shown me."

Spirits sank back into the greenery at her words. Torin's teeth flashed bright in the white of his beard. "You have never ceased to impress me, granddaughter, but in this you are wrong. The altar was real. This is real. Whether or not what you see is physical, does not make it any less important."

"Then if I take the throne?"

"You do so in the physical world as well."

She blew out a breath and weighed her options. Queen was a heavy title to bear, and not one she'd ever intended to have. She hadn't considered what a relationship with Eamonn would turn into, hadn't wanted to. His choices were his own, and she couldn't control him.

Sand tipped through the hourglass of her mind and she saw their time together dim.

Torin placed a hand back on the throne. "What kind of king will he be without you?"

"A better one."

"Do you believe that?"

She didn't. She had already seen what he could do, had heard of his battles, and seen the mark of each sword slash upon his skin.

Sighing, Sorcha picked up her skirts and walked towards the throne.

"I never thought I would agree to be queen with a dirty hem."

"I wouldn't expect anything less from you." The cold touch of his hand passed over her forehead. "But there is far more symbolic regalia for you to wear."

Magic shimmered down her body like a cold splash of water. Gasping, she looked down to see her dress had disappeared.

Thick green wool swayed around her hips with golden threads embroidered in the shape of leaves falling to the ground. A leather corset hugged her ribs, ending just below her breasts. The long sleeves of the green underdress hooked around her middle finger, triangles of fabric leaving her hands warm and green.

A magnificent silver fur covered her shoulders, soft and infinitely warm. She tossed her head, red curls falling freely to her waist.

Arching a brow, she looked up at her grandfather. "Furs and wool?"

"The regalia of our people."

Thank the gods he hadn't put her in a faerie outfit. She turned with a sigh. All the other druid souls watched her, their faces painted blue and their eyes hopeful.

What was she getting herself into?

"You walk in the footsteps of Ethniu," Torin said. "This throne does not make you a Queen, but your actions from here on out. Do you accept this title?"

"I do."

She lowered herself onto the throne with a troubled mind. Was she ready for this? Sorcha could say with near certainty she wasn't. Responsibilities already weighed heavy upon her mind. And now she had even more people to take care of.

A great cheer lifted in the throne room, but she hardly heard it. Vines closed over her wrists, thorns dug into the sensitive skin of her biceps.

"Torin?" she called out. "What's happening?"

"Now, we test your lover."

"What? No! Stop!"

Leaves stuffed into her mouth and roses bloomed over her eyes. She pulled against her bindings, flexing her arms and wiggling her legs until thorns dug into her skin. Blood slicked across her biceps as the vines tightened and pinned her down.

"Eamonn!"

"Sorcha!"

The vines dragged her through the wall and he could do nothing about it. Her warmth still heated his palms.

He growled, lifted his blade, and hacked at the green leaves. They did not move, nor did they break as the sharpened metal slid across them

"Magic," he spat. "Where have you taken her?"

No one responded. Instead, the leaves bounced as if someone behind them chuckled. Tilting his head back, Eamonn roared as fury turned his blood to fire. How dare they? Ghosts with no form had no right to still be on this land, let alone steal what was his.

He clenched his fists and stilled his breathing. There had to be some sound, some hidden chink in the armor of this place. No faerie had ever built a castle without leaving secrets behind.

The plants snapped vines at him, each thorn dripping green poison. He jerked backwards, holding his blade up as a shield. They left a slick, shiny residue on the Sword of Light. Disgusted, he slid it back into its sheath.

He would have to find another way. He turned and ran his hands over the walls. If it were his castle, he would have put some kind of stone that would shift, opening a door or secret chamber. No magic was completely controllable. Faeries always had an escape plan.

Giggles erupted behind him.

Eamonn froze, hand immediately reaching for his blade. "Where is she?"

"Here."

"She's not here."

"Then she's there."

He turned on his heel. The space behind him was empty other than the shadows which danced upon the walls. Eamonn's lip curled. "Unseelie. Show yourself."

"No."

The Sword of Light sang as he pulled it free again. Its sharp edge glinted as he raised it over his head and pointed directly at the shadows. "I command you to answer me."

The giggles grew louder and one of the shadows pulled off the others. It was human in shape, but he knew how deceptive these creatures could be. When it noticed his gaze, the shadow waved.

"No."

"I command you."

"Oh how lovely. He knows how to use a sword." The shadow twisted into a plant which shook in laughter. "Shame he doesn't know how to deal with ghosts. Turn around."

He spun. There was no longer a wall behind him, but a moor filled with fog and will-o'-the-wisps.

"What trickery is this?"

"Welcome home, brother," a masculine voice spoke in his ear. "Just how long did you think you could avoid me?"

Eamonn twisted, slashing his sword through the air. It passed through Fionn's throat without leaving a single mark.

He narrowed his eyes. "Are you some kind of mirage?"

"Oh, much worse than that."

There was something wrong with Fionn's eyes. Eamonn had seen anger, madness, and fear reflected in those eyes that were eerily similar to his own, but he had never seen such glee.

"You thought you would come here and….what? Take a new throne? Eamonn." Fionn tsked. "That is so petty. What's wrong with mine?"

"I have battled you for five years."

"And you want me to believe you're finished?" Fionn's hair slid over his shoulder, a graceful waterfall of movement and gold. "That's quaint. I know you aren't done. So what are you really up to?"

"Our people have bled long enough."

"That's not why, either," his twin snarled. Leaping forward, Fionn blasted through Eamonn's form in a shower of icy pain. "What are you doing here?"

"I've told you already," Eamonn stumbled to the side and stuck the tip of his sword against the ground. What had Fionn done to him?

"You're still hiding the truth. Half-truths, brother, only succeed in making us both angry."

"I am not angry."

"But you will be." Fionn reached for him, fingers curling in the air just before he touched Eamonn's face. "You and I were close once. As only twins could be. What did you do to us?"

"You know this was not my choice."

"Wasn't it? You were always the favored son, the firstborn. While you were out battling, and killing, and maiming our allies, I was fixing all the bridges you burned along the way," Fionn snarled. "Tell me again, brother, how this was not your doing."

Eamonn's palms slicked with sweat and the pommel of the Sword of Light slipped in his grasp. He didn't have a response to his brother's accusations. They were all true. Eamonn had filled his youth with poor decisions and war. Fionn had spent his learning how to be king, and filling his head with old, outdated prejudices.

"We're both at fault, are we not?" Eamonn finally asked. "I was a poor brother, but you were the one who stabbed me in the back and let me hang."

Fionn rolled his eyes. "We're going back to the 'poor pitiful Eamonn' card again?" He disappeared, reappearing directly behind Eamonn. "You deserved to hang."

"I did nothing wrong."

"You are not fit to be part of this family. Monster."

"I am a good man. I have always been a good man, and I will not allow you to take advantage of our people any longer."

"If you want it that bad, take it." Fionn's hand lifted over Eamonn's shoulder and pointed towards a jagged throne. "Take your new throne, become king of the weak and foolish."

And there it was. The throne of Nuada, blackened by years of warfare. The metal tips curved and split away, sharp enough to slice the throat of anyone who got too close.

It was perfect for Eamonn. That throne had been through more than Fionn could even imagine, more than Eamonn had suffered.

He felt the imprint of his brother's hands upon his shoulders for a brief second before he disappeared. Eamonn glanced once over his shoulder. Mist and fog obscured any shape from his vision. Shivers danced down his spine as he felt the gaze of someone, or something, watching him.

Should he take the throne? In this place, he wasn't sure what would happen.

He worried that he would become someone else. Someone darker, more dangerous, closer to his kin than he wished to be.

His boots struck the ground, solid and comforting in the weightlessness of the bog. The throne was his birthright, and the symbol of everything he had fought for his entire life. He would take it, no matter the cost.

But, as he expected, the spirits were not done with him yet.

The instant his foot touched the first step to the throne, a soft voice echoed behind him. "Eamonn?"

"No," he groaned. "Not that. Anything but that."

"My son?" Queen Neve, the most beautiful Seelie faerie to ever exist, walked out of the mist. He stared at her, pain splintering through his chest as if someone had run a sword through his heart. "My beloved boy."

"Please don't do this," he moaned.

"What are you doing in this place, my shield?"

The childhood nickname made him squeeze his eyes shut. "You aren't real. You aren't here with me now."

"Eamonn, of course I am." He flinched as her hands touched his cheeks, gently tracing the outlines of wounds that had smoothed with age. "What have they done to you?"

Though he knew it was a trap, his resolve shattered. With a ragged sound, he folded around his mother and drew her into his arms. She was so small, so delicate, in his strong grasp. He worried he might break her.

"My shield," she said as she stroked his hair. "Hush now, Eamonn. I am here."

"This is impossible, Mathair. You cannot be here in this twisted place."

"I came as soon as I felt your presence. What are you doing here?" She pulled back to stare up at his face, and something inside him healed when she did not flinch away.

"Fionn must be stopped, Mathair."

"Your brother is doing his best. It is all we can ask of him."

"His best is not enough."

"So you come here? Of all places?" Neve looked around, worry lines forming between her eyes. "I never understood your obsession with your grandfather. He and I never got along."

He remembered. Their arguments were quiet, as his mother had always been, but powerful enough to push everyone from the room. She had kindness bred into her, but she was one of the Tuatha dé Danann who supported the old ways.

"My grandfather was a good man and brought about much change for our people."

"Until we removed him from the throne," she replied. "Eamonn, don't do this."

"I must."

"If you take this throne, how long do you think you will stay upon it? You will show our people it is possible to dethrone a king. They will do it over and over again until the Otherworld is reduced to ruin. Let things stay as they are. It is safer that way."

Eamonn's lips twisted to the side. She had said the same things to him long ago before his twin had carved the future into Eamonn's flesh.

Her hands upon his jaw turned him back towards her. He drowned in her pity, in the sadness of her eyes. "My son. Do not sit upon that sullied throne."

Every word she said cut him to the bone. He pulled her close and pressed his lips against her forehead. Squeezing his eyes shut, he said against her, "I love you so much. Memories of you kept me alive for so long after I was banished. I remembered you brushing my hair as a child, singing lullabies, whispering stories in the dark after father had grown angry. I wish I could tell you all this in person."

"You are."

"You aren't really here." He squeezed her. "But whoever you are, you will need to do a lot better than this."

His mother dissolved into thin air.

Eamonn ground his teeth together and spun in a circle. Spreading his arms wide he called out, "What else? What further evil do you have planned?"

Fingernails clicked as they wrapped around a spike of the dark throne. Ready to pull his blade, to run it through whatever phantom they called upon, he turned on his heel with a snarl.

He fell silent as Sorcha stepped around the throne.

They had clothed her as a princess of his people. Fine feathers slid across her curves, each dipped in gold and carefully sewn into the dress.

Flakes of gold stuck to her fingers, tangled in her hair like stars, and dotted across her shoulders.

She was so beautiful.

His expression crumbled, and he twisted away from her. This was worse than his mother, worse than this twin. These spirits had no right to twist her form like this.

"Eamonn?" Sorcha asked. "Why do you turn from me?"

"You are not Sorcha."

"Is this not to your liking? This is the form you desire most, is it not?"

He almost groaned. Her hands stroked his biceps, circling him until she stared up at his face. This was a truly talented trickster. She looked exactly the same.

"Eamonn," she tilted her head to the side. "Kiss me."

"No."

"Do you no longer want me?"

"You know that would be impossible."

"Then why won't you kiss me?"

"Stop this." His voice was little more than a croak. "Why must you torment me?"

Her hands smoothed over his chest, dipping into the crevices and circling the numerous wounds. "Sometimes tormenting is fun. Come with me, my love, let me show you."

Her love. He bared his teeth in a grimace. "You aren't playing fair."

"I never said I would." She looped an arm over his neck and pulled him down. "Come, my love, my life, come with me from this awful place."

"You are not my Sorcha."

She couldn't be. Every person so far had not been the person he expected them to be. Why his mother and Sorcha were solid, he did not understand. But he knew this stunning phantom was not the woman his heart beat for.

"Let go of me," he growled.

"Why? Don't you want me?"

"Where is she?"

"Who?" Sorcha tilted her head to the side. "Don't you mean me?"

"You are not Sorcha."

"I could be, if you wanted. I would grovel at your feet, press kisses against your lips and worship the ground you walk upon."

"That is not what I want."

"Isn't it? Why else would you choose a human woman? If you wanted an equal, you would have chosen a faerie." She tsked and stepped back, smoothing her hands down her chest and stomach. "You wanted a druid, a forbidden creature to taste and sample until Sorcha grew old and frail. Leave the weak girl behind, Eamonn. Take me instead."

"Never."

"Why not?"

"She is not a weak woman, nor is she less because she is druid," he snarled. "Her name on your lips is blasphemy."

"You claim to care for her?"

"Her bravery, courage, and unwavering loyalty to my people captured my heart from the moment she first washed up on Hy-brasil."

"Prove it. Prove that you care for her, more than anything else."

"How?" He would do it. He wouldn't hesitate to prove that she was the reason he drew breath.

"Choose." She lifted a hand and pointed towards the throne. "Which future do you want, Eamonn?"

Another throne appeared next to his. Tangled vines and thorns stuck out in all directions from the roses blooming, but it was the shape that held his attention. Red hair peeked through the gaps of greenery, streaked with blood and sap.

A choked sound slipped off his tongue. He stumbled forward, but hesitated when he remembered that everything had been an illusion thus far. "Is it really her?"

"Of all the things you've seen, that is the only truth." The other Sorcha leaned against his side. "You have two futures before you. One as king, seated upon your throne knowing she is safe and sound. Beside you, yes, but also kept safe from all you fear. The other future is that she is free to wander on her own."

"Why wouldn't I choose the second?"

"You can't control her if she wanders free. Sorcha will continue to grow into her own power, finding her history, her family, her culture. Everything you love may change and grow into something else." She traced a circle on his chest. "Just how much do you want to ensure your future, High King?"

To be certain she was safe would be a pleasure he had never considered. Consorts of kings had suffered worse, at least she would be alive.

"Can she see?" he asked, voice cracking.

"No. She is awake, but not. Dreaming without sight, sound, or touch."

"So she isn't really alive under all that."

"An offer for you, Eamonn of the Seelie Court. If you leave her here, she will join with the rest of her ancestors. She will live among the roses for all eternity at your side."

For all eternity, the words echoed over and over again. She wouldn't die. He wouldn't have to watch her grow old, crumbling to dust in his hands. Centuries of loneliness spread out ahead of him without her. He could keep her safe and preserved.

But it wasn't his choice. She was a fiercely independent woman and Eamonn had no right to make these decisions for her. He could only keep her safe for so long.

"No," he said, shaking his head. "She is not mine. She is her own being and I will not take that from her."

The Sorcha beside him flashed a feral grin. "Then go to her, High King. Free your bride and remember that we told you not to take this throne."

"Why?"

The thing burst into shadows and rushed away, giggling so loud that the halls echoed with its screeches.

Halls.

Mist and fog disappeared. Eamonn stood in the same place he had when Sorcha disappeared through the wall.

He spun to the wall of roses, seeing only an open space where the plants had once stood. Charging through, he rushed into the throne room with the giant glass sun while shouting, "Sorcha!"

Two thrones stood at the end of the hall. One black, the other covered in red roses. She sat upon the queen's throne, bound into place by the very beauty that set her apart.

He blew out a horrified breath and ran to her. His eyes did not stray to Nuada's throne, to his birthright, to anything other than her.

She needed him.

Falling to his knees, he ripped at the thorns that tore his flesh. Crystals flashed into view, peeking through tiny holes in his hands. The fine bones of his wrists creaked with stone that sent shivers of magic pulsing through his veins.

"Hold on," he growled as he pulled at the plants. "I'm here, Sorcha. I'm here."

The sound of her exhalation was music to his ears. He yanked her hands free and pressed them against his face.

"Can you hear me?" he asked.

She did not respond.

Frantic, he stood and ripped vines away from her head. The flowers shrieked as they pulled away. There were leaves in her mouth, he realized.

He scooped his fingers between her lips, pulling handfuls of plants out. Over and over again, he yanked leaves and vines away until she let out a moan and then gasped.

"Eamonn!" she cried out.

"I'm here," he pulled her out of the throne and wrapped his arms around her. His soul settled, peace finally easing the tension in his neck. "I'm here, mo chroí. I am so sorry."

"This was not your fault," she coughed as she spoke. "This was mine."

"Do not blame yourself."

"I should never have brought us here. You were right, this is a dangerous place."

"We will find another castle." He pressed his lips against her forehead and tightened his hold. He had almost lost her. Again. "We will leave this cursed place and never return.

"I cannot."

"We can, Sorcha. This is not the only option for us."

"I cannot, Eamonn!" She pulled away, her green eyes dark and haunted. "This castle echoes with the souls of my people. Druids, like me. I told them I would stay, I took the throne."

"You did what?"

He stumbled backwards, looking at her as if he had never seen her before. He had fought against the demons of his past, denied his birthright, and she had taken the throne?

"Why are you looking at me like that?" she asked. "Eamonn?"

"They told me not to take the throne."

"Who?"

"Your people."

She licked her lips. "These are the thrones of Nuada and Ethniu. They wish us to walk in their footsteps, following the path they carved together."

"Does that future not belong to me as well?"

"It was a test," she said. Her eyes were as large as the moon. "They were testing you, Eamonn."

"And what was the test?"

She believed the words she said. He could see the truth in her eyes and taste it on the air. But what could such a test prove? That he had a weakness?

Another voice joined them, deep and unfamiliar. "A test you passed, my boy."

The man was old. He wore a wrap of fur and balanced upon a cane, but Eamonn was certain the ancient exterior hid powerful magic.

"Did I?" Eamonn asked. "And what was the test?"

"That you would take care of my granddaughter."

"Granddaughter?" Eamonn looked from Sorcha to the new man. "I see no family resemblance."

"Then you are far less capable than I thought you to be. She is mine, and if you wish to take her, then I needed reassurance you would treat her well."

"Have I not thus far?"

"You have ignored her. You have fostered a fear of her own magic and controlled your people while not listening to her words. You are a Tuatha dé Danann. You must excuse me, High King, but I do not trust you."

Other words echoed underneath the deep tones. Suggestions of punishment should Eamonn make a mistake. But something else as well. Something older, and so powerful that it resonated in his tones.

Eamonn narrowed his eyes. "Just how old are you, grandfather?"

"Old enough to know when a boy is trying to back me into a corner."

Sorcha reached out and touched Eamonn's arm. "His name is Torin."

"This is the druid who found you in the glade?"

"I am," Torin replied.

"You are not what you appear."

Eamonn pulled Sorcha into his arms, tucking her behind his broad back as he pieced the stories together. "How many generations have passed since you were her grandfather?"

"Seven."

Although surprised Torin would respond so easily, Eamonn recognized the game. "You said you were a druid?"

"Yes."

"Were you something else before?"

"Yes."

Sorcha pulled against his arm. "What are you doing, Eamonn? He's my family!"

"That is Ethniu's throne behind you, is it not?"

Torin lifted a brow and placed a hand upon the back. The roses twined around his wrist as he nodded. "It is."

"And you sat upon that throne yourself, didn't you?"

"Clever boy," the ancient man chuckled. "Take care of her."

A blast of air pushed them back as Torin disappeared from the room. The thrones remained, symbolic but still pulsing with power.

"You know who he is," Sorcha exclaimed.

"I do."

"Who?"

"Ethniu's father, King Balor."

"I thought he was dead?"

"We all think the ancient ones are dead, but they exist in some manner." Eamonn glanced down at her, brows furrowed in worry. "You are King Balor's granddaughter?"

"And you are Nuada's grandson."

He had grown up with the legends of Balor, the Fomorian god. His third eye would open and cast destruction wherever it looked. He had been the only one capable of defeating the original Tuatha dé Danann on the battlefield. A great king, a horrible enemy, and the father of the druid race.

And now, he looked upon the fearsome creature's granddaughter with new eyes.

"Do you fear me now?" she asked. "I did not know who I was."

"No, mo chroí. I am in awe of you."

"Good. I would not want you to see me differently because of this."

"Come here." He yanked her forward and pressed his lips against hers. "We will weather this storm, as we have all others."

"Is this a storm? Who my family is?"

"It is a sign. We bring together families, people, races that have never existed side by side before. We are the beginning of a new age, Sorcha. Together."

He swept her into his arms and carried her from the haunted place. Spirits fled from his shadow as he brought them into the light. And in that moment Eamonn made a vow to himself that he would protect her from everything.

Even herself.

CHAPTER SEVEN
THE SWORD OF LIGHT

Faeries filled the banquet hall, their laughter and joyous shouts echoing from the rafters. They had made it to the castle. A new home, a new future, and the promises of new hope.

Rows lined the hall, each sturdy table filled to the brim with whatever food they could scavenge. Oona was in her element, bustling to each person who lifted their empty goblets, asking for more drink.

The wine cellar was still full. The dwarves had returned with their arms full of elixir, chortling at their find.

After all they had been through, Sorcha thought they deserved a few nights of merriment.

She sat with the others of her new family. Pooka leaned over the table and reached for bread, his hands already sticky with honey.

A dwarf passed by and handed off a cup to Cian. "It's not the usual."

Cian grinned and downed whatever the new drink was. "My thanks!"

The merriment was contagious. She could hardly hear a word over the din, and loved every second. How could she not? These were her people, and they were so happy after their struggles.

She ducked as a chicken flew by, its feathers bursting into the air. Oona waved her hands and raced after it. The clucking squawks only added to the laughter.

There were many colors, people, and vibrant sounds. She hadn't seen such a gathering since the Samhain festival. Sorcha leaned her elbow against the table and watched their antics with a grin.

The door to the banquet hall slammed open and silence rang louder than the laughter. A cup dropped to the floor, shattering with a crash.

Shadows crawled in from the hall. The candles beyond had long since burned down to their bases, blinking out any light which might have shown.

She recognized the silhouetted figure. Eamonn, their fearless leader who had brought them all this way. Sorcha wondered where he had stolen off to.

It was difficult for him to be here when there was so much merriment. His thoughts grew clouded, responsibilities, family, and centuries of solitude distracting his mind.

The faeries were silent. They did not cheer for him, nor did they stand. They seemed to be holding their breath.

Sorcha waited until she could no longer stand it. He stood in the doorway with his hands loose at his sides, conflicted and incapable of movement. She would not stand by while his own people rejected him.

She stood and passed each of the faeries who acted as if they were stuck to their benches. Her footsteps were soft, but they seemed loud to her ears. Each step was a choice. A confirmation that he was hers, and she was his.

She held out her hand for him to take. "Welcome, king."

The shadows obscured his relieved expression from the others, but she could see it bright as day. "Good evening, Sunshine."

"Have you come to join us?"

"If I am welcome."

"You are always welcome among your people."

He took her hand and pulled her closer. The shadows enveloped her, along with his strong arms. "Are you so certain of that?"

"Come and eat with them and we shall find out."

The crystals at his throat bobbed as he swallowed hard. "I have no wish to ruin their dinner."

"You never did while we traveled."

"A general is something entirely different than a king. They should be afraid of me on the battlefield, and they will take orders from anyone who will bark at them. But now? This is different."

"How so?"

Eamonn squeezed his eyes shut. "They want a man, now. A king who can sit at the table and be regal. The king who inspires courage and honor, settles the worried mother and calms the wounded soldier. I am not that man."

"That is not who they expect you to be." She reached up and stroked his cheek. "They know who you are, Eamonn, that is why they follow you. If they wanted a king to sit at a table and look nice, then they would pledge their allegiance to Fionn."

"They are here."

"Exactly. They don't want you to change! So come eat with us, drink with your men, and tease your women. They are your people, now. Not his."

The tension eased from his shoulders and his expression softened. "Lead the way, my queen."

Shivers danced down her spine. His queen. Did she want to be? His yes, but all the others?

She wasn't so sure.

Sorcha tangled her fingers with his and drew him into the banquet hall. The dwarves watched with wide eyes as the dangerous warlord who had led them through battle calmed at the touch of a druid woman.

Sharp eyes caught the moment when Eamonn reached out and hooked a finger through one of her curls. The long length swayed at her waist, and coiled around his finger as if it knew he needed its strength.

They made their way to one of the remaining tables where only a few sat.

Eamonn tugged on her hand, "Why here?"

"Let them come to you," she said as she sat down. He let her draw him to her side.

"Will they?"

"I watched a master horseman break a stallion once. It had spent its entire life wild and free, but this man never gave up. He sat in the pen with the horse for hours upon hours so it would grow used to his presence. No whips, no shouting words, no ropes to ensnare it. The horse grew to love him merely because he was there."

"You think the dwarves are like horses?"

"I hope they are," she said with a soft smile. "It's how I'm hoping they will come to like me."

"Then let us both eat our meals and perhaps they will join us."

He leaned forward, piled food on his plate, and tucked in. Eamonn did not look at the others, nor did he waste any time waiting for them.

As if he felt the weight of her stare, he looked up at her. Mouth full, he paused. "Everything all right?"

"Yes."

"You sure?"

"I am."

He gestured at her plate. "Are you eating?"

"I've already eaten a little, but I'll pick at this."

"And it's to your liking?"

"Yes."

She had missed this, Sorcha realized. Eating with him, talking to him. The mundane things that meant so much.

He saw the change in her eyes. The softness that seeped through from her soul into her eyes. Eamonn reached out and took her hand, his thumb smoothing over her knuckles. "I missed you, too."

Warmth sparkled through her veins like falling stars. She sighed and squeezed his fingers, words impossible to find.

Oona bustled towards them and slumped down onto a bench with a huffed sigh. "My goodness! I didn't think it was possible for faeries to drink so much!"

"They're dwarves, Oona," Eamonn said with a chuckle.

"And they need to worry about their addiction!"

"They deserve to have some revelry after all the fighting."

"That they do." Oona pulled her skirts up and swung her legs underneath the table. There were so many layers of skirts, Sorcha couldn't decipher where they stopped and the faerie started. "Are we to be staying here then?"

"I don't see why not," Eamonn said. He shoveled more food into his mouth and gave Sorcha a look that suggested she continue the conversation without him.

"It needs a little bit of love," she rushed to fill in. "But I think it has the possibility of being a home for us all."

"The dwarves included?"

"Of course," Sorcha moved the food on her plate around in a circle. "I think they'll be useful in the coming months. I cannot imagine sending them away."

"Sending them home, you mean."

"I'd rather call their families here." The idea had seemed impossible as it left her lips, but Sorcha saw the merit of it. Bringing women and children here would only make it more of a home.

There would be maids to help with the cleaning, children to help with the farming. Eamonn looked up at her, a question in his eyes.

"Families?" Oona asked.

"Yes. Spread the word that the dwarves are welcome to bring their people here. The intent of this castle was to create a stronghold for those who stand against Fionn. That means making it a haven for all, not just soldiers."

"Can we support that many people?" Eamonn asked.

Cian lumbered over, his bulk pushing aside a few dwarves who had stood. "That we can. The gardens are wild after so many years untended, but they're still producing enough to feed many. We've got quite a few hunters here, and even more who'd like to learn."

"And bedding?" Sorcha leaned forward, excitement rushing her words. "We have to put them somewhere. I know the castle needs a lot of work, but what about the surrounding buildings?"

"I can send a few people out to check on them tomorrow," Oona said. "There's a few women interested in cleaning the place up. The outbuildings are in better shape than the castle."

"Then this is possible?" Eamonn glanced at the three of them. "Are we prepared to add another potential hundred mouths to feed?"

"Hundred?" Sorcha laughed. "Eamonn, your army is easily over two hundred men and women. Their families are likely an additional three people, if not more than that. We're considering many more than a hundred people."

His stunned expression made her grin. Sorcha reached out, pressed a palm against his cheek, and chuckled. "When you started this journey, you knew you would become a king."

"I did not think that would include so many people."

"You're planning to rule all of Seelie. Starting with a small empire is not a bad thing."

"Empire," he repeated and shook his head. "What have you gotten me into?"

"Exactly what you wanted." She looked over at Oona and Cian. "Is this something we can start soon?"

"Yes."

"Do you think the dwarves will be botterested?" Her worries dug at her hope with sharp claws. "I know there is always a concern about bringing family to war, but I would like to make this place more than just a place to feed an army."

"I think the dwarves miss their families just as much as we would," Oona replied. "They will be happy to have their spouses and children at their sides."

Sorcha thought about children running through the halls of this haunted place. She glanced around and saw all the cracks where plants grew and the shards of glass that littered the ground.

It was not a safe place yet, but it would be. This castle would shine before she would let any children wander around. She imagined maids rushing through the banquet hall with brooms and washcloths. Men with large beams on their back walking amongst them, ready to fix broken walls and cracked floors.

This castle had been a home to her ancestors once, and now she would make it a home for her people again. She wanted to hear the rooms filled with laughter, the kitchens filled with the aroma of cooking food, and the grounds brimming with marketplaces.

They could do it. This was just the first step.

"Let us begin then," she said. "Oona, Cian, spread the word amongst the dwarves we are making this castle our own. Bring their families and all those who wish to work for their keep."

She met Eamonn's gaze and blushed at the awe she saw in his eyes. She reached out and took his hand.

"Are you ready for this?" he asked her.

"Absolutely. It's time to make this place our home."

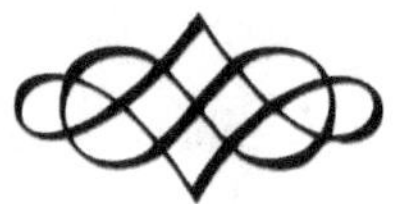

Sorcha loved watching the dwarves sing stones to life. They lifted their hands in song, palms raised to the sky, and let their voices fly free. The land listened to them, as she had never understood before.

Boulders shifted, rolling gently into place. Carefully carved statues pieced themselves back together and sealed old wounds with quiet grumbles. Brick and mortar rose into the air and glided back into their places.

She had explored as much as she dared. There was something sinister about this place, far more than Hy-brasil had ever been.

Sorcha worried all the rooms would be dangerous until she found a hidden corridor and a quiet place. The plants didn't move when she walked by, the stained glass windows were still intact, and moss covered the cold ground. Sorcha enjoyed the cushion against her weary feet.

She worked with the others when she could. She gained peace from helping, even though the dwarves were loath to let her anywhere near them. The tiny bearded woman who'd first spoken to Sorcha was not the only one who held prejudice in her heart for the druids.

The giant window let her watch them without interfering with their work. They would likely stop if she stepped outside, similar to how the other faeries had reacted to her presence.

Now, she knew how to coax them into liking her.

"I thought I might find you here."

She smiled. Eamonn always knew where to find her, no matter how she tried to hide from him.

His arms wrapped around her shoulders, pulling her back against his warm skin. She brushed her fingers over his forearm. The smooth crystals were not the same as she remembered from so long ago. She found herself touching him more now, familiarizing herself with this new version.

"Did you sleep well?" she asked.

"Better if I had woken up with you beside me." He planted a kiss on top of her head. "Why are you not in bed?"

"I wanted to watch them."

"You enjoy the dwarven songs?" He snorted. "It is early for them to be up."

"I think they want to finish as soon as possible. The rains have slowed them far more than they wish."

She let her head tilt to the side as his fingers tangled in the curls above her ear. He frequently pulled on the coils, letting them bounce back into place before doing it again. She thought he enjoyed seeing something so vibrant in his life.

Blue light splashed over his forearm, the stained glass window giving new colors and life to all the light touched.

"Come back to bed," he said with a chuckle.

"We have much to do today."

"We?"

"Oona has asked me to help clean out the kitchens."

"You are the lady of this castle. You don't need to clean."

"I want to," she said. Spinning in the circle of his arms, she planted her hands against his chest. "It's important for me to be useful, Eamonn."

"I will never turn you into a royal, will I?"

"Why would you want to?" She smiled up at him, stretching for the kiss she knew he would give her. "I'm just fine the way I am."

"Fine isn't the word I would use," he said, pressing a kiss against her forehead.

"No? Then how you would describe me, High King?"

"Well," his lips feathered over her cheek, moving over her nose to the other. "Exquisite. Thoughtful. Kind."

He tilted her chin with gentle fingers, pressing a chaste kiss against her lips.

"Those are good words."

"There are not enough in the world to accurately describe you, mo chroí."

"Your nobility is showing," she replied, playfully tugging on his ear. "When you speak like that I can see the king in you."

"Only then?"

Sorcha rolled her eyes and pulled away. "What would I know? I've never met a king before you!"

"You've met my brother."

"Are we calling him a king now? I was unaware."

"Sorcha," he growled. "Come back here."

"I'd rather not."

"Now."

A delightful shiver ran down her spine. She loved it when his voice took on that hard edge. The grating sound that suggested he was a hair's breadth from losing control.

She bit her lip and shook her head.

The crystals in his throat glowed a mere moment before he lunged forward. She let out a happy shriek and leapt over the bench behind her. Skirts tangled in her legs, the distraction giving him just enough time to reach out and snag the back of her dress.

He tugged, a warning he had caught her, and then let her go. He wanted the chase, her warrior king.

Spinning, she held her hands loose at her sides and darted her gaze around the room.

"Are you looking for an escape?" he growled. "There is none."

"There's a particularly strong looking vine behind you."

"You plan to climb it?"

"I plan to tangle you in it. That will give me enough time to slip out the door and find a far more suitable place to set up camp."

"High ground," he advised. "If you're battling an opposing army, you always want the high ground."

"The towers then."

"And then what? Do you face me and fight?"

"No," she muttered as she looked around for a better escape. "You are much larger than me, so I do not face you. I look for anything I might throw or distract you with."

"While?"

"While shouting for someone who is more skilled with a blade to come and help. They will arrive from behind if we are on the tower stairs, and then we will flank the enemy."

"Good," Eamonn nodded. "Now come here."

Sorcha stooped and upturned the nearest bench. It crashed against the floor and gave her enough time to sprint past him.

But he was no green warrior, and she was an untrained human. He snagged her arm, spun them so he wouldn't hurt her, and lifted her up into the air.

"I have taught you well," he said as he pressed his lips against her collarbone.

"That was the point, wasn't it?"

"You're a quick study."

"I have a good teacher."

She brushed his hair back from his face, smiling down at him. Her heart was light in moments like this. When a smile crinkled the edges of his eyes, and his lips twisted with no sarcasm. He truly was a handsome man when he wasn't so severe.

His expression fell. "I have to go."

"Go? Are there more buildings to plan?"

"I have to leave the castle grounds."

"What?" She shook her head in confusion. "Why?"

"Our city is growing, and there are many more mouths to feed. I am taking a small battalion to hunt."

He let her slide down his body. Each inch scraped over grooves underneath his clothing she had not noticed. Armor.

"Eamonn," she grumbled. "I thought we agreed you wouldn't fight anymore."

"I am not looking for a battle. Even you cannot disagree that there are many more people to feed."

She sighed. This was an argument she knew well, and she understood why he was so antsy. Eamonn was a man of action. The many years on Hy-brasil hadn't helped that. Now that he was home, he wanted to do everything he could to help his people.

It was grating on her nerves.

"We should focus on bringing more people here. You can turn the

Seelie Fae away from your brother without bloodshed. Force his army to see you are the better king. The one who will take care of them, their families, their livelihoods. You don't have to do that by spilling more blood upon the ground."

"I'm not going to," he said with a chuckle. His finger slid underneath her chin, tilting her gaze to his. "I am getting food, so we might bring even more people to this castle. I'd like to see more Fae than dwarves."

"You won't fight?"

"I will not look for a fight with Fionn."

She searched his eyes for the truth. There was something off-putting about the way he spoke. As if he was hiding something.

Faeries couldn't lie. She had to trust he wasn't twisting his words, and he'd given her no reason to feel wary.

A slow smile spread across her face. "I rather like the dwarves."

"No you don't."

"I do! They're steadfast and hard workers. That's something rather difficult to find these days."

"They ignore you."

"So did the other faeries," she said with a shrug. "There's nothing I can do about that. They don't trust me. Yet. I'm working on it."

"I have no doubt they will fall in love with you." He pulled her into a tight hug. "I won't be gone long. Only a few days."

"Be careful."

"I should say that to you."

"I'm safe behind castle walls. You'll be avoiding your brother's army, all while trying to hunt down enough food to feed a large village."

He chuckled and released her from his hold. "Do me a favor? Don't speak to any ghosts while I'm gone."

"I don't plan to sit on the throne either."

"Good girl."

She watched him leave the room and told herself the pit in her stomach was foolish. He would be fine. He didn't leave with a fight on his mind, nor was his plan to confront his brother's forces.

But she couldn't shake the feeling that he wasn't telling her everything. Troubled thoughts dug at her.

Eamonn wasn't the type to wander. He was clearly mad about her, far more than any of his people had ever seen him before. Sorcha didn't worry that a tiny dwarven woman had caught his eye. And if she had, then good for the dwarf.

The only thing remaining to worry about was that he still wanted to fight. That battle ran through his veins and he was sneaking off hoping Fionn might find him.

She hoped not. Five years of war had been enough, his people grew tired of fear and hardship. There were only so many deaths that the Seelie Fae could sustain. Birth was difficult for their kind, and she feared she was the only midwife in the Otherworld.

Worry made her mind wander. She stood in the same place, she did not know how long, staring at the door as if he might return.

"Are you going to stand there all day?" A rough voice barked. "Or are you going to do something?"

"Excuse me?" Sorcha looked over her shoulder at the female dwarf who had berated her soundly. "Who are you?"

"'Course you don't remember me."

"No, I remember you from the campfire. That doesn't mean I know *who* you are."

The female dwarf tossed the tail of her beard over her shoulder and crossed her arms. "Well? Why 'aven't you done it yet?"

"Done what?"

"You're a druid. They always do something sneaky to get out of situations like this. So go on. Do whatever it is you do."

"I'm a Weaver."

The dwarf snorted. "As if. There aren't any more of those left, we killed 'em all when we sent your lot off. I bet you talk to plants. I've seen 'em reach out to touch you."

Sorcha narrowed her eyes at the rude dwarf. Bravery such as this was foolish. She didn't know what Sorcha was capable of, and she still provoked as if there was no danger.

Stinging from Eamonn's abrupt departure, Sorcha focused on the dwarf.

Weaving had become easier here in the Otherworld, even more so in this castle. Druid souls fed her power, their ghostly hands stroking her arms and guiding her mind.

Plucking the name out of the dwarf's skull was almost too easy. She pulled just the slightest amount and a strand of shimmering light hovered just above the dwarf's ear. No one could see it but Sorcha, and perhaps the druid souls who whispered excitedly in her ear.

"Yes," they said. "That's it. Pull it a little bit, don't let her notice."

Sorcha sighed. "That is enough, Caitlyn."

The thread hummed, revealing that the dwarf preferred the name Cait.

The dwarf crossed her arms. "That's a good trick. Guessed that one, did you?"

"No. It's what Weavers do."

"And I'll tell you again, we killed the lot of them in the last war. There ain't any Weavers left. You'd be wise not to call yourself that, there are dwarves 'ere who would want to kill you."

The fine thread of patience Sorcha clung to snapped. She tugged hard, words spilling from her lips like fine wine. "They would kill me? Then perhaps I should be more prepared. What other names do you have stored in that little head of yours?"

Another swift tug of her mind revealed a few names, but nothing important.

"Hey!" Cait shouted. "Get out of my head!"

But she wasn't quite done yet. Sorcha pulled once more, smiled, and tilted her head to the side. "There it is. You were a lucky girl to be taken in by Angus, the man who would become king of the dwarves."

"That's not your name to have." Cait growled.

"And my life is not yours to take."

They stared each other down, neither wanting to let go of the anger that burned behind their eyes. Sorcha's tension eased when Cait shrugged and sighed.

"Fine. So you've got a little bit of fire in you. That's not a bad thing. Now, how do you plan on protecting yourself?"

"Against who?"

"Everyone. The dwarves. Faeries who don't want a human in the Otherworld. Your lover's twin who obviously wants you gone," Cait ticked off fingers as she spoke. "Seems to me like everyone wants you dead."

Sorcha blinked. The dwarf flitted from emotion to emotion so quickly that even the heat of the air changed. "Why do you want to know?"

"Because it's important that people know how to protect themselves. And you've proven to me that you plan on keeping yourself alive, even though that little escapade with the king was embarrassing to watch. What do you know?"

"Eamonn has been teaching me to fight from the high ground."

"Fight? With what?"

She repeated what she had told Eamonn only moments ago, slowing as Cait shook her head. "What? Why are you making that face?"

"What do you do if no one comes to help you?"

Sorcha didn't have an answer to that. "I fight them myself I suppose."

"And what happens if they grab you?"

"Then I struggle."

"With what?"

"Kicking and screaming until they let me go."

"Right," Cait snorted and crossed her arms. "Let me tell you how that will go. You'll scream, they'll slap you so hard you taste blood and then once more just to make sure you see stars. Then they'll pin you down, and you won't be able to move. You'll be lucky if they kill you at that point. So let's start again. How are you going to fight?"

The dwarf had a point. She had argued a similar fight with Eamonn, who refused to even entertain the idea that he would be so far away he couldn't protect her.

And then he left her here alone.

She straightened her spine. "I don't know."

Cait snapped her fingers and pointed at Sorcha. "That's the right answer. Come on then."

"Where are we going?"

"I'm going to teach you how to fight."

A part of Sorcha hesitated, wondering why the dwarf would helping when she obviously didn't like druids. But another part wanted desperately to know how to protect herself.

Perhaps that was the druid coming out. She had only felt the strange yearning in her heart a few times, but each instance was a powerful one. There was a creature inside of her that longed to be stronger than ever before.

"All right," Sorcha said. "When?"

"Right now, unless you want to stare at the door for a little while longer."

She didn't. Sorcha narrowed her eyes and said, "No. We can go now, if you are prepared to teach me."

"Come on then, out into the yard with you. What weapon do you 'ave experience with?"

"None."

They moved past dwarves singing to their stones. Not a single one faltered in their work, but their gaze burned against her back. Perhaps they were merely curious about who she was. More likely, they wondered why she was walking with one of their own.

Cait shoved a dwarf aside that stood in their path. "That won't do. Swords?"

"I don't own one."

"Can't make you one any time soon in this pit. Knives?"

"Just the kind that carve food."

"That's a start," Cait jabbed at the air as if she were stabbing a person. "People are a little bit like meat. A little more sticky. We can work with that, and every woman should have a 'idden blade. Bow and arrow?"

The mere thought of stabbing someone made her queasy. She had dedicated her entire life to helping and healing, not harming. "I used to hunt with my father when I was young."

Cait perked up, bouncing. "Did you ever get anything?"

"No."

"Oh. Well then you don't know how to shoot a bow."

"I was a good shot."

"You could hit still targets you mean. Moving ones are a lot different."

She imagined they were. Sorcha treated such wounds before, and knew that an arrow stuck in bone sometimes. She shuddered at the memories.

"Don't get squeamish on me now," Cait said with a chuckle. "We'll get you ready for anything that might come our way."

"I have to ask again, why are you interested in helping me?"

"The way I see it, you're right on the way to becoming our queen. I already don't like the man who's trying to make himself king. The last thing I want is two royals who have little sympathy for my people."

"Eamonn cares," Sorcha said. She skirted past a dwarf who stepped in her way, his song deepening for a moment in disapproval. "That's why he's working so hard to take back the throne. To give your people a voice."

"Funny, that's not how we see it."

"Then how do you see it?"

They walked into a training yard. Only a few dwarves lingered in this area, most of them choosing to work with stone rather than practicing their battle skills. Sorcha found it strange for an army to not train every second they could.

Cait kicked a bale of hay as they passed it. "How do we see it? Just more of the same. Another noble who thinks he can make a difference because his ideas are a tad different than the last one's. Nothing ends up happening, no matter who is on the throne."

Sorcha had seen a very similar situation in her own world. The peasants, those who worked all day to make their living in life, had never cared who was king. They did what they wanted, worked hard, gathered food and water for their families, and the royals lived entirely separate lives.

"That's disappointing," she said. "It is similar in the human world. Royalty has no connection to the people. I always wished they did, but those of us who lived hard lives never even saw them."

"You want me to believe you ain't royalty?" Cait snorted. "Right."

"I'm not. I was raised in a brothel and became a midwife to heal my sisters and prevent them from filling the brothel with children."

"You were raised with whores?"

Sorcha winced. "It's a rather cruel word, but yes. My sisters made a good living and kept us all alive. I value them greatly, no matter their choice of employment."

The more she spoke, the further Cait's jaw dropped. "You don't care at all that they sell their bodies to whomever will pay the most?"

"Not in the slightest. What they do with their own flesh is none of my business."

"And you don't judge 'em for that?"

"Not unless they get with child, and that would only happen because they didn't take the tea I gave them. If they were foolish with their bodies, their hearts, their minds, then yes. I would judge them. But they are highly intelligent women. I have never once thought less of them for their choices."

"You know, I could like you."

Sorcha's jaw dropped. "That's all it took?"

"Guess so."

"How?"

Cait turned and rummaged through a few of the sacks lying on the ground. "Dunno. Guess you're more of a person now then you were before."

"I wasn't a person?"

"Royals ain't people. They don't know how to be people."

"Fair enough."

Sorcha glanced around the yard that the dwarves had repaired. A short knee wall surrounded three sides, the remaining side abutted the cliff peak which stretched up two men's height. Targets leaned against the wall, not yet set up or used. She recognized a few of the straw dummies. Eamonn had used them in his own training yard.

Hay littered the ground, not yet disturbed by footprints. Everything was pristine, perfect, exactly how it would be when they were first made.

"Are you not practicing?" she asked. "Everything seems to be untouched."

"We ain't an army, that's why."

"What?"

Cait walked over and handed her a bow taller than she was. "Dwarves don't have an army. We don't like to fight, other than brawls in pubs. That we'll do. Now take the bow, 'ere's your arrows, and shoot that target."

"What do you mean dwarves don't fight?"

"Shoot the target."

Sorcha could hear the iron in the dwarf's voice, and didn't know how to take it. Faeries didn't lie. There wasn't any reason for Cait to twist the truth. But what did she mean that dwarves didn't have an army?

What had Eamonn done?

She took the offered arrow, notched it, and lifted the bow. She could hear her father's voice in her ear. Breath out before the arrow is released. Sight the target with one eye. Keep the arm straight.

She exhaled and released the arrow.

It sang as it shot through the air and struck the edge of the target. Letting out a whoop, she turned to Cait with a grin. "I hit it!"

"Well that's just great, princess, but if that had been the size of a person then you'd have missed them entirely. There's a giant red dot on that target for a reason. Again."

"I thought that was all right for someone who hasn't picked up a bow in years."

"I don't care if you're all right. Just aim again, would ya?"

Sorcha grumbled and lifted it to her eye. "Are you qualified for this, if you aren't a soldier?"

"I can teach a person to fight. Not to be in an army and march in a line towards their death. Dwarves fight to stay alive. That's how you should fight too."

She exhaled and let her next arrow fly. This one was closer to the center, although it stuck weakly in the bottom, drooping towards the ground.

Cait tossed her hands into the air. "Well this will take all day. Again!"

Sorcha met with Cait every day, setting up lunch in the training yards and eating in the dirt. At first, the dwarven woman seemed nervous and uncomfortable around the consort of a would-be king. But, the more Sorcha showed she didn't care about the state of her skirt, the quality of her hair, or getting mud on her hem, the more the dwarf loosened up.

On the third day, she arrived in the courtyard with her bow already strung, Cait pointed at her dress and shook her head. "That won't do."

"What won't?" Sorcha looked down. "It doesn't matter if I get it dirty. There are hundreds of these musty things in the castle."

"Skirts will only trip you up. I already talked with Oona, she's waiting in the kitchens."

"In the kitchens? With what?"

"Your clothes." Cait hopped up onto the fence of the training grounds and tossed her beard over her shoulder. "Go on then. I'll wait."

Sorcha narrowed her eyes and pointed. "You'll let me braid your beard?"

"Why would I ruin a good beard by doing that?"

"Agree, and I'll wear whatever clothes you want."

"Fine. Just hurry up, I don't 'ave all day to waste training you."

"That's exactly what you've been doing!" Sorcha called out with a laugh.

She left her bow and arrows with the dwarf, racing to the kitchen with laughter ringing in her ears.

Of all the time she had spent in the castle, these few days training had been her favorite. She missed Eamonn and even Cian, who had gone with him. But there was something so refreshing about learning new things, using her hands and body as they were meant to be used.

Her hands were already strong from healing, her arms larger than most women. Every night she went to bed with aching muscles and a smile on her face. She wasn't a delicate creature, nor had she ever wished to be.

Banging open the kitchen door, she sauntered in, calling out, "Oona!"

"Here, dearie!"

Sorcha brushed aside a large sheet hanging up to dry. The pixie was elbow deep in soapy water, but grinning from ear to ear.

Sorcha smiled. "There you are. Cait said you had something for me?"

"It's long past time you accepted the faerie way of dress!"

"Please tell me it isn't made of spiderwebs, I'll tear it the first second I put it on."

"Oh no, dearie. It's much better than that." Oona nodded towards a table. "I think you'll be able to figure it out, but let me know if you need help. I'll dry my hands off!"

Sorcha stood stock still when she saw the clothing laid out on the table. Leather leggings, so smooth and supple that they were perfect. A loose tunic, split over her hips for ease of movement, and a leather corset. Twin wrist guards sat atop the small pile.

"These?" she asked.

"I know they're considered men's clothing in your world, but they're much more comfortable."

"You wear skirts."

"I'm no warrior. I work in the kitchens and I'm not expected to do anything other than that. You need speed on your side, whether you're working as a midwife or fighting. It'll make your druid ancestors proud."

Sorcha could feel it was true. Hands smoothed over her shoulders, tightened on her bicep, and pushed her forward.

"Grandfather?" she asked.

Fingers tapped on her shoulder in agreement before pressing down on the cloth, leaving a handprint behind. Even the druids wanted her to wear the outfit.

Sighing, she gave up her sense of propriety and took the clothes with her to change. Sliding the leather leggings over her skin brought a strange sense of self-reliance. She shed the dresses and petticoats with relief, and became a new woman dressed in men's clothing.

Smiling, she walked into the kitchen and gave Oona a small twirl.

"Well would you look at that," Oona said with a giggle. "What a pretty faerie you would make."

"Don't my ear tips qualify me as one?"

"Doubtful, but we'll let it slide. You really are beautiful, dearie. Eamonn won't know what to do with himself when he returns."

Sorcha's smile dimmed. "It's been quite a while."

"It can take a bit to find the deer. Don't you worry that pretty head of yours, I'm sure nothing has happened to them. Now off with you."

Sorcha saw the worried expression that Oona carefully hid. A part of her wanted to push, to see whether her newfound power could force Oona to speak. The faerie was hiding something.

They all were. Shaking her head, she wandered back out to the training grounds where the dwarf sat.

"What's the matter?" Cait asked immediately.

"Nothing."

"You look like you just watched someone kick a child. Don't give me that bullshit."

Sorcha let out a frustrated groan. "I feel as if everyone is hiding something from me! No matter how much I try to get everyone to give me a clear answer on why it's taking Eamonn so long."

"Oh well that's easy."

"Is it?"

"They don't want you to know that he took out a whole troop of dwarves to find more people to force into his army. And if they happen to find some of Fionn's forces along the way, well, that's all the better."

Stunned, she blinked a few times. "Thank you for the honest answer, but you can't possibly be right."

Eamonn couldn't have lied to her, could he?

Cait gave her a look that suggested he could. "Fine, if that's what you want to believe. I'm just training you."

She released arrow after arrow, her mind a turbulent sea of crashing waves. She didn't want to believe he had bent the truth. They had only just found each other again, and they had agreed this was the best course of action.

There wasn't another choice. Fionn had to be stopped, but the real concern was the people of the Seelie Fae. They didn't need to go through another war. It had been five years already, and that tactic hadn't worked.

Eamonn had understood her point of view. He'd agreed with it, acted as if he was relieved. Was he that good at deceiving her?

The sun arched overhead and dipped down to kiss the horizon. Still, she didn't stop. A frown furrowed her brows, her biceps trembling from the stress. Her tongue swelled, mouth dried, body ached for water.

Her mind wasn't done yet. She wasn't done processing that he might have betrayed her. That he might still think she was a foolish little human girl who couldn't understand Faerie politics.

"Sorcha!" Cait's voice cut through the fog of her mind. "You're still here? Enough!"

She couldn't —wouldn't — stop until he returned. Until she could look him in the eye and accuse him of all the wrongdoings Cait said he had done.

"Enough!"

The bow flew out of her grasp, clattering across the stone ground and scattering the hay. Breathing hard, Sorcha whirled to glare at Cait.

"I'm not done yet."

"Yes, you are."

"You have no right to order me," Sorcha pivoted and reached for the bow.

"Stop it! You're bleeding, can't you see that? You've practiced enough today."

She could see her hands now. Fingers raw and blistered, blood dripping from beneath the nails and landing in fat droplets atop the discarded bow. When had she begun to bleed?

Pain seeped through her skin. The gut-twisting ache immediately stiffened her fingers, locking them in place.

Crying out, she fell onto her knees and held out her hands. Foolish, she berated herself. Now all her training would go to waste.

Cait reached out, at eye level now that Sorcha sat upon the ground. The dwarf grasped her hands and winced. "I should have known it would upset you. I apologize, Sorcha. This wasn't the time, nor the place, to voice my concerns."

"Was it true?" She looked at the dwarf with hope in her eyes. "Please, tell me it was just rumor."

"You'll have the ask the king for the truth."

"Then you don't know?"

"I know where the men went, and why they packed their armor. I know they all expected to meet an elven army on the road because the path chosen is a known trade route. Can I say that the High King chose this with full knowledge? No. I cannot read his mind."

Sorcha's shoulders slumped forward in defeat. "He knew."

"How can you know? Can you read faerie minds, druid?"

"He wouldn't go, otherwise. Eamonn is meticulous in his decision making. He knew."

"I'm sorry," Cait said. She patted Sorcha's arm with a firm smack. "I know it's not the easiest thing to hear, especially when you thought you knew him."

When you thought you knew him.

Did she? Sorcha wasn't certain anymore. They had spent many hours together, but all of them superficial at best.

Was it even possible for a human, so limited in years and knowledge, to understand the full breadth of a faerie life?

"Chin up. You'll have your moment to ask him for clarification soon."

"What?" Sorcha glanced over the dwarf's shoulder, towards the castle gates. "They're returning?"

"We could see the trail of dwarves an hour ago. I called out to you, but you weren't responding. I figured it was best to let you go rather than interrupt."

"I can't see him like this."

"Good thing dwarves are always prepared."

Cait pulled a small jar from her pocket. She smeared the salve over Sorcha's hands which miraculously healed before her eyes. The cuts sealed, blood dried, and the bruises faded to yellow.

Holding her hands up to the dying light, she shook her head in wonder. "Remarkable."

"Useful, ain't it?"

"Why doesn't everyone use it?"

"Because it's dwarf magic, and not everyone has access to it." Cait nudged Sorcha's shoulder. "Go on with you. Go and greet your man."

"I don't know if I want to."

"He'll know something is wrong if you don't."

"Then I'll remain here."

Cait shuffled. "The others will know there's something wrong as well."

"And?" Sorcha looked down. "They don't care for me."

"You're growing on us. The consort of a king plays an important role in the well-being of the Fae. If you're upset, we'll likely be upset."

She wanted to say then so be it. Eamonn could deal with an upset group of dwarves on his own. But the other half of her said it was her duty to comfort the others.

Sorcha had never spread fear before, nor had she perpetuated it. She would not start now.

Squaring her shoulders, she rose to her feet with a groan. "That salve wouldn't be good for muscles, would it?"

"You're on your own with that. Good luck."

She would need it. Sorcha trailed across the training grounds, hardly noticing her feet touching the stones. Her heart raced, her palms grew sweaty with the mere thought of confronting him.

Would she scream? She certainly wanted to. Words built up at the back of her throat, pushing against her tongue, longing to spray acidic anger. Her palm already stung in anticipation of a resounding smack.

She climbed the steps up to the battlements. Wind whipped her hair loose from its tie until it tangled around her arms and shoulders.

There they were. The long tail of dwarves, not together as they should have been, but loosely spread across the mountain. They had not yet reached the bridge, their pace sluggish and weak.

White banners of makeshift bandages spread among the crowd. Some wore the fabric around their heads, others their waists and hands. The anger drained from her body as she saw a few litters, bodies lying limp upon the rickety frames.

They had fought, and they had lost.

Her gaze caught on the tallest figure. Eamonn picked his way over craggy rocks and sparse heather. His torn cloak revealed new crystals, wounds and slashes decorating his skin.

He glanced up and their gazes caught.

Many emotions sizzled between them. Relief he was alive, even though so many were dead. Happiness they had returned, for she had missed them all. And disappointment he had lied to her.

One of the dwarves on the wall hummed. His voice carried on the wind like the steady beat of a drum. Others joined in, their haunting call a hymn to their fallen brothers and sisters.

A hauntingly beautiful voice soared overhead. Tenuous at first, then growing in strength, Cait's voice carried the souls of the dwarves from their bodies deep into the earth.

Tears dripped down Sorcha's cheeks as she counted the fallen. Eight litters. Eight men who had died because Eamonn had not kept his promise.

The dwarves looked to her, their gazes solemn. What would the lady of the castle do? How would she treat the returning warriors?

It was the first time she had to make a decision worthy of a queen. Druid souls pressed against her spine, their hands supporting her when she might have faltered. They drew her straight, pulled her shoulders back, tipped her chin up.

"Good," a voice whispered in her ear. "That is how a queen stands."

Sorcha squeezed her eyes shut for a moment. She could do this. She could walk in the footsteps of so many women before her. Druid women who had made such a decision hundreds of times before.

Cait's voice trembled and fell silent. The deep thrumming bass silenced until all that remained was the wind whipping in her ears.

Her eyes found Eamonn's again, his begging her forgiveness. He wanted her to understand his decision. Try as she might, she couldn't.

Heart breaking, Sorcha turned her face from him and the warriors who had drawn their blades. She stepped back down the stairs, refusing to look back.

"M'lady?" Cait called out, the first time she had ever given Sorcha a title of respect.

"They know their way home." Her voice was icy and iron hard. "Tend to the dead, but let the wounded see to their injuries themselves."

"Are you not our healer?"

"I am." She glanced around to find the dwarves had followed her off the battlements. No one remained to greet the returning soldiers. "Hear me now! I will not lift a finger to help anyone who has dedicated their lives to bloodshed. There will be no more *war*."

Cait pushed to the front of the crowd, her eyes brimming with tears. "We cannot go against the orders of our king."

"You all have a difficult decision before you. Follow your high king, and lose your healer. Follow me, and lose your king."

She headed towards the castle, stones crunching underneath her feet. She would not look back, would not see whether he made it across the bridge in time to see her leave.

The brush snagged in her curls, catching upon leaves and tangles that were always in her hair. She had changed out of her new clothing and tucked the articles away in a drawer she wasn't certain she would open again.

He hadn't seen her in them. Now, she wasn't certain that he deserved to.

Her white nightgown was another relic found in a treasure chest. Simple, plain, and sturdy, it serviced her desire to feel something from home. All the velvets and silks made her head spin. She wanted was something simple, and the only thing she could find was a nightgown.

She tugged hard on the brush, stoically bearing the angry sting of her scalp.

Night had fallen long ago. The rest of the castle residents settled into bed, their snores and quiet dreams angering Sorcha further. He hadn't come up to their room yet.

He had a right to be nervous. She still wasn't certain what she would say, or how she would say it. Anger simmered underneath her skin like the ragged edges of claws.

He was likely drinking. She had heard that soldiers did that after returning from war. The alcohol would wipe their memories of blood and death, and then they would return to their wives.

"Not me," she vehemently told her reflection in the mirror. "I will not be that wife who will service a man making foolish decisions. He has no right!"

He should have *listened* to her! Did he think her incapable of forming a plan that would adhere to faerie politics? Or did he think her incapable of anything in the realm of Fae?

The door creaked open just enough for shadows to creep in. He paused, frozen as soon as the spear of her candlelight slashed into the hallway.

"Eamonn." It was not a question. She knew who lingered at her door.

"You're still awake."

"I was waiting for you."

He sighed and pushed the door open the rest of the way. She wanted to berate him, to scream and shout and throw her brush at his head.

But bruises spread across his cheeks, a ragged edged crystal slicing down his neck. It spread from the old wound, and she knew someone had tried to take advantage of the weakness. They wouldn't know it was his strength.

She sighed and put the brush down.

"You're going to yell," he said. His shoulders squared as if he were preparing for the worst. "I deserve it. It was a horrible idea, and I didn't listen to you."

"Yes, it was."

"We lost good men out there, because I thought we were prepared. I was wrong."

"Yes, you were."

"Our people saw you turn from me. The army is already on the verge of deserting, and seeing your reaction certainly didn't help. I'm not saying it wasn't the right thing to do. It likely was."

She stared back at him, silent in her regard.

"Why aren't you yelling yet? I can see you have plenty to say."

"I don't need to yell at you, Eamonn. You're already doing it for me."

Her words broke something within him. A low breath hissed through his teeth and he rushed towards her, dropping to his knees at her feet. The tension drained from his body, shoulders falling forward in defeat.

He placed his head in her lap, wrapping his arms around her waist with a low moan. "Yell at me, mo chroí. Be angry, break pottery and statues. Do something other than this, I beg you."

"What good would it do?" she said, stroking his head. "You know what you did, and how wrong it was."

"I am lost." He pulled the length of her nightgown up to her thigh, breath whispering over her skin as he pressed crystal lips against her. "Everything I thought I knew is wrong. This world is one I remember, these people familiar faces, but I cannot find the man I once was."

"You don't need to find him. The warrior prince is no longer who you are, nor what this land and people need."

"Who do they need?"

He looked up and their gazes locked. She wanted to say that the world needed him. They needed the kind soul that existed inside who wanted to help his people. But the longer she was here, the more she realized that faerie culture was beyond her.

"I do not know," she said. "I might have once said they need a kind king."

"And now?"

"They are looking for someone to lead them, but also for someone to understand them." She thought of the dwarves and their steadfast ways. They didn't want to fight, other than the occasional tussle, yet here they were. "They trust you, in their own way. But they fear you will follow in your brother's footsteps."

"Blood calls to blood."

"No." Sorcha dug her fingers into the crystals of his cheek. "You will not become Fionn."

"How can you be so sure? I can feel it, the old ways sinking underneath my skin."

"The old ways are not the best ways. You were the first to believe that, Eamonn." She stroked a thumb over his lips. "No more of this. No more fighting, blood, and death. Your people deserve to rest."

"I cannot stop." The torment in his eyes nearly shattered her heart. "He will come here next, and he will not stop. Fionn has no care for our people or how many people must be sacrificed to make his point."

"Which is?"

"I am not worthy to be king."

"No man ever is," she said with a soft smile. "You can only try your best to be a good king. You will never win over the hearts of every single one of your people. But you can provide for them, ensure their lives are rich, and their bellies full."

"How do you know this?"

"I was one of those people wishing that my king only knew that we were hungry." She stood, pulling him with her until he rose to his great height. "Have you bathed?"

"No."

"Has anyone tended to your wounds?"

"There is no need. My wounds do not bleed."

Sorcha winced. She wanted to remind him that not all wounds were external, that sometimes a person could heal through physical touch. His gaze caught hers, holding her locked within blue crystals as sharp as a sword and deep as the ocean.

He knew, she realized. He knew what she wanted to tell him and still he did not want her to say it.

"Come with me." She held out a hand for him to take.

"Sorcha…"

"Take my hand, Eamonn. Let me tend to your wounds."

"I don't deserve your forgiveness."

"I have yet to meet anyone who didn't." She let her hand hover in the air, waiting for him.

He fought with himself. She watched a battle rage behind his eyes until he finally sighed and took her hand.

"I don't deserve you."

"No, you don't. Now come into the bath and let me show you what the dwarves have created."

The room behind their bed was a modern work of art. The dwarves had brought to life an old washroom by tapping into the geothermal vents underneath the castle. A slight twist of a knob, and hot water rushed into the large iron tub they had carried up the stairs.

Sorcha had already used it more times than she should have. Her practices with Cait had made her muscles ache and her body tremble. The warm water had soothed those aches, as she hoped they would for

Eamonn.

He stopped in the center of the room, and she ran her hands across his shoulders. Standing on tiptoe, she reached for the clasp of his cloak and let it fall to the ground. The soft sound echoed in the tight room.

"You don't have to do this," he said, searching her gaze for an answer she did not have.

"I do."

As angry as she was, Sorcha needed to feel his ribs expand under her fingertips. Life coursed through his veins, strong and violent as a churning river. He had been wounded, but survived.

It was all that mattered.

A sigh slid through her lips as she tucked her fingers underneath his tunic and lifted the fabric up. He stooped to help her slide it over his head, sinking to one knee.

Again, she curled her fingers over his hair. Snarls tangled and tugged, but she patiently worked each and every one loose.

"Stand, warrior."

He looked at her as if she were his world. Eamonn rose to his feet, powerful chest broad and scarred.

Sorcha hooked her fingers at his breech waist, tugging until he was completely bare. She pressed a kiss against the newest scar. It was an angry thing, ragged and raw with crystal so sharp they pressed against her lips.

"Let me take care of you tonight, Eamonn. Tomorrow, we will wage a battle of our own."

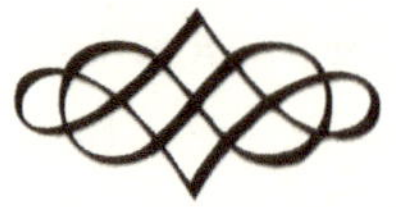

Sorcha couldn't sleep. Her mind whirled with possibilities and the screams of dying men.

War flickered to life behind her eyes. Memories that were not hers, but those of druid women. Blood coated their hair, bodies painted blue as they screamed out their rage. She couldn't understand the power of their anger. It bubbled over their soul until they became a beast, no longer human.

Eamonn shifted behind her. His arm slid from her waist and he rolled onto his side. Distance. It kept growing between them, further and further until she wondered if they slept in the same bed at all.

She swung her feet over the edge of the bed and slipped from beneath the furs. Glancing over her shoulder, she waited until he settled again.

Did he know how beautiful he was? Eamonn was a vision of power. Crystals glinted in the moonlight, decorating his skin like thousands of stars.

It hurt to look at him when she was so angry.

She couldn't yell at him for making a decision that felt right. He had made his choice, and they fundamentally did not agree on how to handle this war. She only wished he would listen more carefully.

The floor was cold against her toes, bitter and icy. Her white nightgown suddenly seemed flimsy against the cold night air that wiggled beneath the door and sank claws into her skin.

She pulled the fur from a nearby chair and slipped out onto the balcony.

The full moon smiled down at her. Silver light gave mist a magical quality as it swirled through the courtyard below. The dwarves had built a pattern into the stones they replaced. A triskele, she realized with a smile. They honored the old ways.

"Shouldn't you be in bed?" The warm voice was recognizable, and one she had not heard in a very long time.

"Bran," she replied, warmth imbuing her voice with happiness. "It has been a long time."

"Yes, I suppose it has."

"Where have you been?"

"My life is not all about meddling in Seelie affairs."

She grinned and turned towards the raven man. "Just recently?"

He looked exactly as she remembered him. The strange dark feathers that smoothed along his cheekbone and forehead. A raven eye filled one socket, too large in comparison to the other and restless in its movements. One side of his head was still shaved, although a new growth filled in the pale skin of his skull.

"You look well," she said.

"As do you. Something has changed within you."

"I discovered I am a druid."

"No it's not that." He leaned forward and lifted a lock of her hair. "You appear more confident."

"I am."

"You're carrying yourself far more regally than before."

"I have learned to do so."

"But you're still dressed like a peasant." He let his hand drop. "Eamonn has not yet beaten his brother, I take it?"

"Do you really think I wouldn't dress like this if I was Queen?"

Bran shook his head, a severe look marring his handsome features. "No, you are far too connected to the earth to be swayed by jewelry and silk."

"I wouldn't be able to keep it clean."

"And how would you fight?"

She frowned and leaned back against the banister. "You've been watching me."

"I have not."

"You cannot lie, so what are you omitting? You would never know that I was training to fight."

"A raven has many paths to fly across. If I saw you training with that fiendish little dwarf, that was merely by mistake. A traveler sees much, but does not watch others specifically to gain knowledge."

"You've been practicing that for centuries, haven't you?"

He chuckled. "I have."

Sorcha gestured towards the stairs leading from the balcony. They ended at another protrusion, this one far more precarious than the first. The dwarves had yet to add railings or safety to it. Still, she was quite certain it would hold their combined weight.

Like the gentleman he pretended to be, Bran gestured for her to go first. Pulverized stone coated her fingers as she glided them down the railing. Settling on the very edge of the rock, she let her legs dangle high above the ground.

Bran sat down next to her. "Your mind is troubled."

"Is that why you took human form? Bran, I'm touched."

"What happened?" He nudged her shoulder with his. "Regardless of the fact that I dislike rules, nor do I follow any form of law, I still prefer to know what others are doing. And I find myself growing fond of you."

She blushed. "Eamonn is still battling Fionn for control over the Seelie throne."

"And is this a bad thing?"

"His people have had enough dying. They deserve at least some kind of break."

"It hasn't been that long of a war."

"It's been five years!" Sorcha exclaimed. "How much longer should it go?"

"Faerie wars last centuries. We fight, that's part of living in the Otherworld."

"Don't you ever tire of that?" Sorcha could hear the exhaustion in her own voice.

And she was tired. She didn't want to see the horrified expression on the dwarves faces. Oona had aged greatly. Cian resorted to kindness just to make people feel better. It was unnatural for any of these creatures to undergo such stress.

Bran watched her, his raven eye spinning. "You want to care for them."

"Don't you?"

"No. Faeries look out for themselves, and if they can't, then they are not training the next generation to be hardy."

"What if you didn't have to be hardy anymore?" Sorcha turned towards him and grasped his hands in hers. "What if you lived in a land where war was nothing more than memory? Where food and water was abundant, and people worked for their own living. No more slaves. No more lesser Fae."

"It would be a utopia."

"It would. It would be a beautiful place to live, and one that was inclusive and kind to all who lived there."

He tapped her nose with a claw tipped finger. "That is not the Fae way."

"Why can't you change?"

"We have changed much in the many centuries since our people began. But we are not human, Sorcha. You continue to give us human traits, and forget that faeries are more beast than man. We want to fight. We want to argue and meddle. These are parts of us you have to accept if you want to remain here."

"Why are you so intelligent?" she asked. "Every time I ask a question, you not only have an answer but find a way to make me look like a fool."

"You are not a fool. You are an extremely kind hearted woman who wants to save the world. It's admirable."

"He's forcing them to fight." She looked down at the ground. It was so far away and obscured by the shadows of night that she could almost imagine it wasn't there at all.

"Forcing?"

"I don't know how. Cait, the dwarf you called fiendish, told me that the dwarves no longer wish for war. They did not make the choice for battle and they are tired. I don't know how he's convincing them to continue if this is true but…" She shrugged. "How could it not be true? Faeries cannot lie."

Bran leaned back on one hand and stroked his chin. "You think Eamonn is coercing them or forcing them?"

"I hope neither."

"And yet, you are still talking about it."

"Something isn't right."

"Do you think it will make everything better for these dwarves to no longer fight? Do you think without an army, Eamonn will stand a chance against Fionn?"

"I don't know." She looked over at him, her shoulders slumped in defeat. "Do you?"

"Fionn is unpredictable. He sees the world in black and white, right and wrong, the classic definition of Seelie Fae. It's why he's made a relatively good king."

"Good?" Sorcha's jaw dropped open. "How is enslaving his own people and perpetuating class structure considered a good king?"

"It's always worked for the Seelie before."

"You cannot honestly believe that."

Bran held his hands up. "I believe nothing. I think the Seelie race in general is a waste of breathing space. Even your lover, whom I consider a friend, would better the world by not being here."

"What are you getting at, Bran?"

"Eamonn and Fionn are two very different men. One favors the old ways, which certainly puts a grouping of faeries at a disadvantage. But, the others brings a large amount of change. That can be just as dangerous as not changing at all."

"You're speaking in riddles."

"That's what faeries are good at."

She rolled her eyes and looked towards the sky for guidance. He was right, in a way. There were so many ways this could go wrong. But could she stand by and watch others die?

No. She couldn't. It went against every fiber of her being to allow a war as senseless as this one to go any further.

"I know Eamonn will make a good king."

"Why is that?"

"Because I will be at his side."

The words vibrated through her with enough power to weaken her knees, if she had been standing. Sorcha sucked in a breath. She had meant it. He would be a better king because she would never let him be anything else.

"Good," Bran said. "That's exactly what I wanted to hear."

"What?"

"These lands have been without a Queen for too long. Faeries are volatile creatures. We have a lot of emotions, but rarely show them until they are overpowering. It's why we love with all our being and why we fight wars until everyone is dead.

"A King encourages faeries to be who they are. He teaches the younglings to protect themselves, tells the old to pass on traditions. His role is important, for his is judge, jury, and justice.

"The Queen is different. She is the gentle soul that passes through the lands, healing injuries, and breathing life into wombs. She is the softness in a world that is as hard as steel. Without that gentle mother, our people quickly descend into chaos."

Sorcha exhaled. "There's nothing I can do to help. I will not lie with Fionn, and Eamonn has not yet been successful at taking back the throne."

"I think you're doing all the right things."

"And Eamonn?"

Bran chuckled and rose to his feet. "He's doing his best. It's been a long time since he's been home. There's an adjustment period."

"Is there any way I can help him?" Sorcha looked up at the dark man standing before her. "Is there any way I can help his people?"

Bran hesitated for a brief second, and in that moment she knew.

There was something he wasn't telling her. Something that could stop all this madness.

"What do you know?" she asked. "What is it that you have discovered?"

"Do you trust that Eamonn will be a good king?"

"Without doubt."

"And you believe that Fionn will not come and find him with an army?"

"There are more secrets in these castle walls than you know. An army would have a difficult time finding us."

Bran licked his lips, fingers twitching as she shifted side to side. "I shouldn't tell you."

"I thought you liked to manipulate the story." She toyed with his natural desire to meddle. It was a cruel trick, but one she thought necessary.

He blew out a breath. "It's the sword."

"Which sword?"

"The Sword of Light, midwife, what else could it be?"

"Nuada Silverhand's sword?" She gaped at him. "What does that have to do with this?"

"It's how he's controlling the army. That sword controls anything that it points at. Eamonn is ordering the army to fight for him, and if he gets the chance, he's likely ordering Fionn's army to kneel."

"Then why hasn't he stopped everyone in their tracks? He could have avoided all this entirely if he simply ordered the men to return home."

Bran shrugged. "That's not the Seelie way. Honor demands that he defeat them without the help of magic. It's likely that Eamonn is ordering the dwarves to fight, but giving both armies a fair fight."

Sorcha's mind raced. Her hands shook as she realized what Eamonn had done. "Cait was right," she whispered. "They really don't wish to fight."

If he was forcing the dwarves to become his army, then what else was he capable of? It was no wonder that he carried so much guilt on his shoulders. He had done the unthinkable and took the choice away from his own people.

"How do I stop it?" she asked.

"Destroy the sword."

"I suppose you meant that to sound easy. Destroy the sword of Nuada? Just how do I do that?"

"I'm sure your little friends will help," Bran said. He winked at her with a roguish grin. "The druids always knew how to destroy faerie objects."

"Bran."

"I'm not telling you anymore. You said to meddle with the story, and now I have. You're a smart woman. I have full confidence you'll figure this out."

A rush of wind swirled around his body. Clothing fell to the ground and dissolved. Feathers sprouted from his skin as his form shrank into that of a raven with one human eye. Bran cocked his head to the side, croaked at her, then spread his wings and flew away.

"Destroy the sword of Nuada," she grumbled. "That's the only way to stop this?"

Warm air surrounded her. Hundreds of hands pressed against her shoulders and legs, no longer strange or discomforting. They were her family, her past, and her future. The druids would assist if they could. They wanted the war to end just as much as the faeries.

Sorcha wished she knew why.

CHAPTER EIGHT
The Wisdom Of Ethniu

Sorcha sat at the head table with Eamonn and marveled over the changes the dwarves had wrought in such a short time. The banquet hall was far more than the ruin it had once been. They even repaired the stained-glass windows, although she was not certain how.

Simple chandeliers hung from the ceiling. Candles stuck to their metal rings, melted and glowing merrily. They lit the entire space with ease. Wall sconces glimmered at the edges of her vision, giving light to even the darkest of shadows.

The tables were sturdier now that the dwarves had built them to last. There were a few extras, though many of the dwarves no longer ate in the hall.

Hundreds of dwarves had arrived in swarms. They refused to swear fealty to Fionn, and as such, left their mountain abodes to seek shelter from the coming winter. Each family chose where they wished to live, and the rest gathered by trade.

It was quiet and peaceful among the dwarves.

Sorcha wished it was in her life as well.

She clutched the spoon in her hand so tightly she worried the metal might bend. He hadn't said a word to her since their late night when he returned from battle.

Eamonn made himself scarce. He fought, trained with the dwarves ate dinner, and then disappeared during the nights. She did not know where he went.

"Eamonn," she began.

He lifted a hand to silence her. "All is well."

"We have not spoken in some time."

"I have dedicated myself to repairing the castle. There is much work to oversee."

"And at night?"

"There are secrets within these walls I need to uncover. I will not rest until I am certain this castle is safe for all who live within it."

"The ancestors have assured me that everyone is safe." They whispered secrets in her ears when she could not fall asleep. Stories of the old days, recipes for spells and magic. Anything that would keep her mind occupied while she waited for him. "You need not worry."

"I do not know your ancestors, nor do I know the world they came from. What is not dangerous to druids may prove deadly for the Fae."

"They would tell me if it was."

"Would they?" He glanced towards her. "The druids have never been fond of my kind."

"I am."

She watched him struggle to find the words to respond to her. He knew she wasn't lying. She had proven herself time and time again to all the people of this castle. Sorcha was a trustworthy woman who wanted to help them.

He knew that. He understood it as well, but he still held prejudices against the ghosts of her past.

It was a shame he couldn't trust her.

Sighing, she stirred her soup and slowly nodded. "So, that is the way of it then."

"Sorcha, I'm not angry with you."

"No, I suppose you are not. But you are still distant. You have been since I returned here."

"I don't know how to change that."

"Spend time with me."

Eamonn tossed his cutlery to the table with a loud clatter. "I have so many things I have to do, I'm hardly finding time to sleep. And you want me to find more time to spend it with you? I am only one man, Sorcha. And there is only so much time in the day."

"Then include me. Give me something to do, so I might report my successes. Then at least we are working together!"

"I—"

The banquet hall doors opened, cutting off Eamonn's exasperated words. Cian made his way through, arms pumping as he raced towards the head table. "My lord! Visitors!"

"Who?" Eamonn stood.

His shoulders squared and his legs spread wide. He crossed his arms over his thick chest, muscles bulging as he pressed them forward. Sorcha shivered as he changed from her lover to the high king who fed off the energy of war.

"I do not know." Cian gulped. "They are not familiar to me."

"Let them pass."

"And if they mean harm?"

"Then let them come."

She watched Eamonn place a hand against the Sword of Light. It rarely left his person although she had noticed it disappeared while he was assisting the dwarves on their repairs. She simply didn't know where he left it.

Sorcha reached out and caught the fist resting upon the pommel of the blade. "No violence."

"If they come here intending to harm, I will not stop."

"You will. These people may seek shelter, and they do not know you. Your reputation as the man who kills precedes you. Do not give them reason to spread such a rumor any further."

"They should be afraid of me."

"Only in battle. When you are in your home, peace must reign."

She waited until his fingers relaxed and released his hand.

A small troop of faeries entered the room. Their foreheads were overly high, eyes so large they reflected the light, their bodies thin and lithe. Twig like hair smoothed back and hung in dreadlocks down their backs. Moss grew upon their shoulders and arms while leaves covered their bodies where clothing might have been. Flowers bloomed on a few of them. The females, Sorcha assumed.

"Peat faeries," she said in awe. "I didn't know they still existed."

"They don't in your world. Humans killed them off, along with the will-o'-the-wisps. Their kinds have warred for centuries."

"They're beautiful."

"They're dangerous. Too many of their kind have turned Unseelie."

"That is a personal choice, so you've said. It's not bred into species whether they are Seelie or Unseelie. They make a choice to uphold the honorable ways, or they do not."

"That does not mean they are trustworthy."

She glared at him and stood. Turning towards the faeries who hesitated before their table, she forced herself to smile. "Hello, and welcome travelers."

"Thank you, lady," one of the flowered faeries said. She stepped forward, large eyes blinking rapidly. "We come seeking shelter."

"From whom?"

"That of the king. We no longer wish to have our homes trampled by the High Fae and their ilk."

She had suspected this would happen and was pleased to see she was correct. News had spread fast that the High King had returned and was taking his subjects back one by one. To prove a point, she asked, "How did you find this place?"

"The legends speak of a Stone King who provides shelter for those who seek it. We have journeyed far to understand the truth of this legend." The woman's eyes dipped towards the ground. "I see the rumors of his ferocious nature were not exaggerated."

Sorcha glanced over her shoulder to see Eamonn's hard expression. He was trying to scare them and succeeding. Rolling her eyes so only he could see, she turned back to the faeries. "He is fierce on the battlefield and unparalleled by any warrior. But he is also a protector of his own."

"We would like to swear our allegiance to him."

Again, she looked back at the large man standing behind her. Lowering her voice, she asked, "Is this what you wish?"

Eamonn replied directly to the peat faerie. "Your people have feuded with many. There will be no fighting amongst mine."

"We have no wish to fight any more than we already have."

"I will hold you to that. The first person who lifts a finger in anger will be measured by my judgment."

A shiver raced through all the faeries. Their leaves turned over, revealing silver veins underneath the vibrant green. "We understand and acknowledge your warning."

"Good. Then you may stay within the castle walls."

"With all due respect," the faerie said, "we would prefer to stay in the peat bogs on the other side of the bridge. We are happy to sound an alarm if anyone approaches."

She could see Eamonn was considering it. "It may be of use," she murmured. "There is merit to knowing when someone is arriving, rather than when they get to the bridge."

"Every faerie here has a use," he declared loudly. "If you will provide us with a watch, then we will gladly provide your food. My dwarven army will also provide you safety should any issues arise."

"Thank you, High King." The peat faerie and her kin dipped into low bows. "You are most gracious."

"Do not forget my warning, for I will not."

"Thank you," they said in unison again.

They turned to leave the hall on trembling legs. Sorcha stared at their backs with a troubled expression.

"What?" Eamonn grumbled as he sat back down. "I know that expression, you think something is wrong."

"I don't think you should rule through fear."

"How else should I rule?"

She shrugged. "I've never been a queen, I do not know."

"Then sit back down, Sorcha. I'm doing my best."

"That's all one can ask." Her words trailed off as her eyes caught upon a bright, vibrant color laying upon the floor.

She left the high table without thought. Her feet whispered across the stone floor and the din of the crowd fell silent as she walked to the center of the room. She felt the eyes of a hundred dwarves on her back like a physical weight.

Kneeling, Sorcha scooped up the bright pink blossom that smelled like sunshine and sweet wine. Its oversized petals drooped over her fingers, limp and forgotten.

One of the peat faeries would miss this, she knew it in her heart that a flower was as much a part of them as their vines. She cupped it as gently as possible and rose to her feet.

A soft sound made her look up.

The smallest peat faerie stood before her, wringing its hands and staring at the flower.

"Is this yours?" Sorcha asked.

The tiny female nodded.

"You don't have to be afraid, I don't plan to keep it." Sorcha held it out for the faerie to take. "It's the most beautiful flower I've ever seen."

"Thank you, druid."

At the word, Sorcha's vision skewed. She could see all the threads that tangled around the peat faerie. Golden loops that tied her back to her family and far beyond Sorcha's vision. A thread that Sorcha could tug so easily, and secrets would spill from it like water from a basin.

She did not tug, instead, choosing to leave the faerie privacy.

"You are safe here," Sorcha said. "All of you are safe."

"That is all we have ever desired."

"It is what all of us strive for every day. If you have need of anything, please reach out to me."

"Thank you, lady."

She watched the peat faeries leave. The small one affixed the flower back to her person, just above her heart. The head female patted her on the head and glanced back at Sorcha with a soft smile on her face.

All would be well, Sorcha could feel it deep in her bones.

Turning back to Eamonn, she sighed at the scowl on his face. There would be many more battles to fight with him. The faeries were still dangerous to her and to his people. But he needed to understand that this was the path towards growth.

He would come around, she decided.

She walked back to their table and sat down. "They will be a good addition."

"Are you so certain?"

"Yes."

He lifted his goblet to his lips and nodded. "Then they will stay."

"Just like that?"

"You are the one with the golden heart, mo chroí. I trust your judgment even more than my own."

She relaxed. "You made me worried."

"That I would not accept them?" Eamonn shrugged. "The more you speak, the more I see the light. You have taught me much, Sunshine, and I would be a fool not to listen."

The clang of hammers striking stone echoed throughout the castle. Sorcha's head pounded, pain blooming in the center of her forehead and radiating out in pulsing circles.

"I have to go," she said to Oona. "I can't stand this incessant noise any longer."

"Are you ill, dearie?" Oona reached forward and pressed the back of her hand to Sorcha's forehead. "You feel a touch warm."

"I'm fine."

"Have you been sleeping well? I know it's been a stressful time for all of us."

"Really, I am well. I just need to get away from all this noise."

Otherwise, the headache behind her eyes might explode. She couldn't stand the constant movement of the castle, the watchful eyes of the faeries, the dwarves who made constant jokes. They were wonderful in small doses, but Sorcha desired a single moment of pure silence.

"There's a garden behind the castle which needs tending," Oona said. "I'm uncertain anyone has looked at it. The vines have created quite a mess, and the thicket is large enough to hide a human."

"Thank you." Sorcha's chair squeaked she stood up so fast.

"I understand the desire for freedom, dearie. Get yourself off and enjoy the quiet."

"Do you need anything before I go?"

Oona gave her a bright smile, lifted two oversized pieces of cotton, and stuffed them into her own ears.

That would certainly do the trick.

Sorcha grinned and slipped out of the kitchen, heading to the one place where she might find a little peace. She knew which garden it was. They had all seen the ominous, overgrown area. It was impenetrable, axes couldn't hack through the tangled roots and weeds.

There was a small path leading into the center. A few of the younger dwarves had dared each other to race to the center. Sorcha had watched them jostle around, but none had actually attempted the frightening adventure.

Now, it was her turn, and she refused to hesitate.

The ancient castle door shrieked as she pushed it open. The wild scent of autumn air bit at her arms and lifted the hairs. She had missed this most of all. Sorcha enjoyed being outside, away from the stifling, thick air inside of the castle.

Rustling leaves filled her ears with music while chirping crickets overpowered any remaining hammer strikes she might have heard.

"Thank goodness," Sorcha said, relieved by the cool touch of silence.

Finally, she could hear herself think. She appreciated the little moments when she could be alone.

Brushing aside tangled ivy, she peered into the shadows. It was a perfect place for a lover's tryst, or for a Fomorian to hide.

Twigs crunched underneath her feet, snapping and cracking as she trod over their fallen limbs. Light disappeared as the thorns and vines arched overhead. The thicket was dark even when the sun was at its peak.

A hand pressed against her back, ghostly and smoother than any she had felt before. It was a comforting touch.

Sorcha wasn't certain the exact moment she had grown used to the druid souls that clustered around her at any given moment. They were as much part of her daily life as the dwarves. She was just as grateful for their presence as the faeries who toiled throughout the castle.

At the center of the wild garden, a natural altar grew. Purple amethyst and quartz crystals jutted from the land. Each peak was hewn flat, creating a table bare of offerings.

Her heart thumped painfully. No altar should be left untended. It reminded her too much of the faeries her own people had forgotten, and how much the land had suffered.

The gentle hand pressed against her spine again and smoke swirled around her. "Honor the dead," a calm voice whispered. "Wake them."

She didn't hesitate. Sorcha walked up to the altar and sank to her knees.

Her fingers curled into the dirt at the base. "I ground myself through the earth," she began.

She tilted her head back and breathed in the crisp, clean air. "I fill my lungs to clear my mind."

The brittle thorns shifted, letting a spear of sunlight play across her features. "I connect with the fire of the sun and link it to my own."

A single drop of water fell from a rose that bloomed above her head. "I heal all wounds with the water of life."

Her soul settled. Each word pieced together a part of her she hadn't known she was missing. Sorcha had gone to her own forest altar at least once a week, more if she was feeling stressed. That part of her life had disappeared, and now, returned.

The rituals made her feel whole.

"Well met, daughter." The warm voice from before was one she did not recognize. "See what your offerings have begat."

Sorcha blinked her eyes open and stared up at the altar. The crystals had changed form. They grew and stretched towards the sun, creating a figure who was more beautiful than anyone she had ever seen.

The woman wore a druid ceremonial garb. Furs graced her shoulders, a tunic touched the tops of her knees, and a headdress made of deer antlers sat atop her head. But it was her face that captured Sorcha's attention. It was beautiful, perfect in every way and form.

"It is a fair likeness," the voice said. "Although I always think they are too kind."

Sorcha glanced over her shoulder at the real life version of the crystal woman.

Beauty, so overwhelming that it was painful to look upon, made the newcomer all the more otherworldly.

Dark hair curled in waves down to her shoulders. Her face was pointed at the chin, delicate with perfect, smooth skin. Vibrant green eyes, so close to Sorcha's own, glittered with a smile.

"Ethniu?" Sorcha asked.

"Yes, granddaughter. It is I."

"You're alive? Or are you dead like grandfather?"

"I am neither. I exist in a world between life and death, a place where you could never find me." She reached out and brushed a hand over Sorcha's head. "But I am real enough to touch you."

"How is this possible?"

"You look very much like your mother," Ethniu said. "She was one of my favorite students. So talented, bright, capable, the kind of woman who could take the world by storm."

"She honored the old ways."

"And they burned her because of it. Humans can be unnecessarily cruel."

"They dislike what they cannot understand."

"To horrible ends."

Her grandmother wandered over to the altar and pressed her hands against the smooth surface. The ancient Tuatha dé Danann did not hesitate to show themselves to her, now the Fomorians also spoke with her.

"We visit our grandchildren," Ethniu said with a chuckle. "Even Nuada has visited Eamonn."

"Did you read my mind?"

"Being ancient has its perks. Druid minds are fragile, easy to peek into."

"You found nothing that disappointed you?"

"How could I?" Ethniu smiled at her, brilliantly white and blinding. "You are everything I ever desired. The druids were meant to be like you. Kind creatures who looked out for the humans in our absence."

"Were they not?" Sorcha heard the sadness in her grandmother's voice. "The old druids?"

"No one can control their creations. We didn't expect the druids to be so unpredictable, but they are two races with anger and pride in their blood. The Fomorians, my people, were beastly and cruel. The Seelie Fae, Nuada's people, are thoughtless and rule with iron fists."

"And the combination made druids dangerous. They desired

power," Sorcha replied. She had heard the legends from the other faeries.

"They did," Ethniu agreed. "And some, like you, were wondrous. They did great things, created empires, healed small creatures, and then they died quietly along with the small miracles they wrought."

"Witches."

"Druids. Men and women connected to the earth as no human had ever been before. I am glad you became exactly what I meant for your race to be. The druids were banished from the Otherworld because they wanted to rule. They survived in this castle for a few hundred years, but eventually the faeries overran them. Banished to the human world where the druids nearly disappeared. They were burned at the stake or unable to pass along their knowledge to children capable of great magic."

Her grandmother reached out, hands hanging in the space between them.

Sorcha took Ethniu's hands. "I do not know what you wanted me to be. I can only continue to live by my own morals."

"Healing?"

"And spreading love."

"This is why your mother was my favorite. She, too, thought the world could change just by a little healing energy sent out the window every night."

"I remember that."

Tears welled in Sorcha's eyes as a memory long forgotten surfaced in her mind. Her mother used to hold her hands out the window as if she were cupping hands full of water. When Sorcha asked, her mother would laugh and say she was letting happiness drip through her fingers.

Eventually, she would toss her hands into the air as throw good feelings out into the world. Sorcha used to find it a rather odd, but entertaining ritual.

Now, she knew it was real.

"Why are you here?" Sorcha asked. "I have not had luck with Tuatha dé Danann telling me things they want me to do."

"Ah, but I am Fomorian, and I want nothing from you."

"Then why are you here?"

"I wanted to meet my granddaughter, face to face."

"Just as Balor did?" Sorcha's voice grew hard as stone. "I do not trust him, and you must forgive me for having difficulties trusting you as well."

"My father is a difficult man to trust. He has caused so much heartache in this world he no longer knows how to prevent himself from doing so. You should not trust him, but ask the right questions."

"Why?"

"The Fomorians are a proud people. We gather knowledge as the Fae gather art. I sometimes wondered why they are so enamored with beautiful things when there is so much more out there. Knowledge is a power that can be turned against anyone. Beauty is merely a talent."

Sorcha arched a brow. "A talent? Or a gift from birth?"

"Anyone can be beautiful if they love themselves, but not everyone can be intelligent. Which do you want to be?"

Sorcha didn't know the answer to the question. When she was younger, she would have chosen beauty. Making men fall to their knees because she was the most beautiful woman in the world made her knees tremble.

But then the knowledge of every living creature and thing would provide her with everything her soul needed. Beauty was fleeting, but intelligence meant that her name would remain on people's lips for thousands of years to come.

"Knowledge," she answered. "I would choose knowledge."

"Why?"

"If I measured my worth in beauty, I would live a life full of riches and happiness. If I am valued for the knowledge I impart on the world, then I live forever."

The smile that bloomed on Ethniu's face warmed Sorcha's soul. "Yes, you are correct, my granddaughter. I am proud that you are of my blood."

"And I thank you for it. I did not come to this grove to meet you, but I am glad that is the path my future took."

She leaned forward and pressed her forehead against Ethniu's. They leaned against each other, fingers linked atop the crystal altar and the remains of a once great empire around them.

Sorcha breathed in the magic that crackled around her grandmother like lightning. Ethniu was beautiful in a hard way. Perfect, lovely, but so smooth that she seemed made of stone. It was fitting for a creature who had come from a difficult familial line.

"Sorcha," Ethniu breathed, "There is so much to say. I would give you wisdom if you will listen."

"Always."

"Nuada and I did not have an easy life. We made decisions that angered each other and changed the course of the Otherworld. There are things I have done that I regret. But I never feel guilt for staying true to what I love, and the people I hold in my heart."

Sorcha understood what she was trying to say. Love came in many forms and underwent much stress throughout the course of time. She stayed silent as Ethniu continued.

"I know what it is you seek. The Sword of Light has changed many people's lives. Though it can bring an army to its knees, destroy an entire race of people with a single word, it can also do much good. My husband used it in such a way, and I would not see you destroy it."

"I have to. How else can I prevent Eamonn from turning into his brother? He's hurting his people because he is so blind to his own rage."

"Then hide it. Leave it in the waters of the ocean, throw it from the cliff and give it back to my capable hands. Let the sword sink to the ocean floor where it will remain until the next generation has need of it. But do not destroy a relic that is one of the few remaining pieces tying our people to the original race."

The words dug into her heart and twisted. These people had lost enough over the centuries. They wanted to hold on to whatever they could from the old days, the good days, the ones where they had ruled over everything.

Now, their children continued to fight and quarrel like vultures picking through bones.

"I want no one to use it," Sorcha admitted. "In my generation or the next. No one deserves the power to control."

"Like you?"

"I will not use my power against the Fae. I do not want to control them, and I see no reason why I should. They are intelligent creatures with the capability to love greater than any other."

"You want to appeal to their good senses," Ethniu said with a chuckle. "You know that won't work."

"It has to."

"Fionn has no reason to give you any time to speak. He will listen to your pleas and then he will strike you down."

"I won't let him."

"By controlling him?" Ethniu leaned back and squeezed her hands. Vibrant eyes stared into hers with more knowledge than any person should hold. "You've already controlled him once, Sorcha. He knows what you are capable of and that is why he is so frightened."

"If he truly knew what I was capable of, then he would not be afraid. I will not hurt anyone."

"Throw the sword off the cliffs of the castle, and I will hide it in a place where it will not surface again."

"Where?"

"I will give it back to my husband. The Tuatha dé Danann have no desire to change the course of this story. We're enjoying watching you. Druids are unpredictable in their choices, and you far more than the rest."

"There are others?" Sorcha blinked, her heart squeezing as hope lifted her chin. "Are there are other druids who live?"

"Yes, although you are all spread out. I do not know if you have ever met another, but I feel as though you may some time in your life."

"Will you take me to them?"

"That would meddle with the story, and unlike your Unseelie friend, I dislike meddling."

Ethniu stood, the furs on her shoulders touching Sorcha's hands. They were impossibly soft, smooth, like that of a rabbit rather than a sheep. But Sorcha had never seen a rabbit large enough to create a seamless shoulder piece.

Where was this giant woman from?

"Thank you, granddaughter, for sparing a relic of the Tuatha dé Danann. For that, I will look after you in the coming days."

"What is coming?" she asked.

"War. Violence. Death. All the things you have feared, they follow your lover's footsteps like a loyal dog."

"Is there any way to shake him free from that grasp?"

"Not that I know of," Ethniu breathed. "But I believe you may find a way."

Sorcha closed her eyes as sorrow coursed through her veins. She wanted this to end. Everything. Every bit of hatred and anger that spread through the Fae like wildfire through a dry forest. They deserved happiness.

She deserved happiness, and it wasn't fair they weren't allowed to have it. After all she had been through, after all she had given up, she was still stuck here waiting for the moment when her life would begin again.

"Ethniu," she called out, "I need your guidance. He is so much like his grandfather, warlord more than politician, that I do not know what his next step will be."

Silence was her answer. Sorcha opened her eyes and glanced around the grove which had fallen so quiet. Ethniu had disappeared.

A cricket strummed a tentative tune, growing louder when it

realized nothing would speak again. It was as if the meeting had never occurred.

Cold air brushed across her skin, lifting the tiny hairs until Sorcha rubbed at her arms. The Fomorian had been far more unsettling than the Tuatha dé Danann.

What did that mean? Was she so unsettled by her own people?

"Yes." She let the word fly into the wind, in case Ethniu was listening to her thoughts. "I am."

All she knew was there was now a step to take. A beginning to the end in the form of a sword and a cliff.

She had to find it.

"I'm not telling you, girl. Off with you!"

"I healed you, Cian! You must pay with something."

He blew air at her, flabs of skin turning bright red in anger. "If I had known the payment for healing would betray my master, then I would have gone elsewhere!"

"You're not betraying him! Stop being dramatic."

"I am! You don't want that sword for just anything, I know you girl." He waggled a finger at her. "You're up to something."

"I am not."

"Yes you are."

"I'm sorry, did you somehow learn to read minds while you were off on your adventure? If I tell you I'm not up to anything, then I'm not!"

Oona opened the door to the kitchen with a loud crash. Her arms were full of carrots, so large they piled nearly above her head. "Are you two arguing again?"

"Bartering," Sorcha corrected. "Do you need help?"

"No, dearie, I'm just dropping these off before I go back out. Those dwarves grow the most impressive vegetables!"

She dumped her armload in the corner of the room with a loud bang. Dusting her hands on her skirts, she turned back to them and shrugged.

"Do they?" Sorcha asked. "Strange, I thought gnomes were renowned for gardening."

Cian hopped up to smack her shoulder. "We are!"

"You made nothing so impressive. I wonder if size difference matters?"

"Excuse me?"

She'd never seen the gnome look so angry. His face turned tomato red, and every roll jiggled as he held himself in check.

Peals of laughter filled the room. Oona leaned against the table and wiped tears from her eyes. "Do you think it's because he's so small, dearie?"

"Well the height difference certainly makes me consider that the dwarves, with a few extra inches, may have a significant advantage."

"It's a good thing to be closer to the earth!" Cian shouted. "That's where all the plants are!"

"I'll stop teasing if you tell me where it is."

"Absolutely not."

"Oona? Have you ever heard the joke about the gnome and the dwarf who met the same lovely elven lady? She said she would only sleep with one, but that it all depended on how large the faeries was. So, both men turned and pulled down their trousers—"

"Enough!" Cian shouted.

Oona looked as though she might burst. Giggles shook her form until her wings rattled. "What is it that he's hiding from you, dearie?"

"I want to know where Eamonn is keeping the Sword of Light."

"In the treasury, love. It's the safest place for it."

"Oona!" Cian shouted. "The girl is up to something! Don't tell her where it is!"

"Thank you, Pixie." Sorcha dropped a kiss to her cheek as she passed. "That's exactly what I wanted. Cian, if you follow me I will drop you in a bin you won't be able to climb out of."

"You wouldn't dare!"

"Try me. I'm all too happy to see what happens when you stuff an angry gnome in a barrel."

"Fine then! You can handle Eamonn when he finds you."

She absolutely would. The man might be intimidating, but he knew what she was like when she wanted something. Sorcha didn't know how to stop.

She left the kitchen with a smile on her face. One step closer to her next goal. Life was turning around.

In the cold quiet of the hall, she took a deep breath and reached deep into the well of power inside her. It still felt unnatural. Almost as though there was something else inside her, a woman she didn't quite know yet but could feel.

"Ancestors?" she asked. "I need to know where the treasury is."

They didn't answer her immediately. The longer she remained in the castle, the more they saw fit to leave her alone. Sometimes she went days without feeling their hands on her skirts.

The ghosts were kind, but odd. They didn't react to things the way normal people did. A tea kettle shrieked, and they flew out of the room in a panic. Swords striking against each other would invigorate them to beg Sorcha to train. Horses pawing the ground almost made the ancestors visible.

She had yet to discover the key to what frightened them and what they liked.

The halls were quiet this time of day. Every dwarf in the area dedicated their attention to finishing the castle as soon as possible. Eamonn was in the training yard with those who were working and Bran, who had shown up again.

Sorcha grinned. The Unseelie continued to say he didn't like them all that much, and that they were more work than they were worth. Yet, here he was. This time training with the dwarves and teaching them all the ways to fight dirty.

A voice whispered in her ear, "The Unseelie throws them to the dirt and laughs."

"He's teaching them how to fight his way."

"The Seelie are honorable in their battles. This dark newcomer is not."

"Is war honorable?" Sorcha turned down a dark hallway. She picked her way over the cracks and craters left by a battle long ago. "I have never seen a battle where the soldiers took the time to be polite."

"There is an etiquette to fighting."

"And I'm supposed to place a napkin in my lap before eating, yet I rarely do."

Sorcha didn't have time for the druids to whisper their opinions in her ear. She didn't want to be distracted while wandering the castle. The Sword of Light was far more important than debating the properties of war.

"Is the treasury this way?" she asked.

"Yes."

"How far?"

"To the right and down the stairs."

"It's in the dungeon?" She had only seen the dark underbelly of the castle once. The memories of screaming victims left imprints. She had left when their screams became too much for her.

"It is beneath the dungeon."

"There's further to go?"

The voice chuckled. "The castle stretches deep into the heart of the mountain. You will find much within its belly."

"Well that's not ominous at all," she muttered.

The ragged edges of ripped vines hung in front of the dungeon. Plants were already taking back the areas where Eamonn and his men had slipped through. Moss covered the footprints they left behind, only the faintest hint of a divot revealing she was still in the same doorway.

Mist curled out of the opening. Sluggish and thick, it was more magic and ghostly essence than water.

A blast of cold air rushed from the bowels of the dungeons, bringing with it the echoing call of screams.

"I don't want to go down there," she said.

"It's the only way."

"Why would Eamonn put the sword in the most terrifying place?"

"No one goes into the dungeons."

"No one but foolish women who want to help," Sorcha corrected. "After all, why else would any sane person walk through this haunted place?"

"You traveled through the Unseelie court."

She shuddered. "Yes, I did. And it was eerily similar to this place."

"The Unseelie gather souls like gemstones. They let them wander through their dark castle hallways so they never truly die. They like to watch the specters relive their death over and over again."

"Of course they do. That fits with all the things I remember," she said as she brushed aside a vine and started down the long stairwell.

Each step squelched underneath her booted feet. The moss covered steps were dangerously slippery, but no railing guided her way. Instead, Sorcha placed her hands on the walls and made her way while holding her breath.

Slipping and falling would end poorly. No one would know where she was, other than Cian and Oona. She didn't see them often enough for them to raise the alarm.

She repeated all the ways she could help a head injury to herself. "Check the pupils to ensure they are not dilated. If they are, keep the patient awake for as long as possible. Wrap the wound with white fabric so the bleeding will stem, and to create an easy way to monitor any potential wound. Pack with yarrow and mugwort to stem the bleeding and prevent internal bleeding."

She recited another directive on how to help injured people with each step. It calmed her. She remembered how to heal, and that meant she had not changed. Druid blood ran through her veins, faeries worked around her, but Sorcha was still the same person.

She could say it over and over again, but she wasn't certain how true the thought was.

Reaching the bottom, she pressed a hand against her chest in relief. "There. Now where do we go?"

A druid soul wrapped around her bicep. "Past the cells."

"Really?" Sorcha groaned. "I don't want to go all the way back there."

"You want to go to the treasury?"

"Yes."

"Do you want to climb the cliffs?"

"I don't think I know how to do that."

"Then you go forward."

Sighing, she started forward with her shoulders set. If she had to walk by all those deranged souls, she would. But she refused to look as if she was afraid.

A clanging started up as soon as she moved. The souls liked to throw stones, rattled their cages, anything they could do to get her to look at them.

Sorcha wasn't sure if the others could see them. Eamonn hadn't reacted when a faerie soul who's jaw hung limp from its socket billowed through him. She had seen it, gasping in shock and horror.

He had looked at her as if she had gone insane. Sorcha knew what she had seen, the green glowing light of the dead man hadn't been magic. It was the fiber of what made him live.

Souls shouldn't pass through solid bodies.

She told herself not to look. The cells weren't filled with real people, these were the last remaining pieces of souls that replayed over and over again. She could do nothing to help them.

But she looked. Sorcha glanced over at the nearest cell and immediately regretted her decision. A dryad, masculine and covered in bark, grinned at her. There was a gaping hole where his heart should be and sap oozed down his skin in tiny rivers.

"Hello, pretty girl," he said, the muscles on his face twitching. "Want to help a man out?"

"You're dead," she told him. "You have no place in the land of the living."

"It is my job to remind people like you what waits for them at the end of the dying light. Join me. Share your beauty and I will save you from the darkness."

"Be gone."

A druid pressed its ghostly against her spine, smelling like pine and earth. "Weaver, use your magic."

Could she? She looked over at the spirit of the faerie and wondered just how far her power stretched. She could compel him to keep his mouth shut.

But there were better things to do.

The ghostly guidance of her ancestors helped pull thread from her flaxen magic. She spun it in her mind and wove it around the thread of the dryad spirit. Tugging lightly, her fingers danced in the air.

His eyes widened. "What are you doing?"

Sorcha didn't know. Her magic and everything she was capable of felt new and shiny. Fingers gracefully swaying in the air, she mimicked sewing a thread through a tapestry.

"I release you from this realm," she said. The magic needle between her fingers dipped. "Go home to your ancestors and family. Tell them of your journey and adventures, feel peace in the comfort of their arms."

"How?" The spirit looked down at his arms which were slowly losing form. "This is impossible."

"You have earned the right to death, warrior. Find your eternity."

"What have you done?" He looked her in the eye, horror and fear glimmering in their depths.

"I have released you."

"Thank you."

He dissolved into thin air. She felt the pull of his soul disappearing even as the energy left her own body. Every time she controlled a faerie, she felt it deep in her gut.

"You did well," the druid whispered in her ear. "Far better than expected."

Sorcha didn't respond. Controlling even the remnants of a soul felt wrong. It was the reason she was in this dungeon. Preventing others from controlling the free will and mind of faeries meant more to her than life itself.

And then she used such power herself.

The floor grew slick with moss and algae. The souls shook the bars of their prisons, screaming their rage and anger into the air until Sorcha's headache blossomed again. She did not stop and help any of the others.

"There," the voice proclaimed. "The treasure room is ahead."

She saw the door now. Gemstone encrusted hinges fairly glowed in the dim light. A sweeping movement had recently disturbed the dust on the floor.

The door handle was molded into the shape of a snake. It reared up with an open mouth, waiting for her to place a hand upon its metal surface. Gritting her teeth, Sorcha tentatively grasped the silver metal and pulled the door open.

Faint light filtered through slits on the walls which let salty air stir the room beyond. Roots hung from the ceiling, tangled and gnarled. Bats squeaked above her. Sorcha could just barely make out their small, fuzzy forms.

Graceful archways were carved with legends and myths, Tuatha dé Danann battling back beasts. Hallways split off from the main chamber, suggesting rooms upon rooms of ancient knowledge and treasure.

She was not here for the riches.

"Where is it?" she asked the druid souls.

"Clasped in the hands of the most ancient king."

"Which king?"

"Walk towards the center."

Movement in the shadows caught her eye. She glanced over to see the ghostly specter of her grandfather. Beads embellished his full beard and a sparkle in his eye made her worried.

"Grandfather," she acknowledged.

"Are you certain this is the path you wish to take?"

"There are many ways to alter the future. I wish to walk the path with the least death."

"Then you have chosen correctly. Towards the back of the room is my own tomb. You will find the sword in my corpse's hands."

"You really are dead?" Balor seemed like he was impossible to kill.

"Even the most ancient of beings must die, my dear child."

A stiff breeze passed through him, and he faded away into green light. Sorcha took a deep steadying breath and made her way across the wide antechamber.

The tomb was relatively simple for a god who had made such an impact. A rectangular stone with a plain cover. No carvings marked him as anything other than one of many soldiers who had died in this land.

For that, Sorcha felt her heart soften towards Balor the great. She ran her hand over the top, noting the crumbled stone at her feet.

"You chose a plain coffin?" she asked.

"It is not my place to ask for grandeur in death."

"You made a good choice."

"I like to think so."

Perhaps she was more similar to her grandfather than she gave herself credit for. Sorcha leaned her weight into the cover and pushed hard. It groaned, scraped, screamed in her ears until it fell from its base and crashed upon the floor. The heavy stone cracked in two.

King Balor lay with hands crossed over his chest. A golden crown circled his skull while all the flesh had withered away long ago. Skeletal hands clutched the hilt of the Sword of Light.

"Why would he put it with you?" she asked. "This is not your sword and giving it to you would anger Nuada."

"Nuada does not know. And if someone was searching for the Sword of Light, they would not look in my grave."

He had a point. She wouldn't have looked in Balor's tomb for it was far more likely he would raise from the grave than hold the legendary Sword of Light. His brittle fingers wrapped around the hilt, gemstones glittering on each skeletal finger.

"Do I—" she hesitated and gestured towards his corpse, "pull it out?"

"It won't hurt." Amusement warmed her grandfather's voice.

"I don't want to break anything."

"What harm could you possibly do to my body? I'm dead."

"Good point."

It still felt wrong to touch his corpse. Swallowing hard, she reached out to touch the dust covered hands. Mummified skin slid off the smooth bones at her touch, sloughing off like parchment paper piled too high. She gagged.

"I didn't expect you to have such a weak stomach, granddaughter."

"Have you touched a corpse before?"

"Many times."

"I don't want to know why."

His bones creaked as she pulled back the fingers, snapping and cracking until one hand released its hold. She gently set it aside while her stomach muscles clenched.

"Don't think about the corpse moving," she said. "The body is dead, the soul is what makes it move."

"Are you reassuring yourself?"

"Hush."

She peeled back the second hand, wincing when one of the fingers broke off between hers. This was not how she wanted to find the sword. Why had Eamonn hidden it so thoroughly?

The wolf's mouth gleamed in the dim light, rubies dripping like blood from its jaws. Magic swirled around the blade. Tendrils of mist too thick to be water coiled around it like snakes.

She didn't want to touch the cursed blade. Nuada may have been a strong enough faerie to handle such magic, but she had no desire for it to touch her life. Steeling herself, she grasped the hilt and pulled it from the tomb.

It was heavier than she expected. The sheer power of the sword weighed her down until her arms shook and the tip touched the ground.

Her biceps quaked. Did she want to throw the sword over the edge of the cliff? She could take it with her instead, force them all to bend a knee to Eamonn and stop the war now. There didn't need to be any more fighting. It could end with her.

"The future hangs in the balance," Balor mumbled. "It is your choice now. Destroy the sword, use it, or throw it away for later generations."

She saw the threads of magic wrapping around her. Unlike her own woolen threads, these were coarse and improperly spun. They weren't right, and they couldn't control her.

She snapped the threads hanging onto her mind and straightened. "Where is the cliff where Ethniu waits?"

"There is an opening to the waters below." Balor pointed down a hall near her. "Do not fall."

"I don't plan on it."

The sword suddenly felt much heavier. It dragged on the ground, sharp tip sparking red hot embers as it screeched across the stone. She did not stop even though the sound made her ears bleed.

"I don't care if you want to stay," she growled at the blade. "You've caused enough trouble for me and mine. Wait for the next desperate generation."

Sorcha swore the sword grew even heavier. Gripping the hilt with two hands, she threw her back into carrying it and pulled it down the hall where light filtered into the cave.

Salt spray coated her skin long before she reached the edge. The salt stung the scrapes on her arms from the thorns she battled in the garden and filled her mouth with the bitter taste. Waves crashed and foam flooded the front of the cave.

Sorcha did not hesitate this time, flexed her arms, and heaved the sword over the edge. It spun wildly in the air, rubies shining sunlight in her eyes.

Just before it hit the surf, an arm shot out of the waves. Graceful fingers caught the hilt of the sword, holding it aloft for a few moments before sinking back into the depths.

"And good riddance," she muttered, kicking a stone into the surf for good measure.

She froze when Eamonn's voice rang out behind her.

"What have you done?"

CHAPTER NINE
The Invitation

Eamonn watched her heave the sword over the edge and felt his resolve shatter into a thousand pieces. His grandfather's sword, his legacy, now gone.

He'd seen the hand raise from the waves to grasp the blade. If she had simply thrown it into the sea, he might have recovered it. But he knew the claw-tipped fingers. A Fomorian had swayed her and taken the relic for itself.

"What have you done?" he asked.

"What you should have done a long time ago."

"That sword was the only assurance we had at winning this war!"

"Do you really believe that?" She spun on him, the cloud of her red hair billowing in her anger. Her cheeks stained red as she glared him down.

His woman was a fearsome creature when she grew angry. Almost enough that he didn't want to scold her, to shake her hard enough that her teeth rattled. Why had she done this? Now of all times?

"Sorcha, that was a relic of the Tuatha dé Danann! It can force Fionn to his knees. We will win with that blade on our side!"

"And you were using it against your own people. I will not stand for it!"

Her words flew at him, tearing at his heart and shoving him a step backwards. "You think I used that against our people?"

"Perhaps you were not aware that you use it, I told Cait that—"

"Cait?" He shook his head, running his fingers through the loose crop of his hair. "Sorcha, Cait doesn't want to be here!"

"None of them do!"

"Is this what you think of me?"

It all made sense now. He had been busy, there were too many things for him to oversee. He understood that she wanted to be with him. Eamonn missed her with every fiber of his being, but he could not allow his focus to wander.

Every time he was near her, his soul drifted. He wanted to touch the beloved locks of her hair, trace the outline of her stubborn pout, ease the nightmares he knew plagued her.

But he couldn't. He saw his mistake in pulling away.

Eamonn went to her, clutching her cold hands and pressing them against his heart.

"A chuisle mo chroí," he breathed. "Pulse of my heart, the folly is mine. I have done nothing to control the dwarves. They wish to be deep within their mountain halls with no one to tell them what to do. There are plenty of soldiers who wish to fight Fionn, and those who do not. I would never force a soldier onto a battlefield. That is a certain way to kill them."

"Then why did you fight Fionn when I asked you not to?"

He smoothed the tangled curls away from her face. "I am a general, and I make mistakes. I thought a small war party would convince him that I was not retreating. I was wrong."

"What did you plan to do with the sword?"

"I would have forced Fionn to abdicate the throne. He would have no choice when the sword of Nuada commanded him."

Her green eyes searched his, questions forming within their emerald depths. He knew her well enough to expect the question before she voiced it. "Is that really how you want to win?"

No. He wanted to battle until his brother fell onto his knees. He wanted to shred Fionn's face, strip everything from him and send him out to the wilds.

"I can't hurt him," he admitted. "He is my brother. My blood."

She tucked herself into his embrace, her tiny cold hands pressed against his chest. "I couldn't harm my siblings either."

"And now I have no choice."

"You still do. Eamonn, we can do this together. He doesn't have to fight us!"

He shook his head. "You don't want to get involved with faerie politics, Sorcha. Trust me."

"Why not? You were raised among them! You must be able to prepare us for what might come."

"That is what you want?"

He didn't want it. A part of his wounded soul never wished to return to the castle where they had stripped him of all rights. They despised him, feared him, hated him because he was no longer the handsome man he had once been.

Eamonn knew the dangers of the court. They would latch onto Sorcha with sharp teeth and claws, desperately trying to drag her down into their bitter anger at the world. His pure sunshine would slowly be corrupted.

He squeezed her tighter, holding her against his heart where she belonged. He wouldn't lose her. They wouldn't get their greedy hands on her as long as he drew breath.

She looked up at him, green eyes shimmering with tears. "Eamonn?"

"If this is the path you wish to walk, then I will walk beside you mo chroí."

"Then what do we do?"

"The correct way to address the king is to request an audience."

"That doesn't sound like something Fionn would respond to." Tiny wrinkles gathered between her eyes. "He seems more likely to ignore it, or deny that it ever reached him."

"Especially if it comes from me."

"What do you suggest?"

He arched a crystal brow. "Are you asking me for advice on how to approach this difficult situation?"

"Of course I am."

"You threw away the only relic which could have taken the throne from Fionn with no blood."

"Eamonn," she bit her lip. "I can control the Fae."

"You are the most beguiling creature I have ever met, but you cannot control everyone."

"I am a Weaver. I never told you what that meant. There is a particular kind of druid which can reach into a faerie's mind and order them to do whatever it is they please."

His mind raced through the old tales, the reasoning behind why they cast the druids from the Otherworld. "That is true?"

"Yes."

"And you can do it?"

"I can."

"You won't do it to me?" He only halfheartedly meant the words, although it was a slight concern. Sorcha had never shown any tendency to cajole faeries into doing what they didn't want to do.

"Eamonn," she scolded.

"I had to ask, mo chroí. Are you saying you can control Fionn?"

"If I'm close enough, I believe I might be able to. I tried in the dream when he visited me, but I wasn't fantastic at it. I did overpower him though."

"I imagine younger faeries are easier." Eamonn shook his head. "We are trained from a young age to shield our minds. Faeries do it naturally by the time we are adults. Too many of our kind can peek into others thoughts, it's easier to ensure that no one can pick up on what you're thinking."

"So that's why he was more capable than I."

"Have you practiced?"

"No."

"Not at all?" He could taste her lie upon the air. "Sorcha."

"Only a little! With Cait, who insisted I prove to her that I was actually a druid. That's all I've done."

"You need to practice far more than that if you plan to walk the halls of the Castle of Light."

He already knew the tactics he wished to take. Though he was still angry over the loss of the sword, this was no longer the end of all he knew. Sorcha was a hidden power in her own right, and one his brother might not suspect.

He would make her stronger than she ever imagined. They would train noon and night until she could control even him. Then, he would know for certain she was ready.

Sorcha must have recognized the calculating expression on his face. She shook her head and said, "No. Eamonn, whatever you are thinking, no. I will not be used as a tool to end this war."

"How else are we going to defeat him?"

"We will exhaust all other options before we force him to his knees."

He couldn't think of any other way which would seat him on the throne.

Eamonn knew she believed that faeries were good. He saw it every day as she healed their scrapes, ignored their quips and predisposed fear of her people. Even the dwarves, for all they had grown to tolerate her, whispered stories about her behind her back.

Sorcha didn't let any of it bother her. She went about her day giving and giving until she fell exhausted into bed. It was one thing he loved dearly about her and hated at the same time.

He wanted her safe and happy. The only way that would happen, was if he were king.

"What do you suggest?" he asked with a sigh.

"Let us speak to him first. What harm could there be?"

"Then I will send a missive." He released her from his arms and shook his head. "I cannot believe I'm allowing you to convince me to do such a thing."

"Why wouldn't we at least try?"

"He will ignore it. And then we will be back to sneaking you into the castle."

"If he ignores it, then I will train." The troubled wrinkles returned to her brow. "Though I would not choose such a course."

"Swear it."

"What?" She stared at him in shock.

"Give me your vow that if this fails, you will agree to do what I say to overthrow Fionn."

He held his breath, knowing without a doubt that she would argue. She always did.

But sometimes, Sorcha surprised him.

"I vow it."

Cool night air drifted over Sorcha's shoulders as she made her way down the stairs. She awoke to an empty bed with the sheets thrown back and the sheets cold. He had left, and she wasn't certain why.

Although, that wasn't entirely true. They had mended their ways after she threw the Sword of Light into the ocean. So she thought.

But he was still distant. She often caught him wrapped up in his own thoughts, staring off into the air even as the dwarves shouted and lifted their glasses to toasts.

As more faeries joined them, Eamonn retreated further and further into his own mind. It worried her. Was this partly Sorcha's fault? Had she unknowingly made all of this worse?

Her nightgown swished around her ankles, the white fabric fluttering in the wind as she stepped out of the stairwell and into the wide expanse of the great hall.

Moonlight streamed through the stained glass. The giant sun reflected on the stone, silver and cold thought it should have been warm.

Eamonn sat in the dark throne, his head resting on his fist.

She paused. How many times had she seen him sitting exactly the same way? He liked to be where people expected the most of him, even when no one was around.

Her stomach rolled with nerves, and she blew out a breath.

"It is late," she said, breaking the still quiet. "What plagues your thoughts?"

"Many things." His deep voice rumbled through her, sending shivers down her spine.

Eamonn never ceased to be both a sensual and terrifying creature at every turn. He wasn't like the other Fae. He moved in an otherworldly way, but he did not show the natural, lithe grace the others had.

It was why she loved him so much.

Love. It seemed strange that her heart had called out to him almost immediately upon meeting him. She didn't know if it was normal, perhaps not, but there had never been a question in her mind.

Once her stubborn heart decided it wanted him, she had no other road to travel. Where he went, so did she.

His fingers twitched, beckoning her to his side. Sorcha's footsteps made soft shushing sounds as she glided across the stone floors.

"It is late," she said with a soft smile. "We should be resting."

"I find it difficult to rest these days."

"Your mind is busy."

"Among other things." He patted his knee for her to perch upon.

She was so tiny, she could sit on his thigh and not worry about her weight or his discomfort. Sorcha found it easier to forget his size now that she was in his presence so much. But he was incredibly large compared to her.

His massive hand smoothed down her spine. "Nightmares have plagued my sleep."

"About?"

"I worry you did not make the correct choice. Fionn will come, ravage this land and these people, and I will lose again."

"We must have faith, my love." She rested her head against his shoulder. "I still believe there is a better way. That we can still change the path towards something more kind. We shape the future with our actions. I would have it be a good future."

He sighed. "You are right, but that does not mean I do not worry."

"No, I imagine it doesn't."

She worried about them as well. War put people on edge, forcing them to realize that their time walking the earth was limited.

No one was ready to die. Many years stretched out into their future. Years which could be filled with happiness and life. Family, animals, a small house where one might farm or grow crops. To have those years be questioned was no easy thing.

Sorcha lifted a hand, tucked it underneath the loose lapels of his shirt and rubbed his smooth chest. "You have gathered a capable group of people. It is admirable that you worry for them, but I believe they can take care of themselves."

"It is not just my people I worry about."

She heard the warble in his voice. "You're worried about me."

"I do not know what I would do if I lost you again."

"Would you fight for me?" She leaned back with a mischievous glint in her eye. "If Fionn stormed the castle and stole me away, my knight in shining armor?"

Eamonn did not want to tease. His brows furrowed, and he reached forward to stroke the high peak of her cheekbone. "If Fionn captures you, he will not keep you alive for long. You are one human, with a life that is unnecessary for his plans."

"He will not kill me."

"He will do much to get back at me."

"Eamonn!" She sighed in exasperation. "When are you going to put an end to this foolish battle? You're brothers, you should be able to work this out."

"Faeries do not work the same way as humans."

"No, but they should."

He chuckled. "Ah, my fierce love. You see the world with such a light in your heart. I wish I could."

"You can," she vehemently declared. "You just have to try."

"I am, mo chroí. I am."

He drew her into his arms and tucked her head underneath her chin. Crickets chirped their midnight song, and the air was no longer cool with him touching her. Sorcha dipped her fingers into a crevice of stone, chewing her lip as thoughts danced through her mind.

"You're thinking," he grumbled in her ear.

"I don't know how to help you."

"This is not something you can heal. Worry and anxiety are not physical wounds."

"I don't like it that I can't help you."

His heart beat against her ear, steady and strong. Each thump reminded her that he was alive, but their time was limited. That of all the things they had survived together, all the things they had suffered, they might still be cut short.

His fingers stroked through her hair. Sorcha smiled at the slight tugging, for she knew he was coiling individual strands around his fingers and unraveling them again.

"Why do you do that?" she asked.

"What?"

"You wrap my hair around your fingers over and over again."

"It helps me think."

"Does it?" Sorcha tucked her face into the hollow of his collarbone, grinning from ear to ear.

"Why, does it make you uncomfortable?"

"Not at all."

"Good," he rumbled. "I don't want to stop."

Sorcha would never forget moments like this. She didn't need wondrous declarations of love, romantic scenes in front of other faeries. She wanted a quiet evening hidden away from others where they could privately enjoy each other.

But there was much left unsaid.

"Are you mad at me?" she asked. "For the sword?"

"Mo chroí, there is too much going on in the world to say mad for long."

"Is that a yes?"

"I will always be a little angry about that. But I will never let it stand between us."

She swallowed hard and nodded. "If you say so."

"Sorcha," he groaned while rubbing her back. "What must I do? I will not let this stand between us, not when I know what life is like without it."

"Like a piece of you is missing?"

"I wasn't myself without you at my side. I do not wish to ever repeat that again."

"I wasn't the same either," she admitted. "I am far more giving when I know you will be there to stop me should I go too far. I didn't know what I could or not do while I was home. Even my father commented on it. That part of me was something I left here."

"I was cold," he replied. "Losing pieces of myself over and over again as a kind of punishment. I forgot there were people out there who loved me, who cared whether I lived or died."

"I've never felt this way about anyone before."

"The Tuatha dé Danann believe in soulmates. Do humans?"

"My mother did," Sorcha said with a soft smile. "She used to say I would meet someone who meant more to me than my own life."

"A wise woman."

"A good woman who died far too soon."

She felt the hitch in his breath as she mentioned death. Perhaps it was too soon, he was still worried about her. She shouldn't have said anything so dark.

His hands clenched on her shoulders. "The Tuatha dé Danann are not like humans. We do not have priests to marry us, nor chapels to ring bells."

"You know of that?" She tilted her head on his shoulder so she could stare up at his severe profile, outlined by moonlight. "Why were you gathering information about human marriages?"

"I tried to find a priest who we could safely bring into the Otherworld, but there were none near faerie circles for the past week. They do not seem to support the old ways."

"No, they avidly stay away from anything of the old religion. They don't believe in it." Sorcha wrinkled her nose. "Eamonn?"

"I want to keep you safe. If I die, you should have everything of mine without question."

Everything clicked into place. She lunged back, slapping her hands on his shoulders. "Are you asking me to marry you?"

"In a rather awful way, I suppose I am."

"You suppose?"

"Is this not the right way to do it?"

She groaned and tossed her head back to stare at the ceiling. "No, this is a horrible way to do it."

"What should I do?"

"Men get on their knees! They plan accordingly to ask a woman in a romantic way! They don't ask in the middle of the night because she happened to find him."

"I would have asked tomorrow morning, but now seemed like an opportune time."

"Did you even get me a ring?"

"A ring?" His brows furrowed. "Did I need one of those?"

"Generally."

"Then I ask we postpone this until I may ask in a more appropriate way."

Sorcha huffed out a breath, half laugh, half frustrated sigh. "Well, I already know what you're going to do now."

He reared back in shock. "Is this usually a surprise for women?"

"Sometimes we have an inclination that it may happen soon."

"You do not talk about marriage beforehand?"

"Some do, but many women are surprised when the man proposes."

"That sounds horrible," he scoffed. "Such a decision should be a mutual agreement. If it's a surprise, then how can the man ever be certain she didn't make her choice under duress?"

"I don't know."

"I will not do that to you." His lips set in a thin line of determination. "You know of my intentions now. I would like to marry you, and I apologize you were not aware of my thoughts. Please, take all the time you need to make your decision."

This man would be the death of her. She shook her head. "I know how I want to answer."

The alarm in his wide eyes nearly made her laugh in his face. "Well I'm uncertain I wish to know what such a quick response is."

"Do you think I will say no?"

"I never have any idea what you might say."

"Yes," she said immediately. "A thousand times yes."

"That I don't know what you'll say, or that you wish to marry me?"

"I will marry you in whatever way you wish. I do not need a priest, I am satisfied with the Fae tradition."

"That's much easier."

He sank his hand in her hair and pulled her forward for a kiss that rocked her soul. She gasped as his lips smoothed over hers, teeth and crystals nipping.

"I pledge my soul to you," he growled. "My heart, my mind, my life are now yours."

Somehow, she knew she was supposed to say the words. "I pledge my soul to you, my heart, my mind, and my life are now yours."

"Good," Eamonn called out. "Again!"

The young dwarves all stood in formation, squaring their shoulders and attempting to stand like he did. It was the sincerest form of flattery and one that did not escape his notice. The boys were learning fast. He wouldn't put them in a war soon, but they didn't need to know that.

Dwarves were talented in many areas of war. Their arms were strong from manual labor and lifting stone. Their punches were enough to cause Eamonn's teeth to crack. The right handed hook a few of them dealt made him see stars.

They were a better army than he remembered the Tuatha dé Danann being. Perhaps it was because they were so eager to learn.

Sorcha had forgiven him in the eyes of their people. She ate with him every night, scooped food from his bowl and stoked his arm when the others were looking. Although they were still learning their way around each other, the dwarves had relaxed.

When the king and queen were happy, so were their people.

"Raise arms!"

The dwarven boys and girls held their swords horizontal over their heads, freezing in place while waiting for his next order.

He held out just long enough for the weakest few to tremble.

"Attack!"

He paired them off in twos and threes. Individual sparring for those who were not confident in their abilities, and larger groups for those who had fought with him longer. Their parents trained in the afternoon.

He was slowly turning this castle into an army full of legendary warriors. Untried, but capable in every way he could make them.

Ghosts of the past haunted his steps. Eamonn couldn't shake the feeling that something bad would happen. He wanted to be present for as long as he could.

"Again!" he shouted.

They didn't need to train even more than they already did. These men and women were no longer children. They could step onto the battlefield confidently and know they could protect themselves.

"You work them too hard," Sorcha's soft voice echoed through his being. A shiver trailed down his spine, and he reminded himself to pay attention to his pupils.

"They need it."

"They need water and food."

The amusement he heard made him glance over his shoulder.

She wore a plain linen dress that hugged her arms and waist while leaving her legs free to move. The style was far more dwarven than he liked. But on her? It was magical.

Sorcha had taken to wearing her long curls free. They waved in the breeze and stretched towards him as if begging for his touch.

He groaned. "You are distracting me."

"That was precisely the point. Come, mo chroí. It's far past time for us to take our lunch."

"Our lunch?" He lifted a brow. "We do not have a lunch."

"We do now."

She lifted a small wicker basket. The lid was closed, revealing nothing but a small corner of red fabric.

"You brought me food?"

"I brought *us* a picnic. I thought we might disappear for the afternoon."

"I need to train the adults."

"They know how to fight, Eamonn." She ducked underneath the training ground fence and waltzed towards him. Her hand brushed against his chest, sending shivers down his spine once more. "They can practice without you for one day. Let us go and enjoy ourselves."

"Have we heard any response from Fionn?" The letter hung over him like a dark cloud.

"No, not yet."

"How much longer are we waiting until you begin your training?"

"Enough talk of work! Let us go and enjoy ourselves for the afternoon. It is the last warm day of the summer before the rains catch us. And then it will be winter, and we'll be stuck inside the castle all day!"

He felt time bearing down on his shoulders. He should be a king. His people needed him to drive them until they were better fighters than he.

But she wanted to play in the fields. The smile on her face was as tempting as a warm summer breeze.

Finally, he relented. "All right. Get out of the training yard while I finish up here."

"Hurry, please. I have plans for us."

"Plans?" He didn't like the wicked glint in her eyes. "Sorcha, what plans?"

"They're a surprise!"

"I don't like surprises."

He tried to catch the tail end of her dress as she whirled from him, but she was already gone. The woman was likely to be as much pixie as druid.

Eamonn growled in frustration, torn between duty and desire.

"Enough!" he shouted to his students. "We are done for the day!"

He expected complaints and worried noises. That was what he was used to from the soldiers in his previous company. The children did not make any sound he recognized.

Casting a calculating glance over them all, he saw how tired they were. Their shoulders slumped forward and they let their swords hang in the dirt if they hadn't dropped them entirely. Their eyes were drooping, a few even listing to the side.

Not a single one had complained throughout the entire training.

His heart warmed. "You've all done well today! You've earned your supper. Enjoy your afternoon with your family and forget training for the time."

"Are you going off with your lady friend?" One of the boys called out.

"I am."

The boy was nearing his teenage years. He might even travel with Eamonn's company if the war came to that. For a dwarf, he was tall and broad. His face was handsome, beard already thick and lush.

While the others left the training yard in a hurry, this handsome child stayed behind. Eamonn recognized a youngling who wished to speak. He lingered and waited for the dwarf to come to him.

Like a wild horse he wished to break, he remembered Sorcha proclaiming.

"My king?" the boy asked.

Eamonn glanced at him but did not speak.

"I have a question for you that I did not want to ask my Pa."

This had already gotten off to a bad start. Eamonn propped himself up against the fence, crossed his arms firmly over his chest, and tried not to appear worried. "Go on with it."

"It's just…" The boy scuffed his feet in the dirt. "There's a girl I like, you see. She's one of the peat faeries that comes in here now and then. I thoughts, seeing as you and your lady aren't the same species, that maybe you'd be able to help. I don't even know how to talk to her."

The tips of Eamonn's ears heated. Was the boy asking him for relationship advice? Him?

Years ago he might have been capable of giving the dwarf good advice. Women had flocked to him just because he would be king and was as handsome as his twin. For some, the fact that they were twins had been most of the appeal.

Now? It had been centuries since he had even thought about a healthy relationship with a woman. Not until Sorcha came along.

Clearing his throat, he shifted his weight onto the opposite leg and gave the question good thought. "You like this girl already?"

"Yes?"

"Is that a question or do you know you're interested in her?"

"I know, sir."

"How do you know if you haven't talked to her yet?"

"Well," the dwarf scuffed a path of grass with his toe. "She's awful pretty."

Eamonn nodded wisely. "That is why most of us find ourselves enamored."

"And she's smart!" The boy appeared insulted to be categorized with all the other men who found themselves infatuated. "I've seen her figure out problems that none of the other dwarves could figure out."

"She sounds like a good catch."

"She is."

"You must talk to her."

That blew all the wind out of the dwarf's sails. His shoulders sagged and his chin dipped towards his chest. "I don't know how."

"I didn't know how with Sorcha either."

"You didn't?"

"Not at all. The first few times we spoke, I picked fights with her. Every time I opened my mouth, something rude would come out. I didn't know if my tongue was broken or if I would become a mute."

The boy snickered. "So what did you do?"

"I forced myself to keep talking. I figured that eventually, something nice would come out."

"Did it?"

"It did. And once that first sentence was said, I could talk to her without hesitating."

The boy's lips screwed to the side as he pondered the revelation. "So you're saying I should just talk to her?"

"It's a good place to start."

"What if she doesn't like me?"

"Then you keep talking. Be polite, listen to what she has to say, and she'll come around. If she still doesn't like you, then respect that. We can't win them all, boy."

Eamonn watched as the boy's face turned bright red. He stammered something about needing to find his friends and bolted from the training yard. Small puffs of dust kicked up underneath his heels.

He felt her gaze on his back, the cause of his own trials and tribulations. Sighing, he turned. "How much did you hear?"

"Enough," she said with a soft smile. "Just keep talking?"

"That's how I won you over."

"I don't remember you talking much at all."

She had a point. Eamonn pointed to his crystal eye with exaggerated care. "I talk with my eyes."

"Sure you do." Her laughter was music to his ears.

It was why he had to stay away from her so much. He would give anything to hear her laugh over and over again until the world ended.

Eamonn swung his leg over the fence and landed lightly on his feet. "So, where are we going for this surprise?"

"I can't tell you, that would ruin it."

"I don't like surprises."

Her eyes sparkled. "So you've said."

She was a siren, calling him to crash upon her rocks. And he fully intended to.

Eamonn followed her as if in a dream. He was a lucky man, for all that she annoyed him or overstep her bounds. Few women would walk into the Otherworld and not grow to despise the strange creatures or their world.

Sorcha thrived here. She stood straighter than she had when she first arrived to the isle. Her eyes sparkled with life and a vivacity that he knew were from helping his people. She showed love to everyone she passed with bright smiles, blown kisses, and a gentle touch that shook the foundation of his being.

She was a gift he did not deserve.

They walked out of the castle onto the cliffs at the back. The sun was weak this time of year, the usually unbearable heat tempered by a crisp autumn breeze.

Salt spray stung his cheeks, but invigorated his soul. Eamonn had always loved the ocean. It was the only part of his banishment to Hybrasil that made it slightly tolerable.

Seagulls soared overhead, their screaming cries quiet compared to the hush of waves crashing against the shore far below them. He hadn't realized the cliff on the other edge of the castle was so dangerous.

"Here we are!" she exclaimed. "Isn't it lovely?"

"It is."

He was no longer looking at the surf or the stunning cloud formations. He was staring at her.

The wind brushed her curls over her cheeks, her full lips parted in appreciation of the beauty all around them. The half smile he so loved quirked her lips to the side. He'd seen them frown, grin, speak rapidly, everything that a person could do. And he would never stop watching her until the day she died.

Her linen dress fluttered in the delicate breeze. She had to be cold, but she didn't shiver at all. Instead, she caught him staring and laughed.

Sorcha lifted her arms to the side, dropped her head back, and let the sun play across her face. The wind scooped underneath her arms, trailing along the length of her sides. She was beautiful, wild, and all his.

Unable to resist, he stepped behind her and followed the path the wind had taken. The dip of her waist was so intriguing although he could not understand why. His fingers spread over her belly and he stooped to breathe in her scent.

Strawberries and sunshine. She always smelled the same, no matter what she had gotten into that day. How was it possible for a woman to work all day and still smell like sugar?

She spread her fingers over his. Each tiny imprint seared through the back of his hand and deep through the crystals that spread throughout his body like wildfire.

They were growing again. He wasn't certain to tell her or if he even should. She would only worry.

Eamonn had always known that the crystals would continue to harm him. He had never truly thought about how they worked. They pieced him back together when he was injured and that was enough.

Now, he wondered just how far they would heal. A poisoned blade would sink into his bloodstream and spread throughout his entire body. Would the crystals follow that path? Would he be reduced to little more than a statue?

He rested his head atop hers, stooping slightly to accommodate for her small size, and focused on what was around him. There were so many things to be thankful for. He would be a fool to not appreciate them while he had them.

He sighed, stirring the sprigs of red curls. "What did you have planned?"

"A lunch with just the two of us."

"It sounds wonderful."

"I had hoped it would be." She looked up and caught him with her gaze. "You'll have to let go of me."

He didn't want to. She belonged within his embrace and nowhere else. But he also understood these weren't rational thoughts. With a sigh, he released her.

She sank onto her knees and opened her woven basket. The scrap of red fabric was a blanket she spread across the ground, patting gently to remind him that he could also sit.

It all seemed strange.

Eamonn frowned, but sat down next to her. "We're eating on the ground?"

"Yes."

"There are perfectly good tables within the castles."

"Don't you remember taking women out into the wilds? To eat among the birds?"

"Vaguely." He leaned back on an elbow and hooked his ankles. "That was back when I thought I could woo a woman with pretty words."

"Really?" Sorcha made herself busy sorting through the basket, but he could see she was intrigued. "Were you quite dashing?"

"All faerie men think they are poets."

"I cannot imagine you as a poet," she said with a chuckle.

He was almost insulted. Plucking a blade of grass from nearby, he stuck it between his lips and stared her down. "Why's that?"

"You don't seem the kind of man who would take the time to string together words. You're more the type to back a woman into a corner and kiss her senseless."

"It's what I did with you."

"Precisely."

She thought she knew him so well. He almost wanted to let her believe it of him, for that was who he was now. Eamonn had become that man after three hundred years in faerie courts. His father once said that men had to sow their wild oats long before they became intelligent royals.

"I trained as a general my entire life, but I was not always on the battlefield."

"You weren't?" Her jaw dropped. "I thought you weren't like your brother."

"We both went through similar training when we were children and young men."

"How young?"

"Three or four hundred years, give or take a few centuries I cannot remember."

"What did you do then?" She gave up on the basket and turned completely towards him. Her legs crossed, skirts akimbo as she leaned forward for a story. "Tell me, Stone King, what kinds of poetry would you use to woo a woman?"

"I have no use for those words any longer."

"Of course you do! I want to hear them Eamonn."

He didn't want to speak them. His ears heated, turning bright red under her scrutiny. "You'd laugh."

She clapped her hands on her thighs in disappointment. "So you aren't good with words then. You'd wax on about her cornflower eyes and laughter that sounds of bells, wouldn't you? The same poetry every man thinks will win a woman's heart."

"You know these tricks?"

"Every man has tried to use them on my sisters or I." Sorcha rolled her eyes. "They never work."

"You compare me to human men?"

"What else should I compare you to? I haven't heard any faerie men recite poetry."

He pursed his lips. She thought he was similar to any man she had ever had before? It was a pity these humans were so pathetic.

Eamonn grabbed her hand so quickly that she gasped. Her eyes wide, she stared at him as he brought her knuckles to his lips.

"When I was young, I would have told you that I heard your voice in the song of the sea. That in your absence, the scent of strawberries filled me with yearning for your hair, your lips, the white moons of your fingertips." He stared down at her hand in his, stroked her palm gently with his nails.

"Eamonn—"

"I am no longer the faerie prince with soft words. My poetry for you is a vow. The world may burn down around us, but nary a flame shall touch thy beloved flesh. The ocean may swallow the land, but I shall be your ship and feed you sweet air. A sword may try to cut you down, but I will bear all your wounds. I have lived a thousand years in the dark, waiting for the rays of your sunlight."

Her ragged breaths filled his heart with a longing he could not explain. He desired her, but not her body. He wanted her thoughts, her dreams, her wishes, her future. Every bit of her was his, and he wanted to mark it all.

"That was beautiful," she murmured.

"I told you all faerie men are poets at heart."

"That was not poetry. That was *you*."

Their gazes caught, and he forgot what they were even speaking of. Her eyes blazed, singing her love. He wished he was as good as the best faerie poet.

She deserved every sonnet he could write. Those days were long gone, but Eamonn wished he could go back. Even for a few moments.

Clearing his throat, he nodded towards the basket. "What did you bring, mo chroí?"

"Oh." She dragged it towards her. "A little something I thought you'd appreciate."

Sorcha pulled out a loaf of bread, warm steam still puffing from its surface. A small jar of honey and cream, more for him than her. He knew she didn't like the sweet gold. And finally, she pulled out a small wrapped bundle that she revealed to hold fresh strawberries.

He leaned forward and pulled one out of her hand. "Where did you get these?"

"I asked Cian for a favor."

"He grew you strawberries out of season?"

She shrugged. "I might have pushed for them."

"You wicked thing." He bit into the soft flesh, savoring the sweet taste that danced over his tongue. Nearly as lovely as her, but not quite so satisfying.

He felt her eyes on him. The memories they shared lit a fire deep in his belly.

"Are you not eating?" he asked.

"I was enjoying the view."

It was almost too easy to pluck a strawberry from her grasp and hold it to her lips. "Bite."

For once in her life, she did not argue. He nearly groaned as her white teeth bit into the red flesh, soft lips barely touching his fingertips.

As the first time, a small trickle of wine red juice trickled from her mouth and traveled over her chin. It ran down the long column of her neck to nestle in the hollow of her collarbone.

"I thought I would die the first time you ate strawberries," he groaned. "Now I am certain of it."

"Why is that?"

She knew. She had to know why he was so enamored with a woman covered in his favorite taste. Woman and forbidden fruit.

A growl vibrated in his throat. He pushed her until she lay on her back, hair splayed out like a sunset. Leaning down, he licked from the valley of her neck to the base of her chin.

"You are a dangerous woman."

"Am I?"

"You consume my thoughts."

"You poor man."

"I cannot even train my soldiers without wondering what you are doing, who you are with—" He fisted his hand in her linen skirt, tugging hard enough to make her gasp. "What you are wearing."

"Likely hand-me-downs."

"The most tantalizing clothes I have ever seen on a woman."

"I borrowed them."

"As long as you wear them, I don't care," he moaned. His fingers moved, bunching the fabric in his palm so that it rose higher and higher over her milky white thighs. "You could wear a blood soaked cloak and I would still want you."

"Oh, don't say that my love, I may test you."

"Test all you want, but not today."

He pressed his lips against her shoulder, moving the fabric of her dress as he went. He knew she enjoyed the way his crystals scraped against her skin. The tiny movements she made were the ultimate victory.

Eamonn had always thought a woman in the throes of passion to be a wondrous sight. He spent centuries learning every inch, every trick to pleasure them. But each one was a unique pearl. A book that must be read, correctly and frequently to fully understand. He was a very attentive student.

Letting the rough edge of his lower lip drag just below the rise of her collarbone, he breathed onto the damp trail he had made.

She whimpered.

"I love how sensitive you are," he said while pressing kisses lower and lower. "No matter what I do, you react."

"You've done little to disappoint."

"I am flattered."

He trailed his hand up the rise of her hip, pressed his palm flat against her belly, and slid between her breasts. Front ties held her dress together. He sent a prayer to whatever god had looked out for him.

"Eamonn," she gasped. "What if someone sees?"

"Let them look, mo chroí. They will not bother us on the one afternoon we have together."

She must have planned this the entire time. The knots were loose at the front and came free easily. He parted the fabric and bared her to his eyes.

"Exquisite," he said. "It was the first thing I noticed about you."

"My breasts?" She sounded almost angry.

Eamonn shook his head and bit his lip. "No, mo chroí."

He smoothed his hands over the pale, smooth skin of her shoulders. He dug in just enough to squeeze her muscles. The fine bones captivated him.

"You are a storm of a soul contained in a glass bottle. So fragile and easily harmed, yet powerful in every other way." His shoulders rocked in a shudder. "You take my breath away."

She clutched at his biceps, tiny nails digging into his skin with sudden fervor. "Eamonn, do *something*."

"As my lady commands."

He dipped down, nibbling at the delicate swells laid out before him like a banquet. She writhed beneath him. He knew she was ready, but he was not done tormenting his own little prize. Not just yet.

Reaching for the woven basket, he uncorked the bottle of honey. She gasped as the soft liquid spilled over her chest.

"What are you doing?"

"Enjoying the meal you've provided."

"What?" Her voice sounded hazy. "I didn't—"

"Hush, Sorcha."

His tongue swirled through the golden elixir, coating his tongue with sugar and woman. She had no way of knowing what honey meant to the Fae. That this substance was as much an aphrodisiac as it was food.

He sucked a rosy bud into his mouth, spreading the honey until he couldn't tell where she began and where the sweet started. It didn't matter in the end. She shivered underneath him. Her thighs dropped open, and he filled the void with a surge of motion that brought her tighter against him.

Releasing his prize, he turned to the other with a growl that rivaled an animal. He could hardly believe how much he desired her. His heart throbbed his chest, lungs heaved with movement, and he strained against the tight fabric of his breeches. It had never been this way with a woman before.

Only her.

She arched her back, demanding his attention with a subtle movement he understood. Her body was a language he was dedicated to learning.

He brushed her skirts to the side and slid a hand between them. Her core throbbed, slick and satin soft as he had always remembered it. His entire body shook with the force holding him in check. Groaning, he released her and shook his head.

"You turn me into little more than an untrained boy! I should torment you for hours."

"I would surely die!"

They were the words he had hoped to hear. Eamonn fumbled desperately with the ties of his breeches, freeing himself with a relieved sigh.

He would need to be mindful of his crystals. He reminded himself every time that she was delicate, her skin easily breakable, her bones fragile. But she dug her nails into his shoulders and moaned for him to hurry.

How was a man to keep his head?

He flexed his hips and eased into the slick heat of her. They both threw their heads back in ecstasy. She moaned his name, and he clenched the muscles of his jaw so hard he heard his teeth creak.

Sorcha was home. Every inch of her, whether he was inside her, beside her, or so far away that he could no longer catch the scent of her on the wind. Home had been a place he had fought and searched for. Centuries had passed with many people and places passing by.

Eamonn had never realized home could be a person. He hadn't known how a single smile, a curl wrapped his finger, a graceful arch of a foot could change his life forever.

He moved, slowly drawing them both closer and closer to the peak.

But it wasn't right, not yet.

He leaned down and smoothed the hair away from her forehead. Her beautiful eyes opened, meeting his stern gaze without fear.

"I pledge myself to you." His breath fanned across her lips as the tempo of their bodies quickened. "Everywhere you go, I shall follow. You are the only light in my life, the beacon at the end of a long and winding road. Together we will be more than lovers, husband and wife, king and queen. We are a thousand years of want and desire and love. So much love."

"Together," she repeated and pressed a delicate kiss upon his lips.

A jolt of fire and lightning raced through his body until he pressed his forehead against hers and joined her as they burst into a thousand stars. He imagined that in the wild rush of passion that he sewed her stars into his own to create a cloak of midnight that would forever keep him warm.

"Mo chroí." He pressed a kiss against her lips, her cheeks, her eyes. "My heart beats for you."

They lounged on the cliff edge until the sun set and the stars blinked to life above them. Sorcha didn't want to leave. Every second that they had together was infinitely precious.

She shivered. Cold air sank through the thin fabric of her dress and dug claws into her bones. She tucked herself deeper into his embrace and sighed.

"Do we need to go inside?" he rumbled.

"It is growing cold."

"Delicate little human."

"Druid," she reminded him. He rolled her onto her back, smiling down at her with a soft expression she never tired of seeing.

"Druid," he agreed. "How could I ever forget?"

"It's rather easy when you're so distracted."

"Am I?"

She followed the ragged edge of a crystal fissure from his forehead down to his lip. "Perhaps not as distracted as you were this afternoon."

He nipped at her fingers. "Don't tempt me."

Temptation was the definition of him. Her heart throbbed every time she looked at him. They were different here in this castle than they had been on Hy-brasil. Responsibilities filled their lives and finding time together was difficult.

The time they found was rare, and therefore all the more special.

She shivered again and laughed. "I'm sorry, mo chroí. I need to warm up. Unless you magically have a jacket?"

"No jacket."

He rolled to his feet and held out a hand for her. "Then let us find you a fire."

"Or a bed with blankets."

"Not yet satisfied?"

"Thoroughly satisfied, but finding myself still hungry."

He scooped her up into his arms and carried her back through the castle. She laughed as he struck the door like a battering ram. The sheer power of his body was impressive, yet he was infinitely gentle with her.

They raced through the halls, hiding in the shadows when a faerie passed them. His hearing was far stronger than hers. He listened for their footsteps, for the sound of their breath, and ducked behind drapes to avoid them.

He hushed her when she giggled. "We're hiding!"

"Why?"

The glint in his eye suggested he was enjoying himself.

She was so glad to see him happy. Bubbles of incandescent joy lifted through her being and spilled out in waves. She stroked whatever bit of him she could reach. His jaw, his hair, his shoulders, the ragged edges of his throat.

"Master!" Oona's scolding shout made them freeze.

They had just reached the stairs, so close to freedom. Eamonn's sigh stirred her hair. Responsibility called.

She stroked the back of his neck and smiled. "We had an afternoon."

"And a lovely afternoon it was."

He let her legs swing down onto the ground. Sorcha kept hold of his shoulder as they turned towards the pixie, wanting to stay connected to him as long as possible.

Oona's brows furrowed and the tips of her elongated ears drooped. "Master?"

"Yes, go ahead Oona."

"It's…" She swallowed and held out a small square of parchment. "A letter arrived."

"A letter?"

Sorcha's stomach dropped to her feed. Nerves traveled through her veins in electric currents as she stared at the too white paper. She knew what it was, what it had to be, and couldn't force her feet to step forward.

Eamonn released her hand and walked forward as if in a trance. She watched his expression, the crestfallen way he stumbled and gently took the letter in his hand.

He smoothed his fingertips over the edges but did not open the envelope.

She didn't notice she had moved until she placed her hands over his. "We'll open it together."

"It is the first time I have spoken to them in centuries."

"Them?"

He turned the letter over and revealed gold wax stamped with the curled lines of a tree. "It is the royal marker. This is not just from Fionn."

It was from his entire family. Tears stung her eyes until she could hardly see the sigil. They had condemned him, hung him, banished him, and still he desperately wanted to speak with them.

"Give it to me," she said.

He handed it over without complaint.

Sorcha slid her nail underneath the wax. It popped open with no magical seal or warning sign. At least they weren't trying to poison him.

She slid the letter out and ran her eyes over it, reading through the note with disappointment. This wasn't handwritten by anyone in his family. She suspected they hadn't even looked it over.

"All it says is that our formal request has been accepted. In three moon's time we are to arrive at the palace where rooms will be prepared for us to meet with the king and his court." Sorcha looked up. "What is this? We asked for a private audience, not an assembly."

"So that is how he will play this," Eamonn growled. "So be it."

"What does it mean?"

"Oona, prepare the dwarves. They will need to create court acceptable outfits for the both of us. We leave tomorrow afternoon."

The pixie shifted. "Is that enough time to reach the castle?"

"We will ride all night if we have to."

Oona raced down the hall towards the servants quarters. They would need to be up all night to piece together outfits that Eamonn deemed acceptable.

Worried, she grabbed his arm as he started away from her. "Eamonn! What is going on?"

"We're going to court." Pity filled his eyes. "We will need to prepare ourselves for the worst, and hope that my brother has not completely lost his mind."

CHAPTER TEN

The Seelie Court

They left the castle just as the sun kissed the horizon the next day. Oona and her faeries worked until their fingertips bled. The clothing they made was stunning, golden threads running throughout the black cloth that looked like starlight.

Eamonn grunted when he saw them, but Sorcha saw the appreciation in his gaze. Oona did as well. The pixie's cheeks flushed bright red in pleasure.

They decided that only a limited amount of their people would travel with them to Cathair Solais. They had no way of determining what Fionn was up to, and in the end, it wasn't worth risking the lives of their people.

The army would remain behind. Only Oona, Cian, and a few select dwarves travelled with Sorcha and Eamonn.

Eamonn wanted to leave her behind, saying that the castle required a queen. She argued that he required a queen far more than the dwarves, who had never had a queen before.

She won.

Eamonn set a grueling pace that quickly made everyone regret going. He lashed the faeries to their horses so they could sleep while they travelled. Rather than tie her down, Eamonn held Sorcha on his own horse and allowed her to sleep against his chest.

They did not rest until the castle was in their sights.

She blinked her eyes at the golden light that nearly blinded her. "Are we here?"

"We'll get a good night's sleep first. We'll all need our wits about us when we enter the palace."

She wouldn't argue with that. Sorcha waited for him to slide off his horse before following him on rubbery legs. He caught her against his chest, giving her time to find her footing before stepping away to untie the faeries. Sorcha started on Oona's ties first.

"We're stopping?" Oona slurred her words, exhaustion tying her tongue. "Why aren't we continuing? We're so close."

"Eamonn wants us all to have a clear mind when we arrive at the castle."

"Oh," Oona slid down and braced her hands on Sorcha's shoulders. "That's probably a good idea."

"Can you get yourself settled?"

"I'll help the others."

"No. Get your bedroll and lay down. We'll get the others."

It only took a few minutes to free the rest of the faeries who piled on top of each other and fell asleep in a giant heap. They were so tired that they were silent and still.

Eamonn spread a blanket out on the hard ground and sighed. "It's not the luxury we're used to."

"We're used to luxury? And here I was thinking we were living in a haunted, crumbling castle." She placed a hand on his arm, gentle and kind. "It will suffice."

They lay down together, his arm curved over her waist, her hands tucked against his chest. He was warm enough that she didn't ask for a fire.

She breathed in his woody scent and sighed. "Are you ready for tomorrow?"

"No."

"We can turn around now. There is no need to take back your family's throne now that you have your own."

"Nuada's old throne is not real," he replied. "There is no substance to the claim, and the faeries will eventually remember that. If I am to save our people and change the old ways, then I must take back the Seelie throne."

Sorcha understood his desire to take it back. She had seen in the Unseelie mirror all that Fionn was capable of. The Lesser Fae deserved a life equal to that of the Tuatha dé Danann. Eamonn saw that when others did not.

But she worried what they were walking into. The tense way Eamonn held her suggested he was also troubled by the possibilities. Fionn had never been a man to trust before.

What horrors awaited them?

She sighed and tucked her head underneath his chin. Of them all, she would need her wits about her. A human was little more than a plaything to these creatures. The others would watch her back, yet they all remembered what she really was. A druid was capable of far more than a simple human.

Sleep claimed her until the early morning light. Her arms were freezing and held close to her chest. He had left her some time ago without waking.

Oona crouched in front of Sorcha, holding out her hand. "It's time to wake up, dearie."

"Thank you." She rolled onto her side, shaking out the long mane of her hair and yawning. "How much longer do we have?"

"Not long. I'm to get you ready and then we will ride into court."

"We? Are you coming with us?"

"We're to be your court."

"Do we have a name?" Sorcha stood up and stretched her spine, loud cracks easing her tension. "The Seelie, the Unseelie, who are we?"

Oona did not respond.

Sorcha glanced at her and caught the haunted expression in the pixie's eyes. "Oona?" she asked. "Are you all right?"

"It's the first time I've been back."

"Oh." Sorcha didn't know how to help the kind woman. Pixie deserved the world laid at her feet for her giving nature and her sweet disposition. These people had not cared that she existed at all, and then Eamonn had dragged her to an isle far away.

Sorcha cleared her throat, "Oona, I realize I have been remiss in getting to know you. I don't even know if you have family here."

"No, dearie. I never had the opportunity. Pixie families are rather small, and my parents left this world a long time ago." She gestured to the bundle in her hands. "Let's get this dress on you and I'll see what I can do with your hair."

"Did you want children?" Sorcha couldn't help but ask.

"Yes."

"Why didn't you have them?"

"Lesser Fae in the service of Tuatha dé Danann cannot have children unless their masters permit them."

"Who was your master back then?"

Oona glanced over her shoulder as Eamonn strode towards them. "His father."

"We have little time," Eamonn called out. "Get her ready!"

"Yes, master."

Sorcha's heart clenched. She reached out and caught Oona's hand that held the glimmering fabric. "You don't have to call him master anymore."

"I do. That is what he is."

"He doesn't want that to be the reality for Lesser Fae anymore."

"I know, dearie. But I won't stop calling him that until that becomes truth for us all."

This was why she was here. Sorcha stepped away from the men and hid between the horses as Oona stripped her of clothing. She let the silken fabric slide over her skin, barely noticing the fine quality and cool touch.

Nerves made her stomach clench. She stared off into the distance as her mind wandered. Would they be as cruel as Fionn? Was she walking into a court where they would all attack?

Would she lose the people she loved today?

"Worrying will get you nowhere," Oona soothed. "Clear your mind and show them you are more than just a weak human."

"Humans are not weak."

"They are compared to us. But you are a druid priestess, a Weaver who is capable of great things. The granddaughter of Ethniu, Fomorian and mother of the druid race. You have nothing to fear."

"And everything to lose."

"Arms up."

She lifted her eyes for Oona to clasp delicate gold mesh over the top of the sleeves. The entire gown was made of yellow silk that clung to every inch of her body. Oona affixed bands around her arms, her waist, and her collar.

"This is uncomfortable," Sorcha complained.

"Beauty is not comfortable. Can you breathe?"

"Yes."

Oona synched the metal corset tighter. "And now?"

"No," Sorcha wheezed.

"That's perfect then. Let me see what I can do with your hair."

"Leave it down."

"It's not in style."

"I don't care if it's in style. I want them to remember that I am not Fae. Even if I'm trying to look like one."

It felt important to remind the Seelie Court that Eamonn and his consort were not the creatures they expected. He had grown much in the years since leaving them. She was an unknown creature they would underestimate. She wanted to use that to their advantage.

Rounding the horses, she carefully picked her way across the ground, avoiding mud puddles as she went.

"I'm ready."

Eamonn had donned his armor. Clean and oiled, it still bore the marks of war. Dents and cracks turned the metal chest plate into a dimpled mess. Crystals poked out where swords had crushed the armor against his skin and shattered the plates.

He looked every inch the warlord, and she was thoroughly pleased.

"You are beautiful," he said. "They won't know what to think of you."

"Ideally nothing at all. I would prefer to stay in the shadows. I'm better at listening then I am at politics."

"No, we have not had the time to train you." He tucked a strand of her hair behind her ear. "Let me do the talking while we are there."

She didn't argue.

Eamonn lifted onto his own horse rather than letting her ride separately. He swung up behind her, wrapping an arm firmly around her waist and pulling her back against him.

They were all quiet on their ride to the castle. The few dwarves who had traveled with them were on high alert. They scanned the distance as if waiting for an army to appear out of thin air.

Sorcha assumed it wasn't such a far-fetched idea. She held her breath, waiting.

They reached the main road without incident. The buildings around the castle were just as splendid. Gold poured from the roofs as if the rain were molten metal. Filigreed pieces so fine they must have been made with magic decorated the outsides of building like the finest of wallpaper.

Faeries milled through the streets, far more beautiful and impossible than Sorcha had ever seen. A woman with ebony skin walked by their horses, a red cloak covered her head and tiny dots of gold flecked over her cheekbones and forehead. She bought a strand of gemstones from a man covered in so much jewelry that Sorcha couldn't tell where he began. Perhaps he was made entirely out of gold and gems.

No one even glanced at them as they rode by.

Sorcha leaned back and whispered, "Why aren't they looking at us?"

"We are the banished. We do not exist."

"They *can* see us, can't they?"

"If they cared to look up, yes, they could see us. It is forbidden to acknowledge that any of the banished exist."

"How do they know we were banished?" she asked.

"They were warned."

So this was how Fionn would tear at Eamonn's confidence before he even reached the castle. Not soldiers. Not bloodshed.

Sorcha had forgotten how painfully intelligent Fionn was. The king wouldn't take the risk of making Eamonn angry. His pride could be wounded long before anyone needed to fight. A man with no surety in himself would fall without Fionn lifting a finger.

She lifted her chin. "Let them know we are not ashamed then. They may not remember our faces, but they will remember we walked through this crowd without fear."

The dwarves lifted their chins with her and Oona's ears tipped up. Sorcha refused to allow any of them to feel unwanted. They were dearly wanted by *her*, and if the Seelie Fae could not appreciate them, then she would.

"Sing the stones," she whispered.

One of the dwarves glanced at her in surprise. "M'lady?"

"Sing the stones. Let them hear us coming, we have nothing to hide."

Eamonn's arm tightened around her waist, but he did not silence the dwarves. They lifted their deep voices high into the air and let the wind carry their ancient song. Faeries flinched all around them, some lifting startled eye towards the newcomers before violently turning away.

Good, Sorcha thought. Let them know the high king traveled among them.

The dwarven song echoed through the streets, bouncing off stone and statues. Fionn's people scattered. Soon, the streets were empty of all but a brave few who refused to budge or look.

Sorcha watched them as they ducked their heads and kept their eyes trained on the ground.

"They look as though they are bowing," she observed.

"They are not."

"Do your kind not realize that looking a leader in the eyes is the greatest show of defiance?" A faerie nearby lifted his green-haired head. But he still did not meet her gaze. "It is a shame there is so little bravery amongst your people."

At that, the faerie looked up and meet her gaze. She smiled, cold and sharp edged, until he looked back at the ground.

They reached the steps of the castle and Eamonn did not hesitate. He clucked his tongue, urging the horse to continue. Sorcha leaned forward, gripped Eamonn's forearms tight, and took a deep breath.

The large doors opened.

Cathair Solais was as beautiful as she remembered. Polished floors, open ceilings that filtered the sky through emerald green leaves, tall columns made of the whitest marble with no veins to speak of.

This time, faeries filled the castle. They lined either side of the great hall which lead to a massive throne. Three stories high, billowing red fabric stretched as far as the eye could see. A great tree grew behind it, nearly as tall as the castle. And seated in the center, Fionn the Wise watched them approach.

Eamonn leaned down and said, "So it begins."

The crowd remained silent, their eyes staring towards the throne and not the newcomers who dared parade horses through the hallowed halls of the king. Sorcha nearly gasped in shock as they grew close enough to see the throne in detail.

There were two chairs on lower levels, upon which the previous king and queen sat.

"Eamonn." Her nails dug into his arms.

She felt the moment he saw them. His body tensed, his spine straightening and his breath sawing unevenly.

What torment he must feel! She wanted to close her eyes to banish the image of Eamonn's parents who did not even look at him. They too, kept their eyes on the floor. Fionn was the only person in the entire room who met Eamonn's gaze.

Stone hands gripped the reins and tugged hard. The horse chuffed, tossing its head in discomfort.

"So," Fionn's voice echoed through the great hall. "The banished prince returns."

"I have come to take back what is rightfully mine."

Eamonn's powerful message sent a ripple of shudders through the crowd. Sorcha hadn't expected him to declare his intent immediately, but she agreed with his decision. They needed to be strong because Fionn expected them to be weak.

"It is a shame I must disappoint you." Fionn leaned back in his throne, crossed his legs, and gestured at the hall. "None of this is yours."

"This is when we dismount." He leaned down so only Sorcha would hear him. "Get down before me, mo chroí."

She swung her leg over the horse's side. Her skirts rode up her smooth thighs, but she didn't cover herself. No one was looking.

Eamonn followed, standing powerfully behind her. She could feel the electric power of his anger and disappointment in his brother.

"Fionn," he projected through the great hall. "You have ruled in my stead for long enough."

"Have I? If there is any faerie in this court who wishes to desert and go with my brother, please, make yourself known."

Sorcha stared at the crowd who remained silent and still. Not even a cough echoed, nor the shuffle of feet against stone.

She wanted to scream at them. Were they all cowards? Was this the faerie court she had dreamed about as a child? Nothing more than meek followers of a king who wasn't even frightening.

A smile spread across Fionn's face. "So you see? No one wants to go with the banished prince who returned uninvited."

"They would not state their opinions in so public a setting."

"Why not?"

"They are afraid of you, brother."

"Stop calling me that."

Eamonn patted his horse, the soft sounds startling a few of the faeries nearby. Their fearful gazes lifted to the high king. "That is what we are, whether you choose to admit it or not."

"You have no place here."

"You are sitting on my throne."

Gasps echoed again. The audacity of a man to walk into a king's court and level such a bold taunt! Sorcha could feel their horror, curiosity, and wonder growing with every second.

Fionn stood, his great height nearly as imposing as his brother. But he lacked the muscular build that suggested a hard life. Instead, Fionn was lean and tall. His body was everything Eamonn's might have been. Smooth lines, gentle curves, graceful hands that made women beg for a single touch.

He floated from the throne like a feather on the wind. Waist-length gold hair shimmered in a perfect swath of color. Fionn walked directly to Eamonn and stared him in the eyes.

Sorcha winced at the similarities between the twins. She had seen them both individually, but together they were a sight to behold.

They were mirror reflections of each other. She knew the stubborn set of Eamonn's chin, the curve of his jaw, the tiny marks at the edge of his eyes when he smiled. They were all on Fionn's face, right down to the exact wrinkles caused by worry between their eyes.

Where Fionn was stunning, Eamonn was not. Crystals and geodes ruined the beauty he might have born. Handsome couldn't begin describe the grace with which they moved, the whispered sounds of their body shifting even as they stood still, and the gentle inhalations that lifted their chests and flared their nostrils.

"You have no right to be here," Fionn growled.

"You had no right to banish me."

Fionn tilted his head to the side, lips curled in a snarl and eyes flashing hatred. What had caused such a rift? Sorcha refused to believe it was jealousy, for that was an emotion that dulled with time. Eamonn had nothing left. What more could Fionn find to hate him for?

The Seelie King's face wiped of all emotion and he turned towards Sorcha with a smile that made her shiver. "Sorcha of Ui Neill, it is a pleasure to be in your presence again."

He reached for her hand and she had no choice but to allow him to kiss her fingers. "I wish I could say the same."

"Are you not pleased to see me? Your king?"

"You are not my king."

Eamonn and the crowd stiffened, but Fionn laughed. "No, but no man is your king. Are they, little druid?"

"You do not know me, Fionn the Wise." His hand clenched around hers at the mention of his name. "You sit upon a stolen throne, and as such you have no right to it."

"And just what are you going to do?"

She leaned forward so the crowd could not overhear her words. "I argued for a peaceful treaty rather than an army at your doorstep. You should be grateful."

"You think I'm afraid of a dwarven army?"

"Have you not yet learned that underestimating a druid is dangerous?"

"Oh, I remember that very well." He leaned close, trying to intimidate her with his body. Sorcha did not back way even though she could feel his breath against her forehead. "But now you are in my court, and I have a thousand guards who would like nothing more than to run a sword through your chest."

"Careful, brother," Eamonn growled.

"And what will you do? Banished prince that you are?"

"You know what you made me."

"Immortal?" Fionn shook his head. "No, it is possible to kill you."

Sorcha's eyes widened at the revelation. What did Fionn know that they did not? She looked over at Eamonn who's troubled expression only made her more nervous.

Throughout it all, the dowager queen and king remained silent on their thrones. Fionn walked up the steps and gently touched the arms of their thrones. They did not speak, they hardly even moved but to acknowledge the son they had chosen.

Anger planted a seed in her chest that burned. Sorcha rubbed her throat and told herself to remain silent. This was not her battle.

Not yet.

Fionn sat back down and lifted a hand. "I granted you an audience, banished prince, not a scene. As you can tell, there are already many who wish to speak with me. Your antics and dramatics are not appreciated by those who already have waited for days to voice their pleas. You will remain in your quarters which I have graciously provided until the time of your audience. My guards will see you there."

Clanking armor echoed as a veritable army of golden soldiers advanced upon them. Sorcha's pulse jumped as the army separated her and Oona from the others.

"Eamonn!" she shouted.

He did not respond, only glared at his brother as the guards shoved his chest and pushed him out of the great hall.

"Fionn!" her voice carried through the hall so loudly that the king had to look at her. "Where are you taking me?"

"It wouldn't be proper to allow an unwed couple to stay in the same quarters, now would it?"

She couldn't tell him they were married, and Fionn knew he had her cornered. He was up to something, and she refused to play along with this game.

"They didn't even look at him!" Sorcha shouted as she ripped the golden bangles from her arms. "Did you see that? They're his parents and they didn't even have the decency to glance at their son whom they have not seen for centuries!"

"It is the faerie way," Oona said in a quiet voice.

"It is a *stupid* way!"

Sorcha threw the bangles at the wall. The crashing sound only made her feel slightly better.

"They will not look upon his visage until he is no longer banished," Oona said.

"And who can do that?"

"Only the king."

"Right." Sorcha balled her hands into fists. "He will never do that."

"No, Fionn is unlikely to choose that path. He wants Eamonn to remained banished for as long as he reigns."

"Do we have no other recourse?" she asked. "How are we supposed to do this?"

She slumped down on the bed and put her head in her hands. Fionn already had them by the throat. Eamonn's plan had been ironclad. He was so certain he could waltz in and his people would support him.

They hadn't. They wanted nothing to do with the banished king, especially when his own parents wouldn't even look at him.

How cruel were these Fae?

She couldn't imagine forsaking her own child. No matter what they did, they would be in her heart for the rest of her life. But these people didn't hesitate to disown a child for merely being different. Ugly. Strange.

Eamonn wasn't any of those. He was a kind and capable man, one who saw the differences in others and accepted them for those differences. He understood that what made these people strong were their differences.

Oona knelt in front of Sorcha, her knees creaking. "My sweet girl, all is not yet lost."

"What else is there?"

"The audience with the king may go differently than we expect."

"How could it?"

"We cannot know the future." Oona reached up and brushed a strand of hair behind Sorcha's ear. "We can only hope that the future remains bright."

"We cannot even see the men, Oona."

"Then we shall plan on our own, we have no need of men."

"He will banish Eamonn again, or worse."

A rustling from the window broke through their conversation. "He's already banished me, he cannot do it again."

Sorcha lifted her head so quickly her vision spun. Eamonn threw one leg over her windowsill, the other dangling over the sheer drop towards certain death.

"How did you get there?" she shouted as she stood. She raced to his side and gripped his arm, terror coursing through her veins. "Get inside you foolish man! You'll tumble to your death!"

"Mo chroí, have a little more faith than that."

He grinned, and she lost her breath. Had she ever seen him this happy? The wild abandon of joy that danced across his features with the breathless excitement of near death. She kept finding new sides of him, new stories that his body told, new whispers of the man he used to be.

She squeezed the hard edges of his bicep. "What are you doing here?"

"I didn't like Fionn keeping us apart."

"Why didn't you use the door?"

"There are guards posted outside both our rooms. He wasn't making it easy on us, mostly just to spite me."

Sorcha shook her head. "How would that spite you? He doesn't think highly enough of me to consider my thoughts or plans a threat."

"He knows I will worry about you, and not about my audience." Eamonn swung his leg over the edge of the window and slid into her room. "Now, I can focus."

He pulled her into his arms and cupped the back of her head. She felt a sigh lift his chest as he tucked her further into his embrace.

Oona cleared her throat. "I'll find us some food then."

"A bath as well, Oona."

"Master?"

"We've been traveling for a very long time. I'd like to be clean when I stride into that faerie pit again."

"As you wish, Master."

Sorcha grinned and rested her head against his chest. "You don't want the bath just to clean, do you?"

"It's your first night in Cathair Solais. You should enjoy all the pleasures of faerie life."

"Which are?"

"The bath water here is mixed with ambrosia straight from the enchanted flowers. If I know Fionn, he will have too much added to the bath water Oona requests."

"What will that do?" Her brow wrinkled with worry as she leaned back to stare at his face. "Why don't you seem concerned about that?"

"Ambrosia in small amounts relaxes the body. In large amounts, it acts as an aphrodisiac."

"Ah." Her cheeks flamed red. "You said you didn't want to be distracted."

"I am in my childhood home for the first time in centuries, with the woman I love more than life itself. A man would have to be insane to not wish for distractions at a time like this."

"You may regret that come morning."

"I shall never regret a single moment of your time." His hands smoothed down her ribs to the dip in her waist. "If this is our last night, then I wish it to be a night our souls remember in the ancestral halls."

Eamonn swept down and claimed her lips. He pressed his body against hers, delved into her heart with his tongue, whispered promises against her skin all night. Promises they both worried he couldn't keep.

"Are you ready?" Eamonn asked.

Sorcha watched Oona tighten the remaining straps of his armor, checking each one to make certain she had gotten them all. He could have worn the regalia of faerie royalty. It was the chosen outfit laid out for him by Fionn's men.

Eamonn had refused. Instead, he pulled out the armor which he wore like a second skin. Sorcha didn't know whether she approved. On one hand, giving his people a chance to see him as something other than a warlord was potentially good. On the other, he shouldn't change simply because they were used to a king who did not fight by their side.

She would be soft for the both of them. Oona had dressed her in an ephemeral dress that floated like a cloud. Green as sea-foam, it pooled around her legs and moved on its own. The sleeves were so fine, they appeared as if made of smoke. Gems dripped from her throat and wrapped around her arms in coiled chains.

"No," Sorcha replied. "I am not ready. My stomach is in knots, and I can't stop thinking something horrible is going to happen."

"We cannot plan for what might happen."

"What did he mean when he said you weren't immortal?" Sorcha stared at him with wide eyes. "The crystals stop every blade. What does he know?"

"I cannot fathom what he might be up to. He will not kill me, Sorcha."

Oona finished tightening the straps and Eamonn strode towards Sorcha. Confidence echoed in each step. He took her hands and pressed his lips against the backs.

"How can you be so sure?"

"He is as much a part of me as I am of him. Twins are two sides of a coin. To kill me would be to kill himself."

"You want to kill him," she said.

"And I am prepared to kill myself to end this war. Fionn has never been so selfless."

As he turned, she reached out and grasped his hand. "Do not kill yourself for this. There are other ways."

He looked back, emotions dancing in his eyes like the flipping pages of a book. "I have much to live for. I have no intentions of letting him take that from me."

She followed him out of the room, into the safekeeping of twenty guards, and back to the great hall.

For all Fionn's blustering when they first arrived, he had not made them wait long. A single night in the golden rooms of the Seelie castle could hardly be considered an extended stay. He had wanted to throw them off, make them uncomfortable, and then force them to return.

He showed them that his word was law by simply making them go away and then he would see them on his own terms. Their plans were foiled that easily.

It made her worried.

Every inch of this castle spread fear throughout her mind and soul. What would Fionn do? What madness could he bring to life?

Eamonn's square shoulders did not waver as he stepped into the throne room. Sorcha locked her eyes on his form, the only rock that grounded her. He did not let fear rule him. Neither should she.

Faeries filled the hall again. Why? Fionn had made it seem as though they were waiting to speak with him, but she recognized many of their faces. These were the same faeries as before. Beauty, so powerful that it hurt her eyes, spread across his court.

She glanced at Oona. "They are faerie nobility, aren't they?"

"They are."

"Why are they here?"

Eamonn strode towards the throne, halting mere feet from his parents. "My petition was for a private audience."

Fionn reclined on his throne, rings glittering on his fingers. "And it is within my right to deny that request. Your petition will be public."

"Are you certain you wish to do this, brother?"

"You have nothing to say."

Eamonn bowed his head. "Then I shall address both you and your court."

"You may begin."

The faeries looked up as one and met the gaze of the high king. The firstborn son who should have ruled them, but had fallen from grace.

Sorcha's throat clenched. They *looked* at him. All it took was a few words from Fionn and suddenly Eamonn existed again. But why? Why now would he allow it?

Her beloved hesitated for a brief moment as he met individual gazes.

"My people, you have suffered long enough. The throne has always passed to the firstborn of the king and queen, never the second unless the first dies. I am not dead. Many of you have fought beside me on the battlefield, some have saved my life. Others, I have saved.

"You knew me from when I was a little boy. You watched me grow with confidence and honor, you loved me as one of your own.

"This deformity was not my choice, but neither was beauty yours. Your king caused this wound and all others you see upon my face. What you look upon is your own face, your fears, your temptations, your nightmares. I may be ugly, but I am far more worthy a king than the one who sits upon your throne.

"Faeries should not be slaves. We have a chance in this moment, to change our world. To live with tolerance of each other, to grow stronger together. I will not rest until I sit upon that throne and bring our people together once and for all."

His words were beautiful. They brought tears to Sorcha's eyes and were spoken like a true king. One who would take the burdens of his people and carry them upon his shoulders.

But did they see it?

She looked over the crowd of people and her heart fell. They did not care for his words. No one moved, blinked, or breathed as they stared him down.

Fionn scoffed. "And so you have had your petition, banished prince. Your people have given their answer."

Eamonn did not respond. He kept his gaze locked upon the men and women who scorned him so easily. His expression did not change, the set of his shoulders did not move. He watched them and waited.

She sucked in a wavering breath, telling herself not to cry.

The king sighed. "Yours is not the only petition I accepted."

Eamonn turned and stared. "What?"

"You sent a request with two names, and I accepted both."

"Whose?"

"Mine," Sorcha said. Her voice carried line the peal of a bell. "I signed my name on the letter."

He twisted towards her. "Why would you do that?"

"I don't know."

Hundreds of faerie gazes burned. They waited for the druid woman to say something that might change their minds. Something that would rock the very foundation of their world.

And she couldn't find a single word.

Fionn gestured for her to step forward. "Come here, Sorcha."

Her feet carried her without her knowledge. She watched the faces as she passed by and wondered what she could say that would change their minds. They already knew what decision they would make. They had condemned him years ago and didn't want to alter their thoughts.

She stopped next to Eamonn and brushed her pinky against his. She wouldn't disgrace him by taking his hand.

"Not there," Fionn said. "Approach the throne."

What games did he play now? She looked up at Eamonn who stared down at her with worry in his eyes. But she had no choice. The king had summoned her to his side.

Each step felt strange. The stairs weren't right to walk upon. A king should be level with his people, should eat at their table, fight by their side. He shouldn't sit above them and cast his judgment throughout a crowd.

The dowager queen made the slightest of sounds as she passed. A hum, a hymn, a whispered prayer that skittered down Sorcha's spine.

"There you are." Fionn licked his lips. "You're such a pretty little thing for a human."

"Thank you." Her words slid between her clenched teeth.

"So polite! Since when do you curb your tongue?"

"I have been learning self-control."

"I bet you have." He leaned forward and stroked a finger down her arm. She felt the heat of him burn through the fabric, her body's confused response to a man who was Eamonn but not. "Why don't you tell us why Eamonn is more worthy of this throne than I?"

"It is not my place to suggest such a thing. Faerie politics are beyond me."

"Even you shall not stand beside my brother? If his own lover will not claim him worthy then why should we?"

She swallowed. "I care little whether he sits upon this throne or the one he has already claimed. The name of the castle or seat means little, it is the people who decide where their allegiance lies. I have watched all those who seek shelter from your mistreatment arrive at our doorstep.

"And we have taken care of them. Each faerie who was neglected, whose family hungers for food. We cared for their wounds, filled their bellies, provided a warm place to sleep. Whether you continue on as Seelie king or not, matters little to me. We will continue to save those you have wronged. And you will continue to wrong them."

Fionn's brows lifted. "Banished prince, your lover speaks quite well for a gutter rat."

"She is a queen. You would do well to show her respect."

"A queen?" Fionn burst into laughter along with a few of the faerie court. "She is a druid. We ran them out of the Otherworld long ago, and for good reason. I should send her back to the human realm now."

"She would only find another way to return. She already has once."

"Then you choose him?" Fionn asked her directly. "There are many gifts I can give you. Many wonders you might behold in this court without the presence of a faerie prince that will amount to nothing."

"He is your brother," she said with a hitched breath. "How can you be so cruel? He is a part of you."

A shadow passed across his face. The same sadness she had seen on his face when he looked at Elva. "I cut out that part when I stuck a dagger in his back, little midwife. There is no mending that wound."

She didn't think anyone but her had heard his admission of guilt. Regret rang in his voice, saturated his words with heavy oil. He hated himself for what he had done. But he was not willing to back down.

They were so much alike. Eamonn would never let his brother rule at his side, and Fionn would never apologize. They were two pillars of hatred and jealousy which had grown so solid they could never break.

"You have this moment to change the future," she whispered. "You can take this step towards mending your life and his. It will not belittle you, nor will it make you appear weak. Two great men are stronger than one."

"Your words are so pretty." He reached forward and touched her cheek. "And your soul is so bright. He does not deserve your devotion."

"He has earned it wholeheartedly. Again and again."

"If only the world was filled with more women like you."

"Where is Elva?" she asked quietly.

He shut down, his expression smoothing into porcelain and hands gripping the arms of his throne so tightly that they groaned. "You have made your plea, midwife. Return to your lover's side for my judgment."

"Judgment?" her voice rang out. "We are not here for punishment. We came to you for an audience, king to king."

"I do not recognize another king in the Seelie Court. Nor will my people."

"They already have!" She backed down the steps, her soul screaming for justice. "They flock to us by the hundreds, and thousands more will come."

"You have fled from Hy-brasil in clear defiance of banishment."

"You have no right!" Sorcha screamed even as she reached Eamonn's side. "Your judgment means nothing!"

"I find you guilty of breaking the laws of our people and treason."

Sorcha clenched her fists. "You are not their king! The true High King of the Seelie Court stands before you, and you are blind to see it!"

"Sorcha," Eamonn caught hold of her shoulders. "Silence."

"I will not be silent while these fools call him king!"

"Mo chroí," he leaned down and pressed his forehead against hers. "We have failed."

"I will not accept that."

Fionn's voice boomed. "Guards, remove the midwife."

Hands grabbed her arms and yanked her from Eamonn's hold. He growled, palming the blades at his side and jerking forward. Two other guards held him in place.

She watched the blood drain from his face as he was forced to stare at his brother.

Fionn shook his head. "Release him."

The gold clad hands fell from Eamonn's shoulders. Sorcha twisted and turned, trying to break the solid hold upon her. One of the guards wrapped his arm firmly around her waist.

"You knew what the punishment for such blatant disregard for our rules was, and still you came here," Fionn said.

"Hang me again, brother. I will swing from the cord for as long as you wish, but I will come back here when that rope breaks."

Again, the darkened expression Sorcha recognized crossed Fionn's features.

"No," she breathed. Her gut clenched, her hands shook, her eyes watered. She didn't know what Fionn was going to do, but she could see his heart breaking.

"You forced my hand, brother." It was the first time Fionn admitted his familial ties to Eamonn. "And now you will remain here, for all to remember what happens when they defy their king."

"I am to be a prisoner then?" Eamonn scoffed. "You truly are a fool. Eventually, they will hear what I have to say as truth. Abdicate the throne. End this."

"You are not the only one to find the old relics."

Time slowed as Sorcha watched the scene unfold before her. Eamonn's eyes widened and for the first she saw fear. Raw and ragged, it shredded his quiet visage, and he gripped the sword at his side.

But Fionn was faster. He reached through the folds of his robe and pulled out a bejeweled handle. At the press of a finger, it extended into a wicked spear with an edge so sharp it was blinding.

Fionn turned so quietly her eyes could not track his movements and sank the blade through Eamonn's armor, between his ribs.

He couldn't die, the crystals would stop it. She waited for the telltale clink and shattering sound of metal breaking against earth. It did not come.

A choked sound echoed through the hall which was suddenly silent as the grave. Eamonn coughed again and Fionn twisted the spear. He pushed until the tip split through Eamonn's back and gleamed in the light. No blood tainted its tip.

Rattling breath mirrored her own. Fionn stepped back, wiped a hand across his mouth, and ascended the stairs to his throne.

Eamonn fell onto his knees and would have sprawled onto the floor if the spear had not caught on the stairs. It held him up, balanced on the very thing which plunged through his heart.

A wail split through her head, screaming and crying in pain. It was the scream of a bean sidhe, the thundering of a heart breaking, the shattering of a soul.

She made that sound. Screaming out her rage and fear until her throat vibrated, and she tasted blood. Sorcha wasn't certain if she said words, or if the sound was merely the raw, violent edge of agony.

The guard loosened his hold just enough for her to break free. She ran towards Eamonn and cupped his face, tilting his head until she could look into his eyes.

Crystals spread from the wound on his chest. They climbed down his arms, solidifying his stomach until he couldn't move.

Tears slid down her cheeks and her hands trembled.

"No," she moaned. "No, my love. You will not leave me!"

"I—" The crystals traveled up his throat and locked his words within his body. His eyes tried to say what his lungs could not. But all she saw was the fear and sadness. Their life had been taken from them. It was always taken from them.

"Mo chroí, fight for me."

His lips moved but crystal sprouted from his tongue. They rose out of his mouth and spilled into her hands. His eyes roved, sightless, until they too stilled.

She no longer held a man in her hands. No heart beat, no lungs drew breath, no eyes spoke of his love. He was nothing more than a man made of crystal, a symbol of all those who fought against Fionn.

Sorcha drew air into her lungs, threw her head back, and screamed. Her agony was so great it cracked the surrounding stone. Great fissures that spread like spider legs across the floor towards the hated faeries who had condemned him to this fate.

She would kill them all. They would die a thousand deaths for taking him from her.

One brave soul linked an arm through her waist but she would not let Eamonn go. She refused to leave him here where so many hated people would look upon him and laugh. They had no right to keep him.

"Sorcha!" Cian shouted in her ear. "Sorcha, we must leave!"

"I will make them regret ever drawing breath!"

"We will, love. But we must go!"

She opened her eyes and saw that the throne room was in shambles. Faeries tore at each other and the guards. Screams and shouts echoed her own though she did not recognize those who fought.

Fionn fled from the room with a small army of guards trailing behind him. They ushered the dowager queen away who stared at Sorcha with pain in her eyes.

Sorcha pointed directly at her. "You have no right to mourn him."

The queen flinched and fled.

"Now, Sorcha! We cannot risk being caught in the dungeon! All our work will be for nothing!"

"I cannot leave him."

"He doesn't know anymore." She heard the anguish in Cian's voice. "He doesn't know, Sorcha. We have to go."

Trembling, she pressed a kiss against Eamonn's cold, stone lips. "I will find you again. In this life or the next."

Heart numb, she stood and left with what remained of Eamonn's people. Her soul screamed out a vow.

She would destroy his house and pity the fool who tried to stop her.

CHAPTER ELEVEN
THE DRUID QUEEN

"The king is dead."

The words rang throughout Nuada's stolen castle. The dwarves and Seelie Fae who found shelter in the ancient walls watched with wide eyes.

They had arrived two weeks ago. Broken, bleeding, and dragging Sorcha as she screamed and fought their hold. Once calm, she told the others to still their tongues. She would tell their people once the words no longer stuck in her throat.

She hadn't known it would take this long. Madness danced at the edges of her vision for longer than she cared to admit. Sorcha had not thought herself so weak.

Bran's words danced in her mind. Find something else to fill her time, to give her purpose, to force her life in another direction. She had survived without him before. She could do again.

But she hadn't thought losing him a second time would destroy her.

Now, she stood before the crowds of people with a clear mind. She had a purpose, and it was to provide a home for every faerie that sought shelter from the bitter storms of Fionn's wrath.

Sorcha said it again, forcing herself and them to realize the truth. "The king is dead. Fionn plunged the Spear of Lugh through his chest, the only weapon that could kill our crystal king."

"Where is his body?" A dwarf called out.

"Fionn kept him as a symbol of what would happen to all those who defy him."

Murmurs lifted into the air. The faeries' minds grew troubled, wondering what would happen next. They had defied the king. Living in this castle, following Sorcha and Eamonn's people, all decisions that went against the king's orders.

"We will prevail," Sorcha called out. "This place is our home. The people next to you are your family, by blood and by choice. Our lives remain as he would have wished them to. Free."

She buried her hands in the folds of her dress. Tears pricked the edges of her vision, but she couldn't let them fall. How many tears could a single person have?

"We will stay in this castle. We will continue to build our people."

"Will we go to war?" A peat faerie shouted.

"No," Sorcha shook her head. All her energy drained and her posture sagged. "I have no intention of leading our people to war. I make these decisions based on what he would have wanted. You were more important to him than his own life. We could not have known what Fionn planned, but we do know Eamonn's intention. We will not fight until we are forced to."

She left the great hall as the murmur of the faeries lifted into the air. They could think what they wished, but she was done fighting.

Her hands shook as she pushed the door open. Her stomach tensed as she walked down the hall. Her knees quaked until she pushed into one of the rooms and slammed the door shut behind her.

He is gone.

A sob shook her shoulders, rocking her body back and forth. *He is gone.*

What was she supposed to do when her ribs were cracking open, exposing her heart to the frigid expanse of her soul? She had lost everything, over and over again. And now she was alone.

She slid to her knees and pressed her forehead against the door. Their people needed her to lead them, to guide them forward and all she could do was fall into thousands of pieces.

Eamonn had never failed them. Even the loss of their love had driven him forward. His own family hung him, and still he found the strength to lead the people on Hy-brasil, the courage to return home and look them in the eye.

She couldn't even stand.

Hands pulled at her shoulders, ghostly hands that chilled her skin.

"Sorcha," they whispered. "Let us comfort you."

"I do not want comfort. I want to feel the pain."

"You should not have to bear this weight alone."

"He shouldered my burdens. He comforted my worries and lifted my soul. Who am I without him?"

"You are Sorcha of Ui Neill."

"No longer. I left that life behind when I abandoned my family."

"You are the Druid Queen of the Seelie Fae."

"What is a queen without a king?" She licked her lips and turned into the green mist of her ancestors.

"A dark, powerful creature with no man to temper her steel. You shall wield a sword as your crown, a whip as your jewels, and armor as your gown."

"I have no more wish to fight."

The mist stirred and parted. Dark hair and billowing clothing covered Ethniu's graceful body, but her feet were bare. She had cloven hooves, tiny goat-like feet that tapped against the stone floor.

"Granddaughter," she said and opened her arms wide. "My girl, I am so sorry."

Sorcha scrambled to her feet, launching herself into the waiting embrace. Ethniu smelled like a rose garden. She breathed in her grandmother's sweet scent and sobbed into her shoulder. "I don't know what to do."

"Let us help you, child. You are not alone."

"I am. I have no family, no lover, no one but people who expect me to lead them when all I wish to do is curl up in bed."

"You have us," Ethniu said with a smile.

A deep voice echoed the words. "You have always had us."

Sorcha turned her face against Ethniu's shoulder and stared at her grandfather. Balor, Torin, the unnamed druid who had helped her through so much. "What can you do? Can you bring a man back from the dead?"

"I warned you," he said with a sad shake of his head. "Without the sword, the story changed. Sacrifices have to be made, and that is not always easy."

"I didn't know I would lose him. I didn't know that was what I traded."

"Your heart is so big. If I had known it would hurt you thusly, I would have prevented you from throwing it away."

Ethniu squeezed her. "All is not yet lost. You have found your people, and they deserve a leader like you. One who is kind, good, honest; who cares for them."

"He did," she replied. "He cared for them as no one else ever did. He understood them in ways I never will be able to."

Balor and Ethniu shared a troubled glance over her head. Ethniu guided Sorcha deeper into the mist. "My sweet girl, let me tell you a story."

"I have no need for a story, grandmother. I have need of a miracle."

"Stories can be that." A bench materialized before them. Ethniu sank onto it, skirts puffed around her. "You know that Nuada and I were married?"

"It is a legend I know well."

"The human stories never do it justice. Nuada and my father had battled for centuries. They ravaged this land, and all who lived in it. The

Fomorians did not want to give up the Otherworld, and the Tuatha dé Danann refused to allow them to remain.

"The easy solution was to unite our people through marriage. I had seen Nuada before. He was handsome and powerful and everything I had ever desired in a man. Even to the Fomorians, the Tuatha dé Danann are beautiful creatures. I desired him like no other, and it blinded me to all his faults.

"I married him on a cold spring day. He pleased me for a time, and I gave him many sons. There were other women far more beautiful than me. Not cursed with animal features, but gifted with beauty that only the Tuatha dé Danann have."

Sorcha swallowed. "Are you saying his attentions wandered?"

"Wandered is the kind way to say it. I might use such a term if it were but a handful of women. He found pleasure in the arms of many before I discovered his infidelity."

"Why are you telling me this story?"

"You cannot trust the Tuatha dé Danann. They are a strange lot who see themselves as lords above all. You have seen it with your lover, how he refused to see reason even when his people were fighting to the death."

"He explained that to me. It was their choice."

"The fires of war can be fanned with the slightest of breaths."

Sorcha stood and shook her head. "No. I will not think ill of him. He was a kind man, he wanted the best for his people, and though I did not always agree with his decisions, the motives behind them were pure."

"No one can know the intentions of a faerie."

"I will not let you twist my mind!" she shouted. "I love him!"

Ethniu reared back. "We're not try to twist your mind, Sorcha. We're trying to ground you."

"By insulting him?"

"By telling you his lineage. Even the greatest of them all had his faults. That is why I left Nuada. That is how you were created. There are a great many things in this world you do not know."

"I know that I trusted him and he was far more capable than any other to rule his people."

"Would he have been alone?" Balor asked. "Or was he great because you stood at this side?"

"Both. The answer you seek is that we were both better when we were together."

The two Fomorians shared a glance and Ethniu smiled. "She sounds so much like me."

"She is more than you were, more than you are."

"She believes in him, where I did not believe in Nuada."

"Then we will help you." Balor turned to Sorcha. "Your lover is not a man easily liked, nor do I respect his family line. But I do respect you. If he has earned your trust, then he has earned mine as well."

"Thank you," she said. "I did not know I was trying to win your approval with the haunting memories of my dead husband."

"You weren't. We came here because your soul cried out for help, and you must forgive us for blaming him. We have not had good experiences with those of Fae blood."

She slowly sank back onto the bench. "It seems that not many have. Even their own people are distrustful of each other."

"With full right. Fionn the Wise sits upon a throne he has built from lies and rivers of blood. His twin would have helped for a small amount of time before he too turned towards the wickedness existing in his soul."

Sorcha recognized the words of a prophet. Balor could see the future, or perhaps he knew one who could. Her mind whirled, and she said, "That is what the Unseelie Queen saw in my future."

"Your path has always dripped blood."

"What would have happened if I hadn't thrown away the sword?" The Fomorians did not even blink at her question. "Balor, what would have happened?"

He hesitated for a brief moment before relenting. "What dripped blood would become a river. A war unlike any other would spread across Tir na nOg. The Unseelie would join the battle after fifty years when the refugees spilled into their lands."

"And Eamonn?"

"He would be known as the Bloody King. His armies would win the war after you died of old age."

Sorcha's mouth went dry. "The Unseelie Queen was right. The fate of the Fae rested upon my decisions."

"It always has."

"What now? Nothing has changed. Eamonn is dead, Fionn sits upon the throne, and the Seelie Fae have seen no positive change."

Ethniu leaned forward and grasped her hands. "They have seen change. They have seen *you*."

"I am not Fae."

"The Fae do not need a faerie leader. They need someone who will guide them through this difficult time, who will right the wrongs, and fight on their behalf."

"I don't want to fight anymore."

"Sometimes that is not a choice," Ethniu said. "We must do what is right for our people. And your people are still spread across Tir na nOg with no one to bring them together."

Sorcha's hands shook. She did not want to be the person who did this. Eamonn's dream was to lead his people. Hers was to be a healer, not a queen.

"I am not ready to lead the Fae."

"We will help."

She couldn't help but feel suspicious of the druid souls swarming around her. "Why would you want to help? All your lives you have tried to control the Fae. I wonder if you are just trying to fulfill that desire."

Balor scoffed. "We are dead. Even if we control the Fae through you, what good will it do? We want to see one of our lineage repair the rift between our species. A single person has a difficult time healing old wounds throughout all the Fae. But a queen? A queen could convince all the Fae that Druids are worthy to return."

"I ask again, grandfather. How many Druids still breathe?"

He pondered her question for a few moments as though he were reaching out to the remaining souls that still flared bright with life. "Many. Although most do not know they are Druid."

"Where are they?"

"Spread across the lands, handling magic as much as they can without humans growing suspicious."

A plan laid out in her mind. She wanted to help Eamonn's people, but she desired her own as well. "If I do this, if I lead these people, you think they will become more tolerant towards druids?"

"Yes."

"I need you to guide me. To help me in every choice I make because I desire to bring our people together. Both druid and Fae."

"That will take a long time."

"Then I suggest you bring me more water from Dagda's Cauldron."

Resolve settled into her soul like a sword sliding free of its scabbard. She had a purpose again. A reason for living. Even if Eamonn was gone, she could continue his work.

Balor shifted. "You wish to become immortal? Even though your lover is gone?"

"I will not share my body with another, and I trust no one other than my own line to continue my destiny. Bring me the waters, Balor, and I will devote my life to bringing home our kind. I will see these halls filled with Druids once more."

Ethniu lifted her hand and souls tangled around them. Sorcha saw their faces in the green hued smoke. Men, women, even children staring at her with approval or fear.

Her grandmother smiled. "Then we will whisper in your ear and guide your hand as you lead your people. But first, you must gather your armies. Spread word that though Eamonn is dead, you remain.

The crowd teemed with faeries. Dwarves, pixies, will-o'-the-wisps, and countless others who feared for their lives. They did not know whether they should stay when the king had disappeared.

A month had passed, then another. One entire season since Eamonn had lost his life, and they became leaderless. Their queen remained in the castle, her wails carrying on the wind. They mourned with her, shrouding their bodies and homes in black. But the time for mourning had ended.

The queen called for them.

Sorcha stood on the ramparts. The wind whipped her hair, creating a swirling mass of red like a cloud of blood. She waited for them to quiet. Their jostling ceased, their whispers ended, and they all stared up at the woman they knew to be sweet, kind, and giving.

"The king is dead." Her voice lashed across the crowd, carried by magic and souls of Druids who repeated her words to the far reaches of the crowd. "But his work is unfinished. A usurper sits upon the throne of the Seelie Fae while his people toil and die. We will not stand for this."

She felt the excitement of the crowd like an electric current. They stared up at her with hope in their eyes, and she finally understood what Eamonn felt when he walked into battle. This was a heady feeling, one which could run away with her senses.

"We have spent months in mourning. A full moon of regret, sadness, and fear. No more! Now is the time for action, and we will not let this attack upon our people go without response."

A few will-o'-the-wisps trilled, dwarven hums joining their

approving song.

"Let it be known, I call for war."

Her people began to shout. They lifted their hands into the air, some brandishing swords already. They desired revenge just as much as she.

Sorcha curled her hands into fists and the druid magic grew stronger as they lifted her voice even louder.

"I call for blood. I call for vengeance. Fionn the Wise shall know our names and feel the ground tremble beneath his feet as our armies march towards his city. We will destroy the nobility and replace them with our own!"

They screamed unlike anything she had ever heard before. The resounding shout of a people who'd suffered their entire lives.

Sorcha understood their desire; she felt it boiling in her own breast. She needed them to feel it too, and then she needed them to understand the truth of their situation.

"But we will make smart, calculated decisions in every step we take. I will not lose a single one of you to men and women who do not care we exist." She stared at all her people and sighed. "You follow a druid. I know many of you personally, and some I do not. I say to you now, I am not human."

Ethniu had suggested a show of power, and Sorcha had not been pleased with the idea of it. The faeries needed to trust her, not be frightened. In the end, all the druids had agreed. Sorcha was not one of them, and they would fear only what they did not know.

The crowd silenced again, staring up at her in expectation of something great.

She breathed in and pulled on the threads she could see connecting them all. It was the slightest of tugs, the kind they wouldn't even feel. And then she tied all their threads to herself.

Sorcha argued this was the gravest of insults. She took all their names, all their memories, all their dreams and threaded them through herself. Weaving them into her very soul, knotting the tapestries of time. All without their knowledge.

Now, she saw that it wasn't harming them at all. The warm glow from her own soul, the part that still wanted to heal, spread throughout the crowd. It lifted their hearts, eased the torment and fear, breathing life into faeries who were very much afraid of the future.

They felt it. The crowd stirred, spines straightening, faces lifting to look at the woman who stood apart from them. The same place she had judged Fionn for taking.

"I cannot do this alone," she said. "I am a midwife from the human world who has no experience in war or battle. Ordering you without such knowledge would lead to devastation. I ask two things of this crowd.

"First, any of your leaders who wish to join my council are welcome in my great hall. For the rest of this moon I shall plan our attack upon Fionn and his castle. All who come to advise will be heard, fed, and housed.

"Second, all others must spread the word. Our army is already great, but I wish for it to be a thunderous wave crashing down upon the golden army. We will snuff out every inch of the Castle of Light and fill it with our magic. Tell others there is a haven for them here. The wounded and the weak shall be healed. The old shall find a safe place to rest their heads. All others will train for war."

Exhaustion sank nails into her bones. She stood strong and regal on the ramparts as her soul crumbled even further.

Eamonn would have loved to see this. The crowd screaming out as their champion spoke for them. As they took steps towards reclaiming what was theirs.

She had led him wrong. These creatures didn't want political talks. They wanted blood, gore, and death.

Sorcha felt more distant from them than she ever had before.

Turning from the crowd, she descended the stairs and made her way towards the great hall. She would remain there for as long as it took.

Oona and Cian waited for her. Their faces wrinkled with worry, for they knew what this meant.

The pixie held out a cup of tea. "Here, dearie. For your nerves."

"Thank you," Sorcha took the offered drink and drank it in one fell gulp. It burned her tongue and the roof of her mouth, but the pain was welcome. "Will they come?"

"I believe so. They desire retribution from the king who took Eamonn's life."

"Have I made a grave mistake? I do not wish for them to think me weak, but I cannot do this without them."

"They will decide upon your character once they have met in your war council. If you appear weak there, then they will believe you weak. If you do not, then they will support your decisions."

"Wonderful," Sorcha sank onto a table. "There is little I can do to control that outcome. If their suggestions are overly cruel, I will not support them."

"And if you do not support them, then they will fight without you."

"There are many factions of Fae," Sorcha said with a sigh. "They do not all fight together very well."

"No, they do not." Oona agreed.

Cian stepped up onto the bench seat and then onto the table. He sank down beside her, short legs dangling. "It's the first step towards doing anything at all. They are likely to be feral. And will want to test you."

"I expect that."

"Do not give in to all of their whims. They are good people at their core, but they wish for their people to be safe."

"Did I agree to another century-long war?" she asked.

"I do not know. You won't last for more than a century, so for your sake I hope you are not an old woman fighting a battle that may never be won."

Sorcha reached into her pocket and palmed the small vial of liquid the druids had left at her bedside. She had never thought she would drink it. It could heal thousands.

Drawing it out, she lifted it to the light and watched the rainbow reflections of the milky moon. "What if I didn't have to worry about age?"

"Is that–?" Oona gasped.

Cian gaped at the bottle. "Where did you get that?"

"Does it matter?"

"The relics of the Tuatha dé Danann disappeared before we even had the second generation of kings. When the first generation disappeared, they took their relics with them. Dagda was very careful where he hid that cauldron."

"The druids have it. I suspect they always have."

"Why?" Cian shook his head forcefully. "Why would he give it to the druids?"

"Maybe he trusted them. They've kept it secret for all these years, and no one knew they had it."

"Now they give it to you? For what purpose?"

Sorcha palmed the bottle, squeezing gently. "The first time they gave it to me, it was to cure the blood beetle plague. They told me it would heal thousands, or make one person immortal."

"Immortal?" Cian blinked rapidly. "You could become long lived? Like us?"

"I think it's more than that."

"Why would Dagda give that to the druids? Foolish faerie, they would only use that against us! They would become all powerful!"

"They didn't." Sorcha breathed out a long sigh. "They didn't use it all. Only in gifts to those who would alter the future in a positive way. There is so much mending needed between our people."

She stared into the glass for a moment, popped the cork, and drank deeply. Like the first time in the druid hallucination, it bubbled in her throat and settled cold in her belly. She didn't feel any different. The world looked the same through her eyes.

But she wasn't the same anymore.

Cian cleared his throat. "My apologies, m'lady. I don't mean to speak ill of you or your people."

"I will help in whatever way I can to restore this world to its original purpose. Kindness, honor, respect. All the laws that Seelie Fae live by have been twisted to suit Fionn's vision. I want to see it go back to the way it was originally intended."

A new voice joined them, booming and deep. "Bravo. I couldn't have said it better myself."

Sorcha leapt to her feet. The newcomer was handsome, tall for a dwarf although still not quite to her shoulder. Beads decorated his fashionably short beard. A golden crown sat atop his head.

She nodded. "Master dwarf, it is a pleasure to meet you. Have you come to join the war council?"

"Indeed I have. If you are to lead my people into battle, then I would have a say."

"Your people?" She glanced at the crown. "You are the dwarven king?"

"I am. But you, pretty thing, may call me Angus."

"And you may call me Sorcha."

He raised his eyebrows. "I've never met a human who so willingly gives her name to a faerie. You know that might cause trouble in the wrong hands."

She tugged on his thread, enough that he lurched forward in surprise. "I have my own tricks up my sleeve."

"Weaver," he breathed. "I thought all of your kind were dead."

"Many thought the same. It is not so."

"And glad I am of it. My father had many friends among your kind. We were frightened of them, but always pleased when they fought on our side."

She inclined her head and gestured towards the tables. "Shall we?"

"Are the others here yet?"

"I was unaware there were others." She tucked her hands behind her back as they made their way towards the makeshift war council. "Has there already been talk?"

"I profess, I do not know. It is my assumption that many will wish to have their hands in such a declaration of war. We have been waiting for a very long time to take on Fionn."

"Strange, I heard you did not wish to send your troops."

"Not to Eamonn." He cleared his throat. "My apologies, m'lady. I understand you were close. However, I fought next to him on the battlefield and I know how he fights. The man was reckless, without care for his own life. It served him well, but I had no wish to pledge my people to one who cared little for their lives."

"He changed. Eamonn was focused far more on the lives of his people than his own in the end. It's why he took the risk to visit Fionn."

"Ah," Angus nodded. "Then sorry I am to have judged him wrongly. What is your plan?"

"There are many, and I would have the opinion of my war council before I decide."

"I think you'll find there are many opinions."

The dwarf sat himself down, braced his elbows on the table, and looked her in the eye. "Shall we begin?"

Though she appreciated their candor, Sorcha would never have anticipated the faerie leaders to be so vocal.

She held her head in her hands and stared at the worn wood of the table while the men and women shouted over each other. A headache pounded between her eyes, racing down the long column of her neck with every heartbeat.

They couldn't agree on anything. Each leader had their own opinion on how to attack, what to do with the armies, where to come from, what day to fight.

And there were more leaders every day. Sorcha hadn't expected the swarm of faeries who rushed to the castle. The cooks grew overwhelmed, the fields wilted, fights broke out in the bars nearly every night.

She tried to tie them all to her, but there were too many to keep track of. Every time she broke free from the war council to wander the streets, she would find yet another who she hadn't attached to her expanding web of faeries.

She breathed out a slow, controlled sigh. Every moment was another second to remind herself that she had asked for them. These people were here on her request, and she owed them respect.

They had led their people for a very long time. They knew these lands as she could not. Yet, she still wondered just how much they actually knew.

Druids voices whispered in her ear.

"We could have made these decisions hours ago."

"Let us guide you, Sorcha. The Fae are only slowing down the process."

"It takes longer as more arrive. Make your choices now and tell the others they were too late."

She squeezed her temples. "I cannot do that. They deserve to have a choice in their future."

"This will only end poorly, Sorcha. You must control them."

"I will not use my powers to sway their opinions."

"Then you will be long dead before they agree!"

"So be it!" Sorcha stood and slammed her fists down on the table. The faerie leaders fell silent, staring at her in surprise. "We have argued enough."

"We still have not decided," the brownie hissed.

"Then I urge you to decide soon, or I decide for us all."

"You have no right," the pixie grumbled. "You are not a faerie, merely the catalyst for a war which has been in the making for centuries."

Sorcha rolled her eyes.

One of the peat faeries clawed at the table. "I did not agree to follow the whims of a Druid!"

"You agreed to that the moment you walked through those doors and sat down at *my* war council!"

"How dare you!"

The shouts started again. Some argued that Sorcha was the only reason they were there. Others agreed that she had no right to be their leader.

Sitting back down with a hard thump, she watched the proceedings and wondered where she had gone wrong. Was she not supposed to assume these creatures were capable of rational thought?

"They aren't," a druid angrily said in her ear. "Why do you think they banished us all those years ago?"

She ached for Eamonn. He would have known what to do. Worse, they never would have become unruly when he was here. They would fear for their lives and what torture he would force them to live through.

"M'lady!" Oona's shout echoed through the outside halls before the doors burst open. "I tried to stop her, but she would not listen!"

"Who?" Sorcha stood and placed her palm on the knife at her hip.

The woman who entered the room was so painfully beautiful that she was difficult to look at. Hair, so golden it rivaled the sun, spilled down her shoulders to her waist. Sunlight blossomed from her skin, making her glow with an otherworldly light.

Sorcha glanced down at the woman's fingertips, pleased to see the stains had turned gray. Elva had shaken the addiction, so it seemed. Or at least had not partaken in such activities while she traveled.

"Royal consort," Sorcha greeted her. "I did not expect to see you here."

"I ask for a private audience."

The faeries stared at her, and Angus chuckled loudly. "Sorry, we're not able to afford you that. Not when we asked for the same and you killed our king."

"I did not kill him, and I request you respect my station, dwarf."

"What station? That of a sheath for our bastard of a king?"

A pink blush spread across Elva's cheekbones, and Sorcha knew it wasn't from embarrassment. There was a certain sense of panic radiating around the faerie. She was here without permission, Sorcha guessed.

"Go," she said to the faeries. "Leave us."

"M'lady, I cannot agree to such folly."

"Out, Angus. All of you, get out."

She half expected them to refuse. But they stood as one, reluctantly filing out of the room. Angus was the only one to remain.

"You too," Sorcha ordered.

"With all due respect, m'lady, I intend to stay. Someone should remain as your guard."

"Oona will stay."

"A pixie?"

"They are surprisingly capable of protecting those they love. Please, inquire with the pixie leader and see if she disagrees."

He grumbled, but left the room. She caught the way he hesitated to close the door. He watched them for as long as he could before the doors boomed shut.

Oona shook in the corner, her body locked tight as she stared at the woman she had helped raise. Sorcha caught her gaze and nodded.

The pixie launched herself forward and wrapped her arms around Elva's waist. Tears dripped down her cheeks, and her lavender wings beat so hard the wind knocked a cup off the table.

"Oh dearie! I never thought I'd see your face again!"

"Hello again," Elva hesitantly said. Her hand hesitantly pressed against Oona's back. "It is good to see you."

"I am so sorry. I should have kept you. I should have run away with you and never looked back. But that mother of yours was so certain you would become queen! She didn't let you be a child, and she certainly didn't want me around you too much. I should have tried harder!"

"Oona, there was nothing you could do to alter my future." Elva gently set the pixie aside, grimacing at the tears streaking Oona's cheeks. "I dislike being touched."

Sorcha watched from her seat at the head of the table, elbows propped up and her chin on a fist. "Yours is a story I would very much like to hear. But not now."

"No, there is little time for reliving the past," Elva agreed. "Thank you for offering a private audience."

"As private as one might get in such times. Please, have a seat. I would offer you food and drink, but I suspect you would not take it."

Elva sank into the chair across from Sorcha, arranging her skirts neatly. "The others did not?"

"Many choose not to eat until they have become invested in the cause. Once they realize we are talking about war, they are more likely to gorge themselves on my gardens."

"I did not realize midwives were capable of such greatness."

Sorcha's grin was feral. "I did not realize consorts traveled without permission."

"I see your tongue is quicker than I remember." Elva ducked her head. "It is true, Fionn does not know I am here."

"How long will it take him to realize where you have gone?"

"I imagine he already knows I have left, but he will never suspect I came here."

"Why not?"

"He still believes I love him."

Sorcha leaned forward, steepled her fingers, and pressed them against her lips. "Did you ever?"

"Love him? No."

It was a shame. Sorcha had seen how attached Fionn was to the beautiful faerie. Though it hadn't seemed possible, he was gentle with his consort. Almost kind.

Elva saw the emotions flicker across Sorcha's face. "It is true, he loves me."

"How is that possible?"

"Did you think him incapable of it? He is just a man, like the others."

"He admitted his guilt to me before he killed Eamonn."

Elva nodded. "He has nightmares about that night. He dreams of the blade plunging between his own shoulders and everything being taken from him while Eamonn watches."

"That was his plan."

"I suspected it was. They gave each other no choice."

"They could not see past their own differences."

"Both were set in their ways."

Sorcha felt a kindred spirit in the Tuatha dé Danann before her. They both knew the dangers of meeting, but both understood why the events had unfolded the way they had. They both mourned for the pain the twins had inflicted upon each other.

"Why have you come?" Sorcha asked.

"To offer my aid."

"You wish to go against the king? To help build an army which will defeat him?"

"I wish for my freedom," Elva corrected. "I wish to make decisions for myself, which I have never done before."

Freedom. It was a concept they all fought to possess. Sorcha wanted nothing more than her own freedom as well, yet she was now queen of a people who were not her own. At the very least, she could help Elva.

"Then you are welcome within my walls. I'm certain you will understand my hesitation at having you here, and that I will assign a personal guard."

"Understood."

Sorcha leaned back in her chair. "All right Angus, you can come back in."

The doors immediately burst open, and the dwarf sauntered into the room. "I knew you'd have need of me, m'lady."

"You were listening at the door. I don't take kindly to those who do not know when they are needed and when they are not."

"I wanted to be sure you would not be harmed. The queen needs a protector."

Sorcha forced her eyes to remain still. "This queen does not. You will assign a personal guard to attend to Elva. Please, remind the others she is here as a guest, not as a prisoner."

"It will be my pleasure."

"Take care of her and keep her safe."

Elva stood, brushed her hands down her skirt, and hesitated.

"Yes?" Sorcha asked. "Is there more?"

"I thought you would like to know. He keeps Eamonn next to the throne, a crystal figured twisted in pain and anguish."

"As a reminder to his people what happens when they go against the King."

"No." Elva shook her head. "I think it is a reminder for himself."

"Of what?" Sorcha asked.

"I do not know."

The thought was unsettling, and the last piece of information Sorcha needed to hear. She wished that Fionn was one of the evil characters of old. The man who wanted nothing more than to maim and torture, who needed to be put down.

He simply followed the old ways and trusted that they were the right decision for his people. Blind and foolish, he made decisions he might not agree with because they should be the right ones. Fionn was a complicated man.

Almost as complicated as his brother.

Sorcha nodded. "Angus, please show her to one of the guest rooms. Send Oona to attend to her and post two guards outside her door. She is to have whatever she wishes. Tomorrow morning, bring her to the war council."

"Understood."

The door closed behind them with a final bang that eased the tension from her neck. She lifted her hands and massaged the muscles, sighing as the headache faded away.

Balor appeared in one of the seats, leaning forward to grab a goblet of wine. "You did well today."

"Did I? I cannot say anything was accomplished."

"No, but you're earning their trust."

"By letting them scream and shout?"

"They need to get out their frustrations. The future is tenuous, and that makes people nervous."

Sorcha nodded. "And nervous faeries seem to have knee jerk reactions."

"That they do."

She leaned back and watched as he inhaled the sweet scent. She had yet to see him or Ethniu eat, and suspected they couldn't, but he still enjoyed smelling the food and drink.

"What would you do?" she asked him.

"I would have gone to war long ago."

"How many people would die?"

"Thousands. The land would be decimated, crops ruined, ground burned, grass trampled underneath the feet of my armies. We'd have cut down all the trees for lumber, killed all the animals for food, destroyed the mines so the other army couldn't get more resources."

"So, you would have killed Tir na nOg along with Fionn?"

Balor nodded. "The old ways were cruel."

"Are they the only ways?"

"That is up to you, my dear. These people deserve at least one battle.

See how you like that first and then make your judgment."

She leaned back in her chair and stared at the ceiling. It was a large decision to make and one she did not anticipate would end well.

Free from the war council for a few hours, Sorcha stood on the edge of the cliff where Eamonn had recited poetry. Her soul ached. It was a bruise she did not know how to heal.

"There are so many people here," she said to the wind, hoping it would carry her words to his soul. "Dozens of leaders, hundreds of clans, thousands of warriors all ready to stand in your name. I wish you were here to see it, my husband."

He would have been proud. He would have stood at the top of the mountain with her and stared down at the sea. Likely made a joke about how they could still run away and leave this place.

She smiled. He would have trailed a hand down her head and tangled curls around his fingers. He had always loved her hair.

Stones crunched from the crack in the wall behind her. It was almost completely fixed when she asked them to let it remain cracked. Though it was a weakness should an army climb the cliffs, she couldn't let them take this place away from her.

"Oona," she sighed. "I asked to left alone."

"Then it is a good thing I am not Oona." The deep voice sounded like the stamp of hooves. The fresh scent of grass drifted to her nose.

Sorcha stiffened. "Macha."

"Yes."

"You have not spoken to me in a very long time."

Why did the faerie come now? Of all times, why did the Tuatha dé Danann arrive just as the battle was about to begin?

Stones shifted back on her heels. Macha stood beside her, staring out over the crashing waves with her hands clasped behind her back. Their red hair tangled together until Sorcha could no longer tell whose curls were whose.

"You have done well," Macha said. "Far better than I expected from a human girl."

"Druid."

"As you wish. Druid."

Sorcha licked her lips, refusing to glance up at Macha. "I did not uphold our deal. Have you come to collect my debt?"

"No. You have exceeded my expectations and done the impossible. While Eamonn was not returned to my children, the outcome was exactly what I hoped."

Sorcha looked at her then, eyebrows lifted in surprise. "You wished Eamonn to start a war?"

"That was the intent of bringing him home. I expected he would fight my children for a time, but then he would agree that returning to Tir na nOg was the only way to save his people. I did not anticipate he would fall in love with you and wish to take back the throne on his own."

"He didn't really want the throne," Sorcha hesitated, "he wanted a home."

"Yet, he found that with you."

"I believe he realized that too late." She looked back out to sea. "And because of that, he paid dearly."

"It is always sad when we lose one of our own. I am sorry you must bear the weight of his loss."

"I bear more than that," Sorcha whispered.

"An army waits outside these walls for your orders. It is strange how time changes. I remember when we ran the druids out of the Otherworld for fear they would destroy us. Now, we all wait with bated breath as a druid determines whether or not she will catapult us into a time of blood and fear."

"You gave me this power."

"No," Macha shook her head. "I would love to take that credit, but you took this power all on your own."

Sorcha supposed she was right. If she had gone to Hy-brasil and done what she was told, then she would likely be back home with her father and sisters.

She sighed. "Did your children ever have the cure?"

"No."

"Did they know of it?"

"They knew ways to prevent a person from contracting the beetle plague, but not any way to cure those who were already ill. They also knew the druids had it, but with no way to contact them, they would not have told you."

"Could they have killed the beetles?"

"No."

Sorcha nodded. "Then you and your children misled me."

"We needed you to get Eamonn, and I knew he would follow you."

"Why?"

"He always had a weakness for pretty girls. Even more so for humans. I remember when he was a child, he used to watch your people through that mirror of his. He was fascinated by the choices you made, the stories you told, and the world you had built."

She could believe it. Eamonn had been too comfortable with her, too easily swayed when the others still did not trust her. They respected her, but they would not allow her to stay in their homes.

"Why did you lie about the cure?" Sorcha asked.

"It was not a lie. We would have given you whatever we could and then told you that there was no true cure. Only bandages to wrap around a gushing wound."

"You were wrong."

Macha curled her hands into fists. "I could not have known the druids hid a relic."

"They didn't hide it. They kept it safe for all these years because your brother asked them to."

"My brother has much to answer for, but that is not why I am here."

Sorcha spun, her feet confident and sure on the edge of the cliff. "Then why are you here? The great Macha, one of the trinity which makes up the Morrighan, stands upon a cliff side with a midwife. What could you possibly have to say to me?"

"That I am proud of you."

"I do not want your pride!" she screamed. "You and your people took everything from me. My life is in ruins, and you say you are proud? Do not be proud that I have discarded all sense of self."

"I have watched you grow from a child, to a woman, to a queen." Macha reached out, her hand hovering in front of Sorcha and then closing into a fist. "You are more than the midwife I found in a glen with honey on her hands and rosemary in her hair. Look at you!"

Sorcha hated it that the Tuatha dé Danann was right. She wasn't the same person she had been at the beginning of this journey. She had changed so much that she barely recognized herself.

And she expected that. Who wouldn't? Making a deal with a faerie was bound to affect the way she saw the world. The way she saw herself.

She could never have seen this future for herself. If she was being truthful, she had dreamed of a quiet cabin on the edge of the forest. A family who loved her, a tiny baby that bounced on her husband's knee.

Macha looked at her with pity. "You wanted a family."

"I wanted a life."

"Is being queen not a life?"

"No," she shook her head. "It is living a life for others. And while I do not resent them, I wish to be selfish, to live by my own choices without affecting so many others."

"There is no such life."

"Yes, you are right," Sorcha said with a sigh. "I didn't think I would walk this path alone."

"Are you alone? There are hundreds of souls standing around you, even now."

"The support of the dead is not the same as a loving touch, nor can they warm my bed at night."

She missed him with every breath she took. Though he would have been proud to see her accomplishments, Eamonn could not.

And now he stood as a trophy at his brother's throne. She wanted to bury him. To plant roses on his grave and tend to them every day. Sorcha would gently guide them into blooming all year, through snow and sun. She could do the impossible for him.

Tears pricked her eyes, and she cleared her throat. "It does not matter now. I have no choice."

"I cannot gift you a relic of the Tuatha dé Danann," Macha said. "I cannot even fight beside you on the battlefield as I am not supposed to alter faerie lives. But, if you will accept my final gift, I would give you all the knowledge I have."

"How is that possible?"

"I have watched thousands of battles, killed more men and women than those that walk this earth. It is my penance and my desire to see you win."

It could only help, although she did not want more screams of the dying in her head. She sighed. "It is another choice I make for others. Yes, Macha, I accept your gift."

The red haired woman reached out, tapped a finger to Sorcha's forehead, and all her battle knowledge flowed between Sorcha's eyes.

She understood the formations which worked and those that didn't. She saw through the eyes of the dying and the victors. Blades formed as red hot hammers struck them. Shields dented before her great strength, and blood flowed like a waterfall from her palms.

Sorcha landed on her knees with her hands outstretched. "Take it back," she cried out. "Take it back, I do not want it!"

"You will need it to protect yourself and your people. No matter how hard it is to bear."

She hated it. She hated the screams, the guilt, the wonder if the warriors had families. Macha didn't feel this worry. She saw the cold, hard truth of war and filtered it away.

How did the Tuatha dé Danann carry all this within her?

Macha knelt and took Sorcha's hands. "You must not let it overwhelm you. War is dark and dangerous, there are many who fall prey to its nightmares. But you will not let it devour you. That is not your destiny."

"I do not want to know all this."

"You must know it and use the knowledge well. You will carry your people into battle and you will fight by their side as a leader should."

"I will only slow them down."

"Not with this knowledge. You will wield a sword, you will fight with a shield that will drip with blood, and you will make your next decisions knowing you have done it their way."

Sorcha heard the hidden words in Macha's speech. She looked up through eyes ringed red with tears. "You do not want us to go to war."

"I have seen the outcomes of countless battles. I have seen what the Fae are capable of. I believe you need to see it too."

"Are the memories not enough?"

"You may share my memories, but you still have not experienced it for yourself. War tears at the strongest of creatures and breaks them into raw materials. You will only find your true self once you are in the heat of battle."

Sorcha searched her gaze for an answer. "And if I don't like what I find?"

"No one likes what they find at the end of a blade. But it will help you decide for yourself what the future of the Seelie Fae must be."

Macha stood, dusted her skirts, and held out a hand for Sorcha to take.

She wanted no more of the faerie's help, but realized she was being petty. Sighing, she reached out and let Macha lift her to her feet.

The scent of grass was overwhelming this close. It smelled of home, of kind things, of summer days that never ended. These were not memories Sorcha had the time to dwell upon.

"Are you ready, child?" Macha asked.

"No."

"But you will be."

"Yes."

"When will you give your army the answer they wait for?"

Sorcha looked up at the sky and saw the sun was already dipping below the horizon. "Tonight, at the feast they have prepared. They will expect such news to be announced then."

Macha nodded and released her. "And so the Druid Queen begins her war."

CHAPTER TWELVE

THE BATTLE TO END THE WAR

"Oh, dearie," Oona said as she tightened a strap of Sorcha's armor. "Are you certain of this?"

No. She wasn't certain of anything. But Sorcha knew she could not stand by while her people fought. She refused to stand atop a hill and watch people die when she should fight with them.

She was a queen now. That was her duty.

"Yes," she finally said. "I will fight by their sides."

"He wouldn't have wanted this."

Sorcha chuckled. "No, he would've tucked me in a corner and told me to wait until the screaming stopped. That isn't me, Oona. And you know that even if he were alive, I would have found a way to go."

"But you would have been healing people, not fighting with them."

"I will admit that is the difficult part of this. I wish very much to heal, not harm. However, this is my only choice. I took these people as my family, as my wards, and I will not be a coward in their eyes."

Oona smoothed her hands down the ornate breastplate covering Sorcha's chest. They had chosen an armor to rival all others. Hammered swirls created a pattern on the flat plate covering her chest and belly. Interlocking pieces lay smooth over her arms, shoulders, and thighs.

It did not hinder her movement, the most important part of a good piece of armor. They found the set hidden deep within the bowels of the castle, and Oona claimed to remember it from long ago. It was not faerie made, but the Druids had worn such armor long ago.

"Dearie, someone has come to see you."

Sorcha glanced over her shoulder, expecting to see a member of the war council. Instead, Elva stood in the shadows of the doorway.

"Enter."

She gracefully stepped into the light, and Sorcha locked her jaw. Elven armor covered Elva in gold from head to toe. She remembered it well from the attack upon Hy-brasil.

"Are you joining us then?" Sorcha wanted to ask if she were joining Fionn's army, wearing their symbol so blatantly.

"I am. I wanted to send a message to my beloved consort."

"Which is?"

"I may bear his name, his marks, and his love, but I am not his."

The fire blazing in Elva's eyes was enough to set an answering flame crackling in Sorcha's own breast. She nodded firmly. "Then select your weapon."

"Thank you Oona, I can prepare her from here on."

The pixie ducked her head and left the room.

Sorcha watched the elf circle the room, testing the weight and balance of sword after sword. "My council has warned me not to be alone with you. They do not believe you are to be trusted."

"I am certain they believe I am here to assassinate you."

"Could you?"

"Easily." Elva selected a rapier thin blade and tied the strap over her shoulder so the sword hung between her shoulders. "I have no wish to kill you."

"You say you are here to gain your freedom. How does starting a war with Fionn gain you that?"

"I am not starting a war. I am ending a war." Elva's gaze locked with hers. "Eamonn and I were very close in our youth. He protected me even though I didn't want him to. He was like an older brother, and then someone I could put a pedestal and fall in love with."

"And then Bran showed up." Sorcha said, thoroughly pleased with the shocked expression on Elva's face.

"How do you know that?"

"Eamonn mentioned something of your back story, and I pieced it together. Bran was here, you know."

Elva nodded slowly, ducking her head until shadows blanketed her expression. "A long time ago, he and I would have made a powerful pair."

"A long time ago?"

"I am weary of men. Their hands are grasping, their needs are great, and my mind no longer wishes to bend to their will."

"I do not believe Bran would ask that of you," Sorcha declared. "He seems an honorable man for all he is Unseelie and his family is unsavory."

"It is a good word for them." A small smile spread across Elva's face. "I wish I had become a different person as I aged, but I did not. The woman residing inside this physical form no longer wishes for the attentions of any man. Even one I might have loved."

Sorcha vividly remembered the state Elva had been in. The opium stains on her fingers, the glassy eyed expression, her fear when she thought Fionn might return. Although Fionn loved her, she had still been abused.

Stepping forward, Sorcha reached out an armored hand and grasped Elva's. Metal scraped against leather in a harsh grind. "When I was little, a woman on the street told me that women were created to suffer. It was the card life dealt us, no matter our station or purpose. I never believed it, and I see now we make our own path in life."

"If we choose to."

"You have made that choice, Elva. I will fight at your side for your freedom. I will support your choices after this war is over and will let no one stand in your way."

Sorcha meant every word with a power that vibrated through her body.

Elva nodded firmly, squeezed her fingers once more, and stepped back towards the weapons. "Have you selected a weapon, Your Majesty?"

It was the first time someone had addressed her as queen. Sorcha's spine straightened. "No. My skills lie with the bow, but my war council has advised I must also adorn myself with a sword."

"It is good advice. A bow is superb for long range combat, but a sword is the only thing that can protect you once his armies reach ours." Elva pulled a small sword from the rack. "This will suit you well."

It was much smaller than the sword Elva had chosen, but it felt good in Sorcha's hand. It was not too heavy as many of them were. She slashed through the air.

"I like this one."

"As I expected you would. It is a Druid blade."

Sorcha tested the weight in her hand again. "It feels right."

"That's what you want in battle."

"Have you fought in many?"

"Every Tuatha dé Danann has fought in many battles. We are a warring society. It is what we are good at."

"That's sad," Sorcha said.

"Is it? Our men test their worth through blood and fire. Our women learn kindness through small acts of kindness."

"Do any of you know how to love without the need to harm?" Sorcha shook her head. "I count my blessings that Eamonn was banished to that isle. For all the harm it did, he is a better man for it." She caught herself. "*Was*. He was a better man, but no longer."

Elva winced. "I envy you. At the very least, you carry him with you wherever you go."

"Love is like that."

"No," Elva shook her head. "I didn't plan to fight with you until I walked past you in the hall. There are two heartbeats inside you."

Sorcha blinked, not quite comprehending what Elva said. "Excuse me? Are you suggesting magic is at work?"

"Magic in the most earthly way. You are a midwife, Sorcha. I thought you would have recognized the signs before I did."

It wasn't possible. She couldn't be carrying his babe, could she?

She tried remembering the past few months, but all she could think of was the stress and fear. Her spells of nausea were brought about by the yelling of the war council, the memories of Eamonn's death, the responsibilities that rested on her shoulders. Not from a child.

"How is that possible?" she asked, pressing a hand against her armored belly.

"I suspect much in the same way my child happened."

"But I am not Fae."

"That has never stopped children from being born. There are plenty of half breeds, even in the Otherworld. Eamonn comes from a lineage of Fomorian and Tuatha dé Danann, as do you."

A dizzy spell made Sorcha's head spin. "I need a few moments."

"Of course, Your Majesty." Elva paused as she walked by and placed a hand on her shoulder. "I will fight by your side, to protect both you and the babe. Nothing will touch you. You have my word."

Her hand slid from Sorcha's shoulder and the door closed quietly behind her.

Sorcha stared at the racks of swords, the hanging crossbows, the shields leaning against the wall. A loud sob echoed through the weaponry, and she pressed a hand against her mouth to hold in any further sound.

A child? She was to bring a child into this life?

Still, it was the last bit of him she had left. She stumbled backwards and leaned against the wall.

"I am so sorry," she sobbed as she pressed her fingers to her belly once more. "You deserve so much more than this life. So much more than war and violence. You deserve a father who loves you and a mother who will kiss your bruises."

She couldn't fight now. She couldn't go into battle with thin armor and expect her child to live. What kind of mother would do that?

Rustling caught her attention, slicing through her fear and anguish. Looking up, her tear streaked cheeks turned cold as she saw a glimmering portal open on the ceiling.

A long, bristled leg reached through. It held a small clay pot in its claws, which it let drop onto the nearest hay bale.

The Unseelie Queen's voice boomed through the portal. "A queen makes many hard decisions, and you will not be the first pregnant woman to march into battle. We fight many wars. With our bodies, with our minds, with our words. Go and be safe, Druid Queen."

Sorcha watched the leg withdraw and the portal disappear.

Scrubbing her cheeks free of tears, she lurched towards the pot and wrenched off the top. Blue powder coated the inside. She recognized this, although she did not remember why. Sorcha dipped a finger into the substance and rubbed her index finger and thumb together. They both stained bright blue.

A druid voice sighed in her ear. "It is the symbol of our people."

"Why did the Unseelie Queen have it?"

"None know the reasons why the Unseelie Queen collects anything. Woad has always been a druid symbol of anger and war. Our women and men paint their faces and bodies before battle. It brings the ancestors with them."

"You will come with me to war?"

"We will guide your hand."

Sorcha blew out a quiet breath.

She could make the choice in this instant to fight. Her people would charge towards Fionn's and meet with them fierce pride, with or without her at their side.

But they would fight powerfully if she was with them. She would lift her blade and champion their injustices. The offending armies would fear the Druid Queen, rumored to control the whims and minds of the Fae.

She couldn't force them to do anything. She hadn't been able to since Eamonn left.

Sorcha dipped her fingers into the pot and swiped one across the high peak of her forehead. She glimpsed herself in the reflection of a shield. Each pass of blue paint made her anger grow stronger, louder, and all the more fierce.

Her hair tied up, swinging at her shoulders, she lifted a helm and placed it on her head.

As she stepped from the armory, all who saw her felt fear in their hearts. Gone was their healer queen. A warrior stood before them, hair like a waving banner of blood, and war in her heart.

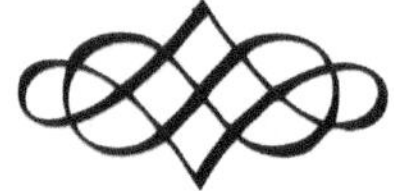

Their banners snapped as loud as a drum. Sorcha's horse shifted beneath her, restless for the battle to begin. It wanted to paw at the air, to crush skulls beneath its hooves, to race down the hill towards Fionn's army and begin.

She sat and stared down at the golden army, measuring each breath, forcing her movements to remain calm and still.

"M'lady," Angus said from behind her. "It is too late to turn back now."

"I have no wish to turn back, dwarf king. I am merely allowing them to look at us as we look at them."

"Why?"

"I want them to see our faces. To see the sheer number of faeries who disagree with their king."

"It will not change their opinion of him."

She shook her head. "I am not yet ready to believe these are not intelligent men and women. If they are not courageous enough to leave their king, then I want them to see those who were brave enough to do so. I want them to quake with fear before we even begin."

Angus fell silent and stared down at the army with her. This would be a bloody battle. Each army had sent a massive amount of soldiers. Fionn's was clearly well armed, but she knew they did not fight for the right reasons. They would falter because they were not angry enough.

The white stallion next to her huffed out a breath. Elva tightened her grip on the reins. "Will you give a motivational speech?"

"Is that necessary?"

"It is tradition for the leader to scream out a cry for their warriors."

"Then I shall."

Sorcha kicked her heels against the horse's side, moving out from the army and riding parallel to their ranks. She racked her brain for something to say, anything which would give these men and women a reason to be here. A reason to lose their lives.

There was none. There was never a reason to take a life or give their own, nothing worthy of their soul.

She drew her horse still and looked out over the people she loved. The last of her family, the last of Eamonn's great ambition.

The wind picked up, catching her hair and snapping it out like the red banners they all held. The Druid Queen—the Rose Queen—sat atop her mighty steed. She knew how small she looked, how small she felt.

In the end, the words came to her without the hard edge of steel, the metallic taste of battle, or the bitterness of war.

"Be safe!" she shouted. "Be well! And if you are not, I shall meet you in the halls of our ancestors with wine and stories to tell. We fight to take back what is ours, and we will not rest until we scream victorious in the halls of Cathair Solais!"

A cheer lifted into the air. Not enough, not nearly enough to strike fear into the hearts of the army behind her. Sorcha was too soft, too weak, too much a healer. She hardened her tender heart and screamed out a battle cry.

She was not a weak human. She was not faerie to hide behind armor and steel. The woad was her message, and it had been heard.

She reached up and pulled off her helm as green smoke swirled around her arms. The souls of druids dipped into her armor and would guide her hands as she fought.

The faeries fell silent as they stared. Blue woad covered one side of her face, patterns drawn across the other. She was an otherworldly creature, now. A being from their history who stepped out of time itself.

Her feral grin split the paint. "Let our swords feast this day! May your shields hold, your arrows fly true, and your battle cry resound through the Seelie courts from this day forth!"

The faeries screamed out. They lifted weapons into the air and cried out, for the Druid Queen rode with them.

Sorcha wheeled her horse around and stared down at the golden army readying themselves for war. Elva and Angus urged their steeds forward, their legs pressing against hers.

She could hear each breath she took, each beat of her heart thumping loudly against her ribs. The castle gleamed behind the army, so bright it burned her eyes. That was her goal, her destiny, where this would all end. Sorcha lifted her runic blade, inhaled, and shrieked, "Faugh A Ballagh! Clear the way!"

The horse's hooves sounded like thunder as they raced down the mountain. Clanging armor beat against her ears and her thighs gripped tight to her mount.

Fionn's army raised spears, ready to catch the horses the moment they reached them. But Angus had planned for that.

"Dwarves! Ready yourselves!"

They lifted great maces above their heads, swinging them wildly and releasing them at Angus's command. The spiked weapons bashed through the lifted spears, shattering the staffs into thousands of shards. The faeries only had a moment to stare at their broken weapons before the horses struck them.

She heard nothing at first. Then, the ringing in her ears dimmed.

They were screaming. Men, women, and horses all screaming as their lives drained from their bodies.

Dwarves lifted heavy hammers and brought them down on the heads of those who were not riding horses. The great thuds sounded like gongs as the Tuatha dé Danann dropped to the ground. Pixies threw knives into the air, catching underneath armor and digging into flesh.

She flinched as a golden soldier swung his massive sword and cleaved a peat faerie's head from its shoulders. He advanced towards her only to meet Elva's double blades.

"Sorcha!" she screamed. "Behind!"

She whipped around at the last moment and lifted her sword. The blades locked, vibrations jolting down her arm and zinging through her nerves. The soldier staring back at her knew exactly who she was. A grin spread across his lips as he swung the sword back again.

A spray of blood splattered across her face. Sorcha cried out, but the soldier slumped forward on his horse which raced away.

Angus lifted his hammer in salute and turned to swing at yet another man.

There were so many people. All she could hear were the screams of the dying, the aching pain and agony that stretched throughout the battlefield.

This was only the start.

She lifted a hand and touched the blood on her cheek. None of it hers, her people wouldn't allow that.

Elva screamed her rage into the air. She wielded dual blades, said she didn't need a shield, and Sorcha could see why.

The fair woman was not just stunning in person. She used her body like a weapon. Leaping and striking out from the air. Her horse was long gone, groaning on the ground and kicking its legs to kill any who came near it.

Sorcha was infinitely glad she had forced Cian and Oona to stay at the castle. They did not need to see this.

A soldier fell to his knees beside her horse. He reached for her ankle and she flinched, but the golden soldier did not try to pull her off.

She looked down and lost herself in his eyes. He was dying, he knew, and wanted a small bit of comfort as his soul leaked out of the gaping hole in his chest. She reached out a hand for him to take.

Cold metal met her fingertips for a brief moment before he fell onto his side. The final sigh of his breath echoed so loudly that she swore it was the wind.

On and on it went, the dying screaming out for mercy, for help, for anyone to hear their pleas. Both her people and Fionn's, all the same and yet infinitely different.

The Lesser Fae were brutal. They had so much anger built up over centuries and they showed no pity. The High Fae grew more and more angry that those who they believed beneath them would dare rise up.

She watched the ground grow slick with blood. Her heart beat slower and slower even as she refused to lift a blade.

A large man broke through her personal guard's ranks. His chest heaved, and he rushed towards her with his sword lifted. She heard the angry cry of the dwarves, the sad wail of Elva as they all watched him charge forward.

Sorcha was so tired of death. She lifted a hand towards the great man and called out, "Enough."

He stumbled but his sword remained in the air.

"Enough," she cried out. "There has been enough death!"

He took one more step towards her and let the blade dip towards the ground.

Sorcha slid from her mount, armored feet touching the ground so lightly they did not make a sound. She walked towards him with her hands at her sides.

The fighting slowed in the small pocket around them. Lesser Fae watching in fear as Sorcha risked her life. The High Fae staring with stunned expressions, horrified their largest soldier was hesitating to kill such a small girl.

"Be at peace," she said calmly. "You are not my enemy, and I am not yours. We did not choose this destiny, but we can change it. I do not wish to harm you."

In the blink of an eye, he lifted his sword and jabbed it towards her. Sorcha cried out, her voice mingling with his shout, and waited for the pain. It did not come.

A sword split through the front of his armor and he staggered to the side.

"No," she sobbed. "No more of this."

Sorcha reached out and caught him as he fell to his knees. She pulled off his helmet and smoothed her hands over his handsome face.

Shock reflected in his eyes even as blood dripped over his cheek.

"You did not deserve this," she said. "I am sorry."

He lifted a shaking hand lifted even as Elva cried out a warning. "You are not what I expected."

"Rest easy warrior."

"You should not be in war."

The life drained from his eyes as tears slid from her own. She smoothed her hand down his face, closing the vacant stare.

"M'lady!" Angus shouted as the Tuatha dé Danann advanced upon them. "Get back on your horse."

"No," she growled as anger sparked in her veins.

The green smoke of her ancestors swirled through her armor. They knew what she wanted to do. That she would no longer lift a blade towards these men and women who should be her people as well. They were Eamonn's family, and they would be hers.

"Enough."

The word carried across the battlefield. A druid tugged hard on her armor, "More, Sorcha. You must do more."

She imagined a distaff in her hand and remembered in startling clarity her mother's voice as she taught Sorcha how to weave.

"No, Sorcha, be patient. You'll create bumps in the wool!"

"We're just going to knit it anyways!"

"Silly girl, weave the flax around the distaff so it doesn't get tangled as we work. That's it, hold it like that, all the unspun fibers will keep still and then you can spin them into thread. Good. See? You were capable of it all along."

A tear slid down her cheek and Sorcha wove all the unspun magic and souls in the air into a fine thread strong as steel. She wove it into the air, knotting and untangling until she had created a tapestry of this moment in time.

"Sleep," she told the faeries on the battlefield. "Rest until this is done."

Releasing her hold on the thread, she heard every Fae drop to the ground. Their breathing was even and synchronized, creating a hushed wind that brushed against her ears.

She was so tired. She wanted to sleep with them, to curl up with the dead soldier and let her mind wander. It had been a long day. And she had spent so much energy to calm their minds.

"No, Sorcha. Our work is not yet finished," druids whispered in her ears. "You cannot sleep yet."

She had to go to *him*. Once Eamonn was put to rest, she could finally sleep in peace.

A quiet chuff blew on her face. When had she closed her eyes?

The air puffed again, brushing against her cheeks and reminding her of a time when a selkie had awoken her on a beach. Was she back there? Would he still be alive if she opened her eyes? Had this all been a bad dream?

Sorcha lifted her gaze and flinched at the sight of red fields. The stench of death filled the air and clogged her lungs.

Breath washed over her and brought with it the salty scent of the sea. Sorcha inhaled deeply, clearing her mind and lungs of war.

A kelpie stood before her. His dark eyes spoke of pity and forgiveness.

"You," she said in wonder and reached up to touch his velvet soft nose. A drop of water splattered on her forehead. "I remember you."

He bounced his head in agreement.

"You were at the waterfall on Hy-brasil. How did you get free?"

His eyes seemed to say that kelpies could were wild creatures. The waters of the earth wove together like her magic, and he had come because she needed him.

The kelpie shifted, slowly getting to its knees and waiting for her to pull herself onto his back.

She stood, her knees crying out in pain and her back aching. Her hands glided over his seaweed mane and the bumps of his spine.

"Eamonn said you would drag me down into the depths and drown me if I tried to ride you."

The kelpie's eyes said otherwise, the same as they had at the waterfall.

She swung a leg over its side and pressed herself against the cool wet skin. "Bring me to the castle, faithful friend."

The guards at the gate did not hesitate to open them for the warrior queen who rode alone into Cathair Solais. They could see the army laying on the field and wondered if they were dead. What had this witch woman done? What powers did this druid possess?

She balanced herself on the kelpie's back and planned what she would say. She would call for peace, she wouldn't give Fionn an option, she would force him to understand.

But then she rode directly into the palace and all words drifted from her mind.

They were having a ball. Gorgeous men and women swirled in colors she could not comprehend. Wine flowed from statues and laughter bubbled towards the ceiling.

The faeries wore fine masks, the metal so thin it looked like wire. Their dresses were pristine and their movements graceful.

They were so drunk they didn't notice she had arrived.

Anger burned so hot that Sorcha couldn't control herself. She leaned down, stuck her hand under a plate a passing waiter carried, and upended all the glasses onto the floor. The shattering made even the musicians shriek to a halt.

They saw her now.

The crowd parted, and she locked eyes with Fionn who relaxed on his throne.

"There is a war on your doorstep, Wise King," she mocked. "Or had you not noticed the blood coating your stairs?"

"Kings do not fight in wars."

"No, but apparently Queens do." She swiped at the blood on her cheek and pointed at him with a hand that dripped seawater. "I have come to claim what is mine."

"You think to take this throne?" he said, chuckling. "You are a mere human."

"I care little for a chair. The crystal man beside you is mine, and I intend to take him back."

"No." Fionn stood and gestured with the glass of wine in his hand. "Guards, remove this woman."

None moved.

"Guards! Take this human from my sight!"

Sorcha growled. "Sit down, Fionn."

"You cannot order me, midwife."

"I said, sit down."

"No!" Anger mottled his face with red splotches. "You have no right to be here, to interfere with anything! You should be on your knees when you greet me!"

"It is you, false king, who will *kneel*"

Her scream echoed through the great hall. The threads in her mind flared bright, and she tugged them hard, grabbing them in her fist and twisting cruelly. She wanted them to feel the pain and torment in her soul.

Each and every Fae dropped to their hands and knees.

Breathing hard, Sorcha clenched her hands into fists and slid from the kelpie's back. Her armored boots clacked against the stone as she advanced towards Fionn. Anger, so vivid and raw it blew hot breaths against her neck, beat through her mind and screamed for release.

There was so much pain inside her that thunder echoed in her ears. She walked up the stairs to Fionn and fisted a hand around his throat. Souls tangled around her arm, giving her inhuman strength. She slammed him against the back of the throne and squeezed.

"Your time is up," she growled.

"Never," he croaked.

Not releasing her grasp on his neck, she reached over her head and pulled out an arrow from the quiver at her back.

"You have been tried and found guilty, Fionn the Wise. Your crimes are slavery." She sank the arrow into the throne next to his head, reached for another, and continued. "Brutality." This one just missed his ear. "And lies."

She whipped the crown from his head and sank the last arrow so close that it cut through his hair.

Sorcha met his gaze with burning eyes and held the crown up for him to see. "This is not yours."

Turning to the crowd of faeries behind them, she brought the crown down on her knee and broke it in half. The two pieces fell to the floor and tumbled down the stairs. She met the gaze of each guard, saw the fear in their eyes, and felt it resound in her own chest.

Sorcha snapped her fingers and yanked hard on the threads of their existence. "Bring your king to the dungeon and wrap him in iron chains."

"No!" Fionn shouted. "Do not listen to this woman!"

"If he screams overly loud, tell me. I will ply him with herbs that will swell his tongue until he can hardly breathe."

The guards linked their hands underneath Fionn's armpits and dragged him from the room. His protests were ignored.

But then the faeries couldn't do anything other than ignore him, could they? She hadn't given them a choice.

Sorcha dropped into Fionn's throne with a heavy sigh. "Get out. All of you."

The faeries scrambled to their feet and left in such a rush that in three heartbeats she was alone.

A sob cut through the silence. Her agony rushed to the forefront.

"I have become everything I did not want to be," she cried out.

Her hands shook, and she stopped breathing as she finally turned her head and stared into Eamonn's cold, vacant eyes.

"My love," she sobbed. "I have come for you."

Pulling herself from the chair, she wrapped her arms around his shoulders and pressed her lips to his. Cold crystal bit at her flesh. So familiar and yet not at all. His chest did not move, his heart did not beat, and his eyes did not fill with the tenderness she had grown to expect.

Sorcha pressed her mouth against his again, "Would that I could save you. My love. My heart."

Tears dripped from her eyes and splattered against the cold stone.

Rage poured through her again. It wasn't fair. It wasn't right that she was so close to him, and yet so far. He would never look at her with love again. Never touch her shoulder, wrap her curls around his finger.

It was a cruel and angry jest that the world played on her.

She whipped around and cleared the food and wine from Fionn's side table. Screaming out her rage she fell to her knees beside him and gripped the Spear of Lugh.

"This does not belong here," she cried.

As if the spear understood what she wanted, the staff shortened, no longer propping Eamonn up. Yanking with her entire weight, she pulled the spear out of Eamonn's heart.

It clattered to the floor and all her anger drained, leaking from her eyes as tears slid from her cheeks. What was she to do with him? Bury him in the earth? Place him at the front of the castle like a watchful gargoyle?

She whimpered and wrapped herself around him once more. "Please, mo chroí. I want to hear your voice one last time. I love you."

At first, she didn't notice that her lips were pressed against silken hair. Then she heard the cracking of crystal as his fingertips moved.

Stumbling back, she landed on her behind and watched with wide eyes as the crystal shattered. It fell from his body in great shards, leaving behind warm caramel skin. He shook the stones from his shoulders, twisting away from her to rip off his armor and lift his hands to his face.

A chunk of crystal fell to the ground, the piece which had covered his face. Cold, blank eyes stared back at her, as if he had simply taken off a mask. Sorcha gasped and pressed her hand to her lips, watching with wide eyes as he stared down at his hands, then turned to face her.

He was perfect. Ragged and tired, but free from all blemishes. His face was smooth, his throat unmarked. Not a single crystal remained, not even a small one poking through his shredded shirt.

She watched his throat work as he swallowed.

"Sorcha?"

She moaned and scrambled to her feet. Launching herself in his arms, she tucked her face against his now smooth neck and breathed in his scent. "I thought I'd lost you."

"I thought I was dead." Eamonn pressed his lips against her

shoulder and crushed her in his embrace. "How is this possible?"

"I do not know, but I thank every god who ever existed that they brought you back to me." She leaned back and traced her fingers down his face, foreign now but just as beloved. "It's really you."

He said nothing. Eamonn palmed the back of her head and pressed their lips together. Warm and safe and wondrous, she framed his face with her palms and counted each of her many blessings.

CHAPTER THIRTEEN

THE CORONATION

Sorcha couldn't let go of him. She had to feel the smooth skin to believe he was really here, that somehow, some way, the disfiguring marks were magically gone. A god must have smiled upon them and healed all their wounds.

It was difficult to believe.

As they stumbled from the throne room, arms wrapped around each other, she realized how weak he was. His muscles trembled, legs quaked, and he leaned on her for support. This was not the king she remembered, but he would be.

He stepped out of the palace and lifted a hand to block the sun.

Faeries spread out on the grounds before them. All having stayed to see what the Druid Queen might do next. They gasped when they realized she wasn't alone.

"Fionn?" Someone called out.

"No," Eamonn replied. "Your high king."

Sorcha felt the tremble run through his body at the name. He glanced down at her.

"What happened?"

"Your crystals, Eamonn. They're gone."

"Gone?" He ran a hand down his face, shaking as he touched his throat. "Are they truly gone?"

"I don't know how, or why, but you are reborn a new man."

He swallowed, and Sorcha didn't know whether she would get used to see his Adam's apple move. How strange it was to see so much skin after all this time.

She linked her arm through his and pulled him through the crowd. There was more for him to see, more that needed to be explained, and all these Fae didn't deserve to see him at his weakest. They had condemned him long ago. They would now wait to hear what their fate would be.

They paused at the gate to the castle. His eyes widened in shock as he stared out over a battlefield of thousands all lying on the ground.

"You went to war?"

"And I ended it."

"You?" He tore his gaze away from the bodies and met her gaze. "You killed them all?"

"They're not dead, just sleeping."

"Do they know what happened?"

"No."

He blew out a breath. "I will confess, mo chroí. I can hardly handle this right now."

"We can wait to wake them."

"We shouldn't. Where is your horse?"

"No horse," she said with a smile. The wet suction of feet pattered on the ground behind them. "Just a kelpie."

His expression was almost comical. "You rode that? Alone?"

"I told you he didn't want to hurt me."

"The kelpie from the waterfall?"

"Not everything is black and white," she said as she stroked the kelpie's forehead. "I don't know why he helped me, but I know I'm forever grateful. I'm not sure I would have made it here otherwise."

Her own legs were trembling now. They both desperately needed to lie down in each other's arms and rest.

How long had it been since she'd slept in his embrace? Too long. Months, weeks, days, even hours were too long for Sorcha to bear.

He nodded. "Let's get this over then. Thank you, my friend. You have earned honor for the race of kelpies."

The sea horse bent to its knees and waited until both Sorcha and Eamonn were safely on its back. It surged forward and raced towards the battlefield. She could smell the sea air, hear the cries of seagulls, and the whispering crash of the waves.

Gods, how she missed the sea.

His arms tightened around her. She traced her fingertips over his forearms and realized she would have to learn him all over again. The sway of his body, the sparse spray of chest hair, the taste of skin rather than stone.

Breath stirred the curls at her temple. "How was I blessed with such a woman?"

"Is there an answer for that?"

"The gods smiled on me when they created you. I am a well-loved man."

"You are." Sorcha dug her nails into his arms and sent a silent prayer towards the sky.

But she knew it wasn't the gods who had helped. Whatever deity was out there had only set the wheel in motion.

The kelpie picked through fallen bodies as Eamonn guided it towards a rise which would give them the highest peak to call out to the armies. As they walked, she saw the faces of her ancestors hovering above the Fae. Each woad painted face smiled at her. They kept the faeries still and quiet.

Macha stood at the edge of the battlefield, her sword lifted in greeting. Beside her, Balor and Ethniu held their arms around each other and grinned.

Sorcha nodded to them and leaned further back against the wall of strength behind her. She finally had him. The only thing she'd wanted since starting this journey was a place to call home, a family who loved her, and to feel as though she belonged.

She would never have guessed she'd find it all in a single person.

The kelpie's feet touched the highest rise and shook its head. She jostled forward with a gasp, Eamonn pressing against her spine.

He groaned and pressed a kiss between her shoulder blades. "Just a little longer, mo chroí."

They moved like ancients, sliding from the kelpie's back while wincing. A headache throbbed between her eyes. It was over and yet not… for her.

Eamonn caught her as her knees gave out. He pulled her against his chest and smoothed the hair back from her face.

No crystals caught her hair.

"Let them go. Let them awaken and we shall greet our people."

She sighed, tucked her head against his chest, and released her grip on the threads. She could feel the druid souls disappear into the mist. A great weight she hadn't realized pressed down upon her lifted. She sagged against Eamonn, her head lolling to the side in relief.

"Good." He pressed a kiss against her temple, breath tickling her neck. "You've done remarkably well, mo chroí."

Sorcha nodded, incapable of responding in any other way.

He held her against his side and stepped forward to watch as the faeries rolled to their sides, some to their knees. Soldiers pulled their helms off to shake their heads in confusion.

Eamonn waited only a heartbeat before he called out, "Faeries of the Seelie Court! Behold! Your new king and queen!"

The golden army froze. A few looked up at the couple, torn clothing, blood splattered, and strangely alive.

No one could mistake Eamonn for Fionn on a battlefield. He stood with his legs spread wide, his chest rounded and spine straight. This was his domain.

"What did she do to us?" someone called out.

"I made you sleep," she said. "No more fighting, no more battle, just dreams."

"And our king?"

"He stands before you," Eamonn growled. "The Usurper sits in my dungeon until I decide what I wish to do with him."

Those who supported Fionn fell silent. Sorcha's people grabbed their weapons and corralled them until they stood in a great mass before their new king and queen. He squeezed her shoulders, tilted her chin, so she met his gaze.

"What shall we do with them?"

"If they wish to join our family, to support us, then they may."

"And if they don't?"

A spark of anger fired in her mind. "Then they can join their king who forced so many into slavery and more into starvation."

The armies heard her words loud and clear as druid souls echoed her words. One by one, the golden soldiers bent a knee. Not a single one remained standing.

Sorcha smiled. "I think they are afraid of me."

"In truth, so am I." But he lifted her hand and pressed his lips against her fingers. "My Druid Queen, I am sorry I could not battle beside you."

"I hope we will never have the chance."

"Angus!" Eamonn shouted. "Take care of things for me! I'm taking my queen home."

The dwarf saluted. "My pleasure!"

Eamonn swung her onto the back of the kelpie and they raced away from the Castle of Light. The kelpie swung his head, huffing out a breath, and mist formed beneath its feet. Faster and faster they rode until Sorcha threw her head back against Eamonn's shoulder.

"What is happening?"

"A kelpie can travel anywhere they wish, so longer as the water hears them."

"Then where are we going?"

"Home."

They sank into the earth and raced on rivers of magic to the small crevice in the back of Nuada's castle which Sorcha refused to fix. They carefully dismounted as the moon laved them with silver light.

Eamonn swung her into his arms and turned to the kelpie. "Thank you, my friend."

It bowed and leapt from the cliff into the sea.

He carried her through the shadows to give them a few moments of peace. The castle was silent, its residents sleeping with quiet dreams.

He tucked them into bed and wrapped himself around her. Just before she shut her eyes, she watched as he lifted her hand and stared at it in the moonlight. "You are a miracle, mo chroí."

"I am yours," she whispered.

They slept tangled up in each other, alive and finally at peace.

Feather light touches pressed across her cheeks and lips. She furrowed her brow, desperately trying to hold onto the warm grasp of sleep.

"Stop," she murmured. "It's not time yet."

"Mo chroí, if we wait any longer they will fear we died. Again."

Her eyes snapped open at the deep baritone so familiar it made her heart hurt. She blew out a breath as her gaze met bright blue eyes.

"Eamonn?" She lunged forward and wrapped her arms around his neck. Yanking him down on top of her, she breathed in his woodsy scent while tears trickled down her cheeks. "I feared I dreamt it all."

"I am here."

"You are *here*!"

He chuckled against her throat. "Yes, I am. Although I'm uncertain how much longer if you keep choking me."

"You're too stubborn to die by my hand. Let me hold you for a few moments longer. Please."

"A man cannot deny such a tempting argument." He rolled them over and wrapped his arms and legs around her. "Be at ease. We survived."

She couldn't stop crying. Tears splattered onto his chest, mingling with the short hair there. *Hair!*

Sorcha tugged on it. "Since when did you have chest hair?"

"Eh?" He ran a hand down his chest, craning his neck to look down at himself. "I didn't. Or I haven't, for a very long time."

She sucked in a breath and traced a circle around a hole she hadn't noticed before. A star shaped wound over his heart Tiny crystals scattered around it, hardly comparable to his previous crevices and cracks, but still there.

"Look," she said.

He held his hand over hers. "I'm pleased to keep it. It's a good reminder of how precious life is."

"It is." Sorcha leaned up and pressed her lips against his, making a face when she pulled back. "You have morning breath."

"I have *what?*"

"Morning breath!"

"I've never had morning breath in my life."

"You have now." Still, she kissed him again just to enjoy it. "Eamonn, there's something I have to tell you."

A fist pounded on the door, Cian's angry voice shouting through the wood, "Ain't no servants meant to be in those rooms at this time of day! If you're canoodling in the master's chambers, I'll flay you myself!"

Sorcha bit her lip and shook her head. "It can wait."

"I don't mind telling him where he can find the whip."

"Eamonn," she giggled. "We have to tell them sooner or later."

"A few more hours alone couldn't hurt." He ran his hand suggestively down her spine.

"You were the one waking me up and saying we needed to go."

"I changed my mind."

"Are you certain you're up to it?" She winced as her hip popped when she moved.

"Ah, we're both still aching. Perhaps we should wait."

She didn't want to, but knew she would regret it if they found time for each other. She wanted to run her hands over this new body of his and rediscover every piece of him. But her body creaked when she moved and trembled at the mere thought of stretching.

It would have to wait, as he said, but she wasn't happy about it.

"Shout for him then," she grumbled. "I hadn't thought to reintroduce you in our bedroom. But so be it."

Eamonn cleared his throat. "Cian! You mangy bastard open the door!"

The gnome's bellow echoed through the hall nearly as loud as the banging door which slammed off its hinges. There was so much hope in Cian's eyes as he looked at them, wrapped up in the cream sheets with gossamer curtains all around them.

And then rage so red it burned turned the gnome to stone.

"So that's how you're repaying him?" he growled. "The master's only been dead for three months and you crawl into bed with his brother?"

Eamonn moved, a sword flinging through the air so swiftly that it embedded halfway through the door just above Cian's head. "You'll be careful talking to my queen that way, gnome. We might have a history, but I won't stand for that."

"I won't have the false king in this castle."

"Then it's a good thing you don't have him."

Cian crossed his arms firmly over his lumpy chest. "You aren't the master."

Sorcha pulled the sheets up to her chest and sat up. "I appreciate your loyalty, but you must be blind if you cannot see this is Eamonn."

"Have you been tricked girl?"

Clattering steps echoed up the hall and Oona shouted, "What is it Cian? Did one of the will-o'-the-wisps get stuck again?"

She burst into the room, froze when she saw them, and crumpled into tears. "Oh my stars! Master!"

She threw her arms wide and leapt onto the bed. Sorcha choked as Oona's elbow hooked over her throat and dragged her back down to Eamonn's side.

Oona blubbered, "Oh my dearies! I never thought to see your faces again! And Master! You're so handsome, not that you weren't before, but look at you!"

She pulled back enough to pat his face with her violet hands.

"Oona!" Cian scolded. "That isn't the master! That's his brother, Fionn. Look at his face!"

"You dolt! Don't you recognize our boy when you see him?"

Cian's face paled. "Eamonn?"

"I tried to tell you," he grunted. "Instead you made me put my sword through a perfectly good door."

The gnome launched himself across the room and wrapped his arms around Eamonn's shoulders. "You're alive!"

They all laughed and held onto Eamonn until he turned bright red and attempted to shove them away. Neither Oona nor Cian would let go. He looked over their heads at Sorcha with wide eyes.

"They're in our bed."

"They missed you."

He sighed. "Ah well, we'll have a new bed soon."

Oona pulled back and stared at Sorcha. "You succeeded?"

"We conquered Cathair Solais and its previous king now rots in the dungeon until we decide what to do with him."

"Dearie, that is wonderful. And now the true king can take the throne."

Eamonn grinned, but Sorcha winced.

"They won't like me with you, Eamonn. You may wish for me to step aside for a while, just until you are comfortably king."

"Why would I want that?"

"There's a reason my people were cast aside. They fear me, even more so now that I proved what I can do. I can control them so easily. They are right to be afraid."

He reached out and took her hand. "They fear what they do not know. You've already captured the love of half the Seelie Court, and that's far more than any king has ever managed."

Sorcha lost herself in his gaze. He believed in her so much, it made her heart swell. She could do anything with him by her side.

Oona cleared her throat. "Then we go back to the Castle of Light?"

"As soon as possible."

Cathair Solais was abuzz with movement. For the first time in hundreds of years, a new coronation was being held. No one knew much about the mysterious king and queen who had fought through the golden army and won.

But all were curious. And all were invited to see the momentous crowning.

Servants rushed through the halls, Lesser Fae and High Fae alike. Some of the High Fae enjoyed their new lives. Working gave a purpose rather than constant balls, drugs, and alcohol.

Others chose not to have a respectable life, and they had the right to that choice. Old money would sustain them for a time, but eventually, they too would need to earn their keep.

"M'lady!" A shout echoed down the hall. "That's for the ceremony!"

"Oh it'll be fine, Ada! Shh."

Sorcha giggled at the startled expressions. The servants had yet to grow used to her strange behavior. They expected her to be like the countless other queens and princess they had seen. Stoic, demure, kind to a fault.

She stuffed the sweet pastry in her mouth and waved her fingers at them. Someday she might act like a queen, but certainly not within her own quarters.

Wiping sticky fingers on her skirts, she wiggled away from the wall of servants and rushed towards her room.

She still couldn't believe that an entire wing of the castle was dedicated to her. She had looked at the woman who ran the castle with wide eyes and asked why on earth she would need an entire wing.

Apparently, most queens thought they needed that much room.

Sorcha wanted a painting of the woman's expression when she had said to give the servants the bottom three floors. It was as if she'd suggested keeping farm animals inside her rooms.

"Sorcha!" Oona called out. "If you aren't in your coronation gown, I will come and stuff you in it myself!"

Her eyes went wide. Right, she needed to get into her dress, and wait patiently for the hairdresser.

She heard the tell-tale whoosh of Oona's wings and spun on her heel to race up the stairs.

"I can see your skirts!" Oona shouted. "Get dressed!"

The servants had to get used to their relationship as well. No one would dare speak in such a way to any previous queen. But Oona was nearly a mother to Sorcha, she could say anything she wanted.

Feet flying up the spiral stairwell, she made her way to the highest tower. Why had she insisted on this room? Her breath sawed out of her lungs and dizziness threatened to throw off her balance.

She slipped through the door, screeching when arms wrapped around her waist and lifted her off her feet.

This was why she had insisted on a tower room. Eamonn yanked her back against his chest and peppered kisses over her shoulders.

"You're supposed to be in a gown made of sunlight," he growled and bit down on her neck. "I don't see a gown, I see a milkmaid hiding from the scolding fishwife."

"Did you just call Oona a fishwife?" she laughed.

"She shrieks loud enough to have earned the name."

"Did you call me a milkmaid?"

"Oh, is that only in my fantasies?" He spun her around to capture her lips.

Sorcha shook her head, laughter bubbling through her lips. "You have fantasies about me as a milkmaid? Of all things, Eamonn!"

"What? There's something rather entertaining about the idea of returning from war, hungry, aching, tired. And there you are, on a hillside among the heather with your hair down and a smile on your face." He tugged at her dress. "And skirts that aren't too tight to toss."

She rolled her eyes. "That's more what I expected. Are you trying to distract me? We have a coronation to go to."

"And we're the king and queen! We can make them wait." He backed her towards the bed, tugging at the laces of her bodice.

Sorcha laughed again, slapping at his hands. "Stop that! You're only tangling them further!"

"I'm helping."

"You are not!"

"Sorcha, I've undressed more women in my lifetime than you have yourself. Stand still!"

It was to this playful scene that Oona barged in on. She pressed a hand to her mouth and blushed bright red, but Sorcha knew she had seen far worse.

"I see the master has taken it upon himself to get you into the coronation gown."

Sorcha shrugged and yanked the strings out of Eamonn's hands again. "It seems as though everyone is working against me."

"Into the gown with you." Oona pointed at Eamonn with a severe expression. "And if you delay her any longer, I will take a switch to your backside, boy."

"You haven't done that for centuries."

"Don't think I won't!"

She left the room and Eamonn glowered at the empty space. "We shouldn't have given her so many airs. She speaks to us as if we're children!"

"We are to her," Sorcha said with a chuckle. "More than that, we're her children. So don't take it away from her."

"Hm. Maybe just a little?"

"No!"

She let him spin her around and start on the clasps at the back of her dress. There was something quiet and sweet about the way he undressed her. Whether he had a particular goal in mind, or was helping after a long day.

Eamonn was always so gentle with her. And she still had a hard time believing this was her life.

Such a short time ago she was a peasant girl living in a brothel. The old religion was her escape from the mundane world of her life. And now? She sat on a throne with a man she would have claimed a god.

One of the Fair Folk loved her. How was she so lucky?

"I'm the lucky one," he said against her shoulder as he let her outer layers drop to the floor.

"Was I speaking out loud?"

"No, I could read it in your expression, mo chroí."

"Then we shall both be the lucky boxes, for we have surely been blessed in this life." She spun around, shoved her hands against his shoulders, and forced him to sit on the bed. "Eamonn, I've been wanting to tell you something for a while now, and I refuse to have a crown placed on my head without you knowing."

"You were married before you came here."

"What? No!"

"You killed a man on the battlefield."

"No."

"You've been cursed to shout 'toad' whenever you see my twin?"

She burst into laughter again. "No! You foolish man, none of that."

He palmed her hips and dragged her forward until she stood between his thighs. Pressing a kiss against her collarbone, he breathed, "Then what is it? It surely will not make me love you any less."

"No I suspect it will make you love me quite a bit more."

The words were hard to find, and nothing would do it justice. Instead, she took his hand and guided it over her lower belly where the slightest of bumps had formed.

He took a moment to understand what she meant.

Sorcha watched as each emotion danced over his features. His brows drew down in stubborn concentration as he worked thoughts through the feel of her belly. His eyes widened as he realized what she meant. Then, his hand flexed ever so gently over their child.

She had never seen Eamonn so stunned, or so moved. Tears filled his eyes and a rapid exhale took all the air from his lungs.

"Ours?"

Tears pricked her own eyes as she laughed. "Could it be anyone else's?"

Beside himself and without words, Eamonn slid from the bed onto his knees before her. He pulled her close and pressed his forehead against her belly. She felt the slow glide of his nose as he nuzzled closer.

"You are loved," he growled, both to her and the child. "You will be great and honorable and good. You will have your mother's flaming hair and your father's stubborn chin. I will rock to sleep at night, and your mother will kiss you awake every morning."

She pressed one hand to her trembling lips and the other to Eamonn's head. She held him against her, close to their child who seemed so much a miracle in the midst of such darkness.

Voice choked, Eamonn looked up at her. "How long?"

"I can't be so certain. Six moons, maybe a little longer."

"Is it a girl?"

"I don't know," she chuckled. "Don't you want a son?"

"I want anything you can give me and hundreds more." He lurched to his feet and drew her so gently into his arms she wondered if he thought she were now made of glass.

"Hundreds?" she chuckled. "That's too much to ask, high king."

"Not enough. I can't ever have enough of you."

She lost herself in his kiss, in his embrace, as he held her against his heart.

"Are you ready?" Eamonn asked.

They stood just outside the throne room, fully garbed in the most uncomfortable clothing Sorcha had ever seen. He looked wonderful. Dressed all in white and gold, the long tail of his braid left free to swing as he moved. Ocras swung from his hip and a large starburst pendant from his neck.

Sorcha's high necked dress made her want to scratch. It splayed out around her chin like a wave from the ocean, and in theory was stunning. The bell sleeves touched the floor if she let her arms dip too far. Gemstones studded the metal corset and sprayed down the heavy skirt in fine, embroidered stitches. Her hair piled heavy on top of her head, braided so tight she could feel the skin at her temples pulling back.

It was too bad the whole thing made her feel as if she were an antique on display.

"Sorcha?" Eamonn asked again.

"Yes, yes I'm ready."

"Are you certain?" He reached out and touched a hand to her belly.

"We can always postpone if you wish."

"I'm no different than I was before, and you didn't treat me like glass then. Besides, we've already made them wait too long."

"It will be overwhelming."

"Why should it be? They will be silent as the grave and wondering just how much we will change."

He smirked. "You'll see. Guards, open the doors."

The two men in silver armor, Eamonn had insisted the uniform change no matter how much Sorcha argued it was wasteful, swung open the doors to reveal the crowd of faeries.

They saw their king and queen and burst into boisterous cheers. She forced her mouth to remain shut at their enthusiasm. She had thought they would remain reserved, unsure of their new rulers who had taken the kingdom by storm.

They were not. Some faces she recognized, dwarves from the battlefield, pixies in the air, peat faeries in the shadows with bright smiles on their faces. But others, she did not. Tuatha dé Danann, dryads, brownies, those who had remained faithful to Fionn until the bitter end.

Even they were pleased to see Eamonn and Sorcha at last.

She gripped his forearm tighter and glanced up at him. "I had not expected this."

"The Fae are much used to changes in their lives. The royalty moves, pieces changing, switching as the game is played. They hope we shall be better than the last, and if we are not, that we will be overthrown just as quickly."

Sorcha blew out a breath. "That is a lot of pressure."

"It is, but we will be a good king and queen."

"How can you be so certain?"

He looked out over his people, a soft smile on his face. She was struck by the ease he stood among them. The simple way he could switch from warlord to king seamlessly.

"This is what I was raised to do, Sorcha. I saw the injustices our people were forced to bear, but it was you who convinced me they could truly be changed. We will make a great difference in this world, unite our people, and give this land much needed peace."

She looked up at Eamonn and smiled. They made their way up the steps towards their thrones. One jagged edged, burned, and foreboding. The other with roses blooming over every inch.

A voice shouted, "Thus ends the era of Fionn the Wise and so begins the reign of the Stag King and the Rose Queen!"

Two of the oldest Tuatha dé Danann stood, carrying gilded crowns that made Sorcha's heart pound. Was she ready for this? Could she ever be ready to be Queen?

She looked out over the crowd and saw faces she loved, people she trusted, and she knew that if it were her destiny to become queen, then she would wear such a destiny with pride.

The strange creatures were a myriad of color and textures. Wings, horns, glittery appendages, all blended together to creature a patchwork of magic and wonder.

Except one single person, who stood out like a sore thumb.

She gasped out a wrenching sob. "Papa?"

Eamonn squeezed her hand and nudged her back towards the crowd. "The crowning can wait."

She didn't care what her people thought of a queen who fled from her throne and burst into the crowd. She threw her arms around her father's shoulders and sobbed into his neck.

"Oh, Papa! I didn't think I would ever see you again!"

"Neither did I, my sweet girl." He held her close, laughing in her ear. "But your husband found me far too easily, and here I stand."

"And my sisters?"

"Waiting in our room. I'm afraid they were much overwhelmed by the Otherworld."

"And you are not?"

"No, I'm too ornery to fear these creatures." But he looked around them and gulped. "Besides, it's not every day a father gets to watch his child crowned queen."

Sorcha tightened her hold around his neck. "I must go and do that, father. But I wish to speak with you immediately afterwards."

"Aren't you supposed to be having some kind of ceremony?"

"They can wait. My family is far more important than stuffy old traditions."

He chuckled. "I believe your husband feels the same way."

"He does."

It took quite a bit of effort to release her hold on her father's neck. She missed him terribly and hadn't realized the hole in her heart that came from him not being here. Sliding from his embrace, she smiled brilliantly before turning back to her husband.

Eamonn. The man who had not only saved her life and convinced her to become something far more than a midwife, but who catered to her every whim and desire.

She walked back up the steps and reached her hands out to him. "You did this."

"I knew you wouldn't want to go through it without at least one of your family members."

"I would never have asked. I don't even know what you must have done to bring him here."

"You don't want to." He pulled her close to him and feathered a kiss over her lips. "But I would do anything for you, mo chroí."

"Then let us be crowned and get this over as soon as possible. I wish you to meet them."

He whirled her around so her skirts flew in a bell shape around her knees. The faeries cheered, and he sat her down in her throne, taking his beside her.

The herald cleared his throat and began again. "We crown thee the Stag King! May you rule with honor, confidence, and a sure hand."

The faerie behind Eamonn lowered a crown which twisted and

turned, pockmarked like the tines of an antler.

"We crown thee the Rose Queen! May you rule with kindness, nobility, and forgiveness."

She felt the thin gold crown nestle in her hair. She knew without looking that delicate roses had been crafted by the finest artisans in all the land. Looking out over the crowd of her subjects, she smiled at them and prayed she would never let them down.

Eamonn reached for her hand and squeezed it. "Together."

She looked over at him and felt her heart swell. "Together."

"Are you certain you're up to this?" Eamonn asked.

"Would you stop asking me that question today?"

"It's just in your delicate condition—"

"If you say one more word about me being pregnant and fragile, I will set the drapes on fire."

"You wouldn't dare."

Sorcha glared up at him. "I most certainly would."

"Your sisters sound…" He glanced at the door as shrieks of laughter blast through the thick wood. "Exhausting."

"They are. But they are very kind and have good heads on their shoulders. I think you'll find that they are wonderful women who love me very much."

"They let you go."

"Because it was what I wanted." She put her hand on the doorknob and grinned. "You'll be all right, won't you?"

"Just open the door."

Sorcha turned the knob and threw her arms wide. "Sisters!"

"Sorcha!"

The shrieking group of thirteen women surrounded her. They

passed her around for hugs, tears, and blubbering words incapable of being understood. They didn't need to know what the others had said, the love was already in the air.

Each woman had missed Sorcha so much that it boiled over into a cloud of happiness that tasted of salt and relief.

Eamonn leaned against the door with his arms crossed. Sorcha's father walked over to him and stood watching the teeming mass of females.

"It's rather intimidating, isn't it?"

Eamonn glanced down. "That's one way to put it."

"Her family loves her very much."

"It is a rare gift. She appreciates it."

"Do you?" Papa glanced up with a stern expression. "I won't have my daughter taken away from me by the Fair Folk."

Eamonn found it strange that such a small man was threatening him. Humans were tiny compared to the Tuatha dé Danann, and yet Sorcha's father had no hesitation. He understood what those words meant but did not curb his tongue.

Inclining his head, Eamonn replied, "I have no intention of keeping Sorcha from her family."

"Good, that is good."

Sorcha glanced up and gestured for Eamonn to join them. "Mo chroí! Let me introduce you to my family!"

He shouldn't have to steel himself to manage a group of Sorcha's sisters. But Eamonn found himself more nervous than the eve of battle.

Straightening his waistcoat, he stepped forward. "Ladies."

They tittered. *Tittered* and giggled like little schoolgirls and ducked their heads to whisper to each other.

Gods help him.

Eamonn glanced behind him, hoping Sorcha's father would provide some much needed guidance. The old man simply shrugged.

Some use he was. Eamonn clenched his fists and lowered himself onto a tiny couch with women flocking all around him.

"Sorcha! I thought he was supposed to be beastly! That's what all the stories say."

"Stories?" Sorcha blinked at them. "What stories?"

"Well once we knew you went to Hy-brasil, we searched for any rumors! Everyone was talking about the ugly brute on the isle, but this man… Oh, he's not ugly at all."

He wanted to remind them that he could hear them. But the ladies were enjoying themselves, and he hadn't had a crowd of women admiring him for a very long time. What harm could find him from allowing himself to find peace?

Sorcha's eyes flashed with jealous anger.

Right. That's where the harm could come from. Sighing, he wrapped an arm around her shoulders and pressed a kiss against her temple. "It's been a pleasure, ladies. But I have other business to attend to. I trust you will take care of my life?"

"Your wife, you mean?"

"No," he corrected. "My life. She is the very reason I draw breath and is worth far more than just a title."

One of the sisters listed to the side with her hands pressed against her heart.

He stood immediately, catching Sorcha's eyes to make sure she was all right. She nodded with more glee in her expression than he had ever seen. If all it took to make her happy was having her family around, then he would keep them.

What would the old Tuatha dé Danann say to that?

Grinning, he strode from the room. He did not run. No one would dare say that the new king of the Seelie Fae would ever run from a group of women.

But he may have rushed.

The servants bowed as he walked by, and Eamonn didn't have the heart to tell them to stop. So many things were already changing. They needed something to remain the same so their world didn't completely upend.

He looked just like his brother. Some of them still slipped and called him by Fionn's name, turning white as a bean sidhe when they realized what they had done.

He wouldn't hurt them for the small slip. He understood why they were concerned, but didn't have the heart to punish them. These people had suffered enough.

Or perhaps they hadn't. Some of them had liked having Fionn has their king. Eamonn didn't know what to make of that.

The dungeon was a dank, dark place. Water dripped from the ceiling in a never ending stream of sound that would have driven him mad. Some of the prisoners had already lost their minds.

Eamonn had personally reviewed their records. Some he let go, Lesser Fae who had broken the law only to feed their families. Others stayed where they were. Just because the king changed didn't mean murder was acceptable.

At the far end of the dungeon, far away from the others, Fionn waited. His arms stretched out at his sides, chains digging into the skin. His beautiful hair dripped water and hung lank to the ground. They removed most of his clothing, leaving him in nothing more than dirty breeches.

Eamonn nodded at the guard who opened the door.

Fionn did not even look up.

He knelt beside his fallen brother and sighed.

"You told me I forced your hand when you plunged the Lugh's spear through my heart."

The chains rattled, but Fionn remained silent.

"So I say to now, you have also forced my hand. I wish it could have been different between us, brother. I would have liked to rule with you by my side."

Eamonn tipped Fionn's face up, staring at his sunken eyes and the bruises on his jaw. It was like looking at a mirror image of himself. And so painful that Eamonn forgot how to breathe.

"Are you going to kill me?" Fionn croaked.

"No. I'm banishing you to the human lands and denying you all ties to the Otherworld. No faerie shall speak with you, no Wild Hunt shall find you. I gift you life, brother, but nothing else."

"It's a fate worse than death."

"Perhaps you think so now. But I promise you, someday you'll realize these people are capable of love in a way we never imagined. You have never been alone, Fionn. Now you will be." Eamonn stood. "I look forward to watching you, and how you change your story. Or how you don't."

As he walked out of the cell, Fionn lifted his voice once more.

"And Elva?"

"She doesn't love you, brother."

"It doesn't matter. I love her, and I would know she is safe."

"Elva has taken her life into her own hands." Eamonn clasped his hands behind his back and turned towards Fionn. "She travels to an isle far north, dedicating her life to the art of war. No man may step foot on those lands. I would be surprised if she ever leaves it."

He turned away from the tragic expression on Fionn's face. The fallen king was more affected by the loss of his consort than he was his own fate. A shame, because his brother didn't know what real love was.

The chains rattled, and Eamonn blew out a breath. The head of his army waited at the top of the stairs. The tall elf worked closely with Angus who had returned to his home under the mountain.

"Your Majesty?"

"You heard my judgment?"

"Yes. Do you wish to wait and speak with the queen?"

Eamonn shook his head and clapped a hand on the elf's shoulder. "No. She need not be a part of this. Keep the information from the dowager king and queen, they are to be confined to their quarters for the remainder of their lives. Banish Fionn, take care of the gates, and ensure all faerie rings reject him. I want no chance that he will ever return to the Otherworld."

"Consider it done."

He already did. And perhaps that was why his heart ached.

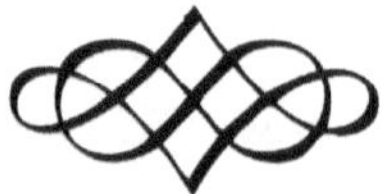

Much later, Eamonn awoke from his dreams. The wind brushed through the windows of the high tower, cooling his skin. Groggy and half awake, he reached for Sorcha only to find her spot cold.

He grumbled as he rolled over to stare at their balcony.

The moon silhouetted her figure, sheer white fabric billowing over her body as the wind kissed her curves. How he loved her.

A man's legs shifted, perched on the railing. Eamonn also knew who that would be. Damned Unseelie, they never knew when to stop meddling.

He swung his legs over the edge of the bed and strode towards her. Shirtless, he pulled her back against his chest and pressed a kiss to the top of her head.

"Bran," he grumbled.

"Your Majesty." A distinct tone of mockery was in the Unseelie prince's voice.

"Jealous?"

"Never. The throne is not my destiny."

"Don't say that. The ancestors have a way of meddling in our lives."

"I wish they'd stick to humans."

Sorcha scoffed. "Keep your bad luck to yourself, thank you."

She was warm and soft, everything he had always desired his wife would be. He couldn't remember ever seeing a Tuatha dé Danann woman quite like her. They were always regal, put together, tall and broad shouldered. Sorcha was tiny and so hot she burned like a furnace.

He spread a hand wide over their child and the ever growing bump of her belly. "What were you two talking about?"

"The future," Sorcha replied.

"And?"

"We think it will be very good."

"Is it? Why do you think that?"

Bran chuckled. "My mother said so."

"Ah. Then it will be."

Eamonn felt the last chip of his soul slide back into place. His life had never been blessed with love, family, friends. He'd always been alone.

Now, with this woman who was never alone, he found himself and a future filled with laughter and love.

Sorcha's hands pressed against his, and a firm kick pressed against his palm.

"Was that–?"

"Your daughter is restless, Athair," Sorcha said with a smile.

He didn't care that Bran was watching. Eamonn spun her around and dropped to his knees. He pressed his lips against her belly and felt the slow roll of his child between her hips.

"Just a little while longer, nighean, daughter. Soon our family shall be together at last."

Sorcha threaded her fingers through his loose hair, and Eamonn suddenly realized what it was like for all to be right in the world.

AFTERWORD

And thus ends the second part of Socha and eamonn's story.

What a journey with these two! I thoroughly enjoyed writing this book, and I hope you enjoyed reading it as well!

The series of the Otherworld will continue in another character's story, with a new fairytale. I think it's safe to say, I can tease you that the story will be the Swan Princess!

Please make sure to keep in touch on my social media (Facebook, email, etc) as I will continue to update you on all the exciting new stories and books!

Well met, and blessed be.

ACKNOWLEDGMENTS

There are so many people to thank for this book that I couldn't possibly write them all down. If I forget you, I am sincerely sorry and yell at me later.

Nata - Again, the cover. I mean SERIOUSLY I am so lucky to have found you and your wonderful talent. This artwork embodies everything I want people to see in these characters. Their strength, their virtue, and their ability to overcome all odds. I can't thank you enough.

Amy - The fearless editor who has no problem telling me when something is stupid, or just not up to my usual standards. You're a saint.

Renee and Emily - The fearless duo who have helped me get through writing in general. Thank you for never letting me get too far down in the dumps, and for taking the time to listen. It means the world.

Mom and Dad - Is there any way to thank you? For all the bruises, scrapes, nights crying, headaches, and crap you put up with, I love you and appreciate you more than words can express.

To my Readers - Every book you buy, every review you leave, every message you send means the world. (Didn't that sound like it was going towards a Police song? Everything breath you taaaake)

This is for you.

BRIDE OF THE SEA
EMMA HAMM

Copyright © 2018 by Emma Hamm
All rights reserved.

Cover by: Magdalena Korz
Editing by: Amy Cissell
Formatting by: AB Formatting

No part of this book may be reproduced in any form or by any electronic or mechanical means, including information storage and retrieval systems, without written permission from the author, except for the use of brief quotations in a book review.

GLOSSARY OF TERMINOLOGY

Tuatha dé Danann - Considered to be the "High Fae", they are the original and most powerful faerie creatures.

Seelie Fae - Otherwise known as the the "Light Fae", these creatures live their lives according to rules of Honor, Goodness, and Adherence to the Law.

Unseelie Fae - Considered the "Dark Fae", these creatures follow no law and do not appreciate beauty.

Máthair - "Mother"

Bean sídhe - Also known as a banshee, their screams are echoing calls that herald the death of whomever hears them.

Hy-brasil - A legendary isle which can only be seen once every seven years.

Merrow - Also known as a Mermaid, merrows have green hair and webbed fingers.

Merrow-men - The husbands of their female counterparts are considered horribly ugly with bright red noses, gills, two legs, and a tail.

Kelpie - A horse like creature who lives at the edge of a bog. It will try to convince you to ride it, at which point it will run underneath the water and drown the person on its back.

Selkie - A faerie which can turn into a seal, as long as it still has its seal skin.

FOREWORD

This is the first Companion novel in the Otherworld series. What is a Companion novel?

This story and all others with the "Companion" tag will be about characters in the main stories who might not have gotten a voice otherwise. These are non-royal characters given life in their own stories. They are standalone retellings and can be read in any order.

As always, I'm not a historian and as much as I wish I was, this is a work of fiction.

PROLOGUE

Once upon a time, when the world was new, a tiny seashell washed ashore. She was small and rough, for only a small snail had lived inside her. But she was strong enough to withstand the heaviest of storms and the crushing weight of the ocean.

Alone and insignificant, she rested on the sands and waited. The seashell didn't know what she was waiting for, but she was certain it was something big. The land was not quiet like the ocean. People shouted, the ground thundered, the animals were noisy, and the world was very frightening.

The brave little seashell waited in the sand, buffeted by gentle waves and softened by their wandering touch until she shone like a pearl. She waited and waited until a man stopped right beside her.

His foot came so close to crushing her that she cried out in fear! He paused—a bear of a man with so much hair she thought him an animal—stooped down and picked her up. Tossing her back and forth between his meaty fists, he stared at her shimmering surface.

"Hello," he murmured. "It's good luck to find such a pretty seashell."

She stared up at him in awe. "You think I'm pretty?"

"I think you're beautiful."

At that moment, the tiny seashell fell in love. She decided his furry face wasn't quite so loathsome, his booming voice wasn't too loud, and the bright flash of his smile wasn't too blinding.

"Will you come home with me? I shall place you by my bed on a tiny pillow which will keep you safe from all harm," he asked.

"Yes," the tiny seashell whispered. "Yes, I will."

He placed her in his pocket which had a tiny hole at the seam. Through the opening, she peered out at the world. It was wondrous and great, far more than a seashell could comprehend.

The animal-like man placed her atop a velvet pillow and kissed her shiny surface.

"Thank you for the good luck, little shell. I must go to sea, but when I return, I promise to turn you into a necklace and keep you with me forever."

She waited—she was good at that—and waited some more.

A spider wove her web across the door. The tiny seashell watched her weave, capture food, create a family, and then die. Soon, another spider took her place and unraveled all the work she spent her entire life creating.

The tiny seashell watched dust settle on the home and on her velvet pillow. The windows cracked in a storm and tiny birds nested in the rafters. Mice tore at her pillow and pulled out the stuffing for their nests.

And still, the man did not return.

CHAPTER 1

THE MERROW AND THE PIRATE

Seagulls screamed overhead, their rasping cries echoing in the fresh salt air. The sea rolled in gentle heaves which did not disturb the ship bobbing atop its surface. A faint breeze cooled overheated skin, but it was not enough to fill the sails hanging limply from the mast.

Manus shaded his eyes staring out at the horizon. It was always the same. A small sliver of hope, the slightest glimpse of land, and a ship that wouldn't move.

Such was the life of a sailor. The sea tossed and turned, storms tore at ships and men, and dehydration tore at their bodies. They all did it for one reason.

Adventure.

Danger dogged them at every corner, yet each man returned month after month to climb atop the great ship and set sail for new horizons.

He lifted his face to the wind and breathed in the salty air. It didn't matter to Manus that they were sitting ducks on the ocean, that their water supply ran low, nor that their food was slowly disappearing.

As long as he was on the ocean, he could take any beating. Always did, even when he was a child. The old sailors used to call him the street rat born in the arms of the ocean. The boy who was meant to live on a ship.

"Manus!"

He glanced over his shoulder at the boatswain. The sturdy man was intimidating on a good day, frightening on a bad one. Oisin knew how to order the men about and get them moving without complaint. It was a talent Manus intended to learn someday.

"Get yer arse moving, sailor! The wind is bound to blow again!"

The wind wouldn't move anytime soon. Manus had always felt the weather deep in his bones. Faerie touched, some might call it, although he would never admit to having any marks on his soul. Faeries hadn't mingled with his family line in a long time.

But there was one grandmother whose tipped ears made people question how truthful he was when he denied having faerie blood. The ancient crones remembered his loving gram spending hours making certain everyone was well-fed and content. They still thought she was cursed and wanted nothing to do with her, even though she'd bent over backwards to make them happy.

Shaking his head, Manus tossed the long mane of his hair back and made his way up the netting.

"Wind," he grumbled as he climbed up the mast. "As if there will be any wind in these waters."

Not for a few more weeks, at best. He'd suggested last night they put all the men's backs to use and row. The other sailors nearly shoved him overboard for that proposition.

The ropes tugged hard, and his feet slipped from their hold. He grasped the horizontal post, glared down at the laughing shipmate, and swore under his breath.

Manus had bribed his way onto the ship, and now everyone knew because a loud-mouthed shipmate had shouted it during a drunken revelry. He laughingly revealed Manus wasn't meant to be here at all, but the Captain let him stay for a little bit of coin.

All chances of a fair trip had shattered at that moment.

No one wanted a man aboard who didn't know his way around a ship. Manus told them, time and time again, he knew how to sail. He'd known since the first moment his mother dipped his toes into the water and pressed a kiss to his head.

They didn't believe him.

There was also the slight problem of Manus's big mouth. He didn't take shit from any man and solved problems with fists rather than words. On the streets of Uí Néill, it was far easier to push and shove his way out of a bar.

On a ship? That was a different story altogether.

He heaved himself to the top of the mast, wrapping his legs around the smooth wood to anchor himself in place. His ribs protested as the stretching movement pushed against the raw bruises blooming across his dark skin.

Another beating, another day. How many had he endured so far?

He couldn't count that high.

If this was how they wanted to deal with him, then so be it. But, he would be back for the next trip, and the next. When the Captain wouldn't have any more of him, he would look for another ship.

The sea called to him like a siren. It wanted him to ride her great swells and feel the kiss of sea spray against his skin.

Manus whipped a cloth out of his waistband and scrubbed the mast. It wasn't doing anything. The boatswain kept saying how it was good to clean the mast of salt, but Manus knew it wasn't that.

They wanted to keep him away from the real work. Scrubbing the deck put him in the way of everyone. He was a big man, and a ship wasn't a place for big men. So, they sent him as high up as he could go, out of their line of sight and their hair, told him to clean, and forgot he was there.

He didn't mind too much. If anything, this was where he wanted to be. He could see every bit of the water spread out like a blanket around them. Seagulls soared above his head, dolphins leapt into the air with chattering cries, and the clouds created patterns only he could decipher.

Who wouldn't love this life?

Manus spent the rest of his day in the crow's nest, only descending when the sun dipped below the horizon.

The rest of the crew slept beneath the deck, other than a single man on watch who sat at the bow and stared out to sea. Manus recognized his face. The only man who didn't take part in the regular beatings that made Manus's ribs creak.

He silently crept up the main deck, readying himself to grab the other man.

"Don't, Manus. I don't have the humor for it tonight."

Sighing, Manus slumped next to him on deck. "And why not, Arturo? The world is a grave enough place without people losing their sense of humor. Where shall you go when you can no longer laugh?"

Arturo sighed, scraggly blonde hair dipping in front of his eyes. "I wished to be home a week ago."

"We can't all have our wishes granted."

"My wife was with child when I left. I should be by her side."

Manus stared at the dirt underneath his nails. "Why? That is women's work."

"Just because I cannot help her doesn't mean I shouldn't be there." When Manus didn't reply, the sailor leaned down and cuffed him. "Take note! Someday you'll have your own wife to tend to."

"I don't expect to marry."

"Whyever not?" Arturo exclaimed. "Women are wondrous creatures, and they give us a reason to return after a long voyage."

"Like what?"

"A warm bed at night, a willing woman after a long trip, children, food, a clean home. What more shall I tell you?"

"I can find all of that at a brothel."

Arturo rolled his eyes. "Aye, you could. But none of those women are yours. They belong to every man who presses a coin to their palm, and there's something sweet about knowing a woman is yours alone."

"Is it worth that much? I don't care if a woman stays true, as long as she's there when I return."

"You don't understand," Arturo replied, shaking his head.

Manus gestured to the sea, the ship, and the sky. "What more is there? We're all here for a reason. The ocean calls to us. She is our mistress and our wife! Why would I need another woman in my life?"

"Because the sea cannot give you sons!"

He scoffed. "I have no need of sons. I don't plan to leave anything behind and wouldn't be able to give them a comfortable life as children deserve. My father was a brute with a heavy hand. I will not continue the cycle."

"Why should you? Stop the cycle and become a good man."

"That isn't an option for me."

"Isn't it?" Arturo looked him in the eye. "Why not?"

"The same reason I just said. The sea is my mistress."

He heaved himself up and leaned over the edge of the ship. Manus reached out a hand, imagining icy spray numbing his fingertips as it did when they sped across the sea with sails full.

"The sea isn't a real woman," Arturo grumbled. "The older you get, the more you'll realize that."

"A woman deserves a faithful husband. I would run away at every chance, just to let my mistress rock me to sleep at her breast."

"You haven't slept on the right woman's breasts," Arturo said with a chuckle. "You wouldn't be saying that if you had."

They laughed, making certain the others didn't hear. The sailors would put an end to it if they knew.

Shaking his head, Manus patted the sailor's shoulder. "Why don't you get some sleep? I'll keep watch tonight."

"The captain won't like it."

"He won't know, now, will he? Go, sleep. You look like you're about to keel over, my friend."

Arturo lumbered below deck, and Manus stared out at the still sea.

He meant every word he said. The ocean was more a person to him than many he'd met in his lifetime. Frightening, consuming, and wondrous, it was his life's calling to devote himself to salt waters.

Manus stared down into the murky depths and felt a tension ease inside him.

Sometimes, in the very dead of night, he wondered what was beneath the waves. The great unknown of the ocean was baffling and frightening. There could be creatures staring up, looking right at him even as he stared down into the abyss.

Saoirse stared up at the silvery light filtering through the surface of the ocean. Its rays pierced through the depths until it was swallowed by the ocean and disappeared. She wished it didn't.

Moonlight was so beautiful and less dangerous than its sunny counterpart.

Merrows weren't supposed to go to the surface. Too many things hunted them there; humans, ships, sharks, even the occasional faerie would attack the delicate little creatures.

She nudged aside a strand of hair that floated in front of her eyes. The strand was so inky dark that no one would ever know it was green. Her father called it a shame. She would have been infinitely more beautiful if she had hair like her mother and sisters.

Saoirse much preferred her dark hair to the vibrant green of her people. She didn't like the way theirs looked like seaweed waving in the shallows, and besides, she stood out in a crowd.

The other merrow men didn't seem to mind her oddities. In fact, most found her differences thoroughly interesting. They lifted their webbed hands to touch the strands whenever she passed.

Saoirse did her best not to shiver in disgust, but the merrow-men were not attractive creatures. Their giant red noses were a beacon that attracted attention to their frog-like faces. Webbed hands and feet kept them firmly at the bottom of the ocean, though their strong tails could propel them forward when needed.

In contrast, merrow women were beautiful. Their long sleek tails came in a variety of colors, and their smooth skin shimmered in the sunlight. Rainbows danced in the slick webbing between their fingers, and the green hue of their hair mingled with vibrant fish that swam through the long locks.

She drifted on the currents, letting them drag her deeper and deeper into the abyss. That was where she lived, where her father and his many children waited for her to return.

Warmth faded from the waters. An icy chill wound around her shoulders and pulled harder, deeper, until darkness covered her vision and even her sensitive eyes were blind.

This was the part of the ocean that frightened her. Squid could tangle her in their tentacles without her ever seeing them. Saoirse had bumped into whales a few times, terrifying her so much that each time it happened, she remained in her undersea home for a very long time after.

But she always returned to the surface.

A tiny light bloomed in the darkness, small but enough that she knew precisely where she was.

Long ago, when she was very little, Saoirse had stolen a tree sapling and dragged it down with her. The scraggly, dying thing didn't stand a chance in the deep salt water. Her mother had felt such pity for the daughter who longed for a tiny piece of the land, that she wove a tapestry of magic around an abandoned grotto.

White pillars surrounded the small outcropping, the remains of a once great kingdom. A barrier held the ocean back between the pillars. Within that tiny space, her mother coaxed glowing coral to grow. She breathed life into the sapling, planted it in the center, and taught her daughter how to will the tree to stretch its roots and lift branches towards the sky.

Now, the great oak reached the ceiling of the grotto and spread wide leaves almost as large as Saoirse's head. Her mother kept saying she needed to tell the tree to slow down, but Saoirse couldn't.

It was an impossible thing growing at the bottom of the ocean. She would never tell it to change.

She didn't hesitate as she swam towards the grotto. Her shoulder slammed against the surface of the shield which made an audible pop and spat her to the ground. Landing hard on her arms, she blew out a relieved breath.

Grace certainly wasn't required to enter the grotto. She shook her head and winced as her legs tingled. Exposure to air caused an immediate reaction. The silver scales of her tail melted into a thick mucus that slid from her smooth skin.

Legs were such strange things. Saoirse didn't know how humans and merrow-men could stand having two appendages. They moved separately from each other, independent and infinitely difficult to control.

She stumbled to her feet, groaning with frustration before finding her balance.

The tree glowed in the dim light of the coral. She sighed in happiness and stepped towards the worn bark. She knew it as well as her own skin.

Its rough texture abraded her palm as she slid her hand down it. Saoirse reached up and framed the branches with her arms. They were nearly as thick as her new legs.

"Hello," she whispered.

Sometimes, she thought she heard a whispered greeting from the old tree. It would bend just so, as if a wind blew past. It was, perhaps, a rather fanciful thought, but she liked to think the tree knew her as well as she knew it.

She swayed side to side, getting used to her new body. Saoirse was fascinated by the changes merrows could undergo with little pain.

Magic was a strange thing. It allowed her to become something new and allowed this grotto to exist. It was wonderful, and fanciful, and so bright.

Saoirse closed her eyes and hummed under her breath. If she hit the right tone, faint and quiet, it almost sounded like there was wind. She could mimic birds as well.

The tree liked that. She was certain he stretched his roots deeper into the earth when she made bird sounds.

Pursing her lips, she trilled a few notes and stared up at the tree as if it were a man. She wouldn't mind kidnapping a person and bringing them down here.

Once in a great while, a ship would pass through their waters. She'd only seen a few men in her life, but they captivated her.

Their bodies were so different from her own and from the merrowmen. Humans grew hair in the strangest of places. Their arms were far stronger than she would have expected, and their bodies trim and muscular. It was a shame their skin was so strange. Pale white and faintly blue, they swelled as soon as they touched the ocean.

Granted, she'd only seen them after they were dead. The guardians wouldn't let them get too close to any ship that carried harpoons.

The great guardians, larger than most whales, traveled with the merrows when they left their homes. They escorted them from place to place, sometimes even just to stretch their tails.

They were kind, sweet, and thoughtful in a way most things under the water weren't. Saoirse loved them dearly. It was a shame her father didn't.

She glanced over her shoulder at the tree and saw instead a strong man with hair as dark as hers, reaching out his arms. Dark thoughts forgotten, she batted her eyelashes and asked, "Who? Me? Dance? Why I haven't danced in years."

She didn't really know what dancing was. A passing merrow, who had once shed her tail at the surface, spoke of humans tapping their feet to music.

Dancing wasn't the merrow way, and not likely something she would ever participate in.

Instead, merrows listened.

She had seen hundreds of females all gathering around a whale singing its haunting song. They floated, still as death with their hands pressed against their chests, listening as quietly as possible.

Why would anyone stomp their feet and not hear the music?

Still, it seemed rather interesting. She stamped her feet against the ground a few times, humming a tune that echoed the whale song. It was too slow, too simple, too quiet.

Frustrated, she shook her head and looked back at the tree. "I can't do it. You must have seen dances, even in your young life. What were they like?"

The tree seemed to sway, bowing to her.

"Oh! Were they all so polite? Did the men look at the women with their hearts in their eyes? Did the women sway?" Saoirse lifted her hands into the air and spun. "What do human women look like? Their men are quite handsome, so I cannot imagine what they must be. Are they ethereal creatures whose beauty burns?"

It was the only life she knew. Merrows were painfully more attractive than their counterparts. Humans must be the same, otherwise, what kind of creatures were they?

She bit her lip, looking the tree up and down. "Were you a handsome prince? If you were, tell me, right now. I simply must know!"

She didn't expect it to respond, not really. But there was always a bit of hope in her breast that someday she would meet a real prince. That he would sweep her off her feet, fall in love, and save her from marrying a merrow-man.

The tree didn't respond. Instead, all she heard was the sound of someone's muffled laughter.

Saoirse spun around so quickly her ankles tangled together.

Tripping into a heap, she landed in the roots of the tree with her long hair wrapped around her body. She pushed the dark length away and stared between two of the closest columns.

Her brother and father hovered just beyond the border. Their ugliness made her wince in pity. Her father was covered in warts, his froggish feet so large they were longer than her arm. Her brother was slightly more attractive, for a merrow-man, at least his nose wasn't quite as bulbous as the others.

He chuckled again, bubbles frothing from between his hands pressed against his mouth. "Saoirse, really?"

"What?" she asked defensively. "Mother gave this to me to do as I wish."

Her father shook his head. "You are too old to be playing pretend."

"I am not that old."

"You are well beyond the age of marriage. I have been looking for you all day, and here I find you with this damned tree."

"It's not a damned tree!" She pressed her hand against the bark. "It's mine and it means something to me."

"I should have had your mother take these walls down a long time ago. They have made you fanciful."

"I am allowed to have something which is mine and mine alone."

"You won't for long!" he thundered. "You are going to have to accept marriage sooner or later, Saoirse. Most girls your age are already married, and still you will not pick a husband!"

She should have known that was why he was here. Her father wanted her to marry more than anyone else, although she couldn't understand why. There were other sisters for him to focus on, seventeen to be precise.

Her mother and father were prolific, desiring to be the family with the most children so they might have more bride prices. It wasn't difficult as a merrow. They had the choice to carry their children within them, or within an egg sack which was anchored to the bottom of the ocean.

Most tried to keep the babe within them. But, if one wanted many children, it was easier to place the eggs on the ground and forget until they hatched.

Saoirse helped take care of the eggs when she could. The number of her siblings were ever growing.

"I have no wish to marry," she informed her father, tight lipped and angry. "I have already told you this."

"And I have told you it is not acceptable. You *will* marry, and if you do not choose a husband soon, I will choose one for you."

Saoirse stumbled to her feet, cheeks flushed with anger. "You can't do that!"

"I can, and I will!"

"Athair!"

"Enough!" Her father held his webbed hand forward, treading water with an unreadable expression on his wart covered face. "Listen to me child and listen well. You will be married by the next turn of the tides, whether you wish it or not. I would suggest you choose a husband soon."

He swam away, frog-like legs kicking rapidly as he fled the sadness in her eyes.

Saoirse pressed her fingers to her face, the remaining short webs glistening with her tears. She had never noticed the leak when she was underwater. Tears mixed with the sea until everything tasted like salt.

Not so when she was in her little grotto. Her sorrows were all the greater when the ocean did not cradle her in its embrace.

Her brother chuckled and floated closer to the grotto. "Little sister, when are you going to learn that arguing with Athair is a waste of time? He always gets what he wants."

"Not if I can help it."

"What are you going to do? Run away?" He gestured towards the surface. "Do you think life above the sea will be any better than it is down here?"

She turned away from him, sniffing loudly. "How would we know?

"The rumors aren't true, you know. All those fanciful, romantic tales you whisper to yourself at night. Our sisters hear you, Saoirse. They listen to them and think you are foolish. Humans don't care about us, and they certainly don't care about the sea."

"You don't know that."

"I do!"

She flinched as his heavy fists struck the magical bubble holding back the ocean. The sound echoed through her head, then stilled as he pushed hard and slid through the shield.

The wet slap of his feet sent shivers down her spine. The merrow men were ugly in the water, but without the buoyancy of the salt water, they were monstrous.

Saoirse steeled herself and glanced over her shoulder. Flesh sagged from his form, dripping down his body like the slimy glow worms she'd seen in caves. Grayish green skin did little to enhance his appearance.

She swallowed hard. "What are you doing, bràthair?"

"Enjoying your little haven. Mother built it for all of us, after all."

"You've never liked this grotto."

"I think anything from above is not worth our time." Water dripped from his shoulders to land with wet plops on the moss she had carefully cultivated. He glanced slyly over his shoulder. "You know father will pick the worst of them."

"He wouldn't do that. I'm his favorite."

"You like to think that, but he thinks you're too wild. A husband with a heavy hand is needed to control you, we all think so."

"A heavy-handed man would break me. I am more delicate than Athair knows."

"Is that so?"

Her brother padded around her, peering around the tree with unnaturally dark eyes. "Who do you think he'll pick, piuthar? Craig? His hands are large enough to crush your skull."

"He wouldn't dare."

"I always thought he would make a good match for you."

She liked Craig even less than the rest of them. He enjoyed the hunt too much. Saoirse couldn't count the number of times she had caught him floating in a blood-stained current. He liked to inhale the metallic scent.

"No, it won't be him."

Her brother arched his brow. "That almost sounds as if you're considering choosing."

She didn't like the shrewd look in her brother's gaze. He was too smart for his own good and read her too easily. He had no right to know her thoughts, but she was bound to tell him.

As a faerie, she couldn't lie. Her tongue twisted into knots the moment she tried. But, she could twist the truth. And she *was* fragile, she felt like the thinnest of shells beneath the weight of the ocean.

This world wasn't for her. She longed for the sun, for waves, for seagulls screeching above her head. The darkness and silence didn't fit the glowing light of her soul.

"You've made it perfectly clear I have no other choice."

"What are you planning?"

"Nothing at all. I am trapped, though you didn't say it in so many words. If I do not choose, I will be forced. And I will not submit to whatever brute father chooses for me."

"This is unlike you."

Saoirse sniffed. "Perhaps you do not know me as well as you think."

"No, I know you better than any of our siblings. I'll be keeping a close eye on you, Saoirse. You won't do anything foolish to compromise this family."

With a hard look, he stepped back through the bubble of magic and into the water. She waited until he disappeared into the murk before huddling against the tree. Her shoulders shook with the force of her emotions.

Married? To one of those disgusting creatures?

Her mother would say that looks weren't everything. Saoirse needed to set up her future so she would be happy and comfortable. A lone merrow in these waters didn't have the protection they all required.

She hated it. She hated them.

The mere thought of a merrow man touching her skin made her shudder. Her scales weren't thick enough to shield her from their warts and wrinkled skin. What was she to do?

A few leaves floated down from the branches above her head and gently rested against her shoulders. She plucked one off and rotated it. The weak light from the coral shone through the fine leaf and made the veins glow.

"You're right," she whispered. "There is always another way."

She stared through the bubble towards the surface. Darkness obscured her vision, but she knew it was up there. The sun would touch her skin again, and it didn't matter that her brother thought her foolish.

If they would force her to marry, then she would see the sunlight one more time.

CHAPTER 2
OF SEAS AND STORMS

The rocking waves lulled Manus deep into sleep. Dreams danced through his head, each wilder than the last.

His mother's voice whispered in his ear, "Manus! My boy, where have you been off to?"

"The sea, mother!"

"You visited her again?"

"She told me stories."

"Stories?" his mother said with a laugh. "What stories did she tell you this time?"

"She told me stories of merrow women with seaweed hair."

"Oh!" He heard the shifting sound of fabric and the trickle of water as she washed her hands after a long day of work. "Merrow women are a strange lot. They're beautiful and kind, but their husbands are terrifying to behold."

"The merrow men can't come out of the water, though."

"No, but you must be careful to never anger them. They will tear a ship apart with their bare hands just to take back their brides."

The dream shifted, swelling and cresting with the waves. His mother's quiet voice shifted and warped, changing to a desperate cry.

"Manus! Manus, wake up!"

He jolted upright, sweat staining his brow and sticking his shirt to his chest. Nightmares weren't frequent in his life, particularly about his mother. Her soul remained in the afterlife where it belonged.

Manus blew out a sigh and wiped his forehead. It came away not sticky with sweat, but cold and gritty with dried salt.

"What?"

His groggy mind thought for a moment he was sweating seawater.

Slowly, he pulled himself from the strange dream and glanced up at the planks above his head. Water leaked through, dripping down on his forehead in solid and heavy drips.

He shook his head. "Arturo?"

The man who shared his bunk snorted and turned over in his sleep.

"Arturo," he growled. "Wake up."

"Is it time for our watch?"

Manus watched as the drops became a steady stream, pouring through the cracks on the ceiling to the floor in a quiet trickle. "The deck is leaking."

"The deck doesn't leak."

"It does now."

Arturo rolled over onto his back, stared up at the drips, and scrunched his face. "So it does."

"Doesn't seem good, does it?"

"Probably not."

"Should we go topside?" Manus questioned.

"I'm not sure that's wise." Arturo's hand flopped over the side of the bunk and waved. "It's probably just a bad storm, and if it isn't, we're safer down here."

Manus wanted to agree with him. The ship rolled over the heavy waves, but there was something strange about the way the hull moved. It shouldn't be bouncing like this.

He remembered the strange dream and his mother's voice whispering in his ear.

"Arturo?"

"Aye?"

"Where did the captain say we were headed?"

"Out into the Great Ocean. A passing tale caught his attention, that if he turned the ship into the wind when the sea grew still, that he would see the land of plenty."

Manus swore. "Fools! The land of plenty? You mean Tir na nOg?"

He watched as the sailor's eyes grew wide with fear. "That's another way to think of it."

"All you bastards should listen to the old tales," he spat as he swung his legs out and leapt onto the deck. "I'll see if I can fix this, or if we're too far gone."

"Gone?"

"We're heading straight into faerie waters!" Manus shouted as he grabbed ahold of the ladder leading out of the belly of the ship. "They'll sink the ship!"

A sudden shift sent him toppling sideways. His strong hands grasped the rungs, preventing a nasty fall. He swung himself upright and made his way to the deck.

The storm raged above them. Unnaturally colored lightning struck the mast, flaring bright and leaving bright spots in the center of his vision. Stumbling to the side, Manus caught himself on the stairs.

"Captain!" he shouted. "Captain!"

"Get down below deck, boy!"

"No!" He pulled himself hand over hand, up the railing and stairs to the captain's side. He flung himself onto the wheel of the ship. "You don't know what it is you do!"

"I do, boy! We sail towards riches."

The rain lashed against the captain's cheeks, but he didn't seem to feel it. He stared with blank, dull eyes into the heart of the storm. His coat flapped in the wind. Fabric cracked against his side with harsh smacks, but he did not react.

It was as if he were under a spell.

White with fear, Manus held the wheel still. "You'll kill us all."

"It's just a small storm. We can get through it."

"We can't without faerie protection!"

"Who says we don't have that?" The captain's eyes moved a fraction, settling on Manus. "We have one of faerie blood to keep us alive."

"Me?" Manus shook his head. "You think they care for a drop of faerie blood in an ocean of human?"

"It's more than any of us."

"It's only enough to tempt the sharks."

Lightning cracked again, flaring so bright Manus thought he would never see again. The mast creaked in warning and fire spread across the sails.

"It's an omen!" he shouted. "We must turn back!"

"Just a bit further."

"No!"

The captain wasn't listening. He stared through Manus as if he didn't exist at all.

What had happened?

Manus let go of the wheel and raced towards the back of the ship. There were lifeboats there, he could gather as many men as possible, toss them into the dingy and….

And what? Where else could they go?

The waves swelled, spilling water over the edge, causing him to slip and slide across the boards. His heart thumped in his chest, a terrible feeling, foreboding and dark. Would they die here?

Arturo poked his head out from below deck. His eyes narrowed as saltwater sprayed in his face.

"Get out!" Manus shouted. "We have to get off the ship!"

"Why? We're safer here!"

"No one is safe in this storm!"

A deep bellow echoed, sending vibrations travelling through his feet and deep into his chest.

"What was that?" Arturo asked, his expression grim.

Manus wanted to tell his friend it was likely nothing. A whale, the groan of churning ocean waves, thunder on the horizon. But it was worse than that.

Much worse.

"Go!" he shouted, sprinting towards the lifeboats himself. "Run!"

He didn't have enough time to take even a few steps. A wave larger than the ship swelled beside them, arched overhead, and crashed down upon the deck.

Salt water pounded down on him, throwing his body to the planks and rolling him into darkness. Wood cracked against his ribs, splintering the bones. Pain ricocheted through him until Manus couldn't tell what hurt. Everything felt shattered.

He hit the ocean with a sharp slap that ruptured his eardrums and sent his senses reeling. His lungs burned, but he didn't know which way was up and which was down. Was he even swimming?

A bolt of lightning struck the surface of the water, illuminating the carnage underneath the waves.

Men floated in the sudden silence between muffled cracks of thunder. Their arms hung limp at their sides, hair billowing in almost graceful tendrils. Manus peered at their faces, recoiling at the vacant expressions in their eyes.

They had drowned. And there were so many of them.

Lightning struck again, and this time he stared straight up into the sky. Swimming to the surface was nigh impossible. His arms ached, his lungs squeezed, and small dots of darkness obscured his vision.

He burst into the air with a gasp. Coughing and choking, he called out, "Arturo! Arturo, can you hear me?"

A groan echoed in the air, so loud that Manus was certain it was a beast of the waves. But it wasn't. He stared in horror at the burning mast of the ship which tilted down… down…

Swearing, he set his body into motion and swam. The burning wood barely missed him as it crashed into the water sending ripples and waves splashing over his body

He inhaled, coughing so hard he dipped underneath the surface again. Manus was a strong swimmer and even he was having a difficult time finding his bearings. Swimmers needed to be calm and let the ocean do the work for them.

And yet, it felt very much like the ocean was working against him.

Hands grasped his ankle, and he shuddered. Had the faeries come? He had known they wouldn't allow humans to enter their lands without retribution, but he hadn't expected them to be so cruel.

To sink a ship needed magic. And there were only a few creatures in the ocean with magic strong enough for that.

The hands clawed up to his thigh, his chest, and then a head burst out of the water. Dark hair plastered to his skull, his beard stuck over his mouth, but Arturo was alive.

Manus grabbed onto him, forcing Arturo to stay above the waves. "You're alive!"

"Not for long. Look at the ship."

He had seen the ship. The crumbling pieces, the burning sails, the hole in the side which hadn't been there before.

"What could have caused this?" Arturo asked. "What madness lives in these waters?"

"No madness," Manus replied. "Just the Fae."

"The faeries did this?"

"I tried to tell the captain to turn around. There was only one way for this to end."

And now they would all face the mercy of the sea.

He cursed the captain and his foolishness for thinking he could enter faerie lands and steal their cursed riches. What had possessed him to think he could claim it?

"Manus," Arturo gasped. "Manus, what's the plan?"

"Plan?"

He didn't have a plan. He might like the ocean as his mistress, but he didn't want to rest in her arms forever.

Manus glanced around, finding a small bit of debris within reach. The plank wouldn't float forever, but it would ease Arturo's exhaustion. He pushed the other man up onto the board and tried to grin.

"See? We'll be fine. I'll get you back to your wife in no time."

"If I don't make it—"

"I won't hear it, Arturo."

"You have to find my wife—"

"Stop talking."

"Tell her I love her and that the child would have meant more than the world—"

"Enough!" The shout was too harsh, too ragged, but he couldn't listen to his friend plan his own death. "We're going to live, Arturo."

"We're in the middle of the ocean with a ship that's slowly sinking. I'm not going anywhere." Arturo shook his head ruefully. "But you? With that faerie blood, you might stand a chance."

"You know better than to put trust in rumors."

Faeries didn't care if he was the bastard son of a bastard son. They didn't care there was a drop of their own kind in him.

Still, it wasn't the time nor the place to dash Arturo's hopes.

Manus nodded. "Aye, I'll tell her."

"Good."

"But I'm staying with you until we figure out what we're going to do."

Arturo's teeth chattered. His expression said he didn't believe Manus for a second, but he gave a firm nod all the same.

There had to be something they could do. The mistress of the ocean took away their ship, and she would give them something in return. That's how it always worked.

Manus just had to find what she had exchanged.

"Manus?"

"Yes, Arturo?"

"Do you ever see shadows in the water?"

"Sometimes."

"Large moving shadows?"

He stilled as cold fear trailed down his spine. "How large?"

"Bigger than a ship. Bigger than a whale."

He'd only heard of such things in myths and legends. Old sailors whispered of creatures so large that the ocean could barely contain them. Creatures that patrolled the faerie waters and removed any who did not belong there.

A guardian.

Swallowing hard, he patted Arturo's shoulder. "Stay alive, sailor. I'll take a look."

"You be careful."

"Faerie blood, remember? I'll be fine."

He likely wouldn't be. Manus couldn't imagine what a guardian would do to him, the stories never went that far. The sailors always said they had seen the beast but couldn't describe what it looked like. Or even what it really was.

Just a faerie in the water who was larger than life. Not exactly helpful.

Manus took a deep breath, ducked underneath the surface, and opened his eyes. The murky darkness revealed no secrets, no oddities, no guardian. The burning sails fell and landed not too far away.

Whale oil spread across the surface of the ocean, carrying with it orange light. Spears of fire sank beneath the waves and bounced off the surface of an ink dark hide.

He followed the line of the body that floated near the wreckage of the ship. It was like a whale in texture, smooth, supple, no scales to deter from the sleek body. A large hand shifted. It reached through the water and grabbed the remains of a lifeboat.

His stomach clenched. It was big enough to palm a lifeboat?

Smaller shadows moved all around the strange creature. Sharks? Beings it had at its beck and call?

The guardian paused, hesitating for a moment before he realized it had a head. Not just a whale head, but a *human* head. She wasn't a beautiful thing in the slightest, with hair shaved close to either side of her skull and lacking a nose. But those eyes were eerily human, and they were staring directly at him.

Manus gulped and kicked to the surface. It had seen him. The guardian had seen him, and now what was he going to do?

He looked over at Arturo with fear racing through his veins. "I'm sorry, old friend. I don't think I'll be taking that message to your wife after all."

"What is happening? Manus, what did you see?"

The image of the guardian seared into his mind for all time. What could Manus say? That he had seen a beast which lurked in the depths of the ocean? That this creature shouldn't exist, shouldn't be possible, yet it had stared back at him with eyes as black as hell?

No. He couldn't tell Arturo any of that. Not when he felt the waves lapping at his neck and knew the guardian was coming for them.

Humans had no place in faerie waters. They should never have come here, and though it hadn't been their choice, the guardian wouldn't care. There would be no reasoning with a creature meant to hold the gates of faerie oceans closed.

He gulped. "Think of your wife. Picture her face in your mind and don't let go of her image."

Arturo licked his lips. "We're going to die."

"It'll be quite a story to tell if we survive."

The wave swelled and crested over their heads. Manus tumbled beneath their weight, shoved deeper and deeper into the dark depths.

He threw his arms wide, pushing and punching against the wall of water until he stilled. Floating far beneath the surface, he stared up at the meager light. It disappeared as the guardian passed overhead.

She paused and stared down at him with an eye so large he saw his entire torso reflected in it. Spots danced in his vision as she swam by. With one flick of her tail, she pushed him even farther down into the heart of the sea.

Saoirse held her breath and watched as the ship sank. It was a rare sight for a merrow. Ships rarely traveled into faerie waters.

Especially unmarked ships.

Her heart clenched as she saw her sisters dart through the waters, grabbing the bodies of fallen sailors who hadn't known any better. The humans didn't understand that yellow was a soothing color to the guardian who then would allow them to pass. Why didn't they know to paint the hulls for smooth passage?

Another merrow swam past, her tail flicking aggressively as she swarmed with the others. They would take the bodies of the sailors to their homes. Humans made good food for the bottom feeders, and they would help keep small fish and snails alive.

She understood why they needed to die. Humans were the ones who had chased the faeries out of Uí Néill long ago. They only knew how to fight and rage at the world.

They didn't look like the rage-filled creatures of lore as their limp bodies drifted with the currents.

Saoirse could easily picture her father's livid expression when he found out she had come with the guardian. She was supposed to be searching for a husband, speaking with all the merrow men who were interested.

There were less than her father had expected.

She knew she shouldn't feel pride in that, but she did. Saoirse wanted to be an old maid. She wanted to live on her own, in peace and quiet, passing her days in the grotto with her tree.

Why was that so hard for him to understand?

The guardian sang out, her melancholy song marking the end of their battle. Not that it was ever a battle when a guardian was involved. No one could stop the sheer power her dearest friend wielded with a blithe smile.

Merrows flashed by. Their scales glimmered in the dim light, feral smiles on their faces as they dragged their prizes down into the depths. They called out for Saoirse to follow them, but her gaze caught on a dark shadow.

A silhouette hovered in the crystal-clear water, suspended above slowly sinking planks and great swaths of sails.

She bit her lip. The guardian swam overhead and traced a gentle finger down Saoirse's spine. She knew what the message was.

Go home, little merrow. Back to safety and family.

Angry thoughts bubbled in her head. If she were to marry an ugly, mean creature who wanted to beat her down with a heavy hand, then she would do as she wished while she was still free.

Casting a defiant glance at the guardian, she swam towards the man. He floated, long dark hair billowing like ink around him. It was sad he had died. He was handsome.

The current shifted his clothing, lifting his shirt to reveal ridged bumps that trailed down his stomach and disappeared under the fabric of his pants.

She cocked her head to the side. His legs weren't as repulsive as the merrow men's, although she still found it strange that he had two. They weren't as frog-like and they certainly weren't scaled.

He was handsome, in a chiseled kind of way. A long nose, strong jaw, and dark piercing eyes all melded together to create a pleasing face. His skin was burned to a dark, earthen color by the sun.

Saoirse reached up and marveled at her pale skin in comparison.

She looked like the moon, silver and pale and shimmering with an inner light, whereas he was dark and swarthy, like the night sky.

Temptation's song was too much for her to ignore. She touched the high peak of his jaw, her expression softening. He felt just like she did, soft and warm.

Her brows drew down. Warm?

The man's eyes snapped open, staring directly into her dark gaze.

She flinched back, swinging her tail up to cover her face and vulnerable torso. But he did not attack as she had expected. Instead, he lifted a hand towards her. Then, his entire body jerked. The spasm rocked down his entire frame and his eyes rolled back in his head before he went limp.

Saoirse pressed her hands against her mouth. He was alive! How was it possible that the guardian had missed him?

Or had she? Perhaps the guardian hadn't wanted Saoirse to go back at all. Perhaps she wanted the tiny merrow to meet a human for the first time.

Resolve settling on her shoulders, she surged forward, slid her arms underneath his body, and swam to the surface. Her strong tail propelled them; his added weight was nothing in the water.

Would he like that? Would he be frightened of her because she could hold his weight? She knew nothing about humans.

They broke into the air with a wild splash. Saoirse tilted his head up, cupping the back and helping his body float.

He wasn't responding. Weren't they supposed to do something other than lie there?

"You're supposed to breathe," she whispered. "Humans are supposed to breathe."

She pressed her hands against his cheeks, patting gently. His head lolled to the side and dipped beneath the surface before she could grab it.

"No," she groaned. "It's not supposed to be like this. Wake up!

Please wake up."

Water bubbled between his lips, frothing over his cheeks, and then he coughed. Coughed so hard he slipped from her arms, but she quickly yanked him back to the air.

"That's it," she encouraged. "That's it!"

His body curled away from hers. Each wracking cough sounded painful to her ears. Was he hurting himself? Could humans do that with such a simple thing?

Saoirse panicked. She didn't know the first thing about human anatomy. What if he coughed himself to death?

She shivered, pulled him close to her chest, and swam. There was an island nearby. Small, nothing that would sustain a man for a lifetime, but enough he might live for a little while.

Her father would be livid if he heard about this, so she would need to keep him secret. Her human was still weak, and no one needed to fight with a merrow man when they weren't well. And her father was a very large merrow man.

The man's body scraped against her scales. Saoirse winced as a few wiggled loose and floated on top of the waves. They would grow back, but she hated the itchy feeling as they healed.

He slowly stopped coughing, but his body fell limp again. She hovered a hand over his mouth to make sure he was still breathing. Strong gusts of air buffeted her palm.

Good. He would live.

Setting her jaw, she turned her attentions to the faint outline of an island far away. It wasn't Tir na nOg, even she wasn't foolish enough to bring him to the realm of the Seelie Fae. Nor was it Hy-brasil, she didn't want to imprison him with the unruly prince.

No. It was a quaint little place with only Lesser Fae to bother him. She would bring him food, scoop fresh water from the depths of the ocean and bring it back to him. He would stay alive.

For her.

Though her tail trembled, she pulled him through the waters. She desperately wished they could travel underneath the water. Waves splashed in her face, confusing the gills on the side of her neck as they tried to suck in air while her lungs breathed.

Soon, she was coughing as well. How did humans do this? The air was confusing. There were too many things she could inhale. The water was easy, she breathed through her gills and it filtered out anything she didn't need. Human lungs were useless.

Every gurgle from the depths sent adrenaline spiking through her veins. No one could know what she had done. Especially not the sharks, notorious gossips who had never liked her very much anyway.

Just as her tail shook in exhaustion, she felt sand brush the tips of her fin. It was enough. She relaxed and released her hold on the man in her arms.

As much as she wanted to rest, the hard part was ahead of her. He couldn't stay in the ocean.

She caught her breath for a few moments and then pushed. He would have to survive the dunks under the water as she rolled him onto the sand. Up and up he went until his torso was firmly on land.

"Just a bit more," she grunted.

Dragging herself herself onto land was far different than hauling him. Merrows were naturally graceful creatures, and far more acclimated to land than selkies. But it wasn't easy.

She coiled her tail and launched herself onto the soft white sand next to him. Saltwater slid from her scales. They softened and slid away from her pale skin. Her legs felt different above the surface with the sun stroking her limbs.

Thoughts danced through her mind, all the possibilities of the paths her life could now take. What if a ship came to find him? What if she could flee her father, her brother, all the merrow men who wanted to grasp at her flesh until it turned black and blue?

She looked at the sailor in a new light. He could be her salvation.

The remaining mucus of her tail slid off her legs as she leaned over to peer down into his face. He was still breathing. The broad expanse of his chest lifted and fell in a hypnotic rhythm.

Gently, she touched a single finger to the intriguing muscles of his chest. A necklace hung in the valley of his chest, accentuating the broad musculature. Light from the pink sunrise reflected off the round single pearl at the end of the chain.

"Who are you?" she murmured. "How did you end up in faerie waters? Didn't you know it was dangerous?"

He couldn't answer her questions, but it made her feel better to ask them. A second finger joined the first, walking up his sternum to touch the long column of his suntanned throat.

The muscles worked beneath her touch, shocking her. He was so similar to her, and yet so different. The pale skin of her hand fairly glowed against the darkness of his.

Trailing up his neck, she touched the bristly hairs that made up his coarse beard. It was softer than she expected although still strange. The merrows who had gone to land said humans brushed their hair. Did he brush this as well?

Her fingers caught on a golden bead tangled in the long strands. Decorations? Adornments? Did it mean he was important?

"Are you a prince?" she asked.

He groaned low in his throat.

Saoirse flinched back, drawing her hand away from the beard which parted to reveal rows of blinding white teeth.

"Water," he rasped. "Water."

She didn't have water he could drink. Saoirse knew humans didn't drink saltwater. Their bodies couldn't filter it the way merrows could, which was why so many sailors died at sea when the winds fled and the ocean called for their souls.

Instead, she curled herself around him and brushed her fingers through the long, tangled snarls of his hair.

"Shh," she murmured. "Rest easy, my prince. Go to sleep and all shall be well."

He didn't seem to believe her. Delirious and blinking, he stared directly into her eyes.

Dark eyes, like hers. But the more she looked at them, the more she realized there were colors of the ocean in his eyes. They appeared brown at first, like the dirt they dug up for her tree. But flecks of yellow, green, blue, every color she had ever seen, all existed within his gaze.

Lust speared through her chest and stole her breath. He was so handsome that she couldn't even think.

"Who are you?" His voice warbled with strain. "How did you find me?"

"You should be resting."

"I have no wish to rest. I was drowning."

She hesitated, licking her lips at the harsh tones in his voice. He was frightening while awake and she much preferred him asleep. "The ocean is a cruel mistress; she wanted your soul for her own."

"Why didn't she get it?"

The question in his eyes was one she couldn't answer. Saoirse knew the sea wanted him. It wanted to drag him down into the depths so that his sailor body would feed her children and his spirit would wander the currents for all eternity.

Her expression softened, and she tentatively brushed her finger over the frown lines on his forehead.

"I did not want her to take you." She shouldn't say it, but she couldn't stop herself from blurting out the admission.

His brow wrinkled. "Why?"

"I wanted to meet you first."

His brow furrowed even more, flexing behind her fingers.

Saoirse smiled and bit her lip. "I have ever been a selfish thing. I desire that which I cannot have."

"You can have me anytime you want, beautiful." His voice shivered across her skin, deep and sensual.

Her cheeks burned red. Was she ill? She reached up and touched the pads of her fingers to the heat, realizing quickly that it was a reaction to his words. Was she embarrassed? Was this how human bodies reacted?

"I should go," she quickly replied. "Stay well, prince."

"Go?" He moved to sit up. "Where are we?"

She couldn't afford for him to sit up. He would know she was a merrow and then all her plans would be ruined. Humans didn't know what to do with faeries, let alone those that came out of the sea.

Launching herself at his chest, she pushed him back into the sand.

A warm hand pressed against her spine, holding her close to the heat that billowed from his skin in waves.

She stared down into his strange eyes and swallowed. "You almost died."

And she couldn't bear the thought of it. The lament of death was a song she knew well. It was a song she did not want to sing for him.

"I feel much better now."

"I can see that."

His fingers shifted over the bumps of her back. "I hadn't noticed you weren't wearing much."

"Much?" She wasn't wearing anything. Merrows didn't, it wasn't in their nature. Bodies were bodies, and they weren't embarrassed by them.

"It was your hair," he murmured. "I must not be as awake as I thought. Your hair was covering you and I thought it was some kind of headdress."

"I said, you should rest."

"Am I dreaming?" He leaned back slightly, lifting a strand of her wet hair to the light. "I've never seen hair such as this."

"Never?" She shook her head, dislodging his warm hand and the confusing feelings it evoked. "I should go."

Saoirse fought her way out of his arms. Her legs didn't want to listen to her orders, not surprising considering she still hadn't gotten used to the strange limbs, but they were even more unruly around him. Knees shaking, she whimpered as she stood.

Embarrassing. This entire situation had been embarrassing. He must think her a weak little thing, incapable of even standing on her own.

"Wait."

His words made her freeze just at the edge of the water. Trembling, she tucked her hands close to her heart and stared out to sea. "Yes?"

"Will you come back?"

"I want to." More than anything else in the world. Her soul already ached at the mere thought of his loss although she didn't understand why. No man had ever wiggled underneath her skin. Not like this.

"That isn't a yes," he said. Amusement warmed his voice to sweet wine.

"I don't know if I'm allowed."

"Do you always do what you're told?"

The tone of his voice made her turn, curious what this strange human could be suggesting.

He laid out on the sand, his head on his hand and his legs crossed at his ankles. The shark-like grin on his face made her shiver.

"Well?" he asked. "Do you always follow the rules, my strange female friend?"

She shook her head. "No."

"Show me."

She stooped down, grasped the rock hidden beneath the water, and tossed it as hard as she could. It struck his head with a solid thump and knocked him flat on his back. Tiny puffs of sand burst into the air.

"Oh," she muttered. "That might have been too hard."

Breath brushed her hand when she leaned down and pressed it against his mouth. He was alive, and she was still the foolish one.

Saoirse pressed her fingers firmly against his lips. "You can't know I'm a faerie. You can't know anything about who I am, or you won't take me with you when you leave."

Humans knew merrow men were dangerous to deal with. Stealing a merrow from them was as good as signing a death warrant. And though she felt guilty tricking him into stealing her away, she didn't think he would mind much.

Casting one last glance at the intriguing human, she slid beneath the waves and deep into the heart of the sea.

CHAPTER 3
EILEAN AN FHAERIE

Manus thrashed through the underbrush, cursing the leaves that stood in his way. What were these strange growths? He'd never seen a plant in the middle of the ocean grow so tall, so wide, nor so large.

But they did here.

Leaves as large as his head reached towards the sky and slammed down on him every time he tried to walk around them. It made for slow progress, and all he wanted to do was explore a little.

The isle did not want to relinquish its secrets. He had looped around it multiple times in the days since he had awoken. It took exactly half a day to come back to the same place where he'd first opened his eyes.

He knew, because he left a line of rocks from the edge of the jungle all the way to the water lapping at the pristine, white sand.

And what a lot of good it had done. All he knew was that it took half a day to round the entire isle.

Every time he tried to go into the interior, the vegetation stopped him. From the giant leaves, to the strange flowers, and spine-chilling growls, everything seemed to work against him.

He fought with plants until the sun dipped below the horizon, and only then did he go back to his line of rocks. A small bit of food awaited him every night, along with a pitcher of fresh water.

Huffing out a frustrated breath, he turned around and stared at the waves. Nothing yet, but the sun was close to skimming the western horizon. Whoever brought him the food would reveal themselves soon, or he wouldn't eat.

Somehow, he didn't think they would let him go hungry. They had gone through a lot of trouble to keep him alive.

Then there was the mysterious woman he remembered. Her eyes haunted his dreams. Big and black like the deepest point of the ocean, but so kind it made his chest burn.

He'd never seen a woman who looked like that before. He'd never seen a woman who made him *feel* like this before.

Manus assumed she lived on the isle and spent many of his first days looking for her. It didn't take long before he realized she wasn't anywhere near him, no one living was, and that she must have come from another isle nearby.

The problem was that he didn't think there was another nearby isle. He'd scaled a palm tree and stared out at the horizon for hours. There was no land nearby, nothing but water and waves.

He glanced over his shoulder again.

No food, no water, no small platter made of gilded metal that was far too fine for the likes of him. This place was strange and his mysterious benefactor even more so.

"Let's see who you really are," he muttered.

If he had to resort to trickery, then he would. Manus punched a leaf so hard it flew up into the air. Using the opportunity, he ducked beneath the small space revealed for a split second before the it snapped back down.

The dim light made it difficult to see what might be around him. He could smell the earthy loam, the decaying plants, and the faintly sweet scent of flowers. His bare feet sunk into the wet soil where he curled his toes.

If he had to wait all night, he would. Whoever was providing food and water would arrive. He was certain of it.

Manus waited for what felt like hours. The sun froze, the waves slowed, everything hesitated with bated breath. Would the mysterious person arrive? Would it be the woman with dark eyes and hair so black it shone green like whale oil on water?

No one arrived. Darkness fell over the isle, and the moon showed its silver face.

Manus frowned. He hadn't expected them not to arrive. Why wouldn't they show up? It had been five nights, and every night someone had left food and water for him.

Strange.

His knees creaked as he stood. He'd bed down in the sand again tonight. The sun's heat didn't leave it until late into the night, and the air was strangely warm here.

Slumping to the ground, he wrapped his arms around his knees and stared at the waves lapping at the shore. Just when he thought he had it figured out, his strange circumstances changed.

Where was he?

A soft sound danced down his spine. Not the quiet sound of someone hidden moving. A whine, like that of a wounded animal.

The last thing he needed was to discover he wasn't alone here. If there were beasts that hunted, then he had little to protect himself with.

He curled his hands into fists and glanced down the shore. A white form slumped half in the ocean and half out of it.

"What?" he muttered.

It looked like a dog or some semblance of one at least. The long muzzle was familiar. He'd seen wolfhounds as a boy, used to play with them outside the butcher's who had used them as guard dogs. They were fiercely loyal and dangerous, but kind to those who treated them with respect.

Slowly standing, he approached the animal as quietly as he could.

"Easy boy." Manus poured honey into his voice, calming and

peaceful. "Did you wash up on shore as well?"

The mutt whined again. It only had enough energy to turn its head towards him, then let its jaw rest against the sand.

"Let me guess. A strange woman brought you here? Hair the color of oil on water?"

An ear pricked forward.

"You're a good wee beastie, aren't you? You won't bite me."

He stepped too close, and the dog curled a lip. Manus carefully watched the dog, unsurprised that it would feel threatened.

The closer he got, the more he realized this was no normal dog. Its fur had a slightly green tint to it although he thought it might be a trick of the moonlight, and it was far too large. Almost as big as a half-grown cow, it would fit just underneath his arm if it stood up.

"Cù sìth?" Manus exclaimed.

The dogs were said to be a legend. They were faerie born, the faithful companions of only a few Fae who proved themselves worthy.

For humans, they were the harbingers of death. They walked at the sides of bean sídhes, waiting for the moment when their faerie would cry out at the taste of carrion in the air. The dogs were rumored to then steal human souls.

He shivered but shook his head. "You aren't here to kill me, are you boy? You're just as unlucky as I."

Stooping just out of the dog's reach, he hunkered down and cocked his head to the side.

It was an intelligent enough creature to know it was being watched. Manus guessed the cù sìth was male. It was larger than the legends claimed, and the growl in its throat was deep.

"Easy there, friend. What shall I call you?"

The beast snorted.

"When I was a boy, I used to be obsessed with Manannán mac Lir, god of the sea, and king of the ocean I love. I shall call you Mac Lir in honor of the Tuatha dé Danann who gave you to me."

He heard a tiny sound behind him. Something another might have missed, but Manus was a very perceptive man. He listened for the slightest of sounds which may be important—like the slight clink of a plate hitting gilded edges.

It took everything he had not to whip around. The person who had taken care of him was there, close enough he might be able to run and catch them.

Was it the woman? Did she row a boat all the way out here just to feed him? Was she hiding from someone?

His mind drifted towards the possibility of a husband causing her to run away into the ocean. There must be a mainland somewhere.

He lifted his voice but spoke to the cù sìth. "Do you know the story of mac Lir?"

The faerie dog twitched its ear, one forward and one back. Its eyes were not focused on him, but on something behind him.

"He was a great and powerful Tuatha dé Danann. Half druid, half Fae. Some say he was more powerful than Nuada himself. Now, that is not an observation I might make, but he is an incredible figure in our mythology.

"You see, mac Lir had the ability to call upon the mists. He would wrap them around himself and his armies until no one could see them. I've seen such magic out in the middle of the ocean. One moment you can see, and the next? The mist is so dense you can't even see your own hands.

"He would wrap these mists around him like a great shroud." Manus lifted his hands, gesturing as if he wrapped a cloak over his shoulders. "Once, invaders almost saw the isle—perhaps similar to this one—that he lived on. Mac Lir called upon the mists and the isle disappeared."

The dog gave him a disbelieving look.

"I'm just telling you about your namesake, boy. At least enjoy the story, would you?"

If anything, the cù sìth enjoyed it less. The Fae beast turned its head away from him and heaved a great sigh.

"Come now! You don't want to hear anymore? It's said mac Lir is the greatest of all sea gods and that even the merrows love him."

"That's not true." The voice was the quiet drip of water against stone, the echo of ice gurgling. It was beautiful and haunting at the same time.

He held his breath and glanced over his shoulder at the most beautiful creature he had ever beheld.

She stood outlined by moonlight. The sheer white dress she wore plastered to her skin as if she had swum to the isle. Long, dark hair stuck to the fabric, covering her breasts, and brushing the tops of her thighs.

And her face was surely made by the heavens. Her dark eyes were like a storm brewing in the west. Her lips were stained wine dark, her skin the color of starlight. But it was her voice that captivated him. It carried the promise of fulfilled boyhood dreams.

"Is it not?" he asked. "I think I'm the one telling this tale."

"If you're going to tell a story, then you should tell the right one."

He could see she was uncomfortable. She rocked back and forth on her heels, her fingers toying with the ends of her long hair.

"What is the right one then, beauty?"

Her brows furrowed. "I don't like it when you call me that."

"Why not?"

"It feels as if that is all you see."

"That's a strange thing to say," he muttered and turned to face her. "What would you like me to call you?"

"Well, I'm not sure."

"Why not?"

"No one has ever asked me that before."

She was a strange woman, far stranger than he had expected. Manus rose from his crouch and crossed his arms. "You must tell me what you want me to call you."

"Saoirse," she blurted it out so quickly he raised a brow.

"That's a name."

"It is mine."

"But I want to call you by a nickname."

She cocked her head to the side. "Why?"

"They're a form of endearment."

"Surely you don't consider me dear to you?"

Again, he asked, "Why not?"

"Because you hardly know me."

"I don't know you at all."

Saoirse grinned, the smile so brilliant it nearly knocked him off his feet. "There, you see? You've admitted it as well."

"Just because I don't know you, doesn't mean I can't find you compelling, intriguing, or someone I'd wish to keep at my side for a while."

"Then you're judging entirely upon my appearance."

He knew the look on her face. A frown mixed with furrowed brows that suggested she was about to throw the largest fit known to womankind. At least now he knew she was just the same as any other woman he'd ever known. Manus was good with women.

"Now who's judging who?" he asked. "Seems like you appeared out of nowhere, soaking wet right to the skin as if you swam all the way out to this isle. If I'm an intelligent man, and I like to think I am, you're also the one who's been bringing me food and water. I've got a right to call you whatever I want."

"Why?" She sucked in a deep breath, her hands fisted at her side. "Why does taking care of you give you any right to treat me as you wish?"

"Oh, I never said that. I'll treat you how you wish, Saoirse, and I intend to do that by starting with an endearment, so you know when I use it I'm focused on you. And only you."

Manus had seen plenty of beautiful women in his life. He liked to track down the prettiest whore and pay a hefty price for her. But even the most renowned prostitutes in all of Uí Néill couldn't hold a candle to the mysterious woman who stood in front of him.

Saoirse.

Her name rolled off his tongue like sweet honey and burned his throat like the finest of whiskey. She had kept him safe all this time, saved him from the ship, and why?

Manus watched her fists unclench and waited for the soft sigh he knew she would heave.

"All right," she murmured. "So be it. If you must find something to call me other than my given name, then I request it be something from the sea."

"The sea?"

She looked up, catching his gaze with those dark eyes, and stole his soul from him. "The ocean is my mother. Her waves rock me to sleep at night and her will keeps me alive. I would honor her gifts in the way you honored Manannán mac Lir."

A woman who appreciated the ocean as much as he? Manus thought perhaps mac Lir himself was looking down on him, saw his strife, and sent him a bride that would wipe all others from his memory.

Cheeks red, he cleared his throat. "Ah, well then. That's much harder to think up."

"Is that so?"

"The sea is my life. I spent every penny I had getting out here in the first place, but I was one with the ocean the moment my mother first dipped my toes into saltwater. Such endearments have stronger meanings."

"Precisely why I requested one."

She had him there. The girl had spunk, something he couldn't remember any woman other than his mother having.

He was used to simpering smiles and hidden knowledge beneath lids that coyly cloaked true emotion. He was used to women who knew the game between the sexes and played it well.

This woman didn't seem to know there was such a thing. The ends of her hair shifted in the breeze, already drying from the trip she had made. Manus realized with startling clarity he wanted to know more about her. *Everything* about her. And he couldn't remember the last time that had happened.

He cleared his throat and rubbed the back of his neck. The cord of his mother's necklace tangled in his fingers, the tiny white stone bouncing against his chest. "Pearl."

"What?"

"Pearl, that's what I'll call you."

"Why?"

The vehement way she asked suggested his answer was important. That this was a turning point he could never return from if he got this answer wrong.

"Pearls take a long time to make. Even longer to find."

She waited to respond, her eyes suggested she thought he might continue.

He didn't.

"What does that have to do with me?"

"Someday I'll explain it to you, my pearl. But that is not today. What have you brought me for dinner?"

The swift change of subject confused her. She backed away a few steps as he strode forward, stuttering and tripping over her words. "I-I-It's just a bit of a fish and a few oysters I found—"

"You already know my favorites," he interrupted. He lifted the food off the gilded plate and inspected the fine craftsmanship. "I've never seen anything like this before."

"It's just something to put the food on."

"Oh, I know that. What I don't understand is how you found it all the way out here. This should be in a nobleman's house." He glanced up at her. "You aren't a noble, are you?"

"Royalty? Me?" Her jaw snapped shut so fast she didn't seem able to open it. Instead, she shook her head.

"You've got a royal look about you."

"What?"

"Perfect skin, perfect teeth, not a single callous or blemish on you. The only people who can afford to look like that are royals."

"I live a different life," she replied. "I don't think it's fair to judge someone because they don't look like you."

"Ain't that the truth. Come here," he said and patted the sand beside him. "Share dinner with me."

"Why?"

"I haven't spoken to anyone but myself in five days. I'd like a little company tonight, if only to save my sanity."

She hesitated.

Manus wanted to warn her. It wasn't safe for a woman so painfully beautiful to be alone with a man like him. She should run. That's what he would have said if he were her father. But he wasn't, so he smiled like the wolf he was and waited for her to sit.

Saoirse sat just out of arm's reach, her whole body tense as if he might spring at her. He might. He was strung tighter than a drum and he didn't have a clue why.

She was just a woman. The same as any other. Yet his body wanted her like a dying man wanted water.

He cleared his throat. "What brings you here?"

She did not respond.

"How did you get here? I couldn't find any land nearby, at least not that my eyes could see. And I don't see a boat. Did you swim?"

Again, she did not provide him any response.

He plucked at the oyster, pulling at the shell with his fingers even though he knew he would need a knife to eat it. Padding footsteps slapped against the sand and Mac Lir raced towards them. He settled onto the sand and stared at the oyster with such intensity it almost made

Manus laugh.

"You want some?" he asked the dog.

"They don't eat oysters," Saoirse replied. "It's not good for them."

"How do you know that?"

Again, she remained silent. He noted her curled fingers, the way she held tight to the thin fabric of her dress and breathed out a sigh.

"You don't want to answer any questions about yourself, do you?"

She shook her head.

"I didn't think so. Smart, that. You don't know me from the next strange sailor on a ship, and it would be a sad shame for a woman like you to trust too easily." He grunted, straining to rip open the oyster.

"Here," she said, holding her hand out for the oyster.

Now what did she think she was going to do with it? If Manus couldn't get it to open, a slip of a girl wouldn't be able to.

Curious, he handed it over.

Saoirse ran her fingers along the seams. She didn't pull, didn't rip, did nothing other than hum under her breath and stroke the outer shell. It opened a small bit, and she gave a quick yank.

Just like that, he had an oyster to eat.

"Neat trick."

"Not a trick," she replied, and handed the sweet meat back to him. "The ocean provides, one need only to ask."

How many times had he said the exact same thing? Manus tilted his head back and let the salty oyster slide down his throat. It was his favorite delicacy although most sailors never got the opportunity to eat them.

Yet another reason he thought it likely she wasn't who she said she was. Oysters? Raw fish? A gold plate?

"You saved me from the wreck, didn't you?"

She averted her eyes.

"You can say it. I know it was you, I remember."

"Memories can be strange things. Perhaps you only dreamt of me."

"No, I wouldn't forget eyes like those. You pulled me out of the abyss, dragged me to this isle, and then brought me food. Who are you?"

Again, she did not provide him any answers. She stared at the waves lapping her toes and remained silent.

"Arturo would love you," he muttered. "He'd tell me I'm finally getting what I deserve."

"Who?"

"A friend." Pain twisted his chest, an ache he knew all too well. Loss never got easier to bear, he just became a harder man. He rubbed his chest. "Gone now, I suppose. He was on the ship with me. A shame, too. He had a wife back home and a new babe."

"A baby?" she whispered. "That's so sad."

"Such is the life of a sailor. We all know the risks that come with our line of work."

"Your life is so fragile."

"Everyone's is. A man can die from a cut on his hand, a cough, a sting of a bee. Why not live a life of adventure? There's no guarantee life won't be cut short without it."

"I'm not sure I understand what you mean," she replied. Her toes curled in the sand. "If you're always sailing from one adventure to the next without fear of pain or hardship, how are you safe? How do you care for the life you're living?"

"I care. I care about the experiences, the adventure, the things I've seen that no one else has seen."

"And have you?"

"I've seen things that would make your heart race. Strange beasts that shouldn't exist. Lands so far away the people look entirely different. I've brought back furs of animals that are taller than me with claws the size of my hand."

Her lips parted, eyes locked upon him. "What is it like?"

"Sailing?"

"No. Going wherever you want, whenever you want."

"Now, that's a sad thing to hear you ask, my pearl." He handed another oyster over, silently asking her to open it. "There are men out there who don't think women should travel. They want to keep them under their thumb, so to speak, and prevent them from experiencing the world. I know it, and I think you know it too."

She petted the oyster and chewed her lip. "Why do they do that?"

"I think for some, it keeps them powerful. In their minds if they limit the knowledge of their women then they always have the upper hand. But they forget an important thing."

"What's that?"

"Women always have the upper hand. You have something we want, and we'll do anything to get it."

Saoirse froze, the oyster peeking out to gently touch her finger. Her eyes slanted towards him. "What is it men want?"

"Oh, that's a loaded question and not one I should be answering."

"Why not?"

"We're alone on an isle in the middle of the ocean, and as much as I like to think I'm a good man, I'm not."

"You seem like a good man."

"There's a difference between a good man and a patient one."

He could see her pulse fluttering in her neck. It called out to him like the song of a siren. She was just as affected as he was.

"I have to go," she blurted, scrambling to her feet in a flurry of sand and water.

"Where are you going?"

"Away!"

He lunged to his feet, holding out his hands because he didn't trust himself to touch her. "Will you come back?"

Saoirse froze, her back to him. "I don't think I could stay away if I wanted to."

They were exactly the words he wanted to hear. Grinning, he clenched his hands into fists and forced himself to back away from her. "All right then. Go on with you."

She raced down the sand and disappeared from sight, likely towards some unknown home at the interior of the isle.

Manus licked his lips.

"Patient," he muttered. "I am so full of shit."

"Saoirse! Where is your mind today?"

Her sisters gathered all around Saoirse, plucking at the floating strands of her hair. Her family had been a terrible bother lately. It wasn't unusual for their sister to disappear. She did so regularly, choosing to be alone rather than with them. Why did they think it strange now?

She groaned and jerked her head to the side. "It is here with you."

"No, it isn't. We've been talking to you for minutes and you've been staring at the stone!"

"Perhaps the current topic is one I share no interest in."

"You've always liked the whales, what changed?"

"*Nothing.*" Saoirse lurched up, propelling herself through the small cave they shared. "Why are you so bothersome today?"

"Why are you so testy?" Her eldest sister giggled. "Is it because father has decided you shall marry?"

Another sister pretended to swoon. "Has our youngest sister already chosen her groom?"

"How could I?" Saoirse shook her head at their antics. "There is not one merrow man in the entire ocean who could capture my attention."

"That's a shame, considering you are also a merrow."

"Can you willingly say there is one you like?"

"Craig has an interesting look."

"Craig?" Saoirse swallowed. "He has a heavy hand. One that likes to find its way towards innocent creatures."

"Oh, that's just a rumor."

It wasn't. Saoirse had seen it herself when she was coming home from gathering crabs for dinner. He had backed a woman into a crevice, speaking in low tones and lifting his fist. The look of terror on the merrow's face would stay with her for the rest of her life.

She shivered. "I would rather not tempt fate."

"I think she's found a man," one of her sisters giggled. "That's where she's been sneaking off to!"

Perhaps it was easier to let them think so. They could question it all they liked, but Saoirse was planning her escape. There were only a few more weeks until the full moon. Her father was already pressing her to give an answer, but she persisted that he had given her a fair amount of time.

If her plan worked, she would be long gone before then.

"Please," she clasped her hands, "don't tell Athair. I don't want him to know. It would be best if it were a surprise."

"Go on then, sister. But when you return, promise you'll tell us who it is?"

She shook her head and launched herself out of the cave mouth. They would never know who it was. And they would remain the only thing she regretted about this entire foolish plan.

Her sisters were as much a part of her as her gills. They might be foolish creatures, vain and sometimes silly, but they had hearts the size of the seven seas. She didn't want to see anything evil change that.

She shook her head and flexed her tail. Now was not the time to be thinking such morose thoughts. She still had to figure out how to get the human off the isle.

Jellyfish slid past, trailing their long tendrils against her skin. The faint electric sting made her muscles twitch. The larger ones posed a threat even to merrows. She grinned and batted one away. The small ones were kinder than their brethren.

Her smile faded. She supposed she could say the same about merrows and their kin. The guardians weren't likely to let her human leave any time soon. Even with her on a ship, they would want to tear it apart for trespassing.

Could she stop them? Was it even possible to reason with a guardian?

She had never tried. As far as Saoirse knew, no one had ever tried. They let the giants do as they pleased and were glad their homes were safe.

Could they even talk? No one had whispered rumors of conversations between any sea creature and a guardian.

Saoirse would need to know all these things before she let her plan unfold. The human needed to understand the danger he was in. He would need to trust her, to understand she had his best interests in her heart.

She shook her head ruefully and sped through the waters. He wouldn't trust her easily. He didn't seem like a foolish man.

"A patient man," she whispered, bubbles floating from her lips.

What had he meant by that?

There were too many questions in her head, and she needed them answered before *she* could trust *him*. It wasn't as if she had any choice. He was the only escape she could see.

Otherwise, she would end up in the arms of a merrow man for all eternity. Gooseflesh raised on her arms at the mere thought. Whether it was Craig or any other, she couldn't see herself marrying a frog.

The human? That was an entirely different story.

His matted locks were strangely appealing. The frown perpetually furrowing his brows made her want to smooth the anger away. Even his body was intriguing, so unlike her own even when she didn't have her tail.

Saoirse bit her lip. Did he think the same of her? She liked to think he did. The heat in his gaze suggested he was interested. But was that enough for him to take her far away from here? So far that the sea would never touch her again?

Her heart hurt at the mere thought.

The isle stretched its roots in the distance. The earth rose to meet her, lovingly sculpted by the hands of old gods. Coral glowed far beneath her, fish and sea life appearing as if by magic.

Poking her head above the waves, she eyed the beach. He didn't appear to be on this side of the isle at all. Worry ate at her. This was where she usually found him. Why wasn't he here?

She circled the land twice but didn't see him at all. The isle wouldn't let him go into the heart, would it? Those were faerie lands. Magic lands humans weren't allowed to see.

But apparently, it had.

Only those with faerie blood could pass through the sentinel plants which had a taste for blood. She'd watched him beat at them for hours before, when she couldn't keep herself away from the sight of him.

What had changed?

She dove beneath the waves. A small tunnel at the base of the isle was the only way for sea creatures to get to the heart. She peered into the darkness and swallowed hard.

She hated tight spaces.

Wiggling herself in, she used her hands to pull forward. Scales scraped against stone, loosening until she felt the telltale sting she had lost some.

Her father would notice that. He noticed everything that might mar her beauty even though her looks were considered "strange" compared to the other merrow women. Saoirse grunted and yanked herself forward.

Now, she would have to come up with some kind of story. He'd already noted her lost scales from the last time she swam with Manus. She couldn't make the same mistake again.

Maybe she'd been daydreaming and ran into something? He might believe that. His youngest daughter was often called the foolish one. The story would need to be as tight as a clam shell.

Light filtered through the water ahead. The tunnel ended in a fresh water pool so clear it was like looking through air. Green plants carpeted the bottom and brightly colored fish darted through the waving fronds.

She hesitated, not wanting to appear if he were looking straight into the water. What would she say?

Saoirse knew she would have to tell him what she was. Merrows weren't a bad faerie. Humans used to like them quite a bit until the rumors started that they sang men into rocks. They weren't trying to kill men back then. They were trying to *warn* them.

Humans were foolish. They thought the beautiful women were beckoning them closer and dashed their ships against the ragged stones.

Hooking her fingers over the edge, she pulled herself forward just enough to stare up at the surface.

A foot nearly touched her head.

Clapping a hand over her mouth so no bubbles rose, Saoirse ducked back into the tunnel. He was *in* the water? Why was he in the water?

She twisted her body so she could lay against the stones and stare up at him. He wore nothing but his skin and treaded water as naturally as she did.

Human males were not as she expected. Their parts were so different! Long legs, not at all frog-like, although dusted with hair. That made her uncomfortable. What were these hairy creatures? Were humans part beast after all?

He swam away from her, to the edge of the pool where his toes flexed, and he stood with practiced balance. Fish nibbled at his feet, the larger ones brushed against his thighs, but he didn't react.

She tried to see his face, but the water warped it. One moment, she thought he smiled. The next, she thought it might be a frown.

It didn't matter all that much, she still found him rather handsome. Never before had heat blossomed deep in her belly when looking at a male.

Humans were so lucky. There would always be a male out there they found handsome, beautiful, strong. Merrows were stuck with frogs and shark-like men who were always drunk and cared little for their female counterparts.

"How am I going to tell you what I am?" she whispered as she stared up at him. "Will you despise me? Will you think I am an animal to lock away? Or worse, a fish you might eat?"

Something grabbed onto the delicate membrane of her fin so hard she yelped, flexed the appendage, and shot out of the tunnel.

Her fear was so great she couldn't stop her momentum. Saoirse propelled herself through the pool and smacked her back against his.

The man.

She froze. He froze. They remained with their spines against each other's.

He was so warm. The heat from his body sank into hers, even through the scales. The ocean was a cold place to live. Her skin was used to the frigid waters of the deepest abyss. Touching him felt the same as lying in sand with the sun dancing across her skin.

"Pearl, is it?" he murmured. "I'm afraid you caught me in a compromising position."

"I could say the same."

Saoirse tried to keep her tail away from him. The long, eel like appendage must make him uncomfortable. But she couldn't keep herself above the surface without moving it. She winced as her scales rasped against his knee.

"Ah," he said. "So that's the way of it."

Her tongue tied in a knot. What was he going to say? Did she catch a hint of disgust in his words? She had never felt so self-conscious about being a merrow.

He waited for her to speak. His ribs expanded with each measured breath, calming her jarring gasps.

When she didn't respond, he continued. "I knew you weren't human. No average woman could pull me out of a shipwreck in the middle of the sea, swim with me to an isle, and then disappear into thin air. I just didn't know what you were."

"You do now."

"I do."

She gritted her teeth and waited.

"Merrows are rare where I come from," he finally said. "We call them good luck. Sometimes they help sailors when they're in a bad way."

"I've heard of such things."

"Is that what you were doing for me? A bit of charity?"

"No," she shook her head. "No, I couldn't let you die."

"Do you usually?"

"I've watched men drown and dragged their bodies into the depths with my sisters, yes."

"Why didn't you let me?"

"I don't know." Saoirse's voice elevated, rising to a high pitch that voiced her panic. "I saw you there in the water and I couldn't bring you down with the others. I couldn't watch the crabs feast on your body until there was nothing left but bone."

"*Why?*" he pushed.

"I wish I knew the answer."

They both remained silent, breathing together. She had never felt so close to a man, and so far away at the same time. She could touch him. Feel his heartbeat against her spine. Yet she did not know what he was thinking.

"I'm going to turn around now, Saoirse."

"I'd rather you didn't."

"That's not an option."

"Can't it be? Just for a few moments longer."

"'Fraid not."

She kept her back turned to him even as the warmth of his skin disappeared. She didn't want to see his expression when he saw what she really was.

It wasn't as if she knew him. Saoirse shouldn't be as attached as she was. He could think whatever he wanted of her. It shouldn't matter.

But it did. Her heartbeat thumped hard against her chest at the mere thought he might dislike her.

His hand touched her shoulder. Fingers sliding across the sensitive tendons, pulling her hair away from her skin to reveal the glistening sparkle of her skin.

"Are you going to turn around?"

"No."

"I can already see you."

"I'm certain you can, that doesn't mean I will turn."

He didn't seem disgusted. His voice was as warm as the rest of him, not frightened or tight with dislike. Perhaps he didn't mind after all.

"Saoirse," he chuckled. "No woman as beautiful as you should hide her face."

"I thought you said you didn't care about beauty."

"I never said that. Any man cares about beauty, but some of us see it inside a woman just as much as outside."

She melted. It didn't matter he might be lying to her, or that perhaps he was good with words. He had said the right thing to ease her nerves.

Her tail fluttered in the water, fine membranes glistening from the small of her back and tapering down to her wide fin. She flicked the end and turned towards him.

He stared down at her with an expression of awe. His eyes devoured every detail, starting at the top of her head and meandering down below the water. She couldn't imagine that he didn't feel at least a little apprehensive about her existence, but he didn't seem surprised at all.

"May I?" he asked.

Saoirse didn't have the faintest idea what he meant. Captivated, she nodded in response.

He reached down, lifted her hand, and tilted it into the sun. He pressed his thumb against the sensitive bones, forcing her fingers to spread wide and reveal the thin webbing. Rainbows danced over the membrane, making her hand appear to be made entirely of magic.

"You know," he murmured. "I never told you my name."

"It isn't customary for humans to tell faeries their name."

"I thought that goes both ways."

She blushed. "I am a foolish merrow. I speak with my heart before I think with my mind."

"I'm glad of it."

"Why?"

He ran a gentle finger across her webbing. "I would rather know your name than my own."

"You're very charming."

"It's working then?"

She lifted a brow and met his gaze with silent questions.

He chuckled. "I'm trying to charm you."

"You're doing very well."

"Any suggestions?"

"For what?" Saoirse shook her head, uncertain what he was asking.

"Improvement."

She blinked. "Not at the moment."

"You'll have to tell me if you think of anything."

"Why are you trying to charm me?"

"I've never met a merrow before."

"What does that have to do with anything?" Saoirse frowned. "Are you trying to avoid the question?"

"My name is Manus."

The words echoed in her mind, over and over again. She tasted the sweet whiskey of his true name that exhaled like a lover's sigh. A knot loosened in her soul, one she hadn't realized was there but had been since the moment she met him.

So, this was what it felt like to be the keeper of a human name. It was a heady feeling. Her fingers flexed against his, whispered possibilities overtaking her. She could order him to do anything. She could force him to help her leave.

Would she ever forgive herself? Saoirse wasn't sure. He deserved to make his own decisions, no matter how desperate she was.

"Manus," she repeated.

He visibly shivered, her words dancing across his skin and her control sinking deep into the vessel of his soul. He met her wide stare with an expression so heated she felt it burn. "That's a strange feeling."

"It doesn't always happen."

"What is it?"

"A bond. A tie between faerie and human."

"What does it mean?"

"We are linked forever, you and me. Like the ocean knows each creature that lives within it, we shall always know how to find each other."

He cleared his throat. "And if we don't want to be found?"

"I don't know. I've never met another faerie who made a bond with a human."

"Why not?"

"We don't like to be far from those with whom we are linked."

His eyes slanted away from hers and his hand tightened on hers. "I didn't ask for that."

"Neither did I. I might have prevented such a bond if I had an idea it might happen, but as I said, it is unusual for such a thing to occur."

"Why are you here, Saoirse?"

Not Pearl. He did not call her by the endearment she had come to enjoy. Strange. What had upset him? The bond? It wasn't anything she could change. The moment they heard each other's true names, the knot had loosened in her. Perhaps it had tightened in him.

She pulled at his hold. "I hadn't intended on seeing you."

"Ah, yes. The isle didn't want me in the interior. Is it because this is your home?"

"I do not live here."

"That's not an answer."

She hissed. "It is my only answer."

"Then why did the plants allow me here for the first time, and then you showed up?"

"I don't know."

"You say that a lot, and I think you're lying."

"Faeries cannot lie."

Her kind were truth tellers, no matter how much they wished they could lie. Faerie words could be twisted. Even Saoirse was adept at saying one thing and meaning another.

Surely, he knew? She wracked her brain, trying to find an answer to his question. She didn't want him to be mad at her. Frantic, she blurted out the first thing she could think of.

"Only faeries may come into this oasis. It is why it wouldn't let you in before."

"I'm still not a faerie." He hesitated before he said the words, just enough for her to notice.

"Why did you pause?"

"I didn't."

"You did. I heard your hesitation. I may not be able to lie, but I can tell one when I hear it."

He licked his lips and let her hand drop from his grasp. "My grandmother was rumored to have faerie blood."

"A changeling?"

"Not so much as that. Just a few drops of faerie blood that made her more likely to garner their favor."

Saoirse giggled at the thought. "Faeries don't care if humans share some of their blood. Those that we give our favors to are simply good people."

"Are you so certain of that?"

"The Unseelie Court may be different, but the Seelie Fae live with honor. They do not provide their aid to those who do not deserve it. If they deem their descendants unworthy, then they do not help them."

"Then the isle finds me worthy?" He snorted. "It wouldn't be the first to be wrong."

She stared up at his strong features, wondering what he looked like without the strong beard and tangled nest of dreadlocks. Were his features just as strong as she imagined? With such dark skin, she thought he looked much like the tree in her grotto.

"You say that so often. Are you trying to convince yourself it's true?"

"What?" He looked at her with raised eyebrows.

"It's just…" She looked down, afraid he might think her foolish. "Of all the men I've met, you are the last person I would say was unworthy."

"Have you met many?"

"Just merrow men." Were her teeth chattering? The thought of her own kind caused such a visceral reaction, and she couldn't control it. "They are not kind."

"All of them? I find that hard to believe."

"All of them."

He couldn't understand. It wasn't her species that was the issue. It was their life. Merrow men were stuck at the bottom of the ocean. They were so slow compared to merrows, incapable of protecting themselves against sharks or squid. Merrows were fast, darting through the ocean without a care.

Alone, forced to remain in the dark depths, merrow men turned to alcohol to ease their troubled minds. It made them ugly, angry, and they were even worse when they drank.

He watched every thought reflected on her face. She felt his gaze as if he touched her.

He hummed deep in his throat. The tones sounded like that of the great whales that passed by at night. Their haunting songs sometimes crept into her dreams, reminding her that the world was large, and she was nothing more than a small merrow.

"If that's the way of it, then I am glad you are here," he said. "It is a long and difficult road to walk when those around you are not willing to be kind."

"You know this life?"

"Most children do when they grow up on the streets."

Her heart bloomed again, opening like a flower to bask in the acceptance of his tones and the understanding she heard within his words. "Then you understand why I am here."

"Perhaps too much, my pearl."

She stared up at him as if he hung the stars in the sky. He understood her? He understood the things she had fought over again and again.

Manus cleared his throat, a blush spreading from his chest up his neck. "Are you staying then?"

"I would like to."

"Good."

CHAPTER 4

JOURNEY TO THE DEPTHS

Manus lay on his back in the sand, wondering when and how he got so lucky. A merrow? They were creatures of good fortune, at least for sailors who worried the ocean would swallow them up at any minute.

Mac Lir must have looked kindly upon him. Little Saoirse would be a talisman for him. A confirmation he would never die on the sea.

He grinned up at the clouds that spun like churning waves above him. Just how far would this luck go? Would she bring him fortune? The legends said merrows cast their favors upon men easily enough. They liked a quiet-spoken husband who took care of them.

Her story hadn't surprised him. Anyone who knew of the Fae knew merrow men were poor excuses for faeries. They all liked their drink and disliked any man who stepped in their way.

The voice of his mother whispered through his memories. She had loved to tell stories of creatures under the sea.

"Never fall in love with a merrow," she whispered in his ear. "They are kindly and beautiful creatures, but their husbands will hunt you down and kill you without a thought."

He must be a foolish man because he was willing to take the risk.

How could he not? She was more beautiful than any woman he had ever seen, and she had saved his life. Manus had never met a woman who could do that although Arturo was likely to laugh at him.

"That's the point of a wife, boy," the spirit of his friend crowed. "They would die for you. They take the chance with every child they bring into this world and yet they do it again and again for the men they love."

Foolish thoughts, all of them. He hadn't ever desired a wife, and it made little sense he would want one now.

Manus lifted a hand and rubbed at his chest. The sting of magic still lingered there, deep underneath his ribs and wrapped around his heart like a thorny vine. She murmured his name with a tongue dripping honey and eyes so large they held the entire night sky in their depths.

She owned a part of him now even though he didn't like it one bit. He hadn't given it willingly. She snatched up the bright light inside his heart and swallowed it whole.

Merrows were dangerous, he agreed with his mother. This one could bring him to his knees with a smile.

A soft clinking sound echoed from waves lapping the sand, and he smiled. She had returned, as promised, although he worried what it might cost her.

"Not your business," he grunted, reminding himself that she wasn't part of his life. Not yet.

If he had it his way, he would take her all the way back to Uí Néill and sit her in a quiet little cabin all to themselves. She would look good by a fire with a cat curled at her feet.

He rose up on his elbows, staring down the length of his body at the merrow lying in the waves. She had her head on her fists and her tail curled out of the water, flipping back and forth.

"Hello," she said.

"Welcome back. Safe trip?"

"As safe as most."

"I'm glad to hear it." The sun reflected off the small pile of objects in front of her. Raising a brow, he sat all the way up and pointed. "What did you bring?"

"Things I thought you might find interesting."

"Well bring them here then."

"I'd rather you come get them."

He thought for a moment she was flirting. It surprised him. She had proven to be an innocent little thing, and far too curious for her own good, but he quickly realized no flirtatious tones heightened the trill of her voice.

Her hands clenched into tiny fists. Her tail stopped flipping, instead, it lay still underneath the water. Even the shimmer of her scales dulled as her eyes dropped from his. She was uncomfortable, he realized, or perhaps even embarrassed.

That was something he could fix. Manus was a charming man when he wanted to be, and women were easy for him to understand. He read their bodies like a well-loved book.

He shot towards her, kneeling in the sand and tucking his finger underneath her chin. She was chilly but not cold and shivering as any other woman would have been. Her eyes met his, albeit slowly, and a muscle in her jaw bounced against his thumb.

"What is it?" he asked. "What chases the light from your eyes?"

"Merrows change outside of water. You've seen me without the tail but the transformation…" she hesitated. "It is not a pleasant sight."

"Why?"

"The body of a merrow is like slime when it is no longer attached to me."

"Like a jellyfish?"

"If we must draw comparisons, yes, similar to that."

"It will not startle me," he murmured.

She didn't seem convinced. Chuckling, Manus stroked the soft skin of her jaw and told himself not to marvel at the silken flesh. She was a woman, not a goddess, and he refused to put her on a pedestal.

"Truly," he continued, "I will not be disgusted or startled by anything you do, my pearl. I want to know you, every part of you."

"I don't know how you could."

Neither did he. A woman melting into a jellyfish turned his stomach, but if this was what the merrow needed from him, then he would school his thoughts and ensure that was what she got.

He glanced down at the pile of glinting gold and his jaw dropped. "What did you bring me?"

"Oh!" Happiness sparked in her gaze again and she looked down at the treasure. "Just a few things I found at the bottom of the ocean. Do you like them?"

Like them? These were priceless treasures! Golden crowns, heavy jeweled necklaces, even a goblet fit for a king. He could make so much coin from these if he found the right person to peddle them.

"These are stunning, Saoirse. Are there more?"

"More?" She shrugged. "There's more of them I suppose. We throw them out, so there is likely plenty along the bottom of the ocean. I could find others if you don't like these."

She moved to scrape the treasures back into sea. With a great shout, Manus leapt forward and pulled it all back towards him.

"No! No, I need no more than this. I was just curious. For humans, this is a considerable amount of wealth."

"Really?" She stared at him in shock. "But it's *trash*. What use could you possibly have for such things? Food or water I could understand, but these are just metal."

He watched her clink them together, smashing precious gold against delicate jewel. Perhaps she was right. They were useless objects in the long run, but he wasn't about to let go of a small fortune. If he ever got off this isle, he would make himself a wealthy man.

"Humans rarely make sense," he said. "But if we ever leave, we could live like kings and queens with that treasure."

"Leave?"

So that was what she wanted. He eyed the merrow with new found interest. She was using *him*, not the other way around.

Manus couldn't let her know he had discovered her plan. Let her play him while he wooed her. He intended to take the little merrow all the way home with him. If she cooperated and thought it was her idea, then it would only make his plan easier.

He would need to convince her of his interest though.

Swooping down, he lifted her tail and all into his arms. "Come on, out of the water with you."

She squealed, in happiness and delight he was certain. "Manus!"

The name zinged down his spine. "Saoirse."

"What are you doing?" she asked with a shiver.

"Bringing you to the sand, little merrow."

"I thought you wanted more treasure?"

"I do, but first I want you to be certain that nothing you do will ever disgust me."

"Oh," she whispered.

"Now, let's see how long you take to change back to the long-legged lass who captured my attentions long before she became magic."

Saoirse collected more "treasures" in the small bag she had made from Manus's shirt. He seemed to like them, and she enjoyed making him happy. The creases at the corner of his eyes made something in her belly quiver. His hearty laugh echoed through her soul until she dreamed about the sound.

Manus was slowly becoming a part of her. She held the knowledge of him in the deepest parts of her heart, hiding him from other merrows.

Her sisters commented that she seemed so much happier than she ever had before. Her smile was brighter, her laughter lighter, even the way she swam was much more graceful than they remembered.

They couldn't understand it. They didn't understand the concept of love at all.

Saoirse was certain this feeling was the elusive gift that only humans understood. she loved him. Nothing else could explain the lightness of her being whenever she looked at him.

Treasures stuffed his shirt so much that she feared it would rip. Perhaps that was all she would need. He couldn't ask for much more, how else would he carry it away?

He talked about leaving all the time now. She spent most nights at his side, watching the stars and listening to his stories. The land was a wondrous place full of people she would soon see.

He said he would take her with him. Saoirse was certain he wouldn't lie about such an important thing. He must love her though he hadn't said it. Manus looked at her with such gentle eyes, touched her with loving strokes, but never inappropriately.

She wrapped her arms around her waist and twirled. Her hair funneled above her in a coiling mass of dark green.

"Love," she whispered. "What a strange emotion it is."

It made her sick and happy at the same time. She sometimes couldn't feel the tips of her fingers because of it.

A shadow passed overhead cast by a massive dark form blotting out the sun.

She flinched. "Hello, guardian."

The beast did not respond, but when did they ever? Instead, the large female paused and stared down at Saoirse with a massive eye.

"Do you need me for something?"

Silence echoed in the water, but Saoirse could almost feel the creature's thoughts. Guardians never spoke, yet Saoirse was certain their emotions were strong.

Disappointment radiated in great blasts that stirred the waters to churning. The guardian didn't like Saoirse disappearing so often, and it knew where she went.

"He loves me," she whispered, toying with the frayed strings of the shirt. "He wants to take me away from this place."

The deep hum echoing around her suggested the guardian did not agree with her.

"He wouldn't lie to me." Saoirse called out. "He couldn't. It's not within him to be so cruel."

But they were all cruel, the guardian sang in her mind. All humans had the ability to be cruel and were regularly. It was human nature, and they could not swim from that. Saoirse needed to be careful before she left the ocean for good.

Twitching her tail, Saoirse floated up and touched the guardian's large cheek. "I will be careful," she said. "I promise. I will not give my heart to someone unworthy of it."

Her heart stuck in her throat as the song changed. Be careful, the guardian reminded her. Be careful and be wise as so many merrows are not.

Saoirse pressed a kiss to the guardian's cheek. "Don't worry. Even if I go to land, I will always return home to visit you."

She hoped. She twisted away and flowed through the water as quickly as she could. What if she couldn't return to the ocean? What if in leaving, she was also saying goodbye forever?

Saoirse was young. The idea of an adventure and a new love was tantalizing. She hadn't considered that she might never see her family again. The taste of salt on her lips, the songs of whales so far away she couldn't see them. Would those all disappear from her life forever?

She wasn't sure what she would do if that were the case. Saoirse frowned and skimmed the bottom of the ocean. She was close to the isle, close to where she would need to decide what to do about Manus.

She reached out and touched her fingers to the sand. It plumed in great scattered clouds, obscuring her vision. She was used to the weightless quality of the ocean. She'd discovered life on land was harder. Her body easily tired, weary from days fighting against the pull of the earth. She struggled to walk, to run, to move.

In the ocean, she was graceful. Her body moved like that of the dancers she heard of in stories. She could do anything she wanted under the water. Speed through the waves, leap into the air above them, or dive into the dark depths.

Would she be able to continue that?

No, she knew she wouldn't. The land would suffocate her. It was what the land did. It took everything from the creatures who lived there and devoured them whole. The land even ate them after they died, worms and bugs feasting upon the bodies until they were little more than bone. Somehow, it felt different when those creatures were fish that then provided for merrows.

The sight of their own grisly deaths terrified humans. Saoirse remembered well a sailor who had seen a skeleton upon rocks. The horror in his gaze haunted her dreams for many years.

She clutched the bundle of treasures to her chest.

"It won't be like that," she told herself. "You won't be alone. Manus will be with you, and he is part of you now. He is part of your soul. You are part of his. Together, there will be no fear, no hunger, no ache."

She had to believe it. Otherwise, what good was life?

Saoirse flexed the strong muscles of her tail and pushed herself towards the surface. Maybe seeing him would make her feel better. He would understand her thoughts; he must experience very similar ones himself. She would talk with him, let him pet her hair as he so loved to do, and calm both their minds.

She poked her head above the surface and searched the beach for him.

There. Where he always was. Lying in the sand like a great sea lion, the sun playing across his features and darkening his skin to a deep chocolate.

Butterflies took flight in her belly. They fluttered up her throat until she swallowed, hoping to still their beating wings for fear they would erupt from her lips and reveal everything she felt. That she was mad about him. That he invaded her dreams and even in those he smiled with those crinkled eyes and said the same words over and over again.

"I want to know everything about you, and I will find nothing disgusting."

He hadn't. Even the slime from her tail dissolving hadn't resulted in anything more than a simple shrug.

"It's part of you, Saoirse. If I am uncomfortable, it will only be for a few moments. I am pleased that you exist, my pearl. Do not fret."

And she hadn't. For an entire week she hadn't thought a single angry word at all. Until today. He had to know their time was limited. That she only had three more sunsets before she had to choose a husband, and unfortunately a human was not in the running. If they were going to flee, they had to do it soon.

She swam to shore and tossed her findings next to him. He sat straight up with his fists raised, the loud clanking sounds startling him.

Saoirse pressed her fingers against her lips, giggling through the crevices. "I'm sorry, I thought you knew I was coming."

"You're a silent swimmer, my pearl."

"I splashed!"

"The ocean splashes regularly, that doesn't mean it's you." But he wasn't angry at her. His eyes crinkled at the edges and he bit his lip as he looked her up and down. "Are you coming out of the ocean today?"

"No."

"No?" He raised an eyebrow. "Why ever not?"

"I thought you would like to come into the ocean with me."

"I'm not as strong a swimmer as a merrow."

"No one is. But there is much I would like to show you. The world under the waves is a beautiful place, and it would be selfish of me to keep it to myself."

He pondered her words, tapped a finger against his chin, and eyed her carefully. "Where are we going?"

"The place where I found most of our treasures."

His eyes slashed towards her, gold shimmering in the depths of his dark eyes. "There's more?"

"There's always more."

"You've captured my attention, my pearl. How far beneath the ocean is this trove?"

"Not far. There are pockets of air within, I believe you will make it to the shipwreck if you are a strong swimmer."

"Didn't I tell you the ocean is in my blood?" he asked with a snort. "A wreck you said?"

"An old ship."

"Any markers?"

She hadn't ever looked. Human markers meant little to her. They put something on everything, little details that claimed ownership over yet more material objects.

She shrugged. "Not really. It's filled with these though," she gestured at the golden coins. "And it was dangerous to swim through the first few years. There was too much fabric."

"Silk?"

"I don't know what that is."

Saoirse didn't understand why he was so interested in the cloth. It was annoying at best even though she had yanked a dress out of a sunken ship just a few nights ago. He was distracted by her nudity, at least that's what he told her.

Maybe he was excited for the adventure. She plastered a bright smile on her face and shook off the ominous feeling. "Are you ready?"

"You want to go now?"

"The sun is up, the water is warm, and the wreck is waiting for us."

She held her breath as he looked her up and down. "How strong of a swimmer are you, my pearl?"

The question was strange, but one she was proud to answer. Flexing the muscles of her spine, she lifted her fluke and let it slap down on top of the water. "Very strong."

His grin was the sun, the moon, and the stars. It split across his features and warmed the usually hard expression that always made her wonder whether he was angry. Creases formed at the edges of his eyes, his shoulders shaking with some unknown mirth.

"Good," he said with a nod. "So am I."

Without hesitation he stood, stretching his arms over his head. The movement was graceful as if he was already diving underneath the waves.

Saoirse sighed and planted her chin on her fist. His beauty still stunned her. Merrows were used to their own feminine beauty, but never that of masculine perfection. And how could she not admire him? The ridges of his strong body were made by years of hard labor. Each scar told a story, each bump a tale of hardship and endurance.

A shiver danced down her spine. He was a fine specimen of a man, and it was a shame her sisters couldn't admire him.

That would open a can of worms. They didn't need to know the possibilities the rest of the world held. It would only make their own life that much harder.

The waves stroked his feet, his strong calves, and then delicately to his thighs. Manus flexed his muscles, rubbing his shoulders to prepare for cold water and Saoirse lost her breath again. His sun darkened skin poured over the muscles of his body like liquid bronze.

Could it be possible he wasn't a man at all? A prince? Or perhaps he was a god of the ocean, like his stories, come to steal her away.

She shook her head and pushed herself away from the shore. Dwelling on such fantasies was a child's game. She shouldn't put him up on such a high pedestal, she would only find herself disappointed.

Peering up through the waves, she saw the flash of his grin before he dove beneath the surface to join her.

His hair floated up, the knotted tendrils reminding her of the dark kelp which grew in the depths. He hovered in the crystal-clear water, sand billowing in great puffs from his kicks, with a smile revealing blinding white teeth. The golden hoops in his ears flashed, and the beads in his beard echoed with a clack.

Could he hear things the way she did?

Saoirse clutched sand in her fists, staring up at him with her heart in her throat. His eyes were the deepest of oceans. Dangerous, but exciting at the same time.

He kicked with his powerful legs and shot towards the surface. It broke the spell he held upon her. The membranes along her spine flattened as embarrassment turned her fingers cold. She was acting like a lovesick child.

Twisting, she rose to meet him. Her dark hair slicked back from her face and water dripped down her cheeks. She licked the droplets, enjoying the taste of salt on her tongue.

Saoirse hadn't thought it possible, but his gaze heated even further. His eyes traced a burning line from her lips to her eyes.

"Which way?"

"Follow me."

She dove deep into the waiting cold of the water. It was a chilling splash, one that reminded her above all else she was just a merrow. He was a human man. He wouldn't live as long as her; they never did.

Manus swam above her, his shadow merging with hers until she could pretend he had a tail as well.

"Foolish," she muttered, bubbles floating from between her lips. "If he were a merrow, then he'd be just as ugly as the others."

She couldn't survive his beauty being stripped away from him. Disturbed by her own thoughts, Saoirse flicked her tail and sped through the water.

White sand blasted in her wake, leaving a trail of sparkling light she could see over her shoulder. A brightly colored fish swam in front of her and she marveled at its scales glimmering like the most precious of gems. At the sound of her bubbling laugh, a starfish lifted an arm and waved.

Manus kept up with her. He hadn't lied when he said he was a strong swimmer. His body cut through the waves easily, and his shadow never left hers. Not even for a second.

As they rounded the isle, Saoirse reached out her hand and traced the outline of his. He had reached one hand forward in his strokes, leaving it jutting out.

Curious, she flipped over and stared straight up at the surface.

He was watching her. Dark eyes locked upon her form and powerful legs did most of the work. The raised arm shifted, moving until his shadow traced along her cheekbone. Saoirse held her breath as the faint outline of his hand moved down her throat, between the valley of her breasts, and down to the curve of her hip.

She didn't know how to respond. Was this what men and women did on land? Was every interaction so visceral they couldn't breathe?

The fluke of her tail flicked involuntarily, sending her shooting away from the temptation he presented. He didn't need to touch her at all, she was already captivated.

His smile flashed again. Bright, like the side of a tuna when sunlight strikes its scales, and so blinding it seared into her mind forever. He lifted his head to the air and the spell shattered.

Her heart thundered against her ribs, pounding so hard she could hear it. She pressed her hands to her chest. They trembled so violently she feared she might have harmed herself.

Had she? Saoirse thought long and hard, trailing her thoughts down her body but could identify nothing physically wrong. Yet, the trembling would not cease.

The shipwreck loomed before them. Jagged edges of wood lashed out at the ocean, their points like swords ready to catch any that ventured too close. A once great mast had long ago snapped in half, tilting over the edge of the ship and pointing down into the abyss. Barnacles covered the hull, and eels stuck their heads out of their holes, watching the newcomers with black eyes.

Saoirse might have once been afraid of the dark place and the shadows that lingered in the belly of the ship. Now, she only saw the beauty hidden within.

Propelling herself to the surface, she silently revealed herself next to Manus. "Found it."

He let out a loud curse and spun around.

She giggled. "I'm sorry, I thought you were watching me."

"I was, but I lost track of you. I was staring at the monstrosity below us."

"Isn't it beautiful?"

He glanced through the water towards the ship. "I don't know if I'd call it beautiful. Ancient comes to mind."

"Old things are beautiful too," she replied. "Didn't you want to see all the treasure?"

"Of course I do, but are you sure there are air pockets? There doesn't seem to be much left of the ship."

She nodded, albeit a little slowly. It had been some time since she explored the area of the ship where the air pockets had been. It was difficult for her to climb to those sections, and she hadn't wanted to.

In any case, it wasn't that far down. A child could swim to the bottom and back in record time, surely he could do the same.

"We'll be careful," she replied. "If there aren't air pockets, we'll come back up."

If he was worried, Manus didn't reveal it. He rolled his shoulders, nodded, and breathed deep through his lungs.

Saoirse panicked for a moment. He was breathing so quickly and so deeply that something had to be wrong. At her panicked noise, he gave her a wink, and a flashed grin, then dove.

Shocked, she ducked her head and watched him cut through the water like a spear. His powerful body dove deeper and deeper with no hesitation at all.

He hadn't lied. Only a creature who came from the sea could swim that well.

With a grin on her own face, she followed him into the depths with a bright flick of her tail. It was easily five lengths of a man to the ship, then they needed to find an entrance. She should have scouted ahead for air, but he rushed head first into the ocean with little fear.

She liked that.

Excitement bubbled in her chest, foaming and frothing until it popped in her heart as the brightest of glee. She spiraled around him, her tail glimmering in the light and her hair a riot of dark color that tangled over his shoulders.

He grinned, powerfully pulling himself through the weight of the water with his strong arms. No wonder ropey muscles crisscrossed his body. It was so much more work for humans underneath the waves!

She admired his determination. It was a long way down, and not once did he hesitate.

Saoirse reached the ship first, catching the edge in her hand and peering into the nearest hole. No air, just a sea slug and a few clams that opened their mouths at her arrival.

Frowning, she pushed herself down the side, searching for a small bit of air where he could catch his breath. Otherwise, he wouldn't be able to see all the wonders of the ship! And she desperately wanted to prove to him that her world was just as beautiful as the surface.

He knew it. Saoirse had seen the longing in his eyes when she told him stories of swimming beside whales and their hunts for deep sea squid. He deserved to experience it first-hand.

Determined, she pulled at a rotting piece of wood and ripped it from the side. A few bubbles escaped. They weren't much, just a few, but that had to mean there was air.

She turned, but Manus was already swimming towards her. He closed strong hands on the side of the ship and disappeared into the opening she'd made.

"So brave," she observed, shocked by his lack of fear as she slipped in after him.

It was dark, and it took a while for her eyes to adjust to the dim light. Blinking, she glanced up where Manus had pressed himself against the ceiling. The faintest line of air created a space barely the width of her finger.

Saoirse's heart stopped beating for a fraction of a second. It wasn't enough air to keep him alive, it might not even be enough to get him to the surface.

He ducked back into the water, his gaze meeting hers with a surety that felt too final for her liking. He knew he wouldn't make it back to the surface, couldn't without a lungful of air.

That wouldn't do.

Saoirse's brows lowered in determination and she launched towards him. Spearing through the water with a flick of her powerful tail, she struck him like a stone plummeting towards the bottom of the sea. Her momentum pushed him backwards, but the wall would stop them.

Grasping his cheeks, she turned his head and closed her mouth around his. She inhaled deeply through her gills, fronds spreading open wide in her gasp, filtering the water into crystal clear air. They snapped shut as her body switched the air into her lungs, which she then poured between his lips.

He grew slack in her grasp. Was he dying? Had she done something wrong?

Saoirse's gills flared again, and she took another deep breath. Bubbles created a curtain between them as she tried to get him to take more air, but it billowed out of his mouth. She was frightened he'd passed out and didn't feel him move until his hands found her hips and drew her closer.

Even in the water, his touch burned like fire. This incredible man tugged her into his arms and wrapped her in his embrace. She exhaled again, and he drew air from her lips as if he were sipping the finest of wines.

He stroked his fingers down the indent of her spine. They lingered at the small of her back, dipping in the curve and stroking the scales that met the sensitive area. Feather light and gentle, he cupped the back of her head with his other hand and angled it up.

His lips softened against hers. She couldn't begin to fathom what he was trying to do, but it wasn't unpleasant.

Saoirse let her own mouth relax, allowing him to explore, and discovering him in return. Her chest bumped his and his legs tangled around her tail. She didn't know where he began and she ended.

Her eyes drifted shut and she let him take the lead. Manus pressed tiny kisses against the corners of her lips, drifting in the faint current as if they didn't have a care in the world. When he needed air, he brushed his fingers over the slits of her gills. They flared at his touch and she fed him air from her own lungs.

Every inch of him was warm. The firm plane of his chest held her comfortably while his hands calmed her every movement. It was as if he was in her head, like he could read her mind.

Eventually, he drew back with lungs full of air and a grin on his face. He lifted a brow at her stare.

Of course, they were supposed to be finding treasure.

Her shoulders shook with a shiver, but she gestured for him to follow her. Saoirse grasped the ragged edge of a doorway and pulled herself deeper into the ship.

The light filtered through holes in the sides, revealing the treasures she cared about. Eels slithered through the shadows. Silver fish darted through the window, their formation breaking around Saoirse. Their smooth sides brushed against her and sent her hair swirling in a coil.

Grinning, she beckoned Manus forward into the dark room.

He didn't hesitate, following her into the darkness and catching her by the neck. Surprised, she didn't stop him when he pressed his lips against her again and sipped air from her lips.

Bubbles floated from her mouth, the tip of his tongue stroking the outline of her bottom lip. Startled, she pulled back and swam towards the treasure.

But the taste of him remained. Salty, like the ocean, like the oysters she had shucked for him. And sweet, like the finest of jellyfish, rare and only tasted on special occasions.

It was a taste she could become addicted to, and she couldn't understand why.

Merrows did not press their lips together. Saoirse had seen humans do it, even men on ships found their way towards each other. It never made sense to her. Mouths were for eating.

At first, she thought they were animals. The pressing of lips must be some kind of attack, a threat, a way to warn off other creatures. But they continued to do it. Repeatedly, and they always smiled afterwards. As if they enjoyed it.

She pressed her fingertips against her mouth and tucked her newfound secret deep in her soul. If it were a kiss he gave her, not just the exchange of air, then he had given her a gift. No other merrow that Saoirse knew could say they understood this human pleasure.

A smile spread across her face. She lifted her hand again, gesturing for him to follow her. There was another secret to this ship although she wasn't supposed to show it.

Every now and then, merrows found themselves captivated by gold. She never understood the desire. The ocean provided far more than any human could ever make. But those who enjoyed the secrets of humanity, carefully hid them away.

She hadn't planned to show him, there were other treasures he could see. Yet, the kiss lingered on her lips and clouded her mind.

The tunnel extended through the bottom of the ship. Deep into the earth it bored, twisting and turning until it emerged in a cave system. She remembered air and a great pile of gold.

How did she express he needed to trust her? It would be a frightening journey for a creature who couldn't see well in the darkness, and who couldn't breathe unless she helped him. And yet, she was willing to take the risk to see the look in his eyes.

Saoirse reached out and grasped his hands, pulling him into her arms so she could stare into his eyes.

"Trust me," she said, not knowing whether he could hear or understand her. "I promise, I will keep you safe."

If he understood, he made no movements.

Hesitantly, she leaned forward and pressed her lips against his again. The kiss was meant to be calming, to ease any worry he might have. He changed it, forcing more of his heat into her body until even the surrounding waters warmed.

Saoirse pulled him even closer, wrapping her arms around him and tucking his head underneath her chin. He stiffened but allowed her to control his body. She ran a hand down his back and curled his arms around her. With her tail, she nudged his legs closer, curved her spine, and dove backwards into the dark tunnel.

He immediately clenched his body around hers. Bubbles echoed, his question lost in the water as they passed by. She caught only one word.

"What—"

Perhaps it was cruel, but her teeth flashed in the darkness. She pulled him up her body and pressed her lips against his. She flexed her tail, propelling them through the tunnel with ease.

His heart thundered against her chest, and she needed to give him air three times before she saw the faint light.

"Just a bit more," she told him, although he couldn't possibly understand her. "It will be worth all the fear."

One last powerful undulation and they burst free from the tunnel, into the air.

Manus spluttered, coughing and flailing his arms. She held him up while dodging his kicks.

"Manus!" she shouted. "Manus, we're here!"

"Here? Where is here? You couldn't have warned me?"

"I didn't think I'd take you here."

"You know humans can't breathe underwater, don't you?"

"I do," Saoirse chuckled. He finally stilled in her arms, hair hanging in limp strands across his forehead. "I kept you alive, didn't I?"

"Barely! What if you hadn't known I needed air?"

"You were taking care of that," she murmured. Her eyes strayed to his lips, the thin slashing lines turned down in displeasure. "Or perhaps you were entertaining yourself in other ways."

"Ah," he shook his head. "I shouldn't have taken such liberties."

"I hope you will continue to take them."

"You deserve someone better than me."

"I know you claim you aren't a good man," she said. Saoirse met his gaze with a heated stare. "Has it occurred to you I am not searching for a good man, but one who will break all the rules to have me?"

He groaned. "You shouldn't say such things, Saoirse."

Her name strummed through her veins like pure magic. It bubbled, foamed, popped in her heart until all she could think of was him.

"Did you kiss me?" she asked. "Or were you using me for air?"

"Both," he admitted in guttural tones. "Each time."

Her skin heated with the admission. He had kissed her. *Her.* A simple merrow, from a simple family, with nothing to her name but a family who desired her to marry.

This man surprised her around every corner, and she refused to hide her feelings any further.

Saoirse slid her hands along his shoulders, up his neck, to the back of his head where his hair tangled in her fingers. Coarse and thick, the kelp-like dreadlocks reminded her of the deepest oceans that lingered in his eyes.

"Kiss me again," she whispered, "when there is no danger of life or death. Just a man and a woman, with nothing else between them."

Her words snapped whatever control he held upon himself. Manus kissed her as if he were a drowning man and she his salvation. With teeth, lips, and tongue he devoured her.

She hardly remembered to keep them afloat, wanting to drift back into the embrace of the ocean where she knew they would both be loved. They were two halves of the same shell. Creatures born outside of their true element, linked by their love of the sea.

He drew back enough to breathe, his breath fanning across her face like a sea breeze. "Was that enough?"

"Never."

"Didn't you have something to show me?"

It didn't matter anymore. She didn't care about the golden treasure anyway; couldn't they continue to kiss? This newfound desire was difficult to force from her mind.

But his eyes were curious, and his fingers drummed a beat against her throat.

"Yes," she replied. "Turn around."

The cave was lit by a rare species of worm which grew from the ceiling. Their spit was bioluminescent and cast a blue light around the cave.

Saoirse helped him turn by holding onto his ribs. His back rested against her bare chest and she wrapped her arms around his shoulders.

"The gold is here," she said. "Do you see it? It's a merrow hoard, a rare one in these parts as most of us live in the abyss."

And what a hoard it was. The few merrows with the addiction carried handfuls whenever they could. Coins, crowns, goblets, all mashed together in a mountain of wealth that spilled into the water.

He pulled away from her, swimming to the edge and clambering up onto the mountain. His eyes were large with awe as he stumbled and fell onto his knees.

Saoirse watched him grab fistfuls of the coins. They trickled through his fingers and clinked, cascading down into the water and glinting as the blue light reflected off their shiny surfaces. Mouth agape, he turned back to her.

"How did all of this get here?"

"There are many shipwrecks in these waters, and some among us gather up the pieces."

"You?"

Saoirse shook her head. "No. I have only added one thing to this cave."

"What is it?"

She blushed. Would he think it was foolish? A child's desire to add something to the hoard but not seeing the meaning behind it all?

Yet, he had asked, and she was loath to deny him anything. Saoirse pointed behind him and up, towards a small rocky ledge that jutted out from the cave way. "There."

He stood and made his way over the mountain towards her one contribution. It was a golden statue, small enough to easily hold and barely larger than her hand.

Perhaps it was some country's prince, a ruler known throughout the human world. She thought the smooth lines of his face were too intricately made to let him wallow in the depths. The crown on his head was sharply pointed, and the sword on his hip made her dream about the wars he had fought.

And won.

She dreamt about that prince throughout most of her childhood, and even into her adult years. He was handsome, kind, a king that would make all other kings appear foolish. His intelligence was known throughout the lands and all the royal women wanted to be his bride.

The stories she made up in her mind fueled her happiness. Now, Saoirse found she was afraid what Manus would say. Was he a made-up figure? Just a man an artist sculpted on a whim with no real roots?

Manus turned it over in his hands and nodded. "Cú Chulainn. One of the greatest kings in all the legends, son of Lugh and a mortal woman. It is a good omen to keep such a talisman. He'll keep you safe."

"He was a protector then?"

"Of everyone he loved and one of the most unfortunate men in history."

She swam closer, placing her elbows on the mountain of gold and staring up at him. "Tell me?"

"A story?" he asked, his voicing lifting in surprise. "Now?"

"Please."

"Won't the other merrows return and be angry we've invaded their treasure?"

"It's unlikely." She shifted, sending more gold tumbling into the saltwater. "I dearly love stories, and you tell them so well."

"Are you staying in the water?"

Saoirse looked at the piles of gold dubiously. "Yes."

He glanced at the wealth around him one last time and sighed. "All right then."

Manus settled onto the pile. He wiggled until his body created an indent in the coins, placed his hands behind his head, and cleared his throat.

This was her favorite time with him. He'd told stories at night when the moon was full and held its breath along with Saoirse. She liked to pretend she was in his stories, living the moments with the people who adventured, battled, and loved.

"Cú Chulainn is known throughout the lands as one of the most powerful men who ever lived. He's the son of Lugh and took after his father in battle. It is said when the ríastrad overtook him, the battle frenzy turned him into a completely different man. A beast. And he was handsome, so handsome that all the other lords worried that he would steal their wives and daughters away from them."

Saoirse sighed and laid her head on her forearms. "Did he take a wife? Was she as beautiful as he?"

"No," Manus shook his head and grinned. "He was too wild for that. He never took a wife, and the others resented him for that. In an attempt to get him away from their women, and to give their own sons a chance at marriage, the Forgall Monach suggested that Cú Chulainn was not as legendary a warrior as he claimed. Any warrior worth his mettle would train with the Scáthach of Alba, a woman more powerful and more deadly than any man alive. She lived in Dún Scáith, the Fortress of Shadows, far away in the Isle of Skye."

At the name, Saoirse sat back up. She leaned forward gleefully. "I have heard of Scáthach! Her daughters traveled here once, long ago."

"Her daughters?"

"They were as fearsome as she. Wondrous creatures wearing the armor of men and the helms of animals. The guardian threatened them, but they screamed battle cries so loud that we heard them in the deepest parts of the ocean. They earned the right to pass through our waters."

His cheeks paled. "I wonder what kind of creature would frighten a guardian."

"Frighten? No. They didn't frighten the beast, they were a kindred spirit." She pressed her hand against her chest. "The guardian knows the pain of a woman wronged. They are born from the souls of the drowned and exist only to help prevent any from experiencing such heartache again."

Her soul ached to be held in the careful grasp of a guardian. They were kind, and although capable of much destruction, they harmed nothing without reason. Saoirse loved them so much that it hurt.

Could he ever understand that? Did he know the tearing feeling in a woman's heart at the chance a man might not love them in return?

He couldn't, she surmised, but she would not think less of him for it.

Saoirse lifted a hand and gestured for him to continue. "Cú Chulainn, what became of him when he went to the isle?"

"He trained long and hard with Scáthach and her daughters. He learned all the techniques which were known only to the women of the isle. But as a handsome, virile man, he could not keep his eyes from the women themselves. They were strong, brutal creatures who sometimes appeared more man than woman.

"Cú Chulainn found himself captivated by one, whose rival, Aife, became bitter and jealous. In a fit of rage, she challenged Cú Chulainn to a duel."

Saoirse gasped. "She did?"

Solemnly, Manus nodded. "She did. They fought for days on end, with blade and fist. The sun rose, and the moon sank over and over until the battle was finally won. Cú Chulainn pressed his sword against her throat, a victor as he had always been. In return, he requested to lay with her and got her with child."

Tears filled Saoirse's eyes immediately. She swallowed and lifted a hand to make him pause. "I thought you said he was a good man. A hero?"

"So the story goes."

"But he forced a woman to lie with him? The battle was already won, and yet he waged another with her body?"

Manus took a deep breath, his brows wrinkled. "I hadn't ever thought of it like that, but I believe you might be right."

"I don't believe he's a hero. Not anymore."

"And perhaps you are right. Even the old legends remind us that these stories are tales of men, not gods. Men make mistakes."

"Tell the rest of the tale, Manus. I would like to know what became of this Cú Chulainn." Fires burned in her chest, rage so pure and angry she didn't know what to do with it.

He shifted and rolled onto his side, so he could watch her expressions. "After learning all the skills he could, he left the Isle of Skye and returned home. He stormed a fortress of a man who wronged him, took his castle, his men, and his lands, and became a lord of his own right.

"The prophecies of Cú Chulainn always said he was a man whose fate was to be known in name, but to die young. With such knowledge riding on his shoulders, it's little surprise that the day an intruder arrived at his doors, he was nervous.

"Cú Chulainn called out to the man, 'Who goes there?' and there was no response. Again and again he asked until he issued a warning. 'If you do not respond, I shall fight you, and I shall kill you.'

"The intruder did not respond. They began a duel that was brief, brutal, and bloody. The unknown man lay dying on the ground, and Cú Chulainn's curiosity got the better of him. He knelt beside the body and pulled the helm off the intruder's head.

"His own face stared back at him, young with vivid green eyes like his mother's. As his son lay dying in his arms, he whispered to his father, 'I came to carry the flag of Ulster to the gates of Rome and beyond with you.'"

The ending words of the story echoed in the cave. Saoirse reached up and wiped a tear from her cheek. "Then he did not have a happy story after all."

"No," Manus said, though he sounded confused. "I always thought he was made of legends, but now…no. I do not believe he had a kind or happy story."

"How did he die?"

"In a battle with Queen Medb, Cú Chulainn grew arrogant, and broke many geasa, taboos. Each was another nail in his coffin. Her champion, Lugaid, made three magical spears, designed and spelled to kill kings. First, he killed Cú Chulainn's charioteer, the king of all chariot drivers. Then, he killed Cú Chulainn's horse, Liath Macha, king of all horses. And last, he threw the spear straight through Cú Chulainn.

"The hero tied himself to a standing stone in the middle of the battlefield so he could die on his feet. A crow landed on his shoulder, the Morrighan come to guide his soul to the afterlife. Lugaid cut off his head, and in one final movement Cú Chulainn's sword fell and chopped off Lugaid's hand."

"And so Cú Chulainn got his revenge, yet again."

"He did many great things as well."

"Your heroes are men of great and terrible deeds."

He held out the figurine for her to take. The metal was cold on her fingers.

"That is the way of men, little pearl. We are cold and callous creatures. We come screaming into this world already dying. It is little wonder we are such selfish beasts."

Saoirse turned the prince over, staring down into the face which had graced her dreams for such a long time. She traced a finger over the prominent brow, the kind eyes, the hawk like nose, and stubborn chin. He had been good to her in her dreams.

Dreams were nothing more than the fancies of children. Real people were flawed, and it was the most painful lesson she had ever learned.

She let the figurine fall from her hands and sink to the bottom of the cave. It teetered on the edge of the tunnel that delved deep into the abyss and then fell into the darkness.

"I don't know if I like your world," she whispered. "It is angry and frightening."

"It is. But it is also beautiful and free."

"What is freedom? Is it something we dream about at night? Something our hearts dream up even though our minds know it's not real?"

"Ah, if you give up dreaming then all the possibilities of the world disappear. Whether or not they exist."

She swished her tail through the water, waving it back and forth as she thought about his words. Dreaming was important. It had kept her alive and happy for so long, removing it from her life would be difficult. Would she be the same person without her dreams?

Unlikely.

Saoirse chewed on her lip and nodded. "You are a wise man and a good man, Manus."

"Don't give me any compliments, little pearl. You don't know me all that well."

"I know you. I know your soul, your kindness, your trust. There is a good man beneath whatever walls you have built around yourself."

She looked up, her heart in her eyes and her stomach rolling like the sea in a storm. After baring her soul, she hoped he would return the sentiments. Instead, his gaze was focused on the water behind her.

Manus stilled. Even his breathing stopped for a few moments as he stared through the dimly lit water.

"Saoirse," he growled. "Get out of the water."

Her spine stiffened, and her fingers grasped the coins. "Why? What is behind me?"

She felt the soft brush of a large body against her fins. Smooth and silky, she recognized the texture.

Shark. Likely a bull shark considering the size of it, and one of the most aggressive species.

It could only mean one thing. The merrow men had somehow heard she was here, or worse, that she had brought a human. Sharks always worked with the nasty drunkards under the sea.

"We have to go," she gasped. Saoirse reached for Manus, holding her arms high and gesturing for him. "Come!"

"Saoirse, get out of the water!"

"Get *into* the water we have little time!"

He gaped at her. "Get into the water with the shark? No! I won't let you risk your life!"

"The merrow men are coming, we don't have much time!"

He let out a snarl that shook her bones but eased into the water beside her. The bull shark circled them, slow and calculated, its movements deliberate but not threatening. It made her nervous.

What were the merrow men up to? Did they know she had hidden a human man from them? Or were they threatening her only to force Saoirse to return and make her decision?

She grabbed Manus's arm and looped it over her neck. "Hold on."

Saoirse held him tight to her breast, the dark tendrils of their hair linking to create a barrier between the shark and them. It eyed her tail, hunger flashing in its dark eyes.

Teeth flashed in a grin. There were secrets in the water, tainting it like blood and bringing the monsters to feast. She clutched Manus tighter and launched into the dark tunnel.

The echoing crack of the shark's jaws clamping just beyond her fin rang in her ears. She raced forward, scraping her shoulders and tail on the jagged stone walls of the tunnel. Their flight was not graceful. Fear spiked through her body in a wave of heat and nausea.

Sharks didn't attack like that unless they were told to. And though it had not hurt her, it had forced her into the tunnel.

Was it herding her?

She rounded the loop, forcing Manus's mouth to hers and exhaling air. He spluttered, bubbles frothing all around them, but she didn't have time for such foolish behavior. He needed air, and she needed to rush.

Saoirse dug her fingers into his cheeks, forcing him to breathe.

They burst into the dim light of the shipwreck so quickly that she almost didn't catch them before they burst through the side. Saoirse caught her breath and stared around the wreckage, hoping she wouldn't see a merrow man through the cracks.

She was not so lucky.

Their bulbous eyes stared at her through each torn board. Red noses leaked mucus into the water while they swiped at their faces and overly large eyes. Webbed hands ending in claws shook, preparing for a hunt as never before.

Frog-like legs stroked to keep them afloat, although she could see some merrow men in the distance walking on the bottom of the sea floor. Hundreds of shadowy figures marching up from the abyss. All to kill the man she held in her arms.

Manus touched the side of her neck, tilting her face towards him and taking in her horrified expression. Brows furrowed, he nodded and touched his lips to hers.

It was as much a kiss, the newfound thing which made her soul take flight, as it was a sharing of air. He stroked the soft curve of her cheeks with fingers light as the softest of breezes. He sipped from her tongue and gently gifted the quietest part of himself. A subtle touch, a breath of life, and a promise of adventure.

She felt like the name he had given her. The small pearl who hadn't realized she was more than a plain grain of sand until he plucked her from her shell.

Manus pulled back with a soft smile, placed his hands on her shoulders, and shoved.

The push sent her careening backwards until the wall stopped her. It was a far enough distance that he could grasp a splintered piece of wood and pull himself out the nearest window.

She lost all sense of reason. He put himself directly into harm's way, and for what? They wouldn't hurt her! They would hurt him.

Hands shaking, heart already bleeding, she shot out of the shipwreck and into the open water. She frantically searched for him, for anything that wasn't a teeming mass of green skin covered in warts and lesions.

Where was he?

"Manus!" she shouted. Her wailing call echoed like the shriek of a guardian, like the song of a whale. It flowed over the merrow men who flinched back from the sheer agony in its tones.

A form shot up from the ocean floor. Strong, powerful, and oh so handsome, he fled the merrow men with blood streaking behind him like a red banner. His makeshift weapon was gone, and she fiercely hoped it was buried in a merrow man's chest.

Determined to save him, she streaked through the water like a falling star. She reached her arms out for him, scooped him up, and spun around.

Never before had she swum so fast. The long muscles in her tail burned, her heart thumped hard against her ribs, and her gills worked overtime to get him to the surface. He'd be safe there, she was certain of it. They couldn't catch him once he swam, Manus was too fast.

A clawed hand closed on her tail fin, sinking through the thin membrane and yanking. She cried out as pain sent icy nails up her spine.

In one last attempt to save Manus, she shoved him towards the surface.

The merrow man dragged her back down to the ocean floor where the others waited. Manus broke through the surface, his legs kicking wildly as he kept himself afloat.

Just before she sank too far down, he ducked under the waves to stare down at her. If she had been on land, tears would have streaked down her cheeks. Instead, the entire ocean became a symbol of her sorrow.

She reached her hand out for him even as the merrow men pulled her into the abyss.

CHAPTER 5

A Ship on the Horizon

Manus crawled onto the white sand shore, coughing up mouthful after mouthful of water. The sea had tried to take him again, and this time he hadn't thought he'd evade her. However, once again, his mistress sent him back to the land.

He curled his fingers in the earth.

"Where did they come from?" he coughed. "And where did they take—"

He spun, sat hard on his hip, and looked out to sea. The waves were calmer than he remembered, lapping gently at the land. It was such an innocent scene although he now knew the face of the danger the ocean hid.

Guardians. Merrow men. What other horrors lurked just out of reach?

A wave splashed foam onto his foot. Skin crawling, he backed up until he was far away from the tide. Manus wasn't certain he would ever look at the sea the same way again.

Saoirse hadn't exaggerated when she called the merrow men ugly. They were monstrous creatures. Their wide gaping mouths, eyes popping out of their heads, leathery skin, and claws that scratched at his arms.

Absently, he rubbed a hand down his bicep and flicked away the watery blood. He would heal unless their claws were tipped with poison, which he doubted. Though the creatures were frightening, they appeared more brutish than evolved.

He shivered again and drew his legs to his chest.

Saoirse's face flashed in his mind. She reached for him as they dragged her down, and she was so afraid. Manus had tried to protect her, but they were many and he was only one.

He'd failed her. They took her back to wherever horrid creatures like that came from. What could he do?

If he were a better man, he would swear to go find her. He would trawl the oceans with a net searching for the next merrow man he could find. He'd track down a guardian and force it to take him down to her kingdom so he could fight her father with a sword.

But Manus was none of those men. He valued his own life far too much to risk it for a merrow.

Even one who had saved his life.

A quiet snort echoed in his ear and a warm weight settled against his side. Manus lifted his arm and draped it over the eerie green and white shoulders of the cù sìth.

"Hello, Mac Lir. I wondered where you had gone off to."

The fae snorted again and stared out to sea.

"Yeah, me too." Manus glanced in the same direction, but nothing disturbed the strangely still seas. "We'll keep watch for her. Maybe she'll escape from them."

She didn't.

Manus waited for three more weeks with the faerie dog at his side. They would each leave in intervals, gathering food and water from whatever they could find. Without the merrow providing for them, it was far more difficult to stay alive.

The isle allowed Manus to pass through to the interior. He found little food, less fresh water, and nothing useful for escape. Every now and then, he would hear a strange chirping sound, but he couldn't find the owner of the sound.

The Fae were toying with him. He knew this isle must be overrun with their kind, invisible and impossible to catch even if he tried.

At the last moment when his strength was about to break, he stumbled from the brush to find the cù sìth standing with its hackles raised. Its lips rose in a snarl, bright teeth shining in the sunlight.

Manus shaded his eyes and nearly fell in shock. Outlined far in the distance was the clear shape of a ship. He would know the tall masts anywhere.

Something in his being heated. Though the sea was dangerous and its creatures wild, his blood called for adventure. For freedom. For something other than this gods-forsaken isle, and a lost merrow who haunted his dreams.

"Mac Lir, enough!"

The faerie stilled, growling deep in its throat.

"Go get 'em boy. Bring them to me."

The faerie charged forward and dove beneath the waves. Manus didn't know if it were possible for a cù sìth to communicate with any man. He hoped it was.

Exhaustion weakened his knees. He fell onto his hands and reminded himself to inhale. His lungs would work if he forced them. His stomach would quiet if he bade it, and the shaking muscles would build back up if he found salvation.

A ship. There was a ship.

He only needed to stay alive for a little while longer.

Heartbeats passed, and still Manus stared into the sand. His arms shook, but he refused to fall onto his face. He would wait on hands and knees for the men from the ship. He would not sink any farther than that.

He didn't know how long he waited, but eventually his ears pricked at sounds. Oars dipped into the water nearby, sprinkling droplets as they hit the surface. The hull of the boat scraped against sand in a harsh grinding sound. Boots hit the water, followed by the grunt of a man as he pulled the small boat ashore.

Manus listened to the crunching sounds of a man walking towards him. Heavy, sure, strong.

All the things he would have been if he hadn't starved for three weeks.

He heaved himself onto his haunches with the last of his energy, listing backwards as his head lolled. His hands settled on his thighs and he watched the large man approach.

Strange, he hadn't thought to see a man with such coloring. The sailor was tall and broad, blonde-haired and blue-eyed. The mane of gold shook around his head like that of the lion Manus had seen once in his life.

The stranger crouched, looked Manus up and down, and said, "Are you dead yet?"

"No."

"Can you make it to the ship?"

"I can."

"And you'll work?"

"I've done so my entire life."

The behemoth of a man nodded. "Then you're lucky a cù sìth is willing to help you. The mutt stays here."

"That's the one thing I will not allow," Manus croaked through cracked lips. "Mac Lir stays with me."

The other man arched a brow. "The god of the sea?"

"I named him myself."

"An accurate name if the beast approached you in the same way." He stared at the faerie and shrugged. "He's your responsibility if you take him on this journey. We sail for Uí Néill, and you'll be dropped off there."

"That's good," Manus said with a tired nod. "That's home."

"You're a lucky man."

He knew it. Manus had always been blessed with luck, from the first beating at the hands of another boy who tripped on his own feet and fell off the docks. He might be broken and starved, but Manus always came out on top.

Manus groaned as the blonde man wedged a shoulder underneath his arm and yanked him to standing. The ocean grabbed at his feet, stroking gentle waves along his calves.

He imagined it was apologizing.

I'm sorry for hurting you.

I'm sorry for killing your friends.

I'm sorry for taking her away from you.

If he were a stronger man, he would tell the sea they were over. Done. He couldn't remain loyal to such a woman who would take everything he loved. Repeatedly, the sea took and took. Yet, here he was.

The blonde grunted, shoved the boat from the shore, and leapt into the it. "There's a blanket at your feet. If you're a smart man, you'll grab it."

Manus did not move.

"Either stubborn or dumb then, which are you?"

"Why did you come?"

"Dog didn't give us much of a choice."

"Why?" Manus repeated.

He looked up and met the icy gaze of the Nord. Viking, by his guess. Now that his mind was clearing with fresh salt air, he could see the twisted braids and beads in the man's beard. It was too far south for such a ship. And yet, here they were.

The Viking nodded. "In my land, a creature such as that is wild. I wanted to meet the man who tamed the faerie."

"It's not tame."

"It comes at your beck and call."

"I asked; it agreed to help."

"That's a dangerous game to play with the Fae," the Viking chuckled. He picked the oars up in massive hands and rowed. "You know they like to hold favors over our heads?"

"I know the old legends well."

"You should not have made a deal with the cù sìth."

"It's my business, Viking."

"It's your head," he corrected. "I don't know you, you don't know me. But if you're going to be on my ship, you keep that dog away from my men. I'll have no faeries bringing bad luck onto my journey."

Manus nodded. He didn't want to share he too carried faerie blood. Was that why he was still alive?

Arturo's voice whispered in his mind, "*They'll spare you boy, you're a faerie. Like them. Just tell my wife and child I love them, and your debts will be paid.*"

He had a feeling that the debts on his soul could never be repaid.

The ocean swelled and guided the boat towards the Viking ship. His vision blurred, and for a moment he thought he saw her in the water. Dark hair like seaweed and a smile on her face that would break any man's heart.

"How did you get past the guardian?"

"The water beast?" The Viking grinned, and his teeth appeared pointed for a moment. "They know better than to attack a Viking ship. We do not pass through often, but we have tasted their hide too many times for them to attack us."

"They fear you?"

"I like to call it mutual respect."

Manus wasn't so sure about that. The Vikings didn't seem the respectful type, even as they hauled him onto the ship. They grasped his clothes with hands that were too strong. They were too tall, too large; they had more mass to them than any man he'd seen before.

For a few moments, he feared he wasn't aboard a ship with Vikings at all. He worried they were Tuatha dé Danann, faeries who were here to steal him away.

Then they clapped each other on the back, swore, pissed off the side of the ship and he knew they were men. And men he knew how to deal with.

Manus sank onto a pile of drying nets. Mac Lir leapt out of the small boat and into the waters. The Vikings shouted, pointing at the Fae beast swimming in the middle of the sea.

But Manus saw something else entirely. He watched the beast's eyes change color, become more human and infinitely old.

"Thank you, Manannán mac Lir," he murmured.

The dog sank beneath the waves and he wondered whether or not it was a beast at all. Faeries were shape shifters at heart. Was it possible Manannán mac Lir himself had guided Manus towards Saoirse?

He sank his fingers into the thick netting and tried not to stare into the ocean again.

Monsters lie in wait there. Monsters with no form, eyes, face, nor mouth. The worst monster lurking in those depths was that of his own guilt.

"What have you done?"

"Athair, please."

"Do not speak! It was a question I did not want answered."

Her father slashed his hand through the water. The current pushed her back into her brother's chest.

Saoirse flinched forward so she wouldn't feel the rough skin against her back. The warts, the lesions, the hated scales that weren't human at all. She'd had a taste of beauty and wanted nothing to do with their tainted forms.

"You were with a human," her father growled. "You know our laws."

She twisted her fingers in front of her. Silent, as he wished her to be.

"You've pushed me too far, Saoirse. I would have given you the choice of any merrow man you desired. But this? I will have no more of this foolish behavior."

"I have no desire for any merrow man."

"What did you say?"

His face turned mottled green.

Saoirse heard the gasps of her sisters, some covered their faces in fear of the resulting outburst from their father. Yet, she couldn't stop now.

"I will not marry a merrow man. I love someone else."

"Love? Love is a figment of human imaginations to make marriage more palatable."

"I know love is real. I felt it when I was with him, and I will not survive without it."

"You will survive just fine," he spat. "No daughter of mine is so weak that she cannot survive marriage. Take her away. Lock her up so she cannot run before her marriage to Craig."

"Craig?" she gasped as her brother's arm locked across her shoulders. "I will not marry him. I will not marry anyone!"

"You will do as I say."

"Athair! You cannot do this to me! Please!"

She expected him to yell, to argue, perhaps even to hit her. But he did none of the things she expected.

Her father turned his face from his youngest child and held up his hand so he could not see her beg. "Take her away."

"Wait." she whispered. "Athair, you must look at me."

Warts scraped across the delicate skin of her chest. She struggled against her brother's grip, her tail wildly writhing.

"Athair! You will look at me if you condemn me to a life of unhappiness! Athair!"

Her father turned his back, straightened his spine, and remained silent.

Saoirse struggled the entire trip out of the cave. She bit at her brother's arms, drawing blood and spitting green ooze into the water like an animal. Drool hung in strands around her shoulders, leaking from his oversized lips. Milky white and mucus thick, they reminded her where she was.

Underwater. In the depths of the ocean where no one could hear her scream.

Her sisters trailed along behind them. They wept into their hands but watched her with heated gazes. They wanted to know the story of her love. What it felt like, how it had happened, what manner of beast had infected her with such an emotion.

Love wasn't real. Any merrow knew that. Love was something that merrows liked to dream of. It was a fairytale, something that perhaps the High Fae experienced but Lesser Fae knew was impractical.

It led down paths that were dangerous. People did foolish things while drunk on love, bitter spats, fights, arguments, and eventual death because the longing that came with it was equally horrible.

Her sisters likely thought she would die. And perhaps she would.

Saoirse could feel the burning pain of loss deep within her chest. It seared through her flesh and bone until she was certain everyone could see the embers glowing. She hated them. She hated every creature that stood between herself and Manus.

A sob rocked through her until she curled up in a tiny ball with a limp tail trailing like a banner of defeat. Her brother didn't care. He thought she was reckless, just like her father.

And perhaps she was. If she hadn't saved the human, then she might be happy with the idea of a merrow man like Craig. He would provide for her. He would take care of her in his own way.

She would never need to worry about food. She wouldn't miss her family because he brought her to land.

But she would never experience adventures or the world above the waves.

"It's not that bad," her brother grumbled. "You'll be like the rest of the merrows. Married with children and lots to do. You'll forget all about your human as soon as you're busy with your own family."

"I don't want to forget. I want to remember him for the rest of my life."

He snorted. "No, you don't. You'll hold onto the memories for a while, but then they'll fester. Old wounds either bleed until you run dry, or you heal them up and only pick at them when you want to feel the pain."

"Speaking from experience?"

Saoirse said the words with poison laced in their tone. She meant to hurt him. To make him bleed as she was bleeding.

She never expected the answering hum that twisted in her gut and echoed through her spine.

"You aren't the only one who has experienced loss, little sister. Now grow up and bear it like the rest of us."

Individual currents wrapped themselves around her. They hugged her with a gentleness that brought tears to her eyes. Even the ocean wanted to apologize for taking part in her loss.

What kind of life did she live? Her people were suffering from hatred, and she could do nothing about it. They continued to feast upon hatred, anger, loss, and there was no stopping the addiction. It spread from parent to child, generation after generation.

She was only one among many who would feel the pain of the merrows spread through her veins.

Bars made of stone loomed in front of them. They only used the cage for the worst of their kind. For merrows who stole, who harmed, who killed.

Thankfully, no one else was inside. She remembered a hard time in their existence, when she was just a little minnow, when there had been no space at all between the bars. Flesh, fins, and knobby arms had stuck between the bars, searching for the smallest amount of space possible.

That wouldn't be her fate.

Saoirse sighed and allowed her brother to push her into the cage. The quiet thunk of the lock turning in place made her flinch.

"Just stop getting into trouble, Saoirse," he grumbled. "You're making it worse for all of us."

He turned and drifted away until she could no longer see him.

Shivering, she gripped her arms and sank down onto the sea floor. Coral bit between her scales, but she didn't care. Her life was about to change forever, and she had no say at all in it.

What was she to do? She couldn't escape from the cage. She couldn't change her father's mind. Her future turned dark and gray.

She wasn't certain life was worth living like this, not when she'd had a taste of what it could be.

Nails clinked against the bars, tapping incessantly until she looked up.

A cluster of her sisters floated nearby. They waited for her eyes to meet theirs and then their faces split into bright, sunny smiles. But then again, they wouldn't know they were sunny. Many of them would never see the sun in their lifetime.

"Sister, what is it like?"

"We want to know!"

"Love? Is it real?"

"It couldn't possibly be real! Look at her, all curled up like that, there's not a chance in the ocean that love is real."

"But what if it is? I want to know what it feels like!"

Saoirse held up a hand. "Stop."

"You must tell us!"

"Stop it, please. I don't wish to speak of it."

"Saoirse. You're being so selfish! We want to know what the human affliction feels like!"

"It's not an affliction," she murmured, drawing tighter into herself. "It feels like the first time an oyster opens its mouth. Fearful, shy, it takes its time to reach out into the saltwater and taste the sea on its tongue. And then it realizes the world is wide and great, but not so fearsome after all. It lets the dirt get sucked between its shells willingly and it works them round and round to create a pearl all for itself."

Her sisters remained quiet through her speech. The eldest drifted forward and pressed herself against the bars. "But Saoirse, we eat oysters."

"You wouldn't understand. It's not like food, or water, or even the delicacies of the sea. It's unlike anything I've ever felt before."

"Then why do you look like you're in pain?"

"Because I am," she whimpered. "I am so far away from him, and I know I shall never return to his side. The knowledge is killing me."

They flinched back from the cell, grasping each other's shoulders and creating a ball of shuddering merrows. "Are you ill? Is it truly a sickness then?"

Some cruel part of Saoirse opened wide. Its dagger-filled mouth gaped open like the bottomless pit of the sea. They would never understand her pain. They would never understand what they had watched happen and did not even try to stop.

She glanced up at them with cruelty in her heart. "Yes. Yes, it is an illness that spreads like an infection you have never seen before. It rots from the inside out until your beauty is gone, and all that is left is a ragged shell of a creature. Love makes you ugly when you lose it."

Their shrieks were music to her ears. Great blasts of water pushed her against the back of the cell as they fled from her words. She couldn't bring herself to care. Let them think love was a dangerous, barbed thing. Perhaps it would save them the brutality of what she was experiencing.

Curling back into a ball, Saoirse breathed in the saltwater and tried desperately not to think of the next morning.

Craig.

Strong, wart covered hands stroking her skin.

A merrow man with complete and utter control over everything she did.

She shuddered.

At the very least, she would always have her memories. She could feel the press of his lips against her shoulder, against her lips. The sound of his laughter unhindered by the weight of the ocean. The sparkle of appreciation in his eyes every time she left the waves and raced into his arms.

Saoirse sighed and pressed her fingertips against her lips. Sleep would come late on this night, but she would drift into dreams filled with his image. As she would for the rest of her life.

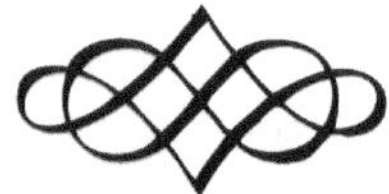

"Saoirse, wake up child."

The voice broke through her dreams of a man who sang songs of the sea but left footprints in the sand. She stirred, uncoiled her tail which lay across her face, and lifted herself onto an elbow.

"Máthair?"

"Child, it's time to go."

"Go? Is it already time for the wedding?"

"No, my dear. You will not get married today."

The words were an electric shock down her spine. "Athair changed his mind?"

"No, I did."

These were the last words she expected to come out of her mother's mouth. Saoirse twisted her body, grasped the stone bars of the cage, and pressed her face close to the openings.

"Máthair?"

"When your father and I first met, I, too wished for a different life. Merrows are born to suffer, child. That is our place in this world." She reached through the cage and brushed her fingers across Saoirse's cheek.

"If you have a chance to break free, then I will do everything in my power to help."

"Won't Athair be mad at you?"

"Likely, but I'm willing to take the risk."

Her mother held up the key to the cell. Life burned in her eyes, so bright it lit an answering spark deep within Saoirse. If even her mother, the perfect example of what a merrow *should* be, could break the rules… surely that meant it was acceptable for Saoirse to do the same.

The key crunched in the coral filled lock. She flinched, holding herself still as if that would make the sound quieter. No one could know she was escaping. No one could know it was her own mother who had set her free.

She rushed from the cage and launched herself into Máthair's waiting arms. Saoirse pressed her face into the crook of her mother's neck, breathing in saltwater and the scent of warmer waters. Her mother had not been born in the depths of the ocean but had come here with her father long ago.

"Where will I go?" Saoirse whispered. "I know nowhere that is safe."

"You will go to my sister, if need be. But I have another idea."

Máthair pulled back and held up a small seashell. It was strangely shaped, like a corkscrew with fine filaments at the end.

"Few merrows know the guardians can speak."

"I've always thought they spoke with me."

"This is different," her mother corrected. "The guardians can *speak*, Saoirse. We just can't hear them. With this in your ear, you can hear their tones and converse with them. Not a one-sided conversation reading body language, but true conversation."

"Oh." Saoirse reached out and reverently held the small shell between her fingers. "I just—"

"Place it in your ear and give it a twist, yes like that. Good job. It doesn't hurt, does it?"

"No, Máthair."

"Good. Find the nearest guardian, ask her to give you passage from our waters and to follow the human ship."

"Ship?" she asked, confused. "Why do I need to find a ship?"

"Your human has gone to safety, chased away by the merrow men. Find the guardian. She'll know which one, they've been watching you for a very long time."

"Why?" Manus had left her? Why would he do that? And why would the guardians care about a merrow girl who was one of hundreds? Saoirse wasn't anything special, other than her dark hair.

"Your soul doesn't belong here with us. They knew it the first moment I brought you to meet them from your egg." Máthair brushed a strand of hair away from Saoirse's face, letting it float behind her head with gentle grace. "They predicted you would leave us at a young age."

"I am not young."

"For a merrow, you most certainly are."

Her mother drew Saoirse into her arms, and it felt very much like the kind of goodbye which lasted forever.

Saoirse drew in a deep breath and squeezed hard. She wanted to remember every instant of this moment when her quiet, withdrawn mother saved her child from suffering the same fate. Saoirse was not alone in her desire for freedom, and that was all that mattered.

"Go," her mother rasped. "Go now, before they have a chance to stop you."

She didn't hesitate. As soon as her mother's arms released, Saoirse shot through the ocean as she had never swum before. Her tail muscles burned, her stomach ached, her hair pulled back so tight her skull screamed as she blasted through the dark waters.

The discomfort was little more than a passing inconvenience. She fled towards freedom, and that was worth a little pain.

Up and up she swam until she saw the beckoning light of the sun. Sunny rays created stunning spears of gold that reached for her with open arms. Just a bit further, and she could turn her face to the open air and the screeching sound of seagulls.

Every instant felt as though someone might grab her tail. That she would hear the enraged shout of her father and a call for a hunt that terrified her to the marrow of her bones. She couldn't afford to lose this chance. Not now.

Saoirse crested the surface and inhaled through her nose. Though water stuck in her throat and her gills gasped, it suddenly felt more natural than breathing underwater.

Shrieks of sea birds and the shushing sound of waves accosted her senses. She'd never been happier in this moment knowing she had made it.

She was free.

A great wave swelled next to her, riding the back of a guardian who had apparently followed her. Its grey skin was marked with scars from countless battles with whaling ships, sharks, and even the occasional faerie. Her great eye tilted up, peering through the water into Saoirse's face.

She had dealt with them enough to know what that expression meant. Sighing, Saoirse sank back underneath the water and faced the guardian's disappointed expression.

"I'm going," she said firmly. "I refuse to linger here when the man I love is out there. It isn't fair I should taste such exquisite ambrosia and not follow it wherever it goes. You cannot stop me."

The shell in her ear quivered, quaked, and rattled with such vigor she worried it would fall out of her ear canal. But then she heard it. The deep, reverberating tones of the guardian.

"I will not try to stop you, child."

"You won't?"

"Saoirse, you were not made for the sea." The guardian swam closer and reached out a finger. It tapped Saoirse above the heart, so gentle for an appendage that was the same width as her body. "You have a piece of it here, in your heart. But the rest of you has always longed for the sun."

"Then you'll help me?"

"I will, but I need you first to know merrows always suffer. It is your purpose in life. If you go to the land, I cannot protect you. No one can."

"I am strong on my own."

The guardian smiled. "You are, I know that. But the land differs greatly from the sea, and I worry you do not understand what it takes to be a human."

"Do you?" Saoirse asked, wrapping her arms around the offered finger. "Can you tell me what it's really like?"

"I have never been to land."

"Have you seen it?"

"I've seen the teeming masses of people. The strange animals when they sink beneath the waves. Humans are cruel and unkind, they do not care for each other as we do under the sea."

"It will be a great adventure." And that was all Saoirse wanted. To see what Manus saw, to understand the world as he did.

"Just be careful, Saoirse. Merrows are young, you in particular have yet to see what the world can do to a person. You love with your whole heart, and I do not want to see you lose it."

"If I let him go, I've already lost it, guardian."

"I know. And that is why I am allowing you to leave. The ship followed the cold current north. Follow it as far as you can until you find the other ships. Uí Néill is where they travel. Hold on to the sides of ships if you must, to listen for their destination. But let no one see your true form."

"I understand." She squeezed the guardian's finger in a hug and pressed a kiss against her knuckle. "I will miss you."

"And I you, child."

With a flick of her tail, she fled from the waters of her home towards the unknown. Saoirse's heart beat rapidly, but in anticipation rather than fear.

She traveled for days on end. Dolphins kept her company for a time. They chattered stories in her ears, making her giggle and laugh even though she was tired. When they needed to leave, a few orcas took their place. They differed from their cousins, more dangerous and solemn. Their stories came from colder waters where blocks of ice floated in the ocean.

Saoirse was rarely alone, even while she slept. Otters tucked their furry bodies under her arms, cuddled along her sides, and helped her float while she rested. A few even let her hold their favorite stones, which they carried with them for their entire lives.

The first week of travel lacked any ship sightings. The second, a few appeared on the horizon.

Saoirse grasped the sides, slick with water and rot, and desperately listened for words that sounded familiar. They were not traveling towards Manus, so she had to let go. Even though her arms and tail shook, they journeyed away from her future.

It was by chance she found the quaint boat carrying only four men. There was one sail, no bottom deck, and one net to its name, but it was plenty for her to hold onto as long as they didn't look behind them too closely.

Thankfully, they all seemed to be in a hurry to get home.

"Did you hear?" one of the men asked. "The Silver Harpoon has a new ale tonight."

"They say that every year, and there's never been a new ale. It's the same old watered-down drink they give us every time we go in."

"No sir! I've heard from very reputable sources that it's the truth this time."

"Do you mean that McDonall fellow you're always going on about? He wouldn't know the truth if it bit him in the ass."

"He's the most truthful man in all of Uí Néill."

Saoirse's fingers clenched on the sodden wood. "Uí Néill," she repeated.

This was the ship which would guide her. Ducking underneath the waves, she trailed it all the way to land. The water grew foggy, and the fish fled, but she continued on.

The guardian hadn't exaggerated. Saoirse peered up towards the docks and held onto the fronds of tall seaweed. There were so many people up there.

She couldn't count the throngs of men and women who shouted and screamed so loudly she could hear them underneath the waves. They waved cloth at each other and wore so much on their bodies she thought they must be tired all the time. And they came in so many different colors.

She searched for him but didn't see the strong jaw and accentuated features she admired. Frowning, she traveled up and down the shore until the light disappeared. Only a sliver of the moon guided her.

"I cannot give up," she whispered. But there was little more she could do.

Saoirse lingered on a single dock far from the city. Her fins drooped, and her arms weighed heavy as she anchored herself on the end of the wood. Laying her head on her folded arms, she watched a small cabin nearby.

It wasn't much, just a tiny shack near the sea. The wood was rotting in places, stuffed with rags to keep the room warm.

The orange light of a flame flared bright, covered briefly by a hand, and touching a candle. She had only heard of such things in stories. The flickering light was enchanting. Like an angler fish, but with far more life.

Who lived in such a place? A small family, with a single child and a mother who loved them dearly? Or perhaps two children, a boy and a girl with a wonderful future filled with faeries and magic?

Saoirse loved to think up stories that would fill the pages of her mind. Someday, she would tell them to others. Perhaps even to Manus, should she ever find him.

A body crossed in front of the candle, throwing a shadow on the wall. Tall and broad, it was a strong outline of a man. His shoulders could hold the world. His aquiline nose was a jagged point, like a hawk or an eagle.

She lost her breath. She knew that profile as well as the small statue of the forgotten king.

"Manus!" Saoirse clapped a hand against her mouth.

What if he didn't want her here? She hadn't thought to question during her entire journey whether he'd left because he had to. What if he'd willingly left her behind?

Could everything have been a lie?

Saoirse wasn't certain what she would do if that were the case. Her heart would splinter into a thousand pieces and her body would disintegrate into sea foam. She would float away on the ocean's current and forget about the cruelty of man.

His shadow turned and disappeared. She clutched the dock with a grip that made the wood creak. The delicate membranes between her fingers ached with the pressure.

The door to the cabin opened, and he held a light above his head. "Hello? Who goes there?"

Her nails scraped the wood. It was him. It was really him. After all she had gone through, all the distance she had traveled, and here he was.

"You there! On the dock!"

"No," she gasped and ducked down into the water.

She couldn't be ready for this, not now! What would she say? She journeyed across the sea to find him? Who did that?

Saoirse wasn't ready to declare her love, and that surely was what he would think when he saw her.

She wasn't even certain she knew what love was. And yet, it sprouted in her breast like the great tree in the grotto under the ocean. It wanted to spread its roots throughout her heart.

And she wasn't inclined to stop it.

Pressing her fingers against her lips, she listened. The padding sounds of bare feet on wood echoed the staccato of her heart.

He was here. He was really *here*.

She reached into her ear and slid the spiral shell out. Tangling it in the strands of her hair, she resolved herself to a life above the waves. He would take care of her. He had to.

CHAPTER 6

By Moonlight I Will Love Thee

Manus lit the candle and watched the flame dance on the wick. It was one of his last matches. He'd have to go to market for more but wasn't certain he'd have the coin.

That was always the hardest part of returning after a long trip. His cabin wasn't secure. No locks barred his doors to prevent scavengers from stealing his belongings, no boards protected his windows. They had been kind this time. He still had blankets on his bed and a table, although they had taken his chairs.

They found his stash of coins and took the lot. That was an issue. He had a few other stashes, but none so big as the missing one. He shouldn't have left the treasure on the isle, although the Vikings might have stolen it anyways.

"Blasted idiots," he grumbled.

Money was the one thing he knew he needed. Manus had to go back out onto the sea. He had to answer the call deep in his chest that already ached, no matter how close to the ocean he lived.

And then there was the added complication of a dark-haired woman with skin like moonlight. She haunted his dreams and now bled into his waking life.

The morning last, he woke and was certain she was at his bedside. Manus could feel the silken strands of her hair wrapped through his fingers. She smiled down at him in that crooked way which was the only flaw to her perfection. And then she disappeared from sight, faded like the mirage she was.

He sighed and blew out the match which burned dangerously close to his fingertips. There was an ocean between them, and it was unlikely he'd ever be able to find her again.

"Let it go," he reminded himself. "She isn't here, you fool. And she never will be."

"Manus!"

The sound was so quiet, he almost didn't hear it. The voice was like that of a song.

"Saoirse?" he whispered, turning towards the door. "No. You're dreaming, man. Let the memories go or you'll drive yourself mad."

He sat down on the end of the bed and tugged his boots off, so he wouldn't chase the siren calling his name. His movements were so harsh that his toes cracked. Each heavy crack of boots striking the floor reminded him he was here. In a cabin by the sea. Not on an isle where the most beautiful of women lay in pure white sand…

"Stop it," he growled.

His leg bounced and finally he gave in. Berating himself the whole way, he lit the candle in his lantern, opened the door, and lifted it high.

"Hello? Who goes there!"

For a second, he thought he imagined it all. There was no one near his door, not close enough to make a sound.

Then he saw the shadow at the end of the dock. It moved so quickly he might have imagined it, but Manus heard the answering splash. Someone was on the end of his dock. Hiding.

"You there! On the dock!"

He would not abide a child lingering in the shadows, or any thief who thought to sneak in and grab the rest of his money. Barefoot and furious, he stomped down the thick, muddy shore and stepped onto the dock.

"I know you're here. I saw you. It's no use hiding."

They would be at the end, likely holding onto the thick posts for dear life. Swimming at night was a dangerous thing!

Manus set the lantern on the end of the dock, leaned over the edge, and stared down into the empty space. No one was there.

"What the bloody hell…"

Something scraped underneath the dock. Quiet and subtle, he might not have noticed the sound if he hadn't been listening so intently. He furrowed his brow, leaned over the dock further, and stared into the water.

His heart stopped. Saoirse's face appeared, lit by moonlight that stroked the planes of her cheeks. She lay on the bottom with tendrils of her dark hair spread out around her in an inky cloud. Her black eyes were wide with shock, and, he hoped, a little with pleasure at seeing him again.

Slowly, he reached out a hand towards the waves.

Saoirse shifted, and her hair slicked back as she floated to the surface. Rivulets of water trailed down her face, tiny pearl drops that traced the beloved features he longed to touch.

She reached out a hand and met his fingers with her own.

"It's you," he whispered. "How is this possible?"

"I came a long way."

"How did you get away from them?"

"It's a long story," she said and licked her lips. "You weren't easy to find."

"We're very far away from your homeland."

"It's a strange place. I am not used to such rocky shores, and everything is very loud."

"Are you staying?"

"If you wish it."

He recognized the hopeful expression on her face, and it nearly crippled him. She thought so highly of him, of the street rat who bought his way onto ships because no one would even hire him as a sailor. And she looked at him as though he hung the moon in the sky, just for her.

It unnerved him.

"You can stay as long as you wish," he blurted.

Because, no matter how much she thought he was a good man, he wasn't. He would put her in his cabin which was falling apart at the seams just so he could have her. He wasn't worthy of her attentions, but he would be damned if he gave her up.

"Do you want me to stay?" she asked again. "I have traveled across the sea to find you, but I will not linger if you do not wish it."

"How could I wish for anything else? I have dreamt of you every night, my pearl. I'm not convinced this isn't still a dream."

Her cheeks turned a pretty shade of red. "Then help me out of the water, Manus. My family has likely realized where I have gone by now, and I would like to be safe."

"And dry."

"For now."

Manus pressed his chest against the dock and held out his arms. She pulled herself part of the way while he heaved her up and into his waiting arms. There were easier ways of doing it, but none that would keep her clean of mud nor safe from the scrape of rock.

He palmed the back of her head with a happy sigh and pressed her against the crook of his neck. She was wet and cold, with her hair plastered against her back all the way to her knees, and he couldn't have been a happier man.

It felt as though he had waited a lifetime to have her in his arms again.

"Absence makes the heart grow fonder," he murmured against her head. "It's what one of my dear friends used to say. He'd go off sailing and miss his wife something fierce after just a few days. Said when he saw her again, it was like the first day they met."

"I believe your friend is right."

She shivered violently, her entire body shaking in his arms. He rubbed her arms briskly.

"Come inside. I'll set you by the fire and give you something to wear."

"To wear?" She pulled back and looked up at him. "Will you put me in the clothing of your women here? It looks terribly uncomfortable."

"What, a corset?" Manus chuckled. "I'm afraid I don't have many of those lying around."

"Why not?"

"I don't live with women."

"I suppose that makes sense."

He tucked her underneath his arm and guided her towards his home. Would she be disappointed? He had no idea what kind of home she lived in before.

"What are merrow homes like?" he asked.

"Not like this," she said, staring at his cabin with wide eyes. "We live mostly in caves. Merrows try to decorate them as much as possible. My mother has strands of pearls strung up across the entryway to her home, seashells affixed to the walls, jellyfish casting light in the dark shadows. But this is so much more than that."

He tried to see the cabin through her eyes but failed. It was a shack. Broken walls, no windows, nothing but ruin covered in mud from the sea.

"More?" he asked. "I'm afraid I don't see what you do, my pearl."

"How could you not? Look at the way the light dances off the wood! And it's not water logged and soft, but strong and whole. Pieces of the trees that grow here so abundantly it makes tears raise in my eyes." She swiped at her cheeks. "Tears, Manus. I couldn't cry where I come from, and here I can. I hope you don't mind tears; they may be rather frequent."

"I only mind if they are tears of sadness." He squeezed her against his side. "Tears of happiness I could get used to."

A woman at his side. When had his life changed so drastically? Arturo must be rolling in his deep sea grave, laughing at his dearest friend who had so recently said he would never take a wife.

A wife.

The words danced through Manus's head until he could think of nothing else. He wanted a wife.

Saoirse wasn't going anywhere, that much he knew for certain. He had lost her once, and he'd be damned if he would do it again. No one could know she was a merrow and therein lay a problem. A woman living with a man without the bonds of marriage was sacrilege.

They would have to get married.

He stared down at her with equal horror and awe. Her bare feet squelched in the mud, leaving tiny footprints next to his large ones. So tiny. So perfect.

The moonlight danced over her bare shoulders and trailed down the smooth skin of her arms. Strands of hair covered most of her nakedness but left little to the imagination. He had seen her like this before but now it felt somehow *more.*

He opened the creaking door and let her step through into the dimly lit shack.

"Oh Manus," she breathed. "It's lovely."

The face he made wasn't gentlemanly, but he'd never pretended to be one. She had a strange way of thinking. Saoirse deserved so much more than a ramshackle cabin by the ocean. She deserved a castle, a stately manor overlooking the sea where she could still be close to the place they both loved.

But he was wandering off into dreams which could never come true.

"Is that so," he said.

"Well, just look at it! You must live like a king."

"A what?"

She pressed her hands to her chest and stepped towards the fireplace. "What is this?"

"A fireplace."

"What do you use it for?"

"To heat the place."

"With what?"

The sheer pleasure on her face made him pause. He had forgotten she spent her entire life underneath the ocean. Everything must be new to her. From fireplaces, to beds, to… his world spun. She'd have to be taught everything.

"Look at me gathering wool," he grunted. "Step aside, my pearl. You'll shiver out of your skin if I don't warm you up sooner rather than later."

"I'm used to the sea, Manus. I'm quite all right."

"There's a shirt on the bed over there. Cover yourself."

"Bed?"

He gestured. "That. The white fabric, pull it over your head."

"All right."

Manus stuffed the fireplace with what little dry wood he had gathered in the few weeks he'd been home. Tinder on the bottom mixed with peat would fill the cabin with a sweet scent he always missed on the sea.

He much preferred peat to heat the home, but it was expensive. It burned far longer than wood and that made it a commodity in this area.

The last match struck, flared bright, and burst the small pile he'd made into flames. Manus held out his hands so the warmth could dance on his palms.

"I think I'm finished!" Happiness bubbled in her voice.

He glanced over his shoulder, a wide grin spreading over his face even before he saw the muddled mess she'd made of his shirt. The sleeves somehow locked her arms against her sides, the fabric was inside out and backwards. But she looked so damned proud of herself.

"Well, you've certainly tried." His knees creaked as he stood and made his way over to her. "But I'm afraid this is all wrong."

"You didn't tell me there was a right way to do it."

"You should be able to use your arms, Saoirse." He tugged on the sleeves, pulling them away from her torso and twisting the fabric. "I don't know how you've done this. It has to come off, Saoirse. We'll start again."

"It can't be that horrendous."

"My dear, I have never seen someone make such a mess of something like a shirt."

He fisted the ends of the shirt and tugged it up over her head.

He lost all the breath in his lungs. This was far different from seeing her on the isle, or even rising out of the ocean like some kind of sea goddess. This was a real woman, standing in the middle of his shack, with nothing but the drying strands of her hair covering a body he intensely longed for.

The peaks of his cheeks heated bright red. He told himself to calm his thoughts. She was little more than a child in this world, didn't even know how to put a shirt on the right way, let alone understand the workings of the world.

And hadn't he realized that on the isle? Saoirse sat too close to him, asked him questions he couldn't answer, cared little for the propriety of things.

"Manus?" Her quiet murmur caught his attention.

"Yes?"

"Well it's just…. I worry things might be different. I understand that you may not have wished for me to come. You left rather quickly, and I know my people can be frightening. But I had hoped you might have missed me."

"You're rather forward."

"I travelled across the seas to find you, Manus. I think I'm afforded that."

"What did you think would happen, my pearl? I cannot read your mind."

She tilted her head back and a dark green lock of hair slid over her shoulder like a dancer in some fancy ballet. "I thought at the very least I might get a kiss."

"A kiss?"

"Is that also forward?"

It was too much. Far more than any woman would ever say in the company of men.

He thanked the heavens that no mortal had ever tempted him, for god had gifted him a woman from the sea who cared little for propriety. She cared for *him*, although he couldn't understand why, and she let nothing stand in the way of that. Not her family. Not the ocean. Not the world itself, for she had travelled across it.

Manus didn't know what god he needed to thank, but he would never forget their kindness.

In a great surge of movement, he yanked her against him and pressed his mouth against hers. She tasted like the sweetest treasures of the sea. Her lips were the softest touch of the tide, and her arms were the gentle grasp of the one being he'd loved his entire life.

A flush of heat spread from the top of his head to the base of his spine. She took all his sense and threw it to the wind, scattering his mind until he was little more than a mess of sensations.

She was so soft, every inch of her body like fine velvet. He flexed his hands on her back and tried to remind himself not to grab her too forcefully. The tiny waist beneath his fingers might bruise, the fragile ribs might break, and he would not leave marks upon her flesh.

His fingers flexed again, and he marveled at the hold she had on him. Somehow, someway, she had completely destroyed his reason.

Manus drew back when they were both breathless and pressed his forehead against hers.

"Marry me," he declared. "Tomorrow, tonight, whenever we might wake a vicar."

"What?"

"Marry me. Please, Saoirse. My life was not the same with you gone, and I wish to never be parted from you again."

"Do you mean it? Now?"

"You have the power to make me the happiest man in the world. My wife straight from the sea."

"How could I say no?"

A surge of elation nearly lifted him off his feet. "Do you mean it?"

"Only if you will kiss me again and again, for the rest of our lives."

"I can promise much more than that," he said, grunting as he lifted her up into his arms so she was eye to eye with him. "A bride of the sea. How did I ever catch you, my pearl?"

"I didn't see a net when I came here. Not one that was yours."

"Your point?"

"You didn't catch me, Manus." She traced a line from his eyebrow to his lips. "I threw myself onto the shore so you might find me."

"And I did, my pearl. I did."

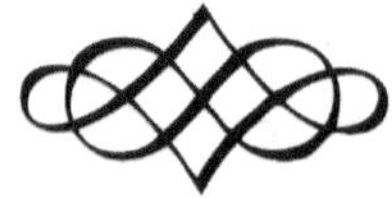

"Saoirse, it's time to wake up."

She snuggled deeper into the warmth that surrounded her. She felt weightless, as if she still floated in the ocean, but it was so warm. The ocean was cold, chilly, sometimes unforgiving in the way it would bite at her skin. This was like sleeping on a cloud.

The most pleasant scent filled her nostrils. Caramel and something raw and earthy, like tobacco, although she'd only smelled it once in her life. Saoirse never wanted to leave this heaven on earth.

"Saoirse, get up. Or have you changed your mind on marrying me?"

"What?" she murmured. "No, I could never change my mind about that."

"I found a vicar. It's very early in the morning, but he was inspired by our romantic tale, so get *up*."

"What is a vicar?"

"The man who'll marry us."

"Aren't we already married? Faeries are not so picky. We've said we want to marry each other, and that is enough."

"That's what I'm trying to do," Manus said with a chuckle. "I even found you a wedding dress."

"A dress?" Saoirse sat straight up, nearly cracking her head on his chin. "What do you mean you got me a dress?"

He pointed towards the foot of the bed, and Saoirse let out a startled gasp so loud she had to cover her mouth. The thing placed at her feet was not like the others she'd seen at the bottom of the sea. The fabric was entirely intact, so delicate it looked as though it were made of sea foam. Lace fell in waves from the neckline and no sleeves would hide her arms.

"Oh, Manus." Tears pricked her eyes. "It's beautiful."

"You seem to think everything is beautiful. It's only half finished, so I got it at a good price. But I figured you wouldn't mind."

"Half finished? What glorious things must this artist create?" She reached out and stroked it with a tentative hand. "It looks like it's made of magic."

"Have you never seen faerie dresses before? I imagine they're much more glorious than this."

"Merrows don't leave the ocean and my father would never let us visit the Seelie Fae. This is the first real dress I've ever seen."

"I'm glad you like it then."

Like it? She would wear the sea; how could she not be instantly in love with the dress he had gotten for her?

She dragged the fabric across the bed and pressed it to her chest. The lace itched her bare skin where the shirt he loaned her dipped below her shoulder. Still, she refused to let it make her think ill of the beautiful thing. Perhaps it would feel better on.

"Is it the same as the shirt?"

"Yes," he said with a chuckle. "You're actually holding this one correctly. That's the front."

"Good."

She scrambled from the bed. Blankets fell onto the floor, and she did not stop them. Grasping the hem of her shirt, she whipped it over her head.

Manus made a strange hissing sound behind her.

She would never understand humans. They acted as though nudity was only acceptable in certain situations. Others, like now, had an effect on him she couldn't understand. Saoirse intended to find out as soon as possible.

The dress slid over her skin like the finest water, trailing over her and molding to her form. She smoothed her hand down her stomach. The inside of the dress was much more pleasant feeling than the outside. Tiny pearls were sewn into the lace, dotting the dress with sea treasures so fine, she was certain they must have contacted the Fae.

"Manus?" Saoirse turned, her smile so wide it made her cheeks ache. "What do you think?"

He sat on the bed and leaned back on his hands, taking his time looking at her from head to toe. Her entire body tingled at his perusal. She desperately wanted to press her hands against the heated burn of her cheeks but held herself still so he might look upon her dress.

"It's incredible, although I think you might give the vicar a heart attack looking like that."

"Why?"

"Any sane man will salivate the moment he sets eyes on you."

Saoirse wasn't certain what he meant, but she knew it was good. He couldn't take his eyes off her.

"Are we going now then?"

Manus blinked, slowly taking his time to lift his gaze to hers. "That was the plan."

"Is it still?"

"I'm trying to be an honest man, my pearl. The things I want to do to you require marriage first."

"I'm not human, Manus. The things you want to do may be perfectly normal in my world."

"I promise you, they aren't." He stood and held out his hand for her to take. "Are you ready?"

She had waited her entire life for this moment. Captivated, she slid her fingers into his. Callouses bit at the delicate skin of her palm, but she had never felt anything as decadent.

Manus led her from the quaint little space and guided her into the night. Moonlight bathed his form in a glow that was almost godlike. He glanced over his shoulder, still holding her hand, and smiled.

They clambered over large driftwood, and up wooden planks hammered together. Stairs, she reminded herself. He called them that, and she would need to remember that if this were to be her life.

Saoirse wanted to stop and stare at everything. The cobblestone path was meticulously laid. Stones fit together almost perfectly, and she wondered who had done the work. Was it possible that humans could also utilize magic? Mortals could never complete such intricate designs on their own.

Buildings rose out of the darkness like great monoliths. Starlight glimmered on the glass windows, blinking at Saoirse as she passed. There were no lights within the great structures.

Unable to contain her curiosity, she tugged on Manus's hand to slow him. "Do people live in these?"

"Yeah."

"How many?" She stared up and up at the four-story building before them. "Are they princes?"

"No, these are communal houses. Falling apart at the seams, but slightly better than my shack."

"Falling apart?"

"You can't see the thatch roof is rotting? Some windows are missing panes, and it looks like the lock was broken off the front door. That's not a safe place to stay unless you know how to protect yourself."

"Oh," she whispered, seeing the home in a new light.

She still thought it impressive. Merrows didn't build things under the ocean. They tended to be more interested in discovering than creating.

And yet, her brother once had strung together a strand of pearls to give their mother. It wasn't anything compared to the building, but it was the start of an intelligent society realizing their hands could do something.

Their father had ripped the necklace apart and her brother never tried again.

Frowning, she let Manus tug her deeper into the port city. The buildings grew, each structure built closer and closer until there was no room at all between them. Her feet became dirty, grit and mud sticking between her toes. She was uncomfortable but didn't dare ask him to stop.

They were going to get married. She wouldn't make him pause for anything other than the world ending. Dirty feet certainly weren't that.

"There," Manus said. He pointed far ahead of them at a gray shape which was just taking form. "That's the church."

"Church?"

"Where many worship God."

She nodded. "It is good to honor the Tuatha dé Danann. They appreciate it when humans remember all the Fae have done."

When he didn't respond, she glanced over at his sharp profile. His brows were furrowed, and he licked his lips before responding.

"They don't honor the Tuatha dé Danann."

"Then who?"

"The Christian God."

"Who is he?"

"I'll explain it to you later."

She tugged again, forcing him to pause. "I want to know what kind of God will be there, Manus. I don't like thinking someone other than my people will sanction this marriage."

"It's my God, Saoirse." He tugged her against his broad, strong chest and tucked a finger under her chin. Carefully, he tilted her head up to look at him. "We're already married in the eyes of your people, aren't we?"

"Yes."

"Then let us marry in the eyes of *my* people."

She couldn't argue with that even though she didn't like the idea of marrying in front of a god she'd never met. What if she didn't like him? Or worse, what if he didn't like her? There were too many questions to answer. She knew what the wrath of a god looked like, and it wasn't pretty.

Shivering, she let him pull her towards the gray shape which grew impossibly taller with each step they took.

The church was terrifying. The high spires jabbed at the air, while solemn looking men stared down at her, wings gracing their backs. She stared at one until it seemed to move. Flinching, she tucked herself again Manus's back.

Fae blood ran in her veins. She should not fear mortal made creations, and yet she did. The things humans created were both wondrous and horrifying.

"Here we are," he murmured. He pushed open a small door near the side of the church which blended into the stone surface. "In you go."

She hesitated for a moment before plunging into the darkness. The stone structure swallowed her whole, and the belly of the beast was even more terrifying than the outside. Meager light filtered through colored glass windows while stone statues glared down at her from great heights.

Was this human god already displeased with her presence?

Saoirse met the gaze of a severe stone man who glowered down at her. He wore a strange hat on his head and held a staff that looked far too easy to clobber people with. He leaned forward just enough that she worried he might take a step onto the floor in the next instant.

The Unseelie Fae used stone statues as warriors. She'd listened to the stories in her youth and swam back to her bed with nightmares already at the edges of her vision. Saoirse never thought she'd see such magic in her life.

She gulped and stepped backwards. Her spine hit what felt like a wall until the flat surface inhaled.

Manus's arm crept around her middle and tucked her back against him. "What is it?"

"The statues."

"What about them?"

"They look as if they are alive."

He pressed a kiss to her temple. "They aren't, my pearl. No magic has stepped foot in this building for a very long time."

"Until me."

"Blessed with the grace of the sea." He pressed another lingering kiss to her hair and then slid his hand down to hers. Warm fingers laced through hers. "Come with me, Saoirse. I'll keep you safe from the statues, and if they step from their pedestals, I shall crush them to dust."

"Promise?"

His brilliant grin was enough of an answer.

Saoirse's shivers disappeared. His eyes crinkled in the corners whenever he smiled, a sure sign he had lived a life where smiles weren't a rare occurrence. The honey gold flecks in his eyes glowed when he was pleased, like the sun dancing across the surface of a black sea.

How could she not be captivated by him? The humans claimed merrow women sang sailors into rocks, but he was the one leading her to trouble. Every sway of his body, every twitch of his lips, every squeeze of his fingers around hers were a siren song she could not resist.

"Father?" Manus called out.

"Father?" she repeated. "This man is your father?"

"No, no. Not mine. It's what we call them."

"Why? That's terribly confusing." Saoirse wrinkled her brows.

"It's just…" Manus sighed and shrugged. "I don't know the answer to that, my pearl. It's how it's always been."

They walked down a long hall with strange, long seats bracketing each side. She wanted to pull on him again and ask what they were for, but he rushed her past the interesting new seats. There were so many strange things here! How would she ever learn them all?

"Manus, you've returned." The voice was quiet and humble. It was a voice she could listen to for hours on end, like the crashing of waves against a sandy beach.

She whipped around, yearning to see who owned such a voice.

The new man stood at the top of a few stairs. There was a table behind him covered with many objects, including a golden man who looked similar to her own. The Father wore white robes, with a black sash around his neck. And though he was not young, he certainly wasn't old. Wrinkles had just begun to form on his kind face, and his eyes sparkled with life.

This was a man she wanted to know, Saoirse realized. He radiated a certain energy she hadn't encountered in any human before. Kindness pulsed in golden light, so vivid she could almost touch it.

"Ah, father, there you are. I've returned with the woman we spoke about."

"This is the lass who has caught your attention? I didn't think it possible to tame your wild soul. Come closer child, I'd like to see the miracle worker."

Saoirse didn't realize he was talking to her until Manus planted a hand against her spine and nudged her forward.

Why did she have to talk to this man who called himself father, but did not have a son? She tucked her trembling hands into the lacy folds of her skirt and stepped forward into the candlelight.

"Ah, you are very lovely, aren't you? No wonder Manus wants to snatch you up. Any man would be honored to have such a woman grace his arm."

"Thank you," she whispered.

All this attention made her uncomfortable. What did this man see when he looked at her? Fidgeting, she tucked her hair behind her ears.

The vicar flinched back immediately. "What is this?"

"Now, father, keep an open mind," Manus interjected.

"An open mind? You've brought a faerie into a holy place!"

"There's nothing wrong with faeries."

The vicar's face grew red. Saoirse couldn't tell if it was in anger or fear. "Faeries have no place in the house of God. I will not perform this marriage, nor will any other sane man."

"You already said you would, father."

"And you *lied*."

"I did no such thing."

"You omitted the truth, which is just as bad." The vicar pointed at Manus, jabbing the air as if his hand were a sword. "I may follow the word of God, but I was raised here, boy. I know the stories of the Fae, and I know what they are capable of. You play with fire! I want nothing of it in my church. Begone."

Their shouts rose into the rafters and echoed back down until she was struck with them over and over again.

Manus flushed with anger, his hands fisting at his sides. "You have no right."

"You raise a hand to a priest and you'll be in more trouble than just a few nights in the gaol."

Saoirse gulped and whispered, "Stop it."

They didn't. She backed a few steps away from them, wrapping her arms around her waist. Did they not understand they were frightening her? She didn't want to be in this terrifying building anymore with its stone guards and angry priest.

They continued on and she pressed her hands to her ears. Their words struck her hands and wiggled between her fingers.

"You think a few nights behind bars frightens me, father? You more than anyone knows where I came from, and I suggest you not be foolish enough to tempt me."

"Temptation is a sin, one I know you over indulge in."

"Don't preach to me of sin as if you are pristine and ready to go to the holy lands! I knew you before you donned the robes—"

"Stop it!" Her shout echoed louder than theirs, fierce and bright as freshly fallen snow.

The two men froze and turned as one to stare at the little merrow. Saoirse watched their lips, waiting for them to move, but they did not. Slowly, she dropped her hands and straightened her spine.

"I don't know what I did wrong," she said. "I'm sorry if I insulted your home by entering it without permission."

The angry lines around the vicar's mouth softened. "Child, that is not why I am angry."

"Then why?"

He stepped towards her, hesitating only when she mirrored his actions in the opposite direction. "What are you?"

"I am one of the merrows."

"My mother used to tell me stories about your kind. How beautiful the women were, but caged underneath the waves by their husbands, or caging others. Is it freedom you seek?"

She nodded.

"Are you certain it is freedom with a sailor you desire?" His eyes turned kind again. "Manus is not one for loyalty. You could have anyone you wanted from the land. A prince, if need be. Your life with him will not be an easy one."

Manus's fists lifted. "You have no right, father."

"I have every right. I will not marry a woman to a man she does not know or understand. She is innocent to this world." He rolled his eyes. "Manus, stop looking at me like that. I may be a priest but I'm an Irishman first and foremost. I was raised with stories of the Fae just as you were."

"She can make her own decisions."

"Can she? Have you told her what you can offer her?" The priest pointed at him again. "The threat of starvation always looming around the corner? No money to buy new clothing, stealing from whoever has loose pockets, wondering if you have enough money to buy peat for the winter? There are better ways for her to live, and you know it. You'll throw her out to the cold as soon as the sea calls you."

"Why you pompous—"

Saoirse could stand this arguing no further. She stepped between the men, her shivers creating ripples down the dress until the lace looked as frothy as sea foam.

"*Enough.* I will not say it again." Their wide eyes met hers at the harsh crack of her words. "I am a grown woman, and I appreciate your concern, but I will not have yet another man making decisions for me. We are already married in the eyes of the Fae. I don't care if you or your god deems us wed."

"You do not know who you are pledging yourself to," the priest sighed. "You are choosing a life of hardship with a man who will always consider you second best to the sea."

Anger flared bright in her chest. "I'm afraid we must not see the same man. It is not that I am blind to his weaknesses, father, I see them clear as day. But I also see a man who acknowledges his faults. There is no such thing as a person without flaws, and I choose to be with a man who knows what he is."

"That's a pretty way of saying it, but it doesn't show you understand what your life will be."

"My life will be what I choose. No more, and no less."

The priest searched her gaze, his eyes delving into the darkness of hers until he found what he wanted. He gave a curt nod, then turned to the altar.

"So be it. If I cannot convince you of your own folly, you will have to learn it yourself."

She didn't think he was right, and she certainly didn't think he would ever prove her wrong. Saoirse reached for Manus's hand and tucked it into hers.

He gazed down at her with pure joy in his eyes. "Are you sure about this?"

"I've never been more sure of anything in my life. I've already pledged myself to you Manus, a thousand times over in my mind and if I must, I will scream it to the sky. I crossed the seas to find you. I would do it again in a heartbeat."

"What did I do for such a creature to find me?" he asked quietly. "I have never been looked upon kindly by any god. Why you?"

Saoirse reached up and pressed her palm to his cheek. "I see the man you keep hidden from the world, and I like him very much. I think, perhaps, you do not. At least not yet."

"See him? Or like him?"

That was a question she couldn't answer for him. Instead, she smiled a secret smile and tugged him towards the priest who patiently waited at the altar.

She knelt beside him and copied his movements. It was a rather easy ceremony. Repeat the words, copy the actions, allow the priest to bind their hands together and proclaim them man and wife. It was more than a faerie wedding, but less than she might have expected from such creatures.

"Do you take this woman as your wife?" the priest asked.

"I do." Manus's voice lifted to the rafters, strong and confident enough to weaken her knees if she had been standing.

"Do you take this man as your husband?"

She looked Manus in the eyes, in those dark earthy eyes with threads of gold and copper.

"I do."

"Then by the power vested in me, I pronounce you man and wife."

Manus lurched to his feet, drawing her with him and tugging her into his arms. He bent low and growled in her ear, "I will not disgrace you before a priest, but you and I are going home right now."

"My lady," the priest called out. "Be careful."

She wouldn't dignify the words with a response. Saoirse might not have been raised a princess, but she felt very much like one as she walked down the steps. Manus waited for her at the bottom with his hand outstretched.

It didn't matter that there was dirt underneath his nails. It didn't matter that he came from nothing, that he lived by the sea instead of with other people, that he had no money or material wealth to his name. He looked at her with the abyss in his eyes and in them she saw home.

He was a prince made of bark and earth, come to life by her wishes and dreams.

Manus rushed them through the streets, not pausing to answer her questions. He didn't seem to even hear her as they raced down cobblestone back to the sea.

The hushed sound of their breath splintered through the air. It mixed with the slaps of their feet as they ran across the mud flats. Manus wrenched his door open, planted a hand against the small of her back, and pushed her over the threshold.

Giggling, she stumbled into the small home, filling her eyes with the golden light of the sunrise. It gilded the edges of every small furniture piece and the edges of his bed.

"Manus, it's morning already."

"I woke you too early," he said. He closed the door with a harsh crack, then wedged a chair against it for good measure.

"What are you doing?"

"Making certain no one can interrupt us."

She lifted a brow. "Interrupt us? What are we doing?"

Manus did not reply. Instead, he picked up a blanket from the bed and tossed it over the window. The room fell into darkness other than a few spears of light from holes in the fabric.

Curious, she peered through one as he struck another match and lit a few candles. The warm light spilled through the shack, turning his skin to burnished bronze.

"Manus?" she asked again. "What are we doing?"

One moment he was on the other side of the room, and the next, she was pressed against the wall with the full length of his body pressed against hers. He leaned down, his lips tracing a line from shoulder to ear.

"Did you mean it?" His voice was hoarse and ragged. "Every word you said to the priest?"

"I did. Faeries cannot lie."

"Ah, yes. I had forgotten." He caught her ear between his teeth, gently worrying the sensitive skin until sparks showered through her body from the pointed tip to her toes. "No one has ever said those words about me."

"Then they are all wrong."

Manus pulled back, and she lost herself in his eyes again. She saw mountains with trees so green they burned her eyes. Waterfalls tumbled from great heights, billowing in clouds of frosted white. Ancient beasts who lifted their many antlered heads with flowers blooming along their spines. She saw the world of the Fae in his gaze, and so much more than that.

"Kiss me," she whispered. "I am yours, Manus of Uí Néill. And I will have no other."

Manus wanted to give her a wedding night that would shift the foundation of her world. He wanted to tantalize her senses, whisper promises in her ear, pretend to be the gentleman he wasn't. She deserved every bit of his control and leashed passions.

But then she said the words that marked her as his forever. A wedding vow meant little when the woman's gaze wandered. This strange woman willingly gifted herself, her life, her soul, everything she was with a promise that stole his heart.

The tethers of his control snapped with a nearly audible crack. He surged forward, pressing his body against her and devouring her lips with an aggression that surprised him. She tasted of the sea.

She stung his soul like saltwater on a sunburn and then soothed his aches with a gentle touch.

Manus lifted his hands and framed her face, tilting her head to plunder her mouth even further. His hands were shaking. He pressed his fingers harder against her cheeks and realized with fear that it wasn't aggression or passion burning in his veins. It was a need so raw and violent that he wanted to brand himself with her touch, with her essence, with her soul.

He would frighten her, and she would be smart to run from him when he was like this. There would be no tender touches, no murmured praise, nothing but a scorching hot flame that would devour her whole.

And yet, he could not stop himself.

He dragged his lips from her mouth, trailing across her high cheekbones and down the graceful column of her throat. Her breath caught, her legs quivered.

"I do not know how to be the man you deserve," he whispered against her skin. "I cannot be a gentle man. I cannot be a good man."

"You are," she whispered, and fisted her hands in the dreads of his hair. "Love me as a man loves a woman, Manus. Do not treat me as if I were made of glass. I am Fae, and I am more than any woman you've had before."

Her words arced through his mind like a lightning bolt. They traveled down his spine and nearly blew out his knees for want of her.

"I want you fiercely," he ground out. "More than any creature I've ever seen before."

His fingers shook as he loosened the tie on the front of her dress.

He tugged at the white bow until it released and fell into a silken puddle on the floor.

The lace parted, fabric held together by little more than a prayer. He nudged it to the side so he might see the smooth skin of her shoulders. She didn't have a blemish on her. No scars, no pockmarks, not even a raised ridge where she might have harmed herself once in her childhood. Saoirse was all milk white skin that turned silver in the moonlight.

He pulled the lace down with a single finger hooked in a delicate swirl. It slithered down, caught at her waist, and she looked as though she were walking out of the sea into his arms.

Manus had seen her pristine skin before. He'd seen her without a shirt or a stitch of clothing to her name, but this was different. It was one thing to see a faerie in her natural habitat. It was an entirely different thing to see her standing in his home as vulnerable as a newborn babe.

"Your hands are shaking," she whispered.

He watched with rapt attention as Saoirse reached forward, grasped his hand, and pressed it to her lips.

"You have no idea what is about to happen," he panted, reminding himself she was fragile.

"You're thinking too much." Her lips turned up in a half smile. "I thought we weren't supposed to think?"

If all were going well, then she wouldn't have a thought in her head other than the taste of him. Manus couldn't breathe. He was staring at perfection and every time he touched her, he worried he would leave a mark.

His dirty fingers didn't deserve to touch a creature such as this, no matter that he had stolen her away. Merrows were myths and legends. She was a goddess, and he was nothing more than a street rat.

She stepped forward on feet that made no sound in the quiet shack. "I don't know what I'm doing, but you'll tell me if I do something wrong. Won't you?"

A shuddering breath escaped him. "Why?"

"Why what?"

"Why would you ever allow me to touch you?"

She smiled and pressed her palm against his cheek. "Why would you ever think a woman wouldn't want you to?"

"I'm only good for whores."

"Who told you that? You're a handsome, honorable man. I do not recognize this part of you, this piece that is self-conscious and can't understand my feelings towards you. It's unlike you."

She was right. Manus was a confident man, one who wooed whores to his bed with little issue. He'd never hesitated with them. They squealed in delight when he came anywhere near their shop.

Maybe that was the reason. He never knew if the ladies of the night were interested in him or his money. Likely the latter, but that meant he didn't have to please them if he didn't wish it. Manus enjoyed paying particular attention to their needs, but after a long day of work, they still got paid. If they were disappointed, he didn't worry.

What if he disappointed her?

Her gaze searched his, and a spark of recognition flared so bright his cheeks burned red. She knew, or at least had guessed some of it.

He bit his lip as she stepped back. Her fingertips caught on the edges of the lace dress, and she pushed it down her hips. It slid to the floor with the soft sigh of a calm sea, and she stood before him as she was meant to be.

Long dark hair framed her arms and made her skin seem even paler than he thought possible. It swayed at her rounded hips, high above slender legs that ended in delicately arched feet.

His gaze lingered upon moon touched skin and the shadows that played over the valley between her hips.

"I don't want to temper you," she consoled. "You are not a blade I wish to dull. I will take you in whatever way I can, Manus. If that is as an animal, then I must ask you to remember that I am part fish."

He chuckled and ran a hand over his knotted locks. "It's not that easy, my pearl."

"Tell me what you desire, my husband, and I will give it to you a thousand times over."

Her husband.

Her husband.

The words rattled through his mind and shattered what little reservation he had left. Manus cursed, stepped forward, and scooped her into his arms. She held onto his neck and let loose a bright bubble of laughter that splintered on the ceiling and showered down upon them in a chorus of bliss.

He laid her down on his bed, whispering that he wished he could give her more. She deserved gold, diamonds, precious gems sprinkled around her body in goddess-like adornment.

Her spine arched into him, and he palmed the silken flesh of her breasts. A groan vibrated his throat in sheer bliss. It was everything he had wished for, everything he had dreamed she would feel like. Soft as satin, warm as a fire in winter, and pliant as the softest of clay.

He leaned down and drew a pebbled peak between his lips. Stroking his tongue back and forth, he waited until her breathing hitched and her fingers curled in the sheets before he moved to the other.

Saoirse was a surprisingly responsive lover. Every swirl of his tongue made her back arch further, every gentle bite of his teeth made her gasp in pleasure. It was music to his ears, and he was all too pleased to oblige the way her body begged for his touch.

The muscles of her stomach contracted as his fingers danced down her soft belly.

"Trust me," he whispered against her heart.

"Always."

He stroked the inside of her thighs, encouraging her to let them fall open. There was no hesitation, only complete and utter trust as she bared herself completely.

She was warm, wet, and all too welcoming for a man's sanity. Manus groaned and pressed his forehead against her collarbone.

"My pearl, I don't know if I can be gentle, and you deserve that."

She pressed harder against his fingers until the heel of his palm was flush against her burning heat.

"I don't want gentle, Manus, I want you."

Saoirse pressed herself into his touch, heat covering her body as never before. He turned her into a creature of the earth. Her blood was molten lava, her body made of rough trees, and her breath the icy north wind.

He rose over her, the long tails of his hair stroking across her sensitive skin. "Do you?"

"Now."

He reached between them, notching himself where his fingers had played. "There will be a little pain—"

She pressed her fingers against his mouth to silence him. "Enough, Manus. We have waited long enough."

The overwhelming sensation of tightness filled her. It was too much, too full, too evocative, and yet she didn't want him to stop.

He was tender and sweet although he said he couldn't be gentle. Each inch that he slid forward caused massive exhalations to dance across her neck and chest. Manus pressed his lips to her throat, obviously holding himself in check until she relaxed around him.

Saoirse hadn't thought it would be like this. She'd seen such acts before. Whales and sea creatures mated with an animalistic fervor she'd never understood until now.

She tangled her fingers in his hair, pressed her lips to his, and waited until he had seated himself fully.

"Enough," she muttered against his lips. "You have been gentle, now give me everything."

The rocking movements of his body increased, each thrust like a tidal wave crashing through her body. He was the ocean and turned her into the many currents that surrounded him, swallowed him, devoured every bit of what he might give her.

Unexpectedly, she shattered. Saoirse tossed her head back against the pillows and stared up at the ceiling, but all she saw were stars. The thousands of glowing lights that decorated the sky. Or perhaps they were the glowing beacons of the underwater cities, bioluminescent and secretive.

She was unmade. Pieces of herself flung into the air by the great release that rode her body, rocking back and forth as he plunged deeper and deeper into her depths.

Manus tossed his head back, the cords of his throat flexing, casting shadows across his form as he let out a guttural groan.

The weight of his body fell onto hers, surrounding her with warmth and safety. Saoirse tucked her arms underneath his and encircled his ribs.

He was not soft, like her, but rugged. Ridges of scars laced across his body, a hard life laid out in a map across his skin. She bumped her fingers over his ribs and traced the laced pattern of scars that crisscrossed all over his skin.

Breath puffed against her neck, and he pressed his lips where the air had chilled her skin.

"Are you all right?"

"Better," she replied with a smile. "Far better than I might have expected."

"I'm glad I didn't disappoint."

"How could you? I'll take any bit of you that I can."

She whispered the words even though she wanted to scream them to the rafters. He was hers, and she was his. They were bound by faerie and human law. No one could take her from him, and she was never returning to her home under the sea.

For the first time in her life, she was completely safe.

It was an overwhelming feeling. Saoirse wasn't certain how to deal with it. She didn't need to look over her shoulder, worried that her father or brother would be there in the shadows. She didn't need to wonder what man she might marry, or what direction her life would take.

Saoirse was her own person although perhaps she was slightly Manus's as well. But that didn't matter much. He was a good man to his core. He just didn't know it yet.

He stirred, pressing his face in the hollow where her neck met shoulder, and sighed.

"It is the beginning of the day. We should get up, and I should try to find work."

"Stay a little longer," she begged.

Saoirse wrapped her arms around him tighter. She snuggled into his chest, inhaling the earthy scent of sweat and man.

"Maybe for a little while longer," he agreed.

He rolled them to the side with his arms wrapped tight around her spine. She let him arrange her as he wanted, draping her leg over his hip and letting him place his chin atop her head.

It was quiet, peaceful, and heady to know that she was cared for. At least a little. They hadn't said the words, but she was certain he felt the same way. He had to.

A rumble of a chuckle spread through his chest.

She smiled, "Yes?"

"What?"

"What's so funny?"

He shook his head, rubbing his chin on her head. "I've never fallen asleep with a woman before."

"Never?" Saoirse leaned back slightly to see him. "Even the priest mentioned that you were well known in these parts."

"I don't stay with them. I enjoy them, they enjoy me, and then I leave."

"Why?"

She furrowed her brow as he hesitated. It made little sense that he wouldn't want to stay. This was wonderful. The feeling of his arms around her made her heart sing a song she'd never heard before but found beautiful.

"I never wanted to," he finally admitted. "Until now."

"Oh. That is acceptable then."

"Is it?"

"Yes." She snuggled back down into his arms and breathed a quiet sigh. "That is perfectly acceptable."

Saoirse did not let herself rest until she heard the peaceful sound of his deep breathing. He fell asleep with her in his arms, and she was pleased to be the first.

CHAPTER 7

BLISS AND AGONY

Saoirse pressed a flower to her nose, inhaling the sweet scent that spun her senses like a top. She hadn't thought it would smell like this.

Lavender wasn't found in the lands that surrounded her underwater home, so this was a rare treat.

"Do you like it?" Manus asked.

He stood on the other side of the stall, his eyes following her every move. She knew how strange she must look. Saoirse rushed from vendor to vendor, grabbing everything she could get her hands on and exclaiming how miraculous it was. They gave her strange looks and tolerated her odd behavior with quick smiles.

"It smells like… like…." Saoirse struggled for the words. "Like far off lands and adventures."

He rounded the stall and plucked the sprigs from her fingers. "That's because it smells like here, and I dare say this is as far as you've ever been."

"I've never been so far in my life!"

"Precisely." He tossed a coin to the woman smiling at them and handed the plant back to her. "It's said to have a calming effect."

"What is? This?"

"The lavender. People place it inside their pillows when they cannot sleep."

"Really?" She looked at the purple flowers, intrigued by the possibilities. "How fascinating."

"Is it?"

He'd asked the same question throughout the day. Was it actually that interesting? Perhaps not to him. But everything was new for Saoirse, foreign and strange, but delightful to every sense.

Glinting colored lights caught her eye. It sparkled like the sun through water. Her heart stopped, and she rushed across the busy street without thought. Manus called after her, but she couldn't stop. Not now that she had seen the newest, captivating find.

She ducked underneath a brightly colored sheet flapping in the wind and then skidded to a halt.

Tiny pieces of colored glass hung on strings, tangled with feathers that shifted in the slight breeze. Clinking glass mixed with the quiet hush of wings. The sun hit the softened edges, sending colors dancing across the wooden stall and spilling onto the ground.

She lifted the hem of her new dress and poked her bare toes into the light. Blue danced over her skin, familiar and yet not. It was like seeing the ocean through new eyes.

One mobile in particular caught her attention. Seashells hung next to shards, the wind singing through them and calling out to her like the ocean waves.

The man behind the counter had a kind smile that reached up into his eyes and twinkled. He wiped his hands with a white rag and stepped forward.

"Can I help you, m'lady?"

"Oh," she murmured and clasped her hands to her chest. "I don't know where to start. These are beautiful."

"They hardly hold a candle to you."

She blushed bright red at his words. The men were charming here, far more than merrow men could ever hope it be. She didn't know how to respond to their teasing, their compliments, or their flirtatious advances.

Manus usually scared them off. But he wasn't here now as the carriages blocked him from her.

Glancing over her shoulder, she spied him searching for her on the other side of the street.

Protection was appreciated, but unnecessary. Saoirse might be a merrow, but she could take care of herself.

She tucked a strand of ink dark hair behind her ear. "How do you make them?"

"Glass is a rare find in these parts. Do you know how we get it?"

"No."

He gestured for her to come behind the stall. "Come around then, I'll show you."

"Won't that keep you away from your other customers?"

"There doesn't appear to be any right now, and it's probably the wrong market to sell my wares. Haven't gotten a single person all day who was a serious buyer. Let me show a pretty lady what I'm capable of. It's a small consolation for such a wasted day."

She took the arm he offered. Muscles flexed beneath the white linen shirt, a promise that this artist was a working man.

Saoirse couldn't imagine how he could create such beautiful objects. Surely it was magic. The hairs on her arms raised at the thought.

She'd only seen a few people capable of magic in her short life. They were marvelous creatures, capable of spinning dreams into reality and worries into fantasy. Her father hadn't wanted her anywhere near them. He said it gave girls fancies.

Saoirse already had more fancies than she could keep ahold of.

"Do you know anything about glass?" the man asked.

"No."

"Some people think it's magic, you know. That it's a gift from the Tuatha dé Danann themselves."

She lifted her gaze sharply, squeezing her fingers on his forearm.

"Is it?"

"No." He patted her hand, both in comfort and as a request for her to relax her grip. "It's a magic from the earth, certainly, but not how you might think. Sit here, and I'll show you."

Saoirse tucked her hands in her lap and reminded herself not to swing to her legs. Manus had tried telling her this morning that she would need to learn how to be human. Swinging legs while seated was not lady like.

The man lifted a wooden crate and set it at her feet. "This is where glass comes from."

With a flourish, he pushed the lid off the crate and her heart skipped a beat. Would it be amazing? Would it be some magical creature she'd never seen before?

She leaned over, stared down into the crate, and blinked. Sand filled it to the brim. White and nearly undisturbed, it might have been sand from her home.

"Sand?" she asked.

"Sand m'lady." He chuckled at the face she made. "Come now, don't look so disappointed! Why don't you stick your hand in there? See what you might find."

Stick her hands in the sand? She'd done it a thousand times. Saoirse almost told him that she'd grown up deep within the ocean, rolling across sand dunes as a child and throwing it in the faces of her sisters. She quickly shut her mouth, knowing that would reveal too much.

The sand was cool against her palms. It slipped and slid through her fingers in a way so familiar it nearly brought tears to her eyes. She had only been gone for a few weeks, and already she missed the sand more than she could admit.

Her fingers bumped against something hard with jagged edges that bit at her skin. Gasping, she yanked her hands from the sand and stared with wide eyes at the man.

"What's in there?"

Glee made his eyes sparkle. "Oh, I don't know miss. Why don't you pick it up?"

"Will it bite me?"

"No, just be careful. I would feel awful if you cut yourself."

Somehow, she wasn't certain he was telling the truth. His eyes were sparkling too much, and he didn't warn her the first time she plunged her hands into the crate.

Saoirse narrowed her gaze and refused to be cowed. He might expect her to flinch away from the discovery, but she had battled sharks. This human man had no idea what he was dealing with.

Again, she sank her hands into the sand and swirled the grains. The sharp object had been in the very corner, farther away so she had to lean nearly into the crate to get it.

Cold shards touched her fingers. It was larger than she expected, and not nearly as sharp as she thought. Tiny spikes dug into her palms but didn't threaten to pierce flesh. The cold surface was smooth, solid, and yet surprisingly delicate.

The artisan must have seen the wonder on her face. He chuckled and gestured with his hands, "Go on then. Pick it up and have a look."

Her biceps flexed as she lifted the surprisingly heavy find. Sand slid off its surface and she gaped at the giant piece of glass between her hands.

It looked like spilled wax, slightly foggy, but stunningly beautiful with its spires of twisted tendrils and thick base.

"Oh," she exclaimed in awe. "Is this what it looks like before you change it? How is it made? Magic? Must you use magic to temper it? How do you turn this into those beautiful prisms?"

He burst into laughter and held up his hands. "One question at a time lady. Although, I can likely answer them all if you'd like to come see how I work."

She nodded, holding the raw glass close to her chest so she wouldn't drop it. This was the most precious substance she'd seen on land so far, and she'd seen lace so delicate it looked like sea foam. What other wonders had these beings created?

The artisan carefully took the glass out of her hands and placed it back in the box. "Come with me."

The hand he offered was covered with callouses. Saoirse realized she had only seen humans with work roughened hands.

Glancing down at her own, she hesitated a brief second before placing her velvet soft hand in his. His eyes widened in surprise for a moment. He'd noticed, she was certain he would, and didn't know how to explain the reasoning behind her untouched hands.

It wasn't that she hadn't worked, she had. She wasn't a royal, nor was she rich. The water had different ways of handling such things. Merrows didn't feel the effects as humans did, and her palms would likely roughen the longer she was here.

Still, it felt almost shameful and embarrassing to have him notice such a thing. She ducked her head and let him lead her behind the row of stalls to where the artisans kept their carts full of wares.

"Lady," he mumbled, "if you are some noble miss masquerading through the market, you should not be alone with the likes of me."

"You aren't the first person to tell me such a thing, and I cannot understand the reasoning behind it." She looked up and met his blue gaze. "Should I not be able to meet and speak with whoever I wish?"

"It isn't proper."

"Says who? Why wouldn't it be proper for someone to meet those who create their wares, their art, the things we use every day? I should know the man talented enough to decorate my home if I was a noble lady."

Relief spread across his face. "Then you aren't?"

"What?"

"You aren't a noble lady?"

"No." She shook her head ruefully. "I don't think I would be any different if I were."

"You're a rare one, aren't you?"

Saoirse wasn't certain the look he gave her was good. It was a thoughtful expression, his brows drawn down and his lips pursed. An expression that made her worry he was wondering who, or what, she was.

"Where are we?" she blurted out, hoping to steer his thoughts away from his curiosity.

Mud squelched between her toes, but she didn't mind too much. Deep tracks were furrowed in the ground from carts traveling over them each day. She saw some vendors rushing back from their small stalls, carrying armloads of new wares back where customers might wish to buy something. White sheets covered most of the carts and protected the goods from the sun.

But not the cart in front of her. This one looked more like a fireplace on wheels. Round as a barrel, with a flame churning within, the strange cart caught her attention immediately.

"Is this yours?" she asked.

"You are astute; it is. Come, I'll show you."

The closer she got, the louder the inferno churned. Saoirse held her hands up to her ears and stared at the artisan. Her fingers shook with fear.

"Is it dangerous?"

"It is if you get too close. Come now, my lady, I won't let you be harmed. Look inside."

Inside? She inched forward. What was he keeping inside that monstrous creation?

"Don't worry," he said with a chuckle, placing a warm hand against her spine. "It won't bite you. Have you never seen a kiln before?"

"A what?"

She peered into the roaring flames and waited for her eyes to adjust. Molten glass pooled in the depths of the fire. It glimmered like starlight, holding its breath for the moment when the artisan would turn it into something new, something beautiful.

At her gasp of surprise, the man chuckled and reached for a metal tool.

"Now step back," he warned, "I don't want you to get burned. Let me show you what else I can do."

The metal tweezers seemed to vibrate in his hand. Perhaps they too realized that something wondrous was about to happen.

Saoirse held her breath as he reached into the kiln and drew out a long strand of glass. It stuck to the metal, dripping like thick honey. He quickly laid it on a small metal table next to the kiln, rolling and twisting it with dual tongs until the glass gave way to a shape.

She could see what he was doing, but still had no idea what he was creating. This was magic, she decided. Not the magic she was used to with glittering lights and powers of unearthly qualities. It was the kind of magic buried so deep within humanity they didn't know they had it.

The artisan grunted, breathed out a sound of relief, and held up the glass piece to the light.

"Come look at it, my lady. Quickly now, I've got to put it in a blanket to cool. I think you'll like this one."

She rushed forward, excitement heating her veins until she felt she might burst.

Within his hand, he held the tiniest merrow she had ever seen. The tail was fine, so delicate, that she could see the bumps of rigid scales down the thick length. Her hair floated around her head, with her arms raised to stroke the tiny fish that darted through the long length.

There was no color, but it didn't need the embellishment. The merrow was perfect in all her clear glory. An homage to the magic which brought them to life, and the beauty underneath the sea. Water would reflect through its surface and give it life with coral reefs, schools of fish, and the echoes of whales.

"How did you—" She glanced up and realized he didn't know what she was. His gaze was on the merrow, not her. Eyes wide with reverence, he stared at his newest creation as if wishing it could come to life.

"It's beautiful," she whispered. "You have a rare gift."

"Thank you. I rarely receive such compliments."

"Do you sell them?" She desperately wanted the tiny merrow for herself, but also knew it would fetch a considerable amount of money. The man deserved to be paid for his efforts, and she had little.

"Few people are interested in such things here. My art isn't practical. It's breakable, and it's difficult for the folks in these areas to buy something they know they can never use, only look at."

"I would fill my home with them if I could."

Her adamant declaration was so forceful that it made him rock back a step. The shock in his gaze warmed to a heat she had only seen from Manus.

This artisan wasn't a terrible looking man. His eyes were blue as the sky behind him, his facial hair carefully combed. Though he wasn't nearly as dark as Manus, he was still intriguing in his own way. His hands had been graceful as they twirled the molten glass and created life with his fingertips.

If she hadn't already been in love, she might have liked this man quite a bit.

Her gaze softened, and he reached forward to tuck a strand of hair behind her ear. "You're a rare beauty, my lady."

"Why do you keep calling me that?"

"Certainly, you are a royal disguised as a peasant. If you are not, then you are one of the Fae masquerading through our streets, and as such deserve all the respect I could possibly give."

"I'm not tall enough to be Tuatha dé Danann," she said with a blush. "If only I were one of the royal Fae."

His fingers tightened on the strand of hair in his grasp. "What—"

"Saoirse!" Manus's voice barked. "There you are."

She hadn't heard such a tone in his voice before. It rang with darkness, rage, and an underlying hurt. He didn't know merrows could hear emotion in voices, it was why their own voices were so beautiful.

Heart pounding, she glanced over her shoulder. "Hello, husband."

Manus stalked towards her, all lethal power and barely controlled aggression. "Hello, wife."

"Wife?" The artisan dropped his hand. "My apologies, sir."

Saoirse thought perhaps Manus's bared teeth would be considered a grin in some cultures, but it made her shiver in fear.

He ground out, "Not your fault. We haven't bought a ring for her yet, how would you have known?"

His hand dropped onto her shoulder and tightened. Had she done something wrong? Was she supposed to announce herself to the world as his wife?

She couldn't. Perhaps he didn't understand the way of the Fae, but ownership over another creature was as good as a name. His name could control her, just as much as her own now that they were married.

Wincing, she patted his hand on her shoulder. "This kind sir was showing me the glass. Isn't it magical?"

"It's just melted sand."

She latched onto his hand and forced him to stay when he moved to leave. "Manus, look at it!"

A muscle on his jaw ticked. She watched the rapid grinding of his teeth until he finally turned. "I've heard there was an artisan here who spins glass like silk. I assume that is you?"

The other man cleared his throat. "I'm not quite so talented, my lord, but I appreciate it."

"I'm no lord."

"I thought—" Again the artisan cleared his throat. "No matter. Have a look before I lay it to rest."

Manus took the offered metal tong and turned the merrow in a slow circle. The winged crinkles at the edges of his eyes deepened for a moment. "She's beautiful. Almost as stunning as the real thing."

"The real thing?" The artisan's eyes darted between them. "Are you… Could you be saying… Sir?"

"Don't think about it too much, you'll hurt yourself."

Manus handed the art piece back to the other man, planted his palm against Saoirse's back, and hustled her back through the stall and onto the street.

"Wait!" she cried out. "I wanted to see if we might take something home!"

"We're not buying anything of his."

"Why not? The glass was beautiful, Manus, and there was the most stunning piece with seashells and all the colors of the sea—"

"Saoirse enough!" Manus's voice was low, but it felt as though he slapped her.

She blinked up at him, willing the tears to remain in her eyes. She hadn't done anything *wrong*, and yet he was yelling at her with all these people looking. All she wanted was something pretty that might remind her of home. She'd given up her home to be with him, to make a new home with him. Did he not see that?

Manus made a pained sound, sighed and stepped away from her. He ran a hand over his hair while his eyes flicked from the tears in her eyes to the ground.

"Did you not see how much danger you were in?" he growled.

"I wasn't in any danger, he is a kind man."

"This one might have been kind, but the next man who pulls you into an alley won't be. Good god, woman! You nearly gave me a heart attack!"

"I didn't mean to."

"Saoirse." He grabbed her arm and swung her around. Cupping her face in his hands, he pressed his forehead to hers. "Humans are not kind creatures. Everyone here is like your merrow men, looking for the next person to take advantage of. You cannot leave my side."

"You shouldn't be so quick to judge others," she replied. "Some of them might surprise you."

He released her with a muttered curse. "I need a drink."

"Manus, your hands are shaking."

She watched his fingers curl into fists that clenched so hard his knuckles turned white.

"Come with me," he grumbled.

They passed by the cobblestoned streets, deeper into the city where gravel and dirt dug into the soft skin of her bare feet. The people were less clean here. Their faces were streaked with sweat, and grime embedded underneath their nails and covered their clothing.

These people made fear dance across her skin with stings similar to that of jellyfish tentacles. Their eyes were hungry, black like a shark and bottomless like the deepest abyss. They weren't on the main street for a reason. She didn't think they had enough money to feed themselves, let alone buy all the wondrous things the vendors had showcased.

A man walked towards them and his eyes traveled from her toes to her head. He let out a slow hiss of breath, a high-pitched whine of a sound that made her flinch. Manus lashed out a hand. He caught the man by the throat and tossed him into the wall.

For a moment, she wondered if they would claw at each other as merrow men might have. But something in Manus's gaze made the other swear and stumble past them.

"Manus?" she called out. "I don't like it here."

"Yeah? No one does, my pearl. Get used to it." He ducked through a door and left her standing on the street.

Saoirse rubbed her arms and swallowed hard. Why was it suddenly cold here? The streets had been warm, full of sunshine and bright smiles. Now, a chilled wind brushed down her arms. It coiled in her palms and whispered dangerous secrets in her ears.

Manus opened the door again and held out his hand. "It wasn't a request, Saoirse. Follow me at all times."

She bristled at his tone but followed him. The street was a dangerous place, and the shadows moved in the corners of her eyes. She didn't want to know what kind of Unseelie lurked in this desolation.

The room beyond was only half full of men and women in various states of disarray. Some women bared their shoulders, something Manus had told her never to do, and others were more sensibly dressed. The men were all covered in dirt and sweat, much like those on the street.

Manus pointed towards an empty table near the large hearth merrily crackling. "Sit there."

She would have to tell him later how little she appreciated his tone. The worn boards were smooth and soft, trailing warm grains against her soles as she made her way towards the rickety seating. Sliding onto the bench, she set her back to the crowd and stared into the fire.

Some things were different here. Far more different than she ever could have imagined. Some humans were wealthy, some were talented, and some were so painfully poor it made her heart ache. Why would they let their own people waste away? Or worse, continue to live a perpetual existence of hardship and strife?

Saoirse shook her head and let it drop into her palms. Maybe someday she would understand them, but for now, it just made her head pound.

The bench across from her creaked.

"Manus, I don't want to be here," she murmured. "I want to go home."

"That'll depend on which home you mean, lassie." The voice sang out, dancing through the air like the trickle of gold coins with the heat of lava pouring from deep sea vents.

Her spine stiffened. Something deep inside of her recognized that kind of voice and answered its call with the burbling of water, the roar of rushing rivers, and the thrum of hidden sea caves.

"Who are you?" She looked up, anger burning in the back of her skull.

The man seated in front of her was surprising. His sheer size was not what she expected although everything was different here in this land. A white shirt strained across his broad shoulders, tapering to a trim waist that spoke of hard labor. A light dusting of freckles spread across his sharply angled face, meeting the hairline of his shockingly red hair.

He wasn't dressed like the others here. His clothing was finer, his hair neatly trimmed, and no hair graced his jaw or chin.

But she wasn't all that surprised that he stood out like a sore thumb. All Fae did.

"I think you know I'm not going to tell you my name," he said with a wry grin. "I won't expect yours either."

"What are you doing here?"

"I could ask the same of you, little merrow."

Her hands clenched on the table. "How do you know what I am?"

"It's not hard to tell. That hair shines green even in this golden light, and you'll forgive me for saying, but a faerie is far easier on the eyes than a human." He leaned forward, interest coiling like a snake within the depths of his dark green eyes. "Now, why are you here?"

"I followed my heart."

"Your heart?" He pointed towards Manus, whose back was still to them. "That one?"

"Yes."

"Oh, little merrow, that was a foolish decision. Humans are entertaining for a time, but they're always disappointing." He leaned back, anchored a shoulder against the wall, and hooked his heels on the table. "Speaking from experience."

"My decisions are my own, and I would prefer it if you kept your opinions to yourself."

"Ah, where's the fun in that lass?" His booted feet shifted side to side. "Do you have any guesses yet?"

"On what?"

"What do you think I am?"

She scoffed. "That's hardly a challenge, leprechaun."

"It is for some. My size is rather confusing, wouldn't you agree?"

"Not at all. Tuatha dé Danann are large, Lesser Fae are not. It's why you and I are both similar sizes to humans, although," she paused and looked him up and down, "you are larger than most men."

"The largest of my entire family. It's a personal accomplishment I'm rather proud of."

"I don't think you can give yourself credit for your size."

He lifted a finger to his lips. "Come now, lass. Don't break a man's heart."

"I don't have time to quarrel with a leprechaun about the size of his flesh. Begone with you."

He wiggled, presumably to make himself more comfortable on the bench. "Not interested in that option. I think I'll stay right here and meet the paragon who caught the attention of a merrow."

"I'd rather you didn't."

Saoirse desperately wanted him to leave. After the way Manus had reacted to the artisan, she couldn't imagine what he might do if he saw this behemoth of a man sitting in his seat.

The leprechaun gracefully gestured, his fingers dancing in the air until suddenly a golden coin appeared between his fingers. It sparkled in the light and forced all her attention onto the single piece.

"Oh," she whispered. "Where did you get that?"

"Just a trick of the light, lass. Now, would you mind answering a few questions for me?"

She couldn't stop staring at the gold coin as he rolled it over and through his fingers. Strange, she didn't feel like herself but didn't mind in the slightest. The coin was too interesting to care that her mind was wandering.

"Good," he continued. "Why are you really here?"

"I followed him across the seas."

"Where did you meet him?"

"He was shipwrecked off my home. I saw him floating in the water and thought he drowned. My heart hurt at the thought, so I saved him."

"Did you heal him?"

"I don't think so." She frowned. That was something important she should remember, but she didn't.

"Try again, little merrow."

"I might have. I didn't want him to die, but he wasn't dead when I grabbed him."

"But you healed him when you brought him back to the isle."

"Perhaps a little? Just with merrow tears, and they aren't supposed to do that much."

He cursed, but it didn't matter. The coin spun over his fingers that flicked so quickly it looked as though they were their own wave.

"Those heal more than you know, merrow. What would you do if I tried to take you from him?"

"I would fight tooth and claw. And if you succeeded, then my heart would rip in two and my blood would meet the waves." She reached out a hand hesitantly, waiting for the moment when the coin would stop. "May I have it now?"

It stopped, hovering just between his middle finger and thumb. "Are you sure you want it?"

"Yes."

He arched a brow. "Just how young are you?"

"I'm close to my first century. May I have it *now*?" Even she heard the petulance in her voice.

"Oh, lass, you are a young wee thing aren't ya?" He spun the coin until it laid flat across his knuckles. "Take it, and I'll give you my name."

"I don't want your name."

"A leprechaun coin is a promise, little one. I'll watch over you as best I can, whenever I can, but you take this coin and I'm as much a part of you as that man hovering by the bar looking like the world is falling down around his ears."

Saoirse hesitated. "I don't want to belong to anyone else."

"You won't. You have my word."

She nibbled her lip, but the golden light was far too compelling. Saoirse lunged across the table and snatched it from his fist.

The coin was warm and heavy, the metal almost soft beneath her fingertips. Its beauty was almost painful so close to her eyes. Etched on the surface, a small merrow swam through golden waves.

Saoirse let out a soft, pleased sigh. "Thank you."

He nodded. "My name is Declan."

"It's a pleasure to meet you, Declan. My name is—"

"Saoirse."

She blinked, looking up at him in surprise. "Yes. How did you know?"

"It tells me a lot more than you'd think." Declan nodded towards the coin in her hand. "You'll have to keep it on you at all times. Leprechaun gold is bad luck if you lose it."

"Oh," she breathed. Saoirse pressed the coin to her chest and held it tight as if her own fingers would let it slip away without permission. "Does it want to be lost?"

"Not as you might think." He leaned forward, the ever-present grin on his face. Saoirse noticed that his teeth were slightly pointed. A little of the real leprechaun was leaking through the glamour he held in place.

"Then I shall be careful with it."

"You sure this is the path you want to walk, little merrow?"

She nodded firmly.

"All right then," he said with a disappointed glower. "I'm not going to say I like it. So, you keep that coin with you at all times. If something bad happens, I'll know."

"Who are you?" she asked. "You don't speak like the others, and you wouldn't be here unless you were banished and yet...."

"Yes?"

The roguish grin on his face sent a shiver running down her spine. "You don't seem like you were banished."

"Let's just say I'm on a little adventure from my home. It's important to get perspective on the world, wouldn't you agree?"

"But *who* are you?"

She searched his gaze for an answer, and her own memories for anything the merrows knew about the leprechauns.

They were traditionally a very secretive lot. The dwarves enjoyed their riches, but leprechauns were a completely different race of Fae. They bled riches. Gold ran through their veins like blood, and gemstones dropped from their eyes like tears. Everything about them was a mountain of wealth and glory.

Leprechauns kept to themselves. She knew there were a few lines of royalty although they were not recognized by the Unseelie court. Saoirse remembered rumors that stretched under the waves.

A prince of the leprechauns, incapable of being controlled by his parents, so wild and free that even the beasts wanted nothing to do with him. They sent him to the human world to learn humility, and to appreciate their origins.

She had heard nothing since, and it would be hard to tell if this was the prince himself. After all, every leprechaun had red hair, freckles, and were built like gods.

Unless….

At her raised brow, his grin widened just enough to reveal a solid gold back tooth.

"It's you," she whispered. "You're the leprechaun prince?"

He winced. "Not my favorite name to go by, but if you must."

"I've never met a prince before." Saoirse leaned forward, keeping her voice hushed so no one could overhear them. "Am I supposed to curtsy?"

"Please don't."

"But I'm supposed to?"

Declan glanced away, and that was all the answer she needed.

"My goodness!" Saoirse lost her breath. "What other things have I done that would get me killed in the Unseelie court?"

"There are several things, little merrow, but you'll find we're far more lenient than our Seelie brethren."

"I've heard they're much more invested in rules."

"Aren't you part of the Seelie court?"

"In a way. My merrow tribe lived on the edges of both kingdoms, but so far away that the customs didn't carry with us."

He breathed out a low whistle. "You're one of the rare wandering Fae? A creature not dedicated to either court?"

"I suppose you could say that. I didn't know we had a name."

"You're more dangerous than I thought."

Two jars slammed down on the table between them. Saoirse recognized Manus's hands, strong and scarred, wrapped around the glasses so firmly she worried they might break.

"Dangerous, is she?" he growled. "I think I could say the same for you, mate."

To his credit, Declan did nothing other than shrug. "It's not every day you meet someone like her, now is it?"

"And why's that?" The dangerous edge to Manus's voice stole the breath from Saoirse's lungs.

"Oh, I think you know why considering you stole her from the ocean and dragged her to this hell on earth. Shall I call you her husband or her captor?"

A snarl twisted Manus's lips. "I'll ask you leave, *friend*."

"But your little lady friend here has made such a good impression. I'll give you one warning because I like her." A coin appeared between Declan's fingers. "You don't know what you're dealing with."

"I think I know perfectly well. A pretty boy like you walks into a bar like this, and he usually gets his teeth readjusted."

Declan nodded with a feral grin that bared teeth sharpening by the second. "So be it. Heads? Or tails?"

He tossed the coin into the air and Saoirse watched it wildly spin between the men. Something important was happening. Something she couldn't understand but knew she should.

It was there, bubbling just underneath the surface of her mind. If she could just reach it, then she could stop whatever was going to happen. But she couldn't *remember*, something to do with a guardian, and with the longing for waves that crashed through her mind until she couldn't think of anything at all except—

Saoirse lunged forward and snatched the coin from midair.

Time slowed. The other people in the bar leaned forward in anticipation but their eyes didn't dance the way they had. Declan slowly turned his head towards her, and that pointed grin spread impossibly wide.

"You're smarter than you look," he mouthed. "Good luck. And if you have need of me, remember the coin."

She blinked, and time started up again. Manus lunged forward. His hands closed around empty space where the leprechaun had sat only moments ago. The coin in Saoirse's fingers disappeared. Vanished, just like its owner.

"Bloody hell," Manus grumbled, running a hand over his head. "What was that thing?"

"A leprechaun."

"What?" His eyes grew wide. Slowly, he sank onto the bench in front of her. His hands were shaking again. "Tell me you jest."

"What's wrong with leprechauns?"

"They're cursed creatures! And you—" he paused, lunged forward, and turned her hands over. "You touched the coin. It's not still on you is it?"

"No."

He must have heard the hesitation in her voice. His gaze snapped towards her, narrowing at her innocent expression. "What aren't you telling me?"

"The coin is gone, Manus. I touched it, but it disappeared with him."

He searched her eyes for a lie that he would never find. Faeries couldn't lie. With a sigh, he slumped back and let her hands drop to the table.

Saoirse sipped at her own tankard of ale. She lamented the frailty of humans and their foolishness. Manus knew faeries, he understood their ways, and even he did not consider she might twist the truth.

The merrow coin heated against her sternum, a reminder that the leprechaun had left his mark, whether Manus wanted him to. There would always be a bond, an undeniable connection.

She didn't want to wonder why she took the offer. Manus could protect her, he had been all day. But there was still an unease that settled deep within her stomach. This wasn't her homeland, and she knew nothing of their ways.

It would be good to have her own kind looking after her.

"We should just go home," Manus grumbled. He tossed the tankard back and let it slam down on the table. "Let's go."

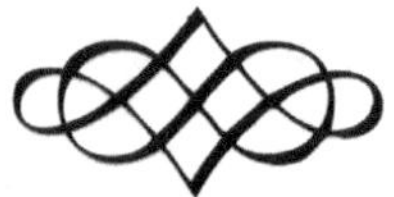

Manus stared at the rotting roof and wondered why it had taken him so long to get here.

He'd made a promise, and he prided himself on being a man of his word. So why hadn't he shown up on this doorstep weeks ago?

Because he was also a coward, he admitted to himself. The thought of telling Arturo's wife he wasn't returning tore at Manus's soul. It wasn't fair. Of all the men to survive that wreckage, Arturo should have been that man.

Instead, his body lay at the bottom of the sea. His bones were likely picked clean by fish and those merrow men who still haunted his nightmares. It wasn't a fitting end for such an honorable, good man.

What was he going to say?

"Your husband was the best man I've ever had the pleasure of sailing with," he tried. "No, that's not right. I wasn't in love with the man."

What else could he tell her? Arturo was like a brother and it was a damn shame he wasn't here anymore.

A cry drifted through the window into the night air. Manus winced. The baby would grow up without a father, and that was even more of a damn shame. He knew the pain first hand. The child deserved someone who loved it.

He straightened his jacket, stepped up the small stairs leading into Arturo's home, and knocked.

It took a few seconds for his wife to open the door, and Manus realized he'd never asked her name.

She was a pretty little thing with a splash of freckles across her cheeks and hair the color of gold. In her hand she held a broom, dust covering her simple gown.

"Can I help you?" she asked.

His tongue refused to work. In her eyes, he saw his own future. A pretty little wife, a babe, a small cottage by the sea. A wife who lived alone because her husband disappeared every chance he could get.

A wife who would inevitably find herself alone and starving.

"Och, you're looking a wee bit pale there," she muttered. "Come in with you."

"I really shouldn't—"

"In." Her stern tone reminded him of his mother.

Manus let himself be pulled into her humble home and almost closed his eyes as a pang of pain struck him in the chest. This was the place Arturo spoke of so often.

It was a quaint little house, as his friend had claimed. Pretty and filled with a woman's touch. Small tapestries hung from the walls, a hand stitched quilt over the small bed. Even the cups were painted with flowers.

The baby cried again, and Arturo's wife raced towards the crib. "Sorry, it's her feeding time and I can't miss it, or she gets grouchy."

He watched her life the tiny bundle into her arms and coo. In his mind, he filled in her image with that of Saoirse. His merrow would look wonderful with a few children, a life.

"It's all right," he murmured as she turned away from him. "Take your time."

"I apologize, I'm usually better with guests. Are you a friend of Arturo's?"

He tripped over his words, "I-Well-Yes. Yes, I was."

Her spine stiffened. "He's not coming back I take it."

This was the moment. His moment to stay true to his word and be a better man. The words stuck on his tongue, his throat closing in anxiety.

"He talked about you all the time," he said. "You were never far from his mind, even in the end."

"Was it quick?"

The baby reached around her mother and took a handful of cloth in her chubby fist. He fixated on the movement and realized he couldn't lie. "No, ma'am it was not."

She sighed. "How did it happen?"

"The ship sank. And I know it sounds crazy, but we sailed into faerie waters. I was the only one who survived, and only because a faerie saw fit to save my life."

Arturo's wife draped a blanket over her shoulder and chest, then turned to look him in the eye. "Why you?"

"I don't know."

"You say a faerie saved you, but the same faerie didn't save my husband?"

"*She* doesn't understand why she saved me. I've asked her a hundred times and every time it's the same answer. She doesn't know."

Silence stung his ears as Arturo's wife looked him up and down. The baby shifted under the blanket, drawing his eyes to the daughter his friend would never see.

Manus cleared his throat. "He said to tell you how much he loved you, and trust me he did. He never stopped talking about you, the child, the life you were going to build together."

"And yet he always went back to the sea," she replied. "He always took his life in his own hands, and I told him it would be the end of him. Of us."

Tears shimmered in her eyes, tearing at his heart until he felt as though he was laid bare before her.

"I'm sorry," he croaked. "For everything."

"It wasn't your fault that he heard sirens calling his name. But I thank you for bringing his message."

He turned on his heel, incapable of walking fast enough. Manus wanted to leave this house filled to the brim with emotions and dark memories.

"Oh, sailor?"

He paused at her doorstep.

"Take care of that lass who has you all tied up in knots. Don't be like my Arturo. Be there for her when the storms come a'calling."

The haunting words rang in his ears as he fled her doorstep and raced towards home.

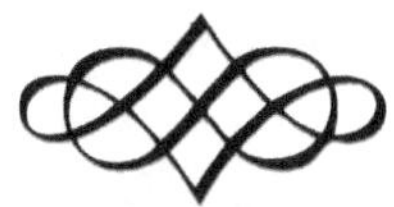

Saoirse stood at the end of the rickety dock, white nightgown whipping around her legs and lashing behind her like the great tail of a guardian. She hugged her arms firmly around her waist. The waves crashed upon the shore in great slaps, bringing with them the silver light of the moon.

Her dark eyes scanned the horizon, searching for something she couldn't name. It wasn't her family. Though she appreciated their memories, she could not condone their lives. The elixir of freedom still flowed through her veins. That life was no longer hers.

So, what was it? What was she looking for? Something deep within her soul yearned for more, but she didn't know what the *more* was.

She dug her fingers into her sides.

A hole ripped open deep inside the fiber of her being. She didn't know what the ache was, couldn't name it or point to the place where it hurt. Yet, there it was. The aching burn of the unknown.

Bare feet padded down the worn planks. Each heavy thump of heel against wood reminded her that she was not alone. That her life was no longer only hers.

Not anymore.

Manus heaved a sigh behind her and wrapped his arms around her waist. His heat sank into her back, easing the tense muscles of her spine instantly. His chin settled on her shoulder as he snuggled her tighter in his arms.

"What is it, my pearl?"

"Hm?" Saoirse hummed the quiet sound. "What do you mean?"

"You're brooding."

"Brooding? I wouldn't even know how to do that." She felt his chest expand in a great sigh that tickled the side of her neck.

"Do you miss them?"

Saoirse hesitated a moment. "I miss aspects of them. Some of them were kind even if their thoughts were backwards."

"Would you go back?"

"Never." She shook her head. "I couldn't go back under the waves after seeing all that I have. This place, with all its dirt and secrets, is still beautiful."

He reached forward and tucked a strand of hair behind her ear, tugging lightly on her lobe. "Your ability to always see the good in things is the first thing I adored about you. Did you know that?"

"Other people can see goodness in the world."

"Not like you do." He squeezed her waist and blew out another breath against her neck. "I should apologize for my behavior today."

"I understand why you yelled."

And she did. Saoirse understood that she was a rare creature in this place. He worried she would disappear with the merest puff of wind. She didn't agree with him but understood why he was nervous.

He had shaken with the mere thought of losing her. That alone told her all she needed to know about his feelings even if he could never verbalize them.

"No," he muttered. "It's not enough. I acted like a cad, and I had no right to do it."

"You were worried about me."

"And there are better ways to handle it. I've never had a… lady."

She turned in his arms and hooked them around his neck. His words vibrated with sadness, fear, and something else she could not name. It tasted like salt water on her tongue and the bitter remains of seashells.

"I don't know what you're trying to say Manus."

"It's just that… Well, fine. I'll just say it and you take it as you will. I've never considered myself a man who might marry. I spent my time with ladies I paid, and none of them were mine. I didn't have to worry about losing them because I never had them in the first place. You understand?"

"I think I'm following," she said, trying her best to keep amusement from her voice.

"When I saw you with that artisan I wanted to spin his head around. He was *touching* you and although I still have no right to say what you can or cannot do, but I wanted to toss you over my shoulder and lock you away from any other man's eyes. I'm not *used* to that, Saoirse."

She watched him struggle to formulate the words. They moved so fast through his lips that she could barely understand them, but it didn't matter. She could feel the words as they brushed through her mind and tingled in the base of her spine.

He cared. He cared so much it turned him into a different person, and he couldn't understand it.

That was okay. She could deal with that.

Saoirse stood on tiptoes and pressed her lips against his. The kiss was chaste and soft, sweet like all the things she did.

"It's okay," she whispered against him. "All is forgiven."

"It is?"

"I could never stay mad at you for too long, Manus. I crossed the seas for you, and nothing will ever change that."

His hands slid down her spine, holding onto her ribs with a touch so gentle it nearly brought tears to her eyes. "What did I ever do to deserve you?"

"You pleased a god."

"Indeed, I must have. For you have a heart large enough to heal the wounded edges of mine." He leaned down and kissed her until her toes curled.

She loved this man. Loved him painfully, achingly, and so thoroughly that it made her worry for her soul.

CHAPTER 8
The Price of Gold

Saoirse blearily blinked her eyes open. She stared up at the ceiling, her mind racing to catch up.

They had lived in the shack for a while, but she was hungry now. Last night, Manus had shaken his head when she asked for a bit of bread. Instead, he'd given her water and tucked her under the covers.

"The water will fill your belly," he'd murmured. "I'll try to figure something out while you're asleep."

But it wasn't better. Her stomach gnawed at itself as if it could eat her body instead of food. It hurt so much that she worried it might kill her.

What had awoken her?

Saoirse restlessly moved her legs, touching a solid warm weight at her feet.

"Manus," she said. "Are you back?"

"I'd hoped to keep you innocent of this," he replied. "I'd hoped to keep you safe."

She tilted her head. He sat with his head in his hands, barely perched on the bed. His spine was a soft curve, coiled in on himself in shame and defeat. She could sense the emotions heavy in the air, so thick it clogged her senses.

"You didn't find food."

"There are no jobs for a man who was born to be a sailor. They all know me. I can't farm, I can't be a shop keep, I don't have any skills."

She reached down and rubbed her hand down his spine. "Then we will find another way."

"There's only one other way, and I am loath to beg you to put yourself in danger."

"Danger? What would put me in danger?"

He turned, gathered her hands in his, and cleared his throat. "On the isle, you used to bring me gold and gems. You'd find all those beautiful coins and treat them as if they weren't important. But they are here. It's how we pay for food, for drink, for everything we have."

"I understand the concept of money, Manus."

"I don't have money." His cheeks reddened. "I think I'm past the point of poor, and closer to just waiting for death. I spent everything I had, and I can't find any way to replace it."

Saoirse blinked, lights flickering to life in her mind. "You want me to find more gold."

"Is it even possible? There cannot be many shipwrecks around here."

"There are always shipwrecks. But Manus, going into the water isn't just dangerous. It's deadly for me. If any of your people see me—"

"They won't. I won't let them see you. We'll take a small boat, row offshore, no one will know what you're doing until we return. And even then, we'll say it's your inheritance."

"My what?" She cocked her head to the side in confusion.

"It's customary for women to have some kind of dowry when they get married. For most in this area it's livestock, but everyone already thinks you're some kind of noble. It wouldn't be a surprise for you to have a treasury to your name."

His eyes were strangely heated as though a fever ran through his veins. She'd never seen him like this before. Not even on the isle when she had brought him fistfuls of sparkling necklaces and priceless jewels.

That her family might find her was a very real danger. It was, however, unlikely they would come this far north. At the least, she might be spotted by a few sharks who would tattle. It wasn't the end of the world.

"It can only be one time," she said. "Once my family catches wind of where I am, then I can't go back in the water."

"Would they already know?"

"I don't think so." She hoped not. Her legs already itched, desperately wanting to free themselves from the confines of humanity. Saoirse wanted to feel the water gliding along her skin again. "We would have seen them by now."

The shack was too close to the water. Merrow men could walk to it, and their strength was still massive on land. Considering they hadn't been raided yet, Saoirse thought it safe to say her father didn't know where she had run off to.

Manus squeezed her hands. "You'd be saving us. I understand it's a lot to ask from you, but Saoirse, we'd be set for life."

"How much do you want me to get?"

"It's just once? You're certain?"

She nodded.

"Then whatever we can find. All of it. I have a few mates from back in the day who have an extra dingy, and we can pay them to keep their silence."

"Manus." She licked her lips. "Where are we going to put it? There's nowhere safe here."

"You let me worry about that. I've got friends in high places, though they won't admit to knowing me yet. Once we have money, people will flock to help us. We just need to get it." He lifted a hand and slid his fingers along her jaw, into her hair. "So, you'll do this?"

"If this is what you want."

"I want to take care of you. I want to give you a life you deserve, but I can't do it alone, my pearl." He tugged the back of her neck and pressed their foreheads against each other. "You are a blessing, Saoirse."

She didn't feel like a blessing. Her entire body ached from hunger, and she knew he was in no better state. Manus's cheeks were gaunt, his ribcage visible, and he moved slower than he used to. They needed something to change.

Apparently, it was her turn to save them.

Swinging her legs over the edge of the bed, she held onto his shoulder to balance herself. "I'll need to be far away from any ships, and even then, you have to make sure no one sees me."

"I can get the boat. Get yourself ready."

They helped each other stand, and Manus rushed out of the door.

Saoirse didn't need to prepare herself. There was nothing here which would assist her in the ocean. The sharp knives in the corner were good for human food, but they wouldn't stand a chance against a shark or an orca.

She bit her lip and twisted her fingers together. Was this a good idea?

So much could go wrong. So much could happen under the surface where Manus couldn't see her. If her family found her again…

No. She wouldn't let herself think like that. Athair would have sent every merrow man he could to retrieve her. Not because she was special or rare, but because she had betrayed him in every sense. If he knew where she was, he wouldn't rest until she was back in the depths, locked away for life.

A shiver danced down her spine. No matter what, she would never allow that to happen. The waters here were cold, the current strong. Merrow men wouldn't be able to find her.

"I can do this," she whispered.

The pounding of approaching feet echoed, and the door opened to reveal Manus's lanky form. "Are you ready?"

She nodded.

"You don't need to change?"

Saoirse looked down at herself, taking stock of the plain blue linen dress, and shrugged. "It's coming off anyways."

His mouth gaped open for a moment before he shook himself. "That's right. Strange how quickly I can forget that you aren't human. For a second I worried you would grow cold."

"The water is my home, Manus. It will never feel cold."

She let him take her hand and guide her from the small shack. An ancient boat was tied to the dock with a frayed rope. It hardly looked safe although she didn't worry for herself. Saoirse could always survive, but he was a little more sensitive to the dangers of the ocean.

"Is it safe?" she asked as she padded down the dock. "It looks as though it should have been put to rest long ago."

"I wouldn't take it out into open waters, but it'll carry us away from the shore safe enough. Give me your hand."

Saoirse took the offered assistance and let him lower her into the belly of the boat. She tucked her legs underneath her, smoothed her skirt, and watched as he clambered in with her.

The oars lifted and settled into the water soundlessly. Each rise sent droplets skittering across the calm waters of the bay. The water streaked pink as the sun lifted its head and kissed the sky.

She thought the waves were calm in slumber, then realized she was wrong. It was holding its breath, waiting for the moment when she would dip her toes in once again. The merrow was returning to the grasp of her great mother. The ocean knew what she was doing, and it watched her with a solemn gaze.

Manus steered their boat through ships with limp sails, past seals which popped their heads out of the water and peered at them. Glassy eyes met hers and Saoirse felt her soul take flight.

She had missed this. The world under the waves was one so rare, so beautiful, that it tore at a person's soul to leave it.

The guardian had been right. Every moment she was away from the ocean felt as though she was inhaling shallow breaths. Her life was dull and colorless.

"Saoirse," his deep voice broke through her reveries. "Here's good enough."

She turned her gaze towards him, and the world bloomed into color. Perhaps she would never understand what it was about him that called to her, but his very existence was a siren call she could not resist. He was color, life, and magic all wrapped in one being who made little sense.

Now, she would dive into the water and risk her life to keep him alive. Nodding, she reached for the hem of her dress, only to pause when he grabbed onto her wrist.

"Just—" he hesitated. "Be careful."

"I'll do my best. The ocean is not a very safe place."

He bit his lip, white teeth worrying at the full flesh. "Come back to me."

Did he think she was going to leave for good? Saoirse could never leave his side, no matter how much she wanted to return to her home. Life wasn't worth living without the other half of her soul.

She reached out and pressed her palm to his cheek. "I will always come back to you, mo ghaol. Never fear that."

My love.

She shouldn't have said it. Her heart was already on the line when it came to Manus. He owned so much of her that Saoirse worried she would completely disappear. And yet, it was the truth.

Love for him shone so brightly within her chest that he must have seen it. Judging by the stunned expression on his face, she doubted he'd even guessed.

"I should have said it sooner," she murmured. "Perhaps in a hundred different ways as well. I don't mean it as a goodbye, I hope you know that."

He said nothing. Instead, he kept staring at her with that dumbfounded expression that set her teeth on edge.

Saoirse took a deep breath and yanked her dress over her head. The light blue linen drifted through the air and landed in Manus's lap as light as a feather. She didn't hesitate. Saoirse dove into the water in a curving arc and created no ripple when she disappeared underneath the waves.

Happiness, so vivid it was almost painful, splashed through her body. It tingled on her skull where her hair lifted up. It effervesced down her spine and lashed her legs together, yet it did not hurt. All she felt was euphoria as scales rippled down into a billowing fluke.

Her tail was powerful and strong. It flexed at the merest whim of her mind and propelled her through the icy ocean. Down and down she went, stretching her arms out so the ocean could stroke more of her body. This was where she belonged. This was where she had been born, and she'd missed it so desperately. She hadn't realized it was the cause of her unhappiness.

Bright bubbles of laughter exploded from her lips. *Home.* She was finally home.

At the bottom of the ocean, she paused and looked back up at the surface where a single small boat bobbed in the middle of a vast nothingness.

It was difficult to be a creature of two souls, she mused. They both longed for the freedom of the ocean and the whip of salty air. And they were both bound by chains. His of desire for wealth and comfort, hers for safety and love.

Her thoughts turned dark, her expression wistful. If only there was a way to save them both. As it was, the only thing she could do was bring back fistfuls of gold.

A pit in the bottom of her stomach suggested this wouldn't help at all. That in the end, all it was going to do boxas create more trouble.

Money was a dangerous thing for humans. She'd seen them spend it wastefully at the market, haggle over prices, buying things they didn't need for people who couldn't care less. Yet, they always bought the thing that meant very little.

Her gills flared in a deep inhale. This was the only way, she reminded herself.

She turned and let the current take her where it wanted to go. Sunken ships always found themselves in the same area. The ocean moved the puzzle pieces beneath the waves wherever it wanted them to go.

Jagged stone jutted out of the ocean floor, bracketed by long strands of kelp that nearly reached the surface. There wasn't as much ocean life here as her home. A few fish wiggled past and brushed against her sides, but there weren't many whales or dolphins.

A jellyfish touched her head with its long tendrils. The zap of electricity made her giggle and bat the strands away.

"Go on," she chuckled. "Off with you, I'm not your newest meal!"

If a jellyfish could look put out, this one did. It sullenly floated away.

Saoirse flexed her muscles and sped through the water. She curved her arms in front of her, spinning as she swam. Barrel rolls were always her favorite trick, and the dolphins loved to watch her spin.

There were no dolphins here; not yet. She could hear their joyous laughter echoing from some far-off space. They were followed by the melancholy cry of a whale and then sudden silence.

A ship loomed in the distance. Its shape was little more than broken masts and dark shadows, but she remembered it from her first trip here. A great beast lurking in the depths.

Saoirse couldn't guess how long ago it was laid to rest. Chunks of the sides were missing, stolen by the ocean and sea creatures. A crack ran down the center of the ship, two halves of a whole spilling out the guts of gold and gems.

She had never felt uncomfortable near a wreck before. The ships were dead—a memory rather than a real thing.

This one sang a song she did not like. It wailed through the currents with forgotten screams and anguished cries. The souls of the dying stayed with this creature of wood.

Floating upright, she hesitated in the foggy water. Was there movement in the depths? She couldn't make out what kind of creature it was but was certain she saw a fin. It didn't look like any sea creature she had ever seen before.

Chests full of gold waited just outside the ship. They must have tumbled from within when the deck cracked in half. She could swim and grab whatever she could hold.

As much as she was enjoying being herself again, Saoirse didn't want to linger in this place. It was terrifying and far too dangerous for her liking.

She pressed her hands against her belly and started forward. Slowly, so as not to frighten whatever lingered within the depths.

Nearby, the ancient sails were flapping in the currents. She could use them as some kind of bag to carry all the gold. It would be a long and arduous journey with so much weight, but it would only need to be one trip. Gritting her teeth, she tugged the fabric free from the confines of dirt and muck. Though it was only a small piece, it would do.

Saoirse hesitated. Fear made her stomach clench, nearly doubling her over with pain.

She rushed forward and thrust handfuls of coins to the center of the sail. She would tie it later, but for now, she needed to rush. A sense of urgency pressed down upon her shoulder, digging into the base of her skull.

"A little one has come to visit?" The voice drifted out of the ragged remains of the ship. "A merrow, perhaps?"

Saoirse froze with her hands on the wealth spilling to the sea floor. Her eyes locked on the shadows moving in the ship. Could it be coiled tentacles? There wasn't a creature with a shape like that, not one that she knew of. Was this some beast even the faeries had forgotten long ago?

Glowing yellow eyes blinked open, then another set, until a horde of yellow eyes stared at her through the writhing darkness. Thick, ropey bodies twisted in a mass. The eels were knotted around each other, clustered so tightly together Saoirse couldn't tell where one started, and where one began.

"Will you not respond?" The voice asked. "I so love a pretty little merrow's voice."

She shivered. "I only speak to those I can see. Who are you?"

"*What am I*, is your real question. Is it not?"

"Few creatures could exist at such depths. I am curious as to what you might be, but I mean no disrespect."

"Move, my lovelies."

The eels undulated in agitation, shifting and snapping their jaws until they parted in the middle like a curtain. Saoirse still couldn't see through the shadows, but she knew something lurked there. Something stared at her through the black mire.

A pale white hand emerged. It clasped the back of a thick eel and flexed. Sharp bones pushed at the thin skin, standing out in stark relief. The creature pulled itself from its home within the nest of eels, revealing long white hair and an emaciated body which was vaguely human although far too thin to boast of such beginnings.

It crawled over the thick eel bodies, grunting as it slid to the sea floor and pushed up onto its arms.

Saoirse had heard of such creatures, although only in legend. The bean sídhes stayed on land. They wailed a warning to all hunted by death. Their haunting cries could be heard in the early light of morning, or the sudden darkness and despair of night.

They were not meant to drown. They couldn't die, not really, but they could rot at the bottom of the ocean for all eternity if they were banished there.

Whatever this woman had done must have been a terrible and grievous crime for such a punishment. And surely it was a woman, for her form might be emaciated but Saoirse could see the sagging skin where curves may once have been.

Clawed hands sank into the muck that squished through the skeletal fingers. "Why have you come here?"

"I wish only to share in your wealth, honored maiden." Saoirse bent at the waist in a bow few merrows could hold.

"My wealth? What use does a merrow have for such a thing?" The bean sídhe pushed herself up onto hands and knees, then stood. She was tall and lithe, perhaps a beauty when she was on land.

"I have a lover, a human who desires to live in comfort."

"Humans are a waste of space. They drove us from our lands, turned us into little more than animals who feast upon their scraps."

"He is not like the others," Saoirse said, twisting her fingers together.

"They're all the same, child." The bean sídhe leveled her with a chastising look. "Don't blind yourself to their flaws."

"I love him," Saoirse blurted. "With all that I am."

"Love? Love is a figment of our imaginations, you know faeries cannot love."

"I think we can. I think we've been told for so long that such a blessing is only for the humans, and we've forgotten it's possible. It's so strong, I feel it in my fingers." She held out her hands as if they might glow from the powerful emotion bursting at her seams. "He is everything."

The bean sídhe tsked. The sound floated in a bubble from her mouth and burst in an echoing call. "I've seen faeries like you before. The stories never end well."

Curiosity dug into the base of Saoirse's skull. She hesitated, her fingers curling in the gold, and finally murmured, "What happened to them?"

A smile curled across the bean sídhe's face. It was raw, ragged, and filled with so much hunger that Saoirse flinched back.

"They died," the faerie replied. "They tied themselves to a human whose life would end someday. You know they only live fifty or so years? A hundred if you're lucky, but those are rare cases. Humans are fragile creatures. One moment they're with you, and then?" The bean sídhe snapped her fingers. "Gone, like a candle snuffed by a careless hand."

"The faeries died?" Saoirse asked. "How is that possible? Surely, they could have returned to their homes, back to where they came from. Did their families shun them?"

"Oh, you're so sweet." An eel untangled itself from the others and draped itself across the bean sídhe's shoulders. "They died of a broken heart, my dear. Faeries love with their entire being, and you said it yourself. He's part of you now, a light that drives you forward. What did you think would happen when he dies?"

She hadn't thought about it. Manus always vibrated with life why would death come for him? But it would, someday.

Saoirse felt like a fool. She should have realized he would die, and the repercussions of that. By falling in love with a human, she had cut her own life short.

The bean sídhe let out a shrieking laugh. "You didn't know? Or you hadn't thought what that truly entailed? Little merrow, you must be the most foolish of creatures to bind yourself to one with limited time."

"No," Saoirse said and shook her head. "I will not regret my decision. I love him, and life without love is meaningless. I would take a short life with him than a long life alone."

The other faerie spun so her back was turned towards Saoirse. Her spine was straight, long white hair floating around her and crackling with electricity. An eel slid around her arm and stared back at Saoirse with a cold gaze.

"I—" Saoirse cleared her throat. "I didn't mean to offend, maiden."

"You did."

"I am frequently careless with my words. I should learn to think before I speak."

"You should." The bean sídhe held up a hand, her shoulders oddly stiff and her body unmoving. "Take what you want and go."

Saoirse tied up the sail and stuffed it to the brim. She hefted the bag over her shoulder, grunting at the weight but not wanting to give the bean sídhe time to change her mind.

"Thank you," she quietly said.

"You are a cursed faerie," the bean sídhe replied. "Your human has a soul, you know. I've seen them. White, ephemeral things that drift through our world for all eternity. But you?"

Saoirse found herself caught in a gaze as black as the deepest abyss. The bean sídhe glowed, her hair emitting a light that illuminated the ship and all its shadows. Thousands of eels twisted and turned, their sharp teeth gnashing and tails whipping.

The bean sídhe bared her own teeth as pointed as the eels. "You have no soul because you are one of the Fae. When you die, you will turn into sea foam in a final death no one can save you from. Remember that when you return to your warm bed."

Emotions she couldn't name rushing through her, Saoirse fled from the cursed shipwreck. The bean sídhe was a cruel creature, lonely and tired after so many years of banishment. Her words were meant to bite and harm.

Unfortunately, they succeeded.

Saoirse felt niggling worms of doubt sinking into her flesh and through her resolve. They punctured holes in the future she had seen for herself until it unraveled like a threadbare sheet.

Death? She'd never even considered it. Fae didn't worry about dying. They were as good as immortal although they could be killed in war. Merrows had very few natural predators and could live thousands of years. She'd known some that seemed as old as the ocean.

She shuddered. Manus would age, it was what humans did. They grew weaker and tired as death slowly sucked away what little life they had.

In bonding with him, she'd given herself the same fate. She would age, she would grow tired, and she would feel hunger so painful it made her entire body hurt.

The physical toll of carrying the heavy bag of gold sent electric pangs skittering from her abdomen to the top of her skull. Unthinking, she grabbed the nearest fish and tore the soft flesh from its side with her teeth. It stopped struggling immediately, part trauma and part weak thrum of death.

She couldn't stop eating it, tearing away until the fish was little more than bones. Only then did the reality set it. She'd killed it and lie bled out from between her fingers.

Someday, she would meet another creature who could kill her. Be that a bean sídhe wailing in the night, the Morrighan herself, or a careless human. No matter what it was, someday she would fade.

"No soul?" she whispered into the murk of the ocean.

Did she really not have a soul? She felt very similar to humans, always had, so certainly there was something? She was a faerie capable of love. That had to count for the god the humans prayed to.

Her meal fueled her muscles and helped propel her to the surface. The sail dug into her shoulder, leaving red welts that might take days to heal. Saoirse gritted her teeth and found Manus's small boat.

It was vaguely where she'd left it, having shifted with the waves and drifted on the currents. The outline was as dark as the shadows in the depths, but somehow filled with a life she could see through the wood.

He leaned over the edge, strong hands grasping the rim of the boat as he tried to peer through the water to find her.

All at once, everything was all right. Her fears abated in the wake of love so powerful it burned her lungs and made her gills flare wide.

It was worth it, losing immortality and the inevitable fear of what might come. It was entirely worth it to know he existed and to feel this tingling emotion of love so vibrant and pure.

Air kissed her cheeks as she surfaced, and sunlight danced across her forehead. Saoirse blew out air to seal the gills flat to her neck. She grunted, lifted an arm, and hooked it over the edge of the boat.

"Manus," she called out. "Come and take this, please."

"Saoirse?"

His beloved face leaned over the side, staring down at her with an expression she couldn't name.

"It's heavy." She lifted a shoulder to show the makeshift pack. "Take it, I think I got more than enough."

He hefted the weight up and off her, shoving it into the center of the ship before leaning down for her.

"Come here," he murmured. "I've got you."

Manus slid his hands underneath her arms and effortlessly pulled her into the boat. His biceps flexed, sunlight bouncing off his caramel colored skin. But it was the warmth she saw in his eyes that made her sigh in happiness.

"Wait," she said. "Hold me on the edge please."

"Why?"

"My tail, it needs to slide off and if we're in the boat, I'm not sure we'll get it out." The mucus wasn't pleasant on the best of days. She couldn't imagine trying to pick it out of the boards.

"Ah," he mumbled.

His arms slide underneath hers and he nudged her backward so she could lean against his chest. He rested his chin against her shoulder while they watched the sun rise.

"Manus?" she asked.

"What is it, my pearl?"

"I'm glad I'm here."

He hadn't asked her if there was danger under the waves. He must have felt her trembling, seen the raw fear in her gaze, understood she didn't wish to give the terrors a voice. Instead, he held her safe and quiet against his heart.

"I'm glad too."

"And someday…" She inhaled a deep salty breath. "Someday, when we're both old and tired, I will look back on this moment and know that above all else, I made the right decision to choose you."

He squeezed her waist, a man of few words and even fewer

emotions. But he understood her. She was certain of it.

"Good," his baritone vibrated in her ear. "Because I'm going to treat you like a queen."

"Where are we again?" Saoirse asked.

She stared up the tall building and tried not to be afraid of the gargoyles standing at attention. The stone steps felt strange against her bare feet. Manus had argued she needed shoes, but no one could see her feet anyways. The dress he poured over her head this morning was so long it brushed the ground. Would someone be lifting her gown to check?

He grumbled but allowed her the freedom to walk barefoot as she desired.

"This is the O'Sullivan manor. They're an old family in these parts, have been in the area for centuries."

"And what are we asking them to do?"

"He manages a bank. They'll be able to help us keep all these riches safe."

"Will he?" Saoirse looked up at Manus. She felt his nerves running through her like the rising tide. "You don't seem as confident as I thought you might be."

"O'Sullivan does not particularly like me."

"Why?"

A red blush stained Manus's cheeks. "I slept with his wife."

"I don't see why sleeping would be an issue." At his pointed expression, she nodded. "Ah. Not that kind of sleeping."

"Most men do not appreciate meeting others who know their wife as intimately as they do."

"Would you like it if another man knew me in such a way?"

He froze with his hand lifted to the door. His brows drew down, his spine straightened, and a ripple of tension spread up his spine into his shoulders. Saoirse watched in fascination as his raised hand curled into a fist and the knuckles turned white.

"I'd kill any man who touched you like that."

"Do you think he feels the same?" She radiated innocence, blinking up at him with large dark eyes.

Saoirse knew what she was doing. Manus thought poorly of people immediately upon meeting them. He could be cruel at times, unthinking in his endless judgment. She softened him with a mere word or comparison.

Manus shook his head. "I don't think O'Sullivan has ever been the killing type. It would get his hands dirty, and he's far too delicate for that."

He pounded on the door three times and took a few steps back.

Saoirse wasn't certain why Manus was so nervous. His fingers tapped against his pant legs and he looked uncomfortable in the tight black suit that hardly fit his broad frame. Her own yellow dress was too tight at the waist and made breathing difficult. Yet, for some strange reason she couldn't understand, he insisted they dress this way.

It made little sense. Why would they willingly wear clothes they didn't like? Why couldn't they be comfortable, like everyone else?

But this was the way of humans, and yet another thing she would need to learn.

The door cracked open and a pinched face appeared. The man stared at them for a few seconds before slowly closing the door.

Manus leaped forward and stuck his foot in the way. "I'm here to see O'Sullivan."

"The master isn't taking any visitors."

"He'll want to speak with me."

"I don't think so, sir. Do you have an appointment?"

Growling, Manus set his shoulder against the sturdy door and shoved hard. Saoirse could hear the man stumble back, strike a solid object, and curse.

"You have no right to force your way into this house—"

"I do when it's O'Sullivan. Tell him I'm here."

"Manus," she chastised, although it was likely too late. The man had already stiffened his spine, sniffed disdainfully, and disappeared around the corner. "Perhaps we might have been a little kinder in our treatment of the poor man?"

"He works for O'Sullivan, he gets worse than that on a daily basis."

"Are you certain? He appeared quite frightened, and I have no wish to harm anyone."

Manus stroked her jaw with a finger. "Let me deal with this, my pearl. These are my people, not yours, and I know how they work. Come with me."

"Where?"

He did not answer. Instead, Manus took her hand and laid it on his forearm. Together, they walked down the narrow hall into a wide room with seating arranged around it. Saoirse stared all around her at the bright splashes of color, the ornately carved chairs, and a large contraption in the back with what looked like wings held down by cords.

A thick carpet cushioned her feet. The pattern was one she did not recognize. Orange, red, yellow, it was a garishly colored piece but one that made the room slightly more welcoming.

"What is that?" She asked, pointing to the strange beast in the corner.

"It's a harp. We play music on it."

"I've seen them before, at the bottom of the sea. The ties were always broken though."

"Strings."

"Hmm?" Saoirse looked up at him with a question in her gaze.

"They're not called ties, they're called strings. You may touch it if you'd like."

"I couldn't. It's not mine." But she desperately wanted to. Her fingers already tingled at the thought. What would it sound like? Deep and sad like whale song? Or high pitched and chattering like that of a dolphin's laughter?

"We're guests here. Besides, we have enough money to replace it if you break it."

She wanted to shake her head, to proclaim she was mature enough to wait until the master of the house gave her permission, but the strings gleamed in the light and the gold curved spine called her like the whisper of a siren. Her fingers tingled until she finally relented.

Saoirse glided across the floor and rounded the harp. She reached out a tentative finger and plucked a string.

The most wholesome tone echoed from the instrument, filling the room with a sound like the beating of butterfly wings. Saoirse's eyes widened, and her soul took flight along with the stunning sound. It made her chest hurt and expand all at the same time.

"You like it?" Manus asked.

She looked up and caught the reverent expression on his face. He stared at her as if she were made of magic. Perhaps she was because she reached out to make the sound again and felt like a goddess.

Settling onto the stool behind her, she scooted as close to the harp as she could. Experimenting with music like this was a rare treat, and one she would consider a gift. Saoirse intended to use every moment to her benefit.

Her fingers danced across the strings, plucking each to create different songs, both tremulous and grand. Once she understood the sounds this strange beast made, she knew how to replicate the music in her mind. She played a merrow lullaby, a whale song, a wail of a sobbing mother, and the sigh of a new bride. The strings hummed against her fingers, urging her to continue.

Finally, she paused. There was still music left inside her, but it didn't want to be released. Not yet. It waited to learn from still silence before creating something anew.

A robust voice broke through the calm. "Bravo! Magnificent, my dear girl."

Her head snapped up so quickly she felt her neck crack. A man stood in the doorway, so large he filled the entire space. His belly stuck out far in front of him and strained the buttons keeping his shirt closed. Strange curled hair graced his upper lip, nearly touching the prominent brows that wisped towards his forehead.

He stepped into the room and Saoirse stared at his oddly thin legs. They weren't proportionate to his body, she mused. Perhaps he was a faerie as well, for he shouldn't be able to remain upright with all his weight in his shoulders and belly.

Saoirse stood, holding herself steady on the harp and swallowing hard. She wanted to apologize but couldn't make the words cross her lips. The music had been so lovely, possibly the most incredible thing she'd experienced thus far on land. She couldn't apologize for finding it.

O'Sullivan flapped a surprisingly small hand in her direction. "Please, my dear, sit back down. Such talent should be rewarded. Manus, I was prepared to throw you out until I discovered this marvelous creature you brought me."

She swallowed and glanced over at Manus, who was clearly having difficulty holding himself together.

"I doubt you could throw me out if you tried, O'Sullivan."

"Is that so? It's been a long time since we rubbed elbows, Manus, but I'm not a poor man anymore. Have you arrived for my wife?" O'Sullivan stared at Saoirse with an angry look in his eyes that made her shiver. "The trade may be agreeable."

"Don't look at her."

"Why not? You couldn't possibly have a claim on such a beauty. She'd have to be mad to waste her time with the likes of you."

Saoirse didn't like the direction of this conversation. Clearing her throat, she made her way around the harp and stood beside Manus.

"Lord O'Sullivan, is it?" she asked.

"You're a sweet thing. I'm no Lord, my dear, but I appreciate the compliment."

Saoirse dipped into a curtsy, as Manus had taught her, and held her breath. He had explained women rarely spoke unless they were spoken to. It was a concept she was familiar with.

Merrow men were like this man with the strange facial hair. They blew up as soon as another male got near them. They wanted to be the biggest, the strongest, the most fearsome male in the ocean no matter what the other looked like.

She could deal with this. This was someone she finally understood and recognized.

"Thank you for excusing our rude entrance to your home," she said in tones dripping honey. "The splendor of this manor is surely enough to grant you the title of Lord."

O'Sullivan chuckled. "Where did you find this little actress, Manus? She's impressively astute. Rise, my dear. Your ploy has reminded me to be a gentleman, for which I thank you."

She rose from her curtsy and focused a bright smile upon the man. "Thank you. And if it pleases you, I should greatly like to address you as my husband does."

The wispy eyebrows lifted to his hairline. "Husband? Good God, what have you done?"

Manus grunted. "Is it so hard to imagine?"

"Frankly, yes. I never thought you'd subject a woman to your company for the rest of her life, let alone one so exquisite. What have you done to the poor girl?"

"Nothing!"

"Are you so certain? No woman in her right mind would agree to live with you—"

Saoirse leapt forward and placed her hand on O'Sullivan's forearm. "Please, pardon my forwardness; I would thoroughly enjoy a tour of your home, O'Sullivan. I have heard many tales of its splendorous attention to detail and would very much like to see it for myself. Was it you who designed such a lovely home?"

He sputtered, mouth gaping open as he tried to respond to her. "I- Well- No my dear, we hired a team of artisans to come and build the entire structure."

"Certainly, you had some say. I can see a man of your intelligence in every piece of this building!"

"Can you?" His mustache twitched.

"Absolutely. And I would love to meet the woman who has captured your heart. Shall we walk and meet her? You can tell me about all the intricacies of this building on the way."

"Manus?" O'Sullivan glanced over her head. "Either she's an incredible actress, or you've caught yourself an angel. Regardless, I find I'm rather unsettled."

"She does that to people."

"Come on, my dear," he said and patted her hand on his arm. "I'll take you through the house and we can meet my wife. I'm uncertain she'll like to see your husband again, but it appears there are topics the men must discuss."

She smiled. "Thank you, O'Sullivan."

"Don't thank me yet. I haven't agreed to whatever request your fool of a husband is about to make."

O'Sullivan guided them through his home, stopping here and there to declare he had assisted in some architecture, he'd designed the parlor, and whatever else he could take credit for. She knew he was trying to impress her, and frankly he did.

She laughed all the way to the small seating room. It was easy to pretend to be this person, the one that cooed at men and calmed their worries. She hated every moment of it.

The banker's wife was a quiet woman, unassuming, with a smile on her face that looked like it might shatter any second. She sat on the couch with a teacup in her hand and trembling hands that clacked the cup against the saucer.

"Husband?"

O'Sullivan waved a hand in the air. "Yes, dear, I am fully aware Manus is here."

"Who is on your arm?"

"His wife." He brought Saoirse forward and gestured for her to take a seat next to his wife. "This is Deirdre, my beloved wife."

"It's lovely to meet you, mistress."

"Decidedly forward, isn't she?" Deirdre glanced at her husband for a moment, and then her eyes turned towards Manus.

Saoirse didn't like the way the other woman's eyes widened in appreciation. Jealousy burned in her chest. This woman had known Manus intimately. In the ways he would kill another man for knowing her.

Why hadn't he thought she might want to kill the woman seated beside her?

Manus followed O'Sullivan to the other side of the room and took the offered glass of amber liquid. Deirdre did not take her eyes off the men.

Saoirse cleared her throat. "I understand you are married to O'Sullivan?"

"The correct way to refer to him is Mister O'Sullivan."

"Ah."

Deidre turned to her with a fiery gaze. "Why are you here?"

"We needed to speak to your husband about a business venture." She repeated what Manus had told her although she didn't understand what it meant. "We believe Mister O'Sullivan might assist us with an investment."

"Manus has no claim to fortune, it was one of his better attributes."

"He does now."

An exclamation from the other side of the room interrupted them.

O'Sullivan set his drink on a warm wooden desk and shouted, "What? You have how much?"

"Keep your voice down, man. There are ladies in the room."

"Where did you get that? I'm not helping you on some get rich scheme where you robbed some poor man blind. Or heaven's forbid, did you *kill* someone for that money?"

"I killed no one, O'Sullivan."

"Then where? You didn't get it riding a ship into the horizon, I'll tell you that. No ships have returned with a cargo that large."

A muscle bounced on his jaw as Manus silently pointed towards Saoirse.

All eyes turned to her. Her cheeks heated in embarrassment, but there wasn't anything she could add. This was the plan. She was the heiress to an immense fortune, one whose father had long ago died and needed a man to marry regardless of his station. She'd added that they'd fallen in love with each other, and Manus agreed.

O'Sullivan cleared his throat. "You? You're the one with the money."

"She's an heiress," Manus explained. "It's old family money, and we obviously can't bury it behind the shack. I must put it somewhere safe, and I'd like to buy a house befitting someone of our station."

"Your station?" O'Sullivan scratched the back of his neck. "You'll have to forgive me, but I cannot reconcile the foolish young want-to-be sailor with a man of wealth and stature."

"Get used to it, old man."

Saoirse stood. "Manus, please. These people have let us into their house and have been perfectly hospitable."

"He's insulting both of us."

"Then let him insult. His words cannot harm us, and I'd much rather he help." She clasped her hands to her chest. "Mister O'Sullivan, any assistance would be greatly appreciated by both of us, no matter what my husband says."

"You want a house and a safe place for your riches," O'Sullivan grunted. "I never thought the day would come."

"Then you'll help us?" Manus asked.

"I'm not pleased about it, but there are a few properties for sale in the area. We could speak to the curators. I'll have to vouch for you."

"And will you?"

Saoirse held her breath, terrified that this man and his wife would turn them down. There were other options, but Manus said O'Sullivan was the most trustworthy. He was a good man at his core.

She heard Deirdre huff out a quiet, sullen breath.

Hands curling into fists, Saoirse reminded herself that she was not human. Merrows did not stoop to the level of human women. She had endured storms, shark attacks, the pawing of merrow men. She could endure the disdain of a woman who had once touched Manus.

Still, every fiber of her being wanted to slash at Deirdre with gnashing teeth and nails.

O'Sullivan nodded. "All right. I'll help you. I want to see where this story goes between the two of you. That's my condition. You stay in touch, Manus."

"Understood."

They clasped forearms, and Saoirse felt a knot unravel in her chest. This was what he wanted, what they both wanted. A normal human life.

Together.

Manus gestured all around, a smile on his face like she'd never seen before. "Well? What do you think? Is it everything you ever dreamed of?"

Saoirse glanced at the gold and white interior. She hadn't ever dreamed of a home, let alone one that made her eyes water. It was too bright. The surfaces were too reflective. Everything about the house was just too much.

But how could she ruin his happiness? Manus loved this home, so much that he already invited people to a dinner party. She didn't even know what a dinner party was.

"It's quite beautiful."

"Beautiful? There are better words that than Saoirse! Magnificent! A feast for the eyes!" He flung his arms out and laughed. "And it's ours. You made this happen, my pearl. I cannot thank you enough."

She made nothing happen. She had stolen from a bean sídhe who didn't need the money any more than they did. Guilt ate at her belly, taking large chunks with each inhale.

"Manus, I think I'd like to go lie down."

"Wait, hold on." He grabbed her arms and held her at arm's length. "I didn't tell you we've hired staff."

"Staff?" Saoirse wrinkled her brows. "What do you mean?"

"People who will work for us. They'll clean the house, manage the gardens, the grounds, everything we need. They'll do it all."

He sounded so excited.

She sighed. "Why do we need people to do all that? We can manage on our own. We have thus far."

"It's not how things are done. I know this is confusing for you, and likely overwhelming. You'll get used to it. I promise." He kissed her forehead, lingering for a few moments. "Now, go on. There's a maid waiting in your room. She'll help you get dressed."

"I want to get *undressed*."

"That's something *I* can help you with." A wolfish grin spread across his face.

"Manus."

"You're right, I have too much to do for such distractions. Go upstairs, I'll see you later tonight."

He spun on his heel and walked out the front door, whistling a jaunty tune.

Saoirse wished she was as happy. The large house felt so empty. The rooms echoed with her steps, so much that she stayed barefoot just for the silence. Statues lined the halls, staring at her with disappointed expressions and vacant eyes.

Now there were more people here? More strangers to wonder where she came from, to pry into her past. She couldn't keep twisting her words and smiling while Manus explained where she came from. Eventually someone would catch her alone, and she wouldn't be able to lie.

Troubled, she made her way up the grand staircase and down the long hallway towards her rooms. She had insisted she only needed one room. Apparently, that was also not done.

Even the doors were different here. Hers had tiny bluebells carved all around it, hand painted and laid with gold leaves.

She paused in front of it and shook her head. It was all too much.

The door opened to reveal another person standing behind it. Saoirse shrieked in surprise, and the other woman let out a gasp, dropping all the clothes in her arms.

"My lady!"

"Who are you?"

The woman ran a hand over her blonde hair and smoothed down her pale dress. "I'm your lady's maid. I thought the master might have told you?"

"Master?"

Saoirse shook her head. Everything was changing, and she didn't know how to feel about it.

The maid blushed. "I'm sorry, did he not inform you I would be here?"

"No, he informed me. I'm just not used to having a lady's maid."

"I can't imagine why not? If the tales are true, you're some far off princess. It's an honor to be waiting on you, my lady."

Princess? Was that what he was telling people now? How was she even meant to respond to that?

Saoirse shook her head and made her way towards the bed. "I would like to rest."

"Of course. Here, allow me to turn down the covers for you. It's rather chilly outside, I can run the coals through the sheets to warm them."

"Please don't. I'll be fine on my own."

"That's what I was hired to do, my lady. Here, let me help with your dress—"

Saoirse couldn't handle this. She couldn't allow another woman to wait on her hand and foot, not while she still had perfectly good hands. "Please. That's enough."

The maid bobbed into a quick curtsy and turned to leave. She hesitated and said, "I appreciate you and Manus hiring me out of the whorehouse. There are some places where the women are treated well, but that was not one of them. This gives me a fresh start."

She disappeared out the door, running as if the Wild Hunt chased her.

Saoirse sank onto the bed. Her bones ached, her heart squeezed, and she felt as though she were ancient. This wasn't the life she had expected. And although there were moments of blooming happiness, there was also a constant river of anguish.

Falling onto her back, she sighed.

This was what her life was supposed to be like, or at least, what her human life should be. She had money, she had a home, she had a doting husband. What more could she want?

All she could think of was a tiny isle with white sand.

CHAPTER 9

PRETENDING TO BE HUMAN

Saoirse hovered in the back of the room, clutching a wine glass close to her chest. There were so *many* people in their home.

Teems of men and women had shown up at the announcement new money had arrived. Already she'd been told their cliff side home was the beloved summer house of a renowned Baron. When his wife had died, he sold the entire plot when his grief grew too powerful for him to survive.

They were saddened by the passing of the Baron and thought it likely his son would wish to buy this land back. Would they be interested in selling?

She'd never met so many rude, noisy people in her life. They flooded into her home, told her how she should look, act, dress, and then swanned off as if they hadn't been insulting.

Finally, Saoirse gave up. She tucked herself into a corner with a glass of port and silently nodded at anyone who tried to speak with her. Let them think she was an uncouth princess, they wouldn't dare start any rumors.

They still thought she was royalty. And apparently that meant more than the quality of her character.

Manus was on the other side of the room talking to a tall man with billowing white hair. They gestured wildly, laughing and swinging their drinks in all directions. It was going well, so it seemed, although Saoirse had no idea who the man was.

She didn't know any of these people, yet she was expected to admit them into her life without complaint.

The port swirled on her tongue, coating her mouth with a heady flavor that calmed her nerves.

"I thought I might find you here." The voice was warm, too forward for any of these strange people who had walked into her life.

She swallowed and glanced up at the tall, red headed man standing beside her. "I didn't think to find *you* here."

"Is it so surprising?" He grinned. "I am, after all, a prince."

He had more of a calling to the title than she did. Declan was dressed as a man of his stature should dress. Tight fitting waistcloth, pale doeskin breeches, a black jacket that barely contained the broad span of his shoulders. Even in the clothes of a noble, he looked more wild animal than most.

"So," she began, "you masquerade as a noble here on earth? Isn't that beside the point?"

"What point?"

"I assume you were sent here to learn a small bit of humility. How are you supposed to learn that if you are still spoiled?"

"I observe them. Humans are a fascinating lot and are so easy to read."

She stared into the crowd filled with swirling colors, wondering just what he saw. Too many of these peoples wore masks instead of faces. They said one thing, but clearly meant another. They whispered behind their fans, pointedly staring at her but refused to explain what captured their attentions.

"I don't know if I agree with you," Saoirse replied. "They seem to hide their true selves, even from those they love. Humans are difficult to understand."

"It gets easier the longer you're among them."

"Does it? I can't imagine understanding them. I prefer our ways."

The feral grin spreading across his face sent a shiver down her spine. Warning bells rang loud and clear. He wasn't one to be trusted, no matter that his glamour was a handsome man. Leprechauns were Unseelie.

She reminded herself not to tempt him. This was the perfect place for an Unseelie to go wild and Manus would be so angry with her.

Declan lifted a hand for her to take. "You have to learn their cues. Human emotions are easily read by the way they use their body, unlike the Fae who are still waters."

"Are you going to teach me?"

"I thought you'd never ask."

She set her glass on a table next to them. "How?"

"We're going to dance."

Dance? She didn't see how that was going to help anything. But she wanted to understand them all, not just Manus. She reached out and placed her gloved hand in his.

Immediately, Declan turned hers over and plucked at the white fabric, pulling it slowly off her hand finger by finger.

"What are you doing?" she gasped. "Manus said it is not appropriate for a woman to be bare handed."

"Precisely. We see their true colors when we challenge their ideals of what is appropriate. Look around us, Saoirse. No, not like that. Don't gape at people as if you don't know what I'm doing, someone will interrupt us. Under your lashes, so no one knows you're even looking at them. Good. Now, how are people reacting?"

She let out a slow breath. "The ladies nearest to us are bright red and holding their fans up so they can talk behind them."

"Are they wildly beating the fans or are they holding them still?"

"Still."

"Good," he said, and finished up removing the first glove. He tucked it into the breast pocket of his jacket and held out his hand for the other. "What of the men?"

"They're watching you rather intently but are not moving."

"And Manus?"

She had to lift her head to find him. Her stomach clenched. "He's still talking to the white-haired man. He hasn't noticed."

Declan pulled off her other glove with a flourish and tucked it away. "Let me summarize for you then. The women wish they were you right now. Their fans are still because they're whispering how scandalous it is that an unmarried man would dare to touch a married woman like this. The men are remaining still because they too are jealous. They have watched you the entire night and thought of doing the same."

"Are you sure?" Saoirse shook her head. "I don't think they care I exist other than as something new to watch."

"That's where you're wrong. And I can prove it to you."

"You can?" She met his heated gaze. "How?"

Declan did not respond. Instead, he peeled off his own gloves with a flourish and held out a bare hand for her to take.

"I couldn't. It's not right."

"You and I are creatures from another world, Saoirse. They can't understand this, nor could they ever understand our connection. We can bend to their ways, or we can show them how faeries dance."

She could already see the imagined anger on Manus's face. Dancing with another man was likely forbidden as well. But Declan sang a siren song she desperately wanted to follow.

Perhaps that was why she felt so out of place. Saoirse was not human. Faeries wouldn't have lied, whispered, and giggled behind fans. They would have had sharpened blades at the ready, perhaps, but at least she would have known their true opinions.

Saoirse reached out and placed her hand atop his.

Warm skin, as smooth as her own, heated her flesh. Declan pulled her onto the dance floor with their hands raised high.

The fans began to flutter, and the men set down their drinks. No one moved yet, but it was painfully obvious the entire crowd held their breath in anticipation. The music played on, the other dancers took their places, and Declan's grin remained in place.

"You knew this would make them unhappy," she muttered.

"Of course I did. Parties like this can only be improved through a little uncomfortable social interaction."

"I have no wish to create waves. Especially not when this night and these people mean something to Manus."

"Manus?" Declan stepped forward as the music started, raising his hand for her to take. "You mean your husband?"

"I don't think there's another Manus in the room."

"Ah, my apologies. I had forgotten he was here."

The words stung. She didn't need to be reminded that her husband had yet to even notice his wife was in the arms of another man. Every turn about the room provided glimpses proving he wasn't looking at her.

"Don't let it bother you too much, love," Declan said. "Human males are so easily distracted."

"And faerie men aren't?"

"I can't say we're perfect, but we certainly know when to pay attention to our mates."

She sighed. "I wish I could agree with you. Merrow men are not fantastic at anything related to their mates."

"Merrow men are barely Fae."

"I think they would disagree with you."

They rounded the line of people, breaking away from each other to new partners for a brief moment. She lifted her hand for a tall, thin man to take, who immediately froze. Bare handed and waiting, she realized he didn't know what to do.

"It's all right," she said, and moved past him into Declan's arms.

"Do you think they know we're different?" He mused. "There has to be a part of their tiny brains that recognizes a predator amongst them."

"Predator? That's a strange way to think of yourself."

"You disagree?"

"I think they would be frightened of anything different. You flatter yourself to think it is because of our species. They don't understand us. If we were human, they would have the same reaction."

"Interesting." His brows furrowed in confusion. "I've never considered that possibility."

"And yet, you proclaim to be talented in reading them."

"Reading them and knowing them are different things, little merrow. Although I'm certain you'll find that out soon enough."

The music stopped, and the partners stepped away from each other. While all others politely clapped, Declan kept ahold of her hand. He forced her to remain close to his side.

"We're done here," she said. "I have nothing else to say to you. Thank you for the distraction, but I don't intend to cause any further scenes."

"You'd rather waste away here pretending to be something you are not?"

"I'm not pretending at all, Declan. This is who I am and always will be. Where I live does not change that."

A gentleman stepped forward, holding his hand against his chest. "My lady, are you quite well?"

"Yes, thank you."

Declan released her hand and took a step back. "Have a lovely evening, my lady."

He strode away without a care in the world. Saoirse wished she felt the same. So many people were staring at her now. She could almost hear their whispered thoughts.

Holding her head high, she moved through the crowd to Manus's side. People parted like a wave before her. None of them said a word, no one tried to catch her attention. They all wondered who she was, this strange creature who was far too beautiful to be likeable. Saoirse was someone they could never understand.

Perhaps Declan was right, in a way. She was trying to fit in, but they weren't likely to ever accept her. They would always sense the faerie in her blood.

She stood beside Manus who did not stop speaking.

"You see, it'll be a good investment for the both of us. The ship will be magnificent, far more profitable than either of us could ever dream. I know the seas—"

"Manus."

"They listen to me. They always have, and if I were captaining your ship, I would take that into consideration. Too many ships are lost because their captain doesn't respect the ocean's power."

"Manus."

The white-haired man nodded at her. "My lady, I'm afraid we have not yet met."

"No."

Manus looked down at her, surprise in his gaze. "Saoirse! I apologize, my pearl, I had forgotten you do not know many people here. May I introduce you to Captain Ramsey?"

She was tired of meeting new people. They were all the same, mistrustful and too curious. Still, she squared her shoulders and forced a smile. "Ramsey is not a name I recognize. I take it you are not from here?"

"My family is from here, but I was raised in the Caribbean."

A warm flood of emotions crashed over her head. Excitedly, she leaned forward and said, "I miss the Caribbean very much. It is a stunning place, and the waters are crystal clear."

The captain lifted his eyebrows. "You've been? I would have taken you as a princess from a much closer province, considering your complexion."

She had said something wrong. He stared at her with suspicious eyes, and Manus rocked back and forth on his feet. But what had she said wrong?

Saoirse glanced up at her husband for clues. When he didn't look down at her, she cleared her throat. "I have traveled all over the world. Although it was not my father's preference that I do so, I believe it important to understand other cultures and beliefs."

It was bending the truth almost to the point of pain. Her tongue pricked with the hints of lies, pain reminding her how fine a line she walked.

Thankfully, the captain seemed pleased with her response.

"Here, here! I see you have married an enlightened woman, Manus. Rare in these parts."

Saoirse heard his quiet sigh of relief. "Yes, indeed. I am a lucky man to have found such a gem."

The captain made his excuses and left to find his wife. The moment he turned his back, Manus spun towards Saoirse. He crowded her through a side window onto a balcony shaded by curtains and the waning moon.

"That was close," he murmured as he backed her against the railing. "A little too close."

"I told you we'd have to worry about that."

"I don't listen well."

Saoirse rolled her eyes. "I can tell."

"Where did you learn to do that?" He touched her cheek with a hand still calloused and rough.

"What?"

"Rolling your eyes. It's not something you've ever done before, and I assume a rather human trait."

"Faeries are able to emote disgust or disapproval. We roll our eyes as well."

He cupped her face and stroked her cheek with his thumb. "I learn something new every day about you and your kind."

"Why were you talking to that captain about a ship, Manus?"

"Why were you dancing with that tall bloke we met in the bar?"

He had her there. Saoirse gaped up at him. "I didn't think you were looking?"

Gently, Manus tugged her against his chest. His hands spanned her waist and stroked the long line of her spine. "I'm always watching you, I can't help it. You looked like a real princess dancing with him. The two of you were almost otherworldly."

She couldn't lie to him. No matter how angry she was, or how much she knew he was trying to distract her, Saoirse thought he deserved to know the whole truth of her life.

"He's not human either," she corrected. "He may masquerade as one of your nobility, but I can assure you, he is not like any of you. Faerie dancing differs greatly from humans."

"I can see that." Manus brushed a strand of hair behind her ear and lowered his head. He pressed their foreheads together, sighing. "Do you regret it? Do you wish you had chosen a faerie lover and run off to the Otherworld?"

"That's a cruel thing to ask."

"Because it's true?"

"Those are two very different futures, incomparable to each other. If I had chosen a faerie, I would have married a merrow man. Even if, by some strange luck, another had fallen in love with me, it's unlikely my life would have been happy. Faeries are cold, hungry, and always desperate for more power."

His fingers stroked the back of her neck. "Then why do you still look disappointed?"

"Humans aren't what I expected. I thought your kind would be more honest, perhaps a little more adventurous. But your nobility is eerily similar to ours. The people in there wear masks instead of faces. They frighten me."

"How could they frighten you? You're a princess from another land, an heiress to a massive fortune, and *my* wife."

Manus spread his hands wide on her back, spreading warmth through her entire body. He slanted his mouth over hers and poured love into her. She tasted whiskey—vivid and stinging — on his tongue.

He pulled back for a deep breath. "Don't dance with too many men, my pearl. I don't think my heart could take it."

"Your heart?" She reached up and traced the swirls of his ears. "Or your pride?"

"Both. You are everything to me, the reason I am here, my wealth, my happiness, my glory. I don't know what I would do if I lost you, Saoirse."

It wasn't a lot, but it was enough for now. She tucked herself under his chin and breathed out a sigh of relief. He cared, she knew it, and somehow she would endure this strange life of servants, secrets hidden behind fans, and houses that moaned in the night.

"I love you." She pressed the words above his heart, willing them to sink into his form and fill his body with magic. His chest expanded, his spine straightened, and she felt a small bit of herself fill the cavity of his body.

Merrow magic was rare and weak compared to all other Fae. She could only give him confidence, health, and impress happiness into his skin like a shield against all that would tear him down.

Even if it cost her life, Saoirse would protect him from the perils of the human world.

Seagulls screamed above the dock, circling the fisheries for any scrap that might fall. The thumping crack of knives against wood tangled with the quiet slap of raw fish striking the ground. Children raced through the crowd, reaching up with quick fingers to pickpocket anyone they could find.

"Stay close to me," Manus said, threading her arm through his. "I'd rather not have to chase a small boy today."

"Are they always boys?" She watched one race through the crowd, a growling man chasing him while loudly swearing.

"The girls usually stand on street corners and beg, they're far cuter for pitying women like yourself. Or—" he hesitated before clearing his throat. "There are other opportunities for poor women, and they aren't ones we should particularly talk about."

"You always say that." Saoirse chuckled. "It's almost as if you were raised a lord, rather than a poor boy running around like this."

"That's because I was."

She froze.

Manus stumbled as she held his arm still, then glanced back. "Saoirse?"

"You never told me that you weren't always a street rat. You've joked so many times about being born on the streets that I always thought…" She shrugged. "I don't know what I thought."

"I wasn't rich or noble-born if that's what you're thinking."

He tried to continue walking, but she tugged on his arm again. "Manus, tell me! I want to know."

"We've got a ship to look over, my pearl."

"This is important. It's part of who you are, and I want to know."

A muscle in his jaw jumped, but he relented. "My mother was a kitchen maid. She wasn't well known, but one of the footmen found her pretty and then I came about. They let her stay in the house while I was a child, but when I started talking they kicked us both out. That's all."

"That's all?" Her mind raced, remembering suddenly how sure footed he was. Manus had bought their house without walking through it. He'd pointed out rooms by name, but she had assumed it was something all humans knew. She shook her head. "You grew up in the house we live in, didn't you?"

Manus licked his lips, obviously uncomfortable with the conversation. "I did."

"Is that why you wanted to buy it?"

"There's a certain amount of justice in my return. I now own the house of the man who threw my mother out onto the streets. If I could, I would have buried him in the backyard to dance upon his grave every night."

She didn't like this side of Manus. The dark edge of his tone was a blade that burned her heart. She had known their house didn't feel safe or loved. They were living in a tomb of bad memories and a past he couldn't let go.

Manus sighed. "Come on, don't put more into it. We have a lovely home, we are both happy. Let the past stay in the past, Saoirse."

"Can you?"

He said no more and dragged her down the docks towards a large ship with clean, white sails hanging limp from three masts. It was an impressive ship, a kind she had only seen once in her life. A royal ship.

Manus opened his arms wide, tossed his head back, and laughed. "Isn't she a beauty? My pearl, Ramsey didn't lie to us. This the most magnificent creation I have ever seen."

"It's beautiful and will weather many storms."

"Storms? I think it could weather a faerie sea itself!"

"I doubt that, my love. It's too small to survive a guardian's wrath." She stood beside him and smiled. "But I think it shall carry us a good distance from shore safely enough."

"Would you like to explore it?"

"I can't think of anything else I'd rather do."

She placed her hand on Manus's arm, and together they stepped onto the ship.

They spent the better part of the afternoon wandering through every nook and cranny. Manus knew ships like he knew his own hand. He pointed out small cracks which would need to be filled with sap, the fine craftsmanship of the carvings, the comfort of the captain's quarters.

This was clearly the love of his life. Saoirse watched him become more confident with every moment he was on the ship. His strides lengthened, his spine remained stiff, his eyes narrowed to catch every detail he might not have seen. He was a sight to behold.

He wrapped his arm around her shoulders at the prow of the ship. "Do you see it?"

"The ocean? It is lovely today. The waves rock us gently, for they know you wish to begin new adventures soon."

"No, not that, my pearl."

She followed the line of his raised arm to the masthead. Ships always had some kind of carved being watching over them. Saoirse had marveled at the carved whales, fish, and warriors. But this one was particularly meaningful.

A merrow lifted her arms into her hair and watched the ocean. Her tail lashed at the waves, warning the ocean to be careful with the men on board.

"Manus," Saoirse breathed. "She's beautiful."

"I asked for her," he replied. He squeezed her tighter. "If I'm going to have a ship, then I'm going to make certain that my faerie looks after me no matter where I am."

"I love it. She's beautiful."

"As are you."

Manus lifted her arm above her head, spun her in a circle, and caught her against his chest as she laughed. "I'm going to name her the *Saorsa*."

"Freedom?"

"That is what she will gift to me, to my men, to all who stand board. And all will know that the ship with the merrow woman is one who shows compassion and ensures all aboard have an equal say in their lives."

"When will they know this?"

"As soon as I hire them."

Laughter bubbled from her chest. He lifted her off her feet and swung her in circles until her head spun. Only when she shrieked did he let her touch the ground again, pulling her close and pressing his lips against her forehead.

"Thank you," he said. "You have made this possible for me, you perfect creature. There is nothing in this world gold could buy which would be a worthy reward for all you have done."

"I need nothing other than your love."

He hugged her tighter, and together they stared out to sea.

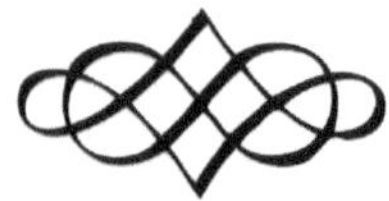

Thunder rolled in the distance, a great storm which would crash upon the shore and crackle with lightning. It rushed across the sea chased by churning waves white with foam.

The rumble vibrated through Saoirse's chest, and she smiled. Storms were rare where she came from. She could hardly hear the sounds so deep underwater, but sometimes she swam to the surface so she could listen to the powerful call. It was lovely and impossible all at the same time.

Lightning flashed and illuminated her room, causing her smile to fall. Her room, private and alone, although it was right across from Manus's. She didn't like being so far away from him, but his response was always the same. It wasn't proper for a man and woman of their station to be together in the same bedroom.

"It simply isn't done, Saoirse," he had said. "If we're going to live like this, we have to fit in."

Humans had strange customs. It made little sense they would insist upon something so ironclad as marriage, but then also require the couples to remain separate.

Her toes twitched as they often did when she was frustrated. A remnant from when her tail would flick side to side in the water, something her brother enjoyed pointing out. Saoirse was easy to read, even for humans it seemed.

She sat up in bed, her hair a wild dark tangle. It was only allowed freedom in her own bedroom. Her maids wouldn't let her outside the room without a tight braid that yanked her face back.

"The lady of the house," she grumbled as she swung her legs over the side of the bed. "Not a single one of them believes I am the lady of this house."

They thought her quaint. Otherworldly. Endearing. Not a woman who ran the household.

In truth, she would likely do a poor job of it. Gardening, cleaning, rearranging furniture, it was all far beyond her knowledge or her interests.

How did human women not die of boredom?

Restless, she padded from her bed to the doors of her balcony. Lightning struck the ocean far out to sea, but from her cliff side home she could see it as if she were standing beside it. The vivid blue light burned her eyes.

The storm was a widow maker. Black rolling clouds threatened any ship which stood in its way. Thankfully, she saw no small dark shadows, bobbing at the mercy of mother nature.

Her nightgown lashed around her legs, twisting through the twin pillars and snapping behind her. Any moment, a maid would yell at her to put her wrap on. A woman would get chilled outside, and what would the master do if his lady fell ill?

Sometimes, she wished she could tell them she was Fae. That a simple cold wasn't something she needed to worry about. Illnesses for the Fae were far different than those humans suffered.

Saoirse wrapped her arms around her waist. She hadn't felt so alone in a while. Manus was easy to be around, and he doted on her when she was near him. But lately, he was always at the ship. He wanted everything to be perfect before they went on their maiden voyage.

She understood the desire. It was the first ship he would captain, and he had coveted the title since he was a child. The sea called to him.

The longer he was away from the waves, the more frantic he became.

Waves crashed against the cliff far below her, echoing out their groan. The sound slid up her spine and exploded in the base of her skull. She couldn't wait to go out on a ship even if she could only feel the water moving its solid base.

Warm hands curved over her shoulders, sliding down her arms and pulling her back against a firm chest. Goosebumps rose as his callouses scraped her sensitive skin. He wrapped them both in a blanket and rested his chin against her shoulder.

"You're still awake."

"I couldn't sleep."

He hummed in her ear. "Ah. Does the storm frighten you? I imagine you didn't get to experience many that far in the ocean."

"No, I like storms. They're beautiful in the way they release their emotions in abandon. I've met nothing like them before."

Lightning struck in the distance. Saoirse held her breath, waiting for the moment thunder would boom. The clouds lit brightly from deep inside the dark masses. It crackled and built until suddenly it released in a line that zagged all the way to the ocean.

"Of all women, I should have known you'd like the storms best." Manus held her closer, rubbing his hands up and down her arms. "Are you not cold?"

"Why does everyone ask if I'm cold?"

"Because they're cold, and we see you standing outside with barely anything on and wonder how you could stand it."

"I'm hardier than humans, so it seems. I grew up in the frigid deep. A little cold air is nothing compared to what I'm used to."

He chuckled. "I look forward to hearing your thoughts about our winters. Even the depths can't compare to snow."

A few fat drops of rain splattered on the stone balcony. Saoirse let him draw her inside though she wished to allow the water to play over her skin. She missed it.

She missed it so much her soul hurt.

Manus slid his finger under her chin, tilting her head up so she was forced to stare at him. "Stop thinking about it. You are *here*, with me, and no one will ever take you from me."

"It's hard not to think about my home."

"I am your home, now. I keep you safe and warm. I heal all your wounds and I dry your tears if they are shed." He lifted her hand and pressed her palm to his heart. "You can feel it, can't you? This is where you belong."

Saoirse spread her fingers wide, feeling the steady beat match her own. "You're still worried I might leave."

"How could I not be when you stare at the ocean as if I stole you from it?"

"This was my choice, Manus."

"And I won't ever let you forget it," he fiercely growled.

Somehow, she had frightened him. Saoirse allowed him to lift her up into his arms and carry her back to bed.

The soft down feathers cushioned her back, so soft it felt as if she were drifting atop the waves. Manus followed her down. He nudged her thighs open, settling against her with a groan that vibrated through her entire being.

"I'm not leaving you," she whispered. Lightning crackled and lit up the bedroom. It gilded the edges of his form in blue and silver while leaving his face in dark shadows.

He was a god among men, looming above her with clear intent. Saoirse couldn't have told him no even if she wanted to. He was everything she had dreamed of and more.

The golden statue of a prince was perfection personified. He was a childish dream of a future filled with fantasy and magic. Manus was real, flesh and blood, bone and marrow. His skin was warm and bent to her will no matter what she demanded of him.

He traced the line of her throat with a feather light touch. "Have I not given you enough to keep you occupied, my pearl? I bought the largest house I could find, hired maids, gardeners, horses, and still you hide in your room."

"I don't like so many people staring at me, wondering who I am and asking questions I cannot answer."

Manus dipped his head and touched his lips to the hollow behind her ear. "I forget you are so innocent. My perfect little pearl, incapable of telling even the smallest lie."

She arched into his kiss. Warmth bloomed from wherever he touched, heating her chilled skin. When had she become so cold? Did it matter? He was a furnace filled with burning passions that would set her ablaze.

His hand trailed down her throat, danced along her collarbone, and settled between her breasts where he could feel her wild heartbeat.

"You are mine," he growled in her ear. "Mine and no other's."

"I am yours."

All at once, he was everywhere and nowhere. His hands slid along her side, his teeth pulled at her ear, his hips pressed into hers. She writhed beneath him.

"Manus," she moaned.

"Say it again. Over and over until it's burned into your memory, my pearl."

"I am yours."

Lightning struck, and thunder rolled at the same time. The storm crashed through the windows, banging the glass panes against the wall. Silver light illuminated Manus in small flickers of life.

She watched each flashing moment as if she wasn't within her body as he pulled her nightgown over her head.

Manus's neck gracefully arched as he pulled a rosy bud between his teeth. The muscles of his back flexed, creating hills of smooth skin like swells of great waves. His fingers dug into the aching muscles of her spine. She bent at his request, allowing him further access to play across the dips of her body.

She pulled at his heat, at the passions so vivid she could almost see them hovering in the air. With each breath, she bound herself to him ever more tightly. The threads of their lives were so entangled they had created a labyrinth from which they would never break free.

Lightning sizzled. She tasted electricity in the air and gasped as Manus delved between her legs. The tangled strands of his hair scraped her inner thighs, but she couldn't focus on anything other than the sensations he created.

Thunder shook the house with a great boom. They could have all been on fire, and she wouldn't have noticed. Electricity flowed through her veins. It buzzed through her mind until all she could hear was the rush of waves crashing against the shore.

Manus trailed his lips up her body, pressing a warm kiss against her lips. "You are mine."

"Yours," she gasped.

He plunged into her like a man possessed. She caught the strained expression on his face in a bright flash of light. He was marking her, claiming her, forcing her to recognize that she was entirely his no matter where she was in the world.

A rumble of thunder trailed up her spine, and she cried out as lightning struck the balcony outside. The room flared bright. Her wicked pirate arched back, driving himself so deep inside Saoirse couldn't tell where one of them ended and the other began.

They cried out together, melding as only two people in love could do. Together they quaked and shuddered, battled the raging sky and shouted their release. They were creatures of passion. Even mother nature agreed tonight and mirrored the weather to the raging inferno inside their souls.

Manus branded his touch onto every inch of her body, worshiping her like a goddess and punishing her like a slave. In return, she allowed her own passions to fly free. Saoirse begged for his touch, murmured encouragement, and sighed happily when he listened.

Throughout the entire night, she wondered whether he was apologizing, convincing her to stay, or saying goodbye.

He dropped to his side and pulled her tight against him. "I want you to be happy here. You know that, don't you?"

"Of course I do." Saoirse pressed a kiss to his slick chest. "I know you want me to be happy."

His body fell lax as sleep overtook him, and she let him rest.

Saoirse didn't have the heart to tell him that no matter how much he *wanted* her to be happy, she couldn't be. Not fully. Not while the sea was out there, waiting for her, and she had made her life on land.

She tucked her head under his chin and pressed her palm against his steady heart. The beat lulled her to sleep, filled her dreams with a quiet drumbeat, and eased the ache in her chest.

Warm lips pressed against Saoirse's bare shoulder. She smiled, her half-awake mind already certain who touched her with such familiarity.

"Manus," she murmured. "Is it time to get up?"

"It's far past that time, my pearl."

She slowly rolled onto her back and opened her eyes. He was seated on the edge of her bed, dressed in soft breeches and a white linen shirt unbuttoned at the throat. He had pulled his dreadlocks back with a leather thong. Beads at the end clacked together as he shifted.

Saoirse stretched her arms over her head. "Where are we going?"

"It's a surprise."

"A surprise?" She yawned. "Manus, I don't like surprises."

He pressed a finger against her lips, eyes twinkling. "Shh, my pearl. You're going to love it. Get out of bed, your maids are waiting to dress you."

"I can get dressed by myself."

"But isn't it so much more fun to have someone else do it?" He winked at her and stood, leaving the door ajar on his way out.

Saoirse covered her face with her hands, groaning at the mere thought of getting up. She was having such lovely dreams. Waves rocking over her body, fish tangled in her hair, a powerful tail propelling her through the water…

"M'lady?"

Saoirse dropped her hands. "Good morning."

The maids bustled into the room, one to stoke the fire and the other to dress Saoirse in whatever clothing the maid picked out. It was as if Saoirse was some kind of elaborate toy. They dressed her, did her hair, powdered her face with makeup, and then set her in a corner to rot while they went on with their lives.

"The master says up, so you must get up." The bedframe shook. "You cannot stay abed all day, m'lady. Unless you are not feeling well?"

"I feel fine." She whispered, although she was exceedingly tired and wasn't certain why. She'd slept well through the night.

"I think you'd look stunning in this lovely sea green. Wouldn't you agree?"

The maid held up the dress which spilled over her arm onto the floor. It was a stunning creation, beautiful in all aspects of the word. It would make her waist look trim, keep her warm with the fur around the shoulders, and yet feminine with the stunning embroidery.

Saoirse couldn't care less.

She sighed and sat up. "Yes, that will do."

The maid tucked her hand underneath Saoirse's elbow and helped her stand. Together, they walked to her small dressing table where they began the arduous journey of placing layer after layer of fabric together.

Saoirse obediently stood still. They could do whatever they wanted with her, not because they had power over her, but because they knew more than she did. Both of the maids had to work on her hair. The long length would be hours to finish if only one person were braiding it.

They had suggested cutting it once. "Just a trim," they had said.

Saoirse's reaction had not been a kind one. They had not brought a knife to her room again.

"How do you get your hair to look like this?" One of the maid's asked. "It's so dark, but it shines almost green in the sunlight. Like whale oil."

"This is my natural hair."

"Surely not! It's not possible to have hair this color."

"I can assure you, it is."

They babbled on, chattering about things Saoirse did not care for. The maids always had something to comment on. The looks of the new gardener, the taste of dinner last night, how the butler thought he was better than everyone else.

They hadn't said a word in the beginning, but quickly realized their mistress didn't care if they spoke. As soon as they realized this, the floodgates opened. They rarely stopped to take a breath between sentences, now.

Saoirse liked it, in a strange way. Their words floated about her and burst in bright bubbles of sound. She didn't care what they said. The words meant little. It was the rhythmic sound she appreciated so much. The same sound that could lull her to sleep and ease her nerves.

"My lady?"

"Yes?"

"I think we're finished. What do you think?"

Saoirse opened her eyes and stared at the creature in the mirror. She looked anything but human. Her eyes were too slanted, her hair oddly colored, her skin milky white perfection. Still, she looked beautiful and the maids would be disappointed if she said anything else.

"You've outdone yourselves, ladies. I don't deserve your talents."

"You shouldn't be saying that to maids, but we appreciate it."

With a soft smile, Saoirse stood. "You deserve all the compliments

I have and more."

She ignored the uncomfortable expressions on the maids' faces. They were strange women. Try as she might, Saoirse would never understand them.

They both dipped into curtsies. "The master said he would wait for you in the stables."

"The stables?" Saoirse sighed. "He knows I don't like to ride."

"I don't believe he was intending to ride milady. A man delivered a carriage today."

"A carriage? Don't those require a driver?"

They giggled behind their hands and slipped out the door in a rush. Likely because they didn't want to answer any more of Saoirse's strange questions.

She smoothed a hand down the bodice of her sea foam gown. It wasn't practical for whatever Manus had planned, but it was something like armor. She was presentable at the very least. As long as she didn't speak, she would remain a paragon of womanly duties.

Now was not the time to dwell on her newly found life. Saoirse straightened her spine, swept down the halls of her home, and out towards the stables. She didn't like horses. They were strange beasts who always watched her and pawed at the ground when she came too close.

They didn't want her anywhere near them either. She was more suited to a kelpie mount who would crash through the waves with a fearsome shriek. Not these imitations of faerie beasts.

"Are you ready, my pearl?" Manus called out. "There are many surprises today!"

He stood next to a glistening black carriage. The wheels were taller than her, and gold curtains covered the windows, barring the interior from her sight. It might have been impressive for a human, but it looked like everything else to Saoirse. Frightening, foreign, and yet another strange thing to endure.

But he wanted her to be pleased. His smiles were rare, and he was grinning from ear to ear today. She wouldn't ruin that.

Saoirse plastered a smile on her face. "What have you acquired, husband? Will this turn into a beetle at sunset or is this truly a carriage made by human hands?"

"Entirely human made. Did you think we were incapable of it?" He pulled black gloves onto his hands with an audible snap. "Are you ready?"

She nodded and marveled at the oddities of her husband. He was a wild beast packed into a suit and tie. His dreads were tied back with a loose leather thong, the heathen hair something he refused to get rid of. Tan breeches hugged his legs so tightly she was certain women would faint when they saw him. A black waistcoat covered the white linen shirt, but she knew it was still unbuttoned.

They were a strange pair. Both wild and tame at the same time.

A crow croaked above them, its eyes staring down with clear intent. Manus mock shivered and gestured for her to come closer.

"The Morrighan watches us my darling, perhaps you should come here. For safety."

"Well, she *is* a faerie. She knows a good story when she sees one."

"A faerie like you or a Fae beast?"

"We're all faeries," she replied. Giggles escaped through her lips in effervescent sounds of joy. "There's no such thing as a Fae beast."

"There's not? Then what are the creatures?"

"Some of us are better at shape shifting than others."

She enjoyed his shocked expression far more than she should have. Saoirse held out her hand for him to take.

"Are we leaving, Manus?"

His jaw snapped shut. "You did that on purpose, didn't you?"

"Did what?"

Lightning fast, his arms lashed out and wrapped around her waist. Saoirse pressed her palms against his chest with a gasp.

"You are a wicked creature, I should have listened to the priest."

He nibbled at her ear as he growled out the words.

"I believe the priest claimed *I* should run from *you*."

"Oh, that's not how I heard it, my pearl. You were always the vixen luring me away with her song and her pretty smile."

"I've never sung to you!"

"You never had to," he murmured against her throat. "Your body sings a song only I can hear."

How could she ever tell him how much that meant to her? That he expressed his love in a thousand and one different ways? She could read him easier than any other human alive.

Saoirse pulled back and ran her finger down the bridge of his nose. "Then I shall hope it continues the song for many lifetimes to come."

He kissed the tip of her finger. "Shall we?"

She thought he would help her into the carriage as she had seen many wealthy women do. They would arrange their skirts just so, nod to their footman, and the door would seal them inside the strange compartment. Saoirse dreaded the mere thought of being entombed.

Perhaps he knew her better than she thought. Manus helped her to the front where the coachman would sit. The board was slightly uncomfortable but cushioned by the thick weight of her skirts.

"Manus? Is this appropriate?"

He sat next to her, the entire carriage rocking with his weight. "Probably not. But this is our day together, and I know you care little for propriety."

"I like this gift already."

Manus reached beneath the seat and drew out a long whip. "Besides, the horses would miss you if I tucked you away."

The nearest horse flicked its tail, glancing back at them with a dubious expression.

"I doubt that," Saoirse said with a laugh. "But I would much rather be here where I can feel the wind in my hair."

He cracked the whip, and they left the haven of their small cliff side home. Saoirse craned her neck to watch the estate disappear behind a line of trees. It was a beautiful home. Though it was a shame bad memories haunted its halls, she hoped someday they might fill it with happy memories of their own.

Rolling green hills filled her vision with emerald. Wind tickled the long blades of grass, sending fields flickering to life like the green fronds beneath the ocean. She was most comfortable here. Strands of her hair broke free from her tight crown braid, tickling her cheeks.

Knee high stone walls bracketed off sections of land. Each square marked where one farmer's land began, and another's ended. Dots of sheep scattered across the emerald hills.

She liked sheep. They were a strange beast, with odd eyes and fuzzy bodies, but they were kind. She could feel their love and devotion even though they kept their distance.

A few horses wandered although they were usually kept in pens, so their owners could find them. Saoirse smiled and waved at a farmer who paused in his work, leaning on a hoe and watching them pass by with a curious expression. He'd probably never seen anyone so rich riding atop a carriage.

He waved back at her hesitantly and returned her bright grin. There was much good she could do here, with all those who needed help. So few wanted to get their hands dirty.

"Manus?"

"Yes, my pearl?"

"Could we perhaps give back to the community?" She pointed towards the farmer's home. "Some roofs look a little worn. We could donate whatever we could to get them ready for winter."

"I like that idea." Manus reached out and grabbed her hand. He pressed a kiss to the back of her fingers. "You'd give up some of our fortune to help others?"

"It's not our fortune anyways. It's a bean sídhe's who didn't mind sharing her wealth with a fellow faerie."

She didn't have the heart to tell him faerie coin was usually cursed. Using the money at all made her uncomfortable, even though she knew it came from humans first. Had it been with the faerie long enough to become cursed?

The carriage rocked to the side, wheels caught in a deep rut. The horses snorted and pulled hard, tossing Saoirse against Manus who held her snug against him.

They rolled into town and she thought they might stop. It was market day. Crowds of people teemed around stalls overflowing with flowers, fabric, food, and more. She loved the colors of market day even though some people were a little pushy.

A few ladies made eyes at Manus, some even waggling their fingers for his attention. Saoirse ignored them as best she could and let out a relieved sigh when they passed through the town onto a small dirt road that led towards the sea.

"Will you tell me what we're doing now?" she asked.

"We're almost there, my pearl. Have a little patience."

She didn't want to have patience. There was no possibility he was taking her for a swim; Manus wouldn't risk her safety to give her what she desperately wanted. But she didn't know what else he might surprise her with.

They travelled over the rise and down towards the white sandy beach. Far at the bottom, a tiny cottage nestled in the yellow seagrass. Smoke curled from the red brick chimney. It was a quaint little cottage, one that radiated the warmth and comfort of home.

Manus drove the carriage up to the front, hopped from his seat, and tied the horses to the neat little fence surrounding the home. Ivy grew up the stone walls, unfurling bright green leaves nearly as large as her hands. Whoever lived here clearly cared for the grounds.

The front door opened, and a man stepped through, wiping his hands on a white cloth. Even with his back turned as he closed the door, Saoirse recognized him.

Eyes wide, she met Manus's pleased gaze.

He grinned. "It's haunted me for a while, my pearl. Now, you shall see everything he has created, and we will commission a piece for our home."

The artisan turned on his heel and froze. "My lord, you're early."

"We made better time than I expected." Manus helped Saoirse down from the carriage and set her down in a flourish of skirts and furs. "Might I present my wife? I believe you have met before."

Saoirse met his gaze with awe. "I had never thought to see you again, artisan. Your talents have remained in my thoughts."

"Oh." He cleared his throat and blushed. "You both look a fair bit different from I remember."

"I imagine we do. I apologize if we deceived you in any way."

"I always thought you were a royal, even with that ragged gown and dirt smudged on your cheek." He tucked the cloth into his breast pocket. "Welcome to my home."

She stepped forward, Manus close on her heels. The gate gave away beneath her hand without even the slightest of squeaks.

The artisan opened the door again, cheeks still red. "I was heading out to check the sands, but I'll find them later. There was quite a storm a few nights ago. Did it reach you up in the big house?"

"Yes, it did," she murmured as she crossed the threshold into his home. "Do you think there will be more glass?"

"There always is, my lady."

It was far warmer inside the house. She hadn't noticed the chill in the air until stepping inside. Without thinking, she toed off her shoes and wandered.

A small stove sat in the corner next to a table, ivy carved onto its legs. Herbs hung from the ceiling, drying for winter and filling the air with a sweet scent. Saoirse filled her lungs and trailed her fingers over the hanging lavender to release more of its perfume.

Trinkets sat on the fireplace. Small glass animals, tiny bottles filled with flowers, and sand dollars from the beach. She touched the mantelpiece with a soft smile.

The men hesitated behind her, the artisan finally breaking the silence. "Does she always make herself at home like this?"

"Not always," Manus replied. She could hear the smile in his voice. "Only the places she likes most."

She glanced over her shoulder to find them both staring at her shoes.

"I remember this," the artisan mused. "She wasn't wearing shoes the day I met her either."

"She tends not to."

"That's strange for a lady of her stature."

"I wouldn't say anything about the lady is normal."

She made a face at Manus. "I'm perfectly normal, perhaps it is all of you who are strange to me."

The artisan cleared his throat. "Considering you were raised a princess in another land, I am quite certain we must all be strange to you my lady."

That silly rumor once again. Saoirse curled her hands into fists, frustrated that she would be trapped in the lie again. Instead of confirming or denying, she gestured to the room. "Why are we here? I appreciate seeing you, artisan, but I am curious about the intent of the visit."

Manus walked to her side and plucked a glass horse from the mantle. "I thought you'd like to see his workroom before we request a commission."

"Is that where you work?" she asked the artisan.

He nodded.

"I would very much like to see that. I haven't seen glasswork like yours before, not even among the richest of houses." Saoirse paused, thoughts whirling in her mind. "Why is that?"

The artisan rubbed the back of his neck. "Well, I'm like your husband, my lady."

"Like my husband?" she repeated the answer. "What do you mean?"

"When I was a boy, my mother set me out in a field because I was ill. A little too old to tempt the faeries in most cases, but even when I was young I had a talent for art. They took me in, healed me, taught me everything I know about glassworks." He sat down at the table and pulled his shirt to the side. Next to his throat was a symbol she knew very well.

Her heart caught in her throat. It was a small flower, barely noticeable and some might think it a scar. The Seelie Fae marked their human slaves. She didn't know whose symbol this was, but she knew what it meant all the same.

"I'm sorry," she breathed. "They should never have taken you."

"It wasn't as bad as you might think. They were kind enough, fed me well, taught me to use my hands in ways I could never have dreamt." He held his hands palm up for her to look at. "Although, they aren't really mine anymore."

Her stomach fell in a pit of dread. She stepped forward and caught his hands in hers. Faint silver lines circled his wrists. She hadn't noticed before, but they were even slightly different colors than the rest of his body.

"I've seen nothing like this before," she murmured. "What did they do to you?"

"It wasn't painful, my lady."

"They shouldn't have done this." The violent tones rocked her body forward.

The artisan widened his eyes, and she knew he had pieced everything together. Quietly, so Manus wouldn't overhear them, he said, "It wasn't you who did this to me."

"I am sorry all the same."

She folded his fingers flat, lifted his hands, and kissed the center of his palms. Merrow magic flowed from her lips to his skin. She pressed compassion, understanding, and healing energies into his body.

He breathed out a shocked tone. "My lady, you don't have to—"

It was too late to stop. The faerie gift glowed along the edges of his stitched hands, and his fingers twitched.

The artisan stared down with wide eyes. "They feel… they feel…"

"Better?"

"*Yes*." The word vibrated with his shock. "Like they know they're my hands."

"Faerie gifts sometimes come with a price. These hands have always known they belonged to another, and they did not want to accept you." She curled his fingers into his palms and squeezed. "Now they do."

"Will it affect my art?"

"I think your craft will only become even better. They'll work with you now, not against you."

"Thank you, my lady. Thank you so much."

She smiled. "It's the least I could do. You've gifted me with so many dreams of wonderful glass figures."

The artisan stood abruptly, energy zinging through his body and crackling in the air. "Then let me bring your dreams to life. You've seen how I work, now come with me. Let me show you what I am capable of creating but could never sell."

She took his offered hand and danced her fingers along the seam. Manus hovered in the shadows, a ball of nervous energy who held himself back. He wouldn't like another man touching her.

Thankfully, he did not step in.

They walked towards the back door. She could see barely glowing runes etched onto the surface. Some she recognized, words of lasting power and hidden secrets. Others she did not. Their fine lines had been painted by a careful hand.

"Magic?" she asked. "Who placed these in your home?"

"A faerie friend. When I returned, all my friends and family were dead. Two hundred years had passed in this world." The artisan gestured at the door. "This was my final parting gift from those who had taught me so much."

She squinted at the top rune, knowing there was something familiar about it. Saoirse gasped in shock. "That's a door to the Otherworld."

"Indeed, it is."

"They gave you a door to Faerie?" She stared up at the artisan with a new appreciation for his skill. "They loved you."

"In a way. The Seelie court was never a friend to me, but they loved what I could do. Come, we will not be bothered."

In any other circumstance, Saoirse would have forced Manus to remain behind. The Otherworld was a dangerous place for even the most astute person. However, she could see sunlight leaking beneath the door and knew the runes of protection.

Whoever had created this door had wanted to keep the artisan safe.

Saoirse stepped forward and pressed her hand to the worn wood. It pulsed with love, desperation, and a longing so pure it made her palm sting.

"She loved you," Saoirse observed. "Quite a bit for a faerie."

"She thought I was special."

"But you couldn't be together."

The artisan shuffled. "No, faerie nobility cannot be with humans. Not in the way we wanted, and nothing else would have sufficed."

"That's where you get all your inspiration. Not from the Otherworld." She turned with her hand still pressed to the enchanted door. "Your inspiration comes from her."

"In everything I create."

Her heart filled with a love so bright it seared her insides. No wonder faeries avoided this emotion like the plague. It hurt even when it was someone else's.

Manus met her gaze. His features softened, his eyes tender as he stared into her dark eyes. He felt it too. She was certain of it.

"Shall we?" she asked.

"After you."

Saoirse pushed open the door and walked into a garden filled with the most spectacular sight she'd ever seen.

Plants of all shapes and sizes bloomed larger than her head. Giant blue hydrangeas surrounded glass sculptures of life-sized people. Women frozen mid dance. Men bowing and offering roses to their beloved. Faeries of all shapes and sizes twirling, singing, playing music. An entire frozen court, each lovingly created out of the finest glass.

Sunlight played off the figures, reflecting rainbows all around the faerie grotto. A soft wind blew tiny seed pods in dancing lines. Faerie lights joined them and bounced around Saoirse. They settled in her hair and trilled high pitched notes.

She pressed her hands to her mouth.

Home. She was home, or as near to it as she could get.

"It's—" Her tongue laced in a knot. She couldn't think, could barely breathe.

Manus stopped beside her and tugged her into his arms. "It's beautiful."

The artisan walked through his garden with his hands clasped behind his back. "It's taken me years to create so many, although not as long as you might think. The hands do a lot of the work for me."

"How many have you made?" she asked.

"Hundreds. Now and then a faerie will come and take one, they always leave something as a gift." He paused beside a small pool. "I know you had intended to request a commission, however, I have a piece I think you will want."

Captivated, Saoirse followed him down a winding path made of seashells and bits of sea softened glass. Each step sang a song in her ears and nipped at her feet with sharp jabs.

The pool was crystal clear. It sank into dark depths so blue they challenged the sky. Salt water stung her nose and filled her with memories. A ring of velvety stones circled the entrance to the sea.

She ached to slide into the water. Her merrow family couldn't be here, not in the Otherworld. They lived on the edge and too far away from the faerie kingdoms for them to know where she was.

Manus's hand clenched on her arm.

He always knew when her mind wandered beneath the waves. She shook herself and politely asked, "Where is it, artisan?"

He pointed towards a shadowed corner where a small stream trickled into the pool.

A glass merrow woman sat on a stone, brushing her hair with an ornate shell. She stared into the distance with a sorrowful expression. The tail was made out of bright green glass, matching the vibrant color of her hair.

She was the most stunning creation Saoirse had ever seen in her life. It was even more lifelike than the others, almost as if she would turn her head to stare at them.

And for some strange reason, it made Saoirse unbearably sad. Tears blurred the edges of her vision and her breath caught in her throat.

"Manus," she whispered. "That's the one I want."

"Are you certain? We could request anything at all to be made. He will happily make anything we desire."

She couldn't be more certain if he had put a blade to her throat. This was the glass creation she needed to have in her home. They would need to hide it from any human viewing as it was clearly faerie made. Even if the statue needed to be kept in a secret cave, she must have it.

Unable to speak, Saoirse nodded vigorously.

Manus frowned at her. He knew something was wrong, he'd always been able to feel that even when she tried to hide it from him.

"Artisan," he said. "We'll take that one home with us."

"I am happy to create any additional commission you would like."

"I have a few I'd like to order, if you don't mind?"

The artisan gestured towards a table surrounded by frozen servants. "Have a seat. We'll sketch out a few ideas and I should have them ready in a few months."

They left Saoirse to stand staring at the merrow.

She couldn't understand the violent emotions flooding through her veins. Happiness, sadness, disappointment, all melding together into one ball that sat in the pit of her stomach. She hated it. She wanted it to disappear altogether and leave her be.

This was a good life. It was a peaceful life where she lived in a land of plenty with a husband who clearly loved her. No matter that she missed the sea, that part of her life was over.

A lance of sadness pierced her heart and sent poisonous tendrils throughout her body.

The glass merrow seemed to turn her head and meet her gaze with sorrow mirrored in her eyes. They were two kindred spirits, this lost creature and the stranded merrow. Without the sea, Saoirse was drowning in her own pitiful sadness.

This was what she had given up. This was the choice she had made.

She turned and made her way towards the table where the men sat. With each step, she heard a faint wailing of a forgotten merrow and a melancholy sea.

CHAPTER 10

GOLDEN LIGHT, ROLLING SEAS

Manus lifted his head from his desk, grumbling as he ran a hand over his face to wipe away the lingering effects of sleep. How long had he been down here?

His eyes caught on the candle spluttering at the base. Apparently a while. The candle had been new when he snuck down here to add the final touches to the document Captain Ramsey had given him. The man was relentless and determined to have a paper trail should Manus turn around and no longer want the ship.

There weren't enough devils in hell to convince Manus not to sail. The crew he'd hired were reliable; he interviewed them all himself and was convinced they'd work hard. He was ready to be lulled to sleep by the rocking waves. The stillness of the ground unnerved him.

He reached forward and pinched the flame. Darkness fell over him like a warm blanket.

Saoirse needed to know. She was too sweet, too innocent, and she'd never understand why he had to go alone.

He couldn't bring her. Merrow men lurked beneath the waves. Their webbed fingers and stretched faces haunted his dreams still. He saw them pulling her out of his arms again and again. That damned hand reaching for him even when they both knew he couldn't save her.

Manus's hands curled into fists. He couldn't do a lot of things but keeping her safe was more important than breathing. If that meant not seeing her for months on end, then he would damned well do that.

Tingles raced up his fingers. He wanted to touch her, brand the softness of her skin to his palms so that he would remember her when he was stuck on a ship full of men for god knows how long.

Would he forget her? *Never.*

Would she forget him?

The thought was unsettling. He liked to think he wasn't an unforgettable man, but he'd caught her staring at the water too often for comfort. She heard the siren call just as he did.

"Selfish," he muttered.

And he was. He kept her here when she wanted to go home, but home wasn't safe, and the world was against them. Two sides of a coin which could never face each other.

He stood from the desk and placed a hand firmly against the small of his back. She'd make a joke that he was getting old, and Manus hoped he was. It was only another marker that they'd made it long enough to grow old. That she hadn't left him, as all merrow wives were wont to do.

Making certain all his paperwork was still stacked in a corner, he slipped from the small study and made his way towards the stairs. A few more signatures could wait. For now, he had more important business to attend to.

The house was eerily silent as he made his way to the grand stairwell. Saoirse stayed in her room, just across the hall, and he stayed in his own. It was a strange custom, but the last thing he wanted was for the servants to start talking.

His palm glided over the soft wood of the banister, soothing his troubled thoughts. Arturo's wife haunted his memories.

"Be there for her when the storms come a'calling."

And the storms would come. Because all sailors heard the call of the sea and all of them died. If he couldn't shake the curse on his soul, then he would make sure she lived in the lap of luxury for the rest of her life.

He wouldn't leave her a broken woman with a child and nothing to her name. He'd do everything he could to keep her safe.

"Master?" a quiet voice whispered from the shadows. "A word?"

"Etain?" Manus turned. "Is something wrong?"

The pretty little maid stepped from the shadows, her fingers twisting in the fabric of her skirt. "No, everything is well. It is a beautiful home."

"I trust it's to your liking."

"My sister and I like it very well, thank you. It is… better."

It didn't escape his notice how she hesitated. He glanced up the stairs towards his own little heaven, sighed, and walked back down towards the maid.

"You seem troubled."

"It just doesn't seem right that we're here, that's all."

"How so?"

"These people," she gestured behind her, "they're not like my sister and I. They were born into positions like this. They've spent their entire lives working in houses like this and I'm just afraid to touch anything. What if I break a vase?"

He tucked his hands into his pockets. "Then I'll buy a new vase."

"Money runs out, Manus, you know that as well as I."

His name slipped from her lips too easily. But then again, they'd grown up together on the streets. He'd stolen bits of bread for her and her sister, even when they both found employment in the whorehouses. They'd kept him safe when his mother died until he could get his feet under them.

She sniffed. "It just don't seem right. We'd like to leave, if it's all right with you. It's just that… Well maybe people like us aren't meant to rise above our station. Right? Maybe there's just people who shouldn't live like this. Maybe we deserved what life handed to us."

"Etain, shut up." He pulled his hands from his pockets and opened his arms. "Come here."

She rushed towards him and let him wrap her in a warm embrace. Her shoulders shook under his hands, her hair tangling in the scruff of his chin.

"Look at what I've done, right? You think I'm staring at all these people thinking I don't belong among them?"

"Of course you are."

He chuckled. "Well, maybe a little. But I've got myself a pretty little piece who worships the ground I walk on. I've got a house that makes even lords envy me, and a ship ready to sail at my command. We *aren't* stuck in the lives that were handed to us. And no one is ever going to make me believe that."

"She loves you," Etain whispered against his shoulder. "Loves you more than any woman has a right to love. Love like that is dangerous, Manus."

"Only if I leave her."

"I've seen it before. Seen someone love another so hard that their soul leaks a little bit every time they see that other person. It drains them, turns them into dust."

He leaned back enough to stare into her eyes. "What are you trying to say?"

"You gotta love her back, or she's going to turn into dust too."

"I love her more than anything."

"More than the sea?"

The question burned. It made his heart hurt and his head spin. "I can't answer that, Etain."

"Someday you're going to have to."

He would, and it wasn't a conversation he relished having. That kind of love terrified him, because Etain was right. The love they shared was powerful, dangerous, dark, and it consumed him.

Manus wasn't the same person he used to be. He saw her and something in him melted. He wanted to touch her hair, stroke her cheek, drag her into his arms and never let her go. But that meant putting her in danger, because he couldn't let go of the sea either.

Had he forgotten how to breathe? He sucked in air, but he couldn't seem to fill his lungs.

Etain stepped back from his arms. "She went for a walk, if you're looking for her."

"She went — what?" He shook his head. "She can't go for a walk, it's nighttime."

"We all go for walks in the nighttime."

He swore. "Not her. She doesn't go outside without me or one of the footmen."

"Why not? You can't turn her into a captive, if she wants go outside, she should be able to."

"Because outside is dangerous." He spun on his heel and stomped towards the front door. "If she gets hurt, it's on your head."

"Why are you so protective over this girl, Manus?"

He whirled, jabbing a finger through the air and pointing at her. "Do you remember the first time you saw a girl? Not the ones we grew up with, but the ones who walked the streets with bows in their hair and smiles on their faces? The innocent ones, the ones who never saw the things we saw. You remember those girls?"

"Of course I do."

"She's one of them. She doesn't know the kind of things we've had to do to stay alive. She's never seen the gutters, never felt a man pawing at her without permission, never saw her mother trying to drink herself into oblivion. She hasn't watched someone die because food was scarce or simply because they didn't want to live this life anymore." He wiped a shaking hand over his mouth. "She's pure, lily white, and glowing like the goddamned northern star. She's all I have, and I won't see her sullied."

He raced out the door, the chilly air penetrating through his linen shirt. He didn't stop for a jacket. Fear sent him sprinting from the manor and frantically searching for her.

Where would she have gone? The sea?

His heart stopped. She wouldn't have gone to the ocean, would she? Even Saoirse wasn't foolish enough to tempt her own safety. She knew the merrow men could crawl out of the ocean and steal her away. She shouldn't even be close to the water.

Manus couldn't think straight. He didn't know where to begin searching for her until he looked up the hill and saw her. Far away but standing on the edge of the cliff with her skirts whipping around her ankles.

She looked like an angel standing up there. So far away from him, yet he knew every detail of her face without being able to see her. He knew the soft curve of her waist, the tiny curl near her ear which always curled in the opposite direction from the others, the dimple on her cheek which only appeared late at night when she was tired.

Gods how she made his chest ache.

It would take him a few minutes to get to her, but Saoirse wasn't moving. She held her arms wrapped around herself and stared off into the distance. He frowned.

She was staring at the sea.

"Damned woman," he muttered. She was always staring at the water and he knew what that meant. He'd heard the stories of sailors with merrow wives who disappeared one night, never to return. He couldn't lose her. He didn't know what he'd do if she left his life forever.

He glanced up at her form again and paused when he saw the male figure walking towards her. At first, he thought it was that damned leprechaun. The faerie was always showing up at the wrong time.

But then he realized the man was obviously trying to be quiet as he approached.

Manus had never felt such fear as when the man raced forward and grabbed Saoirse by the shoulders, whirled her around, and shook her hard enough to rattle her.

He didn't shout for the man to stop, he didn't need to. Manus sprinted towards them. A silent, dark shadow that streaked through the night as though the faeries had given him wings.

His fist flew out, catching the man in the jaw and knocking him to the ground. The thief spat out a wad of blood. He bounced up to his feet a little too quickly and threw a punch of his own.

Manus's breath whooshed out, the man's meaty fist catching him firmly in the stomach. But it gave him the opportunity he needed. Air wasn't required to charge forward, wrap his arm around the man's waist and wrestle him onto the ground.

He straddled the man, slamming his fist into whatever flesh he could find. Face, shoulders, neck, anything.

This thief had dared to touch his wife.

His wife.

"Manus!" Saoirse's voice broke through the red haze of his vision. "Manus enough, let him go!"

His hands were aching, swelling already around bruised bones and blood streaked knuckles. The slight moment of hesitation was all the other man needed to drag himself away and run.

Manus leaned back on his heels, breathing hard and watching the man's quick retreat. This was why he hadn't wanted her alone. This place was dangerous, even in the richest parts.

"Manus?"

Her voice splintered something inside him. A ragged breath tore through him and he snatched her arm. He probably tugged on her too hard, she fell against his chest with a gasp.

"Are you all right?" He traced her body with his hands, over and over again. "Did he hurt you? Did he touch you anywhere other than your shoulders?"

"Manus, please—"

"Saoirse just answer me, for gods sakes."

"I'm *fine.*"

Breath sawed from his lungs and he gathered her closer against his heart. "You scared the life out of me."

"I'm fine." She stroked her hands over his back.

"You're shaking," he muttered. "You are not fine."

"You're here now. I know everything will be okay now."

He thought she was shaking but, as he cupped the back of her head, he realized it was him. He was the one shaking at the mere thought that he might not have found her in time. That she might have been out here alone when that man took her away.

Manus pressed a kiss against her temple and closed his eyes. "You are everything to me, my pearl. Tell me you know that."

"I know."

"Say it again. Please."

"Manus, you're scaring me."

He probably was. He was scaring himself with the intensity of his feelings and the knowledge that he was going to leave her. That she was going to look up at him with tears in her eyes when he said the sea was calling.

A coward, that's what he was. A coward and a fool for ever thinking he could hold onto such a glorious light and not tarnish her with his touch.

He pressed against kiss to her temple and held her close against his heart. A star shot across the sky, falling like the weight attached to his soul, dragging him down into the abyss of self-loathing and fear.

He wished to be a better man. He wished to stay close by her side, to raise a family as he'd always wanted to when he saw those little girls prancing down the street with bows in their hair.

But above all else, Manus wished that she would stay with him just for a few moments longer.

Even if he didn't deserve her.

Saoirse rolled over and stretched her arms over her head. Sunlight filtered through her balcony window while wind brushed the gauzy curtains into rippling movements. The air was chilled now, autumn was in full swing and some said winter may come early this year.

She was excited for winter. Snow was an entirely new and exciting weather for her to see. Some of the kinder servants had told her stories after everyone else had gone to bed.

The faeries danced upon icy winds and scattered thousands of perfectly carved snowflakes upon the ground. They spent the entire year carving each one to be unique in design and creation.

The mere thought of it made her giggle. It didn't seem likely. Faeries would spend that much time and detail into creating something for humans to enjoy, but she hadn't travelled through the Otherworld. It was possible, and she wanted to meet the creatures who dedicated their lives to such a feat.

She rolled onto her side and stretched out her hand, hoping to find Manus on the other side. Cold sheets met her fingertips.

Another night when he slipped away. Propriety be damned, she didn't want him to go back to his room. She didn't like waking to a cold side of the bed while having to wonder where he'd gone off to.

Frowning, she sat up. As she rolled, her hand fell on a small parchment left on Manus's pillow.

Excitement lifted the hairs on her arms. Were they to go on another trip? Had he yet another surprise for her?

She unfurled the scroll and tried to make sense of the scratched marks. It wasn't in any language she'd ever read before. The human writing wasn't easy to learn. They had so many letters, markings, and strange ways of expressing emotion. Manus had given up on teaching her and she grew too frustrated.

A soft knock on the door heralded the return of her maids. They entered quietly as if they did not want to wake her.

"I'm already up," she called out. "Good morning, ladies! How are you?"

They flinched at her voice. One tentatively replied, "We are well, my lady. How are you feeling?"

"Wonderful. It's a beautiful day outside, is it not?"

Saoirse hopped down from the large bed and made her way towards the mirror. They could make her as pretty a doll as they wanted today. Manus had another surprise for her. And though she didn't know what it was, she was certain it would be life changing.

The maids did not reply.

She met their startled gazes in their reflection and furrowed her brows. Something was wrong, but it couldn't be. The sun was shining, the birds were singing, how could anything be amiss?

Hesitantly, she released her grip on the letter and held it up for one of them to take. "Could you read this to me please?"

"Can you not?"

She shook her head.

The maids looked at each other. One blushed bright red, reached out, and plucked the letter from her fingers. "A patron taught me how to read, mistress."

"Start on my hair," Saoirse ordered. She turned towards the mirror and focused on keeping her expression as still as a tranquil pool.

"My pearl, you looked so beautiful sleeping this morning that I could not wake you. Every morning you look the same, and I take all the blame for not telling you sooner. I leave today for—" the maid paused and held the letter out to Saoirse. "My lady I should not be reading this."

"Read it."

"This is personal, perhaps I should get the butler—"

"Read it." Saoirse's tone did not allow for any argument.

The maid winced but returned her gaze to the contents of the letter.

"I leave today for the West Indies. Captain Ramsey has agreed to charter the voyage, so our wealth remains in your capable hands. I apologize I could not tell you this in person, my pearl. I trust you understand why I could not bear to see the disappointment in your gaze. The ocean is not a safe place for you. Be well and know that you will be in my thoughts. Signed, Manus."

Saoirse swallowed, but kept her gaze on the mirror. Her face would not move. She would not show her reaction to these women.

Inside, her heart was breaking. Manus had known this entire time he would never take her on that ship. He hung freedom in front of her, dangling it like a treat, and all the while knew she would never be given that gift.

"My lady," the maid brushing her hair murmured. "We thought you knew."

"What time did he leave?"

"Before the sun rose. He made every effort to make certain you were comfortable in his absence. Being the wife of a sea captain isn't an easy life. They're always gone."

"How long?" The words were strained and rushed. She cleared her throat. "How long are they usually gone?"

She saw the maids exchange a look in the mirror. "You don't know?"

"Manus did not see fit to speak to me about his travels. How long are they usually gone?"

"Months, my lady. The West Indies is a considerable journey that could take a year to complete."

A year? An entire year alone in this gods-forsaken place with only humans to keep her company?

Saoirse's mind spiraled. She lost control over her face which tightened in anger and humiliation. These women knew. They had known the entire time where Manus was going.

She could sense their emotions. Sadness, pity, and the faintest hint of glee.

Words slammed through her lips, rushing forward to set fire to the rest of her life. "Who were you to him? Before he hired you on as my lady's maids?"

"I don't—"

"Tell me."

"We were his favorites," one of them ground out. Saoirse didn't care which one. "At the brothel, there were a few of us who were considered 'special'. Manus always chose one—or more—of us, when he returned from a long trip."

"How long?"

"What?"

"How long has it been since he chose you?"

The maid closest to the door shook her head. "It's not right to be discussing such things. We like our job, my lady. We don't mean to hurt you or the lord, it's just that you asked and—"

"Get out."

They froze, their eyes as big as sand dollars.

The one who had read the letter licked her lips. "My lady, he saved us. The life we led before was not an easy one, and certainly not a safe one. He didn't tell you because it's not important anymore. We can all tell how he feels about you—"

When they did not move, Saoirse whirled around, her fingers clawing into the wooden chair back. "Get out!"

They spun in a whirl of skirts and raced from the room. Pounding feet echoed down the hall, along with shouts of inquiry, then sudden silence. It was as if the entire house waited with bated breath for what their mistress would do next.

Responsibility pressed down on her shoulders. She was supposed to be some paragon for these people. A figurehead for their grounded ship.

How could she possibly be that when she was a creature meant to be wild and free?

She couldn't breathe. Saoirse pressed her hands to her throat and begged her human body to work. Her fingers touched the faint lines where her gills could open, and tears welled in her eyes.

The ocean would help. It would hide all her pain, tears, and frustration. No one could tell she was ripping open at the seams.

Saoirse lurched to her feet, stumbling from the room onto the balcony where she could grip the stone railing and tilt her face towards the sun.

This was what she had wanted. A human life with a human husband in a human house.

She took in a deep breath and held it until her lungs burned. How could she have known what this life would be like? No one had told her.

The stone railing creaked, her grip so strong it threatened to crack the white marble. She stared down at her inhuman hands and wondered how long it would take for them to realize what she really was. In the absence of their master, all attention would be cast upon her.

Would they like having a faerie in their midst? She'd heard tales of humans destroying kind souls who only wished to help. Or worse, elevating them to status of a god.

Someone entered her bedroom, knocking on the door and shuffling their feet.

"My lady?" the butler asked. "Are you well?"

"I wish to be alone."

"Understandable. I wanted you to know we're all here for you."

She turned, seeing his bright red cheeks and the way he wrung his hands together. "Pardon?"

"You must excuse my forwardness, ma'am. But the house staff didn't like the way the master ran off in the early morning. I feared he might not have told you and it didn't seem right."

"Liam, isn't it?"

"It is."

"Thank you for your concern. Please share with the rest of the house that although I am…not pleased, I am well and appreciate their thoughts."

"I will, my lady."

He bowed and closed the door behind him as he left.

Saoirse folded onto the floor of the balcony. Silent sobs wracked her frame while her fingers began to tremble. The desire to leap off the edge and fall into the sea was so fierce, so strong, that she almost flung herself over.

But she didn't. She was the lady of this house, and regardless of what she wanted, this was now her life.

Wind yanked her hair from the tight braid, sending strands lashing across her cheeks and back. The long length flew free and wild in the wake on the oncoming storm.

Saoirse stood with her arms wrapped around her waist, staring at the raging sea. The cliff edge was a few meters from her. Temptation just out of reach. Black clouds boiled in the skies and the ocean churned. A mirror of her emotions and fear.

Winter would soon touch this land with frost and icy winds. The servants explained to her that was why Manus had left in a hurry. The ship would be forced to remain in the harbor until next year if they were caught in the cold.

It had been weeks of waiting. Weeks of trying her best to act human, to be the mistress of a grand house and learn their ways.

Weeks of failure and wasted time.

She had given up. No matter how much she tried to be a lady, there was always something wild in her that rebelled. The women here might hide behind fans, but their fangs were blunt compared to hers. She wanted to tear them apart, to curse them, to fling their pieces to the sharks.

A ragged voice broke through her thoughts. "I am growing weary of your tumultuous emotions, merrow."

"Then stop prying, leprechaun."

Declan crunched through the gravel to reach her. He paused just behind her, his great bulk a wave of heat carrying the metallic scent of gold. "What are you doing out here?"

She didn't respond, merely handed him the letter she held in her hand. The folds were deep, the edges ripped, but she had taken to carrying it, nonetheless. It was the last bit of him she had. And the only thing fueling her anger.

Declan read the words and swore. "That bastard."

"He did what he thought was right."

"You're still justifying his actions? He *left* you."

"And I am still standing." She squeezed her arms to hold in the shiver that rocked through her body. "This was the life I chose, Declan. This and no other."

"You chose it, yes, but you can still change your path. One decision does not create a cage."

"It has for me," she murmured, staring out at the waves. "We are bonded, he and I. There can be no other."

Declan crossed his arms firmly over his chest. "You went through with that nonsense, did you?"

"I didn't think there was a way to stop it."

"Well, you could have just…not bonded with him."

She gave him a censuring look.

"Sorry, love. I know it's probably a sensitive subject." He held out the letter for her to take. "What are you going to do?"

"I don't know." She crumpled the letter and tucked her hands back underneath her arms. "The temptation will always be there. I'm coming to realize that no matter what I do, I will always miss the ocean. And no matter what I say, Manus will never let me near it for fear I will disappear forever."

Declan walked around her, blocking her view of the sea. He filled her gaze with a broad chest, strong arms, and golden rings flickering as he cracked his knuckles.

"Look at me, merrow."

She squared her shoulders and met his gaze.

"If you had a chance, if you were freed from all your ties, would you slip back into the ocean?"

She bit her lip. Would she?

Her shoulders curved forward and her expression fell. "Yes," she whispered. "I would."

"It's not a bad thing to admit it. You should never feel guilty for being as you truly are. Faeries weren't meant to remain in the human world."

"That's not true. This is, and always will be, our first choice."

A flash of anger sparked in his eyes. "They drove us out. We created something better in response."

"Did we? Funny, that's not how I remember the tale."

Declan gestured at the manor behind her. "Is this what you thought it would be? Is this what you wanted? Because I cannot believe that deep under the sea you knew everything this life would bring with it. Responsibility. Servants. Money. Noblemen and their wives staring at your every move and judging you harshly based on them."

"No!" Saoirse shouted. "Is that what you want to hear, Declan? All I wanted was *him*. I didn't care if we had four walls around us. I wanted his love, his attention, his laughter. I wanted to shape my life around him, have a family, grow old together."

"It doesn't look like that's what you're doing. It looks like you're standing on the edge of a cliff, wondering just how long it would take you to hit the water and disappear forever."

He saw right through her so easily it frightened her. Saoirse hadn't even felt herself inching towards the edge of the cliff, but that was what she had done. Step by step, closer and closer to the freedom of the waves.

And the bitter loneliness. The painful end as heartbreak slowly ate away at her sanity until she sank to the bottom of the sea.

A tear slid down her cheek. "Oh, Declan. This isn't the life I thought it would be."

He opened his arms to her. "Come here, merrow. Dry your tears."

She rushed forward and let his warmth envelop her. It wasn't the same as Manus, but she supposed she shouldn't have expected that. No one would ever measure up to the man who filled her heart, no matter what mistakes he made.

Declan smoothed his hands up and down her spine. "It will be okay, Saoirse."

"How could you possibly know that?"

"There's only two options for you. To remain the wife of a human who disappears for months on end or return home."

"I have no home." She sniffled. "I cannot return to my family. They will either lock me up forever or chase me from their waters."

"They are not the only merrows in the ocean."

Saoirse pulled back. "What?"

"There are a few groups around here, they call themselves pods. They're kinder than their deep water cousins. If you ask, they'll take you in."

"My mother mentioned a cousin," she mused. "I didn't know what she meant but perhaps it has something to do with the merrows who live here."

"You'll likely never know. But you'd be with your own people. Safe and sound."

"Do you hate them?"

"Who?"

"Humans. You don't trust them at all."

"When you've seen what I've seen, you can't trust them anymore."

He released her and stepped back. "They lie, cheat, and steal. Humans aren't the paragons we once thought them to be, and every single one of them has the capacity to be cruel."

"I can't believe that. I have seen so much good in them."

"Who? Your little artisan? He's more Fae than human now." Declan lifted his hands and wiggled his fingers. "Or did you think those were human hands they put on him?"

"Now you're just being cruel."

"It's in my nature."

She didn't want it to be in hers. Saoirse understood that many of the Fae were jaded. Most were power hungry, and the humans stole so much from them. But she had thought Declan would have seen the *good* here as well as the bad.

Although she had seen throngs of people with judgmental gazes, she had seen them help each other as well. A woman handing a piece of bread to a hungry child. A servant helping sweep after a long, hard day. Even elderly men and women passing down traditions and knowledge.

All these things made humans worthwhile. They were good people, and she wouldn't forget that.

Her ears burned with the desire to hear true silence once again. She wanted the ocean to press down on her chest. Maybe that would ease the anxiety that stole her breath away.

"My place is here," she croaked. "This is my choice. These are my people now."

"You're fooling yourself if you believe that." Declan shook his head. "I'll stick around for a while. It looks like you may need a man of the house."

"It wouldn't be appropriate."

"We aren't proper, Saoirse. You and I were creatures born of midnight and monsters. The Wild Hunt approaches. We'll need each other if we want to survive it."

He sauntered away, leaving Saoirse to gape at the open sea.

The Wild Hunt. She'd forgotten the Lord and his people who rode across the human lands and collected faeries who should not be there. Would he try to take her?

Would it matter?

She shivered and wrapped her arms back around herself. She should go inside, introduce Declan to the servants, answer the questions they would inevitably have.

Waves crashed against the cliff. Seagulls cried out overhead. And Saoirse remained frozen on the edge of the cliff, listening to the song of the sea.

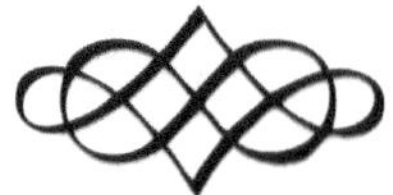

Great bangs echoed through the halls of the manor. Plates and vases shattered on stone. A few murmurs raised in a sudden silence, questions that would not be answered as further bangs rocked the manor.

Saoirse had already shredded her own room. She had tossed the sheets off the balcony, shattered the mirror, ripped apart the bedding in her desperate search. She had stalked across the hall, shoved aside the butler, and started in on Manus's room.

Some might say she wasn't thinking straight. She could hear the servants whispering that she'd lost her mind. It was a shame the mistress was too delicate to live without the master in the home, and who should they contact? She had no family they knew of.

The poor dear needed help.

She snorted and tore through a pillow. Help. As if they would have any idea how to begin to help her.

"My lady?" The butler said, clearing his throat. "You have a visitor."

"I don't have time for visitors."

Clunking footsteps marched into the room. She heard the butler argue as he was pushed from the room, and then the door slammed in his face.

"What in the devil are you doing, Saoirse?" Declan growled. "I'm supposed to be here to keep their attention off you not explaining your eccentricities!"

"I lost something," she murmured, searching the room for her next victim. "I don't know what it is, I can't remember. It's like my mind remembers something but won't tell me what."

"You're not making any sense."

"I know that!" she shouted. "I can feel I'm not making sense, but I also know I don't feel like *myself*. There's something missing. Something I should have."

Declan grabbed her hands. "Saoirse, sit down. Come on, no, you will not look anymore. Sit down."

She slowly sank onto the edge of Manus's ruined bed. Her heart raced, and her eyes flicked around the room, attempting to find yet another hiding place where he could have put... *something.*

"Saoirse, what have you lost? Focus."

She shook her head frantically. "I don't know. I can't remember, it's like everything I knew is filtering out of my head. My memories. My family. I can't... Declan, I can't."

Saoirse buried her face in her hands, sobbing. She was shaking and afraid of the changes she couldn't control. Her mind was supposed to be a temple.

Now, it felt like a prison.

He folded her hands in his, shifting them back and forth until a golden light appeared between their fingers. She watched the soothing movements with rapt attention. Her heart slowed, her head bobbed, and slowly her mind cleared.

Declan opened their hands. A gold coin sat in the center of her palm. The very coin he had given her long ago in the pub.

"Focus on the coin, Saoirse. Let your mind wander. You might not know what you lost, but you know where it is."

She followed the coin as he danced it across his fingertips. The coin wasn't what she desperately wanted, but perhaps he was right. If she relaxed, breathed, centered herself, then perhaps she might *feel* what she wanted.

Saoirse's mind calmed into a trance-like state. Declan skillfully rolled the coin over and over his knuckles.

It was from her home, whatever the item was. She remembered rolling waves, seagulls, but most of all the taste of salt on her tongue. Her family was far beneath her. Hundreds of children, all with tails like fish and hair like kelp. They gathered to sing, but they were horrible at it.

Her lips curved in a soft smile. Not a single one of her sisters could hold a tune. They said they would leave it to the sirens, but she knew it bothered them.

Songs were sacred to merrows, and they dearly loved to listen to music. Sometimes, they would swim towards the surface, hovering together and waiting for the whales to pass by.

Once, when she was very little, Saoirse had swum away from the sounds to explore. And in the darkest depths of the sea, she met a very young guardian who sang a song so pure that it rattled her soul.

"Oh," she whispered. "I remember."

"Where is it?"

"I had it with me when I arrived. But I don't remember where I put it."

"Think harder, Saoirse. Where could it possibly be?"

And then she remembered. Manus had shown her a small music box, his mother's favorite trinket. The song reminded her of the guardian's, so she'd placed it there for safe keeping.

Saoirse sighed. "A music box."

"This one?"

Her eyes snapped open, although she did not remember closing them, and saw Declan held the box in his hand. "How did you know?"

"There's only one music box in the house."

"But where was it?"

He winked. "It's gold, darling. Anything gold speaks to me."

"Open it."

The bright music twinkled from within as soon as he twisted the base. The lid lifted and revealed a tiny dancer spinning in a circle. At the end of the song, a drawer opened at the bottom.

Hidden within was a small spiral seashell.

"Now I remember," she breathed. "This was the gift my mother gave me before I left. How could I forget so easily?"

"The farther he is away from you, and the longer he is gone, the worse you will get." Declan reached out and ran a hand over her head. "Your bond will make you deteriorate even further."

Sudden panic made her push up from the bed and sprint out the door. She careened into the shambles of her room. Sheets tangled in her feet, but she safely stumbled to the balcony.

Breathing in the salt air, she twisted the shell in her ear where it was meant to be.

Song filled the ocean and the sky above it. The guardians cried out for their lost child, mourning a merrow girl who had not returned to their waiting arms. They screamed in rage, sobbed in sadness, and then fell to sudden silence.

Saoirse waited the long heartbeats until they began wailing again.

Declan placed his hand on the balcony next to hers. "He will not return for at least another six months."

"Will I even last that long?" she asked.

"You have a choice. Do you wish to die here, waiting for your human to return? Or do you wish to die in the arms of your own kind?"

"I can't make that decision."

"You will have to soon enough."

"Captain?"

Manus turned, tearing his gaze from the waves for a mere moment to glance at his first mate. "What is it?"

"We've a stowaway."

His curiosity peaked, Manus tilted his head to the side and watched as a small boy was thrown to his hands and knees on the deck. Mangy and young, the boy was hardly of age to be on a ship.

But he remembered being that age and wanting nothing more than to be a sailor.

The boy whimpered as Manus thundered towards him. He'd have to get used to the commanding nature of a captain. Manus couldn't make himself any less intimidating, or the other men would rise against him. Mutiny was something a ship couldn't survive, no matter how new she was.

"How did you manage to hide yourself on my ship, boy?"

The child wiped his nose and glared up at him. "It wasn't all that hard."

"No?"

"I hid myself in a rum casket. Emptied the goods into the sea and your men loaded me on without even checking beneath the lid."

Manus arched a brow. "Really?"

He heard the scuffle of nervous feet. Whoever had loaded the rum onto the ship was likely running off to hide himself for a few days. They'd seen the wrath of their captain already, and he knew they agreed he was a terrifying man. Fair, but lethal.

"I ain't done nothing to you or your men."

"No, you haven't. But you are here without permission, and we are in the middle of the ocean. I meticulously planned to have enough rations for exactly the amount of men on this ship. You showing up means we no longer have the food and drink we require to survive. Do you understand?"

The boy's eyes were as large as dinner plates. "I hadn't thought about that."

"No, I expect you didn't."

"Are you going to throw me overboard?" The boy squared his shoulders and bared his teeth. "I'll fight you."

"I don't think you'd stand much of a chance. But no, I don't intend to throw a child to the sharks."

Manus nodded to his first mate, ignoring the eye roll the other man gave him. The crew would get used to the idea of having a boy around. The child's small fingers would prove useful in the coming months.

"Come with me," Manus ordered. "I have something to show you."

"You sure you aren't going to toss me?"

"We'll give you a trial run on the sea. If you prove to be a good sailor, then I'll allow you to remain. If you aren't, we'll revisit feeding the sharks."

"I'm a good sailor." The boy straightened his shirt. "You'll see."

"Surprisingly, I have no doubt of that."

He saw something of himself in the boy although he was loath to admit it. Manus noted the marks of hard work. Scratches on the child's hands, leathery elbows poking through a threadbare shirt, the slight wince as he stood and the way he pressed his arm against his side.

They walked to the bow of the ship. Manus kept his pace slow and leisurely, making certain to stop and speak with the crew. They needed reassurance just as much as the boy needed to breathe through what Manus suspected were broken ribs.

Once they traveled as far as they could, Manus pointed to the masthead. "Do you know what that is?"

"A merrow. Cursed faeries shouldn't be on boats."

"Who told you that?"

"My pa."

"He the one who punched you in the chest?" Manus chuckled at the boy's startled expression. "I remember the feeling of broken ribs, it's not hard to see it in another."

"What's it to you?" The boy wiped his nose on his sleeve. "Ain't nothing anyways. A bit of bruising is all."

"I'll have the doctor look at you."

"Doctor?"

"I believe every ship should have one, although most aren't willing to pay them. Now why do you say a merrow curses a ship?"

"Faeries are bad luck. Besides, merrows make deals with men and then drown them."

"I don't know about that," Manus replied. He leaned against the railing and looked the boy up and down. "Merrows have always been kind in my experience."

"You've met one?"

"Several. I was one of the unlucky men to meet their husbands too." He made a face. "They were the ugliest creatures known to mankind. So, if the merrows are dragging men to the bottom of the ocean, I suspect they wish to marry *them* instead of their own kind."

The boy stuck out a hand. "Alroy. That's my name."

"Manus." They shook hands as men did, firm and strong. Manus ignored the boy's wince and nodded to the merrow. "Faeries aren't good or bad. They're a little a bit of both. Merrows keep watch over the seas, to make certain no unsuspecting human stumbles into the Otherworld."

"What if we want to?"

"Why would you? The Otherworld is a dangerous place for humans. Faeries aren't particularly kind to us."

Alroy brandished his fists. "I could take 'em. They wouldn't know what hit 'em!"

He mimed punching, throwing out his arms in wild directions. The boy wouldn't stand a chance if a faerie decided he was worth their attentions. Manus suspected it was more likely they would ignore the boy entirely.

"Have you ever heard of the man who married a merrow?"

Alroy frowned. "No. Why would anyone do that?"

"Well, merrows can find gold wherever they are. Shipwrecks, lost jewels, even ancient tombs all buried underneath the ocean. They bring it up for their husbands and let them live a life of happiness."

"Gold ain't worth all that."

"No?"

"People should marry who they want. They shouldn't be forced into it because they want money." Alroy scuffed his bare feet on the deck. "Besides, who would want to be married to a fish anyways?"

"They aren't always fish," Manus said with a chuckle. "But I see your point. In the old stories, the man was always in love with the merrow. She promised to live on land with him as long as he was faithful, and in return, she would give him a son.

"He was good and true. There came a day when he had to travel to market. When he returned, his merrow wife was gone. The boy remained but there was no sign she ever existed."

"Why?" Alroy asked. "Why would she leave without letting him know why?"

"Legend has it the sea calls to them. They desire it so badly, they have to go." Manus stared out at the sea, a troubled worry settling in the pit of his stomach.

Would she leave? He doubted it. Saoirse loved him more than life itself, so it seemed. She wouldn't leave him because he had followed his dreams. Of anyone, she would understand the call of the sea.

Alroy tugged his sleeve. "What happened then?"

"Hm?"

"In the story, captain. What happened to the man and the merrow? Did she ever come back?"

"Oh." He squinted his eyes, trying to remember the story his mother had whispered to him at night. "Aye, they found each other. Ten years later, when their boy was all grown up, they rowed out towards their ship. The merrow woman appeared. She said she had come for her husband now that their son could take care of himself."

Alroy shivered. "What did she do?"

"Nothing. Her husband reached into the water and let her drag him down into the deep."

Alroy raced away. He shouted the story for others to hear, exclaiming that the merrows would certainly find them and drag them into the depths.

It was a fanciful tale. Manus hadn't believed it when he was a boy, and he wasn't about to believe it now.

Still… It had merit.

He reached into the breast pocket of his jacket and pulled out a tiny glass merrow. The likeness to his wife was uncanny. Light reflected on her smiling face, catching the sadness of her eyes. She clutched a seashell in her hands and stared at him as if he had placed her in a cage.

Carefully, Manus folded her in his grasp as he stared at the rolling waves.

Saoirse knelt on an embroidered pillow in the small grotto where they had hidden the glass merrow. Vines framed the cave wall and the quiet rush of the sea echoed throughout. Light reflected the waves on the ceiling, creating a pattern that eased her mind and terrified her at the same time.

She pressed her hands to her chest and breathed out a quiet sigh. "What am I to do?"

Memories faded every day. Important memories that made her who she was. Memories that created the woman Saoirse knew. As they faded, she became confused, complicit, quiet. No one knew what was happening to their mistress.

Declan remained to take care of her. He carried her to bed and pressed cold compresses to her forehead each night. He was tireless in his desire to keep her alive.

But they both knew each day Manus was gone, the more dire her situation grew.

Why hadn't she thought of this? She might have told him, explained to him all that could happen if he didn't bring her with him.

It hadn't felt right. She would have ruined all the good they had built between the two of them. And he would feel trapped. Saoirse could already see the disappointed expression on his face when she told him they could never go to sea again.

No, it was better this way. She would survive until he returned. Only a few more months.

She pressed a hand to the bulge of her belly. Even Declan didn't know this small secret growing inside her.

"We're going to be okay," she whispered. "You and I will survive this."

"Are you so certain of that?" Declan asked from behind her.

"You are supposed to be in the main house. The servants will gossip about where we are."

"They already think you're having an affair. You've heard their whispers just as I have." He settled next to her on the stone floor. "It's not the end of the world if they talk."

"It would be if Manus hears tell of it."

"In the Indies?" He snorted. "He isn't going to hear anything on the other side of the world."

"Don't be cruel."

"You're killing yourself staying here, Saoirse. You know if you return to the sea that you'll have a little more time."

"I can do this."

"For me." Declan reached forward and took her hands. "Do it for me, Saoirse. I'll stay behind, make your excuses, even let your husband know what happened. I cannot stay here and watch you die."

A tentative smile spread across her lips and a bubble of familiar mirth burst in her chest. "Why Declan, that almost sounds as if you like me."

"I'm fond of you. We're in the same situation, you and I, cursed to live on human lands." He squeezed her fingers. "But you can go home. You can live out the rest of your life with your own people, in your own skin, without hiding who you truly are."

"And what will I give up by doing that?" she whispered. "I want to see him one last time."

"He took that from you the moment he set sail from these shores. He won't be back in time, Saoirse. I want to see that babe grow into a beautiful young woman like yourself." He winked. "Maybe she'll be interested in a handsome leprechaun."

Saoirse snorted. "She'll be interested in whomever she wishes. Thousands of men will desire her hand, and she will pick whichever one she desires the most."

"I hope, for your sake, that you are correct."

She stared at the glass merrow and weighed her options.

Manus would return, eventually. There was no way for them to guess how long that might take. Ships traveled as fast as the wind and sea would let them. But it was unlikely he would return for at least another few months, or worse, a year if they were held up in the city where they would trade.

She would drift away until there was nothing left of her at all. Her mind would fracture, her body weaken, and eventually she would answer the pulsating call of the sea. It wanted her to return. It sang for her, the guardians calling for her day and night.

One way or another, she would go home.

Saoirse shook her head, a small sobbing breath puffing between her lips. "I want to be here for him. I want to stay until he returns."

Her eyes burned with the pressure of trying to keep tears from rolling down her cheeks. Declan's expression crumpled in pity.

"I know," he replied. "I know you want to stay here for him, but is there really any other choice?"

There wasn't. He knew that, just as Saoirse knew she was fighting a losing battle. It didn't make it any easier to admit defeat.

She dropped her head and slowly nodded. "What will you tell the servants?"

"That it looked like a rogue wave crashed through the grotto, taking you out to sea before I could grab you. It's close enough to the truth that it's not quite a lie. The waves took you out to sea before I could drag you back." He flashed a grin. "I'm not a faerie who likes to swim."

"Will they believe that?"

"I've enough magic left in me. They won't have a choice." A gold coin flashed between his thumb and forefinger. "It's a believable story. They've never seen you in water before, and with all those skirts it's unlikely even a strong swimmer would survive."

"And Manus?"

The coin disappeared under a clenched fist. "He'll know what happened."

"You'll tell him the truth?" When Declan didn't respond, she pressed with a firm tone, "Declan, you'll tell him the truth."

"He doesn't deserve the whole truth. It would be less painful for everyone if you let him believe the same story as everyone else."

"I won't go knowing he thinks I willingly left."

"You're making the choice."

"I *know*, Declan. I'm doing my best to keep myself together, but I will not allow him to think I don't still love him." She shook her head. "Please, Declan. Please don't take that away from us."

He growled, his glamour slipping to reveal golden skin that glittered in the dim light. Sharp teeth gnashed, but he gave in. "Understood. He'll know the truth. But you understand he'll come after you?"

"It's the only hope I have left. Manus wouldn't let me go without a fight. And if, by some chance, I'm still alive? Then I hope with all my heart he finds me."

She stood, her bones creaking and her head spinning with the effort. Even her physical form hurt now that he had been gone for so many months.

Was this what the bean sídhe had warned her about? That tying herself to a human would slowly eat away at her until there was nothing left?

Saoirse hoped she never had to find out.

Piece by piece, she unwove the layers of clothing her maids had placed on her this morning. Even living with humans this long had not made her self-conscious about her body. Nudity was a normal part of life for faeries. It was humans who were wrong in their shame.

Declan solemnly held each article of clothing until she stood bare as the day she was born. A small pool of water stood behind the glass merrow. It led to the sea through small caverns Manus said he'd played in as a boy. Dangerous pastimes for a human, but he'd had many stories to tell.

A shiver trailed down her spine. Another sign she was weakening by the moment. She had never felt cold in her life.

Until now.

Saoirse reached up and untangled her hair from the winding braids. Pins dropped to the stone floor and echoed in tiny pricks of sound.

"Promise me. Promise me you'll tell him the truth."

"I vow it." Declan's words rang in her ears and bounced off the walls. It was a binding oath, one he would have to fulfil, or he would follow her to the grave.

Giving him one final nod, she stepped into the water and disappeared beneath the surface.

Declan waited until the final ripple subsided. Only then did he stand and return to the main house to give them ill news.

CHAPTER 11
The Return

The sun rose over the horizon and illuminated the port town of Uí Néill. Manus held onto the mast of the ship, far above his crew. It did not befit a man of his station to be up in the sails, but he couldn't care less.

He was finally home.

Tilting his head back, he inhaled deeply. The wind brought with it the fresh scent of salt, the acrid sting of fish, and the burn of smoke rising from the chimneys. It was the scent of his people, and he had missed it.

"Captain!" A voice shouted from below.

"Set down the anchors, boys!" A cheer drowned out his next words. "We're home."

All he wanted to do was get off this ship and back into the arms of the woman he loved. Time away from Saoirse had put so many things in perspective. She could be safe on the waters with him. The waves never crested a height where he might have worried her brethren could be find her location. And if he dressed her like a man, not even the biggest gossips of the faerie world could tell it was her.

His plan wasn't ironclad, but it was enough for him to be comfortable bringing her with him on the ship. There were so many plans to be made. She would want to see the world, and he wanted to show it to her.

Manus had never dreamed of having a wife who would share his love of travel. He had thought it would be hours of arguing, angry fights, lashing words as he went off to sea. It was why he hadn't told her in the first place.

But now he was certain she could come with him. And she would, because Saoirse would do anything for him.

They settled the ship to her bed, laid to rest until the next journey. The men were happy with their share. Manus was generous with their cut. He already had a fortune and knew where to find more if need be. They could keep most of the spoils.

They laughed as they set the boats to the water and tightened the last ropes on the Freedom. Manus patted the railing one last time, in thanks for the safe travels and in hopes for many more journeys to come.

His first mate waited for him in the last of the boats. Together, they watched the line of sailors laughing as they made it to the docks.

"It was a successful maiden voyage," Manus mused.

"To many more."

"Aye."

They stepped into the boat. Manus held himself still. It wouldn't do to show how excited he was to return. Too many sailors believed in superstitions, and a captain who preferred land to sea was a bad omen.

But he very much wanted to see his wife.

"Do you have anyone waiting for you?" he asked the first mate.

"Not particularly, captain. A few ladies in a brothel nearby, and I haven't given much thought to settling down. Do you?"

"I have the prettiest wife in the lands. My personal good luck charm."

"Your fortunes are great then. Few captains have a happy wife waiting for them upon their return."

He chuckled. "I can't say she'll be happy. I slipped out without telling her."

"She might not even recognize you." His first mate pointed to his beard. "You look more beast than man."

Their laughter echoed over the open waters and neither stopped until they reached the docks. Manus stepped out last, taking his first mate's offered hand and leaping onto the worn wood.

"It was an incredible journey, captain. I look forward to many more with you."

"Rest assured, I'll want you by my side on the next adventure."

They parted ways, and Manus made his way through the streets of his childhood. Dirty children raced by, screaming fishwives shook their fists, the tang of fish blood filled the air, and it was all endearing in a strange way.

It had been far too long since he'd wandered these streets. Although a part of him wanted to continue wandering, he also knew someone had likely seen the ship on the horizon. He'd need to rent a horse and get back to the house as soon as possible.

"My lord?" A small voice asked.

He looked down to see a boy, no older than ten, holding out his hand for a coin. "My pa said someone would need a horse from that ship. Be you willing to take this one?"

It was an ancient animal, but it would do. Nodding, he dropped a few gold coins into the child's palm and savored the look of awe.

"I'll take the horse for good. Tell your pa to buy a much better one for his plow."

"Aye, my lord. That'll do."

The boy ran off, little legs pumping to bring the good news to his father. Or to spend the money. Either way, it wasn't Manus's duty to figure out what the child would do.

He mounted the horse and set off at a decent canter. The old nag wouldn't survive a full gallop towards the manor. He didn't mind though; the surrounding landscape was beautiful and the land solid beneath his feet. What more could a man ask for?

Manus thought of his wife and couldn't stop the smile drifting across his face. Saoirse would be so pleased to see him. Even though he had been gone for a long time, there was a part of him that never stopped thinking about her.

Surely she would have felt that? He laid awake at night, staring up at the stars, knowing she was out there looking at the sky as well. He could almost feel her love from leagues away.

The manor appeared ahead of him, the path worn by the feet of thousands who had ridden past it. As a child, he'd marveled at the people who lived within those four walls. Now, those people were Manus and Saoirse. He intended to fill the house with many more family members soon.

The thought spurred him on. Children, he wanted children. Like the child on the ship, a boy who would ride the seas with him. A daughter, whose dark hair and eyes would solemnly watch the waves for faeries.

He rode into the courtyard like a bean sídhe on the wind. The horse foamed at the mouth but galloped upon the stone right to the front door. The butler rushed out and waved his hand.

"My lord! You've returned!"

"I have. And I'd like to see my wife."

"Master, *wait*—"

He didn't pause to listen to whatever the man wanted to prattle on about. Servants were always so focused on what was proper, and he didn't have time for proper. Propriety be damned; he'd waited a very long time to see Saoirse.

And if she was still abed, more the better.

He took the stairs two at a time. His boots cracked against the wood, a staccato beat that echoed the beating of his heart. He was nearly there.

Soon, he would see her again. As much as he hated to admit it, she'd become a part of him. Saoirse, his sweet Saoirse.

Never again would he insist they sleep in separate beds. Never again would he set her aside when there was work to be done. He'd be a better husband and focus less on being a better lord.

Who cared that they had money and station now? If the other nobles wanted to gossip, let them. No one could take away his wealth and they damn well weren't taking his wife.

He set his shoulder to her door and shoved hard. It slammed against the side wall, echoing as he strode in like he owned the place.

"Wife?" he called out. "I have returned."

No one responded to his call. Frowning, he glanced around the room which was oddly put together. She wasn't so tidy. Saoirse had a way of making messes everywhere she went. Her maids could hardly keep up with her, a fact they enjoyed telling him, but Manus liked being able to track her through the house.

"Saoirse?"

The silence was deafening.

Footsteps heralded the approach of an entire servant army. The maids reached him first, their hair in disarray and skirts held up around their ankles.

"My lord, we didn't expect you to return so soon."

"We're so glad you've arrived safe and sound. When we heard no news, we became worried."

His accountant arrived next, pulling off his hat and gloves. "Master, we kept careful watch over your fortune. We can easily continue on in such a manner for a long time. I assure you, we have not misused your wealth in your absence."

The head housekeeper was next, brushing aside the maids with an angry swipe. "It's good to have you home, my lord. There is much I must speak with you about. Plenty of work to be done, I'm afraid."

Manus didn't want to hear any of it. They chattered like hens in a yard until he snapped. "Silence!"

The entire crowd of people fell still. A hairpin might have dropped to the floor and he would have heard it.

"Where is my wife?"

Not a single servant dared to say a word.

"You there." He pointed at the butler who had tried to get his attention upon arrival. "Explain."

"My lord I-I-I'm uncertain that I'm the appropriate person to do so."

"Where is my wife?" Manus thundered.

One of the maids, the whore he'd appreciated most in the brothel, stepped forward and laid a hand on his arm. "Manus, I'm sorry. She's gone."

"Gone where? I'll go and get her. A wife should know to stay and wait for her husband's return."

Anger simmered in his blood. Not at Saoirse, but at the servants who tried to keep his attention away from that which was important. Who cared about the gardens, the money, or the house? He cared about his bride whom he had not had enough time to enjoy.

"No," the maid murmured and shook her head. "She's *gone*, Manus."

"What are you trying to say?"

"She went down by the sea, she often walks at the shore. We thought nothing of it, but her friend...the red headed lord? He came back and said she was swept out by a rogue wave. There was nothing he could do. We looked for her, Manus. We looked for days. I'm so sorry."

They believed it. Every one of his servants believed the most ridiculous tale he'd ever heard before. They thought she was dead.

Their faces fell in sadness. Tears welled in the eyes of the head housekeeper, a woman he knew to be emotionless and cold. They thought he would fly into a rage, blame them for her death, or worse fire them all.

What they didn't know, was that Saoirse could swim. She could swim better than any human and no rogue wave could tear her from his side.

But she could leave him.

His heart clenched, and his palms grew sweaty. She had left him. She had decided that her old life was better than this one.

Gods, he couldn't breathe.

"Leave me," he growled. "Leave me be."

He backed into her room and slammed the door in the faces of all those who remained. They loved him, or some strange semblance of love he couldn't understand. Did he even know what love was?

The only person who had ever loved him had left.

Hands shaking, blood boiling, breath rattling out of his lungs, he turned towards the room which was too put together and let out a rage filled roar. She'd left him? Why?

He swept his arms over her vanity, sending her bottles of perfumes to the floor. They shattered and filled the room with cloying scents, but he didn't care. He only wanted to tear into everything more.

He'd given her a good life. He'd bought her the most beautiful house in Uí Néill, loved her as no man had ever loved a woman before. And she repaid him by leaving?

For hours he raged in her room, shattering furniture, tossing sheets and pieces of her bed over the balcony out to sea. He hoped she was out there in the bay, watching his rage and feeling as though he would do the same to her should she ever return. She had no right to leave him!

Hours later, when his rage died down and the ache in his heart became too strong to ignore, Manus knelt amid the destruction he'd wrought and sobbed.

He'd lost her, and he knew why. It wasn't her fault his soiled hands had touched her perfect flesh. It wasn't her fault his pathetic attempts at winning her heart had failed.

It was entirely his.

Water rushed over Saoirse's shoulders and poured down the hollow of her spine. The ocean caressed her like a lover who'd not seen her in years. It tangled through her hair, sending it flying behind her in a billowing mass of black ink.

Tendrils of kelp brushed her arms and fish rushed past her. Bubbles of laughter erupted from her lips. She rolled over and over, spinning in euphoria like a top set free from its string. The farther she got from shore, the more she felt like herself.

Pieces of her mind fit themselves back into the holes of her psyche. She could breathe again after feeling for months like she was gasping for air.

She smoothed her hands up her sides, feeling the pin prick of scales and the flaps of her gills as she gasped in the sweet, salty water.

This was how she was supposed to live. This was where her life began and would end.

In the arms of the sea.

She needed to find the other merrows, the ones Declan had spoken of. They were likely her mother's cousins. She'd come from these parts, or at least waters that weren't warm with rocky shores. Merrow pods migrated, she had no way of knowing where they would be this time of year.

Saoirse dove deep into the bay, searching for the one person who might be able to guide her in the right direction.

The shipwreck loomed in the distance, dark and foreboding. She didn't want to see the bean sídhe again. The woman's nightmarish visage would haunt her dreams for the rest of her life.

An eel slithered from the darkness. It stretched its neck and hissed as she swam past.

"Just a little further," she murmured.

Tingles slid up her spine as hundreds of eyes blinked open and watched her approach. She settled a hand on the tiny bump of her belly, took a deep breath, and opened her mouth.

"Don't talk," the bean sídhe interrupted her from the mass of eels. "You have returned already. For money or for information, either request will be denied. Begone from this place, cursed merrow."

"I need your help," she blurted.

"And my help is not for sale."

"Please!" Saoirse lurched forward with her arms outstretched. Eels snapped at her fingertips, hissing and coiling in a mass of rage.

The bean sídhe shushed them with quiet hums. She petted their backs, long strokes that calmed their ire. All Saoirse could see was her pale white hands until a gap in the writhing bodies revealed her skeletal face.

"You are desperate," the bean sídhe mused. "Why I wonder? Has your human disappeared into the sea and you wish to find him? You know the ocean keeps her treasures."

"No, I need to find the merrow pod which lives in these waters. Do you know where they are?"

A pale, milky hand reached out to her. "Why are you searching for your own kind?"

"I need to find them."

"We faeries trade in knowledge, merrows. What has sent you back into the arms of the ocean when you know it's a dangerous place for one who has run from it?"

"I'm no longer running." In response, a current pushed against her back, whirling around her tail and trailing up her spine. "I need to find my people for the safety of myself and my child."

"Child?" The bean sídhe's eyes widened. "What have you done?"

Saoirse rubbed a hand against her belly. "Only that which can be born from true love."

"You have condemned an innocent soul to the same life you ran from." The bean sídhe shook her head in disgust. "I will tell you where the merrows are, but only because I know the harrowing journey ahead. That pod differs from the others, you'll see why, and you are not suited for the life they lead."

"But my child will be?"

"Your daughter won't have a choice."

"Daughter?" Saoirse gave the bean sídhe a shy smile. "Can you tell for certain?"

"Humans and merrows can only produce girls." She lifted a hand and pointed towards the darkness. "Follow the whale song. They travel with a pod of orcas who are more likely to bite you than bring you to their favorite merrows. Be careful when you see them and hold your distance."

"How will they know I'm there?"

"Oh, they'll know." An eel stretched out and nipped at the tip of her tail. "Now, go."

She didn't have to be told twice. Saoirse launched herself away from the darkness, from the fearful tomb of undulating flesh.

Hours passed, but she didn't feel the ache or pain of movement. Her muscles longed for use, her tail whipping back and forth in wild abandon. She was free. For the first time in what felt like forever, she was free.

She let herself enjoy the moment. She'd earned a few moments of bliss before the hole inside her chest opened back up.

One thought of Manus, and the ocean swept away the tears leaking from her eyes. He might be home even now, finding the empty bedroom, home, and life he returned to. Would he miss her?

Saoirse knew deep in her heart he would. He would miss her but not a single soul would know.

Had Declan told him yet? She hoped he had been there when Manus arrived. The servants would have so much to say, rumors would start, and she hated to think of what they might come up with.

Hopefully, they all believed she was dead.

Saoirse stroked her belly and shook her head. When had her life degraded to this? It wasn't fair that anyone think she was dead, even less that Manus believe it. It was bad enough he would always question what he did wrong.

Guilt latched onto her heart with gnashing teeth. There was no other way. Declan was right, the ocean had washed away much of the pain his absence had caused. Already, she felt more like herself. The baby stretched inside her, pleased with its new home as much as its mother.

She sighed. If given the choice, she would make the same decision again. She had to choose which future would give her enough time to live for the baby to be born.

Manus had to understand that.

Clicking calls echoed through the surrounding water. She didn't know how long she'd traveled. Hours, days, it was all the same in the depths of the ocean. But these were different cries, not the dolphin song nor familiar whale song.

These sounds were aggressive. They attacked her sensitive ears and warned her to stay still, to freeze, to flee from the predators likely speeding towards her through the murk.

She hesitated, floating in the water and rotating as she tried to find the beasts. They weren't sharks who were easily encouraged to leave merrows alone.

Orcas were highly intelligent and deadly beasts. If they wanted her dead, they would chase her to the ends of the oceans. Their teeth shredded bodies in seconds, their powerful forms sliced through the water with impressive speed, and they liked to play with their prey.

Her gills flared wide. They would not take her. Not yet, not when she had come so far to find the only family she had left.

A black flash skirted past her, buffeting her body with a powerful current of water that shoved her towards another black and white spotted body. But Saoirse was prepared, and she was desperate. Baring her teeth, she flared her fins and lifted her hands into claws.

"You will not take me," she growled. "I am here to speak with your masters, and I will not die before I meet them."

The orcas slowed in their attack. They stared at her, the depths of the ocean reflected in the dark pools of their eyes. She knew they understood her. Why were they not leaving?

Then she saw them. Bodies rising out the depths with spears in their hands. Strong women with muscular bodies and cords wrapped around their biceps with jingling shells hanging to their wrists. They were shadows in the water, warrior women each one.

"Welcome sister," one called out. She swam forward, and Saoirse saw the other merrow's face was tattooed with wave patterns. "You have come a long way to speak with my pod."

"I wish to join you."

The shadows doubled, tripled, then grew in a number so large Saoirse couldn't begin to count them. So many merrows, all together in safety and health. They would be a good family to join if they would have her.

"Why should we allow you to join us?" the merrow asked.

Saoirse thought it likely this was the leader. No other had the tattooed markings, that she could see, and they waited for this woman to speak.

"I have traveled from distant, warm waters. I came here to share my life with a human man." Rumbles whispered across the waves as the merrows drifted closer to each other, their disappointed comments stinging Saoirse's ears. "I love him. He is a good man, but the sea calls to him. I cannot compete with our mother."

"No, I imagine no creature on earth could do that."

Saoirse nodded in agreement. "He travels far from my side, and through our bond, I am fading. I ask not for myself, but for the babe growing within me. Give her the life she deserves."

"Should your child not be with its father?"

She pressed a hand against her stomach, fear dancing along her skin. Some might say the babe belonged with Manus. But she knew this was the right choice. Manus wouldn't know how to raise a merrow child, and the babe would bond to him and likely die while he was off on one of his adventures. He would never know why.

"No. I will not burden him with such a child. Faeries need to raise faeries."

It was the right thing to say. A few of the merrows nodded in agreement, some of them even swimming closer to see the newcomer. Light reflected in their eyes. Pools of glowing green stared at her from the darkness of the sea.

Saoirse swallowed and turned towards the leader. "I request sanctuary from all who would harm me. I do not require you or your family accept me as your own. My time is limited in this world. I ask only for protection from my blood kin until the child is born."

"What would you have us do about your deteriorating mind?"

"Nothing." She answered honestly. "Let me die."

"You do this for a *human*? Why?"

"I love him enough to risk my immortality. I want a good life for the child we have created, one I would approve of, one that is familiar to me."

"Does he know of the babe?"

"No."

The leader decided and gave a simple response. She sternly nodded, slid her spear into its holder, and opened her arms. "Welcome, daughter. You will my join my family for as long as you are with us."

Tears gathered in Saoirse's eyes, but the ocean wiped them away as she raced forward to be folded into the arms of her people once more.

Manus stared into the fires of the great hall, a bottle of rum loosely held in his hand. He didn't care if it dropped to the floor with the others, they'd already done their job. Drunk was an understatement for his current form.

He hadn't wanted to be merely drunk; he wanted to forget he even existed. Two bottles of rum down and already the room was a little hazy. Black dots pricked at his vision, something he likely should worry about, and the entire room listed to the left. But this was how he wanted to be. He couldn't remember anything when he was this drunk.

A sweet scent danced through the air. Salt, sea breeze, the brush of wind against his skin. And suddenly all he could think of was a candlelit night when dark strands of hair brushed across his chest and a voice whispered in his ear, "Manus, my love."

He swatted at the air over his head, trying with all his might to bat away her ghost. She had no reason to linger. She'd left.

And he still couldn't get her out of his thoughts.

Every time he blinked, he saw the way she tilted her head when she had a question. The graceful arch of her neck when she laughed, likely at something he said that embarrassed or pleased her. The dance of her fingers as she walked down the stairs, each fingertip alighting on the railing for brief moments before skipping over the wood.

Every movement was fluid grace, and every glance seared him to the bone.

Her dark eyes haunted him. They stared back from the shadows, swirling in the gloom and glowing with so much love and trust that his heart nearly burst.

The flames crackled and grew tall. He stared into their depths with as much concentration as his foggy mind could muster and swore he saw them coalesce into a single figure. A merrow who swam through the fire.

Snarling, he flung the remainders of the rum into the hearth. It exploded in a wave of heat and broken glass.

Manus stumbled backwards, his hazy mind remembering that fire could burn, but his feet forgetting how to move. He tripped over his boots and landed back in his chair with a loud thump.

"So, this is how the master of the manor spends his days."

He recognized the man walking into his great hall but couldn't pinpoint from where. The tall redhead took up too much room. His face was too handsome, too even, too…inhuman.

Manus bared his teeth. "I didn't give you permission to shadow my doorstep, Fae."

"I don't need permission." The leprechaun sidestepped a pile of bottles and leaned a shoulder against the fireplace. Crossing his arms, he looked Manus up and down. "You look terrible."

"You're smart enough to guess why." Manus reached for another bottle, his fingers hanging limp in the air when he realized he'd already drank it all. "Damn it."

The leprechaun watched as Manus fumbled. His eyes burned, but Manus refused to itch the back of his neck where the faerie's magic seemed to weigh the heaviest.

"Why are you here?" Manus grunted. "Haven't you done enough?"

"What have I done?"

"The servants talk." He waved a limp hand in the direction of the door. "And I'm not blind. I saw the way you looked at her, and I know you had a hand in what happened."

"Do you?" The leprechaun arched a red brow. "Enlighten me."

"I know your kind. I've seen you wandering the streets, complimenting the ladies while giving the men dirty looks. You're a rake, a ruffian, the kind of man who preys on the weak. And you saw my Saoirse as an easy target."

"Your Saoirse?"

"Yes *mine*," Manus growled. "Unless you seem to think she's now yours?"

"I wouldn't claim ownership of another person."

A loud laugh erupted from Manus, cold and cruel. "And here I was thinking Fae couldn't lie."

The silence which followed his outburst stung his ears. The leprechaun stared at him with eyes that delved deep into his soul, and he didn't like it. The man saw too much.

The leprechaun cleared his throat. "You think Saoirse and I were…what? Lovers?"

"Like I said. People talk."

"Yes, she was always worried about that. I happen to enjoy poking fun at your ridiculous ideals, but she was more sensitive to human strife. She didn't want any of you to be unhappy."

The leprechaun was too friendly with his wife, Manus mused. He spoke as if they were friends, dear friends, and those words stung. Saoirse had never once voiced her worries to Manus. She was always bright and happy, no matter what she had seen.

He sighed and pinched the bridge of his nose. "If you make her happy, then I wish you both the best."

"Excuse me?"

"Just take care of her," he ground out. The words were a knife to his gut, twisting and turning with each syllable that fell from his lips. "She's important to me, no matter what you might think. I know she's not dead, and I know she wouldn't have returned to the nightmare of a life she had. That leaves you. So take care of her, or I'll track you down and gut you."

The leprechaun gave him an odd look. "You'd let me have her?"

Manus's hands were shaking. His fingers curled into his palms, fists wanting nothing more than to pound into something. But this wasn't about him. Even drunk and wavering, he wanted to make sure Saoirse was happy. If this man was who she had chosen, then he needed to warn him.

"She's a gentle woman with a heart of gold. Be careful with her, leprechaun."

"But you'd let me have her?" The faerie snapped his fingers. "Just like that?"

"Not *just* like that, she's a person." And she should be able to make her own decisions, but he had to have some control. She had left him.

He got to decide whether she came back. "Just—don't let her forget she was loved by a fool who gave her all the wrongs things to make her happy."

The leprechaun shrugged. "Don't think I'll ever see her again, mate. I don't make it a habit to dive into the ocean and hold my breath. Never liked cold water."

"What?"

"She's off. Who knows where really, just off into the ocean where she belongs."

Manus shook his head, having trouble following what the faerie was saying. "What do you mean you don't know where she is?"

"I mean, I told her to go back to where she belonged but didn't tell her where. I know there's a pod of merrows around here somewhere, but I don't know how to find them."

His vision blurred. "You told her to go?"

"Well you certainly weren't going to." A feral grin spread across the leprechaun's face, full of hidden anger and rage. "Someone needed to have her best interests in mind."

"You're the reason she left me?" Manus lurched to his feet. "You sent her out into the water with no protection, no one she knows, not even a general direction where to look?"

"She's a faerie. She knows how to take care of herself."

"She is my wife!" Manus thundered.

The smile on the leprechaun's face changed. Glamour shivered and fell, revealing a terrifying faerie with golden skin and teeth like knives. He was tall, red headed, and glimmered like molten metal. "Not anymore."

Manus didn't care the faerie was looking for a fight. He didn't care that the faerie was impossibly strong and could use magic to bring him to his knees. This was a matter of pride.

His fist flew through the air and cracked against the other man's cheekbone. Fire blossomed along the ridge of his knuckles. His hand shook, but he wasn't about to stop any time soon.

The leprechaun had said enough. In his drunken state, Manus didn't care that the other man was right. He didn't care that Saoirse deserved to live with her family if that was what she desired. He only cared that this man had admitted to being an instrument in the disappearance of his wife.

And he would hurt for it.

Another punch slammed into the leprechaun's jaw. Manus felt it crack under his fist and the rush of satisfaction as blood splattered on the mantelpiece.

He pummeled the leprechaun, smashing his fist into whatever piece of flesh he could find. It didn't matter if his knuckles split, or his bones cracked, the pain was nothing more than a fleeting memory which was both satisfying and enraging.

He wanted the leprechaun to feel pain. Every crack of flesh meeting bone vibrated through Manus's arm. It rolled around in his head, reassuring him that there was no way the other man couldn't understand his frustration, anger, and the pain violently rocketing through his body.

"I tried to be the bigger man," Manus growled when the leprechaun stepped back. "She deserves a man capable of that."

"Does she? Or have you put your own ideals on her?"

"Shut up." Manus drove his fist down, swift and true.

The leprechaun ducked in an impressive showcase of speed. One moment he was crouched on the floor, bleeding from multiple splits in his face, the next he was five feet away and leaning against the fireplace again.

Manus watched as he swiped at the blood dribbling from his lips and flashed sharp teeth in a mockery of a grin.

"Careful human," the leprechaun warned. "You won't like it if you push me too far."

"I gave you a chance to be the better man."

"Did you now? All I heard was you telling me how things are going to be."

"She deserves someone to look after her. Someone who will take care of her, give her everything she desires."

"Maybe she just wants someone. Period. Maybe she didn't want someone to take care of her. She wanted someone to *be here with her*."

The words flew like arrows and sank their serrated edges into Manus's chest. They dug through his skin, burrowing and tearing until he couldn't breathe. He stumbled back a step and grasped the mantel.

"Is that what she said?" he gasped.

"Not in so many words. She made me promise to tell you why she left even though I disagreed with her."

Manus braced his forearms and stared into the flames. "Then she went back to what she was comfortable with. Back to that place where they locked her in a cage, where they didn't appreciate her for what she was."

"I doubt the merrow pod around here is like that. She left because you two are bonded, and the longer you were gone, the more likely it was for her to die."

"What?" he gasped.

"The bond, you idiot. Do humans no longer speak of it? The further you are from each other, the more strain it puts on her. She exists because you exist." The leprechaun spat blood on his floor. "You've got a mean right hook for such a little man."

"She was dying?" He squeezed the stone mantle until his fingers ached. "Why didn't she tell me?"

"She didn't want you to feel trapped. The land isn't your home, and she'd rather take the pain than take away bwhat you love."

"Until now."

"Until I showed her how stupid she was being. Since you disappeared, she should die in the arms of her family."

"Then she really is dead?" Something cracked in his chest. A chasm opened up with dark eyes staring back at him.

Manus could handle the heartache if she had left him. He'd been left before, and it wouldn't be the first time a woman found him lacking. But to know she was dead?

It destroyed him.

He fell to his knees, gasping through the pain in his chest. How did anyone survive the loss of a loved one? He was barely aware of himself at all. The world fell away, and all that existed was the aching hole in his chest.

Dead.

Her laughter sounded like bubbles breaking on the surface of the water. He had listened to her laugh for hours, trying to make her chuckle or giggle just to hear it again. Had he ever told her how much he loved it?

He would never again see the way she would sweep her hair over her shoulder and stare down at something new she found. It was usually something simple, cutlery, a hairbrush, a small decorative pot. But he had never looked at what she held. All he could focus on was the graceful arch of her neck and how badly he wanted to press a kiss to the curve.

Pain spread its clawing ache further, dancing down his arms and curling his hands into fists. He'd never acted on all the things he wanted to do, because it wasn't *right*. So many things he'd wanted to say, to do, to watch, and he hadn't done them because the world told him not to.

"You're not breathing," the leprechaun said. His words were tentative and curious as if he didn't know what Manus was going through. "You should probably do that."

"How am I supposed to breathe when she no longer does?" He glanced up, fierce and loyal until the bitter end. "What kind of monster are you? Why couldn't you let me continue to think she lived out a normal life? That she left of her own accord?"

"Even faeries have to follow through with unbreakable bonds."

The leprechaun knelt. He stared at Manus with keen eyes, the glamour dropped. If he had been in a better state of mind, Manus might have marveled at the strangeness of the faerie.

His skin wasn't made of metal although it looked as if it was dusted in it. His eyes were cold and hard, his sharp teeth poking through his lips. The leprechaun cocked his head to the side and stared directly into his soul.

"You want her back?"

"How could I not? She was everything."

"You didn't act like she was everything. You left without warning her what your plans were, leaving a note she couldn't read. Her maids read it out loud, did you know that? It embarrassed Saoirse."

The name finally registered in Manus's drunken mind. "You know her name."

"I know everyone's name, Manus of Uí Néill."

He gulped. "Do you know a way to get her back?"

"She might not be dead yet, although it's been months since she slipped back beneath the waves. If you are swift, you may catch her yet."

"Why would you help me?"

The leprechaun shrugged, blood dripping down his chin and hitting the floor with a quiet sound. "You obviously know how to fight, and you care about her. These were facts I did not previously know."

"Had you known, would you have encouraged her to stay?"

"No." The leprechaun shook his head. "The sea was the only way to slow the effects of your bond. If there was a way to save her, I would have taken it."

"You are fond of her."

"Yes."

"You—" Manus paused and licked his lips. "Love her?"

"As only her kind could. Don't worry human, I don't intend to steal her away from you. I have no need of a wife."

"Then, there is a possibility of finding her?" His heart lifted, pain easing for a brief second until he noticed the leprechaun hesitating. "Well?"

"There is a possibility, but I cannot say with any certainty you will be able to find her, or she will be alive and well."

"How? How do I find her?"

Again, the leprechaun hesitated, and Manus knew it would not be an answer he would like. It didn't matter. He would do anything he could to get her back, knowing she had left for her own safety.

He would prove his worth. If she wanted him to live in a cage under the sea, he would do it. Whatever it took to bring her back into his arms.

The leprechaun rolled his lips between his teeth and grunted. "You'll need a swift ship, one that can turn at a moment's notice."

"I have that already."

"And you'll need the courage of a thousand men, because you might not come back from this alive."

"For her, I would do anything."

"Then you need to sail directly into faerie waters and pray she hears your screams."

Manus blinked. "Pardon?"

"Merrows travel alongside guardians. They have a strange relationship, no one can really explain it. However, there are faerie waters near here. A portal into the Otherworld, guarded by fierce merrows and their greatest weapon. If you sail into those waters, Saoirse is sure to hear you. If she loves you, then she might save you."

"That's suicide."

"Maybe. Or she might wait for you."

He'd need to find a crew of men willing to put their lives on the line. He wouldn't put anyone at risk without their knowledge. Were there men like that? Perhaps not in Uí Néill, but there were enough who owed him some kind of recompense for previous grievances.

Manus grimaced. "It's possible. But first, I must know how to fight the guardian in case it attacks."

"You don't fight a guardian." The leprechaun sauntered away, leaving the same way he had entered. "Good luck, human. You'll need it."

Manus raced through the house, not sleeping until he had a crew of men who agreed to travel with him. Days passed, but he did not see the rising or setting of the sun. He had a reason to focus now.

He didn't surface until he was standing on the deck of his ship, staring off into the horizon.

"Captain!" a man shouted. "All sailors aboard!"

Manus glanced at his first mate, lifting an eyebrow. "What say you?"

"It's the foolhardiest trip I've ever been on, captain. I'm not looking forward to seeing a guardian, as it sounds particularly frightening." He cleared his throat. "But none of us would be here if we didn't believe in the cause."

"Gold and treasures."

"And a woman who somehow captured the heart of a wandering man."

"I didn't know you were a romantic." He arched a brow, suddenly wondering if he should know this man. His first mate was a mystery, found on the streets and proving to be a capable man. He hadn't expected loyalty.

"Hardly. I see value in people and actions, captain. Shall we?"

"Give the orders."

His first mate spun on his heel, shouting, "Hoist the sails and bring up the anchors, boys!"

They shared a look of trepidation. "To faerie waters we go."

CHAPTER 12
WATERS RUNNING RED

The merrows gathered together in the never-ending blue of the ocean. Suspended as they were, they could watch for predators from every angle. Each carried a sharpened spear made of coral and lashed to carved stone. The females adjusted their grip, narrowed eyes watching for the slightest movement.

In the center of their protective circle, four women floated. Two supported the middle merrow's arms, keeping her suspended in the water while the other swam in slow circles around her.

"Focus on the pain, Saoirse. Focus on the movement and the feeling of your child."

"I can't!" she grunted as another pulse made her flick her tail wildly. "Please, help me."

"You are doing well. Soon your daughter will enter our world and you shall hold her in your arms. You must embrace the pain."

"I want to sleep," she whimpered. "I want this to stop."

Merrow live birth was difficult as they were not meant to pass a child through their fishlike tails. It was possible although usually excruciating for the mother. Still, like so many others, Saoirse was willing to take the risk.

She had been too late to lay the mermaid's purse where her child might have grown without risking both of their lives. Now, she must go through the gauntlet.

Alannah, the matriarch of the merrow pod, circled her and cast a critical gaze up and down her tail. "You will survive this. You promised me a child in return for your safety. Have I not looked after you? Have I not prolonged your sanity to bring the child into the world?"

Blue tattoos swirled down the merrow's face and disappeared into the long length of her hair. Saoirse knew the waves traveled all the way down to where her tail met her torso. It was a painful process to become matriarch, but well worth it.

She curled her tail up as another wave rocked through her, the fins at her hips fluttering. Her belly was too large for her to tail to move easily.

"I can't do it, Alannah!"

"You can, and you will! Push!"

Saoirse grunted and threw her muscles into the job at hand. She had to bring her daughter into the world. Not because Alannah wanted her, the matriarch was kinder than she pretended to be, but because she wanted to see her. Before she died, she wanted to see the child she and Manus had created.

Her spine arched in pain, her gills sealed shut, and her tail lashed wildly. The merrows holding her arms helped, allowing her to squeeze their hands when necessary.

For hours she writhed in the open blue of the ocean. For hours her blood stained the water in spurting clouds and then, nothing at all.

Exhausted, she fell limp in their hands. "I can't," she whispered. "I can't do this anymore."

Alannah surged forward, strong hands framing Saoirse's face. "Stopping now will only hurt you and the babe further. You have little time, Saoirse."

"I'm trying!" she wailed. "I have tried for hours and I'm in so much pain."

"Just a little more. Just give us a little more or we will intervene."

She knew what the hidden words meant. The worth of merrow lives were measured in years. Saoirse was older, and therefore less necessary than the child within her belly. If she could not bring her daughter into the water on her own, they would slice her open and pull the babe out themselves.

A part of her wanted to ask them to just get it over with. The end was near, and her torment would be over.

The other part remembered the worried expression Manus wore when she stubbed her toe or sliced her finger on the sharp edge of a letter opener. He wouldn't want her to give up so easily.

The waters echoed with a low grumble. Deep and reverberating, the sound was a song she remembered. Almost immediately, Saoirse's body fell limp in the arms of the merrows who parted like a wave for the being swimming towards them.

Her lips parted in a soft sigh as the guardian's hand reached for her. It scooped her from the grasp of the merrows and carried her close to its chest.

"Hello," Saoirse panted. She touched the shell in her ear to ensure it was still there.

The whale song of a guardian filled the waters, quiet and steady as the waves. "Welcome home, little merrow."

"I am in pain. My child does not want to greet the waves."

"Few do." The guardian shifted its fingers, gently rubbing its thumb over the swell of her belly. "Will you accept my assistance?"

How could a guardian help? Saoirse didn't know what it could do but nodded her head. She would accept anything at this point.

"This will hurt, little merrow. Know I am not doing it to cause you pain."

The giant thumb pressed down upon her belly. Pressure swiftly became blinding agony. Saoirse tilted her head back and let out a wail that echoed through the waves. The merrows flinched back, lifting their spears as they prepared to threaten the guardian.

Saoirse held out her hand, palm out and fingers spread. They needed to remain calm. The guardian didn't mean to harm her, it didn't want to, but it also wanted to help save her child.

It pressed harder, just enough that she felt something inside her give. A bloom of red burst, a cloud that preceded the weak cry of a baby.

She reached out her arms, unable to see the child but knowing it was there. Her soul blossomed, spreading petals like the roses she had seen on land. Her daughter.

Her daughter.

"Give her to me," she whispered. "Please, can I see her?"

The guardian's finger shifted, ever so gently, and a tiny body floated towards her on the current.

Saoirse grabbed her daughter and snuggled her close to her chest. She was a tiny little thing, all tail and head with tiny fingers already grasping the strands of Saoirse's hair. Her eyes were open and so dark they looked like the dead of night.

The little one was already swishing her tail back and forth, ready for a hard life under the sea.

Cradled in the guardian's hand, Saoirse could curl around her daughter and hold onto her tiny fingers.

"Welcome to the world," she whispered. "I won't be here long with you, but I want you to know how much I love you."

"Many things change, Saoirse," the guardian sang.

"What do you mean, honored one?"

"There are whispers in the waves. A ship approaches."

Her fingers curled against the baby's back. "A ship? How soon?"

"The wind travels slowly, but they ride the waves with determination. The seagulls say the man who stands upon the bow shouts your name."

"Manus," she breathed. "He has come for me."

"Is coming, little merrow. You will need to hold on for a while longer."

Saoirse held her squirming daughter to her chest and vowed she would stay sane. There wasn't much time left, but she could do it. The knowledge that Manus was coming eased some pressure in her mind.

She wasn't herself, but she could remain alive for a little while longer.

The guardian removed its hands, letting her drift down into the waiting arms of the merrows below. Saoirse floated with her daughter held against her chest.

Coos greeted them.

"Oh, she's beautiful!"

"Look at her, what delicate features."

"Such tiny fingers!"

Alannah pushed through the crowd and reached out her arms. "Congratulations, Saoirse. Let me see my new daughter."

"She is my daughter." Her steely tones made the other merrows freeze. They released their hold on her arms and shoulders, letting her stay upright under her own power.

Alannah's brows drew down. "What?"

"I am not yet dead. This is my daughter until my body turns to foam."

"That was not part of our deal, merrow."

"It is now." Saoirse looked up. She couldn't see the surface, but she could feel he was closer to her now than ever. "My husband comes for me."

"He is not welcome in faerie waters."

"And still, he comes."

Manus would know the dangers of faerie waters. He'd lived it before. Knowing that he would brave such dangers for her warmed the cold corners of her heart, cracking through the ice she had built around herself to remain safe.

Danger awaited him at every corner, and she didn't know how to help. The merrows would attack the ship as would the guardian. Though the gentle giant likely wanted to help, it would do what it was made to do.

Destroy.

She shivered, then turned to meet Alannah's frigid gaze. "This is my family. I came to you for sanctuary, believing there was nothing I could do to mend my grief. I have a chance now to give my daughter a real life. With a father and mother who love her, to help her become a better woman than we can give her in the waters."

Something shifted in the tattooed woman's gaze. She sighed and relented. "You are right. Merrow life is not easy, and I would not wish it upon a child if there was another option. We have already informed your family of your predicament. They have agreed to disown you as you have married a human. If you believe this man is good and worthy of a merrow child, then I will concede she is your child."

"Will you grant him sanctuary in these waters as well?"

The steel returned to Alannah's spine. "If he comes into our territory, we will tear his ship to pieces. It is our way, Saoirse. You know this to be true."

She did. And though it made her shiver, it also set her resolve.

Now she could prepare for the storm barreling towards them. With a child, there was no chance she could meet him. A ship was large, and she was small.

Saoirse's best option was to wait for him to reach her. Then, with what little time she had, she would plan a way to save him.

Their daughter gurgled and tugged on Saoirse's hair. She grinned from ear to ear when Saoirse glanced down at her.

"Your father needs to name you," she whispered.

She was bound and determined that he would.

Manus held onto the railing of the ship, staring fiercely out to sea.

Footsteps behind him cracked on the sodden wood.

"Captain? We're nearing faerie waters."

"I know."

"Do you?" His first mate stood next to him. "Ah. Yes, of course."

A wall of storm clouds marked the edge where it was safe for the ship to travel. Manus remembered this darkness all too well, the terrifying roar of thunder, the bright blasts of lightning.

But more than anything else, he remembered the deep grumble of the guardian, bodies floating beneath the waves, and the gentle caress of fingertips on his cheek.

"Captain?"

"What is it?"

Manus knew what the first mate wanted. He wanted a plan which would ease the minds of the crew. They wanted the reassurance their captain wasn't completely insane.

Sailing into faerie waters was only done by those who had a death wish. Everyone spoke of what happened, the horrifying fear of what might happen to those who tried to make their way into the Otherworld. Death awaited them.

Manus didn't want to disappoint his crew. He spun on his heel and strode across the deck.

"Men! Leave your duties for a moment and gather here with me."

They dropped their ropes, brushes, and brooms, rushing to cluster around the captain few of them knew.

Manus hadn't chosen these men for their talents. He didn't care if they knew a ship up and down, he half expected the ship wouldn't return with them. These sailors needed to be brave, to know about the Fae, and to risk their lives at a moment's notice.

"I cannot promise you a treasure," he said when they had gathered around them. "I cannot promise you glory. But I can promise that you are about to see something few men have seen before. What awaits us in those waters is dangerous, large, and wants nothing more than to kill us."

The men began to shift. Small movements caught Manus's eyes. The twitch of fingers, the bounce of a leg, the drawn down brows. They were afraid of what might happen, and what he might say next.

"Death awaits us, boys. Death and honor and glory. You are here for an adventure of a lifetime, and that I promise you shall see in mere moments. We sail to the edge, kill the sails, and set down the anchor."

"Captain," his first mate interrupted. "The sea is too deep here. The anchor will not halt our progress."

"It's not to stop the ship. It's to give the faeries something to climb."

With that said, Manus turned on his heel and returned to the bow of the ship. They would follow his commands, he'd paid them to do that, and it didn't matter his plan was insane. They weren't technically going into the faerie waters.

Killing a ship in the middle of the ocean wasn't the smartest move. He didn't know if the guardian would think they were too close and grow angry. It was always a possibility.

But there was also a chance he could speak with it. Saoirse spoke of the creature as if it were intelligent. Surely, if that were true, it could also be reasoned with.

The sails fluttered in the sudden wind as his crew turned the ship directly towards the storm. He trusted his first mate to guide them and stood with his arms crossed watching the waters.

Manus needed to be ready. He needed to make sure the crew had a chance at living. He wouldn't be like his previous captain who'd sailed them directly towards death. He knew better.

They slowed at the edge of the storm. The sails slapped as they were drawn down, the anchor chains rattled as men dropped them over the side. Manus savored the splashing sounds and prayed they would work the way he intended.

Everyone held their breath, waiting. The crew stilled; not even the slightest exhale could be heard. They stared towards uncharted territory and prayed their deaths would be swift.

Rain barely touched the deck. It was a wall of splashing movement close enough to touch and obscure their vision.

Manus knew the intention behind the storm. It wouldn't sink a ship, he'd been in enough widow makers to know that. The rain was a warning, the thunder a sign, and the lightning a screaming cry to turn back now.

They didn't have to worry about anything above the waves.

"Captain—"

Manus lifted a hand for silence. He narrowed his eyes and waited just a bit longer.

They didn't have to wait long. A smooth back crested the water in the distance, pale gray and effortlessly graceful. It might have been a whale, the arched spine was familiar, but Manus could see the long tendrils of dark hair flowing down the guardian's back.

A sailor let out a choked sound.

"Get below deck," Manus called out. "Man the port sides and turn the cannons boys. If we have to fight, then we'll give them the fight of their lives."

The slapping feet rushing below deck was enough to set his heart racing. A fight with a guardian wouldn't last long. It was too big, too strong, and he wasn't convinced the guardian he had seen was the only one in the ocean.

A deep groan rocked through the ship. The wood beneath his feet vibrated with the sheer force of her call.

"Captain?" his first mate asked again. "What in the name of God is that thing?"

"That is a faerie."

"Faeries aren't that big."

"Some of them are. Some are terrifying and beautiful, others are just terrifying." Manus lifted a telescope and watched her approach. She raced towards them far faster than any mere whale could. "That is a guardian. She watches over the merrow pods and ensures no humans cross into territories where they shouldn't be."

"Like us?"

"Precisely."

Manus set his jaw and dropped the telescope. The guardian would be upon them in moments, and he needed the ship to remain intact. He had to force it to listen to him, even for a few moments, and perhaps leave his men alive.

He hopped up on the railing of the ship, holding onto the sail ropes to balance himself.

Tilting his head back, he shouted into the wind, "Guardian of the seas, we beseech you to hear our call!"

His shout rang loud and true. It carried through the wind and struck the water as if he had dived into the waves. The guardian did not slow.

Again, he tried, "You have a merrow amongst your charges who belongs to me! I have come to beg her forgiveness!"

Did the guardian slow? To his eyes, it appeared the guardian hesitated for a moment before returning to her charging pace.

"That merrow is my wife! I left her for adventures on the sea, and I was wrong. I wish only to confess my folly and beg her to return to me."

The guardian reached their ship and reared out of the water. She loomed above him, rivers of water pouring off her shoulders and splashing upon the deck.

Her skin was paler than he remembered. Gray, but also with no color. Shadows played across her pronounced musculature, and he shivered when he realized she put most men to shame. Her entire body was made of rip cord muscle.

Scars laced across her shoulders and chest. Small breasts suggested this one was also female although he had no way of knowing for certain. She stared at him with black eyes, no whites to make her appear human. They were so focused upon him he almost didn't notice the lack of nose and wide gill slits upon her neck.

Manus watched in horror as the gill slits slapped against the side of her neck, vibrating with the deep bass he now knew was the guardian trying to speak.

"I cannot understand you, great beast of the deep." He swallowed through the raspy fear in his voice. "I ask you look upon me with pity. My crew is below deck, we have no wish to fight you. But I will do everything in my power to find my bride again."

The guardian cocked her head to the side, throat working as she tried to convey something to him.

Manus wished he could understand her. He wished he knew how to speak to a creature this large, but he didn't. And the reality was if this creature didn't want to help him, then he would do whatever it took to die with honor.

"I will only ask you one more time," he warned. "Where is my wife?"

The guardian did not move. She seemed to be waiting for what he would do next.

He suspected she had never seen cannon fire before. Most ships wouldn't have had a chance to fire at her, they never would have seen her.

It was a shame to attack such a creature. She was beautiful in the same way the sea was beautiful. Strong, powerful, achingly dangerous, but otherworldly.

He nodded. "All right then. You will protect her until the very end, I see that now."

Manus glanced over his shoulder at his first mate who was staring up at the beast with mouth agape.

"First mate." His words lashed across the ship like the crack of a whip. "Fire the cannons."

"How is the babe?" a merrow asked. She swam close to where Saoirse and her daughter were tucked into the edge of a cliff. "It's not often we see a new one born in our pod."

"She is well." Saoirse lifted her finger, the baby's hand wrapped tightly around it. "Already stronger than I expected she would be."

"She's quite beautiful. Like her mother."

"Oh, I think she's strong like her father." She looked down at the child and marveled at how much she looked like them. Manus's strong nose, her own dark eyes, the stubborn set of her jaw likely from both her parents.

The merrow reached out and traced a finger between the baby's eyes. Saoirse's daughter scrunched up her face, not crying yet but warning she might.

Both women laughed at her antics.

"She knows what she likes," the other merrow chuckled. "She will be a handful when she's older. The last merrow who did that when I touched her was Alannah's first daughter."

"Alannah had a daughter?" Saoirse asked in surprise.

"Yes. She lost her long ago. The girl's favorite pastime was deep sea hunting, she had scars on her back from the battles. A giant squid finally got her. They said it was a terrible death, but that she killed the beast on the way down."

"I'm so sorry to hear that."

"It's dangerous to live here." The merrow gave her a stern look. "Just as dangerous as it is to live above the waves."

"It does not surprise me. I lived in a cold water pod, at the bottom of the seafloor. There wasn't much danger there, but the journey to the surface was always tense."

"I suspect it was."

The merrow seemed to hesitate, and Saoirse wondered if she had something to say.

The other merrows had been strange around her for a while now.

They swam close and opened their mouths, then closed them tightly as soon as another cast a glance in their direction. She recognized those who repeated this behavior.

"Do you have something to tell me?" Saoirse asked. "I'm sorry I haven't had time to get to know many of you. But I have seen you looking at me before."

"Saoirse, there are some of us who—"

"Ship!" The cry rocked through the waters. "Ship above!"

Merrows burst into a flurry of movement. Spears were passed between hands while feral grins spread across faces. Tails lashed into movement so quick they reminded her of the bean sídhe's eels.

Alannah raced towards her, pointing her finger and giving her a severe look. "You stay here. That babe's safety is the most important priority."

Saoirse gave a quick nod although she had no intention of staying.

Electricity raced through her veins as if she had touched a man-of-war. Manus was here. She knew it was him, no one else was mad enough to sail a ship into these cursed waters.

Her gills flared, and she watched the merrows leave with wide eyes. A few stayed in the depths, those who were not deemed fit to fight. Saoirse doubted there would be much fighting. The last guardian battle had ended with drowned men before the merrows snatched them up.

She had to see him. She had to *save* him.

Saoirse frantically held her daughter out to the merrow who had not left with the others. "Hold her."

"What? Why?" The merrow took the baby carefully, cupping her head and holding her against her shoulder. "What are you doing?"

"I cannot let them kill him. I won't let him die."

"No one can stop a guardian."

"I have heard tales there were ships allowed to stay in faeries waters. They could pass through without a guardian ever attacking them."

"I've never heard of such a thing!"

"There was only one ship, long ago. Mac Lir's ship." She pressed a kiss to her baby's head. "I need you to look after her."

A current buffeted her as other merrows swam closer. One folded her hands in front of her and blurted, "We want to help."

"You what?"

"We don't agree that all ships should be destroyed. Other merrow pods find husbands and bring them back home. We wish to do the same."

Saoirse stared out over the small number of merrows and marveled at their bravery. They lived in a pod of merrows who would sooner kill a human than allow them close. Yet these women wanted to go against their orders, against everything they were raised to believe, on the chance they might find a husband who loved them.

She knew exactly how they felt.

"In the legends, a guardian will allow a ship with a yellow belly to travel through our waters. That it is a marking of faerie approval."

"How will we do that? There is no way for us to paint a ship."

Saoirse reached out and grasped a small rock. She dug it into the soft flesh of her arm, letting blood flow into the water and press against the stones. Coral grew upon the rocky surface. Magic encouraged it to spread, vibrant colors blooming bright and vivid.

"We can control what grows," she said. "We will cover the ship with yellow coral and the guardian will stop its attack."

"And the other merrows?"

"They will not harm us." Saoirse looked up, meeting the gaze of each merrow waiting with bated breath. "Choose a sailor and keep them safe from harm."

"And bring them back?" a merrow asked.

"Only if they wish it."

The merrow holding her daughter cleared her throat. "Are you well enough for this?"

Saoirse wasn't certain how to answer. She was weaker than she had ever been before. Her spine ached, her heart beat sluggishly, and before this moment she had been staring at her daughter wondering when it would all end.

Now, she had a chance at life. A better life, and the one she had chosen.

She nodded. "I have to be."

Two merrows swam forward and took hold of her arms. It was embarrassing they had to do such a thing. She should be able to swim by herself, to save the man she loved. But Saoirse realized she would never make it to the surface without their help.

She let out a slow breath. "Take care of my daughter. If I do not come back, make sure she is given a life where her own choices are more important than the opinions of others."

The merrow nodded and smoothed a hand down the baby's dark green tail.

Saoirse didn't want to cry. She turned her eyes towards the surface and said, "We need to go now. The guardian will have reached the ship."

They raced towards her husband, clustered together in one mass of women determined to find those who loved them.

She was grateful for her people and wondered how many merrows in her previous pod thought the same way. Had her sisters wanted to free themselves from a future with a merrow man as a husband? Had some of them looked forward to living with the creatures?

Saoirse judged them harshly when she hadn't taken the time to get to know them. Even the women holding her arms were strangers to her.

There were many things she wished she had done differently in her life. She had always prided herself on kindness but had forgotten what kindness entailed.

Determination had her swimming faster than she thought possible. She would start a new life with Manus. They would never be parted, and she would never hide the truth from him again.

He would know what she was thinking, and she would hear his

thoughts. They would understand where the other person was coming from. They would build a life based on trust and truth.

As they should have from the beginning.

Lightning cracked overhead, illuminating the ship hovering above them. A wall of merrows waited, each fierce warrior holding a spear and wearing a smile of hatred and anger.

"Stop!" Saoirse cried out. "Tell the guardian to stop!"

They were too late. Fire flashed on the side of the ship and something impacted the side of the guardian. It struck hard flesh shielded by magic and angered the beast.

The guardian roared in pain and anger. She brought her fist down on the ship and cracked the deck. The sound rocketed through the waters and pushed Saoirse down.

"We have to go now," she gasped. "We have little time left."

"Alannah will try to stop us."

"She won't have time. Let go of me, and swim as fast as you can to the ship. Grow the coral. I'll deal with the guardian."

They split up. Some burst through the rankings of the merrows and flattened themselves to the bottom of the ship. Others hovered in the waters to protect those who were working. They made the right choice as many of Alannah's merrows tried to pull them away.

The merrows were determined on both sides. Saoirse was certain they could grow enough coral to calm the guardian as long as she could capture its attention.

She sluggishly swam towards it, breathing hard and feeling as though her gills weren't working. She ran her fingers down the slits. They were open as wide as they could go, yet she still couldn't breathe in enough.

Saoirse slowed the more she swam until she was struggling to stay afloat. She wriggled in the water.

"Guardian," she whimpered. "Please listen to me."

A deep groan echoed from above the waves. "They hurt me."

"I know they did, and that was wrong."

"He wants to take you away from the ocean, again."

"And you want to protect me, I understand." She clawed at the water with her arms, tail falling limp and threatening to drag her down into the deep. "I need you to protect me now."

The guardian lifted her fist and grabbed one of the great masts. It snapped off in her massive hands and she gave a loud roar. "That is what I am doing."

"I need you beneath the waves! Forget the humans, I am dying, and I need you to be here."

Merrows shrieked as the two groups collided. Saoirse whipped around and watched as more blood filled the water. They did not fight with spears, a small consolation, but with their claws. Each dug at each other, shrieking their anger into the waves.

Alannah propelled herself away from the group. Anger marred her beautiful features, and Saoirse knew why.

If the matriarch reached her, then her plans would be for nothing. She would drag her back down to her child, or worse, lock her away forever. Saoirse would die in these waters and Manus would never know his child.

"Guardian!" She cried out. "Help me!"

For a moment, she feared the creature did not hear her. The boom of cannon fire drowned out her words and the angry cries of merrows filled the sea with rage. The waters boiled with blood and battle.

Just as Alannah reached for her, a giant hand moved between them. The guardian scooped her out of the water and brought her up to its chest.

Saoirse curled up in its palm. With her tail pressed to her chest, she shivered as salt water fell from her body and cold air chilled her skin. She was so near to death she could barely even speak.

"Thank you," she whispered.

"What are you doing, little merrow? Your place is here, with us."

"My place is with him. I wish to see him, guardian. My life and his are bonded for all eternity. I am willing to die in his arms if it is too late or live forever at his side if it is not."

"I don't understand why you would want to leave us. He will not let you return."

"We cannot speak for him. He has traveled all this way to find me, perhaps he has changed his mind."

The guardian looked down at her, thoughtful and kind. A cannon went off again and Saoirse felt its impact on the beast's great form. The guardian did not flinch.

"If you are certain, then I will place you at his side. But be warned, few of our kind think highly of a faerie who would stoop so low as to marry a human."

"Then I have no wish to know them. He is the greatest man I have ever met. And not because of his decisions." Saoirse grinned. "He makes horrible choices. But he loves me, and I love him."

She knew the concept was strange to a creature who could not understand what love was. Guardians were faeries, but they were entirely different from most beasts. Even normal faeries may never discover the blessing as Saoirse had.

"So be it," the guardian sang.

Saoirse held onto the guardian's thumb as she lowered her all the way onto the deck of the ship. Sailors scattered, shouting curses and raising their fists as if that might help.

The guardian deposited her in the center of the ship. "You have only a few moments before I will return."

"We painted the ship yellow," she called out. "Merrows gave their blood to mark this ship as theirs."

"Your sacrifice is not in vain, I shall return to the depths. It was an honor to know you, little merrow."

"And you."

The ship rocked again with the grumble of the guardian as she slid beneath it. The men shouted and pointed. Perhaps they were shocked the beast returned to the deep. Perhaps they didn't understand the way faeries worked.

She wasn't a creature. None of them were. They could be reasoned with as long as they understood why the humans wanted what they did.

Now, Saoirse was alone. Perhaps the other merrows weren't finished yet, or still fought their own kind. She didn't have time to understand why the others weren't on deck.

She pulled herself forward on shaking arms, dragging her useless tail behind her. A sailor flinched away. His eyes were wide and wild with fear. He lifted a broken piece of wood up, brandishing it in front of him as if he needed to protect himself.

"Please," she begged. "Where is my husband?"

"Begone, siren! We will not listen to your cries."

"I will not hurt you. I want my husband."

"You won't find a husband here!" the sailor shouted. "None of us will return with you. We have no desire to find ourselves locked away in a cage far away from land and hope."

"You don't understand."

Why were they afraid of her? Didn't they know Manus was here for her?

Saoirse glanced around at all the men, their suspicious looks making her fear grow like a cloud of blood in the water. They didn't know who she was.

Could this be another ship? Was Manus not here after all?

"Throw her overboard!" One of the sailors shouted.

"Or better yet, kill it and send it back to the sea."

She whimpered and pushed herself back. Her tail wouldn't work, her heart pounded against her ribs, and pin pricks of energy made her hands shake. Saoirse had run out of time.

"Hold!" The shout pierced the air and pounding feet raced towards her.

Dark and swarthy, he raced towards her as if the Wild Hunt chased him down. Blood streaked across his face and splattered down his chest, but he was everything she desired and more. Her husband. Her life.

Manus fell to his knees and pulled her into his arms. "Saoirse," he breathed. "My love."

Relief poured through her body like cold water on a sunburn. "Manus, you have returned to me."

"I should never have left. I love you, Saoirse. I should have said it every single moment you were in my arms. I love you, I love you, *I love you.*" He buried his face in her neck and whispered the words over and again.

Saoirse held him against her until his breathing slowed. He pulled back, brushed her hair from her face and pressed his lips to her forehead, eyes, cheeks. For the first time in months, Saoirse felt all her worries disappear. She lifted her hand and pressed it to his cheek.

"I should have told you everything that was happening."

"I should have loved you as you deserve." He pressed his lips to hers and she tasted salt on his tongue. "I will never leave you again."

Chains rattled, drawing their attention towards the side of the ship. Merrows crawled up out of the sea. They launched themselves at the sailors and for a moment, she couldn't tell who they were. Saoirse held her breath until she realized the women were hugging the men.

They twined their tails around them, holding them in place, and pressing kisses to their necks. As soon as the sailors realized what was happening, stunned laughter spread across the deck.

"Saoirse." Manus's voice echoed in her ears. "What is going on?"

"They don't want to kill you anymore. They want to keep you."

One merrow she recognized. Webbed fingers spread wide over her daughter's back. The merrow pulled herself up with one arm and dragged her body across the deck towards them.

Manus stiffened and placed a hand on the knife at his side.

"Don't," Saoirse warned and held out her arms for her daughter.

"It is our child."

"Ours?" The wonder in his voice made her look up in surprise. "Our child?"

"The leprechaun didn't tell you?"

"No, he said you left because you were dying."

"That is only part of the truth." Her tail melted into thin mucus. Saoirse plucked the baby underneath her arms and tucked her against her chest. "This is our daughter. She was born in the water as both her mother and father were. Now, the choice is yours where she grows up."

"Mine?" He stared at her numbly. "Why would that choice be mine?"

"If you wish me to return with you, then she shall live on land. I will make my goodbyes to the sea, and we will search for some way for me to exist without you—"

He pressed his fingers to her lips.

"Say nothing more, wife. When I said I wanted you by my side, I meant in every possible way. I want to hear your laughter on the wind. I want to see your smiles every morning. I want to feel your skin against mine each night." He leaned forward and kissed her as she had never been kissed before. "I want to love you until the day I die."

Tears pricked her eyes. "And so you will."

EPILOGUE

Sunlight played across the quiet waves and danced across Saoirse's shoulders. She sat in a pool of warm water, sand heating her tail and waves cooling the sting. Fronds of kelp piled in heaps on her lap. She worked to weave them together, creating a strong rope that would last for a few weeks underwater.

"Máthair! Máthair!"

The bright voice calling out made her smile. There was never a day when the sound of her daughter's voice didn't make happiness bubble in her chest.

"Where have you been Orlaith?" she asked with a chuckle. "I thought you were lost in the heart of the isle!"

"There's no such thing, Máthair." The little girl plopped onto the sand. She held something in her grasp, but Saoirse was more concerned about the state of her daughter's hair.

"When did you last brush this?" She tried to run her fingers through the dark locks, but they tangled at her scalp.

"Pirates don't brush their hair."

"Then it's a good thing you aren't a pirate."

"Athair doesn't brush his hair!"

She would have to talk with Manus about that. Although she quite liked the dreadlocks on her husband, her daughter was another story. Saoirse wanted her hair to wave like sea fronds in the water. Not stick straight up like eels.

Orlaith sighed dramatically. "This isn't why I came here."

"Oh? Then why did you come running, my little clam?"

"Máthair!"

Her daughter hated the nickname which had stuck early on in her childhood. Manus claimed their daughter hadn't yet turned into a pearl but would someday become an incredible beauty.

Saoirse tugged on the tangled strands. "Fine, Orlaith. What is it you have?"

"Athair told me to give it to you." She handed a small, golden figure over. "He said you used to have a gold prince when you were little and that you might want this one instead."

She turned the figure over and grinned. It was a small golden pirate with his sword at the ready. It wasn't a prince, not even close, but it was exactly the kind of man she wanted to dream about each night.

"It's lovely, don't you think?"

Orlaith tucked herself underneath Saoirse's arm. "I think it looks like Athair."

"Do you? Why's that?"

"Because he looks fierce and strong."

"That he does." Saoirse held the figure up towards the sun. "Did you know your father fought off a guardian for me?"

"He did?"

"Of course! It was a long time ago, but he wasn't even afraid."

"Not even a little?"

"Well, you must ask him about that. But I remember he didn't even tremble."

She brushed a hand over her daughter's head and sighed in happiness. Her life finally came together. All the pieces she'd missed filled the spaces of her heart.

Waves splashed against the edge of a boat, thunking on worn wood. A secret smile spread across her lips and she looked down the shore to watch her husband navigate his boat towards them. He pulled the oars with strong arms, sun dancing off his caramel skin.

Manus reached them, jumping into the sea spray. "There's my two favorite girls. Are you ready to go?"

"Back to sea?" Saoirse asked. She nudged her daughter's back. "Go get your father."

"Are we actually going?"

"Looks like."

Orlaith stood, shucked her white linen dress, and sprinted through the water. Manus caught her with a bright smile, laughing even as her legs tangled together and merged into one dark green tail. "Hello, my little clam! Did you give your mother our gift?"

"I did! She thought it looked like you, too."

"Did she?" Manus met her eyes, heat reflecting in his. "I thought he was too handsome to look like me."

"You're handsome, Athair!"

"Am I?" He pressed a hand to his chest, hiking their daughter higher in his arms with the other. "Your mother never tells me anymore."

"Máthair!"

Saoirse burst into laughter. "Don't let your father convince you otherwise. He knows I think he's plenty handsome."

"Go get the boat for me, would you little one?"

"Okay!"

Orlaith wiggled from his arms and dove into the water. She was a better swimmer than Saoirse was at that age. She'd taken to her tail like a second skin and had no trouble switching between forms.

Saoirse was so proud of her. She was everything and more.

"Hello, wife." Manus's voice deepened, a husky whisper that sent shivers down her spine. "Are you finished with your work?"

"For now."

He knelt, waves kissing his thighs as he pulled her forward. "I have missed you."

Saoirse sighed as he cupped the back of her neck, pulled her forward, and pressed his lips to hers. He took his time, tasting her as one might a fine wine. His hands stroked the column of her throat while he plundered her mouth until she moaned.

Only then he did pull back, stroking her full lower lip with his thumb.

"I saw you yesterday," she said with a chuckle. "But I don't mind the welcome."

"How was your adventure with your daughter? She refused to tell me anything, only said that your adventures were for merrows to know."

Saoirse chuckled and rolled her eyes. "We found plenty of treasures."

"And?"

She loved it that he wanted more for them. It wasn't about money anymore. Their adventures were to enrich their daughter's life and give the entire family stories to tell at night.

"And we met an octopus who loved her. She still has tiny sucker marks on her shoulders, but he was gentle enough."

"She won't be disappointed coming back to the ship with me?"

"Manus, I think she loves being on the ship with you almost as much as she loves the water with me."

Her words seemed to ease her husband's worry. Manus constantly worried that both his wife and his daughter would leave him. The ocean was too tempting, he would say, how could a mere mortal man attract two equally amazing women?

Every time, Saoirse would tell him they loved him too much to leave. And it was true. No matter how far they traveled, she always wanted him by her side.

Manus pressed his forehead to hers. "Will you follow us in the water?"

"I'd like to stretch my tail for a while."

"Jump a few times for her. She likes knowing where you are."

"I'll let you know if there's any trouble up ahead."

"Trouble? In faerie waters? That's unlikely." He gave her a jaunty wink and splashed through the water towards their daughter. "Orlaith, did you catch that boat yet?"

Saoirse grinned at her adorable family. Manus tackled their daughter and wrestled her onto the small boat. She complained the entire time, saying she wanted to stay in the water for just a little while longer. But they both knew she wanted to get back to the ship.

Orlaith loved being aboard the Freedom. She raced across the deck, climbed the masts like a monkey, and teased the sailors mercilessly. They all adored her.

As her husband and child rowed away, Saoirse slipped under the waves. They had come to terms with the fact that she would always need to be in the water. It didn't matter that their bond was stronger than ever. She had to be in the water every day.

Manus didn't mind, and Saoirse took it as a sign they were growing together.

Schools of fish swirled as they streaked by her, their scaly bodies brushing against hers. A pod of dolphins chattered next to her, leaping from the waves and laughing as they splashed back down.

The deeper they traveled, the less she saw. Humpback whales eyed her on her travels, their song following her for miles.

She felt so good in the ocean. Strong, powerful, and incredibly free.

They sailed towards a faerie isle, one where supposedly the strongest women trained. Manus wanted to trade goods in return for a weapon that would grant them riches untold. He said a faerie had requested it, and she felt certain Declan was the one making the deals.

It didn't matter in the end. She was with the three loves of her life.

Her husband, her daughter, and the sea.

When the sun set on the horizon, Saoirse slowed her pace. The ship would travel slowly now that the stars were their guide. They would set their course for the rest of the evening and let the others rest.

She grasped the handholds Manus had installed on the side of the ship when they were last in Uí Néill. He wanted her to have something to hold onto, something to climb.

Hand over hand, she pulled herself up. Music started up, laughter spilling over the edges in a great wave of happiness and movement. She braced her arms on the railing and laid her head on her forearms.

Manus and Orlaith twirled across the deck. One of the sailors fiddled in the corner and a few of the sailors tapped their feet. Orlaith wore boy's clothing: billowy pants and a white linen shirt falling off her shoulders.

"Saoirse!" A sailor shouted. "I'll get your dress, lass."

They all knew her name and knew to be careful with it. Manus had filled his crew with trustworthy men and put the fear of god in them. He'd kill them if they ever disrespected her.

The sailor respectfully handed her the dress, turning his back to give her some privacy. She tossed it over her head, switching hands on the railing and shaking her legs to free them of mucus.

Manus handed off their daughter to one of the crew who whirled her into a wild jig. She shrieked with laughter and her feet raced across the floor.

Heat blossomed in Saoirse's belly as her husband stalked towards her. He was big, and real, and so powerful he made her shiver.

"Wife," he growled. His hands reached over the railing, surrounded her waist, and lifted her high over the edge.

She tucked herself into his arms with a peaceful sigh. "Husband."

He swayed back and forth, dancing her gracefully across the deck. "You know I love you more than all the stars in the sky?"

"And I love you more than all the fish in the sea."

AFTERWORD

I hope you enjoyed Bride of the Sea as much as I have! This was a journey and an unusual style compared to my other books.

I wanted to challenge myself with this one and create a story that I wouldn't usually write. And I am so incredibly pleased with this story that follows these two characters I love so much.

If you enjoyed this story, please leave a review! They help authors out so much.

<3 Emma

ACKNOWLEDGEMENTS

To all those who want to write, may you find the time to share your worlds with us.

ABOUT THE AUTHOR

Emma Hamm is a small town girl on a blueberry field in Maine. She writes stories that remind her of home, of fairytales, and of myths and legends that make her mind wander.

She can be found by the fireplace with a cup of tea and her two Maine Coon cats dipping their paws into the water without her knowing.

To stay in touch
www.emmahamm.com
authoremmahamm@gmail.com

www.ingramcontent.com/pod-product-compliance
Lightning Source LLC
Chambersburg PA
CBHW031957120726
47898CB00004BA/1108